# Shadow
## of
# Night

ALSO BY DEBORAH HARKNESS

*A Discovery of Witches*

# DEBORAH HARKNESS

# Shadow of Night

VIKING

VIKING
Published by the Penguin Group
Penguin Group (USA) Inc., 375 Hudson Street,
New York, New York 10014, U.S.A.
Penguin Group (Canada), 90 Eglinton Avenue East, Suite 700, Toronto,
Ontario, Canada M4P 2Y3 (a division of Pearson Penguin Canada Inc.)
Penguin Books Ltd, 80 Strand, London WC2R 0RL, England
Penguin Ireland, 25 St. Stephen's Green, Dublin 2, Ireland
(a division of Penguin Books Ltd)
Penguin Books Australia Ltd, 250 Camberwell Road, Camberwell,
Victoria 3124, Australia (a division of Pearson Australia Group Pty Ltd)
Penguin Books India Pvt Ltd, 11 Community Centre,
Panchsheel Park, New Delhi–110 017, India
Penguin Group (NZ), 67 Apollo Drive, Rosedale, Auckland 0632,
New Zealand (a division of Pearson New Zealand Ltd)
Penguin Books (South Africa) (Pty) Ltd, 24 Sturdee Avenue,
Rosebank, Johannesburg 2196, South Africa

Penguin Books Ltd, Registered Offices: 80 Strand, London WC2R 0RL, England

First published in 2012 by Viking Penguin, a member of Penguin Group (USA) Inc.

1 3 5 7 9 10 8 6 4 2

Copyright © Deborah Harkness, 2012
All rights reserved

*Publisher's Note:* This is a work of fiction. Names, characters, places, and
incidents either are the product of the author's imagination or are used fictitiously,
and any resemblance to actual persons, living or dead, business establishments,
events, or locales is entirely coincidental.

LIBRARY OF CONGRESS CATALOGING IN PUBLICATION DATA
Harkness, Deborah E.
Shadow of night / Deborah Harkness.
p. cm. — (All souls trilogy ; bk. 2)
ISBN 978-0-670-02348-6
ISBN 978-0-670-02595-4 export edition
1. Witches—Fiction. 2. Vampires—Fiction. I. Title.
PS3608.A7436S53 2012
813'.6—dc23    2012005843

Printed in the United States of America
Set in Adobe Garamond Pro
Designed by Francesca Belanger

*To Lacey Baldwin Smith, master storyteller and historian,*
*who suggested some time ago that I should think about writing a novel.*

*The past cannot be cured.*

—Elizabeth I,
Queen of England

# Contents

# PART I

# Woodstock:
# The Old Lodge

We arrived in an undignified heap of witch and vampire. Matthew was underneath me, his long limbs bent into an uncharacteristically awkward position. A large book was squashed between us, and the force of our landing sent the small silver figurine clutched in my hand sailing across the floor.

"Are we in the right place?" My eyes were screwed shut in case we were still in Sarah's hop barn in twenty-first-century New York, and not in sixteenth-century Oxfordshire. Even so, the unfamiliar scents told me I was not in my own time or place. Among them was something grassy and sweet, along with a waxen smell that reminded me of summer. There was a tang of wood smoke, too, and I heard the crackle of a fire.

"Open your eyes, Diana, and see for yourself." A feather-light touch of cool lips brushed my cheek, followed by a soft chuckle. Eyes the color of a stormy sea looked into mine from a face so pale it could only belong to a vampire. Matthew's hands traveled from neck to shoulders. "Are you all right?"

After journeying so far into Matthew's past, my body felt as though it might come apart with a puff of wind. I hadn't felt anything like it after our brief timewalking sessions at my aunts' house.

"I'm fine. What about you?" I kept my attention fixed on Matthew rather than daring a look around.

"Relieved to be home." Matthew's head fell back on the wooden floorboards with a gentle thunk, releasing more of the summery aroma from the rushes and lavender scattered there. Even in 1590 the Old Lodge was familiar to him.

My eyes adjusted to the dim light. A substantial bed, a small table, narrow benches, and a single chair came into focus. Through the carved uprights supporting the bed's canopy, I spied a doorway that connected this chamber to another room. Light spilled from it onto the coverlet and floor, forming a misshapen golden rectangle. The room's walls had the same fine, linenfold paneling that I remembered from the few times I'd visited Matthew's home in present-day Woodstock. Tipping my head back, I saw the ceiling—thickly plastered, coffered into squares, with a splashy red-and-white Tudor rose picked out in gilt in each recess.

"The roses were obligatory when the house was built," Matthew commented drily. "I can't stand them. We'll paint them all white at the first opportunity."

The gold-and-blue flames in a stand of candles flared in a sudden draft, illuminating the corner of a richly colored tapestry and the dark, glossy stitches that outlined a pattern of leaves and fruit on the pale counterpane. Modern textiles didn't have that luster.

I smiled with sudden excitement. "I really did it. I didn't mess it up or take us somewhere else, like Monticello or—"

"No," he said with an answering smile, "you did beautifully. Welcome to Elizabeth's England."

For the first time in my life, I was absolutely delighted to be a witch. As a historian I studied the past. Because I was a witch, I could actually visit it. We had come to 1590 to school me in the lost arts of magic, yet there was so much more that I could learn here. I bent my head for a celebratory kiss, but the sound of an opening door stopped me.

Matthew pressed a finger to my lips. His head turned slightly, and his nostrils flared. The tension left him when he recognized who was in the next room, where I could hear a faint rustling. Matthew lifted the book and me in one clean move. Taking my hand, he led me to the door.

In the next room, a man with tousled brown hair stood at a table littered with correspondence. He was of average height, with a neat build and expensive, tailored clothes. The tune he hummed was unfamiliar, punctuated now and again with words too low for me to hear.

Shock passed over Matthew's face before his lips curved into an affectionate smile.

"Where are you in truth, my own sweet Matt?" The man held a page up to the light. In a flash, Matthew's eyes narrowed, indulgence replaced by displeasure.

"Looking for something, Kit?" At Matthew's words the young man dropped the paper to the table and pivoted, joy lighting his face. I'd seen that face before, on my paperback copy of Christopher Marlowe's *The Jew of Malta.*

"Matt! Pierre said you were in Chester and might not make it home. But I knew you would not miss our annual gathering." The words were familiar enough but coated in a strange cadence that required me to focus on what he was saying in order to understand them. Elizabethan English was neither as unlike modern English as I had been taught nor as easily understandable as I'd hoped, based on my familiarity with Shakespeare's plays.

"Why no beard? Have you been ill?" Marlowe's eyes flickered when they spotted me, nudging me with the insistent pressure that marked him unmistakably as a daemon.

I suppressed an urge to rush at one of England's greatest playwrights and shake his hand before peppering him with questions. What little information I once knew about him flew from my mind now that he was standing before me. Had any of his plays been performed in 1590? How old was he? Younger than Matthew and I, certainly. Marlowe couldn't yet be thirty. I smiled at him warmly.

"Wherever did you find that?" Marlowe pointed, his voice dripping with contempt. I looked over my shoulder, expecting to see some hideous work of art. There was nothing but empty space.

He meant me. My smile faltered.

"Gently, Kit," Matthew said with a scowl.

Marlowe shrugged off the rebuke. "It is no matter. Take your fill of her before the others arrive, if you must. George has been here for some time, of course, eating your food and reading your books. He is still without a patron and hasn't a farthing to his name."

"George is welcome to whatever I have, Kit." Matthew kept his eyes on the young man, his face expressionless as he drew our intertwined fingers to his mouth. "Diana, this is my dear friend Christopher Marlowe."

Matthew's introduction provided Marlowe with an opportunity to inspect me more openly. His attention crawled from my toes to the top of my head. The young man's scorn was evident, his jealousy better hidden. Marlowe was indeed in love with my husband. I had suspected it back in Madison when my fingers had traveled over his inscription in Matthew's copy of *Doctor Faustus.*

"I had no idea there was a brothel in Woodstock that specialized in overtall women. Most of your whores are more delicate and appealing, Matthew. This one is a positive Amazon," Kit sniffed, looking over his shoulder at the disordered drifts of paper that covered the surface of the table. "According to the Old Fox's latest, it was business rather than lust that took you to the north. Wherever did you find the time to secure her services?"

"It is remarkable, Kit, how easily you squander affection," Matthew drawled, though there was a note of warning in his tone. Marlowe, seemingly intent on the correspondence, failed to recognize it and smirked. Matthew's fingers tightened on mine.

"Is Diana her real name, or was it adopted to enhance her allure among customers? Perhaps a baring of her right breast, or a bow and arrow, is in order," Marlowe suggested, picking up a sheet of paper. "Remember when Blackfriars Bess demanded we call her Aphrodite before she would let us—"

"Diana is my wife." Matthew was gone from my side, his hand no longer wrapped around mine but twisted in Marlowe's collar.

"No." Kit's face registered his shock.

"Yes. That means she is the mistress of this house, bears my name, and is under my protection. Given all that—and our long-standing friendship, of course—no word of criticism or whisper against her virtue will cross your lips in future."

I wiggled my fingers to restore their feeling. The angry pressure from Matthew's grip had driven the ring on the third finger of my left hand into the flesh, leaving a pale red mark. Despite its lack of facets, the diamond in the center captured the warmth of the firelight. The ring had been an unexpected gift from Matthew's mother, Ysabeau. Hours ago—centuries ago? centuries to come?—Matthew had repeated the words of the old marriage ceremony and slid the diamond over my knuckles.

With a clatter of dishes, two vampires appeared in the room. One was a slender man with an expressive face, weather-beaten skin the color of a hazelnut, and black hair and eyes. He was holding a flagon of wine and a goblet whose stem was shaped into a dolphin, the bowl balanced on its tail. The other was a rawboned woman bearing a platter of bread and cheese.

"You are home, *milord*," the man said, obviously confused. Oddly enough, his French accent made him easier to understand. "The messenger on Thursday said—"

"My plans changed, Pierre." Matthew turned to the woman. "My wife's possessions were lost on the journey, Françoise, and the clothes she was wearing were so filthy I burned them." He told the lie with bald confidence. Neither the vampires nor Kit looked convinced by it.

"Your wife?" Françoise repeated, her accent as French as Pierre's. "But she is a w—"

"Warmblood," Matthew finished, plucking the goblet from the tray. "Tell Charles there's another mouth to feed. Diana hasn't been well and must have fresh meat and fish on the advice of her doctor. Someone will need to go to the market, Pierre."

Pierre blinked. "Yes, *milord*."

"And she will need something to wear," Françoise observed, eyeing me appraisingly. When Matthew nodded, she disappeared, Pierre following in her wake.

"What's happened to your hair?" Matthew held up a strawberry blond curl.

"Oh, no," I murmured. My hands rose. Instead of my usual shoulder-length, straw-colored hair, they found unexpectedly springy reddish-gold locks reaching down to my waist. The last time my hair had developed a mind of its own, I was in college, playing Ophelia in a production of *Hamlet*. Then and now its unnaturally rapid growth and change of hue were not good signs. The witch within me had awakened during our journey to the past. There was no telling what other magic had been unleashed.

Vampires might have smelled the adrenaline and the sudden spike of anxiety that accompanied this realization, or heard the music my blood made. But daemons like Kit could sense the rise in my witch's energy.

"Christ's tomb." Marlowe's smile was full of malice. "You've brought home a witch. What evil has she done?"

"Leave it, Kit. It's not your concern." Matthew's voice took on that note of command again, but his fingers remained gentle on my hair. "Don't worry, *mon coeur*. I'm sure it's nothing but exhaustion."

My sixth sense flared in disagreement. This latest transformation couldn't be explained by simple fatigue. A witch by descent, I was still unsure of the full extent of my inherited powers. Not even my Aunt Sarah and her partner, Emily Mather—witches both—had been able to say for certain what they were or how best to manage them. Matthew's scientific tests had revealed genetic markers for the magical potential in my blood, but there were no guarantees when or if these possibilities would ever be realized.

Before I could worry further, Françoise returned with something that looked like a darning needle, her mouth bristling with pins. An ambulatory mound of velvet, wool, and linen accompanied her. The slender brown legs emerging from the bottom of the pile suggested that Pierre was buried somewhere inside.

"What are they for?" I asked suspiciously, pointing at the pins.

"For getting *madame* into this, of course." Françoise plucked a dull brown garment that looked like a flour sack from the top of the pile of clothes. It didn't seem an obvious choice for entertaining, but with little knowledge of Elizabethan fashion I was at her mercy.

"Go downstairs where you belong, Kit," Matthew told his friend. "We will join you presently. And hold your tongue. This is my tale to tell, not yours."

"As you wish, Matthew." Marlowe pulled at the hem of his mulberry doublet, his nonchalant gesture belied by the trembling of his hands, and made a small, mocking bow. The compact move managed to both acknowledge Matthew's command and undermine it.

With the daemon gone, Françoise draped the sack over a nearby bench and circled me, studying my figure to determine the most favorable line of attack. With an exasperated sigh, she began to dress me. Matthew moved to the table, his attention drawn by the piles of paper strewn over its surface. He opened a neatly folded rectangular packet sealed with a blob of pinkish wax, eyes darting across the tiny handwriting.

"*Dieu.* I forgot about that. Pierre!"

"*Milord?*" A muffled voice issued from the depths of the fabric.

"Put that down and tell me about Lady Cromwell's latest complaint." Matthew treated Pierre and Françoise with a blend of familiarity and authority. If this was how one dealt with servants, it would take me some time to master the art.

The two muttered by the fire while I was draped, pinned, and trussed into something presentable. Françoise clucked over my single earring, the twisted golden wires hung with jewels that had originally belonged to Ysabeau. Like Matthew's copy of *Doctor Faustus* and the small silver figure of Diana, the earring was one of the three items that had helped us return to this particular past. Françoise rummaged in a nearby chest and found its match easily. My jewelry sorted out, she snaked thick stockings over my knees and secured them with scarlet ribbons.

"I think I'm ready," I said, eager to get downstairs and begin our visit to the sixteenth century. Reading books about the past wasn't the same as experiencing it, as my brief interaction with Françoise and my crash course in the clothing of the period proved.

Matthew surveyed my appearance. "That will do—for now."

"She'll more than do, for she looks modest and forgettable," Françoise said, "which is exactly how a witch should look in this household."

Matthew ignored Françoise's pronouncement and turned to me. "Before we go down, Diana, remember to guard your words. Kit is a daemon, and George knows that I'm a vampire, but even the most open-minded of creatures are leery of someone new and different."

Down in the great hall, I wished George, Matthew's penniless and patronless friend, a formal and, I thought, properly Elizabethan good evening.

"Is that woman speaking *English?*" George gaped, raising a pair of round spectacles that magnified his blue eyes to froglike proportions. His other hand was on his hip in a pose I'd last seen in a painted miniature at the Victoria and Albert Museum.

"She's been living in Chester," Matthew said quickly. George looked skeptical. Apparently not even the wilds of northern England could account for my odd speech patterns. Matthew's accent was softening into something that better matched the cadence and timbre of the time, but mine remained resolutely modern and American.

"She's a witch," corrected Kit, taking a sip of wine.

"Indeed?" George studied me with renewed interest. There were no nudges to indicate that this man was a daemon, no witchy tingles, nor the frosty aftereffects of a vampire's glance. George was just an ordinary, warm-blooded human—one who appeared middle-aged and tired, as though life had already worn him out. "But you do not like witches any more than Kit does, Matthew. You have always discouraged me from attending to the subject. When I set out to write a poem about Hecate, you told me to—"

"I like this one. So much so, I married her," Matthew interrupted, bestowing a firm kiss on my lips to help convince him.

"Married her!" George's eyes shifted to Kit. He cleared his throat. "So there are two unexpected joys to celebrate: You were not delayed on business as Pierre thought, and you have returned to us with a wife. My felicitations." His portentous tone reminded me of a commencement address, and I stifled a smile. George beamed at me in return and bowed. "I am George Chapman, Mistress Roydon."

His name was familiar. I picked through the disorganized knowledge stored in my historian's brain. Chapman was not an alchemist—that was my research specialty, and I did not find his name in the spaces devoted to that arcane subject. He was another writer, like Marlowe, but I couldn't recall any of the titles.

Once we'd dispensed with introductions, Matthew agreed to sit before the fire for a few moments with his guests. There the men talked politics and George made an effort to include me in the conversation by asking about the state of the roads and the weather. I said as little as possible and tried to observe the little tricks of gesture and word choice that would help me pass for an Elizabethan. George was delighted with my attentiveness and rewarded it with a long dissertation on his latest literary efforts. Kit, who didn't enjoy being relegated to a supporting role, brought George's lecture to a halt by offering to read aloud from *Doctor Faustus.*

"It will serve as a rehearsal among friends," the daemon said, eyes gleaming, "before the real performance later."

"Not now, Kit. It's well past midnight, and Diana is tired from her journey," Matthew said, drawing me to my feet.

Kit's eyes remained on us as we left the room. He knew we were hiding something. He had leaped on every strange turn of phrase when I'd ventured into the conversation and grown thoughtful when Matthew couldn't remember where his own lute was kept.

Matthew had warned me before we left Madison that Kit was unusually perceptive, even for a daemon. I wondered how long it would be before Marlowe figured out what that hidden something was. The answer to my question came within hours.

The next morning we talked in the recesses of our warm bed while the household stirred.

At first Matthew was willing to answer my questions about Kit (the son of a shoemaker, it turned out) and George (who was not much older than Marlowe, I learned to my surprise). When I turned to the practical matters of household management and female behavior, however, he was quickly bored.

"What about my clothes?" I asked, trying to focus him on my immediate concerns.

"I don't think married women sleep in these," Matthew said, plucking at my fine linen night rail. He untied its ruffled neckline and was about to plant a kiss underneath my ear to persuade me to his point of view when someone ripped open the bed's curtains. I squinted against the bright sunlight.

"Well?" Marlowe demanded.

A second, dark-complected daemon peered over Marlowe's shoulder. He resembled an energetic leprechaun with his slight build and pointed chin, which was accented by an equally sharp auburn beard. His hair evidently had not seen a comb for weeks. I grabbed at the front of my night rail, keenly aware of its transparency and my lack of underclothes.

"You saw Master White's drawings from Roanoke, Kit. The witch looks nothing at all like the natives of Virginia," the unfamiliar daemon replied, disappointed. Belatedly he noticed Matthew, who was glaring at him. "Oh. Good morning, Matthew. Would you allow me to borrow your sector? I promise not to take it to the river this time."

Matthew lowered his forehead to my shoulder and closed his eyes with a groan.

"She must be from the New World—or Africa," Marlowe insisted, refusing to refer to me by name. "She's not from Chester, nor from Scotland, Ireland, Wales, France, or the Empire. I don't believe she's Dutch or Spanish either."

"Good morning to you, Tom. Is there some reason you and Kit must discuss Diana's birthplace now, and in my bedchamber?" Matthew drew the ties of my night rail together.

"It is too fine to lie abed, even if you have been out of your mind with an ague. Kit says you must have married the witch in the midst of the fever's crisis. Otherwise there is no way to account for your recklessness." Tom rattled on in true daemonic fashion, making no effort to answer Matthew's question. "The roads were dry, and we arrived hours ago."

"And the wine is already gone," Marlowe complained.

"We"? There were more of them? The Old Lodge already felt stuffed to bursting.

"Out! *Madame* must wash before she greets his lordship." Françoise entered the room with a steaming basin of water in her hands. Pierre, as usual, trailed behind.

"Has something of import happened?" George inquired from beyond the curtains. He'd entered the room unannounced, neatly foiling Françoise's efforts to herd the other men from the room. "Lord Northumberland has been left alone in the great hall. If he were my patron, I would not treat him thus!"

"Hal is reading a treatise on the construction of a balance sent to me by a mathematician in Pisa. He's quite content," Tom replied crossly, sitting on the edge of the bed.

He must be talking about Galileo, I realized with excitement. In 1590, Galileo was an entry-level professor at the university in Pisa. His work on the balance wasn't published—yet.

*Tom. Lord Northumberland. Someone who corresponded with Galileo.*

My lips parted in astonishment. The daemon perched on the quilted coverlet must be Thomas Harriot.

"Françoise is right. Out. All of you," Matthew said, sounding as cross as Tom.

"What should we tell Hal?" Kit asked, sliding a meaningful glance in my direction.

"That I'll be down shortly," Matthew said. He rolled over and pulled me close.

I waited until Matthew's friends streamed out of the room before I thumped his chest.

"What is that for?" He winced in mock pain, but all I'd bruised was my own fist.

"For not telling me who your *friends* are!" I propped up on one elbow and stared down at him. "The great playwright Christopher Marlowe. George Chapman, poet and scholar. Mathematician and astronomer Thomas Harriot, if I'm not mistaken. And the Wizard Earl is waiting downstairs!"

"I can't remember when Henry earned that nickname, but nobody calls him that yet." Matthew looked amused, which only made me more furious.

"All we need is Sir Walter Raleigh and we'll have the entire School of Night in the house." Matthew looked out the window at my mention of this legendary group of radicals, philosophers, and free-thinkers. *Thomas Harriot. Christopher Marlowe. George Chapman. Walter Raleigh. And—*

"Just who *are* you, Matthew?" I hadn't thought to ask him before we departed.

"Matthew Roydon," he said with a tip of his head, as though we were only this moment being introduced. "Friend to poets."

"Historians know almost nothing about you," I said, stunned. Matthew Roydon was the most shadowy figure associated with the mysterious School of Night.

"You aren't surprised, are you, now that you know who Matthew Roydon really is?" His black brow rose.

"Oh, I'm surprised enough to last a lifetime. You might have warned me before dropping me into the middle of all this."

"What would you have done? We barely had time to get dressed before we left, never mind conduct a research project." He sat up and swung his legs onto the floor. Our private time had been lamentably brief. "There's no reason for you to be concerned. They're just ordinary men, Diana."

No matter what Matthew said, there was nothing ordinary about them. The School of Night held heretical opinions, sneered at the corrupt court of Queen Elizabeth, and scoffed at the intellectual pretensions of church and university. "Mad, bad, and dangerous to know" described this group perfectly. We hadn't joined a cozy reunion of friends on Halloween night. We'd fallen into a hornet's nest of Elizabethan intrigue.

"Putting aside how reckless your friends can be, you can't expect me to be blasé when you introduce me to people I've spent my adult life studying," I said. "Thomas Harriot is one of the foremost astronomers of the time. Your friend Henry Percy is an alchemist." Pierre, familiar with the signs of a woman on the edge, hastily thrust a set of black britches at my husband so he wouldn't be bare-legged when my anger erupted.

"So are Walter and Tom." Matthew ignored the proffered clothing and scratched his chin. "Kit dabbles, too, though without any success. Try not to dwell on what you know about them. It's probably wrong anyway. And you should be careful with your modern historical labels, too," he continued, finally snatching at his britches and stepping into them. "Will dreams up the School of Night as a jab at Kit, but not for a few years yet."

"I don't care what William Shakespeare has done, is doing, or will do in the future—provided he isn't at this moment in the great hall with the Earl of Northumberland!" I retorted, sliding out of the high bed.

"Of course Will's not down there." Matthew waved his hand dismissively. "Walter doesn't approve of his command of meter, and Kit thinks he's a hack and a thief."

"Well, that's a relief. What do you plan on telling them about me? Marlowe knows we're hiding something."

Matthew's gray-green eyes met mine. "The truth, I suppose." Pierre handed him a doublet—black, with intricate quilting—and stared fixedly at a point over my shoulder, the very model of a good servant. "That you're a timewalker and a witch from the New World."

"The truth," I said flatly. Pierre could hear every word but showed no reaction, and Matthew ignored him as though he were invisible. I wondered if we would be here long enough for me to become so oblivious to his presence.

"Why not? Tom will write down everything you say and compare it with his notes on the Algonquian language. Otherwise no one will pay much attention." Matthew seemed more concerned with his clothing than with the reactions of his friends.

Françoise returned with two warmblooded young women bearing armfuls of clean clothes. She gestured at my night rail, and I ducked behind the bedpost to disrobe. Grateful that my time in locker rooms had squashed most of my qualms about changing in front of strangers, I drew the linen over my hips and up to my shoulders.

"Kit will. He's been looking for a reason to dislike me, and this will give him several."

"He won't be a problem," Matthew said confidently.

"Is Marlowe your friend or your puppet?" I was still wrestling my head out of the fabric when there was a gasp of horror, a muffled *"Mon Dieu."*

I froze. Françoise had seen my back and the crescent-shaped scar that stretched from one side of my lower rib cage to the other, along with the star that rested between my shoulder blades.

"I will dress *madame*," Françoise coolly told the maids. "Leave the clothing and return to your work."

The maids departed with nothing more than a curtsy and a look of idle curiosity. They hadn't seen the markings. When they were gone, we all began to speak at once. Françoise's aghast "Who did this?" tumbled over Matthew's "No one must know" and my own, slightly defensive "It's just a scar."

"Someone branded you with a badge of the de Clermont family," Françoise insisted with a shake of her head, "one that is used by *milord*."

"We broke the covenant." I fought the sick feeling that twisted my stomach whenever I thought about the night another witch had marked me a traitor. "This was the Congregation's punishment."

"So that is why you are both here." Françoise snorted. "The covenant was a foolish idea from the start. Philippe de Clermont should never have gone along with it."

"One that's kept us safe from the humans." I had no great fondness for the agreement, or the nine-member Congregation who enforced it, but its long-term success at hiding otherworldly creatures from unwanted attention was undeniable. The ancient promises made among daemons, vampires, and witches prohibited meddling in human politics or religion and forbade personal alliances among the three different species. Witches were meant to keep to themselves, as were vampires and daemons. They were not supposed to fall in love and intermarry.

"Safe? Do not think you are safe here, *madame*. None of us are. The English are a superstitious people, prone to seeing a ghost in every church-yard and witches around every cauldron. The Congregation is all that is standing between us and utter destruction. You are wise to take refuge here. Come, you must dress and join the others." Françoise helped me out of the night rail and handed me a wet towel and a dish of goop that smelled of rosemary and oranges. I found it odd to be treated like a child but knew that it was customary for people of Matthew's rank to be washed, dressed, and fed like dolls. Pierre handed Matthew a cup of something too dark to be wine.

"She is not only a witch but a *fileuse de temps* as well?" Françoise asked Matthew quietly. The unfamiliar term—*"time spinner"*—conjured up im-ages of the many different-colored threads we'd followed to reach this par-ticular past.

"She is." Matthew nodded, his attention focused on me while he sipped at his cup.

"But if she has come from another time, that means . . ." Françoise be-gan, wide-eyed. Then her expression became thoughtful. Matthew must sound and behave differently.

*She suspects that this is not the same Matthew,* I realized, alarmed.

"It is enough for us to know that she is under *milord's* protection," Pierre said roughly, a clear warning in his tone. He handed Matthew a dag-ger. "What it means is not important."

"It means I love her, and she loves me in return." Matthew looked at his servant intently. "No matter what I say to others, that is the truth. Under-stood?"

"Yes," replied Pierre, though his tone suggested quite the opposite.

Matthew shot an inquiring look at Françoise, who pursed her lips and nodded grudgingly.

She returned her attention to getting me ready, wrapping me in a thick linen towel. Françoise had to have noticed the other marks on my body, those I had received over the course of that one interminable day with the witch Satu, as well as my other, later scars. Françoise asked no further ques-tions, however, but sat me in a chair next to the fire while she ran a comb through my hair.

"And did this insult happen after you declared your love for the witch, *milord*?" Françoise asked.

"Yes." Matthew buckled the dagger around his waist.

"It was not a *manjasang*, then, who marked her," Pierre murmured. He used the old Occitan word for vampire—"*blood eater.*" "None would risk the anger of the de Clermonts."

"No, it was another witch." Even though I was shielded from the cold air, the admission made me shiver.

"Two *manjasang* stood by and let it happen, though," Matthew said grimly. "And they will pay for it."

"What's done is done." I had no wish to start a feud among vampires. We had enough challenges facing us.

"If *milord* had accepted you as his wife when the witch took you, then it is not done." Françoise's swift fingers wove my hair into tight braids. She wound them around my head and pinned them in place. "Your name might be Roydon in this godforsaken country where there is no loyalty to speak of, but we will not forget that you are a de Clermont."

Matthew's mother had warned me that the de Clermonts were a pack. In the twenty-first century, I had chafed under the obligations and restrictions that came with membership. In 1590, however, my magic was unpredictable, my knowledge of witchcraft almost nonexistent, and my earliest known ancestor hadn't yet been born. Here I had nothing to rely on but my own wits and Matthew.

"Our intentions to each other were clear then. But I want no trouble now." I looked down at Ysabeau's ring and felt the band with my thumb. My hope that we could blend seamlessly into the past now seemed unlikely as well as naïve. I looked around me. "And this . . ."

"We're here for only two reasons, Diana: to find you a teacher and to locate that alchemical manuscript if we can." It was the mysterious manuscript called Ashmole 782 that had brought us together in the first place. In the twenty-first century, it had been safely buried among the millions of books in Oxford's Bodleian Library. When I'd filled out the call slip, I'd had no idea that the simple action would unlock an intricate spell that bound the manuscript to the shelves, or that the same spell would reactivate the moment I returned it. I was also ignorant of the many secrets about witches, vampires, and daemons its pages were rumored to reveal. Matthew had thought it would be wiser to locate Ashmole 782 in the past than to try to unlock the spell for a second time in the modern world.

"Until we go back, this will be your home," he continued, trying to reassure me.

The room's solid furnishings were familiar from museums and auction catalogs, but the Old Lodge would never feel like home. I fingered the thick linen of the towel—so different from the faded terry-cloth sets that Sarah and Em owned, all worn thin from too many washes. Voices in another room lilted and swayed in a rhythm that no modern person, historian or not, could have anticipated. But the past was our only option. Other vampires had made that clear during our final days in Madison, when they'd hunted us down and nearly killed Matthew. If the rest of our plan was going to work, passing as a proper Elizabethan woman had to be my first priority.

"*O brave new world.*" It was a gross historical violation to quote from Shakespeare's *Tempest* two decades before it was written, but this had been a difficult morning.

"*'Tis new to thee,*" Matthew responded. "Are you ready to meet your trouble, then?"

"Of course. Let's get me dressed." I squared my shoulders and rose from the chair. "How does one say hello to an earl?"

**2**

My concern over proper etiquette was unnecessary. Titles and forms of address weren't important when the earl in question was a gentle giant named Henry Percy.

Françoise, to whom propriety mattered, clucked and fussed while she finished dressing me in scavenged apparel: someone else's petticoats; quilted stays to confine my athletic figure into a more traditionally feminine shape; an embroidered smock that smelled of lavender and cedar, with a high, ruffled neck; a black, bell-shaped skirt made of velvet; and Pierre's best jacket, the only tailored article of clothing that was remotely my size. Try though she might, Françoise couldn't button this last item over my breasts. I held my breath, tucked in my stomach, and hoped for a miracle as she pulled the corset's laces tight, but nothing short of divine intervention was going to give me a sylphlike silhouette.

I asked Françoise a number of questions during the complicated process. Portraits of the period had led me to expect an unwieldy birdcage called a farthingale that would hold my skirts out at the hips, but Françoise explained that these were for more formal occasions. Instead she tied a stuffed cloth form shaped like a doughnut around my waist beneath my skirts. The only positive thing to say about it was that it held the layers of fabric away from my legs, enabling me to walk without too much difficulty—provided there was no furniture in the way and my destination could be reached if I moved in a straight line. But I would be expected to curtsy, too. Françoise quickly taught me how to do so while explaining how Henry Percy's various titles worked—he was "Lord Northumberland" even though his last name was Percy and he was an earl.

But I had no chance to use any of this newly acquired knowledge. As soon as Matthew and I entered the great hall, a lanky young man in soft brown leather traveling clothes spattered with mud jumped up to greet us. His broad face was enlivened with an inquisitive look that lifted his heavy, ash-colored eyebrows toward a forehead with a pronounced widow's peak.

"Hal." Matthew smiled with the indulgent familiarity of an older brother. But the earl ignored his old friend and moved in my direction instead.

"M-m-mistress Roydon." The earl's deep bass was toneless, with hardly a trace of inflection or accent. Before coming down, Matthew had explained that Henry was slightly deaf and had stammered since childhood. He was, however, adept at lipreading. Here was someone I could talk to without feeling self-conscious.

"Upstaged by Kit again, I see," Matthew said with a rueful smile. "I had hoped to tell you myself."

"What does it matter who shares such happy news?" Lord Northumberland bowed. "I thank you for your hospitality, mistress, and apologize for greeting you in this state. It is good of you to suffer your husband's friends so soon. We should have left immediately once we learned of your arrival. The inn would be more than adequate."

"You are most welcome here, my lord." This was the moment to curtsy, but my heavy black skirts weren't easy to manage and the corset was laced so tightly I couldn't bend at the waist. I arranged my legs in an appropriately reverential position but teetered as I bent my knees. A large, blunt-fingered hand shot out to steady me.

"Just Henry, mistress. Everyone else calls me Hal, so my given name is considered quite formal." Like many who are hard of hearing, the earl kept his voice deliberately soft. He released me and turned his attention to Matthew. "Why no beard, Matt? Have you been ill?"

"A touch of ague, nothing more. Marriage has cured me. Where are the rest of them?" Matthew glanced around for Kit, George, and Tom.

The Old Lodge's great hall looked very different in daylight. I had seen it only at night, but this morning the heavy paneling turned out to be shutters, all of which were thrown open. It gave the space an airy feeling, despite the monstrous fireplace on the far wall. It was decorated with bits and pieces of medieval stonework, no doubt rescued by Matthew from the rubble of the abbey that once stood here—the haunting face of a saint, a coat of arms, a Gothic quatrefoil.

"Diana?" Matthew's amused voice interrupted my examination of the room and its contents. "Hal says the others are in the parlor, reading and playing cards. He didn't feel it was right to join them until he had been invited to stay by the lady of the house."

"The earl must stay, of course, and we can join your friends immediately." My stomach rumbled.

"Or we could get you something to eat," he suggested, eyes twinkling. Now that I had met Henry Percy without mishap, Matthew was beginning to relax. "Has anyone fed you, Hal?"

"Pierre and Françoise have been attentive as ever," he reassured us. "Of course, if Mistress Roydon will join me . . ." The earl's voice trailed off, and his stomach gurgled with mine. The man was as tall as a giraffe. It must take huge quantities of food to keep his body fueled.

"I, too, am fond of a large breakfast, my lord," I said with a laugh.

"Henry," the earl corrected me gently, his grin showing off the dimple in his chin.

"Then you must call me Diana. I cannot call the Earl of Northumberland by his first name if he keeps referring to me as 'Mistress Roydon.'" Françoise had been insistent on the need to honor the earl's high rank.

"Very well, Diana," Henry said, extending his arm.

He led me across a drafty corridor and into a cozy room with low ceilings. It was snug and inviting, with only a single array of south-facing windows. In spite of its relatively small size, three tables had been wedged into the room, along with stools and benches. A low hum of activity, punctuated by a rattle of pots and pans, told me we were near the kitchens. Someone had tacked a page from an almanac on the wall and a map lay on the central table, one corner held down with a candlestick, the other by a shallow pewter dish filled with fruit. The arrangement looked like a Dutch still life, with its homely detail. I stopped short, dizzied by the scent.

"The quinces." My fingers reached out to touch them. They looked just as they had in my mind's eye back in Madison when Matthew had described the Old Lodge.

Henry seemed puzzled by my reaction to an ordinary dish of fruit but was too well bred to comment. We settled ourselves at the table, and a servant added fresh bread along with a platter of grapes and a bowl of apples to the still life before us. It was comforting to see such familiar fare. Henry helped himself, and I followed his example, carefully noting which foods he selected and how much of them he consumed. It was always the little differences that gave strangers away, and I wanted to appear as ordinary as possible. While we filled our plates, Matthew poured himself a glass of wine.

Throughout our meal Henry behaved with unfailing courtesy. He never asked me anything personal, nor did he pry into Matthew's affairs. Instead he kept us laughing with tales of his dogs, his estates, and his martinet of a mother, all the while providing a steady supply of toasted bread from the fire. He was just beginning an account of moving house in London when a clatter arose in the courtyard. The earl, whose back was to the door, didn't notice.

"She is impossible! You all warned me, but I didn't believe anyone could be so ungrateful. After all the riches I've poured into her coffers, the least she could do was— Oh." Our new guest's broad shoulders filled the doorway, one of them swathed in a cloak as dark as the hair that curled around his splendid feathered hat. "Matthew. Are you ill?"

Henry turned with surprise. "Good day, Walter. Why aren't you at court?"

I tried to swallow a morsel of toast. Our new arrival was almost certainly the missing member of Matthew's School of Night, Sir Walter Raleigh.

"Cast out of paradise for want of a position, Hal. And who is this?" Piercing blue eyes settled on me, and teeth gleamed from his dark beard. "Henry Percy, you sly imp. Kit told me you were intent on bedding the fair Arabella. If I'd known your tastes ran to something more mature than a girl of fifteen, I would have yoked you to a lusty widow long ago."

Mature? *Widow?* I had just turned thirty-three.

"Her charms have induced you to stay home from church this Sunday. We must thank the lady for getting you off your knees and onto a horse, where you belong," Raleigh continued, his accent as thick as Devonshire cream.

The Earl of Northumberland rested his toasting fork on the hearth and considered his friend. He shook his head and returned to his work. "Go out, come in again, and ask Matt for his news. And look contrite when you do it."

"No." Walter stared at Matthew, openmouthed. "She's yours?"

"With the ring to prove it." Matthew kicked a stool from under the table with one long, booted leg. "Sit down, Walter, and have some ale."

"You swore you would never wed," Walter said, clearly confused.

"It took some persuasion."

"I expect it did." Walter Raleigh's appraising glance settled on me once more. "'Tis a pity she is wasted on a cold-blooded creature. I wouldn't have delayed for an instant."

"Diana knows my nature and doesn't mind my 'coldness,' as you put it. Besides, it was she who needed persuading. I fell in love with her at first glance," said Matthew.

Walter snorted in response.

"Don't be so cynical, old friend. Cupid may yet catch you." Matthew's gray eyes lit up with the mischief born from certain knowledge of Raleigh's future.

"Cupid will have to wait to turn his arrows on me. I'm entirely occupied at present fending off the unfriendly advances of the queen and the admiral." Walter tossed his hat onto a nearby table, where it slid over the shiny surface of a backgammon board, disturbing the game in progress. He groaned and sat next to Henry. "Everyone wants a bit of my hide, it seems, but no one will give me a speck of preferment while this business of the colony hangs over my head. The idea for this year's anniversary celebration was mine, yet that woman put Cumberland in charge of the ceremonies." His temper rose again.

"Still no news from Roanoke?" Henry inquired gently, handing Walter a cup of thick, brown ale. My stomach lurched at the mention of Raleigh's doomed venture in the New World. It was the first time anyone had wondered aloud about the outcome of a future event, but it would not be the last.

"White arrived back at Plymouth last week, driven home by foul weather. He had to abandon the search for his daughter and granddaughter." Walter took a long draft of ale and stared into space. "Christ knows what happened to them all."

"Come spring, you will return and find them." Henry sounded sure, but Matthew and I knew that the missing Roanoke colonists would never be found and Raleigh would never again set foot on the soil of North Carolina.

"I pray you are right, Hal. But enough of my troubles. What part of the country are your people from, Mistress Roydon?"

"Cambridge," I said softly, keeping my response brief and as truthful as possible. The town was in Massachusetts, not England, but if I started making things up now, I'd never keep my stories straight.

"So you are a scholar's daughter. Or perhaps your father was a theologian? Matt would be pleased to have someone to talk to about matters of faith. With the exception of Hal, his friends are hopeless when it comes to doctrine." Walter sipped his ale and waited.

"Diana's father died when she was quite young." Matthew took my hand.

"I am sorry for you, Diana. The loss of a f-f-father is a terrible blow," Henry murmured.

"And your first husband, did he leave you with sons and daughters for comfort?" asked Walter, a trace of sympathy creeping into his voice.

Here and now a woman my age would have been married before and have had a brood of three or four children. I shook my head. "No."

Walter frowned, but before he could pursue the matter further, Kit arrived, with George and Tom in tow.

"At last. Talk sense into him, Walter. Matthew cannot keep playing Odysseus to her Circe." Kit grabbed the goblet sitting in front of Henry. "Good day, Hal."

"Talk sense into whom?" Walter asked testily.

"Matt, of course. That woman is a witch. And there's something not quite right about her." Kit's eyes narrowed. "She's hiding something."

"A witch," Walter repeated carefully.

A servant carrying an armful of logs froze in the doorway.

"As I said," Kit affirmed with a nod. "Tom and I recognized the signs straightaway."

The maid dumped the logs in the waiting basket and scurried off.

"For a maker of plays, Kit, you have a lamentable sense of time and place." Walter's blue eyes turned to Matthew. "Shall we go elsewhere to discuss the matter, or is this merely one of Kit's idle fancies? If it is the latter, I would like to stay where it is warm and finish my ale." The two men studied each other. When Matthew's expression didn't waver, Walter cursed under his breath. Pierre appeared, as if on cue.

"There is a fire in the parlor, *milord*," the vampire told Matthew, "and wine and food are laid out for your guests. You will not be disturbed."

The parlor was neither as cozy as the room where we'd taken our breakfast nor as imposing as the great hall. The abundance of carved armchairs, rich tapestries, and ornately framed paintings suggested that its primary purpose was to entertain the house's most important guests. A splendid rendering of St. Jerome and his lion by Holbein hung by the fireplace. It was unfamiliar to me, as was the Holbein portrait next to it of a piggy-eyed Henry VIII holding a book and a pair of spectacles and looking pensively at the viewer, the table before him strewn with precious objects. Henry's daughter, the first and current Queen Elizabeth, stared at him with hauteur from across the room. Their tense standoff did nothing to lighten the mood as we took our seats. Matthew propped himself up by the fire with his arms crossed over his chest, looking every bit as formidable as the Tudors on the walls.

"Are you still going to tell them the truth?" I whispered to him.

"It is generally easier that way, mistress," Raleigh said sharply, "not to mention more fitting among friends."

"You forget yourself, Walter," Matthew warned, anger flaring.

"Forget myself! This from someone who has taken up with a witch?" Walter had no trouble keeping pace with Matthew when it came to irritation. And there was a note of real fear in his voice as well.

"She is my wife," Matthew retorted. He rubbed his hand over his hair. "As for her being a witch, we are all in this room vilified for something, be it real or imaginary."

"But to wed her—whatever were you thinking?" Walter asked numbly.

"That I loved her," Matthew said. Kit rolled his eyes and poured a fresh cup of wine from a silver pitcher. My dreams of sitting with him by a cozy fire discussing magic and literature faded further in the harsh light of this November morning. I had been in 1590 for less than twenty-four hours, but I was already heartily sick of Christopher Marlowe.

At Matthew's response the room fell silent while he and Walter studied each other. With Kit, Matthew was indulgent and a bit exasperated. George and Tom brought out his patience and Henry his brotherly affection. But Raleigh was Matthew's equal—in intelligence, power, perhaps even in ruthlessness—which meant that Walter's was the only opinion that mattered. They had a wary respect for each other, like two wolves determining who had the strength to lead their pack.

"So it's like that," Walter said slowly, acceding to Matthew's authority.

"It is." Matthew planted his feet more evenly on the hearth.

"You keep too many secrets and have too many enemies to take a wife. And yet you've done so anyway." Walter looked amazed. "Other men have accused you of relying overmuch on your own subtlety, but I never agreed with them until now. Very well, Matthew. If you are so cunning, tell us what to say when questions are raised."

Kit's cup slammed onto the table, red wine sloshing over his hand. "You cannot expect us to—"

"Quiet." Walter shot a furious glance at Marlowe. "Given the lies we tell on your behalf, I'm surprised you would dare to object. Go on, Matthew."

"Thank you, Walter. You are the only five men in the kingdom who might listen to my tale and not think me mad." Matthew raked his hands through his hair. "Do you recall when we spoke last of Giordano Bruno's ideas about an infinite number of worlds, unlimited by time or space?"

The men exchanged glances.

"I am not sure," Henry began delicately, "that we understand your meaning."

"Diana *is* from the New World." Matthew paused, which gave Marlowe the opportunity to look triumphantly about the room. "From the New World to come."

In the silence that followed, all eyes swiveled in my direction.

"She said she was from Cambridge," said Walter blankly.

"Not that Cambridge. My Cambridge is in Massachusetts." My voice creaked from stress and disuse. I cleared my throat. "The colony will exist north of Roanoke in another forty years."

A din of exclamations rose, and questions came at me from all directions. Harriot reached over and hesitantly touched my shoulder. When his finger met solid flesh, he withdrew it in wonder.

"I have heard about creatures who could bend time to their will. This is a marvelous day, is it not, Kit? Did you ever think to know a time spinner? We must be careful around her, of course, or we might get entangled in her web and lose our way." Harriot's face was wistful, as if he might enjoy being caught up in another world.

"And what brings you here, Mistress Roydon?" Walter's deep voice cut through the chatter.

"Diana's father was a scholar," Matthew replied for me. There were murmurs of interest, quelled by Walter's upraised hand. "Her mother, too. Both were witches and died under mysterious circumstances."

"That is something we share, then, D-D-Diana," Henry said with a shudder. Before I could ask the earl what he meant, Walter waved Matthew on.

"As a result her education as a witch was . . . overlooked," Matthew continued.

"It is easy to prey on such a witch." Tom frowned. "Why, in this New World to come, is more care not taken with such a creature?"

"My magic, and my family's long history with it, meant nothing to me. You must understand what it is like to want to go beyond the restrictions of your birth." I looked at Kit, the shoemaker's son, hoping for agreement if not sympathy, but he turned away.

"Ignorance is an unforgivable sin." Kit fussed with a bit of red silk that was peeking out of one of the dozens of jagged slashes cut into his black doublet.

"So is disloyalty," said Walter. "Go on, Matthew."

"Diana may not have been trained in the craft of a witch, but she is far from ignorant. She is a scholar, too," Matthew said proudly, "with a passion for alchemy."

"Lady alchemists are nothing but kitchen philosophers," Kit sniffed, "more interested in improving their complexions than understanding the secrets of nature."

"I study alchemy in the library—not the kitchen," I snapped, forgetting to modulate my tone or accent. Kit's eyes widened. "Then I teach students about the subject at a university."

"They will let *women* teach at the university?" George said, fascinated and repelled in equal measure.

"Matriculate, too," Matthew murmured, pulling on the tip of his nose apologetically. "Diana went to Oxford."

"That must have improved attendance at lectures," Walter commented drily. "Had women been allowed at Oriel, even I might have taken another degree. And are lady scholars under attack in this future colony somewhere north of Roanoke?" It was a reasonable conclusion to have drawn from Matthew's story thus far.

"Not all of them, no. But Diana found a lost book at the university." The members of the School of Night pitched forward in their seats. Lost books were of far more interest to this group than were ignorant witches and lady scholars. "It contains secret information about the world of creatures."

"The Book of Mysteries that is supposed to tell of our creation?" Kit looked amazed. "You've never been interested in those fables before, Matthew. In fact, you've dismissed them as superstition."

"I believe in them now, Kit. Diana's discovery brought enemies to her door."

"And you were with her. So her enemies lifted the latch and entered." Walter shook his head.

"Why did Matthew's regard effect such dire consequences?" George asked. His fingers searched out the black grosgrain ribbon that tied his spectacles to the fastenings on his doublet. The doublet was fashionably puffed out over his stomach and the stuffing rustled like a bag of oatmeal whenever he moved. George lifted the round frames to his face and examined me as if I were an interesting new object of study.

"Because witches and *wearhs* are forbidden to marry," Kit said promptly. I'd never heard the word *wearh* before, with its whistling *w* at the beginning and guttural sound at the end.

"So are daemons and *wearhs*." Walter clamped a warning hand on Kit's shoulder.

"Really?" George blinked at Matthew, then at me. "Does the queen forbid such a match?"

"It is an ancient covenant between creatures that none dares to disobey." Tom sounded frightened. "Those who do so are called to account by the Congregation and punished."

Only vampires as old as Matthew could remember a time before the covenant had established how creatures were to behave with one another and interact with the humans who surrounded us. "No fraternizing between otherworldly species" was the most important rule, and the Congregation policed the boundaries. Our talents—creativity, strength, supernatural power—were impossible to ignore in mixed groups. It was as if the power of a witch highlighted the creative energy of any nearby daemons, and the genius of a daemon made a vampire's beauty more striking. As for our relationships with humans, we were supposed to keep a low profile and steer clear of politics and religion.

Just this morning Matthew had insisted there were too many other problems facing the Congregation in the sixteenth century—religious war, the burning of heretics, and the popular hunger for the strange and bizarre newly fed by the technology of the printing press—for its members to bother with something so trivial as a witch and a vampire who had fallen in love. Given the bewildering and dangerous events that had taken place since I'd met Matthew in late September, I had found this difficult to believe.

"Which congregation?" George asked with interest. "Is this some new religious sect?"

Walter ignored his friend's question and gave Matthew a piercing look. Then he turned to me. "And do you still have this book?"

"No one has it. It went back into the library. The witches expect me to recall it for them."

"So you are hunted for two reasons. Some want to keep you from a *wearh,* others see you as a necessary means to a desired end." Walter pinched the bridge of his nose and looked at Matthew tiredly. "You are a veritable lodestone when it comes to trouble, my friend. And this couldn't have happened at a more inopportune time. The queen's anniversary celebration is less than three weeks away. You're expected at court."

"Never mind the queen's celebration! We are not safe with a time spinner in our midst. She can see what fate has in store for each of us. The witch will be able to undo our futures, cause ill fortune—even hasten our deaths." Kit rocketed out of his chair to stand before Matthew. "How by all that is holy could you do this?"

"It seems your much-vaunted atheism has failed you, Kit," said Matthew evenly. "Afraid you might have to answer for your sins after all?"

"I may not believe in a beneficent, all-powerful deity as you do, Matthew, but there is more to this world than what's described in your philosophy books. And this woman—this witch—cannot be allowed to meddle in our affairs. *You* may be in her thrall, but I have no intention of putting *my* future in her hands!" Kit retorted.

"A moment." A look of growing astonishment passed over George's face. "Did you come to us from Chester, Matthew, or—"

"No. You must not answer, Matt," Tom said with sudden lucidity. "Janus has come among us to work some purpose, and we must not interfere."

"Talk sense, Tom—if you can," Kit said nastily.

"With one face, Matthew and Diana look to the past. With the other, they consider the future," Tom said, unconcerned with Kit's interruption.

"But if Matt is not . . ." George trailed off into silence.

"Tom is right," Walter said gruffly. "Matthew is our friend and has asked for our help. It is, so far as I can recall, the first time he has done so. That is all we need to know."

"He asks too much," Kit retorted.

"Too much? It's little and late, in my opinion. Matthew paid for one of my ships, saved Henry's estates, and has long kept George and Tom in books and dreams. As for you"—Walter surveyed Marlowe from head to toe—"everything in you and on you—from your ideas to your last cup of wine to the hat on your head—is thanks to Matthew Roydon's good graces. Providing a safe port for his wife during this present tempest is a trifle in comparison."

"Thank you, Walter." Matthew looked relieved, but the smile he turned on me was tentative. Winning over his friends—Walter in particular—had been more difficult than he'd anticipated.

"We will need to devise a story to explain how your wife came to be here," Walter said thoughtfully, "something to divert attention from her strangeness."

"Diana needs a teacher, too," added Matthew.

"She must be taught some manners, certainly," Kit grumbled.

"No, her teacher must be another witch," Matthew corrected him.

Walter made a low sound of amusement. "I doubt there's a witch within twenty miles of Woodstock. Not with you living here."

"And what of this book, Mistress Roydon?" George whipped out a pointed gray stick wrapped in string from a pocket hidden away in the bulbous outlines of his short britches. He licked the tip of his pencil and held it expectantly. "Can you tell me its size and contents? I will look for it in Oxford."

"The book can wait," I said. "First I need proper clothes. I can't go out of the house wearing Pierre's jacket and the skirt that Matthew's sister wore to Jane Seymour's funeral."

"Go out of the house?" Kit scoffed. "Utter lunacy."

"Kit is right," George said apologetically. He made a notation in his book. "Your speech makes it apparent you are a stranger to England. I would be happy to give you elocution lessons, Mistress Roydon." The idea of George Chapman playing Henry Higgins to my Eliza Doolittle was enough to make me look longingly at the exit.

"She shouldn't be allowed to speak at all, Matt. You must keep her quiet," Kit insisted.

"What we need is a woman, someone to advise Diana. Why is there not one daughter, wife, or mistress to be had among the five of you?" Matthew demanded. Deep silence fell.

"Walter?" Kit asked archly, sending the rest of the men into a fit of laughter and lightening the heavy atmosphere as though a summer storm had blown through the room. Even Matthew joined in.

Pierre entered as the laughter faded, kicking up sprigs of rosemary and lavender strewn among the rushes laid down to keep dampness from being tromped through the house. At the same moment, the bells began to toll the hour of twelve. Like the sight of the quinces, the combination of sounds and smells took me straight back to Madison.

Past, present, and future met. Rather than a slow, fluid unspooling, there was a moment of stillness as if time had stopped. My breath hitched.

"Diana?" Matthew said, taking me by the elbows.

Something blue and amber, a weave of light and color, caught my attention. It was tightly meshed in the corner of the room, where nothing could fit but cobwebs and dust. Fascinated, I tried to move toward it.

"Is she having a fit?" Henry asked, his face coming into focus over Matthew's shoulder.

The tolling of the bell stopped, and the scent of lavender faded. Blue and amber flickered to gray and white before disappearing.

"I'm sorry. I thought I saw something in the corner. It must have been a trick of the light," I said, pressing my hand to my cheek.

"Perhaps you are suffering from timelag, *mon coeur*," Matthew murmured. "I promised you a walk in the park. Will you go outside with me to clear your head?"

Maybe it was the aftereffects of timewalking, and perhaps fresh air would help. But we had just arrived, and Matthew hadn't seen these men for more than four centuries.

"You should be with your friends," I said firmly, though my eyes drifted to the windows.

"They'll still be here, drinking my wine, when we return," Matthew said with a smile. He turned to Walter. "I'm going to show Diana her house and make sure she is able to find her way through the gardens."

"We will need to talk further," Walter warned. "There is business to discuss."

Matthew nodded and tucked his hand around my waist. "It can wait."

We left the School of Night in the warm parlor and headed outdoors. Tom had already lost interest in the problems of vampire and witch and was engrossed in his reading. George was similarly consumed by his own thoughts and busily writing in a notebook. Kit's glance was watchful, Walter's wary, and Henry's eyes were filled with sympathy. The three men looked like an unkindness of ravens with their dark clothes and attentive expressions. It reminded me of what Shakespeare would soon say about this extraordinary group.

"How does it begin?" I murmured softly. "*'Black is the badge of hell'*?"

Matthew looked wistful. "*'Black is the badge of hell / The hue of dungeons, and the school of night.'*"

"The hue of friendship would be more accurate," I said. I'd seen Matthew manage the readers at the Bodleian, but his influence over the likes of Walter Raleigh and Kit Marlowe was still unexpected. "Is there anything they wouldn't do for you, Matthew?"

"Pray God we never find out," he said somberly.

# 3

On Monday morning I was tucked into Matthew's office. It was located between Pierre's apartments and a smaller chamber that was used for estate business, and it afforded a view toward the gatehouse and the Woodstock road.

Most of the lads—now that I knew them better, it seemed a far more fitting collective term than the grandiose School of Night—were closeted in what Matthew called the breakfast room, drinking ale and wine and applying their considerable imaginations to my backstory. Walter assured me it would, when complete, explain my sudden appearance at Woodstock to curious residents and alleviate questions about my odd accent and ways.

What they had concocted so far was melodramatic in the extreme. This was not surprising given that our two resident playwrights, Kit and George, came up with the key elements of the plot. The characters included dead French parents, avaricious noblemen who had preyed on a helpless orphan (me), and aged lechers intent on stripping me of my virtue. The tale turned epic with my spiritual trials and conversion from Catholicism to Calvinism. These led to voluntary exile on England's Protestant shores, years of abject poverty, and Matthew's fortuitous rescue and instantaneous regard. George (who really *was* something of a schoolmarm) promised to drill me in the particulars when they had applied the finishing touches to the story.

I was enjoying some quiet, which was a rare commodity in a crowded Elizabethan household of this size. Like a troublesome child, Kit unerringly gauged the worst moment to deliver the mail, announce dinner, or request Matthew's help with some problem. And Matthew was understandably eager to be with friends he had never expected to see again.

At present he was with Walter and I was devoting my attention to a small book while awaiting his return. He'd left his table by the window littered with bags of sharpened quills and glass pots full of ink. Other tools were scattered nearby: a stick of wax to seal his correspondence, a thin knife to open letters, a candle, a silver shaker. This last was full not of salt but sand, as my gritty eggs this morning had proved.

My table held a similar shaker to set the ink on the page and keep it from smudging, a single pot of black ink, and the remains of three pens. I was currently destroying a fourth in an effort to master the complicated swirls of Elizabethan handwriting. Making a to-do list should have been a snap. As a historian I had spent years reading old handwriting and knew exactly how the letters should look, what words were most common, and the erratic spelling choices that were mine to make in a time when there were few dictionaries and grammatical rules.

It turned out that the challenge lay not in knowing what to do but in actually doing it. After working for years to become an expert, I was a student again. Only this time my objective wasn't to understand the past but to live in it. Thus far it had been a humbling experience, and all I'd managed was to make a mess of the first page of the pocket-size blank book Matthew had given me this morning.

"It's the Elizabethan equivalent of a laptop computer," he'd explained, handing me the slim volume. "You're a woman of letters and need somewhere to put them."

I cracked the tight binding, releasing the crisp smell of paper. Most virtuous women of the time used these little books for prayers.

### Diana

There was a thick blot where I'd pressed down at the beginning of the D and by the time I reached the last A the pen was out of ink. Still, my effort was a perfectly respectable example of the period's Italic hand. My hand moved far more slowly than Matthew's did when he wrote letters using the squiggly Secretary script. That was the handwriting of lawyers, doctors, and other professionals, but too difficult for me at present.

### Bishop

That was even better. But my smile quickly dissolved, and I struck out my last name. I was married now. I dipped the pen in the ink.

### de Clermont

Diana de Clermont. That made me sound like a countess, not a historian. A drop of ink fell wetly onto the page below. I stifled a curse at the black splotch. Happily, it hadn't obliterated my name. But that wasn't my name either. I smudged the blob over "de Clermont." You could still read it—barely. I steadied my hand and deliberately formed the correct letters.

*Roydon.*

That was my name now. Diana Roydon, wife of the most obscure figure associated with the mysterious School of Night. I examined the page critically. My handwriting was a disaster. It looked nothing like what I'd seen of the chemist Robert Boyle's neat, rounded script or that of his brilliant sister, Katherine. I hoped that women's handwriting in the 1590s was far messier than it was in the 1690s. A few more strokes of the pen and a final flourish and I would be done.

*Her Booke.*

Male voices sounded outside. I put down my pen with a frown and went to the window.

Matthew and Walter were below. The panes of glass muffled their words, but the subject of the conversation was evidently unpleasant, judging from Matthew's harried expression and the bristling line of Raleigh's eyebrows. When Matthew made a dismissive gesture and turned to walk away, Walter stopped him with a firm hand.

Something had been bothering Matthew since he'd received the first batch of mail this morning. A stillness had come over him, and he'd held the pouch without opening it. Though he'd explained that the letters dealt with ordinary estate business, surely there was more there than demands for taxes and bills due.

I pressed my warm palm against the cold pane as if it were only the glass that stood between me and Matthew. The play of temperatures reminded me of the contrast between warmblooded witch and cool-blooded vampire. I returned to my seat and picked up my pen.

"You decided to make your mark on the sixteenth century after all." Matthew was suddenly at my side. The twitch at the corner of his mouth indicated amusement but didn't entirely disguise his tension.

"I'm still not sure that creating a lasting memento of my time here is a good idea," I confessed. "A future scholar might realize there's something odd about it." *Just as Kit had known there was something wrong with me.*

"Don't worry. The book won't leave the house." Matthew reached for his stack of mail.

"You can't be sure of that," I protested.

"Let history take care of itself, Diana," he said decisively, as if the matter were now closed. But I couldn't let go of the future—or my worries about the effects that our presence in the past might have on it.

"I still don't think we should let Kit keep that chess piece." The memory of Marlowe triumphantly brandishing the tiny figure of Diana haunted me. She occupied the role of the white queen in Matthew's costly silver chess set and had been one of the objects I'd used to steer us to the proper place in the past. Two unfamiliar young daemons, Sophie Norman and her husband Nathaniel Wilson, had unexpectedly delivered it to my aunts' house in Madison just as we were deciding to timewalk.

"Kit won it from me fair and square last night—just as he was supposed to do. At least this time I could see how he managed it. He distracted me with his rook." Matthew dashed off a note with enviable speed before folding the pages into a neat packet. He dropped a molten blob of vermilion across the edges of the letter before pressing his signet ring into it. The golden surface of the ring bore the simple glyph for the planet Jupiter, not the more elaborate emblem that Satu had burned into my flesh. The wax crackled as it cooled. "Somehow my white queen went from Kit to a family of witches in North Carolina. We have to believe that it will do so again, with or without our help."

"Kit didn't know me before. And he doesn't like me."

"All the more reason not to worry. As long as it pains him to look upon the likeness of Diana, he won't be able to part with it. Christopher Marlowe is a masochist of the first order." Matthew took up another letter and sliced it open with his knife.

I surveyed the other items on my table and picked up a pile of coins. A working knowledge of Elizabethan currency had not been covered in my graduate education. Nor had household management, the proper order of donning undergarments, forms of address for servants, or how to make a medicine for Tom's headache. Discussions with Françoise about my wardrobe revealed my ignorance of common names for ordinary colors. "Goose-turd green" was familiar to me, but the peculiar shade of grizzled brown known as "rat hair" was not. My experiences thus far had me planning to throttle the first Tudor historian I met upon my return for gross dereliction of duty.

But there was something compelling about figuring out the details of everyday life, and I quickly forgot my annoyance. I picked through the coins in my palm, looking for a silver penny. It was the cornerstone on which my precarious knowledge was built. The coin was no bigger than my thumbnail, as thin as a wafer, and bore the same profile of Queen Elizabeth as did most of the others. I organized the rest according to relative worth and began an orderly account of them on the next clean page in my book.

"Thank you, Pierre," Matthew murmured, barely glancing up as his servant whisked away the sealed letters and deposited still more correspondence on the surface.

We wrote in companionable silence. Soon finished with my list of coins, I tried to remember what Charles, the household's laconic cook, had taught me about making a caudle—or was it a posset?

*A Caudle for pains in the head*

Satisfied with the relatively straight line of text, three tiny blots, and the wobbly *C*, I continued.

*Set your water to boil. Beat two egge yolkes. Add white wine and beat some more. When the water boils, set it to cool, then add the wine and egge. Stirre it as it boils again, adding saffron and honey.*

The resulting mixture had been revolting—violently yellow with the consistency of runny cottage cheese—but Tom had slurped it down without complaint. Later, when I'd asked Charles for the proper proportion of honey to wine, he'd thrown up his hands in disgust at my ignorance and stalked away without a word.

Living in the past had always been my secret desire, but it was far more difficult than I'd ever imagined. I sighed.

"You'll need more than that book to feel at home here." Matthew's eyes didn't leave his correspondence. "You should have a room of your own, too. Why don't you take this one? It's bright enough to serve as a library. Or you could turn it into an alchemical laboratory—although you might want somewhere more private if you're planning to turn lead into gold. There's a room by the kitchen that might do."

"The kitchen may not be ideal. Charles doesn't approve of me," I replied.

"He doesn't approve of anyone. Neither does Françoise—except for Charles, of course, whom she venerates as a misunderstood saint despite his fondness for drink."

Sturdy feet tromped down the hall. The disapproving Françoise appeared at the threshold. "There are men here for Mistress Roydon," she announced, stepping aside to reveal a gray-haired septuagenarian with callused hands and a much younger man who shifted from one foot to the other. Neither of these men was a creature.

"Somers." Matthew frowned. "And is that young Joseph Bidwell?"

"Aye, Master Roydon." The younger man pulled his cap from his head.

"Mistress Roydon will allow you to take her measurements now," Françoise said.

"Measurements?" The look Matthew directed to me and Françoise demanded an answer—quickly.

"Shoes. Gloves. For *madame*'s wardrobe," Françoise said. Unlike petticoats, shoes were not one-size-fits-most.

"I asked Françoise to send for them," I explained, hoping to gain Matthew's cooperation. Somers's eyes widened at my strange accent before his face returned to an expression of neutral deference.

"My wife's journey was unexpectedly difficult," Matthew said smoothly, coming to stand by my side, "and her belongings were lost. Regrettably, Bidwell, we have no shoes for you to copy." He rested a warning hand on my shoulder, hoping to silence any further commentary.

"May I, Mistress Roydon?" Bidwell asked, lowering himself until his fingers hovered over the ties that secured a pair of ill-fitting shoes to my feet. The borrowed footwear was a giveaway that I wasn't who I was pretending to be.

"Please," Matthew replied before I could respond. Françoise gave me a sympathetic look. She knew what it was like to be silenced by Matthew Roydon.

The young man started when he came into contact with a warm foot and its frequent pulse. Clearly he expected a colder, less lively extremity.

"About your business," Matthew said sharply.

"Sir. My lord. Master Roydon." The young man blurted out most available titles except for "Your Majesty" and "Prince of Darkness." These were implied nonetheless.

"Where's your father, lad?" Matthew's voice softened.

"Sick abed these four days past, Master Roydon." Bidwell drew a piece of felt from a bag tied around his waist and placed each of my feet on it, tracing the outlines with a stick of charcoal. He made some notations on the felt and, quickly finished, released my foot. Bidwell pulled out a curious book made from squares of colored hide sewn together with leather thongs and offered it to me.

"What colors are popular, Master Bidwell?" I asked, waving the leather samples away. I needed advice, not a multiple-choice test.

"Ladies who are going to court are having white stamped with gold or silver."

"We're not going to court," Matthew said swiftly.

"Black then, and a nice tawny." Bidwell held up for approval a patch of leather the color of caramel. Matthew gave it before I could say a word.

Then it was the older man's turn. He, too, was surprised when he took my hand and felt the calluses on my palms. Well-bred ladies who married men such as Matthew didn't row boats. Somers took in the lump on my middle finger. Ladies didn't have bumps from holding pens too tightly either. He slid a buttery-soft glove that was much too large onto my right hand. A needle charged with coarse thread was tucked into the hem.

"Does your father have everything he needs, Bidwell?" Matthew asked the shoemaker.

"Yes, thank you, Master Roydon," Bidwell replied with a bob of his head.

"Charles will send him custard and venison." Matthew's gray eyes flickered over the young man's thin frame. "Some wine, too."

"Master Bidwell will be grateful for your kindness," Somers said, his fingers drawing the thread through the leather so that the glove fit snugly.

"Is anyone else ill?" Matthew asked.

"Rafe Meadows's girl was sick with a terrible fever. We feared for Old Edward, but he is only afflicted with an ague," Somers replied tersely.

"I trust Meadows's daughter has recovered."

"No." Somers snapped the thread. "They buried her three days ago, God rest her soul."

"Amen," said everyone in the room. Françoise lifted her eyebrows and jerked her head in Somers's direction. Belatedly I joined in.

Their business concluded and the shoes and gloves promised for later in the week, both men bowed and departed. Françoise turned to follow them out, but Matthew stopped her.

"No more appointments for Diana." There was no mistaking the seriousness in his tone. "See to it that Edward Camberwell has a nurse to look after him and sufficient food and drink."

Françoise curtsied in acquiescence and departed with another sympathetic glance.

"I'm afraid the men from the village know I don't belong here." I drew a shaking hand across my forehead. "My vowels are a problem. And my sentences go down when they should go up. When are you supposed to say 'amen'? Somebody needs to teach me how to pray, Matthew. I have to start somewhere, and—"

"Slow down," he said, sliding his hands around my corseted waist. Even through several layers of clothing, his touch was soothing. "This isn't an Oxford viva, nor are you making your stage debut. Cramming information and rehearsing your lines isn't going to help. You should have asked me before you summoned Bidwell and Somers."

"How can you pretend to be someone new, someone else, over and over again?" I wondered. Matthew had done this countless times over the centuries as he pretended to die only to reemerge in a different country, speaking a different language, known by a different name.

"The first trick is to stop pretending." My confusion must have been evident, and he continued. "Remember what I told you in Oxford. You can't live a lie, whether it's masquerading as a human when you're really a witch or trying to pass as Elizabethan when you're from the twenty-first century. This is your life for now. Try not to think of it as a role."

"But my accent, the way that I walk . . ." Even I had noticed the length of my steps relative to that of the other women in the house, but Kit's open mockery of my masculine stride had brought the point home.

"You'll adjust. Meanwhile people will talk. But no one's opinion in Woodstock matters. Soon you will be familiar and the gossip will stop."

I looked at him doubtfully. "You don't know much about gossip, do you?"

"Enough to know you are simply this week's curiosity." He glanced at my book, taking in the blotches and indecisive script. "You're holding your pen too tightly. That's why the point keeps breaking and the ink won't flow. You're holding on to your new life too tightly as well."

"I never thought it would be so difficult."

"You're a fast learner, and so long as you're safely at the Old Lodge, you're among friends. But no more visitors for the time being. Now, what have you been writing?"

"My name, mostly."

Matthew flipped a few pages in my book, examining what I'd recorded.

One eyebrow lifted. "You've been preparing for your economics and culinary examinations, too. Why don't you write about what's happening here at the house instead?"

"Because I need to know how to manage in the sixteenth century. Of course, a diary might be useful, too." I considered the possibility. It would certainly help me sort out my still-muddled sense of time. "I shouldn't use full names. People in 1590 use initials to save paper and ink. And nobody reflects on thoughts or emotions. They record the weather and the phases of the moon."

"Top marks on sixteenth-century English record keeping," said Matthew with a laugh.

"Do women write down the same things as men?"

He took my chin in his fingers. "You're impossible. Stop worrying about what other women do. Be your own extraordinary self." When I nodded, he kissed me before returning to his table.

Holding the pen as loosely as possible, I began a fresh page. I decided to use astrological symbols for the days of the week and record the weather as well as a few cryptic notes about life at the Old Lodge. That way no one reading them in a future time would find anything out of the ordinary. Or so I hoped.

♄ *31 October 1590    rain, clearing*
*On this day I was introduced to my husband's good*
*friend CM*

☉ *1 November 1590    cold and dry*
*In the early hours of the morning I made the acquaintance*
*of GC. After sunrise, TH, HP, WR arrived, all*
*friends of my husband. The moon was full.*

Some future scholar might suspect that these initials referred to the School of Night, especially given the name Roydon on the first page, but there would be no way to prove it. Besides, these days few scholars were interested in this group of intellectuals. Educated in the finest Renaissance style, the members of the School of Night were able to move between ancient and modern languages with alarming speed. All of them knew Aristotle backward and forward. And when Kit, Walter, and Matthew began talking politics, their encyclopedic command of history and geography made it nearly impossible for anyone else to keep up. Occasionally George and Tom managed to squeak in an opinion, but Henry's stammer and slight deafness made his full participation in the intricate discussions impossible. He spent most of the time quietly observing the others with a shy deference that was endearing, considering that the earl outranked everyone in the room. If there weren't so many of them, I might be able to keep up, too.

As for Matthew, gone was the thoughtful scientist brooding over his test results and worrying about the future of the species. I'd fallen in love with that Matthew but found myself doing so all over again with this sixteenth-century version, charmed by every peal of his laughter and each quick rejoinder he made when battles broke out over some fine point of philosophy. Matthew shared jokes over dinner and hummed songs in the corridors. He wrestled with his dogs by the fire in the bedroom—two enormous, shaggy mastiffs named Anaximander and Pericles. In modern Oxford or France, Matthew had always seemed slightly sad. But he was happy here in Woodstock, even when I caught him looking at his friends as though he couldn't quite believe they were real.

"Did you realize how much you missed them?" I asked, unable to refrain from interrupting his work.

"Vampires can't brood over those we leave behind," he replied. "We'd go mad. I have had more to remember them by than is usually the case: their words, their portraits. You forget the little things, though—a quirk of expression, the sound of their laughter."

"My father kept caramels in his pocket," I whispered. "I had no memory of them, until La Pierre." When I shut my eyes, I could still smell the tiny candies and hear the rustle of the cellophane against the soft broadcloth of his shirts.

"And you wouldn't give up that knowledge now," Matthew said gently, "not even to be rid of the pain."

He took up another letter, his pen scratching against the page. The tight look of concentration returned to his face, along with a small crease over the bridge of his nose. I imitated the angle at which he held the quill, the length of time that elapsed before he dipped it in the ink. It was indeed easier to write when you didn't hold the pen in a death grip. I poised the pen over the paper and prepared to write more.

Today was the feast of All Souls, the traditional day to remember the dead. Everyone in the house was remarking upon the thick frost that iced the leaves in the garden. Tomorrow would be even colder, Pierre promised.

☽ *2 November 1590 frost*
*Measured for shoes and gloves. Françoise sewing.*

Françoise was making me a cloak to keep the chill away, and a warm suit of clothes for the wintry weather ahead. She had been in the attics all morning, sorting through Louisa de Clermont's abandoned wardrobe. Matthew's sister's gowns were sixty years out of date, with their square necklines and bell-shaped sleeves, but Françoise was altering them to better fit what Walter and George insisted was the current style as well as my less statuesque frame. She wasn't pleased to be ripping apart the seams of one particularly splendid black-and-silver garment, but Matthew had insisted. With the School of Night in residence, I needed formal clothes as well as more practical outfits.

"But Lady Louisa was wed in that gown, my lord," Françoise protested.

"Yes, to an eighty-five-year-old with no living offspring, a bad heart, and numerous profitable estates. I believe the thing has more than repaid the family's investment in it," Matthew replied. "It will do for Diana until you can make her something better."

My book couldn't refer to that conversation, of course. Instead I'd chosen all my words carefully so that they would mean nothing to anyone else even though they conjured vivid images of particular people, sounds, and conversations for me. If this book survived, a future reader would find these tiny snippets of my life sterile and dry. Historians pored over documents like this, hoping in vain to see the rich, complex life hidden behind the simple lines of text.

Matthew swore under his breath. I was not the only one in this house hiding something.

*My husband received many letters today and gave me*
*this booke to keep my memories.*

As I lifted my pen to replenish its ink, Henry and Tom entered the room looking for Matthew. My third eye blinked open, surprising me with sudden awareness. Since we had arrived, my other nascent powers—witchfire, witchwater, and witchwind—had been oddly absent. With the unexpected extra perception offered by my witch's third eye, I could discern not only the black-red intensity of the atmosphere around Matthew but also Tom's silvery light and Henry's barely perceptible green-black shimmer, each as individual as a fingerprint.

Thinking back on the threads of blue and amber that I'd seen in the corner of the Old Lodge, I wondered what the disappearance of some powers and the emergence of others might signify. There had been the episode this morning, too. . . .

Something in the corner had caught my eye, another glimmer of amber shot through with hints of blue. There was an echo, something so quiet it was more felt than heard. When I'd turned my head to locate its source, the sensation faded. Strands pulsed in my peripheral vision, as if time were beckoning me to return home.

Ever since my first timewalk in Madison, when I'd traveled a brief span of minutes, I'd thought of time as a substance made of threads of light and color. With enough concentration you could focus on a single thread and follow it to its source. Now, after walking through several centuries, I knew that apparent simplicity masked the knots of possibility that tied an unimaginable number of pasts to a million presents and untold potential futures. Isaac Newton had believed that time was an essential force of nature that couldn't be controlled. After fighting our way back to 1590, I was prepared to agree with him.

"Diana? Are you all right?" Matthew's insistent voice broke through my reveries. His friends looked at me with concern.

"Fine," I said automatically.

"You're not fine." He tossed the quill onto the table. "Your scent has changed. I think your magic might be changing, too. Kit is right. We must find you a witch as quickly as possible."

"It's too soon to bring in a witch," I protested. "It's important that I be able to look and sound as if I belong."

"Another witch will know you're a timewalker," he said dismissively. "She'll make allowances. Or is there something else?"

I shook my head, unwilling to meet his eyes.

Matthew hadn't needed to see time unwinding in the corner to sense that something was out of joint. If he already suspected that there was more going on with my magic than I was willing to reveal, there would be no way for me to conceal my secrets from any witch who might soon come to call.

The School of Night had been eager to help Matthew find the creature. Their suggestions illuminated a collective disregard for women, witches, and everyone who lacked a university education. Henry thought London might provide the most fertile ground for the search, but Walter assured him that it would be impossible to conceal me from superstitious neighbors in the crowded city. George wondered if the scholars of Oxford might be persuaded to lend their expertise, since they at least had proper intellectual credentials. Tom and Matthew gave a brutal critique of the strengths and weaknesses of the natural philosophers in residence, and that idea was cast aside, too. Kit didn't believe it was wise to trust any woman with the task and drew up a list of local gentlemen who might be willing to establish a training regimen for me. It included the parson of St. Mary's, who was alert to apocalyptic signs in the heavens, a nearby landowner named Smythson, who dabbled in alchemy and had been looking for a witch or daemon to assist him, and a student at Christ Church College who paid his overdue book bills by casting horoscopes.

Matthew vetoed all these suggestions and called on Widow Beaton, Woodstock's cunning woman and midwife. She was poor and female—precisely the sort of creature the School of Night scorned—but this, Matthew argued, would better ensure her cooperation. Besides, Widow Beaton was the only creature for miles with purported magical talents. All others had long since fled, he admitted, rather than live near a *wearh*.

"Summoning Widow Beaton may not be a good idea," I said later when we were getting ready for bed.

"So you've mentioned," Matthew replied with barely concealed impatience. "But if Widow Beaton can't help us, she'll be able to recommend someone who can."

"The late sixteenth century really isn't a good time to openly ask around for a witch, Matthew." I'd been able to do little more than hint at the prospect of witch-hunts when we were with the School of Night, but Matthew knew the horrors to come. Once again he dismissed my concern.

"The Chelmsford witch trials are only memories now, and it will be another twenty years before the Lancashire hunts begin. I wouldn't have brought you here if a witch-hunt were about to break out in England." Matthew picked through a few letters that Pierre had left for him on the table.

"With reasoning like that, it's a good thing you're a scientist and not a historian," I said bluntly. "Chelmsford and Lancashire were extreme outbursts of far more widespread concerns."

"You think a historian can understand the tenor of the present moment better than the men living through it?" Matthew's eyebrow cocked up in open skepticism.

"Yes," I said, bristling. "We often do."

"That's not what you said this morning when you couldn't figure out why there weren't any forks in the house," he observed. It was true that I'd searched high and low for twenty minutes before Pierre gently broke it to me that the utensils were not yet common in England.

"Surely you aren't one of those people who believe that historians do nothing but memorize dates and learn obscure facts," I said. "My job is to understand *why* things happened in the past. When something occurs right in front of you, it's hard to see the reasons for it, but hindsight provides a clearer perspective."

"Then you can relax, because I have both experience *and* hindsight," Matthew said. "I understand your reservations, Diana, but calling on Widow Beaton is the right decision." *Case closed,* his tone made clear.

"In the 1590s there are food shortages, and people are worried about the future," I said, ticking the items off on my fingers. "That means people are looking for scapegoats to take the blame for the bad times. Already, human cunning women and midwives fear being accused of witchcraft, though your male friends may not be aware of it."

"I am the most powerful man in Woodstock," Matthew said, taking me by the shoulders. "No one will accuse you of anything." I was amazed at his hubris.

"I'm a stranger, and Widow Beaton owes me nothing. If I draw curious eyes, I pose a serious threat to her safety," I retorted. "At the very least, I need to pass as an upper-class Elizabethan woman before we ask her for help. Give me a few more weeks."

"This can't wait, Diana," he said brusquely.

"I'm not asking you to be patient so I can learn how to embroider samplers and make jam. There are good reasons for it." I looked at him sourly. "Call in your cunning woman. But don't be surprised when this goes badly."

"Trust me." Matthew lowered his lips toward mine. His eyes were smoky, and his instincts to pursue his prey and push it into submission were sharp. Not only did the sixteenth-century husband want to prevail over his wife, but the vampire wanted to capture the witch.

"I don't find arguments the slightest bit arousing," I said, turning my head. Matthew clearly did, however. I moved a few inches away from him.

"I'm not arguing," Matthew said softly, his mouth close to my ear. "You are. And if you think I would ever touch you in anger, wife, you are very much mistaken." After pinning me to the bedpost with frosty eyes, he turned and snatched up his breeches. "I'm going downstairs. Someone will still be awake to keep me company." He stalked toward the door. Once he'd reached it, he paused.

"And if you really want to behave like an Elizabethan woman, stop questioning me," he said roughly as he departed.

The next day one vampire, two daemons, and three humans examined my appearance in silence across the wide floorboards. The bells of St. Mary's Church sounded the hour, faint echoes of their music lingering long after the peals ceased. Quince, rosemary, and lavender scented the air. I was perched on an uncomfortable wooden chair in a confining array of smocks, petticoats, sleeves, skirts, and a tightly laced bodice. My career-oriented, twenty-first-century life faded further with each restricted breath. I stared out into the murky daylight, where cold rain pinged against the panes of glass in the leaded windows.

"*Elle est ici,*" Pierre announced, his glance flicking in my direction. "The witch is here to see *madame.*"

"At last," Matthew said. The severe lines of his doublet made him look even broader through the shoulders, while the acorns and oak leaves stitched in black around the edges of his white collar accentuated the paleness of his skin. He angled his dark head to gain a fresh perspective on whether I passed muster as a respectable Elizabethan wife.

"Well?" he demanded. "Will that do?"

George lowered his spectacles. "Yes. The russet of this gown suits her far better than the last one did and gives a pleasant cast to her hair."

"Mistress Roydon looks the part, George, it is true. But we cannot explain away her unusual speech simply by saying that she comes from the c-c-country," Henry said in his toneless bass. He stepped forward to twitch the folds of my brocade skirt into place. "And her height. There is no disguising that. She is taller even than the queen."

"Are you sure we can't pass her off as French, Walt, or Dutch?" Tom lifted a clove-studded orange to his nose with ink-stained fingers. "Perhaps Mistress Roydon could survive in London after all. Daemons cannot fail to notice her, of course, but ordinary men may not give her a second glance."

Walter snorted with amusement and unspooled from a low settle. "Mistress Roydon is finely shaped as well as uncommon tall. Ordinary men between the ages of thirteen and sixty will find reason enough to study her. No, Tom, she's better off here, with Widow Beaton."

"Perhaps I could meet Widow Beaton later, in the village, alone?" I suggested, hoping that one of them might see sense and persuade Matthew to let me do this my way.

"No!" cried out six horrified male voices.

Françoise appeared bearing two pieces of starched linen and lace, her bosom swelling like that of an indignant hen facing down a pugnacious rooster. She was as annoyed by Matthew's constant interference as I was.

"Diana's not going to court. That ruff is unnecessary," said Matthew with an impatient gesture. "Besides, it's her hair that's the problem."

"You have no idea what's necessary," Françoise retorted. Though she was a vampire and I was a witch, we had reached unexpected common ground when it came to the idiocy of men. "Which would Madame de Clermont prefer?" She extended a pleated nest of gauzy fabric and something crescent-shaped that resembled snowflakes joined together with invisible stitches.

The snowflakes looked more comfortable. I pointed to them.

While Françoise affixed the collar to the edge of my bodice, Matthew reached up in another attempt to put my hair in a more pleasing arrangement. Françoise slapped his hand away. "Don't touch."

"I'll touch my wife when I like. And stop calling Diana 'Madame de Clermont,'" Matthew rumbled, moving his hands to my shoulders. "I keep expecting my mother to walk through the door." He drew the edges of the collar apart, pulling loose the black velvet cord that hid Françoise's pins.

"*Madame* is a married woman. Her bosom should be covered. There is enough gossip about the new mistress," Françoise protested.

"Gossip? What kind of gossip?" I asked with a frown.

"You were not in church yesterday, so there is talk that you are with child, or afflicted by smallpox. That heretic priest believes you are Catholic. Others say you are Spanish."

"Spanish?"

"*Oui, madame.* Someone heard you in the stables yesterday afternoon."

"But I was practicing my French!" I was a fair mimic and thought that imitating Ysabeau's imperious accent might lend credence to my elaborate cover story.

"The groom's son did not recognize it as such." Françoise's tone suggested that the boy's confusion was warranted. She studied with me with satisfaction. "Yes, you look like a respectable woman."

"*Fallaces sunt rerum species,*" said Kit with a touch of acid that brought the scowl back to Matthew's face. "*'Appearances can be deceiving.'* No one will be taken in by her performance."

"It's far too early in the day for Seneca." Walter gave Marlowe a warning look.

"It is never too early for stoicism," Kit replied severely. "You should thank me that it's not Homer. All we've heard lately is inept paraphrases of the *Iliad.* Leave the Greek to someone who understands it, George—someone like Matt."

"My translation of Homer's work is not yet finished!" George retorted, bristling.

His response released a flood of Latin quotations from Walter. One of them made Matthew chuckle, and he said something in what I suspected was Greek. The witch waiting downstairs completely forgotten, the men enthusiastically engaged in their favorite pastime: verbal one-upmanship. I sank back into my chair.

"When they are in a fine humor like this, they are a wonder," Henry whispered. "These are the keenest wits in the kingdom, Mistress Roydon."

Raleigh and Marlowe were now shouting at each other about the merits—or lack thereof—of Her Majesty's policies on colonization and exploration.

"One might as well take fistfuls of gold and dump them into the Thames as give them to an adventurer like you, Walter," Kit chortled.

"Adventurer! You can't step out of your own door in daylight for fear of your creditors." Raleigh's voice shook. "You can be such a fool, Kit."

Matthew had been following the volleys with increasing amusement.

"Who are you in trouble with now?" he asked Marlowe, reaching for his wine. "And how much is it going to cost to get you out of it?"

"My tailor." Kit waved a hand over his expensive suit. "The printer for *Tamburlaine.*" He hesitated, prioritizing the outstanding sums. "Hopkins, that bastard who calls himself my landlord. But I do have this." Kit held up the tiny figure of Diana that he'd won from Matthew when they played chess on Sunday night. Still anxious about letting the statue out of my sight, I inched forward.

"You can't be so hard up as to pawn that bauble for pennies." Matthew's eyes flickered to me, and a small movement of his hand had me sinking back again. "I'll take care of it."

Marlowe bounded to his feet with a grin, pocketing the silver goddess. "You can always be counted on, Matt. I'll pay you back, of course."

"Of course," Matthew, Walter, and George murmured doubtfully.

"Keep enough money to buy yourself a beard, though." Kit stroked his own with satisfaction. "You look dreadful."

"Buy a beard?" I couldn't possibly have understood correctly. Marlowe must be using slang again, even though Matthew had asked him to stop on my account.

"There's a barber in Oxford who is a wizard. Your husband's hair grows slowly, as with all of his kind, and he's clean shaven." When I still looked blank, Kit continued with exaggerated patience. "Matt will be noticed, looking as he does. He needs a beard. Apparently you are not witch enough to provide him with one, so we will have to find someone else to do it."

My eyes strayed to the empty jug on the elm table. Françoise had filled it with clippings from the garden—sprigs of holly oak, branches from a medlar with their brown fruit resembling rose hips, and a few white roses—to bring some color and scent into the room. A few hours ago, I had laced my fingers through the branches to tug the roses and medlars to the forefront of the vase, wondering about the garden all the while. I was pleased with the results for about fifteen seconds, until the flowers and fruit withered before my eyes. The desiccation spread from my fingertips in all directions, and my hands tingled with an influx of information from the plants: the feel of sunlight, the quenching sensation of rain, the strength in the roots that came from resisting the pull of the wind, the taste of the soil.

Matthew was right. Now that we were in 1590, my magic was changing. Gone were the eruptions of witchfire, witchwater, and witchwind that I had experienced after meeting Matthew. Instead I was seeing the bright threads of time and the colorful auras that surrounded living creatures. A white stag stared at me from the shadows under the oaks whenever I walked in the gardens. Now I was making things wither.

"Widow Beaton is waiting," Walter reminded us, ushering Tom toward the door.

"What if she can hear my thoughts?" I worried as we descended the wide oak stairs.

"I'm more worried about what you might say aloud. Do nothing that might stir her jealousy or animosity," Walter advised, following behind with the rest of the School of Night. "If all else fails, lie. Matthew and I do it all the time."

"One witch can't lie to another."

"This will not end well," Kit muttered darkly. "I'd wager money on it."

"Enough." Matthew whirled and grabbed Kit by the collar. The pair of English mastiffs sniffed and growled at Kit's ankles. They were devoted to Matthew—and none too fond of Kit.

"All I said—" Kit began, squirming in an attempt to escape. Matthew gave him no opportunity to finish and jacked him against the wall.

"What you said is of no interest, and what you meant was clear enough." Matthew's grip tightened.

"Put him down." Walter had one hand on Marlowe's shoulder and the other on Matthew. The vampire ignored Raleigh and lifted his friend several more inches. In his red-and-black plumage, Kit looked like an exotic bird that had somehow become trapped in the folds of the carved wooden paneling. Matthew held him there for a few more moments to make his point clear, then let him drop.

"Come, Diana. Everything is going to be fine." Matthew still sounded sure, but an ominous pricking in my thumbs warned me that Kit just might be right.

"God's teeth," Walter muttered in disbelief as we processed into the hall. "Is that Widow Beaton?"

At the far end of the room, standing in the shadows, was the witch from central casting: diminutive, bent, and ancient. As we drew closer, the details of her rusty black dress, stringy white hair, and leathery skin became more apparent. One of her eyes was milky with a cataract, the other a mottled hazel. The eyeball with the cataract had an alarming tendency to swivel in its socket, as though its sight might be improved with a different perspective. Just when I thought it couldn't get worse, I spotted the wart on the bridge of her nose.

Widow Beaton slid a glance in my direction and dipped into a grudging curtsy. The barely perceptible tingle on my skin suggested that she was indeed a witch. Without warning, my third eye fluttered open, looking for further information. Unlike most other creatures, however, Widow Beaton gave off no light at all. She was gray through and through. It was dispiriting to see a witch try so hard to be invisible. Had I been as pallid as that before I touched Ashmole 782? My third eye drooped closed again.

"Thank you for coming to see us, Widow Beaton." Matthew's tone suggested that she should be glad he'd let her into his house.

"Master Roydon." The witch's words rasped like the fallen leaves that swirled on the gravel outside. She turned her one good eye on me.

"Help Widow Beaton to her seat, George."

Chapman leaped forward at Matthew's command, while the rest of us remained at a careful distance. The witch groaned as her rheumatic limbs settled into the chair. Matthew politely waited as she did so, then continued.

"Let us get straight to the heart of the matter. This woman"—he indicated me—"is under my protection and has been having difficulties of late." Matthew made no mention of our marriage.

"You are surrounded by influential friends and loyal servants, Master Roydon. A poor woman can be of little use to a gentleman such as you." Widow Beaton tried to hide the reproach in her words with a false note of courtesy, but my husband had excellent hearing. His eyes narrowed.

"Do not play games with me," he said shortly. "You do not want me as an enemy, Widow Beaton. The woman shows signs of being a witch and needs your help."

"A witch?" Widow Beaton looked politely doubtful. "Was her mother a witch? Or her father a wizard?"

"Both died when she was still a child. We are not certain what powers they possessed," Matthew admitted, telling one of his typically vampiric half-truths. He tossed a small bag of coins into her lap. "I would be grateful if you could examine her."

"Very well." Widow Beaton's gnarled fingers reached for my face. When our flesh touched, an unmistakable surge of energy passed between us. The old woman jumped.

"So?" Matthew demanded.

Widow Beaton's hands dropped to her lap. She clutched at the pouch of money, and for a moment it seemed as though she might hurl it back at him. Then she regained her composure.

"It is as I suspected. This woman is no witch, Master Roydon." Her voice was even, though a bit higher than it had been. A wave of contempt rose from my stomach and filled my mouth with bitterness.

"If you think that, you don't have as much power as the people of Woodstock imagine," I retorted.

Widow Beaton drew herself up indignantly. "I am a respected healer, with a knowledge of herbs to protect men and women from illness. Master Roydon knows my abilities."

"That is the craft of a witch. But our people have other talents as well," I said carefully. Matthew's fingers were painfully tight on my hand, urging me to be silent.

"I know of no such talents," was her quick reply. The old woman was as obstinate as my Aunt Sarah and shared her disdain for witches like me who could draw on the elements without any careful study of the witch's craft tradition. Sarah knew the uses of every herb and plant and could remember hundreds of spells perfectly, but there was more to being a witch. Widow Beaton knew that, even if she wouldn't admit it.

"Surely there is some way to determine the extent of this woman's powers beyond a simple touch. Someone with your abilities must know what they are," Matthew said, his lightly mocking tone a clear challenge. Widow Beaton looked uncertain, weighing the pouch in her hand. In the end its heaviness convinced her to rise to the contest. She slipped the payment into a pocket concealed under her skirts.

"There are tests to determine whether someone is a witch. Some rely on the recitation of a prayer. If a creature stumbles over the words, hesitates even for a moment, then it is a sign that the devil is near," she pronounced, adopting a mysterious tone.

"The devil is not abroad in Woodstock, Widow Beaton," Tom said. He sounded like a parent trying to convince a child there wasn't a monster under the bed.

"The devil is everywhere, sir. Those who believe otherwise fall prey to his wiles."

"These are human fables meant to frighten the superstitious and the weak-minded," said Tom dismissively.

"Not now, Tom," Walter muttered.

"There are other signs, too," George said, eager as ever to share his knowledge. "The devil marks a witch as his own with scars and blemishes."

"Indeed, sir," Widow Beaton said, "and wise men know to look for them."

My blood drained from my head in a rush, leaving me dizzy. If anyone were to do so, such marks would be found on me.

"There must be other methods," Henry said uneasily.

"Yes there are, my lord." Widow Beaton's milky eye swept the room. She pointed at the table with its scientific instruments and piles of books. "Join me there."

Widow Beaton's hand slid through the same gap in her skirts that had provided a hiding place for her coins and drew out a battered brass bell. She set it on the table. "Bring a candle, if you please."

Henry quickly obliged, and the men drew around, intrigued.

"Some say a witch's true power comes from being a creature between life and death, light and darkness. At the crossroads of the world, she can undo the work of nature and unravel the ties that bind the order of things." Widow Beaton pulled one of the books into alignment between the candle in its heavy silver holder and the brass bell. Her voice dropped. "When her neighbors discovered a witch in times past, they cast her out of the church by the ringing of a bell to indicate that she was dead." Widow Beaton lifted the bell and set it tolling with a twist of her wrist. She released it, and the bell remained suspended over the table, still chiming. Tom and Kit edged forward, George gasped, and Henry crossed himself. Widow Beaton looked pleased with their reaction and turned her attention to the English translation of a Greek classic, *Euclid's Elements of Geometrie,* which rested on the table with several mathematical instruments from Matthew's extensive collection.

"Then the priest took up a holy book—a Bible—and closed it to show that the witch was denied access to God." The *Elements of Geometrie* snapped shut. George and Tom jumped. The members of the School of Night were surprisingly susceptible for men who considered themselves immune to superstition.

"Finally the priest snuffed out a candle, to signify that the witch had no soul." Widow Beaton's fingers reached into the flame and pinched the wick. The light went out, and a thin plume of gray smoke rose into the air.

The men were mesmerized. Even Matthew looked unsettled. The only sound in the room was the crackle of the fire and the constant, tinny ringing of the bell.

"A true witch can relight the fire, open the pages of the book, and stop the bell from ringing. She is a wonderful creature in the eyes of God." Widow Beaton paused for dramatic effect, and her milky eye rolled in my direction. "Can you perform these acts, girl?"

When modern witches reached the age of thirteen, they were presented to the local coven in a ceremony eerily reminiscent of Widow Beaton's tests. Witches' altar bells rang to welcome the young witch into the community, though they were typically fashioned from heavy silver, polished and passed down from one generation to the next. Instead of a Bible or a book of mathematics, the young witch's family spell book was brought in to lend the weight of history to the occasion. The only time Sarah had allowed the Bishop grimoire out of the house was on my thirteenth birthday. As for the candle, its placement and purpose were the same. It was why young witches practiced igniting and extinguishing candles from an early age.

My official presentation to the Madison coven had been a disaster, one witnessed by all my relatives. Two decades later I still had the odd nightmare about the candle that would not light, the book that refused to open, the bell that rang for every other witch but not for me. "I'm not sure," I confessed hesitantly.

"Try," Matthew encouraged, his voice confident. "You lit some candles a few days ago."

It was true. I had eventually been able to illuminate the jack-o'-lanterns that lined the driveway of the Bishop house on Halloween. There had been no audience to watch my initial bungled attempts, however. Today Kit's and Tom's eyes nudged me expectantly. I could barely feel the brush of Widow Beaton's glance but was all too aware of Matthew's familiar, cool attention. The blood in my veins turned to ice in response, as if refusing to generate the fire that would be required for this bit of witchcraft. Hoping for the best, I concentrated on the candle's wick and muttered the spell.

Nothing happened.

"Relax," Matthew murmured. "What about the book? Should you start there?"

Putting aside the fact that the proper order of things was important in witchcraft, I didn't know where to begin with *Euclid's Elements*. Was I supposed to focus on the air trapped in the fibers of the paper or summon a breeze to lift the cover? It was impossible to think clearly with the incessant ringing.

"Can you please stop the bell?" I implored as my anxiety rose.

Widow Beaton snapped her fingers, and the brass bell dropped to the table. It gave a final clang that set its misshapen edges vibrating, then fell silent.

"It is as I told you, Master Roydon," Widow Beaton said with a note of triumph. "Whatever magic you think you have witnessed, it was nothing but illusions. This woman has no power. The village has nothing to fear from her."

"Perhaps she is trying to trap you, Matthew," Kit chimed in. "I wouldn't put it past her. Women are duplicitous creatures."

Other witches had made the same proclamation as Widow Beaton, and with similar satisfaction. I had a sudden, intense need to prove her wrong and wipe the knowing look from Kit's face.

"I can't light a candle. And no one has been able to teach me how to open a book or stop a bell from ringing. But if I am powerless, how do you explain this?" A bowl of fruit sat nearby. More quinces, freshly picked from the garden, glowed golden in the bleak light. I selected one and balanced it on my palm where everyone could see it.

The skin on my palm tingled as I focused on the fruit nestled there. Its pulpy flesh was clear to me through the quince's tough skin as though the fruit were made of glass. My eyes drifted closed, while my witch's eye opened and began its search for information. Awareness crept from the center of my forehead, down my arm, and through my fingertips. It extended like the roots of a tree, its fibers snaking into the quince.

One by one I took hold of the fruit's secrets. There was a worm at its core, munching its way through the soft flesh. My attention was caught by the power trapped there, and warmth tingled across my tongue in a taste of sunshine. The skin between my brows fluttered with pleasure as I drank in the light of the invisible sun. *So much power,* I thought. *Life. Death.* My audience faded into insignificance. The only thing that mattered now was the limitless possibility for knowledge resting in my hand.

The sun responded to some silent invitation and left the quince, traveling into my fingers. Instinctively I tried to resist the approaching sunlight and keep it where it belonged—in the fruit—but the quince turned brown, shriveling and sinking into itself.

Widow Beaton gasped, breaking my concentration. Startled, I dropped the misshapen fruit to the floor. where it splattered against the polished wood. When I looked up, Henry was crossing himself again, shock evident in the force of his stare and the slow, automatic movements of his hand. Tom and Walter were focused on my fingers instead, where minuscule strands of sunlight were making a futile attempt to mend the broken connection with the quince. Matthew enfolded my sputtering hands in his, obscuring the signs of my undisciplined power. My hands were still sparking, and I tried to pull away so as not to scorch him. He shook his head, hands steady, and met my eyes as though to say he was strong enough to absorb whatever magic might come his way. After a moment of hesitation, my body relaxed into his.

"It's over. No more," he said emphatically.

"I can *taste* sunlight, Matthew." My voice was sharp with panic. "I can *see* time, waiting in the corners."

"That woman has bewitched a *wearh*. This is the devil's work," Widow Beaton hissed. She was backing carefully away, her fingers forked to ward off danger.

"There is no devil in Woodstock," Tom repeated firmly.

"You have books full of strange sigils and magical incantations," Widow Beaton said, gesturing at *Euclid's Elements*. It was, I thought, a very good thing that she hadn't overheard Kit reading aloud from *Doctor Faustus*.

"That is mathematics, not magic," protested Tom.

"Call it what you will, but I have seen the truth. You are just like them, and called me here to draw me into your dark plans."

"Just like whom?" Matthew asked sharply.

"The scholars from the university. They drove two witches from Duns Tew with their questions. They wanted our knowledge but condemned the women who shared it. And a coven was just beginning to form in Faringdon, but the witches scattered when they caught the attention of men like you." A coven meant safety, protection, community. Without a coven a witch was far more vulnerable to the jealousy and fear of her neighbors.

"No one is trying to force you from Woodstock." I only meant to soothe her, but a single step in her direction sent her retreating further.

"There is evil in this house. Everyone in the village knows it. Yesterday Mr. Danforth preached to the congregation about the danger of letting it take root."

"I am alone, a witch like you, without family to help me," I said, trying to appeal to her sympathy. "Take pity on me before anyone else discovers what I am."

"You are not like me, and I want no trouble. None will give me pity when the village is baying for blood. I have no *wearh* to protect me, and no lords and court gentlemen will step forward to defend my honor."

"Matthew—Master Roydon—will not let any harm come to you." My hand rose in a pledge.

Widow Beaton was incredulous. "*Wearhs* cannot be trusted. What would the village do if they found out what Matthew Roydon really is?"

"This matter is between us, Widow Beaton," I warned.

"Where are you from, girl, that you believe one witch will shelter another? It is a dangerous world. None of us are safe any longer." The old woman looked at Matthew with hatred. "Witches are dying in the thousands, and the cowards of the Congregation do nothing. Why is that, *wearh?*"

"That's enough," Matthew said coldly. "Françoise, please show Widow Beaton out."

"I'll leave, and gladly." The old woman drew herself as straight as her gnarled bones would allow. "But mark my words, Matthew Roydon. Every creature within a day's journey suspects that you are a foul beast who feeds on blood. When they discover you are harboring a witch with these dark powers, God will be merciless on those who have turned against Him."

"Farewell, Widow Beaton." Matthew turned his back on the witch, but Widow Beaton was determined to have the last word.

"Take care, sister," Widow Beaton called as she departed. "You shine too brightly for these times."

Every eye in the room was on me. I shifted, uncomfortable from the attention.

"Explain yourself," Walter said curtly.

"Diana owes you no explanation," Matthew shot back.

Walter raised his hand in silent truce.

"What happened?" Matthew asked in a more measured tone. Apparently I owed *him* one.

"Exactly what I predicted: We've frightened off Widow Beaton. She'll do everything she can to distance herself from me now."

"She should have been biddable. I've done the woman plenty of favors," Matthew muttered.

"Why didn't you tell her who I was to you?" I asked quietly.

"Probably for the same reason you didn't tell me what you could do to ordinary fruit from the garden," he retorted, taking me by the elbow. Matthew turned to his friends. "I need to speak to my wife. Alone." He steered me outside.

"So now I'm your wife again!" I exclaimed, wrenching my elbow from his grip.

"You never stopped being my wife. But not everybody needs to know the details of our private life. Now, what happened in there?" he demanded, standing by one of the neatly clipped knots of boxwood in the garden.

"You were right before: My magic is changing." I looked away. "Something like it happened earlier to the flowers in our bedroom. When I rearranged them, I tasted the soil and air that made them grow. The flowers died at my touch. I tried to make the sunlight return to the fruit. But it wouldn't obey me."

"Widow Beaton's behavior should have unleashed witchwind because you felt trapped, or witchfire because you were in danger. Perhaps time-walking damaged your magic," Matthew suggested with a frown.

I bit my lip. "I should never have lost my temper and shown her what I could do."

"She knew you were powerful. The smell of her fear filled the room." His eyes were grave. "Perhaps it was too soon to put you in front of a stranger."

But it was too late now.

The School of Night appeared at the windows, their pale faces pressing against the glass like stars in a nameless constellation.

"The damp will ruin her gown, Matthew, and it's the only one that looks decent on her," George scolded, sticking his head out of the casement. Tom's elfin face peeked around George's shoulder.

"I enjoyed myself immensely!" Kit shouted, flinging open another window with so much force the panes rattled. "That hag is the perfect witch. I shall put Widow Beaton in one of my plays. Did you ever imagine she could do that with an old bell?"

"Your past history with witches has not been forgotten, Matthew," Walter said, his feet crunching across the gravel as he and Henry joined us outside. "She will talk. Women like Widow Beaton always do."

"If she speaks out against you, Matt, is there a reason for concern?" Henry inquired gently.

"We're creatures, Hal, in a human world. There's always reason for concern," Matthew said grimly.

5

The School of Night might debate philosophy, but on one point they were agreed: A witch would still have to be found. Matthew dispatched George and Kit to make inquiries in Oxford, as well as to ask after our mysterious alchemical manuscript.

After supper on Thursday evening, we took our places around the hearth in the great hall. Henry and Tom read and argued about astronomy or mathematics. Walter and Kit played dice at a long table, trading ideas about their latest literary projects. I was reading aloud from Walter's copy of *The Faerie Queene* to practice my accent and enjoying it no more than I did most Elizabethan romances.

"The beginning is too abrupt, Kit. You'll frighten the audience so badly they'll leave the playhouse before the second scene," Walter protested. "It needs more adventure." They had been dissecting *Doctor Faustus* for hours. Thanks to Widow Beaton, it had a new opening.

"You are not my Faustus, Walt, for all your intellectual pretentions," Kit said sharply. "Look what your meddling did to Edmund's story. *The Faerie Queene* was a perfectly enjoyable tale about King Arthur. Now it's a calamitous blend of Malory and Virgil, it wends on and on, and Gloriana—please. The queen is nearly as old as Widow Beaton and just as crotchety. It will astonish me if Edmund finishes it, with you telling him what to do all the time. If you want to be immortalized on the boards, talk to Will. He's always hard up for ideas."

"Is that agreeable to you, Matthew?" George prompted. He was updating us on his search for the manuscript that would one day be known as Ashmole 782.

"I'm sorry, George. Did you say something?" There was a flash of guilt in Matthew's distracted gray eyes. I knew the signs of mental multitasking. It had gotten me through many a faculty meeting. His thoughts were probably divided among the conversations in the room, his ongoing review of what went awry with Widow Beaton, and the contents of the mailbags that continued to arrive.

"None of the booksellers have heard of a rare alchemical work circulating in the city. I asked a friend at Christ Church, and he too knows nothing. Shall I keep asking for it?"

Matthew opened his mouth to respond, but a crash sounded in the front hallway as the heavy front door flew open. He was on his feet in an instant. Walter and Henry jumped up and scrabbled for their daggers, which they'd taken to wearing morning, noon, and night.

"Matthew?" boomed an unfamiliar voice with a timbre that instinctively raised the hairs on my arms. It was too clear and musical to be human. "Are you here, man?"

"Of course he's here," someone else replied, his voice lilting in the cadence of a Welsh native. "Use your nose. Who else smells like a grocer's shop the day fresh spices arrive from the docks?"

Moments later two bulky figures swathed in rough brown cloaks appeared at the other end of the room, where Kit and George still sat with their dice and books. In my own time, professional football teams would have recruited the new arrivals. They had overdeveloped arms with prominent tendons, enlarged wrists, thickly muscled legs, and brawny shoulders. As the men drew closer, light from the candles caught their bright eyes and danced off the honed edges of their weapons. One was a blond giant an inch taller than Matthew; the other was a redhead a good six inches shorter with a decided squint to his left eye. Neither could be more than thirty. The blond was relieved, though he hid it quickly. The redhead was furious and didn't care who knew it.

"There you are. You gave us a fright, disappearing without leaving word," the blond man said mildly, drawing to a stop and sheathing his long, exceedingly sharp sword.

Walter and Henry, too, withdrew their weapons. They recognized the men.

"Gallowglass. Why are you here?" Matthew asked the blond warrior with a note of wary confusion.

"We're looking for you, of course. Hancock and I were with you on Saturday." Gallowglass's chilly blue eyes narrowed when he didn't receive a reply. He looked like a Viking on the brink of a killing spree. "In Chester."

"Chester." Matthew's expression turned to dawning horror. "Chester!"

"Aye. Chester," repeated the redheaded Hancock. He glowered and peeled sodden leather gauntlets from his arms, tossing them onto the floor near the fireplace. "When you didn't meet up with us as planned on Sunday, we made inquiries. The innkeeper told us you'd left, which came as something of a surprise, and not only because you hadn't settled the bill."

"He said you were sitting by the fire drinking wine one moment and gone the next," Gallowglass reported. "The maid—the little one with the black hair who couldn't take her eyes off you—caused quite a stir. She insisted you were taken by ghosts."

I closed my eyes in sudden understanding. The Matthew Roydon who had been in sixteenth-century Chester vanished because he was displaced by the Matthew who'd traveled here from modern-day Oxfordshire. When we left, the sixteenth-century Matthew, presumably, would reappear. Time wouldn't allow both Matthews to be in the same place at the same moment. We had already altered history without intending to do so.

"It was All Hallows' Eve, so her story made a certain sort of sense," Hancock conceded, turning his attention to his cloak. He shook the water from its folds and flung it over a nearby chair, releasing the scent of spring grass into the winter air.

"Who are these men, Matthew?" I moved closer to get a better look at the pair. He turned and settled his hands on my upper arms, keeping me where I was.

"They're friends," Matthew said, but his obvious effort to regroup made me wonder if he was telling the truth.

"Well, well. She's no ghost." Hancock peered over Matthew's shoulder, and my flesh turned to ice.

Of course Hancock and Gallowglass were vampires. What other creatures could be that big and bloody-looking?

"Nor is she from Chester," Gallowglass said thoughtfully. "Does she always have such a bright *glaem* about her?"

The word might be unfamiliar, but its meaning was clear enough. I was shimmering again. It sometimes happened when I was angry, or concentrating on a problem. It was another familiar manifestation of a witch's power, and vampires could detect the pale glow with their preternaturally sharp eyes. Feeling conspicuous, I stepped back into Matthew's shadow.

"That's not going to help, lady. Our ears are as sharp as our eyes. Your witch's blood is trilling like a bird." Hancock's bushy red brows rose as he looked sourly at his companion. "Trouble always travels in the company of women."

"Trouble is no fool. Given the choice, I'd rather travel with a woman than with you." The blond warrior addressed Matthew. "It's been a long day, Hancock's arse is sore, and he's hungry. If you don't tell him why there's a witch in your house, and quickly, I don't have high hopes for her continued safety."

"It must have to do with Berwick," Hancock declared. "Bloody witches. Always causing trouble."

"Berwick?" My pulse kicked up a notch. I recognized the name. One of the most notorious witch trials in the British Isles was connected to it. I searched my memory for the dates. Surely it had happened well before or after 1590, or Matthew wouldn't have selected this moment for our time-walk. But Hancock's next words drove all thoughts of chronology and history from my mind.

"That, or some new Congregation business that Matthew will want us to sort out for him."

"The Congregation?" Marlowe's eyes narrowed, and he looked at Matthew appraisingly. "Is this true? Are you one of the mysterious members?"

"Of course it's true! How do you imagine he's kept you from the noose, young Marlowe?" Hancock searched the room. "Is there something to drink other than wine? I hate these French pretensions of yours, de Clermont. What's wrong with ale?"

"Not now, Davy," Gallowglass murmured to his friend, though his eyes were fixed on Matthew.

My eyes were fixed on him, too, as an awful sense of clarity settled over me.

"Tell me you're not," I whispered. "Tell me you didn't keep this from me."

"I can't tell you that," Matthew said flatly. "I promised you secrets but no lies, remember?"

I felt sick. In 1590, Matthew was a member of the Congregation, and the Congregation was our enemy.

"And Berwick? You told me there was no danger of being caught up in a witch-hunt."

"Nothing in Berwick will affect us here," Matthew assured me.

"What has happened in Berwick?" Walter asked, uneasy.

"Before we left Chester, there was news out of Scotland. A great gathering of witches met in a village east of Edinburgh on All Hallows' Eve," Hancock said. "There was talk again of the storm the Danish witches raised this past summer, and the spouts of seawater that foretold the coming of a creature with fearsome powers."

"The authorities have rounded up dozens of the poor wretches," Gallowglass continued, his arctic-blue eyes still on Matthew. "The cunning woman in the town of Keith, Widow Sampson, is awaiting the king's questioning in the dungeons of Holyrood Palace. Who knows how many will join her there before this business is done?"

"The king's torture, you mean," Hancock muttered. "They say the woman has been locked into a witch's bridle so she cannot utter more charms against His Majesty, and chained to the wall without food or drink."

I sat down abruptly.

"Is this one of the accused, then?" Gallowglass asked Matthew. "And I'd like the witch's bargain, too, if I may: secrets, but no lies."

There was a long silence before Matthew answered. "Diana is my wife, Gallowglass."

"You abandoned us in Chester for a *woman?*" Hancock was horrified. "But we had work to do!"

"You have an unerring ability to grab the wrong end of the staff, Davy." Gallowglass's glance shifted to me. "Your *wife?*" he said carefully. "So this is just a legal arrangement to satisfy curious humans and justify her presence here while the Congregation decides her future?"

"Not just my wife," Matthew admitted. "She's my mate, too." A vampire mated for life when compelled to do so by an instinctive combination of affection, affinity, lust, and chemistry. The resulting bond was breakable only by death. Vampires might marry multiple times, but most mated just once.

Gallowglass swore, though the sound of it was almost drowned out by his friend's amusement.

"And His Holiness proclaimed the age of miracles had passed," Hancock crowed. "Matthew de Clermont is mated at last. But no ordinary, placid human or properly schooled female *wearh* who knows her place would do. Not for our Matthew. Now that he's decided at last to settle down with one woman, it had to be a witch. We have more to worry about than the good people of Woodstock, then."

"What's wrong in Woodstock?" I asked Matthew with a frown.

"Nothing," Matthew said breezily. But it was the hulking blond who held my attention.

"Some old besom went into fits on market day. She's blaming it on you." Gallowglass studied me from head to toe as if trying to imagine how someone so unprepossessing had caused so much trouble.

"Widow Beaton," I said breathlessly.

The appearance of Françoise and Charles forestalled further conversation. Françoise had fragrant gingerbread and spiced wine for the warm-bloods. Kit (who was never reluctant to sample the contents of Matthew's cellar) and George (who was looking a bit green after the evening's revelations) helped themselves. Both had the air of audience members waiting for the next act to start.

Charles, whose task it was to sustain the vampires, had a delicate pitcher with silver handles and three tall glass beakers. The red liquid within was darker and more opaque than any wine. Hancock stopped Charles on his way to the head of the household.

"I need something to drink more than Matthew does," he said, grabbing a beaker while Charles gasped at the affront. Hancock sniffed the pitcher's contents and took that, too. "I haven't had fresh blood for three days. You have odd taste in women, de Clermont, but no one can criticize your hospitality."

Matthew motioned Charles in the direction of Gallowglass, who also drank thirstily. When Gallowglass took his final draft, he wiped his hand across his mouth.

"Well?" he demanded. "You're tight-lipped, I know, but some explanation as to how you let yourself get into this seems in order."

"This would be better discussed in private," said Walter, eyeing George and the two daemons.

"Why is that, Raleigh?" Hancock's voice took on a pugnacious edge. "De Clermont has a lot to answer for. So does his witch. And those answers had best trip off her tongue. We passed a priest on the way. He was with two gentlemen who had prosperous waistlines. Based on what I heard, de Clermont's mate will have three days—"

"At least five," Gallowglass corrected.

"Maybe five," Hancock said, inclining his head in his companion's direction, "before she's held over for trial, two days to figure out what to say to the magistrates, and less than half an hour to come up with a convincing lie for the good father. You had best start telling us the truth."

All attention settled on Matthew, who stood mute.

"The clock will strike the quarter hour soon," Hancock reminded him after some time had passed.

I took matters into my own hands. "Matthew protected me from my own people."

"Diana," Matthew growled.

"*Matthew* meddled in the affairs of witches?" Gallowglass's eyes widened slightly.

I nodded. "Once the danger passed, we were mated."

"And all this happened between noon and nightfall on Saturday?" Gallowglass shook his head. "You're going to have to do better than that, Auntie."

"'Auntie'?" I turned to Matthew in shock. First Berwick, then the Congregation, and now this. "This . . . berserker is your nephew? Let me guess. He's Baldwin's son!" Gallowglass was almost as muscle-bound as Matthew's copper-headed brother—and as persistent. There were other de Clermonts I knew: Godfrey, Louisa, and Hugh (who received only brief, cryptic mentions). Gallowglass could belong to any of them—or to someone else on Matthew's convoluted family tree.

"Baldwin?" Gallowglass gave a delicate shiver. "Even before I became a *wearh,* I knew better than to let that monster near my neck. Hugh de Clermont was my father. For your information, my people were Úlfhéðnar, not berserkers. And I'm only part Norse—the gentle part, if you must know. The rest is Scots, by way of Ireland."

"Foul-tempered, the Scots," Hancock added.

Gallowglass acknowledged his companion's remark with a gentle tug on his ear. A golden ring glinted in the light, incised with the outlines of a coffin. A man was stepping free of it, and there was a motto around the edges.

"You're knights." I looked for a matching ring on Hancock's finger. There it was, oddly placed on his thumb. Here at last was evidence that Matthew was involved in the business of the Order of Lazarus, too.

"We-elll," Gallowglass drawled, sounding suddenly like the Scot he professed to be, "there's always been a dispute about that. We're not really the shining-armor type, are we Davy?"

"No. But the de Clermonts have deep pockets. Money like that is hard to refuse," Hancock observed, "especially when they promise you a long life for the enjoying of it."

"They're fierce fighters, too." Gallowglass rubbed the bridge of his nose again. It was flattened, as though it had been broken and never healed properly.

"Oh, aye. The bastards killed me before they saved me. Fixed my bad eye, while they were at it," Hancock said cheerfully, pointing to his gammy lid.

"Then you're loyal to the de Clermonts." Sudden relief washed through me. I would prefer to have Gallowglass and Hancock as allies rather than enemies, given the disaster unfolding.

"Not always," replied Gallowglass darkly.

"Not to Baldwin. He's a sly bugger. And when Matthew behaves like a fool, we pay no attention to him either." Hancock sniffed and pointed to the gingerbread, which lay forgotten on the table. "Is someone going to eat that, or can we pitch it into the fire? Between Matthew's scent and Charles's cooking, I feel ill."

"Given our approaching visitors, our time would be better spent devising a course of action than talking about family history," Walter said impatiently.

"*Jesu,* there's no time to come up with a plan," Hancock said cheerfully. "Matthew and his lordship should say a prayer instead. They're men of God. Maybe He's listening."

"Perhaps the witch could fly away," Gallowglass murmured. He held up both hands in mute surrender when Matthew glared at him.

"Oh, but she can't." All eyes turned to Marlowe. "She can't even conjure Matthew a beard."

"You've taken up with a witch, against all the Congregation's strictures, and she's *worthless?*" It was impossible to tell if Gallowglass was more indignant or incredulous. "A wife who can summon a storm or give your enemy a horrible skin affliction has certain advantages, I grant you. But what good is a witch who can't even serve as her husband's barber?"

"Only Matthew would wed a witch from God-knows-where with no sorcery to speak of," Hancock muttered to Walter.

"Quiet, all of you!" Matthew exploded. "I can't think for all the senseless chatter. It's not Diana's fault that Widow Beaton is a meddling old fool or that she can't perform magic on command. My wife was spellbound. And there's an end to it. If one more person in this room questions me or criticizes Diana, I'll rip your heart out and feed it to you while it still beats."

"There is our lord and master," Hancock said with a mocking salute. "For a minute I was afraid *you* were the one who was bewitched. Hang on, though. If she's spellbound, what's wrong with her? Is she dangerous? Mad? Both?"

Unnerved by the influx of nephews, agitated parsons, and the trouble brewing in Woodstock, I reached behind me for the chair. With my reach restricted by the unfamiliar clothes, I lost my balance and began to fall.

A rough hand shot out and gripped me by the elbow, lowering me to the seat with surprising gentleness.

"It's all right, Auntie." Gallowglass made a soft noise of sympathy. "I'm not sure what's amiss in your head, but Matthew will take care of you. He has a warm spot in his heart for lost souls, bless him."

"I'm dizzy, not deranged," I retorted.

Gallowglass's eyes were flinty as his mouth approached my ear. "Your speech is disordered enough to stand for madness, and I doubt the priest cares one way or the other. Given that you aren't from Chester or anywhere else I've been—and that's a fair number of places, Auntie—you might want to mind your manners unless you want to find yourself locked in the church crypt."

Long fingers clamped around Gallowglass's shoulder and pulled him away. "If you're quite finished trying to frighten my wife—a pointless exercise, I assure you—you might tell me about the men you passed," Matthew said frostily. "Were they armed?"

"No." After a long, interested look at me, Gallowglass turned toward his uncle.

"And who was with the minister?"

"How the hell should we know, Matthew? All three were warmbloods and not worth a second thought. One was fat and gray-haired, the other was medium size and complained about the weather," Gallowglass said impatiently.

"Bidwell," Matthew and Walter said at the same moment.

"It's probably Iffley with him," remarked Walter. "The two of them are always complaining—about the state of the roads, the noise at the inn, the quality of the beer."

"Who's Iffley?" I wondered aloud.

"A man who fancies himself the finest glover in all England. Somers works for him," Walter replied.

"Master Iffley does craft the queen's gloves," George acknowledged.

"He made her a single pair of hunting gauntlets two decades ago. That's hardly enough to make Iffley the most important man for thirty miles, dearly as he might covet the honor." Matthew snorted contemptuously. "Singly none of them are terribly bright. Together they're downright foolish. If that's the best the village can do, we can return to our reading."

"That's it?" Walter's voice was brittle. "We sit and let them come to us?"

"Yes. But Diana doesn't leave my sight—or yours, Gallowglass," Matthew warned.

"You don't have to remind me of my family duty, Uncle. I'll be sure your feisty wife makes it to your bed tonight."

"Feisty, am I? My husband is a member of the Congregation. A posse of men is coming on horseback to accuse me of harming a friendless old woman. I'm in a strange place and keep getting lost on my way to the bedroom. I still have no shoes. And I'm living in a dormitory full of adolescent boys who never stop talking!" I fumed. "But you needn't trouble yourself on my account. I can take care of myself!"

"Take care of yourself?" Gallowglass laughed at me and shook his head. "No you can't. And when the fighting's done, we'll need to see to that accent of yours. I didn't understand half of what you just said."

"She must be Irish," Hancock said, glaring at me. "That would explain the spellbinding and the disordered speech. The whole lot of them are mad."

"She's not Irish," Gallowglass said. "Mad or no, I would have understood her accent if that were the case."

"Quiet!" Matthew bellowed.

"The men from the village are at the gatehouse," Pierre announced in the ensuing silence.

"Go and fetch them," Matthew ordered. He turned his attention to me. "Let me do the talking. Don't answer their questions unless and until I tell you to do so. Now," he continued briskly, "we can't afford to have anything . . . unusual happen tonight as it did when Widow Beaton was here. Are you still dizzy? Do you need to lie down?"

"Curious. I'm curious," I said, hands clenched. "Don't worry about my magic or my health. Worry about how many hours it's going to take you to answer my questions after the minister is gone. And if you try to wiggle out of them with the excuse that 'it's not my tale to tell,' I'll flatten you."

"You are perfectly fine, then." Matthew's mouth twitched. He dropped a kiss on my forehead. "I love you, *ma lionne.*"

"You might reserve your professions of love until later and give Auntie a chance to compose herself," Gallowglass suggested.

"Why does everyone feel compelled to tell me how to manage my own wife?" Matthew shot back. The cracks in his composure were starting to show.

"I really couldn't say," Gallowglass replied serenely. "She reminds me a bit of Granny, though. We give Philippe advice morning, noon, and night about how best to control her. Not that he listens."

The men arranged themselves around the room. The apparent randomness of their positions created a human funnel—wider at the entrance to the room, narrower at the fireside where Matthew and I sat. As George and Kit would be the first to greet the man of God and his companions, Walter whisked away their dice and the manuscript of *Doctor Faustus* in favor of a copy of Herodotus's *Histories*. Though it was not a Bible, Raleigh assured us it would lend proper gravitas to the situation. Kit was still protesting the unfairness of the substitution when footsteps and voices sounded.

Pierre ushered the three men inside. One so strongly resembled the reedy young man who had measured me for shoes that I knew at once he was Joseph Bidwell. He started at the sound of the door closing behind him and looked uneasily over his shoulder. When his bleary eyes faced forward again and he saw the size of the assembly awaiting him, he jumped once more. Walter, who occupied a position of strategic importance in the middle of the room with Hancock and Henry, ignored the nervous shoemaker and cast a look of disdain at a man in a bedraggled religious habit.

"What brings you here on such a night, Mr. Danforth?" Raleigh demanded.

"Sir Walter," Danforth said with a bow, taking a cap from his head and twisting it between his fingers. He spotted the Earl of Northumberland. "My lord! I did not know you were still amongst us."

"Is there something you need?" Matthew asked pleasantly. He remained seated, legs stretched out in apparent relaxation.

"Ah. Master Roydon." Danforth made another bow, this one directed at us. He gave me a curious look before fear overtook him and redirected his eyes to his hat. "We have not seen you in church or in town. Bidwell thought you might be indisposed."

Bidwell shifted on his feet. The leather boots he wore squelched and complained, and the man's lungs joined in the chorus with wheezes and a barking cough. A wilted ruff constricted his windpipe and quivered every time he tried to draw breath. Its pleated linen was distinctly the worse for wear, and a greasy brown spot near his chin suggested he'd had gravy with supper.

"Yes, I was taken sick in Chester, but it has passed with God's grace and thanks to my wife's care." Matthew reached out and clasped my hand with husbandly devotion. "My physician thought it would be best if my hair were shorn to rid me of the fever, but it was Diana's insistence on cool baths that made the difference."

"Wife?" Danforth said faintly. "Widow Beaton did not tell me—"

"I do not share my private affairs with ignorant women," Matthew said sharply.

Bidwell sneezed. Matthew examined him first with concern, then with a carefully managed look of dawning understanding. I was learning a great deal about my husband this evening, including the fact that he could be a surprisingly good actor.

"Oh. But of course you are here to ask Diana to cure Bidwell." Matthew made a sound of regret. "There is so much idle gossip. Has the news of my wife's skill spread already?"

In this period medicinal knowledge was perilously close to a witch's lore. Was Matthew *trying* to get me in trouble?

Bidwell wanted to respond, but all he could manage was a gurgle and a shake of his head.

"If you are not here for physic, then you must be here to deliver Diana's shoes." Matthew looked at me fondly, then to the minister. "As you have no doubt heard, my wife's possessions were lost during our journey, Mr. Danforth." Matthew's attention returned to the shoemaker, and a shade of reproach crept into his tone. "I know you are a busy man, Bidwell, but I hope you've finished the pattens at least. Diana is determined to go to church this week, and the path to the vestry is often flooded. Someone really should see to it."

Iffley's chest had been swelling with indignation since Matthew had started speaking. Finally the man could stand it no more.

"Bidwell brought the shoes you paid for, but we are not here to secure your wife's services or trifle with pattens and puddles!" Iffley drew his cloak around his hips in a gesture that was intended to convey dignity, but the soaked wool only emphasized his resemblance to a drowned rat, with his pointy nose and beady eyes. "Tell her, Mr. Danforth."

The Reverend Danforth looked as though he would rather be roasting in hell than standing in Matthew Roydon's house, confronting his wife.

"Go on. Tell her," urged Iffley.

"Allegations have been made—" That was as far as Danforth got before Walter, Henry, and Hancock closed ranks.

"If you are here to make allegations, sir, you can direct them to me or to his lordship," Walter said sharply.

"Or to me," George piped up. "I am well read in the law."

"Ah . . . Er . . . Yes . . . Well . . ." The cleric subsided into silence.

"Widow Beaton has fallen ill. So has young Bidwell," said Iffley, determined to forge on in spite of Danforth's failing nerve.

"No doubt it is the same ague that afflicted me and now the boy's father," my husband said softly. His fingers tightened on mine. Behind me Gallowglass swore under his breath. "Of what, exactly, are you accusing my wife, Iffley?"

"Widow Beaton refused to join her in some evil business. Mistress Roydon vowed to afflict her joints and head with pains."

"My son has lost his hearing," Bidwell complained, his voice thick with misery and phlegm. "There is a fierce ringing in his ears, like unto the sound of a bell. Widow Beaton says he has been bewitched."

"No," I whispered. The blood left my head in a sudden, startling drop. Gallowglass's hands were on my shoulders in an instant, keeping me upright.

The word "*bewitched*" had me staring into a familiar abyss. My greatest fear had always been that humans would discover I was descended from Bridget Bishop. Then the curious glances would start, and the suspicions. The only possible response was flight. I tried to worm my fingers from Matthew's grasp, but he might have been made of stone for all the good it did me, and Gallowglass still had charge of my shoulders.

"Widow Beaton has long suffered from rheumatism, and Bidwell's son has recurrent putrid throats. They often cause pain and deafness. These illnesses occurred before my wife came to Woodstock." Matthew made a lazy, dismissive gesture with his free hand. "The old woman is jealous of Diana's skill, and young Joseph was taken with her beauty and envious of my married state. These are not allegations, but idle imaginings."

"As a man of God, Master Roydon, it is my responsibility to take them seriously. I have been reading." Mr. Danforth reached into his black robes and pulled out a tattered sheaf of papers. It was no more than a few dozen sheets crudely stitched together with coarse string. Time and heavy use had softened the papers' fibers, fraying the edges and turning the pages gray. I was too far away to make out the title page. All three vampires saw it, though. So did George, who blanched.

"That's part of the *Malleus Maleficarum*. I did not know that your Latin was good enough to comprehend such a difficult work, Mr. Danforth,"

Matthew said. It was the most influential witch-hunting manual ever produced, and a title that struck terror into a witch's heart.

The minister looked affronted. "I attended university, Master Roydon."

"I'm relieved to hear it. That book shouldn't be in the possession of the weak-minded or superstitious."

"You know it?" Danforth asked.

"I, too, attended university," Matthew replied mildly.

"Then you understand why I must question this woman." Danforth attempted to advance into the room. Hancock's low growl brought him to a standstill.

"My wife has no difficulties with her hearing. You needn't come closer."

"I told you Mistress Roydon has unnatural powers!" Iffley said triumphantly.

Danforth gripped his book. "Who taught you these things, Mistress Roydon?" he called down the echoing expanse of the hall. "From whom did you learn your witchcraft?"

This was how the madness began: with questions designed to trap the accused into condemning other creatures. One life at a time, witches were caught up in the web of lies and destroyed. Thousands of my people had been tortured and killed thanks to such tactics. Denials burbled up into my throat.

"Don't." Matthew's single word of warning was uttered in an icy murmur.

"Strange things are happening in Woodstock. A white stag crossed Widow Beaton's path," Danforth continued. "It stopped in the road and stared until her flesh turned cold. Last night a gray wolf was seen outside her house. Its eyes glowed in the darkness, brighter than the lamps that were hung out to help travelers find shelter in the storm. Which of these creatures is your familiar? Who gifted you with it?" Matthew didn't need to tell me to keep silent this time. The priest's questions were following a well-known pattern, one I had studied in graduate school.

"The witch must answer your questions, Mr. Danforth," Iffley insisted, pulling at his companion's sleeve. "Such insolence from a creature of darkness cannot be allowed in a godly community."

"My wife speaks to no one without my consent," said Matthew. "And mind whom you call witch, Iffley." The more the villagers challenged him, the harder it was for Matthew to restrain himself.

The minister's eyes traveled from me to Matthew and back again. I stifled a whimper.

"Her agreement with the devil makes it impossible for her to speak the truth," Bidwell said.

"Hush, Master Bidwell," Danforth chided. "What do you wish to say, my child? Who introduced you to the devil? Was it another woman?"

"Or man," Iffley said under his breath. "Mistress Roydon is not the only child of darkness to be found here. There are strange books and instruments, and midnight gatherings are held to conjure spirits."

Harriot sighed and thrust his book at Danforth. "Mathematics, sir, not magic. Widow Beaton spotted a geometry text."

"It is not your place to determine the extent of the evil here," Iffley sputtered.

"If it's evil you're seeking, look for it at Widow Beaton's." Though he'd done his best to remain calm, Matthew was rapidly losing his temper.

"Do you accuse her of witchcraft, then?" Danforth asked sharply.

"No, Matthew. Not that way," I whispered, tugging on his hand to gain his attention.

Matthew turned to me. His face looked inhuman, his pupils glassy and enormous. I shook my head, and he took a deep breath, trying to calm both his fury at the invasion of his home and his fierce instinct to protect me.

"Stop your ears against his words, Mr. Danforth. Roydon might be an instrument of the devil, too," Iffley warned.

Matthew faced the delegation. "If you have reason to charge my wife with some offense, find a magistrate and do so. Otherwise get out. And before you return, Danforth, consider whether aligning with Iffley and Bidwell is a wise course of action."

The parson gulped.

"You heard him," Hancock barked. "Out!"

"Justice will be served, Master Roydon—God's justice," Danforth proclaimed as he backed out of the room.

"Only if my version doesn't resolve the matter first, Danforth," Walter promised.

Pierre and Charles materialized from the shadows, throwing open the doors to shepherd the wide-eyed warmbloods from the room. Outside, it was blowing a gale. The fierceness of the waiting storm would only confirm their suspicions about my supernatural powers.

*Out, out, out!* called an insistent voice in my head. Panic flooded my system with adrenaline. I had been reduced to prey once more. Gallowglass and Hancock turned toward me, intrigued by the scent of fear seeping from my pores.

"Stay where you are," Matthew warned the vampires. He crouched before me. "Diana's instincts are telling her to flee. She'll be fine in a moment."

"This is never going to end. We came for help, but even here I'm hunted." I bit my lip.

"There's nothing to fear. Danforth and Iffley will think twice before causing any more trouble," Matthew said firmly, taking my clasped hands in his. "No one wants me for an enemy—not other creatures, not the humans."

"I understand why the creatures might fear you. You're a member of the Congregation and have the power destroy them. No wonder Widow Beaton came here when you commanded. But that doesn't explain this human reaction to you. Danforth and Iffley must suspect that you're a . . . *wearh*." I caught myself just before the word "vampire" spilled out.

"Oh, he's in no danger from them," said Hancock dismissively. "These men are nobodies. Unfortunately, they're likely to bring this business to the attention of humans who *do* matter."

"Ignore him," Matthew told me.

"Which humans?" I whispered.

Gallowglass gasped. "By all that is holy, Matthew. I've seen you do terrible things, but how could you keep *this* from your wife, too?"

Matthew looked into the fire. When his eyes finally met mine, they were filled with regret.

"Matthew?" I prompted. The knot that had been forming in my stomach since the arrival of the first bag of mail tightened further.

"They don't think I'm a vampire. They know I'm a spy."

6

"A spy?" I repeated numbly.

"We prefer to be called intelligencers," Kit said tartly.

"Shut it, Marlowe," Hancock growled, "or I'll stop that mouth for you."

"Spare us, Hancock. No one takes you seriously when you sputter like that." Marlowe's chin jutted into the room. "And if you don't keep a civil tongue with me, there will soon be an end to all these Welsh kings and soldiers on the stage. I'll make you all traitors and servants with low cunning."

"What is a vampire?" George asked, reaching for his notebook with one hand and a piece of gingerbread with the other. As usual, no one was paying much attention to him.

"So you're some kind of Elizabethan James Bond? But . . ." I looked at Marlowe, horrified. He would be murdered in a knife fight in Deptford before he reached the age of thirty, and the crime would be linked to his life as a spy.

"The London hatmaker near St. Dunstan's who turns such a neat brim? That James Bond?" George chuckled. "Whyever would you think Matthew was a hatmaker, Mistress Roydon?"

"No, George, not that James Bond." Matthew remained crouched before me, watching my reactions. "You were better off not knowing about this."

"Bullshit." I neither knew nor cared if this was an appropriately Elizabethan oath. "I deserve the truth."

"Perhaps, Mistress Roydon, but if you truly love him, it is pointless to insist upon it," Marlowe said. "Matthew can no longer distinguish between what is true and what is not. This is why he is invaluable to Her Majesty."

"We're here to find you a teacher," Matthew insisted, his eyes locked on me. "The fact that I am both a member of the Congregation and the queen's agent will keep you from harm. Nothing happens in the country without my being aware of it."

"For someone who claims to know everything, you were blissfully unaware that I've thought for days that something was going on in this house. There is too much mail. And you and Walter have been arguing."

"You see what I want you to see. Nothing more." Even though Matthew's tendency toward imperiousness had grown exponentially since we came to the Old Lodge, my jaw dropped at his tone.

"How dare you," I said slowly. Matthew knew I'd spent my whole life surrounded by secrets. I'd paid a high price for it, too. I stood.

"Sit down," he grated out. "Please." He caught my hand.

Matthew's best friend, Hamish Osborne, had warned me that he wouldn't be the same man here. How could he be, when the world was such a different place? Women were expected to accept without question what a man told them. Among his friends it was all too easy for Matthew to slip back into old behaviors and patterns of thinking.

"Only if you answer me. I want the name of the person you report to and how you got embroiled in this business." I glanced over at his nephew and his friends, worried that these were state secrets.

"They already know about Kit and me," Matthew said, following my eyes. He struggled to find the words. "It all started with Francis Walsingham.

"I'd left England late in Henry's reign. I spent time in Constantinople, went to Cyprus, wandered through Spain, fought at Lepanto—even set up a printing business in Antwerp," Matthew explained. "It's the usual path for a *wearh*. We search for a tragedy, an opportunity to slip into someone else's life. But nothing suited me, so I returned home. France was on the verge of religious and civil war. When you've lived as long as I have, you learn the signs. A Huguenot schoolmaster was happy to take my money and go to Geneva, where he could raise his daughters in safety. I took the identity of his long-dead cousin, moved into his house in Paris, and started over as Matthew de la Forêt."

"'Matthew of the Forest'?" My eyebrows lifted at the irony.

"That *was* the schoolmaster's name," he said wryly. "Paris was dangerous, and Walsingham, as English ambassador, was a magnet for every disenchanted rebel in the country. Late in the summer of 1572, all the simmering anger in France came to a boil. I helped Walsingham survive, along with the English Protestants he was sheltering."

"The massacre on St. Bartholomew's Day." I shivered, thinking of the blood-soaked wedding between a French Catholic princess and her Protestant husband.

"I became the queen's agent later, when she sent Walsingham back to Paris. He was supposed to be brokering Her Majesty's marriage to one of the Valois princes." Matthew snorted. "It was clear the queen had no real interest in the match. It was during that visit that I learned of Walsingham's network of intelligencers."

My husband met my eyes briefly, then looked away. He was still keeping something from me. I reviewed the story, detected the fault lines in his account, and followed them to a single, inescapable conclusion: Matthew was French, Catholic, and he could not possibly have been aligned politically with Elizabeth Tudor in 1572—or in 1590. If he was working for the English Crown, it was for some larger purpose. But the Congregation had vowed to stay out of human politics.

Philippe de Clermont and his Knights of Lazarus had not.

"You're working for your father. And you're not only a vampire but a Catholic in a Protestant country." The fact that Matthew was working for the Knights of Lazarus, not just Elizabeth, exponentially increased the danger. It wasn't just witches who were hunted down and executed in Elizabethan England—so were traitors, creatures with unusual powers, and people of different faiths. "The Congregation is of no help if you get involved with human politics. How could your own family ask you to do something so risky?"

Hancock grinned. "That's why there's always a de Clermont on the Congregation—to make sure lofty ideals don't get in the way of good business."

"This isn't the first time I've worked for Philippe, nor will it be the last. You're good at uncovering secrets. I'm good at keeping them," Matthew said simply.

*Scientist. Vampire. Warrior. Spy.* Another piece of Matthew fell into place, and with it I better understood his ingrained habit of never sharing anything—major or minor—unless he was forced to do so.

"I don't care how much experience you have! Your safety depends on Walsingham—and you're deceiving him." His words had only made me angrier.

"Walsingham is dead. I report to William Cecil now."

"The canniest man alive," Gallowglass said quietly. "Except for Philippe, of course."

"And Kit? Does he work for Cecil or for you?"

"Tell her nothing, Matthew," Kit said. "The witch cannot be trusted."

"Why, you sly, wee boggart," Hancock said softly. "It's you who's been stirring up the villagers."

Kit's cheeks burned red in twin pronouncements of guilt.

"Christ, Kit. What have you done?" Matthew asked, astonished.

"Nothing," said Marlowe sullenly.

"You've been telling tales again." Hancock waggled his finger in admonishment. "I've warned you before that we won't stand for that, Master Marlowe."

"Woodstock was already buzzing with news of Matthew's wife," Kit protested. "The rumors were bound to bring the Congregation down upon us. How was I supposed to know that the Congregation was already here?"

"Surely you'll let me kill him now, de Clermont. I've wanted to do so for ages," Hancock said, cracking his knuckles.

"No. You can't kill him." Matthew rubbed a hand over his tired face. "There would be too many questions, and I don't have the patience to come up with convincing answers at present. It's just village gossip. I'll handle it."

"This gossip comes at a bad time," Gallowglass reported quietly. "It's not just Berwick. You know how anxious people were about witches in Chester. When we went north into Scotland, the situation was worse."

"If this business spreads south into England, she'll be the death of us," Marlowe promised, pointing at me.

"This trouble will stay confined to Scotland," Matthew retorted. "And there will be no more visits to the village, Kit."

"She appeared on All Hallows' Eve, just when the arrival of a fearsome witch was predicted. Don't you see? Your new wife raised the storms against King James, and now she has turned her attention to England. Cecil must be told. She poses a danger to the queen."

"Quiet, Kit," Henry cautioned, pulling at his arm.

"You cannot silence me. Telling the queen is my duty. Once you would have agreed with me, Henry. But since the witch came, everything's changed! She has enchanted everyone in the house." Kit's eyes were frantic. "You dote on her like a sister. George is half in love. Tom praises her wit, and Walter would have her skirts up and her back against a wall if he weren't afraid of Matt. Return her to where she belongs. We were happy before."

"Matthew wasn't happy." Tom had been drawn to our end of the room by Marlowe's angry energy.

"You say you love him." Kit turned to me, his face full of entreaty. "Do you truly know what he is? Have you seen him feed, felt the hunger in him when a warmblood is near? Can you accept Matthew completely—the blackness in his soul along with the light—as I do? You have your magic for solace, but I am not fully alive without him. All poetry flies from my mind when he is gone, and only Matthew can see what little good I have in me. Leave him to me. Please."

"I can't," I said simply.

Kit wiped his sleeve across his mouth as if the gesture might remove all trace of me. "When the rest of the Congregation discovers your affections for him—"

"If my affection for him is forbidden, so is yours," I interrupted. Marlowe flinched. "But none of us choose whom we love."

"Iffley and his friends won't be the last to accuse you of witchcraft," Kit said with a note of sour triumph. "Mark me well, Mistress Roydon. Daemons often see the future as plainly as witches."

Matthew's hand moved to my waist. The cold, familiar touch of his fingers swept from one side of my rib cage to the other, following the curved path that marked me as belonging to a vampire. For Matthew it was a powerful reminder of his earlier failure to keep me safe. Kit made a horrible, half-swallowed sound of distress at the intimacy of the gesture.

"If you are so prescient, then you should have foreseen what your betrayal would mean to me," Matthew said, gradually unfolding himself. "Get out of my sight, Kit, or so help me God there will be nothing left of you to bury."

"You would have her over me?" Kit sounded dumbfounded.

"In a heartbeat. Get out," repeated Matthew.

Kit's passage out of the room was measured, but once in the corridor his pace quickened. His feet echoed on the wooden stairs, faster and faster, as he climbed to his room.

"We'll have to watch him." Gallowglass's shrewd eyes turned from Kit's departing back to Hancock. "He can't be trusted now."

"Marlowe could never be trusted," Hancock muttered.

Pierre slipped through the open door looking stricken, another piece of mail in his hand.

"Not now, Pierre," Matthew groaned, sitting down and reaching for his wine. His shoulders sagged against the back of his chair. "There simply isn't room in this day for one more crisis—be it queen, country, or Catholics. Whatever it is can wait until morning."

"But . . . *milord*," Pierre stammered, holding out the letter. Matthew glanced at the decisive writing that marched across the front.

"Christ and all His saints." His fingers rose to touch the paper, then froze. Matthew's throat moved as he struggled for control. Something red and bright appeared in the corner of his eye, then slid down his cheek and splashed onto the folds of his collar. A vampire's blood tear.

"What is it, Matthew?" I looked over his shoulder, wondering what had caused so much grief.

"Ah. The day is not over yet," Hancock said uneasily while he backed away. "There is one small matter that requires your attention. Your father thinks you're dead."

In my own time, it was Matthew's father, Philippe, who was dead—horribly, tragically, irrevocably so. But this was 1590, which meant he was alive. Ever since we'd arrived, I had worried about a chance encounter with Ysabeau or with Matthew's laboratory assistant, Miriam, and the ripples such a meeting might cause in future times. Not once had I considered what seeing Philippe would do to Matthew.

Past, present, and future collided. Had I looked into the corners, I would surely have seen time unspooling in protest at the clash. But my eyes were fixed on Matthew instead, and the blood tear caught in the snowy linen at his throat.

Gallowglass brusquely picked up the tale. "With the news from Scotland and your sudden disappearance, we feared you'd gone north for the queen and been caught up in the madness there. We looked for two days. When we couldn't find a trace of you—hell, Matthew, we had no choice but to tell Philippe you had vanished. It was that or raise the alarm with the Congregation."

"There's more, *milord*." Pierre flipped the letter over. The seal on it was like the others I associated with the Knights of Lazarus—except that the wax used here was a vivid swirl of black and red and an ancient silver coin had been pushed into its surface, the edges worn and thin, instead of the usual impression of the order's seal. The coin was stamped with a cross and a crescent, two de Clermont family symbols.

"What did you tell him?" Matthew was transfixed by the pale moon of silver floating in its red-black sea.

"Our words are of little consequence now that this has arrived. You must be on French soil within the next week. Otherwise Philippe will set out for England," Hancock mumbled.

"My father cannot come here, Hancock. It is impossible."

"Of course it's impossible. The queen would have his head after all he's done to stir the pot of English politics. You must go to him. So long as you travel night and day, you will have plenty of time," Hancock assured him.

"I can't." Matthew's gaze was fixed on the unopened letter.

"Philippe will have horses waiting. You will be back before long," Gallowglass murmured, resting his hand on his uncle's shoulder. Matthew looked up, eyes suddenly wild.

"It's not the distance. It's—" Matthew stopped abruptly.

"He's your mother's husband, man. Surely you can trust Philippe—unless you've been lying to him as well." Hancock's eyes narrowed.

"Kit's right. No one can trust me." Matthew shot to his feet. "My life is a tissue of lies."

"This isn't the time or place for your philosophical nonsense, Matthew. Even now Philippe wonders if he has lost another son!" Gallowglass exclaimed. "Leave the girl with us, get on your horse, and do what your father commands. If you don't, I'll knock you out and Hancock will carry you there."

"You must be very sure of yourself, Gallowglass, to issue me orders," Matthew said, a dangerous edge to his tone. He braced his hands on the chimneypiece and stared into the fire.

"I'm sure of my grandfather. Ysabeau made you a *wearh,* but it is Philippe's blood that coursed through my father's veins." Gallowglass's words wounded Matthew. His head snapped up when the blow landed, raw emotion overcoming his usual impassiveness.

"George, Tom, go upstairs and see to Kit," Walter murmured, pointing his friends to the door. Raleigh inclined his head in Pierre's direction, and Matthew's servant joined in the efforts to get them out of the room. Calls for more wine and food echoed through the vestibule. Once the two were in Françoise's care, Pierre returned, shut the door firmly, and placed himself before it. With only Walter, Henry, Hancock, and me there to bear witness to the conversation—along with the silent Pierre—Gallowglass continued his efforts with Matthew.

"You must go to Sept-Tours. He won't rest until he claims your body for burial or you are standing before him, alive. Philippe doesn't trust Elizabeth—or the Congregation." Gallowglass intended his words to bring comfort this time, but Matthew's air of remove remained.

Gallowglass made an exasperated sound. "Deceive the others—and yourself, if you must. Discuss alternatives all night if you wish. But Auntie's right: It's all shite." Gallowglass's voice dropped. "Your Diana doesn't smell right. And you smell older than you did last week. I know the secret you're both keeping. He'll know it, too."

Gallowglass had deduced that I was a timewalker. One look at Hancock told me that he had, too.

"Enough!" Walter barked.

Gallowglass and Hancock quieted immediately. The reason blinked on Walter's little finger: a signet bearing the outlines of Lazarus and his coffin.

"So you're a knight, too," I said, stunned.

"Yes," said Walter tersely.

"And you outrank Hancock. What about Gallowglass?" There were too many overlapping layers of loyalty and allegiance in the room. I was desperate to organize them into a navigable structure.

"I outrank everyone in this room, madam, with the exception of your husband," Raleigh cautioned. "And that includes you."

"You have no authority over me," I shot back. "Exactly what is your role in the de Clermont family's business, Walter?"

Over my head, Raleigh's angry blue eyes met Matthew's. "Is she always like this?"

"Usually," Matthew said drily. "It takes some getting used to, but I rather like it. You might, too, given time."

"I already have one demanding woman in my life. I don't need another," Walter snorted. "If you must know, I command the brotherhood in England, Mistress Roydon. Matthew cannot do so, given his position on the Congregation. The other members of the family were otherwise occupied. Or they refused." Walter's eyes flickered to Gallowglass.

"So you're one of the order's eight provincial masters and report directly to Philippe," I said thoughtfully. "I'm surprised you're not the ninth knight." The ninth knight was a mysterious figure in the order, his identity kept secret from all except those at the very highest levels.

Raleigh swore so vehemently that Pierre gasped. "You keep the fact that you're a spy and a member of the Congregation from your wife, yet you tell her the most private business of the brotherhood?"

"She asked," Matthew said simply. "But I think that's enough talk of the Order of Lazarus for tonight."

"Your wife won't be satisfied leaving it there. She will worry at this like a hound with a bone." Raleigh crossed his arms over his chest and scowled. "Very well. If you must know, Henry is the ninth knight. His unwillingness to embrace the Protestant faith makes him vulnerable to allegations of

treason here in England, and in Europe he is an easy target for every mal-
content who would like to see Her Majesty lose her throne. Philippe offered
him the position to shield him from those who would abuse his trusting
nature."

"Henry? A rebel?" I looked at the gentle giant, stunned.

"I'm no rebel," Henry said tightly. "But Philippe de Clermont's protection has saved my life on more than one occasion."

"The Earl of Northumberland is a powerful man, Diana," Matthew
said quietly, "which makes him a valuable pawn in the hands of an unscru-
pulous player."

Gallowglass coughed. "Can we leave off talk of the brotherhood and
return to more urgent matters? The Congregation will call on Matthew to
calm the situation in Berwick. The queen will want him to stir it up further, because so long as the Scots are preoccupied with witches, they won't
be able to plan any mischief in England. Matthew's new wife is facing
witchcraft accusations at home. And his father has recalled him to France."

"Christ," Matthew said, pinching the bridge of his nose. "What a tangled mess."

"How do you propose we untangle it?" Walter demanded. "You say
Philippe cannot come here, Gallowglass, but I fear that Matthew ought not
go there either."

"No one ever said that having three masters—and a wife—was going to
be easy," Hancock declared sourly.

"So which devil will it be, Matthew?" asked Gallowglass.

"If Philippe doesn't receive the coin embedded in the letter's seal from
my own hand, and soon, he'll come looking for me," Matthew said hol-
lowly. "It's a test of loyalty. My father loves tests."

"Your father does not doubt you. This misunderstanding will be set to
rights when you see each other," Henry maintained. When Matthew didn't
respond, Henry moved to fill the silence. "You are always telling me that I
must have a plan, or else be pulled into the designs of other men. Tell us
what must be done, and we will see to it."

Without speaking, Matthew picked through options, discarding one
after the other. It would have taken any other man days to sift through the
possible moves and countermoves. For Matthew it took only minutes.
There was little sign of the struggle on his face, but the bunching of his
shoulder muscles and the distracted pass of his hand through his hair told
another story.

"I'll go," he said at last. "Diana will stay here, with Gallowglass and Hancock. Walter will have to put off the queen with some excuse. And I'll handle the Congregation."

"Diana can't remain in Woodstock," Gallowglass told him firmly. "Not now that Kit's been at work in the village, spreading his lies and asking questions about her. Without your presence neither the queen nor the Congregation will have any incentive to keep your wife from the magistrate."

"We can go to London, Matthew," I urged. "Together. It's a big city. There will be too many witches for anyone to notice me—witches who aren't afraid of power like mine—and messengers to take word to France that you're safe. You don't have to go." *You don't have to see your father again.*

"London!" Hancock scoffed. "You wouldn't last three days there, *madam*. Gallowglass and I will take you into Wales. We'll go to Abergavenny."

"No." My eyes were drawn by the crimson stain at Matthew's neck. "If Matthew is going to France, I'm going with him."

"Absolutely not. I'm not dragging you through a war."

"The war has quieted with the coming of winter," said Walter. "Taking Diana to Sept-Tours may be for the best. Few are brave enough to tangle with you, Matthew. None at all will cross your father."

"You have a choice," I told him fiercely. Matthew's friends and family weren't going to use me to force him to France.

"Yes. And I choose you." He traced my lip with his thumb. My heart sank. He was going to go to Sept-Tours.

"Don't do this," I implored him. I didn't trust myself to say more for fear of betraying the fact that in our own time Philippe was dead, and that it would be torture for Matthew to see him alive again.

"Philippe told me that mating was destiny. Once I found you, there would be nothing to do but accept fate's decision. But that's not how it works at all. In every moment, for the rest of my life, I will be choosing you—over my father, over my own self-interest, even over the de Clermont family." Matthew's lips pressed against mine, silencing my protests. There was no mistaking the conviction in his kiss.

"It's decided, then," Gallowglass said softly.

Matthew's eyes held mine. He nodded. "Yes. Diana and I will go home. Together."

"There's work to do, arrangements to be made," Walter said. "Leave it to us. Your wife looks exhausted, and the journey will be taxing. You both should rest."

Neither of us made any move toward bed once the men had gone off to the parlor.

"Our time in 1590 isn't turning out quite as I hoped," Matthew admitted. "It was supposed to be straightforward."

"How could it possibly be straightforward, with the Congregation, the trials in Berwick, the Elizabethan intelligence service, and the Knights of Lazarus all vying for your attention?"

"Being a member of the Congregation and serving as a spy should be helps—not hindrances." Matthew stared out the window. "I thought we'd come to the Old Lodge, use the services of Widow Beaton, find the manuscript in Oxford, and be gone within a few weeks."

I bit my lip to keep from pointing out the flaws in his strategy—Walter, Henry, and Gallowglass had already done so repeatedly this evening—but my expression gave me away.

"It was shortsighted of me," he said with a sigh. "And it's not just establishing your credibility that's a problem, or avoiding the obvious traps like witch trials and wars. I'm overwhelmed, too. The broad canvas of what I did for Elizabeth and the Congregation—and the countermoves I made on behalf of my father—that's clear, but all the details have faded. I know the date, but not the day of the week. That means I'm not sure which messenger is due to arrive and when the next delivery will be made. I could have sworn I'd parted ways with Gallowglass and Hancock before Halloween."

"The devil is always in the details," I murmured. I brushed at the sooty track of dried blood that marked the passage of his tear. There were specks of it near the corner of his eye, a thin trace down his cheek. "I should have realized your father might contact you."

"It was only a matter of time before his letter came. Whenever Pierre brings the mail, I steel myself. But the courier had already been and gone today. His handwriting took me by surprise, that's all," he explained. "I'd forgotten how strong it once was. When we got him back from the Nazis in 1944, his body was so broken that not even vampire blood could mend it. Philippe couldn't hold a pen. He loved to write, and all he could manage was an illegible scrawl." I knew of Philippe's capture and captivity in World War II, but few details of what he'd suffered at the hands of the Nazis who had wanted to determine how much pain a vampire could endure.

"Maybe the goddess wanted us back in 1590 for more than just my benefit. Seeing Philippe again may reopen these old wounds of yours—and heal them."

"Not before making them worse." Matthew's head dipped.

"But in the end it might make them better." I smoothed his hair over his hard, stubborn skull. "You still haven't opened your father's letter."

"I know what it says."

"Perhaps you should open it anyway."

At last Matthew slid his finger under the seal and broke it. The coin tumbled out of the wax, and he caught it in his palm. When he unfolded the thick paper, it released a faint scent of laurel and rosemary.

"Is that Greek?" I asked, looking over his shoulder at the single line of text and a swirling rendition of the letter *phi* below.

"Yes." Matthew traced the letters, making his first tentative contact with his father. "He commands me to come home. Immediately."

"Can you bear seeing him again?"

"No. Yes." Matthew's fingers crumpled the page into his fist. "I don't know."

I took the page away from him, flattening it back into its rectangle. The coin sparkled in Matthew's palm. It was such a small sliver of metal to have caused so much trouble.

"You won't face him alone." Standing by his side when he saw his dead father wasn't much, but it was all I could do to ease his grief.

"Each of us is alone with Philippe. Some think my father can see into one's very soul," Matthew murmured. "It worries me to take you there. With Ysabeau I could predict how she would react: coldness, anger, then acquiescence. When it comes to Philippe, I have no idea. No one understands the way Philippe's mind works, what information he possesses, what traps he's laid. If I am secretive, then my father is inscrutable. Not even the Congregation knows what he's up to, and God knows they spend enough time trying to figure it out."

"It will be fine," I reassured him. Philippe would have to accept me into the family. Like Matthew's mother and brother, he would have no choice.

"Don't think you can best him," Matthew warned. "You may be like my mother, as Gallowglass said, but even she gets caught in his web from time to time."

"And are you still a member of the Congregation in the present? Is that how you knew that Knox and Domenico were members?" The witch Peter Knox had been stalking me since the moment I called up Ashmole 782 at the Bodleian. As for Domenico Michele, he was a vampire with old animosities when it came to the de Clermonts. He'd been present at La Pierre before yet another member of the Congregation tortured me.

"No," Matthew said shortly, turning away.

"So what Hancock said about a de Clermont always being on the Congregation is no longer true?" I held my breath. *Say yes,* I urged him silently, *even if it's a lie.*

"It's still true," he said evenly, crushing my hope.

"Then who . . . ?" I trailed off. "Ysabeau? Baldwin? Surely not Marcus!" I couldn't believe that Matthew's mother, his brother, or his son could be involved without someone letting it slip.

"There are creatures on my family tree that you don't know, Diana. In any case, I'm not free to divulge the identity of the one who sits at the Congregation's table."

"Do any of the rules that bind the rest of us apply to your family?" I wondered. "You meddle in politics—I've seen the account books that prove it. Are you hoping that when we return to the present, this mysterious family member is going to somehow shield us from the Congregation's wrath?"

"I don't know," Matthew said tightly. "I'm not sure of anything. Not anymore."

Our plans for departure took shape quickly. Walter and Gallowglass argued about the best route, while Matthew set his affairs in order.

Hancock was dispatched to London with Henry and a leather-wrapped packet of correspondence. As a peer of the realm, the earl was required at court for the celebrations of the queen's anniversary on the seventeenth of November. George and Tom were packed off to Oxford with a substantial sum of money and a disgraced Marlowe. Hancock warned them of the dire consequences that would ensue if the daemon caused any more trouble. Matthew might be far away, but Hancock would be within sword's reach and would not hesitate to strike if it was warranted. In addition, Matthew instructed George on exactly what questions about alchemical manuscripts he could ask the scholars of Oxford.

My own affairs were far simpler to arrange. I had few personal items to pack: Ysabeau's earrings, my new shoes, a few items of clothing. Françoise turned all her attention to making me a sturdy, cinnamon-colored gown for the journey. Its high, fur-lined collar was designed to fasten closely and keep out the winds and rain. The silky fox pelts that Françoise stitched into the lining of my cloak would serve the same purpose, as would the bands of fur she inserted into the embroidered edges of my new gloves.

My last act at the Old Lodge was to take the book Matthew had given me to the library. It would be easy to lose such an item on the way to Sept-Tours, and I wanted my diary to be as safe from prying eyes as possible. I stooped to the rushes and picked up sprigs of rosemary and lavender. Then I went to Matthew's desk and selected a quill and a pot of ink and made one final entry.

> *4 5 November 1590     cold rain*
> *News from home. We are preparing for a journey.*

After blowing gently on the words to set the ink, I slipped the rosemary and lavender into the crevice between the pages. My aunt used rosemary for memory spells and lavender to breathe a note of caution into love charms—a fitting combination for our present circumstances.

"Wish us luck, Sarah," I whispered as I slid the small volume into the end of the shelf, in hopes that it would still be there should I return.

## 7

Rima Jaén hated the month of November. The hours of daylight shrank, giving up their battle against the shadows a few moments earlier with each passing day. And it was a terrible time to be in Seville, with the whole city gearing up for the holiday season and rain just around the corner. The normally erratic driving habits of the city's residents grew worse by the hour.

Rima had been stuck at her desk for weeks. Her boss had decided to clear out the storage rooms in the attic. Last winter the rain had made it through the ancient, cracked roof tiles on top of the decrepit house, and the forecast for the coming months was even worse. There was no money to fix the problem, so the maintenance staff was hauling moldy cardboard boxes down the stairs to make sure that nothing of value was damaged in future storms. Everything else was discreetly gotten rid of in such a way that no potential donors could discover what was afoot.

It was a dirty, deceitful business, but it had to be done, Rima reflected. The library was a small, specialist archive with scant resources. The core of its collections came from a prominent Andalusian family whose members could trace their roots back to the *reconquista,* when the Christians had taken back the peninsula from the Muslim warriors who had claimed it in the eighth century. Few scholars had reason to poke through the bizarre range of books and objects the Gonçalves had collected over the years. Most researchers were down the street at the Archivo General de Indias, arguing about Columbus. Her fellow Sevillanos wanted their libraries to have the latest thriller, not crumbling Jesuit instruction manuals from the 1700s and women's fashion magazines from the 1800s.

Rima picked up the small volume sitting on the corner of her desk and swung a pair of brightly colored glasses down from the top of her head, where they were holding back her black hair. She'd noticed the book a week ago, when one of the maintenance workers had dropped a wooden crate before her with a grunt of displeasure. Since then she'd entered it into the collection as Gonçalve Manuscript 4890 along with the description *"English commonplace book, anonymous, late 16th century."* Like most commonplace books, it was mostly blank. Rima had seen one Spanish example owned by a Gonçalve heir sent to the University of Seville in 1628. It had been finely bound, ruled, and paginated with ornate numbers set in swirls of multicolored ink. There was not a single word in it. Even in the past, people never quite lived up to their aspirations.

Commonplace books like this one were repositories for biblical passages, snatches of poetry, mottoes, and the sayings of classical authors. They typically included doodles and shopping lists as well as lyrics to bawdy songs and accounts of strange and important events. This one was no different, Rima thought. Sadly, someone had ripped out the first page. Once it had probably borne the owner's name. Without it there was virtually no chance of identifying the owner, or any of the other people mentioned only by initials. Historians were far less interested in this sort of nameless, faceless evidence, as though its anonymity somehow made the person behind it less important.

On the remaining pages there was a chart listing all the English coinage in use in the sixteenth century and its relative worth. One page in the back had a hastily scribbled list of clothing: a cloak, two pairs of shoes, a gown trimmed in fur, six smocks, four petticoats, and a pair of gloves. There were a few dated entries that made no sense at all and a headache cure—a caudle, made with milk and wine. Rima smiled and wondered if it would work on her migraines.

She should have returned the little volume to the locked rooms on the third floor where the manuscripts were stored, but something about it made her want to keep it nearby. It was clear that a woman had written it. The round hand was endearingly shaky and uncertain, and the words snaked up and down on pages liberally sprinkled with inkblots. No learned sixteenth-century man wrote like that, unless he was ill or aged. This book's author was neither. There was a curious vibrancy to the entries that was strangely at odds with the tentative handwriting.

She had shown the manuscript to Javier López, the charming yet entirely unqualified person hired by the last of the Gonçalves to transform the family's house and personal effects into a library and museum. His expansive ground-floor office was paneled in fine mahogany and had the only working heaters in the building. During their brief interview, he'd dismissed her suggestion that the book deserved more careful study. He also forbade her to take photographs of it so she could share the images with colleagues in the United Kingdom. As for her belief that the book's owner had been a woman, the director had muttered something about feminists and waved her out of his office.

And so the book remained on her desk. In Seville such a book would always be unwanted and unimportant. Nobody came to Spain to look for English commonplace books. They went to the British Library, or the Folger Shakespeare Library in the United States.

There was that strange man who came by now and again to comb through the collections. He was French, and his appraising stare made Rima uncomfortable. Herbert Cantal—or maybe it was Gerbert Cantal. She couldn't remember. He'd left a card on his last visit and had encouraged her to get in touch if anything interesting turned up. When Rima asked what, exactly, might qualify, the man had said he was interested in everything. It was not the most helpful of responses.

Now something interesting *had* turned up. Unfortunately, the man's business card had not, though she'd cleaned out her desk in an effort to locate it. Rima would have to wait until he appeared again to share this little book with him. Perhaps he would be more interested in it than her boss was.

Rima flipped through the pages. There was a tiny sprig of lavender and a few crumbling rosemary leaves pressed between two of the pages. She hadn't seen them before and picked them carefully from the crevice of the binding. For a moment there was a trace of scent in the faded bloom, forging a connection between herself and a person who had lived hundreds of years ago. Rima smiled wistfully, thinking about the woman she would never know.

*"Más basura."* Daniel from building maintenance was back, his worn gray overalls grimy from transporting boxes from the attic. He slid several more boxes off the beaten-up dolly and onto the floor. In spite of the cool weather, sweat stood out on his forehead, and he wiped it off with his sleeve, leaving a smudge of black dust. *"Café?"*

It was the third time this week he'd asked her out. Rima knew that he found her attractive. Her mother's Berber ancestry appealed to some men—not surprising, since it had bestowed upon her soft curves, warm skin, and almond-shaped eyes. Daniel had been muttering salacious comments, brushing against her backside when she went to the mail room, and ogling her breasts for years. That he was five inches shorter than she and twice her age didn't seem to deter him.

*"Estoy muy ocupada,"* Rima replied.

Daniel's grunt was infused with deep skepticism. He glanced back at the boxes as he left. The one on top held a moldering fur muff and a stuffed wren attached to a piece of cedar. Daniel shook his head, astonished that she would prefer to spend her time with dead animals than with him.

*"Gracias,"* Rima murmured as he departed. She closed the book gently and returned it to its place on her desk.

While she transferred the box's contents to a nearby table, Rima's eyes strayed back to the little volume in its simple leather cover. In four hundred years, would the only proof of her existence be a page from her calendar, a shopping list, and a scrap of paper with her grandmother's recipe for *alfajores* on it, all placed in a file labeled *"Anonymous, of no importance"* and stored in an archive no one ever visited?

Such dark thoughts were bound to be unlucky. Rima shivered and touched the hand-shaped amulet of the Prophet's daughter, Fatima. It hung around her neck on a leather cord and had been passed down among the women of her family for as long as anyone could remember.

*"Khamsa fi ainek,"* she whispered, hoping her words would ward off any evil spirit she might have unwittingly called.

# PART II

# Sept-Tours and the Village of Saint-Lucien

# 8

"The usual place?" Gallowglass asked quietly as he put down his oars and raised the solitary sail. Though it would be more than four hours before the sun rose, other craft were visible in the darkness. I picked out the shadowed outlines of a sail, a lantern swinging from a post in the stern of a neighboring vessel.

"Walter said we were going to Saint-Malo," I said, my head turning in consternation. Raleigh had accompanied us from the Old Lodge to Portsmouth and had piloted the boat that took us to Guernsey. We'd left him standing on the dock near the village of Saint-Pierre-Port. He could go no farther—not with a price on his head in Catholic Europe.

"I remember well enough where Raleigh told me to go, Auntie, but he's a pirate. And English. And he's not here. I'm asking Matthew."

"*Immensi tremor oceani,*" Matthew whispered as he contemplated the heaving seas. Staring out across the black water, he had all the expression of a carved figurehead. And his reply to his nephew's question was odd—*the trembling of the immense ocean.* I wondered if I had somehow misunderstood his Latin.

"The tide will be with us, and it is closer to Fougères by horse than Saint-Malo." Gallowglass continued as though Matthew were making sense. "She'll be no colder on the water than on land in this weather, and still plenty of riding before her."

"And you will be leaving us." It wasn't a question but a pronouncement of fact. Matthew's eyelids dropped. He nodded. "Very well."

Gallowglass drew in the sail, and the boat changed from a southerly to a more easterly course. Matthew sat on the deck, his back against the curved supports of the hull, and drew me into the circle of his arms so that his cloak was wrapped around me.

True sleep was impossible, but I dozed against Matthew's chest. It had been a grueling journey thus far, with horses pushed to the limit and boats commandeered. The temperature was frigid, and a thin layer of frost built up on the nap of our English wool. Gallowglass and Pierre kept up a steady patter of conversation in some French dialect, but Matthew remained quiet. He responded to their questions yet kept his own thoughts hidden behind an eerily composed mask.

The weather changed to a misty snow around dawn. Gallowglass's beard turned white, transforming him into a fair imitation of Santa Claus. Pierre adjusted the sails at his command, and a landscape of grays and whites revealed the coast of France. No more than thirty minutes later, the tide began to race toward the shore. The boat was lifted up on the waves, and through the mist a steeple pierced the clouds. It was surprisingly close, the base of the structure obscured by the weather. I gasped.

"Hold tight," Gallowglass said grimly as Pierre released the sail.

The boat shot through the mist. The call of seagulls and the slap of water against rock told me we were nearing shore, but the boat didn't slow. Gallowglass jammed an oar into the flooding tide, angling us sharply. Someone cried out, in warning or greeting.

"*Il est le chevalier de Clermont!*" Pierre called back, cupping his hands around his mouth. His words were met with silence before scurrying footfalls sounded through the cold air.

"Gallowglass!" We were heading straight for a wall. I scrabbled for an oar to fend off certain disaster. No sooner had my fingers closed around it than Matthew plucked it from my grasp.

"He's been putting in at this spot for centuries, and his people for longer than that," Matthew said calmly, holding the oar lightly in his hands. Improbably, the boat's bow took another sharp left and the hull was broadside to slabs of rough-hewn granite. High above, four men with hooks and ropes emerged to snare the boat and hold it steady. The water level continued to rise with alarming speed, carrying the boat upward until we were level with a small stone house. A set of stairs climbed into invisibility. Pierre hopped onto the landing, talking fast and low and gesturing at the boat. Two armed soldiers joined us for a moment, then sped off in the direction of the stairs.

"We have arrived at Mont Saint-Michel, *madame*." Pierre held out his hand. I took it and stepped from the boat. "Here you will rest while *milord* speaks with the abbot."

My knowledge of the island was limited to the stories swapped by friends of mine who sailed every summer around the Isle of Wight: that it was surrounded at low tide by quicksand and at high tide by such dangerous currents that boats were crushed against the rocks. I looked over my shoulder at our tiny boat and shuddered. It was a miracle that we were still alive.

While I tried to get my bearings, Matthew studied his nephew, who remained motionless in the stern. "It would be safer for Diana if you came along."

"When your friends aren't getting her into trouble, your wife seems able to care of herself." Gallowglass looked up at me with a smile.

"Philippe will ask after you."

"Tell him—" Gallowglass stopped, stared off into the distance. The vampire's blue eyes were deep with longing. "Tell him I have not yet succeeded in forgetting."

"For his sake you must try to forgive," said Matthew quietly.

"I will never forgive," Gallowglass said coldly, "and Philippe would never ask it of me. My father died at the hands of the French, and not a single creature stood up to the king. Until I have made peace with the past, I will not set foot in France."

"Hugh is gone, God rest his soul. Your grandfather is still among us. Don't squander your time with him." Matthew lifted his foot from the boat. Without a word of farewell, he turned and took my elbow, steering me toward a bedraggled huddle of trees with barren branches. Feeling the cold weight of Gallowglass's stare, I turned and locked eyes with the Gael. His hand rose in a silent gesture of leave.

Matthew was quiet as we approached the stairs. I couldn't see where they led and soon lost count of the number of them. I concentrated instead on keeping my footing on the worn, slick treads. Chips of ice fell from the hem of my skirts, and the wind whistled within my wide hood. A sturdy door, ornamented with heavy straps of iron that were rusted and pitted from the salt spray, opened before us.

More steps. I pressed my lips together, lifted my skirts, and kept going.

More soldiers. As we approached, they flattened themselves against the walls to make room for us to pass. Matthew's fingers tightened a fraction on my elbow, but otherwise the men might have been wraiths for all the attention he paid them.

We entered a room with a forest of columns holding up its vaulted roof. Large fireplaces studded the walls, spreading blessed warmth. I sighed with relief and shook out my cloak, shedding water and ice in all directions. A gentle cough directed my attention to a man standing before one of the blazes. He was dressed in the red robes of a cardinal and appeared to be in his late twenties—a terribly young age for someone to have risen so high in the Catholic Church's hierarchy.

"Ah, *Chevalier de Clermont*. Or are we calling you something else these days? You have long been out of France. Perhaps you have taken Walsingham's name along with his position, now that he is gone to hell where he belongs." The cardinal's English was impeccable although heavily accented. "We have, on the *seigneur*'s instructions, been watching for you for three days. There was no mention of a woman."

Matthew dropped my arm so that he could step forward. He genuflected with a smooth bend of his knee and kissed the ring on the man's extended hand. "*Éminence*. I thought you were in Rome, choosing our new pope. Imagine my delight at finding you here." Matthew didn't sound happy. I wondered uneasily what we'd stepped into by coming to Mont Saint-Michel and not Saint-Malo as Walter had planned.

"France needs me more than the conclave does at present. These recent murders of kings and queens do not please God." The cardinal's eyes sparked a warning. "Elizabeth will discover that soon enough, when she meets Him."

"I am not here on English business, Cardinal Joyeuse. This is my wife, Diana." Matthew held his father's thin silver coin between his first and middle fingers. "I am returning home."

"So I am told. Your father sent this to ensure your safe passage." Joyeuse tossed a gleaming object to Matthew, who caught it neatly. "Philippe de Clermont forgets himself and behaves as though he were the king of France."

"My father has no need to rule, for he is the sharp sword that makes and unmakes kings," Matthew said softly. He slid the heavy golden ring over the gloved knuckle of his middle finger. Set within it was a carved red stone. I was sure the pattern incised in the ring was the same as the mark on my back. "Your masters know that if it were not for my father, the Catholic cause would be lost in France. Otherwise you would not be here."

"Perhaps it would be better for all concerned if the *seigneur* really were king, given the throne's present Protestant occupant. But that is a topic for us to discuss in private," Cardinal Joyeuse said tiredly. He gestured to a servant standing in the shadows by the door. "Take the *chevalier*'s wife to her room. We must leave you, *madame*. Your husband has been too long among heretics. An extended period spent kneeling on a cold stone floor will remind him who he truly is."

My face must have shown my dismay at being alone in such a place.

"Pierre will stay with you," Matthew assured me before he bent and pressed his lips to mine. "We ride out when the tide turns."

And that was the last glimpse I had of Matthew Clairmont, scientist. The man who strode toward the door was no longer an Oxford don but a Renaissance prince. It was in his bearing, the set of his shoulders, his aura of banked strength, and the cold look in his eyes. Hamish had been right to warn me that Matthew would not be the same man here. Under Matthew's smooth surface, a profound metamorphosis was taking place.

Somewhere high above, the bells tolled the hours.

*Scientist. Vampire. Warrior. Spy.* The bells paused before the final knell.
*Prince.*

I wondered what more our journey would reveal about this complex man I had married.

"Let us not keep God waiting, Cardinal Joyeuse," Matthew said sharply. Joyeuse followed behind, as if Mont Saint-Michel belonged to the de Clermont family and not the church.

Beside me, Pierre let out a gentle exhalation. *"Milord est lui-même,"* he murmured with relief.

*Milord is himself.* But was he still mine?

Matthew might be a prince, but there was no doubt who was king.

With every strike of our horses' hooves on the frozen roads, the power and influence of Matthew's father grew. As we drew closer to Philippe de Clermont, his son became more remote and imperious—a combination that put my teeth on edge and led to several heated arguments. Matthew always apologized for his high-handed conduct once his temper came off the boil, and, knowing the stress he was under as we approached his reunion with his father, I forgave him.

After braving the exposed sands around Mont Saint-Michel at low tide and traveling inland, de Clermont allies welcomed us into the city of Fougères and lodged us in a comfortably appointed tower on the ramparts overlooking the French countryside. Two nights later, footmen with torches met us on the road outside the city of Baugé. There was a familiar badge on their livery: Philippe's insignia of a cross and crescent moon. I'd seen the symbol before when rooting through Matthew's desk drawer at Sept-Tours.

"What is this place?" I asked after the footmen led us to a deserted château. It was surprisingly warm for an empty residence, and the delicious smell of cooked food floated through the echoing corridors.

"The house of an old friend." Matthew pried the shoes off my frozen feet. His thumbs pressed into my frigid soles, and the blood began to return to my extremities. I groaned. Pierre put a cup of warm, spicy wine in my hands. "This was René's favorite hunting lodge. It was so full of life when he lived here, with artists and scholars in every room. My father manages it now. With the constant wars, there hasn't been an opportunity to give the château the attention it needs."

While we were still at the Old Lodge, Matthew and Walter had lectured me on the ongoing struggles between French Protestants and Catholics over who would control the Crown—and the country. From our windows at Fougères, I'd seen distant plumes of smoke marking the Protestant army's latest encampment, and ruined houses and churches dotted our route. I was shocked by the extent of the devastation.

Because of the conflict, my carefully constructed background story had to change. In England I was supposed to be a Protestant woman of French descent fleeing her native land to save her life and practice her faith. Here it was essential that I be a long-suffering English Catholic. Somehow Matthew managed to remember all the lies and half-truths required to maintain our multiple assumed identities, not to mention the historical details of every place through which we traveled.

"We're in the province of Anjou now." Matthew's deep voice brought my attention back. "The people you meet will suspect you're a Protestant spy because you speak English, no matter what story we tell them. This part of France refuses to acknowledge the king's claim to the throne and would prefer a Catholic ruler."

"As would Philippe," I murmured. It was not just Cardinal Joyeuse who was benefiting from Philippe's influence. Catholic priests with hollow cheeks and haunted eyes had stopped to speak with us along the way, sharing news and sending thanks to Matthew's father for his assistance. None left empty-handed.

"He doesn't care about the subtleties of Christian belief. In other parts of the country, my father supports the Protestants."

"That's a remarkably ecumenical view."

"All Philippe cares about is saving France from itself. This past August our new king, Henri of Navarre, tried to force the city of Paris to his religious and political position. Parisians chose to starve rather than bow to a

Protestant king." Matthew raked his fingers through his hair, a sign of distress. "Thousands died, and now my father does not trust the humans to sort out the mess."

Philippe was not inclined to let his son manage his own affairs either. Pierre woke us before dawn to announce that fresh horses were saddled and ready. He'd received word that we were expected at a town more than a hundred miles away—in two days.

"It's impossible. We can't travel that far so fast!" I was physically fit, but no amount of modern exercise was equivalent to riding more than fifty miles a day across open countryside in November.

"We have little choice," Matthew said grimly. "If we delay, he'll only send more men to hurry us along. Better to do what he asks." Later that day, when I was ready to weep with fatigue, Matthew lifted me into his saddle without asking and rode until the horses ran themselves out. I was too tired to protest.

We reached the stone walls and timbered houses of Saint-Benoît on schedule, just as Philippe had commanded. By that point we were close enough to Sept-Tours that neither Pierre nor Matthew was much concerned with propriety, so I rode astride. In spite of our adherence to his schedule, Philippe continued to increase the number of family retainers accompanying us, as though he feared we might change our minds and return to England. Some dogged our heels on the roads. Others cleared the way, securing food, horses, and places to stay in bustling inns, isolated houses, and barricaded monasteries. Once we climbed into the rocky hills left by the extinct volcanoes of the Auvergne, we often spotted the silhouettes of riders along the forbidding peaks. After they saw us, they whirled away to carry reports of our progress back to Sept-Tours.

Two days later, as twilight fell, Matthew, Pierre, and I stopped on one of these ragged mountaintops, the de Clermont family château barely visible through swirling gusts of snow. The straight lines of the central keep were familiar, but otherwise I might not have recognized the place. Its encircling walls were intact, as were all six of the round towers, each capped by conical copper roofs that had aged to a soft bottle green. Smoke came from chimneys tucked out of sight behind the towers' crenellations, the jagged outlines suggesting that some crazed giant with pinking shears had trimmed every wall. There was a snow-covered garden within the enclosure as well as rectangular beds beyond.

In modern times the fortress was forbidding. Now, with religious and civil war all around, its defensive capabilities were even more obvious. A formidable gatehouse stood vigil between Sept-Tours and the village. Inside, people hurried this way and that, many of them armed. Peering between snowflakes in the dusky light, I spotted wooden structures dotted throughout the enclosed courtyard. The light from their small windows created cubes of warm color in the otherwise unbroken stretches of gray stone and snow-covered ground.

My mare let out a warm, moist exhalation. She was the finest horse I'd ridden since our first day of travel. Matthew's present mount was large, inky-colored, and mean, snapping at everyone who got near him save the creature on his back. Both animals came from the de Clermont stables and knew their way home without any direction, eager to reach their oat buckets and a warm stable.

"*Dieu.* This is the last place on earth I imagined finding myself." Matthew blinked, slowly, as if he expected the château to disappear before his eyes.

I reached over and rested my hand on his forearm. "Even now you have a choice. We can turn back." Pierre looked at me with pity, and Matthew gave me a rueful smile.

"You don't know my father." His gaze returned to the castle.

Torches blazed all along our approach when at last we entered Sept-Tours. The heavy slabs of wood and iron were open in readiness, and a team of four men stood silently by as we passed. The gates slammed shut behind us, and two men drew a long timber from its hiding place in the walls to secure the entrance. Six days spent riding across France had taught me that these were wise precautions. People were suspicious of strangers, fearing the arrival of another marauding band of soldiers, a fresh hell of bloodshed and violence, a new lord to please.

A veritable army—humans and vampires both—awaited us inside. Half a dozen of them took charge of the horses. Pierre handed one a small packet of correspondence, while others asked him questions in low voices while sneaking furtive glances at me. No one came near or offered assistance. I sat atop my horse, shaking with fatigue and cold, and searched the crowd for Philippe. Surely he would order someone to help me down.

Matthew noticed my predicament and swung off his horse with enviably fluid grace. In several long strides, he was at my side, where he gently removed my unfeeling foot from the stirrup and rotated it slightly to restore its mobility. I thanked him, not wanting my first performance at Sept-Tours to involve tumbling into the trampled snow and dirt of the courtyard.

"Which of these men is your father?" I whispered as he crossed under the horse's neck to reach my other foot.

"None of them. He's inside, seemingly unconcerned with seeing us after insisting we ride as though the hounds of hell were in pursuit. You should be inside, too." Matthew began issuing orders in curt French, dispersing the gawking servants in every direction until only one vampire was left standing at the base of a corkscrew of wooden steps that rose to the château's door. I experienced the jarring sense of past and present colliding when I remembered climbing a not-yet-constructed set of stone steps and meeting Ysabeau for the first time.

"Alain." Matthew's face softened with relief.

"Welcome home." The vampire spoke English. As he approached with a slight hitch in his gait, the details of his appearance came into focus: the salt-and-pepper hair, the lines around his kind eyes, his wiry build.

"Thank you, Alain. This is my wife, Diana."

"Madame de Clermont." Alain bowed, keeping a careful, respectful distance.

"It's a pleasure to meet you, Alain." We had never met, but I already associated his name with steadfast loyalty and support. It had been Alain that Matthew called in the middle of the night when he wanted to be sure that there was food waiting for me at Sept-Tours in the twenty-first century.

"Your father is waiting," Alain said, stepping aside to let us pass.

"Have them send food to my rooms—something simple. Diana is tired and hungry." Matthew handed Alain his gloves. "I'll see him momentarily."

"He is expecting both of you now." A carefully neutral expression settled over Alain's face. "Do be careful on the stairs, *madame*. The treads are icy."

"Is he?" Matthew looked up at the square keep, mouth tightening.

With Matthew's hand firmly at my elbow, I had no trouble navigating the stairs. But my legs were shaking so badly after the climb that my feet caught the edge of an uneven flagstone in the entrance. That slip was enough to set Matthew's temper ablaze.

"Philippe is being unreasonable," Matthew snapped as he caught me around the waist. "She's been traveling for days."

"He was most explicit in his orders, sir." Alain's stiff formality was a warning.

"It's all right, Matthew." I pushed my hood from my face to survey the great hall beyond. Gone was the display of armor and pikes I'd seen in the twenty-first century. In their place stood a carved wooden screen that helped deflect the drafts when the door was opened. Gone, too, were the faux-medieval decorations, the round table, the porcelain bowl. Instead tapestries blew gently against stone walls as the warm air from the fireplace mingled with the colder air from outside. Two long tables flanked by low benches filled the remaining space, and men and women shuttled between them laying out plates and cups for supper. There was room for dozens of creatures to gather there. The minstrels' gallery high above wasn't empty now but crowded with musicians readying their instruments.

"Amazing," I breathed from between stiff lips.

Cold fingers grasped my chin and turned it. "You're blue," Matthew said.

"I will bring a brazier for her feet, and warm wine," Alain promised. "And we will build up the fires."

A warmblooded human appeared and took my wet cloak. Matthew turned sharply in the direction of what I knew as the breakfast room. I listened but heard nothing.

Alain shook his head apologetically. "He is not in a good temper."

"Evidently not." Matthew looked down. "Philippe is bellowing for us. Are you sure, Diana? If you don't want to see him tonight, I'll brave his wrath."

But Matthew would not be alone for his first meeting with his father in more than six decades. He had stood by me while I'd faced my ghosts, and I would do the same for him. Then I was going to go to bed, where I planned to remain until Christmas.

"Let's go," I said resolutely, picking up my skirts.

Sept-Tours was too ancient to have modern conveniences like corridors, so we snaked through an arched door to the right of the fireplace and into the corner of a room that would one day be Ysabeau's grand salon. It wasn't overstuffed with fine furniture now but decorated with the same austerity as every other place I'd seen on our journey. The heavy oak furniture re-sisted casual theft and could sustain the occasional ill effects of battle, as evidenced by the deep slash that cut diagonally across the surface of a chest.

From there Alain led us into the room where Ysabeau and I would one day take our breakfast amid warm terra-cotta walls at a table set with pot-tery and weighty silver cutlery. It was a far cry from that place in its present state, with only a table and chair. The tabletop was covered with papers and other tools of the secretary. There was no time to see more before we were climbing a worn stone staircase to an unfamiliar part of the château.

The stairs came to an abrupt halt on a wide landing. A long gallery opened up to the left, housing an odd assortment of gadgets, clocks, weaponry, portraits, and furniture. A battered golden crown perched casually on the marble head of some ancient god. A lumpy pigeon's-blood ruby the size of an egg winked malevolently at me from the crown's center.

"This way," Alain said, motioning us forward into the next chamber. Here was another staircase, this one leading up rather than down. A few uncomfortable benches sat on either side of a closed door. Alain waited, patiently and silently, for a response to our presence. When it came, the single Latin word resounded through the thick wood:

*"Introite."*

Matthew started at the sound. Alain cast a worried look at him and pushed the door. It silently swung open on substantial, well-oiled hinges.

A man sat opposite, his back to us and his hair gleaming. Even seated it was evident that he was quite tall, with the broad shoulders of an athlete. A pen scratched against paper, providing a steady treble note to harmonize with the intermittent pops of wood burning in the fireplace and the gusts of wind howling outside.

A bass note rumbled into the music of the place: *"Sedete."*

Now it was my turn to jump. With no door to muffle its impact, Philippe's voice resonated until my ears tingled. The man was used to being obeyed, at once and without question. My feet moved toward the two awaiting chairs so that I could sit as he'd commanded. I took three steps before realizing that Matthew was still in the doorway. I returned to his side and grasped his hand in mine. Matthew stared down, bewildered, and shook himself free from his memories.

In moments we had crossed the room. I settled into a chair with the promised wine and a pierced-metal foot warmer to prop up my legs. Alain withdrew with a sympathetic glance and a nod. Then we waited. It was difficult for me but impossible for Matthew. His tension increased until he was nearly vibrating with suppressed emotion.

By the time his father acknowledged our presence, my anxiety and temper were both dangerously close to the surface. I was staring down at my hands and wondering if they were strong enough to strangle him when two ferociously cold spots bloomed on my bowed head. Lifting my chin, I found myself gazing into the tawny eyes of a Greek god.

When I had first seen Matthew, my instinctive response had been to run. But Matthew—large and brooding as he'd been that September night in the Bodleian Library—hadn't appeared half so otherworldly. And it wasn't because Philippe de Clermont was a monster. On the contrary. He was, quite simply, the most breathtaking creature I had ever seen—supernatural, preternatural, daemonic, or human.

No one could look at Philippe de Clermont and think he was mortal flesh. The vampire's features were too perfect, and eerily symmetrical. Straight, dark eyebrows settled over eyes that were a pale, mutable golden brown touched with flecks of green. Exposure to sun and elements had touched his brown hair with strands of gleaming gold, silver, and bronze. Philippe's mouth was soft and sensual, though anger had drawn his lips hard and tight tonight.

Pressing my own lips together to keep my jaw from dropping, I met his appraising stare. Once I did, his eyes moved slowly and deliberately to Matthew.

"Explain yourself." The words were quiet, but they didn't conceal Philippe's fury. There was more than one angry vampire in the room, however. Now that the shock of seeing Philippe had passed, Matthew tried to take the upper hand.

"You commanded me to Sept-Tours. Here I am, alive and well, despite your grandson's hysterical reports." Matthew tossed the silver coin onto his father's oak table. It landed on its edge and whirled on an invisible axis before toppling flat.

"Surely it would have been better for your wife to remain at home this time of year." Like Alain, Philippe spoke English as flawlessly as a native.

"Diana is my mate, Father. I could hardly leave her in England with Henry and Walter simply because it might snow."

"Stand down, Matthew," Philippe growled. The sound was as leonine as the rest of him. The de Clermont family was a menagerie of formidable beasts. In Matthew's presence I was always reminded of wolves. With Ysabeau it was falcons. Gallowglass had made me think of a bear. Philippe was akin to yet another deadly predator.

"Gallowglass and Walter tell me the witch requires my protection." The lion reached for a letter. He tapped the edge of it on the table and stared at Matthew. "I thought that protecting weaker creatures was your job now that you occupy the family's seat on the Congregation."

"Diana isn't weak—and she needs more protection than the Congregation can afford, given the fact that she is married to me. Will you bestow it?" The challenge was in Matthew's tone now, as well as his bearing.

"First I need to hear her account," Philippe said. He looked at me and lifted his eyebrows.

"We met by chance. I knew she was a witch, but the bond between us was undeniable," Matthew said. "Her own people have turned on her—"

A hand that might have been mistaken for a paw rose in a gesture commanding quiet. Philippe returned his attention to his son.

*"Matthaios."* Philippe's lazy drawl had the efficiency of a slow-moving whip, silencing his son immediately. "Am I to understand that *you* need my protection?"

"Of course not," Matthew said indignantly.

"Then hush and let the witch speak."

Intent on giving Matthew's father what he wanted so that we could get out of his unnerving presence as quickly as possible, I considered how best to recount our recent adventures. Rehearsing every detail would take too long, and the chances that Matthew might explode in the meantime were excellent. I took a deep breath and began.

"My name is Diana Bishop, and my parents were both powerful witches. Other witches killed them when they were far from home, while I was still a child. Before they died, they spellbound me. My mother was a seer, and she knew what was to come."

Philippe's eyes narrowed with suspicion. I understood his caution. It was still difficult for me to understand why two people who loved me had broken the witches' ethical code and placed their only daughter in magical shackles.

"Growing up, I was a family disgrace—a witch who couldn't light a candle or perform a spell properly. I turned my back on the Bishops and went to university." With this revelation Matthew began to shift uneasily in his seat. "I studied the history of alchemy."

"Diana studies the *art* of alchemy," Matthew corrected, shooting me a warning glance. But his convoluted half-truths wouldn't satisfy his father.

"I'm a timewalker." The word hung in the air between the three of us. "You call it a *fileuse de temps.*"

"Oh, I am well aware of what you are," Philippe said in the same lazy tone. A fleeting look of surprise touched Matthew's face. "I have lived a long time, *madame,* and have known many creatures. You are not from this time, nor the past, so you must be from the future. And *Matthaios* traveled back with you, for he is not the same man he was eight months ago. The Matthew I know would never have looked twice at a witch." The vampire drew in a deep breath. "My grandson warned me that you both smelled very odd."

"Philippe, let me explain—" But Matthew was not destined to finish his sentences this evening.

"As troubling as many aspects of this situation are, I am glad to see that we can look forward to a sensible attitude toward shaving in the years to come." Philippe idly scratched his own neatly clipped beard and mustache. "Beards are a sign of lice, not wisdom, after all."

"I'm told Matthew looks like an invalid." I drew a tired sigh. "But I don't know a spell to fix it."

Philippe waved my words away. "A beard is easy enough to arrange. You were telling me of your interest in alchemy."

"Yes. I found a book—one that many others have sought. I met Matthew when he came to steal it from me, but he couldn't because I'd already let it out of my hands. Every creature for miles was after me then. I had to stop working!"

A sound that might have been suppressed laughter set a muscle in Philippe's jaw throbbing. It was, I discovered, hard to tell with lions whether they were amused or about to pounce.

"We think it's the book of origins," Matthew said. His expression was proud, though my calling of the manuscript had been completely accidental. "It came looking for Diana. By the time the other creatures realized what she'd found, I was already in love."

"So this went on for some time, then." Philippe tented his fingers in front of his chin, resting his elbows on the edges of the table. He was sitting on a simple four-legged stool, even though a splendid, thronelike eyesore sat empty next to him.

"No," I said after doing some calculations, "just a fortnight. Matthew wouldn't admit to his feelings for the longest time, though—not until we were at Sept-Tours. But it wasn't safe here either. One night I left Matthew's bed and went outside. A witch took me from the gardens."

Philippe's eyes darted from me to Matthew. "There was a *witch* inside the walls of Sept-Tours?"

"Yes," said Matthew tersely.

"Down into them," I corrected gently, capturing his father's attention once more. "I don't believe any witch's foot ever touched the ground, if that's important. Well, mine did, of course."

"Of course," Philippe acknowledged with a tip of his head. "Continue."

"She took me to La Pierre. Domenico was there. So was Gerbert." The look on Philippe's face told me that neither the castle nor the two vampires who had met me inside it were unfamiliar.

"Curses, like chickens, come home to roost," Philippe murmured.

"It was the Congregation who ordered my abduction, and a witch named Satu tried to force the magic from me. When she failed, Satu threw me into the oubliette."

Matthew's hand strayed to the small of my back as it always did when that night was mentioned. Philippe watched the movement but said nothing.

"After I escaped, I couldn't stay at Sept-Tours and put Ysabeau in danger. There was all this magic coming out of me, you see, and powers I couldn't control. Matthew and I went home, to my aunts' house." I paused, searching for a way to explain where that house was. "You know the legends told by Gallowglass's people, about lands across the ocean to the west?" Philippe nodded. "That's where my aunts live. More or less."

"And these aunts are both witches?"

"Yes. Then a *manjasang* came to kill Matthew—one of Gerbert's creatures—and she nearly succeeded. There was nowhere we could go that would be beyond the Congregation's reach, except the past." I paused, shocked at the venomous look that Philippe gave Matthew. "But we haven't found a haven here. People in Woodstock know I'm a witch, and the trials in Scotland might affect our lives in Oxfordshire. So we're on the run again." I reviewed the outlines of the story, making sure I hadn't left out anything important. "That's my tale."

"You have a talent for relating complicated information quickly and succinctly, *madame*. If you would be so kind as to share your methods with Matthew, it would be a service to the family. We spend more than we should on paper and quills." Philippe considered his fingertips for a moment, then stood with a vampiric efficiency that turned a simple movement into an explosion. One minute he was seated, and then, the next, his muscles sprang into action so that all six feet of him suddenly, and startlingly, loomed over the table. The vampire fixed his attention on his son.

"This is a dangerous game you are playing, Matthew, one with everything to lose and very little to gain. Gallowglass sent a message after you parted. The rider took a different route and arrived before you did. While you've been taking your time getting here, the king of Scotland has arrested more than a hundred witches and imprisoned them in Edinburgh. The Congregation no doubt thinks you are on your way there to persuade King James to drop this matter."

"All the more reason for you to give Diana your protection," Matthew said tightly.

"Why should I?" Philippe's cold countenance dared him to say it.

"Because I love her. And because you tell me that's what the Order of Lazarus is for: protecting those who cannot protect themselves."

"I protect other *manjasang*, not witches!"

"Maybe you should take a more expansive view," Matthew said stubbornly. "*Manjasang* can normally take care of themselves."

"You know very well that I cannot protect this woman, Matthew. All of Europe is feuding over matters of faith, and warmbloods are seeking scapegoats for their present troubles. Inevitably they turn to the creatures around them. Yet you knowingly brought this woman—a woman you claim is your mate and a witch by blood—into this madness. No." Philippe shook his head vehemently. "You may think you can brazen it out, but I will not put the family at risk by provoking the Congregation and ignoring the terms of the covenant."

"Philippe, you must—"

"Don't use that word with me." A finger jabbed in Matthew's direction. "Set your affairs in order and return whence you came. Ask me for help there—or better yet, ask the witch's aunts. Don't bring your troubles into the past where they don't belong."

But there was no Philippe for Matthew to lean on in the twenty-first century. He was gone—dead and buried.

"I have never asked you for anything, Philippe. Until now." The air in the room dropped several dangerous degrees.

"You should have foreseen my response, *Matthaios*, but as usual you were not thinking. What if your mother were here? What if bad weather hadn't struck Trier? You know she despises witches." Philippe stared at his son. "It would take a small army to keep her from tearing this woman limb from limb, and I don't have one to spare at the moment."

First it had been Ysabeau who'd wished me out of her son's life. Baldwin had made no effort to hide his disdain. Matthew's friend Hamish was wary of me, and Kit openly disliked me. Now it was Philippe's turn. I stood and waited for Matthew's father to look at me. When he did, I met his eyes squarely. His flickered with surprise.

"Matthew couldn't anticipate this, Monsieur de Clermont. He trusted you to stand with him, though his faith was misplaced in this case." I took a steadying breath. "I would be grateful if you would let me stay at Sept-Tours tonight. Matthew hasn't slept for weeks, and he is more likely to do so in a familiar place. Tomorrow I will return to England—without Matthew, if necessary."

One of my new curls tumbled onto my left temple. I reached up to push it away and found my wrist in Philippe de Clermont's grip. By the time I had registered my new position, Matthew was next to his father, palms on his shoulders.

"Where did you get that?" Philippe was gazing at the ring on the third finger of my left hand. *Ysabeau's ring.* Philippe's eyes turned feral, sought out mine. His fingers tightened on my wrist until the bones started to give way. "She would never have given my ring to another, not while we both lived."

"She lives, Philippe." Matthew's words were fast and rough, meant to convey information rather than reassurance.

"But if Ysabeau is alive, then . . ." Philippe trailed off into silence. For a moment he looked dumbfounded before understanding crept over his features. "So I am not immortal after all. And you cannot seek me out when and where these troubles began."

"No." Matthew forced the syllable past his lips.

"Yet you left your mother to face your enemies?" Philippe's expression was savage.

"Marthe is with her. Baldwin and Alain will make certain that she comes to no harm." Matthew's words now came in a soothing stream, but his father still held my fingers. They were growing numb.

"And Ysabeau gave my ring to a witch? How extraordinary. It looks well on her, though," Philippe said absently, turning my hand toward the firelight.

"*Maman* thought it would," said Matthew softly.

"When—" Philippe took a deliberate breath and shook his head. "No. Don't tell me. No creature should know his own death."

My mother had foreseen her gruesome end and my father's, too. Cold, exhausted, and haunted by my own memories, I started to tremble. Matthew's father seemed oblivious to it, staring down at our hands, but his son was not.

"Let her go, Philippe," Matthew commanded.

Philippe looked into my eyes and sighed with disappointment. Despite the ring, I was not his beloved Ysabeau. He withdrew his hand, and I stepped back, well beyond Philippe's long reach.

"Now that you have heard her tale, will you give Diana your protection?" Matthew searched his father's face.

"Is that what you want, *madame?*"

I nodded, my fingers curling around the carved arm of the nearby chair.

"Then yes, the Knights of Lazarus will ensure her well-being."

"Thank you, Father." Matthew's hands tightened on Philippe's shoulder, and then he headed back in my direction. "Diana is tired. We will see you in the morning."

"Absolutely not." Philippe's voice cracked across the room. "Your witch is under my roof and in my care. She will not be sharing a bed with you."

Matthew took my hand in his. "Diana is far from home, Philippe. She's not familiar with this part of the castle."

"She will not be staying in your rooms, Matthew."

"Why not?" I asked, frowning at Matthew and his father in turn.

"Because the two of you are not mated, no matter what pretty lies Matthew told you. And thank the gods for that. Perhaps we can avert disaster after all."

"Not mated?" I asked numbly.

"Exchanging promises and accepting a *manjasang* bond do not make an inviolable agreement, *madame.*"

"He's my husband in every way that matters," I said, color flooding into my cheeks. After I told Matthew I loved him, he had assured me that we were mated.

"You're not properly married either—at least not in a way to stand up to scrutiny," Philippe continued, "and there will be plenty of that if you keep up this pretense. Matthew always did spend more time in Paris brooding over his metaphysics than studying the law. In this case, my son, your instinct should have told you what was necessary even if your intellect did not."

"We swore oaths to each other before we left. Matthew gave me Ysabeau's ring." We'd been through a kind of ceremony during those last minutes in Madison. My mind raced over the sequence of events to find the loophole.

"What constitutes a *manjasang* mating is the same thing that silences all objections to a marriage when priests, lawyers, enemies, and rivals come calling: physical consummation." Philippe's nostrils flared. "And you are not yet joined in that way. Your scents are not only odd but entirely distinct—like two separate creatures instead of one. Any *manjasang* would know you are not fully mated. Gerbert and Domenico certainly knew it as soon as Diana was in their presence. So did Baldwin no doubt."

"We are married and mated. There is no need for any proof other than my assurances. As for the rest, it is none of your affair, Philippe," Matthew said, putting his body firmly between me and his father.

"Oh, *Matthaios,* we are long past that." Philippe sounded tired. "Diana is an unmarried, fatherless woman, and I see no brothers in the room to stand for her. She is entirely my *affair.*"

"We are married in the eyes of God."

"And yet you waited to take her. What are you waiting *for,* Matthew? A sign? She wants you. I can tell by the way she looks at you. For most men that's enough." Philippe's eyes pinned his son and me in turn. Reminded of Matthew's strange reluctance on this score, worry and doubt spread through me like poison.

"We've not known each other long. Even so, I know I will be with her—and only her—for my whole life. She is my mate. You know what the ring says, Philippe: '*a ma vie de coer entier.*'"

"Giving a woman your whole life is meaningless without giving her your whole heart as well. You should pay more attention to the conclusion of that love token, not just the beginning.'"

"She has my heart," Matthew said.

"Not all of it. If she did, every member of the Congregation would be dead, the covenant would be broken forever, and you would be where you belong and not in this room," Philippe said bluntly. "I don't know what constitutes marriage in this future of yours, but in the present moment it is something worth dying for."

"Shedding blood in Diana's name is not the answer to our current difficulties." Despite centuries of experience with his father, Matthew stubbornly refused to admit to what I already knew: There was no way to win an argument with Philippe de Clermont.

"Does a witch's blood not count?" Both men turned to me in surprise. "You've killed a witch, Matthew. And I've killed a vampire—a *manjasang*—rather than lose you. Since we are sharing secrets tonight, your father may as well know the truth." Gillian Chamberlain and Juliette Durand were two casualties in the escalating hostilities caused by our relationship.

"And you think there is time for courtship? For a man who considers himself learned, Matthew, your stupidity is breathtaking," Philippe said, disgusted. Matthew took his father's insult without flinching, then played his trump card.

"Ysabeau accepted Diana as her daughter," he said.

But Philippe would not be so easily swayed.

"Neither your God nor your mother has ever succeeded in making you face the consequences of your actions. Apparently that hasn't changed." Philippe braced his hands on the desk and called for Alain. "Since you are not mated, no permanent damage has been done. This matter can be set to rights before anyone finds out and the family is ruined. I will send to Lyon for a witch to help Diana better understand her power. You can inquire after her book while I do, Matthew. Then you are both going home, where you will forget about this indiscretion and move on with your separate lives."

"Diana and I are going to my rooms. Together. Or so help me—"

"Before you finish delivering that threat, be very sure that you have sufficient might to back it up," Philippe replied dispassionately. "The girl sleeps alone and near me."

A draft told me the door had opened. It carried with it a distinct whiff of wax and cracked pepper. Alain's cold eyes darted around, taking in Matthew's anger and the unrelenting look on Philippe's face.

"You have been outmaneuvered, *Matthaios,*" Philippe said to his son. "I don't know what you've been doing with yourself, but it has made you soft. Come now. Concede the field, kiss your witch, and say your good-nights. Alain, take this woman to Louisa's room. She is in Vienna—or Venice. I cannot keep up with that girl and her endless wanderings.

"As for you," Philippe continued, casting amber eyes over his son, "you will go downstairs and wait for me in the hall until I am finished writing to Gallowglass and Raleigh. It has been some time since you were home, and your friends want to know whether Elizabeth Tudor is a monster with two heads and three breasts as is widely claimed."

Unwilling to relinquish his territory completely, Matthew put his fingers under my chin, looked deep into my eyes, and kissed me rather more thoroughly than his father apparently expected.

"That will be all, Diana," Philippe said, sharply dismissive, when Matthew was finished.

"Come, *madame,*" Alain said, gesturing toward the door.

Awake and alone in another woman's bed, I listened to the crying wind, turning over all that had happened. There was too much subterfuge to sort through, as well as the hurt and sense of betrayal. I knew that Matthew loved me. But he must have known that others would contest our vows.

As the hours passed, I gave up all hope of sleeping. I went to the window and faced the dawn, trying to figure out how our plans had unraveled so much in such a short period of time and wondering what part Philippe de Clermont—and Matthew's secrets—had played in their undoing.

*9*

When my door swung open the next morning, Matthew was propped against the stone wall opposite. Judging from his state, he hadn't gotten any sleep either. He sprang to his feet, much to the amusement of the two young servingwomen who stood giggling behind me. They weren't used to seeing him this way, all mussed and tousled. A scowl darkened his face.

"Good morning." I stepped forward, cranberry skirts swinging. Like my bed, my servants, and practically everything else I touched, the outfit belonged to Louisa de Clermont. Her scent of roses and civet had been suffocatingly thick last night, emanating from the embroidered hangings that surrounded the bed. I took a deep breath of cold, clear air and sought out the notes of clove and cinnamon that were essentially and indisputably Matthew. Some of the fatigue left my bones as soon as I detected them, and, comforted by their familiarity, I burrowed into the sleeveless, black wool robe that the maids had lowered over my shoulders. It reminded me of my academic regalia and provided an additional layer of warmth.

Matthew's expression lifted as he drew me close and kissed me with admirable dedication to detail. The maids continued to giggle and make what he took to be encouraging remarks. A sudden gust around my ankles indicated that another witness had arrived. Our lips parted.

"You are too old to moon about in antechambers, *Matthaios*," his father commented, sticking his tawny head out of the next room. "The twelfth century was not good for you, and we allowed you to read entirely too much poetry. Compose yourself before the men see you, please, and bring Diana downstairs. She smells like a beehive at midsummer, and it will take time for the household to grow accustomed to her scent. We don't want any unfortunate bloodshed."

"There would be less chance of that if you would stop interfering. This separation is absurd," Matthew said, grasping my elbow. "We are husband and wife."

"You are not, thank the gods. Go down, and I will join you shortly." He shook his head ruefully and withdrew.

Matthew was tight-lipped as we faced each other across one of the long tables in the chilly great hall. There were few people in the room at this hour, and those who lingered left quickly after getting a good look at his forbidding expression. Bread, hot from the oven, and spiced wine were laid before me on the table. It wasn't tea, but it would do. Matthew waited to speak until I had taken my first long sip.

"I've seen my father. We'll leave at once."

I wrapped my fingers more tightly around the cup without responding. Bits of orange peel floated in the wine, plumped up with the warm liquid. The citrus made it seem slightly more like a breakfast drink.

Matthew looked around the room, his face haunted. "Coming here was unwise."

"Where are we to go instead? It's snowing. Back at Woodstock the village is ready to drag me before a judge on charges of witchcraft. At Sept-Tours we may have to sleep apart and put up with your father, but perhaps he'll be able to find a witch willing to help me." So far Matthew's hasty decisions had not worked out well.

"Philippe is a meddler. As for finding a witch, he's not much fonder of your people than is *Maman*." Matthew studied the scarred wooden table and picked at a bit of candle wax that had trickled down into one of the cracks. "My house in Milan might do. We could spend Christmas there. Italian witches have a considerable reputation for magic and are known for their uncanny foresight."

"Surely not Milan." Philippe appeared before us with the force of a hurricane and slid onto the bench next to me. Matthew carefully moderated his speed and strength in deference to warmblooded nerves. So, too, did Miriam, Marcus, Marthe, and even Ysabeau. His father showed no such consideration.

"I've performed my act of filial piety, Philippe," Matthew said curtly. "There's no reason to tarry, and we will be fine in Milan. Diana knows the Tuscan tongue."

If he meant Italian, I was capable of ordering tagliatelle in restaurants and books at the library. Somehow I doubted that would be sufficient.

"How useful for her. It is regrettable that you are not going to Florence, then. But it will be a long time before you will be welcomed back to that city, after your latest escapades there," Philippe said mildly. *"Parlez-vous français, madame?"*

*"Oui,"* I said warily, certain that this conversation was taking a multi-lingual turn for the worse.

"Hmm." Philippe frowned. *"Dicunt mihi vos es philologus."*

"She is a scholar," Matthew interjected testily. "If you want a rehearsal of her credentials, I'll be pleased to provide it, in private, after breakfast."

*"Loquerisne latine?"* Philippe asked me, as if his son hadn't spoken. *"Milás elliniká?"*

*"Mea lingua latina est mala,"* I replied, putting down my wine. Philippe's eyes shot wide at my appallingly schoolgirl response, his expression taking me straight back to the horrors of Latin 101. Put a Latin alchemical text in front of me and I could read it. But I wasn't prepared for a discussion. I soldiered bravely on, hoping I had deduced correctly that his second question probed my grasp of Greek. *"Tamen mea lingua graeca est peior."*

"Then we shall not converse in that language either," murmured Philippe in a pained tone. He turned to Matthew in indignation. *"Den tha ekpaidéfsoun gynaíkes sto méllon?"*

"Women in Diana's time receive considerably more schooling than you would think wise, Father," Matthew answered. "Just not in Greek."

"They have no need for Aristotle in the future? What a strange world it must be. I am glad that I will not encounter it for some time to come." Philippe gave the wine pitcher a suspicious sniff and decided against it. "Diana will have to become more fluent in French and Latin. Only a few of our servants speak English, and none at all belowstairs." He tossed a heavy ring of keys across the table. My fingers opened automatically to catch them.

"Absolutely not," Matthew said, reaching to pluck them from my grasp. "Diana won't be here long enough to trouble herself with the household."

"She is the highest-ranking woman at Sept-Tours, and it is her due. You should begin, I think, with the cook," Philippe said, pointing to the largest of the keys. "That one opens the food stores. The others unlock the bakehouse, the brewhouse, all the sleeping chambers save my own, and the cellars."

"Which one opens the library?" I asked, fingering the worn iron surfaces with interest.

"We don't lock up books in this house," Philippe said, "only food, ale, and wine. Reading Herodotus or Aquinas seldom leads to bad behavior."

"There's a first time for everything," I said under my breath. "And what is the cook's name?"

"Chef."

"No, his given name," I said, confused.

Philippe shrugged. "He is in charge, so he is Chef. I've never called him anything else. Have you, *Matthaios*?" Father and son exchanged a look that had me worried about the future of the trestle table that separated them.

"I thought you were in charge. If I'm to call the cook 'Chef,' what am I to call you?" My sharp tone temporarily distracted Matthew, who was about to toss the table aside and wrap his long fingers around his father's neck.

"Everyone here calls me either 'sire' or 'Father.' Which would you prefer?" Philippe's question was silky and dangerous.

"Just call him Philippe," Matthew rumbled. "He goes by many other titles, but those that fit him best would blister your tongue."

Philippe grinned at his son. "You didn't lose your combativeness when you lost your sense, I see. Leave the household to your woman and join me for a ride. You look puny and need proper exercise." He rubbed his hands together in anticipation.

"I am not leaving Diana," Matthew retorted. He was fiddling nervously with an enormous silver salt, the ancestor of the humble salt crock that sat by my stove in New Haven.

"Why not?" Philippe snorted. "Alain will play nursemaid."

Matthew opened his mouth to reply.

"Father?" I said sweetly, cutting into the exchange. "Might I speak with my husband privately before he meets you in the stables?"

Philippe's eyes narrowed. He stood and bowed slowly in my direction. It was the first time the vampire had moved at anything resembling normal speed. "Of course, *madame*. I will send for Alain to attend upon you. Enjoy your privacy—while you have it."

Matthew waited, his eyes on me, until his father left the room.

"What are you up to, Diana?" he asked quietly as I rose and made a slow progress around the table.

"Why is Ysabeau in Trier?" I asked.

"What does it matter?" he said evasively.

I swore like a sailor, which effectively removed the innocent expression from his face. There had been a lot of time to think last night, lying alone in Louisa's rose-scented room—enough time for me to piece together the events of the past weeks and square them with what I knew about the period.

"It matters because there's nothing much to do in Trier in 1590 but hunt witches!" A servant scuttled through the room, headed for the front door. There were still two men sitting by the fire, so I lowered my voice. "This is neither the time nor the place to discuss your father's current role in early-modern geopolitics, why a Catholic cardinal allowed you to order him around Mont Saint-Michel as if it were your private island, or the tragic death of Gallowglass's father. But you *will* tell me. And we definitely will require further time and privacy for you to explain the more technical aspects of vampire mating."

I whirled around to get away from him. He waited until I was far enough away to think escape was possible before neatly catching my elbow and turning me back. It was the instinctive maneuver of a predator. "No, Diana. We'll talk about our marriage before either of us leaves this room."

Matthew turned in the direction of the last huddle of servants enjoying their morning meal. A jerk of his head sent them scurrying.

"What marriage?" I demanded. Something dangerous sparked in his eyes and was gone.

"Do you love me, Diana?" Matthew's mild question surprised me.

"Yes," I responded instantaneously. "But if loving you were all that mattered, this would be simple and we would still be in Madison."

"It *is* simple." Matthew rose to his feet. "If you love me, my father's words don't have the power to dissolve our promises to each other, any more than the Congregation can make us abide by the covenant."

"If you truly loved me, you would give yourself to me. Body and soul."

"That's not so simple," Matthew said sadly. "From the first I warned you that a relationship with a vampire would be complicated."

"Philippe doesn't seem to think so."

"Then bed him. If it's me you want, you'll wait." Matthew was composed, but it was the calm of a frozen river: hard and smooth on the surface but raging underneath. He'd been using words as weapons since we left the Old Lodge. He'd apologized for the first few cutting remarks, but there would be no apology for this. Now that he was with his father again, Matthew's civilized veneer was too thin for something so modern and human as regret.

"Philippe isn't my type," I said coldly. "You might, however, do me the courtesy of explaining why I should wait for you."

"Because there is no such thing as vampire divorce. There's mating and there's death. Some vampires—my mother and Philippe included—separate for a time if there are"—he paused—"disagreements. They take other lovers. With time and distance, they resolve their differences and come together again. But that isn't going to work for me."

"Good. It wouldn't be my first choice for a marriage either. But I still don't see why that makes you so reluctant to consummate our relationship." He'd already learned my body and its responses with the careful attention of a lover. It wasn't me or the idea of sex that made him hesitate.

"It's too soon to curb your freedom. Once I lose myself inside you, there will be no other lovers and no separations. You need to be sure if being wed to a vampire is what you really want."

"You get to choose me, over and over again, but when I want the same, you think I don't know my own mind?"

"I've had ample opportunity to know what I want. Your fondness for me may be nothing more than a way of alleviating your fear of the unknown, or satisfying your desire to embrace this world of creatures that you've denied for so long."

"Fondness? I love you. It makes no difference whether I have two days or two years. My decision will be the same."

"The difference will be that I will not have done to you what your parents did!" he exploded, pushing past me. "Mating a vampire is no less confining than being spellbound by witches. You're living on your own terms for the first time, yet you're ready to swap one set of restraints for another. But mine aren't the enchanted stuff of fairy tales, and no charm will remove them when they begin to chafe."

"I'm your lover, not your prisoner."

"And I am a vampire, not a warmblood. Mating instincts are primitive and difficult to control. My entire being will be focused on you. No one deserves that kind of ruthless attention, least of all the woman I love."

"So I can either live without you or be locked in a tower by you." I shook my head. "This is fear talking, not reason. You're scared of losing me, and being with Philippe is making it worse. Pushing me away isn't going to ease your pain, but talking about it might."

"Now that I'm with my father again, my wounds open and bleeding, am I not healing as quickly as you hoped?" The cruelty was back in Matthew's tone. I winced. Regret flickered over his features before they hardened again.

"You would rather be anywhere than here. I know that, Matthew. But Hancock was right: I wouldn't last long in a place like London or Paris, where we might be able to find a willing witch. Other women will spot my differences straightaway, and they won't be as forgiving as Walter or Henry. I'd be turned in to the authorities—or the Congregation—in a matter of days."

The acuity of Matthew's gaze gave weight to his warning about what it would feel like to be the object of a vampire's single-minded attention. "Another witch won't care," he said stubbornly, dropping my arms and turning away. "And I can manage the Congregation."

The few feet that separated Matthew and me stretched until we might have been on opposite sides of the world. Solitude, my old companion, no longer felt like a friend.

"We can't go on this way, Matthew. With no family and no property, I'm utterly dependent on you," I continued. Historians had some things right about the past, including the structural weaknesses associated with being female, friendless, and without money. "We need to stay at Sept-Tours until I can walk into a room and not draw every curious eye. I have to be able to manage on my own. Starting with these." I held up the keys to the castle.

"You want to play house?" he said doubtfully.

"I'm not playing house. I'm playing for keeps." Matthew quirked his lips at my words, but it wasn't a real smile. "Go. Spend time with your father. I'll be too busy to miss you."

Matthew left for the stables without a kiss or word of farewell. The absence of his usual reassurances left me feeling strangely unresolved. After his scent had dissipated, I called softly for Alain, who arrived suspiciously quickly, accompanied by Pierre. They must have heard every word of our exchange.

"Staring out the window doesn't hide your thoughts, Pierre. It's one of your master's few tells, and every time he does it, I know he's concealing something."

"Tells?" Pierre looked at me, confused. The game of poker had yet to be invented.

"An outward sign of an inward concern. Matthew looks away when he's anxious or doesn't want to tell me something. And he runs his fingers through his hair when he doesn't know what to do. These are tells."

"So he does, *madame.*" Pierre looked at me, awestruck. "Does *milord* know that you used a witch's powers of divination to see into his soul? Madame de Clermont knows these habits, and *milord*'s brothers and father do as well. But you have known him for such a short time and yet know so much."

Alain coughed.

Pierre looked horrified. "I forget myself, *madame.* Please forgive me."

"Curiosity is a blessing, Pierre. And I used observation, not divination, to know my husband." There was no reason the seeds of the Scientific Revolution shouldn't be planted now, in the Auvergne. "We will, I think, be more comfortable discussing matters in the library." I pointed in what I hoped was the proper direction.

The room where the de Clermonts kept most of their books represented the closest thing to a home-court advantage available to me in sixteenth-century Sept-Tours. Once I was enshrouded in the scent of paper, leather, and stone, some of the loneliness left me. This was a world I knew.

"We have a great deal of work to do," I said quietly, turning to face the family retainers. "First, I would ask both of you to promise me something."

"A vow, *madame*?" Alain looked upon me with suspicion.

I nodded. "If I request something that would require the assistance of *milord* or, more important, his father, please tell me and we will change course immediately. They don't need to worry about my small concerns." The men looked wary but intrigued.

"*Òc,*" Alain agreed with a nod.

Despite such auspicious beginnings, my first team meeting got off to a rocky start. Pierre refused to sit in my presence, and Alain would take a chair only if I did. But remaining motionless wasn't an option, given my rising tide of anxiety about my responsibilities at Sept-Tours, so the three of us completed lap after lap of the library. While we circled, I pointed to books to be brought to Louisa's room, reeled off necessary supplies, and ordered that my traveling clothes be handed to a tailor to serve as a pattern for a basic wardrobe. I was prepared to wear Louisa de Clermont's clothes for two more days. After that I threatened to resort to Pierre's cupboards for breeches and hose. The prospect of such grievous female immodesty clearly struck terror into their hearts.

We spent our second and third hours discussing the inner workings of the château. I had no experience running such a complicated household, but I knew which questions to ask. Alain rehearsed the names and job descriptions of its key officers, provided a brief introduction to leading personalities in the village, accounted for who was staying in the house at present, and speculated about who we could expect to visit over the next few weeks.

Then we decamped to the kitchens, where I had my first encounter with Chef. He was a human, as thin as a reed and no taller than Pierre. Like Popeye, he had all of his bulk concentrated in his forearms, which were the size of hams. The reason for this was apparent when he hefted an enormous lump of dough onto a floury surface and began to work it smooth. Like me, Chef was able to think only when he was in motion.

Word had trickled belowstairs about the warmblooded guest sleeping in a room near the head of the family. So, too, had speculation about my relationship to *milord* and what kind of creature I was, given my scent and eating habits. I caught the words *sorcière* and *masca*—French and Occitan terms for witch—when we entered the inferno of activity and heat. Chef had assembled the kitchen staff, which was vast and Byzantine in its organization. This provided an opportunity for them to study me firsthand. Some were vampires, others were humans. One was a daemon. I made a mental note to ensure that the young woman called Catrine, whose glance nudged against my cheeks with open curiosity, was kindly treated and looked after until her strengths and weaknesses were clearer.

I was resolved to speak English only out of necessity, and even then just to Matthew, his father, Alain, and Pierre. As a result my conversation with Chef and his associates was full of misunderstandings. Fortunately, Alain and Pierre gently untangled the knots when my French and their heavily accented Occitan mingled. Once I had been a decent mimic. It was time to resurrect those talents, and I listened carefully to the dips and sways of the local tongue. I'd already put several language dictionaries on the shopping list for the next time someone went to the nearby city of Lyon.

Chef warmed to me after I complimented his baking skills, praised the order of the kitchens, and requested that he tell me immediately if he needed anything at all to work his culinary magic. Our good relationship was assured, however, when I inquired into Matthew's favorite food and drink. Chef became animated, waving his sticky hands in the air and speaking a mile a minute about *milord's* skeletal condition, which he blamed entirely on the English and their poor regard for the arts of the kitchen.

"Have I not sent Charles to see to his needs?" Chef demanded in rapid Occitan, picking up his dough and slamming it down. Pierre murmured the translation as quickly as he could. "I lost my best assistant, and it is nothing to the English! *Milord* has a delicate stomach, and he must be tempted to eat or he begins to waste away."

I apologized on behalf of England and asked how he and I might ensure Matthew's return to health, although the thought of my husband being any more robust was alarming. "He enjoys uncooked fish, does he not, as well as venison?"

"*Milord* needs blood. And he will not take it unless it is prepared just so."

Chef led me to the game room, where the carcasses of several beasts were suspended over silver troughs to catch the blood falling from their severed necks.

"Only silver, glass, or pottery should be used to collect blood for *milord*, or he refuses it," Chef instructed with a raised finger.

"Why?" I asked.

"Other vessels taint the blood with bad odors and tastes. This is pure. Smell," Chef instructed, handing me the cup. My stomach heaved at the metallic aroma, and I covered my mouth and nose. Alain motioned the blood away, but I stopped him with a glance.

"Continue, please, Chef."

Chef gave me an approving look and began to describe the other delicacies that made up Matthew's diet. He told me of Matthew's love of beef broth fortified with wine and spices and served cool. Matthew would take partridge blood, provided it was in small quantities and not too early in the day. Madame de Clermont was not so fussy, Chef said with a sorrowful shake of his head, but she had not passed her impressive appetite to her son.

"No," I said tightly, thinking of my hunting trip with Ysabeau.

Chef put the tip of his finger into the silver cup and held it up, shimmering red in the light, before inserting it into his mouth and letting the lifeblood roll over his tongue. "Stag's blood is his favorite, of course. It is not as rich as human blood, but it is similar in taste."

"May I?" I asked hesitantly, extending my little finger toward the cup. Venison turned my stomach. Perhaps the taste of a stag's blood would be different.

"*Milord* would not like it, Madame de Clermont," Alain said, his concern evident.

"But he is not here," I said. I dipped the tip of my little finger into the cup. The blood was thick, and I brought it to my nose and sniffed it as Chef had. What scent did Matthew detect? What flavors did he perceive?

When my finger passed over my lips, my senses were flooded with information: wind on a craggy peak, the comfort of a bed of leaves in a hollow between two trees, the joy of running free. Accompanying it all was a steady, thundering beat. *A pulse, a heart.*

My experience of the deer's life faded all too quickly. I reached out my finger with a fierce desire to know more, but Alain's hand stopped mine. Still the hunger for information gnawed at me, its intensity diminishing as the last traces of blood left my mouth.

"Perhaps *madame* should go back to the library now," Alain suggested, giving Chef a warning look.

On my way out of the kitchens, I told Chef what to do when Matthew and Philippe returned from their ride. We were passing through a long stone corridor when I stopped abruptly at a low, open door. Pierre narrowly avoided plowing into me.

"Whose room is this?" I asked, my throat closing at the scent of the herbs that hung from the rafters.

"It belongs to Madame de Clermont's woman," Alain explained.

"Marthe," I breathed, stepping over the threshold. Earthenware pots stood in neat rows on shelves, and the floor was swept clean. There was something medicinal—mint?—in the tang of the air. It reminded me of the scent that sometimes drifted from the housekeeper's clothes. When I turned, the three of them were blocking the doorway.

"The men are not allowed in here, *madame,*" Pierre confessed, looking over his shoulder as though he feared that Marthe might appear at any moment. "Only Marthe and Mademoiselle Louisa spend time in the stillroom. Not even Madame de Clermont disturbs this place."

Ysabeau didn't approve of Marthe's herbal remedies—this I knew. Marthe was not a witch, but her potions were only a few steps away from Sarah's lore. My eyes swept the room. There was more to be done in a kitchen than cooking, and more to learn from the sixteenth century than the management of household affairs and my own magic.

"I would like to use the stillroom while at Sept-Tours."

Alain looked at me sharply. "Use it?"

I nodded. "For my alchemy. Please have two barrels of wine brought here for my use—as old as possible, but nothing that's turned to vinegar. Give me a few moments alone to take stock of what's here."

Pierre and Alain shifted nervously at the unexpected development. After weighing my resolve against his companions' uncertainty, Chef took charge, pushing the other men in the direction of the kitchens.

As Pierre's grumbling faded, I focused on my surroundings. The wooden table before me was deeply scored from the work of hundreds of knives that had separated leaf from stalk. I ran a finger down one of the grooves and brought it to my nose.

Rosemary. For remembrance.

*"Remember?"* It was Peter Knox's voice I heard, the modern wizard who had taunted me with memories of my parents' death and wanted Ashmole

782 for himself. Past and present collided once more, and I stole a glance at the corner by the fire. The blue and amber threads were there, just as I expected. I sensed something else as well, some other creature in some other time. My rosemary-scented fingers reached to make contact, but it was too late. Whoever it was had already gone, and the corner had returned to its normal, dusty self.

*Remember.*

It was Marthe's voice that echoed in my memory now, naming herbs and instructing me to take a pinch of each and make a tea. It would inhibit conception, though I hadn't known it when I'd first tasted the hot brew. The ingredients for it were surely here, in Marthe's stillroom.

The simple wooden box was on the uppermost shelf, safely beyond reach. Rising to my toes, I lifted my arm up and directed my desire toward the box just as I had once called a library book off the Bodleian's shelf. The box slid forward obligingly until my fingers could brush the corners. I snared it and set it down gently on the table.

The lid lifted to reveal twelve equal compartments, each filled with a different substance. *Parsley. Ginger. Feverfew. Rosemary. Sage. Queen Anne's lace seeds. Mugwort. Pennyroyal. Angelica. Rue. Tansy. Juniper root.* Marthe was well equipped to help the women of the village curb their fertility. I touched each in turn, pleased that I remembered their names and scents. My satisfaction turned quickly to shame, however. I knew nothing else— not the proper phase of the moon to gather them or what other magical uses they might have. Sarah would have known. Any sixteenth-century woman would have known, too.

I shook off the regret. For now I knew what these herbs would do if I steeped them in hot water or wine. I tucked the box under my arm and joined the others in the kitchen. Alain stood.

"Are you finished here, *madame*?"

"Yes, Alain. *Mercés,* Chef," I said.

Back in the library, I put the box carefully on the corner of my table and drew a blank sheet of paper toward me. Sitting down, I took a quill from the stand of pens.

"Chef tells me that it will be December on Saturday. I didn't want to mention it in the kitchen, but can someone explain how I misplaced the second half of November?" I dipped my pen in a pot of dark ink and looked at Alain expectantly.

"The English refuse the pope's new calendar," he said slowly, as if talking to a child. "So it is only the seventeenth day of November there, and the twenty-seventh day of November here in France."

I had timewalked more than four centuries and not lost a single hour, yet my trip from Elizabeth's England to war-torn France had cost me nearly three weeks instead of ten days. I smothered a sigh and wrote the correct dates on the top of the page. My pen stilled.

"That means Advent will begin on Sunday."

"*Oui.* The village—and *milord,* of course—will fast until the night before Christmas. The household will break the fast with the *seigneur* on the seventeenth of December." How did a vampire fast? My knowledge of Christian religious ceremonies was of little help.

"What happens on the seventeenth?" I asked, making note of that date, too.

"It is Saturnalia, *madame,*" Pierre said, "the celebration dedicated to the god of the harvest. *Sieur* Philippe still observes the old ways."

"Ancient" would be more accurate. Saturnalia hadn't been practiced since the last days of the Roman Empire. I pinched the bridge of my nose, feeling overwhelmed. "Let's begin at the beginning, Alain. What, exactly, is happening in this house this weekend?"

After thirty minutes of discussion and three more sheets of paper, I was left alone with my books, papers, and a pounding headache. Sometime later I heard a commotion in the great hall, followed by a bellow of laughter. A familiar voice, somehow richer and warmer than I knew it, called out in greeting.

*Matthew.*

Before I could set my papers aside, he was there.

"Did you notice I was gone after all?" Matthew's face was touched with color. His fingers pulled loose a tendril of hair as he gripped my neck and planted a kiss on my lips. There was no blood on his tongue, only the taste of the wind and the outdoors. Matthew had ridden, but he hadn't fed. "I'm sorry about what happened earlier, *mon coeur,*" he whispered into my ear. "Forgive me for behaving so badly." The ride had lifted his spirits, and his attitude toward his father was natural and unforced for the first time.

"Diana," Philippe said, stepping from behind his son. He reached for the nearest book and took it to the fire, leafing through the pages. "You are reading *The History of the Franks*—not for the first time, I trust. This book would be more enjoyable, of course, if Gregory's mother had overseen the writing of it. Armentaria's Latin was most impressive. It was always a pleasure to receive her letters."

I had never read Gregory of Tours's famous book on French history, but there was no reason for Philippe to know that.

"When he and Matthew attended school in Tours, your famous Gregory was a boy of twelve. Matthew was far older than the teacher, never mind the other pupils, and allowed the boys to ride him like a horse when it was time for their recreation." Philippe scanned the pages. "Where is the part about the giant? It's my favorite."

Alain entered, bearing a tray with two silver cups. He set it on the table by the fire.

"*Merci, Alain.*" I gestured at the tray. "You both must be hungry. Chef sent your meal here. Why don't you tell me about your morning?"

"I don't need—" Matthew began. His father and I both made sounds of exasperation. Philippe deferred to me with a gentle incline of his head.

"Yes you do," I said. "It's partridge blood, which you should be able to stomach at this hour. I hope you will hunt tomorrow, though, and Saturday, too. If you intend to fast for the next four weeks, you have to feed while you can." I thanked Alain, who bowed, shot a veiled glance at his master, and left hastily. "Yours is stag's blood, Philippe. It was drawn only this morning."

"What do you know of partridge blood and fasting?" Matthew's fingers tugged gently on my loose curl. I looked up into my husband's gray-green eyes.

"More than I did yesterday." I freed my hair before handing him his cup.

"I will take my meal elsewhere," Philippe interjected, "and leave you to your argument."

"There's no argument. Matthew must remain healthy. Where did you go on your ride?" I picked up the cup of stag's blood and held it out to Philippe.

Philippe's attention traveled from the silver cup to his son's face and back to me. He gave me a dazzling smile, but there was no mistaking his appraising look. He took the proffered cup and raised it in salute.

"Thank you, Diana," he said, his voice full of friendship.

But those unnatural eyes that missed nothing continued to watch me as Matthew described their morning. A sensation of spring thaw told me when Philippe's attention moved to his son. I couldn't resist glancing in his direction to see if it was possible to tell what he was thinking. Our gazes crossed, clashed. The warning was unmistakable.

Philippe de Clermont was up to something.

"How did you find the kitchens?" Matthew asked, turning the conversation in my direction.

"Fascinating," I said, meeting Philippe's shrewd eyes with a challenging stare. "Absolutely fascinating."

10

Philippe might be fascinating, but he was maddening and inscrutable, too—just as Matthew had promised.

Matthew and I were in the great hall the next morning when my father-in-law seemed to materialize out of thin air. No wonder humans thought vampires could shape-shift into bats. I lifted a spindle of toasted bread from my soft-boiled egg's golden yolk.

"Good morning, Philippe."

"Diana." Philippe nodded. "Come, Matthew. You must feed. Since you will not do so in front of your wife, we will hunt."

Matthew hesitated, restlessly glancing at me and then away. "Perhaps tomorrow."

Philippe muttered something under his breath and shook his head. "You must attend to your own needs, *Matthaios*. A famished, exhausted *manjasang* is not an ideal traveling companion for anyone, least of all a warmblooded witch."

Two men entered the hall, stomping the snow from their boots. Chilly winter air billowed around the wooden screen and through the lacy carvings. Matthew cast a longing look toward the door. Chasing stags across the frozen landscape would not only feed his body—it would clear his mind as well. And if yesterday was any indication, he'd be in a much better mood when he returned.

"Don't worry about me. I have plenty to do," I said, taking his hand in mine to give it a reassuring squeeze.

After breakfast Chef and I discussed the menu for Saturday's pre-Advent feast. This done, I discussed my clothing needs with the village tailor and seamstress. Given my grasp of French, I feared I had ordered a circus tent. By late morning I was desperate for some fresh air, and persuaded Alain to take me on a tour of the courtyard workshops. Almost everything the château residents needed, from candles to drinking water, could be found there. I tried to remember every detail of how the blacksmith smelted his metals, aware that the knowledge would be useful when I returned to my real life as a historian.

With the exception of the hour spent at the forge, my day so far had been typical of a noblewoman's of the time. Feeling that I'd made good progress toward my goal of fitting in, I spent several pleasant hours reading and practicing my handwriting. When I heard the musicians setting up for the last feast before the monthlong fast I asked them to give me a dancing lesson. Later I treated myself to an adventure in the stillroom and was soon happily occupied with a glorified double boiler, a copper still, and a small barrel of old wine. Two young boys borrowed from the kitchens kept the glowing embers of the fire alight with a pair of leather bellows that sighed gently whenever Thomas and Étienne pressed them into action.

Being in the past provided a perfect opportunity for me to practice what I knew only in theory. After poking through Marthe's equipment, I settled on a plan to make spirit of wine, a basic substance used in alchemical procedures. I was soon cursing, however.

"This will never condense properly," I said crossly, looking at the steam escaping from the still. The kitchen boys, who knew no English, made sympathetic noises while I consulted a tome I'd pulled from the de Clermont library. There were all sorts of interesting volumes on the shelves. One of them must explain how to repair leaks.

*"Madame?"* Alain called softly from the doorway.

"Yes?" I turned and wiped my hands on the bunched-up folds of my linen smock.

Alain surveyed the room, aghast. My dark sleeveless robe was flung over the back of a nearby chair, my heavy velvet sleeves were draped over the edge of a copper pot, and my bodice hung from the ceiling on a convenient pothook. Though relatively unclothed by sixteenth-century standards, I still wore a corset, a high-necked, long-sleeved linen smock, several petticoats, and a voluminous skirt—far more clothing than I normally wore to lecture. Feeling naked nonetheless, I lifted my chin and dared Alain to say a word. Wisely, he looked away.

"Chef does not know what to do about this evening's meal," Alain said.

I frowned. Chef unfailingly knew what to do.

"The household is hungry and thirsty, but they cannot sit down without you. So long as there is a member of the family at Sept-Tours, that person must preside over the evening meal. It is tradition."

Catrine appeared with a towel and a bowl. I dipped my fingers into the warm, lavender-scented water.

"How long have they been waiting?" I took the towel from Catrine's arm. A great hall filled with both hungry warmbloods and equally famished vampires couldn't be wise. My newfound confidence in my ability to manage the de Clermont family home evaporated.

"More than an hour. They will continue to wait until word comes from the village that Roger is closing down for the night. He runs the tavern. It is cold, and many hours until breakfast. *Sieur* Philippe led me to believe . . ." He trailed off into apologetic silence.

"*Vite,*" I said, pointing at my discarded clothing. "You must get me dressed, Catrine."

"*Bien sûr.*" Catrine put down her bowl and headed for my suspended bodice. The large splotch of ink on it put an end to my hope of looking respectable.

When I entered the hall, benches scraped against the stone floor as more than three dozen creatures stood. There was a note of reproach in the sound. Once seated, they ate their delayed meal with gusto, while I picked apart a chicken leg and waved away everything else.

After what seemed an interminable length of time, Matthew and his father returned. "Diana!" Matthew rounded the wooden screen, confused to see me sitting at the head of the family table. "I expected you to be upstairs, or in the library."

"I thought it was more courteous for me to sit here, considering how much work Chef put into preparing the meal." My eyes traveled to Philippe. "How was your hunting, Philippe?"

"Adequate. But animal blood provides only so much nourishment." He beckoned to Alain, and his cold eyes nudged my high collar.

"Enough." Though his voice was low, the warning in Matthew's tone was unmistakable. Heads swiveled in his direction. "You should have instructed them to start without us. Let me take you upstairs, Diana." Heads swiveled back to me, waiting for my reply.

"I have not finished," I said, gesturing at my plate, "nor have the others. Sit by me and take some wine." Matthew might be a Renaissance prince in substance as well as style, but I would not heel when he clicked his fingers.

Matthew sat by my side while I forced myself to swallow some chicken. When the tension was unbearable, I rose. Once more, benches scraped against stone as the household stood.

"Finished so soon?" Philippe asked with surprise. "Good night, then, Diana. Matthew, you will return at once. I have a strange desire to play chess."

Matthew ignored his father and extended his arm. We didn't exchange a word as we passed out of the great hall and climbed to the family rooms. At my door Matthew at last had himself under enough control to risk conversation.

"Philippe is treating you like a glorified housekeeper. It's intolerable."

"Your father is treating me like a woman of the time. I'll manage, Matthew." I paused, gathering my courage. "When did you last feed on a creature that walks on two legs?" I'd forced him to take blood from me before we left Madison, and he'd fed on some nameless warmblood in Canada. Several weeks prior to that, he'd killed Gillian Chamberlain in Oxford. Maybe he had fed on her, too. Otherwise I didn't believe that a drop of anything other than animal blood had crossed his lips in months.

"What makes you ask?" Matthew's tone was sharp.

"Philippe says you aren't as strong as you should be." My hand tightened on his. "If you need to feed and won't take blood from a stranger, then I want you to take mine."

Before Matthew could respond, a chuckle came from the stairs. "Careful, Diana. We *manjasang* have sharp ears. Offer your blood in this house and you'll never keep the wolves at bay." Philippe was standing with arms braced against the sides of the carved stone archway.

Matthew swung his head around, furious. "Go away, Philippe."

"The witch is reckless. It's my responsibility to make sure her impulses don't go unchecked. Otherwise she could destroy us."

"The witch is mine," Matthew said coldly.

"Not yet," Philippe said, descending the stairs with a regretful shake of his head. "Maybe not ever."

After that encounter Matthew was even more guarded and remote. The next day he was angry with his father, but rather than taking his frustration out on its source, Matthew snapped at everyone else: me, Alain, Pierre, Chef, and any other creature unfortunate enough to cross his path. The household was in a state of high anxiety already because of the feast, and after putting up with his bad behavior for several hours, Philippe gave his son a choice. He could sleep off his bad humor or feed. Matthew chose a third option and went off to search the de Clermont archives for some hint as to the present whereabouts of Ashmole 782. Left to my own devices, I returned to the kitchens.

Philippe found me in Marthe's room, crouched over the malfunctioning still with my sleeves rolled up and the room full of steam.

"Has Matthew fed from you?" he asked abruptly, his eyes moving over my forearms.

I lifted my left arm in reply. The soft linen pooled around my shoulder, exposing the pink traces of a jagged scar on my inner elbow. I'd cut into the flesh so that Matthew could drink from me more easily.

"Anywhere else?" Philippe directed his attention to my torso.

With the other hand, I exposed my neck. The wound there was deeper, but it had been made by a vampire and was far neater.

"What a fool you are, to allow a besotted *manjasang* to take the blood from not only your arm but your neck," Philippe said, stunned. "The covenant forbids the *manjasang* to take the blood of witches or daemons. Matthew knows this."

"He was dying, and mine was the only blood available!" I said fiercely. "If it makes you feel better, I had to force him."

"So that's it. My son has no doubt convinced himself that so long as he has taken only your blood and not your body, he will be able to let you go." Philippe shook his head. "He is wrong. I've been watching him. You will never be free of Matthew, whether he beds you or not."

"Matthew knows I'd never leave him."

"Of course you will. One day your life on this earth will draw to a close and you will make your final journey into the underworld. Rather than grieve, Matthew will want to follow you into death." Philippe's words rang with truth.

Matthew's mother had shared with me the story of his making: how he fell from the scaffolding while helping to lay the stones for the village church. Even when I first heard it, I'd wondered if Matthew's despair over losing his wife, Blanca, and his son, Lucas, had driven him to suicide.

"It is too bad that Matthew is a Christian. His God is never satisfied."

"How so?" I asked, perplexed by the sudden change of topic.

"When you or I have done wrong, we settle our accounts with the gods and return to living with the hope of doing better in future. Ysabeau's son confesses his sins and atones again and again—for his life, for who he is, for what he has done. He is always looking backward, and there is no end to it."

"That's because Matthew is a man of great faith, Philippe." There was a spiritual center to Matthew's life that colored his attitudes toward science and death.

"Matthew?" Philippe sounded incredulous. "He has less faith than anyone I have ever known. All he possesses is belief, which is quite different and depends on the head rather than the heart. Matthew has always had a keen mind, one capable of dealing with abstractions like God. It is how he came to accept who he had become after Ysabeau made him one of the family. For every *manjasang* it is different. My sons chose other paths— war, love, mating, conquest, the acquisition of riches. For Matthew it was always ideas."

"It still is," I said softly.

"But ideas are seldom strong enough to provide the basis for courage. Not without hope for the future." His expression turned thoughtful. "You don't know your husband as well as you should."

"Not as well as you do, no. We're a witch and a vampire who love even though we're forbidden to do so. The covenant doesn't permit us lingering public courtship and moonlight strolls." My voice heated as I continued. "I can't hold his hand or touch his face outside of these four walls without fearing that someone will notice and he will be punished for it."

"Matthew goes to the church in the village around midday, when you think he is looking for your book. It's where he went today." Philippe's remark was strangely disconnected from our conversation. "You might follow him one day. Perhaps then you would come to know him better."

I went to the church at eleven on Monday morning, hoping to find it empty. But Matthew was there, just as Philippe had promised.

He couldn't have failed to hear the heavy door close behind me or my steps echoing as I crossed the floor, but he didn't turn around. Instead he remained kneeling just to the right of the altar. In spite of the cold, Matthew was wearing an insubstantial linen shirt, breeches, hose, and shoes. I felt frozen just looking at him and drew my cloak more firmly around me.

"Your father told me I'd find you here," I said, my voice echoing.

It was the first time I'd been in this church, and I looked around with curiosity. Like many religious buildings in this part of France, Saint-Lucien's house of worship was already ancient in 1590. Its simple lines were altogether different from the soaring heights and lacy stonework of a Gothic cathedral. Brightly colored murals surrounded the wide arch separating the apse from the nave and decorated the stone bands that topped the arcades underneath the high clerestory windows. Most of the windows opened to the elements, though someone had made a halfhearted attempt to glaze those closest to the door. The peaked roof above was crisscrossed by stout wooden beams, testifying to the skills of the carpenter as well as the mason.

When I'd first visited the Old Lodge, Matthew's house had reminded me of him. His personality was evident here, too, in the geometric details carved into the beams and in the perfectly spaced arches that spanned the widths between columns.

"You built this."

"Part of it." Matthew's eyes rose to the curved apse with its image of Christ on His throne, one hand raised and ready to mete out justice. "The nave, mostly. The apse was completed while I was . . . away."

The composed face of a male saint stared gravely at me from over Matthew's right shoulder. He held a carpenter's square and a long-stemmed white lily. It was Joseph, the man who asked no questions when he took a pregnant virgin for a wife.

"We have to talk, Matthew." I surveyed the church again. "Maybe we should move this conversation to the château. There's nowhere to sit." I had never thought of wooden pews as inviting until I entered a church without them.

"Churches weren't built for comfort," Matthew said.

"No. But making the faithful miserable couldn't have been their only purpose." I searched the murals. If faith and hope were intertwined as closely as Philippe suggested, then there might be something here to lighten Matthew's mood.

I found Noah and his ark. A global disaster and the narrowly avoided extinction of all life-forms were not auspicious. A saint heroically slew a dragon, but it was too reminiscent of hunting for my comfort. The entrance of the church was dedicated to the Last Judgment. Rows of angels at the top blew golden trumpets as the tips of their wings swept the floor, but the image of hell at the bottom—positioned so that you couldn't leave the church without making eye contact with the damned—was horrifying. The resurrection of Lazarus would be little comfort to a vampire. The Virgin Mary wouldn't help either. She stood across from Joseph at the entrance to the apse, otherworldy and serene, another reminder of all that Matthew had lost.

"At least it's private. Philippe seldom sets foot in here," Matthew said tiredly.

"We'll stay, then." I took a few steps toward him and plunged in. "What's wrong, Matthew? At first I thought it was the shock of being immersed in a former life, then the prospect of seeing your father again while keeping his death a secret." Matthew remained kneeling, head bowed, his back to me. "But your father knows his future now. So there must be another reason for it."

The air in the church was oppressive, as if my words had removed all the oxygen from the place. There wasn't a sound except for the cooing of the birds in the belfry.

"Today is Lucas's birthday," Matthew said at last.

His words hit me with the force of a blow. I sank to my knees behind him, cranberry skirts pooling around me. Philippe was right. I didn't know Matthew as well as I should.

His hand rose and pointed to a spot on the floor between him and Joseph. "He's buried there, with his mother."

No inscription on the stone marked what rested underneath. Instead there were smooth hollows, the kind made by the steady passage of feet on stair treads. Matthew's fingers reached out, fit into the grooves perfectly, stilled, withdrew.

"Part of me died when Lucas did. It was the same for Blanca. Her body followed a few days later, but her eyes were empty and her soul already flown. Philippe chose his name. It's Greek for 'Bright One.' On the night he was born, Lucas was so white and pale. When the midwife held him up in the darkness, his skin caught the light from the fire the way the moon catches her light from the sun. Strange how after so many years my memory of that night is still clear." Matthew paused in his ramblings, wiped at his eye. His fingers came away red.

"When did you and Blanca meet?"

"I threw snowballs at her during her first winter in the village. I'd do anything to get her attention. She was delicate and remote, and many of us sought her company. By the time spring came, Blanca would let me walk her home from the market. She liked berries. Every summer the hedge outside the church was full of them." He examined the red streaks on his hand. "Whenever Philippe saw the stains from their juice on my fingers, he'd laugh and predict a wedding come autumn."

"I take it he was right."

"We wed in October, after the harvest. Blanca was already more than two months pregnant." Matthew could wait to consummate our marriage but hadn't been able to resist Blanca's charms. It was far more than I had wanted to know about their relationship.

"We made love for the first time during the heat of August," he continued. "Blanca was always concerned with pleasing others. When I look back, I wonder if she was abused when she was a child. Not punished—we were all punished, and in ways no modern parent would dream of—but something more. It broke her spirit. My wife had learned to give in to what someone older, stronger, and meaner wanted. I was all of those things, and I wanted her to say yes that summer night, so she did."

"Ysabeau told me the two of you were deeply in love, Matthew. You didn't force her to do anything against her will." I wanted to offer him what comfort I could, in spite of the sting his memories inflicted.

"Blanca didn't possess a will. Not until Lucas. Even then she only exercised it when he was in danger or when I was angry with him. All her life she wanted someone weaker and smaller to protect. Instead Blanca had a succession of what she saw as failures. Lucas wasn't our first child, and with every miscarriage she grew softer and sweeter, more tractable. Less likely to say no."

Except in its general outlines, this was not the tale Ysabeau had told of her son's early life. Hers had been a story of deep love and shared grief. Matthew's version was one of unmitigated sorrow and loss.

I cleared my throat. "And then there was Lucas."

"Yes. After years of filling her with death, I gave her Lucas." He fell silent.

"There was nothing you could do, Matthew. It was the sixth century, and there was an epidemic. You couldn't save either of them."

"I could have stopped myself from having her. Then there would have been no one to lose!" Matthew exclaimed. "She wouldn't say no, but her eyes always held some reluctance when we made love. Each time I promised her that this time the babe would survive. I would have given anything—"

It hurt to know that Matthew was still so deeply attached to his dead wife and son. Their spirits haunted this place, and him, too. But at least now I had an explanation for why he shied away from me: this deep sense of guilt and grief that he'd been carrying for so many centuries. In time, perhaps, I could help loosen Blanca's hold on Matthew. I stood and went to him. He flinched when my fingers came to rest on his shoulder.

"There's more."

I froze.

"I tried to give my own life, too. But God didn't want it." Matthew's head rose. He stared at the worn, grooved stone before him, then at the roof above.

"Oh, Matthew."

"I'd been thinking about joining Lucas and Blanca for weeks, but I was worried that they would be in heaven and God would keep me in hell because of my sins," Matthew said, matter-of-fact. "I asked one of the women in the village for advice. She thought I was being haunted—that Blanca and Lucas were tied to this place because of me. Up on the scaffolding, I looked down and thought their spirits might be trapped under the stone. If I fell on it, God might have no choice but to release them. That or let me join them—wherever they were."

This was the flawed logic of a man in despair, not the lucid scientist I knew.

"I was so tired," he said wearily. "But God wouldn't let me sleep. Not after what I'd done. For my sins He gave me to a creature who transformed me into someone who cannot live, or die, or even find fleeting peace in dreams. All I can do is remember."

Matthew was exhausted again, and so very cold. His skin felt colder than the frigid air that surrounded us. Sarah would have known a spell to ease him, but all I could do was pull his resistant body into mine and lend him what little warmth I could.

"Philippe has despised me ever since. He thinks me weak—far too weak to marry someone like you." Here at last was the key to Matthew's feeling of unworthiness.

"No," I said roughly, "your father loves you." Philippe had exhibited many emotions toward his son in the brief time we'd been at Sept-Tours, but never any hint of disgust.

"Brave men don't commit suicide, except in battle. He said so to Ysabeau when I was newly made. Philippe said I lacked the courage to be a *manjasang*. As soon as my father could, he sent me away to fight. 'If you're determined to end your own life,' he said, 'at least it can be for some greater purpose than self-pity.' I've never forgotten his words."

*Hope, faith, courage*: the three elements of Philippe's simple creed. Matthew felt he possessed nothing but doubt, belief, and bravado. But I knew different.

"You've been torturing yourself with these memories for so long that you can't see the truth anymore." I moved around to face him and dropped to my knees. "Do you know what I see when I look at you? I see someone very like your father."

"We all want to see Philippe in those we love. But I'm nothing like him. It was Gallowglass's father, Hugh, who if he had lived would have—" Matthew turned away, his hand trembling on his knee. There was something more, a skeleton that he had yet to reveal.

"I've already granted you one secret, Matthew: the name of the de Clermont who is a member of the Congregation in the present. You can't keep two."

"You want me to share my darkest sin?" An interminable time passed before Matthew was willing to reveal it. "I took his life. He begged Ysabeau to do it, but she couldn't." Matthew turned away.

"Hugh?" I whispered, my heart breaking for him and Gallowglass.

"Philippe."

The last barrier between us fell.

"The Nazis drove him insane with pain and deprivation. Had Hugh survived, he might have convinced Philippe that there was still hope for some kind of life in the wreckage that remained. But Philippe said he was too tired to fight. He wanted to sleep, and I . . . I knew what it was to want to close your eyes and forget. God help me, I did what he asked."

Matthew was shaking now. I gathered him in my arms again, not caring that he resisted, knowing only that he needed something—someone— to hold on to while the waves of memory crashed over him.

"After Ysabeau refused his pleas, we found Philippe trying to slit his wrists. He couldn't hold the knife securely enough to do the job. He'd cut himself repeatedly, and there was blood everywhere, but the wounds were shallow and healed quickly." Matthew was speaking rapidly, the words pouring from him at last. "The more blood Philippe shed, the wilder he became. He couldn't stand the sight of it after being in the camp. Ysabeau took the knife from him and said she would help him end his life. But *Maman* would never have forgiven herself."

"So you cut him," I said, meeting his eyes. I had never turned away from the knowledge of what he'd done to survive as a vampire. I couldn't turn away from the sins of the husband, the father, and the son either.

Matthew shook his head. "No. I drank every drop of his blood, so Philippe wouldn't have to watch as his life force was spilled."

"But then you saw . . ." I couldn't keep the horror out of my voice. When a vampire drank from another creature, that creature's memories came along with the fluid in fleeting, teasing glimpses. Matthew had freed his father from torment, but only after first sharing everything Philippe had suffered.

"Most creatures' memories come in a smooth stream, like a ribbon unwinding in the darkness. With Philippe it was like swallowing shards of glass. Even when I got past the recent events, his mind was so badly fractured that I almost couldn't continue." His shaking intensified. "It took forever. Philippe was broken, lost, and frightened, but his heart was still fierce. His last thoughts were of Ysabeau. They were the only memories that were still whole, still his."

"It's all right," I murmured again and again, holding him tightly until finally his limbs began to quiet.

"You asked me who I am at the Old Lodge. I'm a killer, Diana. I've killed thousands," Matthew said eventually, his voice muffled. "But I never had to look any of them in the face again. Ysabeau cannot look at me without remembering my father's death. Now I have to face you, too."

I cradled his head between my hands and drew him away so that our eyes met. Matthew's perfect face usually masked the ravages of time and experience. But all the evidence was on display now, and it only made him more beautiful to me. At last the man I loved made sense: his insistence that I face who and what I was, his reluctance to kill Juliette even to save his own life, his conviction that once I truly knew him, I could never love him.

"I love all of you, Matthew: warrior and scientist, killer and healer, dark and light."

"How can you?" he whispered, disbelieving.

"Philippe couldn't have gone on like that. Your father would have kept trying to take his own life, and from everything you say, he'd suffered enough." I couldn't imagine how much, but my beloved Matthew had witnessed it all. "What you did was an act of mercy."

"I wanted to disappear when it was over, to leave Sept-Tours and never come back," he confessed. "But Philippe made me promise to keep the family and the brotherhood together. I swore that I would take care of Ysabeau, too. So I stayed here, sat in his chair, pulled the political strings he wanted pulled, finished the war he gave his life to win."

"Philippe wouldn't have put Ysabeau's welfare in the hands of someone he despised. Or placed a coward in charge of the Order of Lazarus."

"Baldwin accused me of lying about Philippe's wishes. He thought the brotherhood would go to him. No one could fathom why our father had decided to give the Order of Lazarus to me instead. Perhaps it was his final act of madness."

"It was faith," I said softly, reaching down and lacing my fingers through his. "Philippe believes in you. So do I. These hands built this church. They were strong enough to hold your son and your father during their final moments on this earth. And they still have work to do."

High above there was a beating of wings. A dove had flown through the clerestory windows and lost its way among the exposed roof beams. It struggled, freed itself, and swooped down into the church. The dove landed on the stone that marked the final resting place of Blanca and Lucas and moved its feet in a deliberate circular dance until it faced Matthew and me. Then it cocked its head and studied us with one blue eye.

Matthew shot to his feet at the sudden intrusion, and the startled dove flew toward the other side of the apse. It beat its wings, slowing before the likeness of the Virgin. When I was convinced it was going to crash into the wall, it swiftly reversed direction and flew back out the way it had entered.

A long white feather from the dove's wing drifted and curled on the currents of air, landing on the pavement before us. Matthew bent to pick it up, his expression puzzled as he held it before him.

"I've never seen a white dove in the church before." Matthew looked to the half dome of the apse where the same bird hovered over Christ's head.

"It's a sign of resurrection and hope. Witches believe in signs, you know." I closed his hands around the feather. I kissed him lightly on the forehead and turned to leave. Perhaps now that he had shared his memories, he could find peace.

"Diana?" Matthew called. He was still by his family's grave. "Thank you for hearing my confession."

I nodded. "I'll see you at home. Don't forget your feather."

He watched me as I passed the scenes of torment and redemption on the portal between the world of God and the world of man. Pierre was waiting outside, and he took me back to Sept-Tours without speaking a word. Philippe heard our approach and was waiting for me in the hall.

"Did you find him in the church?" he asked quietly. The sight of him— so hale and hearty—made my heart drop. How had Matthew endured it?

"Yes. You should have told me it was Lucas's birthday." I handed my cloak to Catrine.

"We have all learned to anticipate these black moods when Matthew is reminded of his son. You will, too."

"It's not just Lucas." Fearing I'd said too much, I bit my lip.

"Matthew told you about his own death, too." Philippe tugged his fingers through his hair, a rougher version of his son's habitual gesture. "I understand grief, but not this guilt. When will he put the past behind him?"

"Some things can never be forgotten," I said, looking Philippe squarely in the eye. "No matter what you think you understand, if you love him, you'll let him battle his own demons."

"No. He is my son. I will not fail him." Philippe's mouth tightened. He turned and stalked away. "And I've received word from Lyon, *madame,*" he called over his shoulder. "A witch will arrive shortly to help you, just as Matthew wished."

*11*

"Meet me in the hay barn on your way back from the village." Philippe had resumed his annoying habit of appearing and disappearing in the blink of an eye and was standing before us in the library.

I looked up from my book and frowned. "What's in the hay barn?"

"Hay." Matthew's revelations in the church had only made him more restless and short-tempered. "I'm writing to our new pope, Father. Alain tells me that the conclave will announce today that poor Niccolò has been elected despite begging to be spared the burdens of office. What are the wishes of one man when weighed against the aspirations of Philip of Spain and Philippe de Clermont?"

Philippe reached for his belt. A loud clap exploded from Matthew's direction. Matthew held a dagger between his palms, the point of the blade resting against his breastbone.

"His Holiness can wait." Philippe considered the position of his weapon. "I should have targeted Diana. You would have moved faster."

"You must forgive me for ruining your sport." Matthew was coldly furious. "It's been some time since I've had a knife thrown at me. I fear I am out of practice."

"If you are not at the barn before the clock strikes two, I will come looking for you. And I will be carrying more than this dagger." He plucked it out of Matthew's hands and bellowed for Alain, who was right behind him.

"No one should go to the lower barn until told otherwise," Philippe said as he rammed his weapon back into its leather sheath.

"I had apprehended as much, *sieur*." It was as close to a reproach as Alain was ever likely to utter.

"I'm tired of living with so much testosterone. No matter what Ysabeau thinks of witches, I wish she were here. And before you ask what testosterone is, it's you," I said, jabbing my finger at Philippe. "And your son is not much better."

"The company of women, eh?" Philippe pulled on his beard and looked at Matthew, openly calculating just how much further he could push his son. "Why did I not think of it before? While we wait for Diana's witch to arrive from Lyon, we should send her to Margot for instruction on how to behave like a proper French lady."

"What Louis and Margot get up to at Usson is worse than anything they did in Paris. That woman isn't a proper role model for anyone, least of all my wife," Matthew told his father with a withering look. "Unless they're more careful, people are going to know that Louis's carefully managed, very expensive assassination was a sham."

"For someone wedded to a witch you are quick to judge the passions of others, *Matthaios*. Louis is your brother."

*Goddess bless us, another brother.*

"Passions?" Matthew's eyebrow lifted. "Is that what you call taking a string of men and women to bed?"

"There are countless ways to love. What Margot and Louis do is not your concern. Ysabeau's blood runs in Louis's veins, and he will always have my loyalty—as will you, in spite of your own considerable transgressions." Philippe disappeared in a blur of movement.

"Just how many de Clermonts are there? And why do you all have to be men?" I demanded when there was silence once more.

"Because Philippe's daughters were so terrifying we held a family council and begged him to stop making them. Stasia can strip the paint from walls simply by looking at them, and Verin makes her look meek. As for Freyja . . . well, Philippe named her after the Norse goddess of war for a reason."

"They sound wonderful." I gave him a perfunctory peck on the cheek. "You can tell me about them later. I'll be in the kitchen, trying to stop up that leaky cauldron that Marthe calls a still."

"I could take a look at it for you. I'm good with lab equipment," Matthew offered. He was eager to do anything that would keep him from Philippe and the mysterious hay barn. I understood, but there was no way for him to evade his father. Philippe would simply invade my stillroom and harass him there.

"Not necessary," I said over my shoulder as I departed. "Everything is under control."

Everything was *not*, as it turned out. My eight-year-old bellows boys had let the fire go out, but not before the flames had burned too high and produced a thick black residue in the bottom of the distillation apparatus. I made notes in the margins of one of the de Clermonts' alchemical books about what had gone wrong and how it could be fixed, while Thomas, the more trustworthy of my two young assistants, stoked the fire. I was not the first to make use of the book's wide, clean borders, and some of the earlier scribblings had been quite useful. In time maybe mine would be, too.

Étienne, my other errant assistant, ran into the room, whispered in his partner's ear, and received something shiny in exchange.

"*Milord encore,*" the boy whispered back.

"What are you betting on, Thomas?" I demanded. The two of them looked at me blankly and shrugged. Something about their studied innocence made me concerned for Matthew's welfare. "The hay barn. Where is it?" I said, ripping off my apron.

With great reluctance, Thomas and Étienne led me through the castle's front gate and toward a wood-and-stone structure with a steeply pitched roof. A ramp sloped up to the wide, barred entrance doors, but the boys pointed instead to a ladder pushed against the far end. The rungs disappeared into fragrant darkness.

Thomas went up first, making quieting gestures with his hands and imploring me to be silent with facial contortions worthy of an actor in a silent film. Étienne held the ladder while I climbed, and the village blacksmith hauled me into the dusty loft.

My appearance was met with interest, but not surprise, by half of the Sept-Tours staff. I had thought it odd that only one guard was on duty at the front gate. The rest of them were here, along with Catrine, her older sister Jehanne, most of the kitchen crew, the blacksmith, and the grooms.

A softly keening whoosh, unlike anything I'd heard before, captured my attention. The sharp clang and the shriek of metal against metal were more recognizable. Matthew and his father had dispensed with sniping and progressed to armed combat. My hand rose to stifle a gasp when the point of Philippe's sword pierced Matthew's shoulder. Bloody slashes covered their shirts, breeches, and hose. They'd evidently been fighting for some time, and this was no genteel fencing match.

Alain and Pierre stood silently against the opposite wall. The ground around them looked like a pincushion, bristling with a variety of discarded weapons stabbed into the packed soil. Both of the de Clermont servants were acutely aware of what was happening around them, including my arrival. They lifted their eyes a fraction to the loft and slid a worried glance at each other. Matthew was oblivious. His back was to me, and the other strong scents in the barn masked my presence. Philippe, who was facing my way, seemed either not to notice or not to care.

Matthew's blade went straight through Philippe's arm. When Philippe winced, his son gave him a mocking smile. "'Don't consider painful what's good for you,'" Matthew muttered.

"I should never have taught you Greek—or English either. Your knowledge of them has caused me no end of trouble," Philippe replied, unperturbed. He pulled his arm free from the blade.

Swords struck, clashed, and swung. Matthew had a slight height advantage, and his longer arms and legs increased his reach and the span of his lunges. He was fighting with a long, tapering blade, sometimes using one hand, sometimes two. The hilt was constantly shifting in his grip so that he could counter his father's moves. But Philippe had more strength and delivered punishing strikes with a shorter sword that he wielded easily in one hand. Philippe also held a round shield, which he used to deflect Matthew's blows. If Matthew had held such a defensive asset, it was gone now. Though the two men were well matched physically, their styles of fighting were entirely different. Philippe was enjoying himself and kept up a running commentary while he sparred. Matthew, on the other hand, remained largely silent and focused, not betraying by so much as the quirk of an eyebrow that he was listening to what his father was saying.

"I've been thinking of Diana. Neither earth nor ocean produces a creature as savage and monstrous as woman," Philippe said sorrowfully.

Matthew lunged at him, the blade whooshing with amazing speed in a wide arc toward his father's neck. I blinked, during which time Philippe managed to slip beneath the blade. He reappeared on Matthew's other side, slicing at his son's calf.

"Your technique is wild this morning. Is something wrong?" Philippe inquired. This direct question got his son's attention.

"Christ, you are impossible. Yes. Something is wrong," Matthew said between clenched teeth. He swung again, the sword glancing off Philippe's quickly raised shield. "Your constant interference is driving me insane."

"Those whom the gods wish to destroy, they first make mad." Philippe's words caused Matthew to falter. Philippe took advantage of the misstep and slapped him on the backside with the flat of his sword.

Matthew swore. "Did you give away all of your best lines?" he demanded. Then he saw me.

What happened next took place in a heartbeat. Matthew began to straighten from his fighting crouch, his attention fixed on the hayloft where I stood. Philippe's sword plunged, circled, and lifted Matthew's weapon out of his hand. With both swords in his possession, Philippe threw one against the wall and leveled the other at Matthew's jugular.

"I taught you better, *Matthaios*. You do not think. You do not blink. You do not breathe. When you are trying to survive, all you do is react." Philippe raised his voice. "Come down here, Diana."

The blacksmith regretfully helped me to another ladder. *You're in for it now,* promised his expression. I lowered myself onto the floor behind Philippe.

"Is she why you lost?" he demanded, pressing the blade against his son's flesh until a dark ribbon of blood appeared.

"I don't know what you mean. Let me go." Some strange emotion overtook Matthew. His eyes went inky, and he clawed at his father's chest. I took a step toward him.

A shining object flew at me with a whistle, sliding between my left arm and my torso. Philippe had thrown a weapon at me without so much as a backward glance to check his aim, yet it had not even nicked my skin. The dagger pinned my sleeve to a rung of the ladder, and when I wrenched my arm free, the fabric tore across the elbow, exposing my jagged scar.

"That's what I mean. Did you take your eyes off your opponent? Is that how you nearly died, and Diana with you?" Philippe was angrier than I'd ever seen him.

Matthew's concentration flickered to me again. It took no more than a second, but it was long enough for Philippe to find yet another dagger tucked into his boot. He plunged it into the flesh of Matthew's thigh.

"Pay attention to the man with the blade at your throat. If you don't, she's dead." Then Philippe addressed me without turning. "As for you, Diana, stay clear of Matthew when he is fighting."

Matthew looked up at his father, black eyes shining with desperation as the pupils dilated. I'd seen the reaction before, and it usually signaled he was losing his control. "Let me go. I need to be with her. Please."

"You need to stop looking over your shoulder and accept who you are— a *manjasang* warrior with responsibilities to his family. When you put your mother's ring on Diana's finger, did you take time to consider what it promises?" Philippe said, his voice rising.

"My whole life, and the end of it. And a warning to remember the past." Matthew tried to kick his father, but Philippe anticipated the move and reached down to twist the knife still embedded in his son's leg. Matthew hissed with pain.

"It's always the dark things with you, never the light." Philippe swore.

He dropped the sword and kicked it out of Matthew's reach, his fingers tightening on his son's throat. "Do you see his eyes, Diana?"

"Yes," I whispered.

"Take another step toward me."

When I did, Matthew began to thrash, though his father was exerting a crushing pressure on his windpipe. I cried out, and the thrashing worsened.

"Matthew is in a blood rage. We *manjasang* are closer to nature than other creatures—pure predators, no matter how many languages we speak or what fine clothes we wear. This is the wolf in him trying to free himself so that he can kill."

"A blood rage?" My words came out in a whisper.

"Not all of our kind are prone to it. The sickness is in Ysabeau's blood, passed from her maker and on to her children. Ysabeau and Louis were spared, but not Matthew or Louisa. And Matthew's son Benjamin has the affliction, too."

Though I knew nothing of this son, Matthew had told me hair-raising stories about Louisa. The same blood-borne tendency to excess was in Matthew as well—and he could pass it down to any children we might have. Just when I thought I knew all the secrets that kept Matthew from my bed, here was another: the fear of hereditary illness.

"What sets it off?" I forced the words past the tightness in my throat.

"Many things, and it is worse when he is tired or hungry. Matthew does not belong to himself when the rage is upon him, and it can make him act against his true nature."

*Eleanor. Could this be how one of Matthew's great loves had died, trapped between an enraged Matthew and Baldwin in Jerusalem?* His repeated warnings about his possessiveness, and the danger that would result, didn't seem idle anymore. Like my panic attacks, this was a physiological reaction that Matthew might never be entirely able to control.

"Is this why you ordered him down here today? To force him into showing his vulnerabilities to the world?" I demanded furiously of Philippe. "How could you? You're his father!"

"We are a treacherous breed. I might turn against him one day." Philippe shrugged. "I might turn on you, witch."

At that, Matthew reversed their positions and was pressing Philippe back toward the far wall. Before he could gain the advantage, Philippe grabbed him by the neck. The two of them stood, locked nose to nose.

"Matthew," Philippe said sharply.

His son kept pushing, his humanity gone. Matthew's only desire was to beat his opponent, or kill him if he must. There had been moments in our brief relationship when the frightening human legends about vampires made sense, and this was one of them. But I wanted my Matthew back. I took a step in his direction, but it only made his rage worse.

"Don't come closer, Diana."

"You do not want to do this, *milord,*" Pierre said, going to his master's side. He reached out an arm. I heard a snap, watched the arm drop uselessly to his side thanks to the break at the shoulder and elbow, and saw the blood pouring out of a wound at his neck. Pierre winced, his fingers rising to press against the savage bite.

"Matthew!" I cried.

It was the wrong thing to do. The sound of my distress made him wilder. Pierre was nothing more than an obstacle to him now. Matthew flung him across the room, where he hit the wall of the hay barn, all the while retaining a one-handed grip on his father's throat.

"Silence, Diana. Matthew is beyond reason. *Matthaios!*" Philippe barked out his name. Matthew stopped trying to push his father away from me, though his grip never loosened.

"I know what you have done." Philippe waited while his words penetrated Matthew's awareness. "Do you hear me, Matthew? I know my future. You would have beaten back the rage if you could have."

Philippe had deduced that his son had killed him, but not how or why. The only explanation available to him was Matthew's illness.

"You don't know," Matthew said numbly. "You can't."

"You are behaving as you always do when you regret a kill: guilty, furtive, distracted," Philippe said. *"Te absolvo, Matthaios."*

"I'll take Diana away," Matthew said with sudden lucidity. "Let us both go, Philippe."

"No. We will face it together, the three of us," Philippe said, his face full of compassion. I had been wrong. Philippe had not been trying to break Matthew, but only his guilt. Philippe had not failed his son after all.

"No!" Matthew cried, twisting away. But Philippe was stronger.

"I forgive you," his father repeated, throwing his arms around his son in a fierce embrace. "I forgive you."

Matthew shuddered once, his body shaking from head to foot, then went limp as though some evil spirit had fled. *"Je suis désolé,"* he whispered, the words slurred with emotion. "So sorry."

"And I have forgiven you. Now you must put it behind you." Philippe released his son and looked at me. "Come to him, Diana, but move carefully. He still is not himself."

I ignored Philippe and went to Matthew in a rush. He took me into his arms and breathed in my scent as if it had the power to sustain him. Pierre moved forward, too, his arm already healed. He handed Matthew a cloth for his hands, which were slick with blood. Matthew's ferocious look kept his servant several paces away, the white cloth flapping like a flag of surrender. Philippe retreated a few steps, and Matthew's eyes darted at the sudden movement.

"That's your father and Pierre," I said, taking Matthew's face in my hands. Incrementally, the black in his eyes retreated as a ring of dark green iris appeared first, then a sliver of gray, then the distinctive pale celadon that rimmed the pupil.

"Christ." Matthew sounded disgusted. He reached for my hands and drew them from his face. "I haven't lost control like that for ages."

"You are weak, Matthew, and the blood rage is too close to the surface. If the Congregation were to challenge your right to be with Diana and you responded like this, you would lose. We cannot let there be any question whether she is a de Clermont." Philippe drew his thumb deliberately across his lower teeth. Blood, darkly purple, rose from the wound. "Come here, child."

"Philippe!" Matthew held me back, dumbfounded. "You have never—"

"Never is a very long time. Do not pretend to know more about me than you do, *Matthaios*." Philippe studied me gravely. "There is nothing to fear, Diana." I looked at Matthew, wanting to be sure this wasn't going to cause another outburst of rage.

"Go to him." Matthew released me as the creatures in the loft watched with rapt attention.

"The *manjasang* make families through death and blood," Philippe began when I stood before him. His words sent fear instinctively trilling through my bones. He smudged his thumb in a curve that started in the center of my forehead near my hairline, crept near my temple, and finished at my brow. "With this mark you are dead, a shade among the living without clan or kin." Philippe's thumb returned to the place where he began, and he made a mirror image of the mark on the other side, finishing between my brows. My witch's third eye tingled with the cool sensation of vampire blood. "With this mark you are reborn, my blood-sworn daughter and forever a member of my family."

Hay barns had corners, too. Philippe's words set them alight with shimmering strands of color—not just blue and amber but green and gold. The noise made by the threads rose to a soft keen of protest. Another family awaited me in another time after all. But the murmurs of approval in the barn soon drowned out the sound. Philippe looked up to the loft as if noticing his audience for the first time.

"As for you—*madame* has enemies. Who among you is prepared to stand for her when *milord* cannot?" Those with some grasp of English translated the question for the others.

"*Mais il est debout,*" Thomas protested, pointing at Matthew. Philippe took care of the fact that Matthew was upright by clipping his son's injured leg at the knee, sending him onto his back with a thud.

"Who stands for *madame*?" Philippe repeated, one booted foot placed carefully on Matthew's neck.

"*Je vais.*" It was Catrine, my daemonic assistant and maid, who spoke first.

"*Et moi,*" piped up Jehanne, who, though older, followed wherever her sister led.

Once the girls had declared their allegiance, Thomas and Étienne threw in their lot with me, as did the blacksmith and Chef, who had appeared in the loft carrying a basket of dried beans. After he glared at his staff, they grudgingly acquiesced as well.

"*Madame*'s enemies will come without warning, so you must be ready. Catrine and Jehanne will distract them. Thomas will lie." There were knowing chuckles from the adults. "Étienne, you must run and find help, preferably *milord*. As for you, you know what to do." Philippe regarded Matthew grimly.

"And my job?" I asked.

"To think, as you did today. Think—and stay alive." Philippe clapped his hands. "Enough entertainment. Back to work."

Amid good-natured grumbling, the people in the hayloft scattered to resume their duties. With a cock of his head, Philippe sent Alain and Pierre out after them. Philippe followed, taking off his shirt as he went. Surprisingly, he returned and dropped the wadded-up garment at my feet. Nestled within it was a lump of snow.

"Take care of the wound on his leg, and the one over his kidney that is deeper than I would have wished," Philippe instructed. Then he, too, was gone.

Matthew climbed to his knees and began to tremble. I grabbed him by the waist and lowered him gently to the ground. Matthew tried to pull free and draw me into his arms instead.

"No, you stubborn man," I said. "I don't need comforting. Let me take care of you for once."

I investigated his wounds, beginning with the ones Philippe had flagged. With Matthew's help I cleared the rent hose from the wound on his thigh. The dagger had gone deep, but the gash was already closing thanks to the healing properties of vampire blood. I packed a wad of snow around it anyway—Matthew assured me it would help, though his exhausted flesh was barely warmer. The wound on his kidney was similarly on the mend, but the surrounding bruise made me wince in sympathy.

"I think you're going to live," I said, putting a final ice pack into place over his left flank. I smoothed the hair away from his forehead. A sticky spot of half-dried blood near his eye had captured a few black strands. Gently I freed them.

"Thank you, *mon coeur*. Since you're cleaning me up, would you mind if I returned the favor and removed Philippe's blood from your forehead?" Matthew looked sheepish. "It's the scent, you see. I don't like it on you."

He was afraid of the blood rage's return. I rubbed at the skin myself, and my fingers came away tinged with black and red. "I must look like a pagan priestess."

"More so than usual, yes." Matthew scooped some of the snow from his thigh and used it and the hem of his shirt to remove the remaining evidence of my adoption.

"Tell me about Benjamin," I said while he wiped at my face.

"I made Benjamin a vampire in Jerusalem. I gave him my blood thinking to save his life. But in doing so, I took his reason. I took his soul."

"And he has your tendency toward anger?"

"Tendency! You make it sound like high blood pressure." Matthew shook his head in amazement. "Come. You'll freeze if you stay here any longer."

Slowly we made our way to the château, our hands clasped. For once neither of us cared who might see or what anyone who did see might think.

The snow was falling, making the forbidding, pitted winter landscape appear soft once again. I looked up at Matthew in the fading light and saw his father once more in the strong lines of his face and the way that his shoulders squared under the burdens they bore.

The next day was the Feast of St. Nicholas, and the sun shone on the snow that had fallen earlier in the week. The château perked up considerably with the finer weather, even though it was still Advent, a somber time of reflection and prayer. Humming under my breath, I headed for the library to retrieve my stash of alchemical books. Though I took a few into the still-room each day, I was careful to return them. Two men were talking inside the book-filled room. Philippe's calm, almost lazy tones I recognized. The other was unfamiliar. I pushed the door open.

"Here she is now," Philippe said as I entered. The man with him turned, and my flesh tingled.

"I am afraid her French is not very good, and her Latin is worse," Philippe said apologetically. "Do you speak English?"

"Enough," the witch replied. His eyes swept my body, making my skin crawl. "The girl seems in good health, but she should not be here among your people, *sieur.*"

"I would happily be rid of her, Monsieur Champier, but she has nowhere to go and needs help from a fellow witch. That is why I sent for you. Come, Madame Roydon," Philippe said, beckoning me forward.

The closer I got, the more uncomfortable I became. The air felt full, tingling with an almost electrical current. I half expected to hear a rumble of thunder, the atmosphere was so thick. Peter Knox had been mentally invasive, and Satu had inflicted great pain at La Pierre, but this witch was different and somehow even more dangerous. I walked quickly past the wizard and looked at Philippe in mute appeal for answers.

"This is André Champier," Philippe said. "He is a printer, from Lyon. Perhaps you have heard of his cousin, the esteemed physician, now alas departed from this world and no longer able to share his wisdom on matters philosophical and medical."

"No," I whispered. I watched Philippe, hoping for clues as to what he expected me to do. "I don't believe so."

Champier tilted his head in acknowledgment of Philippe's compliments. "I never knew my cousin, *sieur,* as he was dead before I was born.

But it is a pleasure to hear you speak of him so highly." Since the printer looked at least twenty years older than Philippe, he must know that the de Clermonts were vampires.

"He was a great student of magic, as you are." Philippe's comment was typically matter-of-fact, which kept it from sounding obsequious. To me he explained, "This is the witch I sent for soon after you arrived, thinking he might be able to help solve the mystery of your magic. He says he felt your power while still some distance from Sept-Tours."

"It would seem my instincts have failed me," Champier murmured. "Now that I am with her, she seems to have little power after all. Perhaps she is not the English witch that people were speaking about in Limoges."

"Limoges, eh? How extraordinary for news of her to travel so far so fast. But Madame Roydon is, thankfully, the only wandering Englishwoman we have had to take in, Monsieur Champier." Philippe's dimples flashed as he poured himself some wine. "It is bad enough to be plagued with French vagrants at this time of year, without being overrun with foreigners as well."

"The wars have loosened many from their homes." One of Champier's eyes was blue, the other brown. It was the mark of a powerful seer. The wizard had a wiry energy that fed on the power that pulsed in the atmosphere around him. Instinctively I took a step away. "Is that what happened to you, *madame?*"

"Who can tell what horrors she has seen or been subjected to?" Philippe said with a shrug. "Her husband had been dead ten days when we found her in an isolated farmhouse. Madame Roydon might have fallen victim to all kinds of predators." The elder de Clermont was as talented at fabricating life stories as was his son or Christopher Marlowe.

"I will find out what has happened to her. Give me your hand." When I didn't immediately acquiesce, Champier grew impatient. With a flick of his fingers, my left arm shot toward him. Panic, sharp and bitter, flooded my system as he grasped my hand. He stroked the flesh on my palm, progressing deliberately over each finger in an intimate search for information. My stomach flipped.

"Does her flesh give you knowledge of her secrets?" Philippe sounded only mildly curious, but there was a muscle ticking in his neck.

"A witch's skin can be read, like a book." Champier frowned and brought his fingers to his nose. He sniffed. His face soured. "She has been too long with *manjasang.* Who has been feeding from her?"

"That is forbidden," Philippe said silkily. "No one in my household has shed the girl's blood, for sport or for sustenance."

"The *manjasang* can read a creature's blood as easily as I can read her flesh." Champier yanked at my arm, pushing my sleeve up and ripping the fine cord that held the cuffs snug against my wrist. "You see? Someone has been enjoying her. I am not the only one who wishes to know more about this English witch."

Philippe bent closer to inspect my exposed elbow, his breath a cool puff over my skin. My pulse was beating a tattoo of alarm. What was Philippe after? Why wasn't Matthew's father stopping this?

"That wound is too old for her to have received it here. As I said, she has been in Saint-Lucien for only a week."

*Think. Stay alive.* I repeated Philippe's instructions from yesterday.

"Who took your blood, sister?" Champier demanded.

"It is a knife wound," I said hesitantly. "I made it myself." It wasn't a lie, but it wasn't the whole truth either. I prayed that the goddess would let it pass. My prayers went unanswered.

"Madame Roydon is keeping something from me—and from you, too, I believe. I must report it to the Congregation. It is my duty, *sieur.*" Champier looked expectantly at Philippe.

"Of course," Philippe murmured. "I would not dream of standing between you and your duty. How might I help?"

"If you would restrain her, I would be grateful. We must delve deeper for the truth," Champier said. "Most creatures find the search painful, and even those with nothing to hide instinctively resist a witch's touch."

Philippe pulled me from Champier's grasp and roughly sat me in his chair. He clamped one hand around my neck, the other at the crown of my head. "Like this?"

"That is ideal, *sieur.*" Champier stood before me, frowning at my forehead. "But what is this?" Fingers stained with ink smoothed over my forehead. His hands felt like scalpels, and I whimpered and twisted.

"Why does your touch cause her such pain?" Philippe wondered.

"It is the act of reading that does it. Think of it as extracting a tooth," Champier explained, his fingers lifting for a brief, blessed moment. "I will take her thoughts and secrets from the root, rather than leaving them to fester. It is more painful but leaves nothing behind and provides a clearer picture of what she is trying to hide. This is the great benefit of magic, you see, and university education. Witchcraft and the traditional arts known to women are crude, even superstitious. My magic is precise."

"A moment, *monsieur.* You must forgive my ignorance. Are you saying this witch will have no memory of what you've done or the pain you've caused?"

"None save a lingering sense that something once had is now lost." Champier's fingers resumed stroking my forehead. He frowned. "But this is very strange. Why did a *manjasang* put his blood here?"

Being adopted into Philippe's clan was a memory of mine that I didn't intend Champier to have. Nor did I want him sifting through my recollections of teaching at Yale, Sarah and Em, or Matthew. *My parents.* My fingers clawed into the arms of the chair while a vampire held my head and a witch prepared to inventory and steal my thoughts. And yet no whisper of witchwind or flicker of witchfire came to my aid. My power had gone entirely quiet.

"It was you who marked this witch," Champier said sharply, his eyes accusing.

"Yes." Philippe offered no explanation.

"That is most irregular, *sieur.*" His fingers kept probing my mind. Champier's eyes opened in wonder. "But this is impossible. How can she be a—" He gasped and looked down at his chest.

A dagger stuck out between two of Champier's ribs, the weapon's blade buried deep within his chest. My fingers were wrapped tightly around the hilt. When he scrabbled to dislodge it, I pushed it in further. The wizard's knees began to crumple.

"Leave it, Diana." Philippe commanded, reaching over to loosen my hand. "He's going to die, and when he does, he will fall. You cannot hold up a dead weight."

But I couldn't let go of the dagger. The man was still alive, and as long as he was breathing, Champier could take what was mine.

A white face with inkblot eyes appeared briefly over Champier's shoulder before a powerful hand wrested his lolling head to the side with a crack of bones and sinew. Matthew battened onto the man's throat, drinking deeply.

"Where have you been, Matthew?" Philippe snapped. "You must move quickly. Diana struck before he could finish his thought."

While Matthew drank, Thomas and Étienne pelted into the room, a dazed Catrine in tow. They stopped, stunned. Alain and Pierre hovered in the hallway with the blacksmith, Chef, and the two soldiers who usually stood by the front gate.

"*Vous avez bien fait,*" Philippe assured them. "It is over now."

"I was supposed to think." My fingers were numb, but I still couldn't seem to unwrap them from the dagger.

"And stay alive. You did that admirably," Philippe replied.

"He's dead?" I croaked.

Matthew removed his mouth from the witch's neck.

"Resolutely so," Philippe said. "Well, I suppose that's one less nosy Calvinist to worry about. Had he told any of his friends he was coming here?"

"Not as far as I could determine," Matthew said. Slowly his eyes turned gray again as he studied me. "Diana. My love. Let me have the dagger." Somewhere in the distance, something metal clattered to the floor, followed by the softer thud of André Champier's mortal remains. Mercifully cool, familiar hands cupped my chin.

"He discovered something in Diana that surprised him," said Philippe.

"I saw as much. But the blade reached his heart before I could find out what." Matthew drew me gently into his arms. My own had gone boneless, and I offered no resistance.

"I didn't—couldn't—think, Matthew. Champier was going to take my memories—extract them from the root. Memories are all I have of my parents. And what if I'd forgotten my historical knowledge? How could I go back home and teach after that?"

"You did the right thing." Matthew had one arm wrapped around my waist. The other circled my shoulders, pressing the side of my face against his chest. "Where did you get the knife?"

"My boot. She must have seen me pull it out yesterday," Philippe replied.

"See. You were thinking, *ma lionne.*" Matthew pressed his lips against my hair. "What the hell drew Champier to Saint-Lucien?"

"I did," replied Philippe.

"You betrayed us to Champier?" Matthew turned on his father. "He's one of the most reprehensible creatures in all of France!"

"I needed to be sure of her, *Matthaios.* Diana knows too many of our secrets. I had to know that she could be trusted with them, even among her own people." Philippe was unapologetic. "I don't take risks with my family."

"And would you have stopped Champier before he stole her thoughts?" Matthew demanded, his eyes blacker by the second.

"That depends."

"On what?" Matthew exploded, his arms tightening around me.

"Had Champier arrived three days ago, I would not have interfered. It would have been a matter between witches, and not worth the trouble to the brotherhood."

"You would have let my mate suffer." Matthew's tone revealed his disbelief.

"As recently as yesterday, it would have been your responsibility to intervene on your mate's behalf. Had you failed to do so, it would have proved that your commitment to the witch was not what it should be."

"And today?" I asked.

Philippe studied me. "Today you are my daughter. So no, I would not have let Champier's attack go much further. But I didn't need to do anything, Diana. You saved yourself."

"Is that why you made me your daughter—because Champier was coming?" I whispered.

"No. You and Matthew survived one test in the church and another in the hay barn. The blood swearing was simply the first step in making you a de Clermont. And now it's time to finish it." Philippe turned toward his second-in-command. "Fetch the priest, Alain, and tell the village to assemble at the church on Saturday. *Milord* is getting married, with book and priest and all of Saint-Lucien to witness the ceremony. There will be nothing hole-in-corner about this wedding."

"I just killed a man! This isn't the moment to discuss our marriage."

"Nonsense. Marrying amid bloodshed is a de Clermont family tradition," Philippe said briskly. "We only seem to mate creatures who are desired by others. It is a messy business."

"I. Killed. Him." Just to be sure my message was clear, I pointed to the body on the floor.

"Alain, Pierre, please remove Monsieur Champier. He is upsetting *madame*. The rest of you have too much to do to remain here gawking." Philippe waited until the three of us were alone before he continued.

"Mark me well, Diana: Lives will be lost because of your love for my son. Some will sacrifice themselves. Others will die because someone must, and it will be for you to decide if it is you or them or someone you love. So you must ask yourself this: What does it matter who deals the deathblow?

If you do not do it, then Matthew will. Would you rather he had Champier's death on his conscience?"

"Of course not," I said quickly.

"Pierre, then? Or Thomas?"

"Thomas? He's just a boy!" I protested.

"That *boy* promised to stand between you and your enemies. Did you see what he clutched in his hands? The bellows from the stillroom. Thomas filed its metal point into a weapon. If you hadn't killed Champier, that *boy* would have shoved it through his guts at the first opportunity."

"We're not animals but civilized creatures," I protested. "We should be able to talk about this and settle our differences without bloodshed."

"Once I sat at a table and talked for three hours with a man—a king. No doubt you and many others would have considered him a civilized creature. At the end of our conversation, he ordered the death of thousands of men, women, and children. Words kill just as swords do."

"She's not accustomed to our ways, Philippe," Matthew warned.

"Then she needs to become so. The time for diplomacy has passed." Philippe's voice never rose, nor did it lose its habitual evenness. Matthew might have tells, but his father had yet to betray his deeper emotions.

"No more discussion. Come Saturday, you and Matthew will be married. Because you are my daughter in blood as well as name, you will be married not only as a good Christian but in a way that will honor my ancestors and their gods. This is your last chance to say no, Diana. If you have reconsidered and no longer want Matthew and the life—and death—that marrying him entails, I will see you safely back to England."

Matthew set me away from him. It was only a matter of inches, but it was symbolic of so much more. Even now he was giving me the choice, though his was long since made. So was mine.

"Will you marry me, Matthew?" Given that I was a murderer, it seemed only right to ask.

Philippe gave a choking cough.

"Yes, Diana. I will marry you. I already have, but I'm happy to do it again to please you."

"I was satisfied the first time. This is for your father." It was impossible to think any more about marriage when my legs were still shaking and there was blood on the floor.

"Then we are all agreed. Take Diana to her room. It would be best if she remained there until we are sure Champier's friends aren't nearby." Philippe paused on his way out the door. "You have found a woman who is worthy of you, with courage and hope to spare, *Matthaios*."

"I know," Matthew said, taking my hand.

"Know this, too: You are equally worthy of her. Stop regretting your life. Start living it."

12

The wedding Philippe planned for us was to span three days. From Friday to Sunday, the château staff, the villagers, and everyone else for miles around would be involved in what he insisted was a small family affair.

"It has been some time since we had a wedding, and winter is a cheerless time of year. We owe it to the village," was how Philippe brushed aside our protests. Chef, too, was irritated when Matthew suggested that it wasn't feasible to produce three last-minute feasts while food stores were running low and Christians practiced abstemiousness. So there was a war on and it was Advent, Chef scoffed. That was no reason to refuse a party.

With the whole house in an uproar and no one interested in our help, Matthew and I were left to our own devices.

"Just what does this marriage ceremony involve?" I wondered as we lay in front of the fire in the library. I was wearing Matthew's wedding gift: one of his shirts, which extended to my knees, and a pair of his old hose. Each leg had been ripped along the top inner seam, and then Matthew had stitched the two legs together into something vaguely approximating leggings—minus the waistband and the spandex. Some gesture toward the former came from a narrow leather belt fashioned from a piece of old tack that Matthew found in the stables. It was the most comfortable clothing I'd worn since Halloween, and Matthew, who had not seen much of my legs lately, was riveted.

"I have no idea, *mon coeur*. I've never attended an ancient Greek wedding before." Matthew's fingers traced the hollow behind my knee.

"Surely the priest won't allow Philippe to do anything overtly pagan. The actual ceremony will have to be Catholic."

"The family never puts 'surely' and 'Philippe' in the same sentence. It always ends badly." Matthew planted a kiss on my hip.

"At least tonight's event is just a feast. I should be able to get through that without too much trouble." Sighing, I rested my head on my hands. "The groom's father usually pays for the rehearsal dinner. I suppose what Philippe is doing is basically the same thing."

Matthew laughed. "Almost indistinguishable—so long as the menu includes grilled eel and a gilded peacock. Besides, Philippe has managed to appoint himself not only the father of the groom, but the father of the bride."

"I still don't see why we have to make such a fuss." Sarah and Em hadn't had a formal ceremony. Instead an elder in the Madison coven performed a handfasting. Looking back, it reminded me of the vows Matthew and I had exchanged before we timewalked: simple, intimate, and quickly over.

"Weddings aren't for the benefit of the bride or the groom. Most couples would be content to go off on their own as we did, say a few words, and then leave for a holiday. Weddings are rites of passage for the community." Matthew rolled over onto his back. I propped myself up on my elbows.

"It's just an empty ritual."

"There's no such thing." Matthew frowned. "If you can't bear it, you must say so."

"No. Let Philippe have his wedding. It's just a bit . . . overwhelming."

"You must wish Sarah and Emily were here to share this with us."

"If they were, they'd be surprised that I'm not eloping. I'm known for being a loner. I used to think you were a loner, too."

"Me?" Matthew laughed. "Except on television or in the movies, vampires are seldom alone. We prefer the company of others. Even witches will do, in a pinch." He kissed me to prove it.

"So if this marriage was taking place in New Haven, who would you invite?" he asked sometime later.

"Sarah and Em, of course. My friend Chris." I bit my lip. "Maybe the chair of my department." Silence fell.

"That's it?" Matthew looked aghast.

"I don't have many friends." Restless, I got to my feet. "I think the fire's going out."

Matthew pulled me back down. "The fire is fine. And you have plenty of kith and kin now."

The mention of family was the opening I'd been waiting for. My eyes strayed to the chest at the end of the bed. Marthe's box was hidden within, tucked into the clean linen.

"There's something we need to discuss." This time he let me go without interfering. I pulled the box free.

"What's that?" Matthew asked, frowning.

"Marthe's herbs—the ones she uses in her tea. I found them in the still-room."

"I see. And have you been drinking it?" His question was sharp.

"Of course not. Whether we have children or not can't be my decision alone." When I opened the lid, the dusty aroma of dried herbs seeped into the air.

"No matter what Marcus and Miriam said back in New York, there is no evidence whatsoever that you and I can have children. Even herbal contraceptives like these can have unsafe side effects," Matthew said, coolly clinical.

"Let's say, for argument's sake, one of your scientific tests revealed we *could* have children. Would you want me to take the tea then?"

"Marthe's mixture isn't very reliable." Matthew looked away.

"Okay. What are the alternatives?" I asked.

"Abstinence. Withdrawal. And there are condoms, though they're not reliable either. Especially not the kind available to us in this day and age." Matthew was right. Sixteenth-century condoms were made from linen, leather, or animal intestines.

"And if one of these methods were reliable?" My patience was wearing thin.

"If—*if*—we could conceive a child together, it would be a miracle, and therefore no form of contraception would be effective."

"Your time at Paris wasn't a total waste of time, no matter what your father thinks. That was an argument worthy of a medieval theologian." Before I could close the box, Matthew's hands covered mine.

"If we could conceive, and if this tea were effective, I'd still want you to leave the herbs in the stillroom."

"Even though you could pass your blood rage on to another child?" I forced myself to be honest with him, despite the fact that my words would hurt.

"Yes." Matthew considered his words before continuing. "When I study patterns of extinction and see the evidence in the laboratory that we are dying out, the future seems hopeless. But if I detect a single chromosomal shift, or the discovery of an unexpected descendant when I thought a bloodline had died out, the sense of inevitable destruction lifts. I feel the same way now." Usually I had problems when Matthew adopted a position of scientific objectivity, but not this time. He took the box from my hands. "What about you?"

I'd been trying to figure that out for weeks, ever since Miriam and Marcus had appeared at Aunt Sarah's house with my DNA results and first raised the issue of children. I was sure about my future with Matthew but less so about what that future might involve.

"I wish I had more time to decide." It was becoming my common refrain. "If we were still in the twenty-first century, I'd be taking the birth-control pills you prescribed for me." I hesitated. "Even so, I'm not sure the pills would work for us."

Matthew still waited for my answer.

"When I drove Philippe's dagger into Champier, all I could think of was that he was going to take my thoughts and memories and I wouldn't be the same person when I returned to our modern lives. But even if we were to go back right this minute, we would already be different people. All the places we've gone, the people I've met, the secrets we've shared—I'm no longer the same Diana Bishop, and you aren't the same Matthew Clairmont. A baby would change us even more."

"So you want to prevent pregnancy," he said carefully.

"I'm not sure."

"Then the answer is yes. If you're not sure you want to be a parent, we must use whatever birth control is available." Matthew's voice was firm. And so was his chin.

"I do want to be a parent. I'm surprised by how much, if you must know." I pressed my fingers into my temples. "I like the idea of you and me raising a child. It just feels so soon."

"It is soon. So we'll do what we must to limit the possibility until—if—you are ready. But don't get your hopes up. The science is clear, Diana: Vampires reproduce through resurrection, not procreation. Our relationship might be different, but we aren't so special as to overturn thousands of years of biology."

"The picture of the alchemical wedding from Ashmole 782—it is about us. I know it. And Miriam was right: The next step in the process of alchemical transformation after the marriage of gold and silver is conception."

"Conception?" Philippe drawled from the door. His boots creaked as he pushed away from the frame. "No one mentioned that possibility."

"That's because it's impossible. I've had sex with other warmblooded women, and they've never become pregnant. The image of the chemical wedding may have been intended as a message, as Diana says, but the chances of representation becoming reality are slim." Matthew shook his head. "No *manjasang* has ever fathered a child like that before."

"Never is a long time, Matthew, as I told you. As for the impossible, I have walked this earth longer than man's memories and have seen things that later generations discounted as myth. Once there were creatures who swam like fish in the sea and others who wielded lightning bolts instead of spears. They are gone now, replaced with something new. 'Change is the only reliable thing in the world.'"

"Heraclitus," I murmured.

"The wisest of men," said Philippe, pleased that I recognized the quote. "The gods like to surprise us when we grow complacent. It's their favorite form of entertainment." He studied my unusual costume. "Why are you wearing Matthew's shirt and hose?"

"He gave them to me. It's fairly close to what I wear in my own time, and Matthew wanted me to be comfortable. He sewed the legs together himself, I think." I turned to show off the ensemble. "Who knew the de Clermont men could thread a needle, never mind stitch a straight seam?"

Philippe's eyebrows rose. "Did you think Ysabeau mended our torn garments when we came home from battle?"

The idea of Ysabeau sewing quietly while she waited for her men to return made me giggle. "Hardly."

"You know her well, I see. If you are determined to dress like a boy, put breeches on, at the very least. If the priest sees you, his heart will stop and tomorrow's ceremony will have to be delayed."

"But I'm not going outside," I said, frowning.

"I'd like to take you to a place sacred to the old gods before you are wed. It is not far," Philippe said when Matthew drew a breath to complain, "and I'd like us to be alone, *Matthaios*."

"I'll meet you in the stables," I agreed without hesitation. Some time in the fresh air would provide a welcome opportunity for me to clear my head.

Outside, I enjoyed the sting of the cold air on my cheeks and the wintry peace of the countryside. Soon Philippe and I came to a hilltop that was flatter than most of the rounded ridges around Sept-Tours. The ground was punctuated with protrusions of stone that struck me as oddly symmetrical. Though ancient and overgrown with vegetation, these weren't natural outcroppings. They were man-made.

Philippe swung down from his horse and motioned for me to do the same. Once I dismounted, he took me by the elbow and guided me through two of the strange lumps and into a smooth expanse of snow-covered ground. All that marred the pristine surface were the tracks of wildlife—the heart-shaped outline of a deer's hoof, the five-clawed marks of bear, the combination of triangular and oval pads belonging to a wolf.

"What is this place?" I asked, my voice hushed.

"A temple dedicated to Diana stood here once, overlooking the woods and valleys where the stags liked to run. Those who revered the goddess planted sacred cypress trees to grow alongside the native oak and alder." Philippe pointed to the thin columns of green that stood guard around the area. "I wanted to bring you here because when I was a child, far away and before I became a *manjasang,* brides would go to a temple like this before their wedding and make a sacrifice to the goddess. We called her Artemis then."

"A sacrifice?" My mouth was dry. There had been enough bloodshed.

"No matter how much we change, it is important to remember the past and honor it." Philippe handed me a knife and a bag whose contents shifted and chimed. "It is also wise to set old wrongs to rights. The goddesses have not always been pleased with my actions. I would like to make sure that Artemis receives her due before my son marries you tomorrow. The knife is to take a lock of your hair. It is a symbol of your maidenhood, and the customary gift. The money is a symbol of your worth." Philippe's voice dropped to a conspiratorial whisper. "There would have been more, but I had to save some for Matthew's god, too."

Philippe led me to a small plinth in the center of the ruined structure. An assortment of offerings rested on it—a wooden doll, a child's shoe, a bowl of sodden grain dusted with snow.

"I'm surprised that anyone still comes here," I said.

"All over France women still curtsy to the moon when she is full. Such habits die hard, especially those that sustain people during difficult times." Philippe went forward to the makeshift altar. He didn't bow, or kneel, or make any of the other familiar signs of respect to a deity, but when he began to speak, his voice was so quiet I had to strain to hear him. The strange mixture of Greek and English made little sense. Philippe's solemn intentions were clear, however.

"Artemis Agroterê, renowned huntress, Alcides Leontothymos beseeches you to hold this child Diana in your hand. Artemis Lykeiê, lady of the wolves, protect her in every way. Artemis Patrôia, goddess of my ancestors, bless her with children so that my lineage continues."

*Philippe's lineage.* I was part of it now, by marriage as well as the swearing of a blood oath.

"Artemis Phôsphoros, bring the light of your wisdom when she is in darkness. Artemis Upis, watch over your namesake during her journey in this world." Philippe finished the invocation and motioned me forward.

After carefully placing the bag of coins next to the child's shoe, I reached up and pulled a strand of hair away from the nape of my neck. The knife was sharp, and it easily removed the curl with a single swipe of the blade.

We stood quietly in the dimming afternoon light. A surge of power washed through the ground underneath my feet. The goddess was here. For a moment I could imagine the temple as it once was—pale, gleaming, whole. I stole a glance at Philippe. With a bear pelt draped over his shoulders, he, too, looked like the savage remainder of a lost world. And he was waiting for something.

A white buck with curved antlers picked its way out of the cypress and stood, breath steaming from its nostrils. With quiet steps the buck picked his way over to me. His huge brown eyes were challenging, and he was close enough for me to see the sharp edges on his horns. The buck looked haughtily at Philippe and bellowed, one beast's greeting to another.

"*Sas efharisto,*" Philippe said gravely, his hand over his heart. He turned to me. "Artemis has accepted your gifts. We can go now."

Matthew had been listening for sounds of our arrival and was waiting, his face uncertain, in the courtyard as we rode up.

"Ready yourself for the banquet," Philippe suggested as I dismounted. "Our guests will be arriving soon."

I gave Matthew what I hoped was a confident smile before I went upstairs. As darkness fell, the hum of activity told me the château was filling up with people. Soon Catrine and Jehanne came to get me dressed. The gown they'd laid out was by far the grandest thing I'd ever worn. The dark green fabric reminded me of the cypress by the temple now, rather than the holly that decorated the château for Advent. And the silver oak leaves embroidered on the bodice caught the light from the candles as the buck's antlers had caught the rays of the setting sun.

The girls' eyes were shining when they finished. I'd been able to get only a glimpse of my hair (swept up into coils and twisted into braids) and my pale face in Louisa's polished silver mirror. But their expressions indicated that my transformation was weddingworthy.

"*Bien,*" Jehanne said softly.

Catrine opened the door with a flourish, and the gown's silver stitches flared to life in the torchlight from the hall. I held my breath while I waited for Matthew's reaction.

"*Jesu,*" he said, stunned. "You are beautiful, *mon coeur.*" Matthew took my hands and lifted my arms to see the full effect. "Good God, are you wearing two sets of sleeves?"

"I think there are three," I said with a laugh. I had on a linen smock with tight lace cuffs, tight green sleeves that matched my bodice and skirts, and voluminous puffs of green silk that fell from my shoulders and were caught up at the elbows and wrists. Jehanne, who had been in Paris last year to attend upon Louisa, assured me the design was *à la mode.*

"But how am I supposed to kiss you with all this in the way?" Matthew drew his finger around my neck. My pleated ruff, which was standing out a good four inches, quivered in response.

"If you squash it, Jehanne will have a stroke," I murmured as he carefully took my face in his hands. She'd employed a contraption resembling a curling iron to bend yards of linen into the crisp figure-eight formations. It had taken her hours.

"Never fear. I'm a doctor." Matthew leaned in and pressed his mouth to mine. "There, not a pleat disturbed."

Alain coughed gently. "They are waiting for you."

"Matthew," I said, catching at his hand, "I need to tell you something."

He motioned to Alain, and we were left alone in the corridor.

"What is it?" he said uneasily.

"I sent Catrine to the stillroom to put away Marthe's herbs." It was a far bigger step into the unknown than the one that I'd taken in Sarah's hop barn to bring us here.

"You're sure?"

"I'm sure," I said, remembering Philippe's words at the temple.

Our entry into the hall was greeted with whispers and sidelong glances. The changes in my appearance had been noted, and the nods told me that at last I looked like someone who was fit to marry *milord.*

"There they are," Philippe boomed from the family's usual table. Someone began to clap, and soon the hall rang with the sound. Matthew's smile was shy at first, but as the noise increased, it broadened into a proud grin.

We were seated in the places of honor on either side of Philippe, who then called for the first course and music to accompany it. I was offered small portions of everything Chef had prepared. There were dozens of dishes: a soup made with chickpeas, grilled eel, a delicious puree of lentils, salt cod in garlic sauce, and an entire fish that swam through a gelatinous sea of aspic, with sprigs of lavender and rosemary impersonating water plants. Philippe explained that the menu had been the subject of heated negotiations between Chef and the village priest. After the exchange of several embassies, the two had finally agreed that tonight's meal would strictly adhere to the Friday dietary prohibitions against meat, milk, and cheese, while tomorrow's banquet would be a no-holds-barred extravaganza.

As befitted the groom, Matthew's portions were somewhat heartier than mine—unnecessarily so, since he ate nothing and drank little. The men at the adjoining tables joked with him about the need to bolster his strength for the ordeals to come.

By the time the hippocras started flowing and a delicious nut brittle made with walnuts and honey was passed along the table, their commentary was downright ribald and Matthew's responses were just as barbed. Happily, most of the insults and advice were delivered in languages I didn't fully understand, but Philippe clapped his hands over my ears occasionally anyway.

My heart lifted as the laughter and music swelled. Tonight Matthew didn't look like a fifteen-hundred-year-old vampire but like every other groom the night before his wedding: sheepish, pleased, a bit anxious. This was the man I loved, and my heart stilled for just a moment whenever his gaze settled on me.

The singing started when Chef served the last selection of wine and the candied fennel and cardamom seeds. A man at the opposite end of the hall sang out in a deep bass, and his neighbors picked up the melody. Soon everybody was joining in, with so much stomping and clapping that you couldn't hear the musicians trying desperately to keep up with them.

While the guests were busily devising new songs, Philippe made the rounds, greeting everyone by name. He threw babies into the air, inquired after animals, and listened attentively while the elderly cataloged their aches and pains.

"Just look at him," Matthew marveled, taking my hand. "How does Philippe manage to make every one of them feel that they're the most important guest in the room?"

"You tell me," I said with a laugh. When Matthew looked confused, I shook my head. "Matthew, you are exactly the same. All you need do to take charge of a roomful of people is to enter it."

"If you want a hero like Philippe, you're going to be disappointed in me," he said.

I took his face in my hands. "For your wedding gift, I wish I had a spell that could make you see yourself as others do."

"Based on what's reflected in your eyes, I look much the same. A little nervous, perhaps, given what Guillaume just shared with me about the carnal appetites of older women," Matthew joked, trying to distract me. But I was having none of it.

"If you aren't seeing a leader of men, then you're not looking carefully." Our faces were so close I could smell the spice on his breath. Without thinking, I drew him to me. Philippe had tried to tell Matthew he was worthy of being loved. Perhaps a kiss would be more convincing.

In the distance I heard shouts and more clapping. Then there was whooping.

"Leave the girl something to look forward to tomorrow, *Matthaios*, or she may not meet you at the church!" Philippe called out, drawing more laughter from the crowd. Matthew and I parted in happy embarrassment. I searched the hall and found Matthew's father by the fireside, tuning an instrument with seven strings. Matthew told me it was a kithara. A hush of anticipation fell over the room.

"When I was a child, there were always stories at the end of a banquet such as this, and tales of heroes and great warriors." Philippe plucked the strings, eliciting a shower of sound. "And just like all men, heroes fall in love." His strumming continued, lulling the audience into the rhythms of his story.

"A hero with dark hair and green eyes named Peleus left his home to seek his fortune. It was a place much like Saint-Lucien, hidden in the mountains, but Peleus had long dreamed of the sea and the adventures he might have in foreign lands. He gathered his friends together, and they voyaged through the oceans of the world. One day they arrived at an island famed for its beautiful women and the powerful magic that they had at their command." Matthew and I exchanged long glances. Philippe's deep voice sang out his next words:

> *Far happier then were the times for men,*
> *Fondly yearned for now! You heroes, so bred*
> *Of gods in those silver days, favor me*
> *As I call you now with my magic song.*

The room was mesmerized by Philippe's otherworldly bass.

"There Peleus first saw Thetis, daughter of Nereus, the god of the sea who told no lies and saw the future. From her father Thetis had the gift of prophecy and could twist her shape from moving water to living fire to the very air itself. Though Thetis was beautiful, no one would take her for a wife, for an oracle foretold that her son would be more powerful than his father.

"Peleus loved Thetis in spite of the prophecy. But to marry such a woman, he had to be brave enough to hold Thetis while she changed from one element into another. Peleus took Thetis from the island and clasped her to his heart while she transformed herself from water to fire to serpent to lioness. When Thetis became a woman once more, he took her to his home and the two were wed."

"And the child? Did Thetis's son destroy Peleus as the omens foretold?" a woman whispered when Philippe fell silent, his fingers still drawing music from the kithara.

"The son of Peleus and Thetis was a great hero, a warrior blessed in both life and death, called Achilles." Philippe gave the woman a smile. "But that is a tale for another night."

I was glad that his father didn't give a full account of the wedding and how the Trojan War got started there. And I was even happier that he didn't go on to tell the tale of Achilles' youth: the horrible spells his mother used to try to make him immortal as she was and the young man's uncontrollable rage—which caused him far more trouble than did his famously unprotected heel.

"It's just a story," Matthew whispered, sensing my unease.

But it was the stories that creatures told, over and over without knowing what they meant, that were often the most important, just as it was these time-worn rituals of honor, marriage, and family that people held most sacred even though they often seemed to ignore them.

"Tomorrow is an important day, one that we have all longed for." Philippe stood, kithara in his hands. "It is customary for the bride and groom to separate until the wedding."

This was another ritual: a final, formal moment of parting to be followed by a lifetime of togetherness.

"The bride may, however, give the groom some token of affection to make sure he does not forget her during the lonely hours of the night," Philippe said, eyes twinkling with mischief.

Matthew and I rose. I smoothed down my skirts, my attention fixed resolutely on his doublet. The stitches on it were very fine, I noticed, tiny and regular. Gentle fingers lifted my chin, and I was lost instead in the play of smooth curves and sharp angles that made up Matthew's face. All sense of performance disappeared as we contemplated each other. We stood in the midst of the hall and the wedding guests, our kiss a spell that carried us to an intimate world of our own.

"I'll see you tomorrow afternoon," Matthew murmured against my lips as we parted.

"I'll be the one in the veil." Most brides didn't wear them in the sixteenth century, but they were an ancient custom, and Philippe said that no daughter of his was going to the church without one.

"I'd know you anywhere," he replied, flashing me a smile, "veil or no veil."

Matthew's eyes never wavered as Alain escorted me from the room. I felt the touch of them, cool and unblinking, long after I left the hall.

The next day Catrine and Jehanne were so quiet that I slumbered through their usual morning chores. The sun was almost fully up when they finally pulled the bed curtains aside and announced it was time for my bath.

A procession of women with pitchers came to my chamber, chattering like magpies and filling an enormous copper tub that I suspected was normally used to make wine or cider. But the water was piping hot and the copper vessel retained the glorious warmth, so I wasn't inclined to quibble. I groaned in ecstasy and sank beneath the water's surface.

The women left me to soak, and I noticed that my few belongings—books, the notes I'd taken on alchemy and Occitan phrases—had disappeared. So, too, had the long, low chest that stored my clothes. When I asked Catrine, she explained that everything had been moved to *milord*'s chambers on the other side of the château.

I was no longer Philippe's putative daughter, but Matthew's wife. My property had been relocated accordingly.

Mindful of their responsibility, Catrine and Jehanne had me out of the tub and dried off by the time the clock struck one. Overseeing their efforts was Marie, Saint-Lucien's best seamstress, who had come to put the finishing touches on her work. The contributions to my wedding gown that had been made by the village's tailor, Monsieur Beaufils, were not acknowledged.

To be fair to Marie, *La Robe* (I thought of my ensemble only in French, and always in capitals) was spectacular. How she had managed to complete it in such a short period of time was a deeply kept secret, though I suspected that every woman in the vicinity had contributed at least a stitch. Before Philippe announced I was getting married, the plan had been for a relatively simple dress of heavy, slate-colored silk. I had insisted on one pair of sleeves, not two, and a high neckline to keep out the winter drafts. There was no need to trouble with embroidery, I told Marie. I had also declined the outrageous birdcagelike supports that would extend the skirt in every direction.

Marie had used her powers of misunderstanding and creativity to modify my initial design long before Philippe told her where and when the gown would be worn. After that there was no holding the woman back.

"Marie, *La Robe est belle*," I told her, fingering the heavily embroidered silk. Stylized cornucopias, familiar symbols of abundance and fertility, were stitched all over in gold, black, and rose thread. Rosettes and sprigs of leaves accompanied the flower-filled horns, while bands of embroidery edged both pairs of sleeves. The same bands trimmed the edges of the bodice in a sinuous pattern of scrolls, moons, and stars. At the shoulders a row of square flaps called *pickadils* hid the laces that tied sleeve to bodice. Despite the elaborate ornamentation, the bodice's elegant curves fit perfectly, and my wishes on the subject of farthingales had at least been honored. The skirts were full, but that was due to the volume of fabric rather than any wire contraption. The only thing I wore under the petticoats was the stuffed doughnut that rested on my hips, and silk hose.

"It has a strong line. Very simple," Marie assured me, tugging on the bottom of the bodice to help it lie more smoothly.

The women were almost finished with my hair when a knock sounded. Catrine rushed to open the door, turning over a basket of towels on her way.

It was Philippe, looking splendid in a rich brown suit, with Alain standing behind him. Matthew's father stared.

"Diana?" Philippe sounded unsure.

"What? Is something wrong?" I surveyed my gown and anxiously patted at my hair. "We don't have a mirror large enough for me to see—"

"You are beautiful, and the look on Matthew's face when he sees you will tell you this better than any reflection," Philippe said firmly.

"And *you* have a silver tongue, Philippe de Clermont," I said with a laugh. "What do you need?"

"I came to give you your wedding gifts." Philippe held out his hand, and Alain placed a large velvet bag in his palm. "There was no time to have something made, I'm afraid. These are family pieces."

He tipped the bag's contents into his hand. A stream of light and fire poured out: gold, diamonds, sapphires. I gasped. But there were more treasures hidden inside the velvet, including a rope of pearls, several crescent moons encrusted with opals, and an unusually shaped golden arrowhead, its edges softened with age.

"What are they for?" I asked in wonder.

"For you to wear, of course," Philippe said, chuckling. "The chain was mine, but when I saw Marie's gown, I thought the yellow diamonds and the sapphires would not look out of place. The style is old, and some would say it is too masculine for a bride, but the chain will sit on your shoulders and lie flat. Originally a cross hung from the center, but I thought you might prefer to suspend the arrow instead."

"I don't recognize the flowers." The slender yellow buds reminded me of freesia, and they were interspersed with gold fleurs-de-lis rimmed with sapphires.

"*Planta genista*. The English call it broom. The Angevins used it as their emblem."

He meant the Plantagenets: the most powerful royal family in English history. The Plantagenets had expanded Westminster Abbey, given in to the barons and signed the Magna Carta, established Parliament, and supported the foundation of Oxford and Cambridge universities. Plantagenet rulers had fought in the Crusades and through the Hundred Years' War with France. And one of them had given this chain to Philippe as a sign of royal favor. Nothing else could account for its splendor.

"Philippe, I can't possibly—" My protests stopped when he passed the other jewels to Catrine and lowered the chain over my head. The woman who gazed back at me from the murky mirror was no more a modern historian than Matthew was a modern scientist. "Oh," I said in amazement.

"Breathtaking," he agreed. His face softened with regret. "I wish Ysabeau could be here to see you like this, and to witness Matthew's happiness."

"I'll tell her everything one day," I promised softly, holding his reflected gaze as Catrine fastened the arrow to the front of the chain and wound the rope of pearls through my hair. "I'll take good care of the jewels tonight, too, and make sure they're returned to you in the morning."

"These belong to you now, Diana, to do with what you will. As does this." Philippe pulled another bag from his belt, this one made from serviceable leather, and handed it to me.

It was heavy. Very heavy.

"The women in this family manage their own finances. Ysabeau insists upon it. All of the coins in here are English or French. They do not hold their value as well as Venetian ducats, but they will raise fewer questions when you spend them. If you need more, you have only to ask Walter or another member of the brotherhood."

When I'd arrived in France, I was entirely dependent on Matthew. In little more than a week, I had learned how to conduct myself, converse, manage a household, and distill spirit of wine. I now had my own property, and Philippe de Clermont had claimed me publicly as his daughter.

"Thank you, for all of this," I said softly. "I didn't think you wanted me as a daughter-in-law."

"Not at first, perhaps. But even old men can change their minds." Philippe's grin flashed. "And I always get what I want in the end."

The women wrapped me in my cloak. At the very last moment, Catrine and Jehanne dropped a filmy piece of silk over my head and attached it to my hair with the opal crescent moons, which had tiny, tenacious claws on the back.

Thomas and Étienne, who now saw themselves as my personal champions, ran ahead of us through the château and proclaimed our approach at the top of their lungs. Soon we formed a procession, moving through the twilight in the direction of the church. Someone must have been up in the bell tower, and once whoever that was spotted us, the bells began to ring.

I faltered as we came to the church. The entire village had assembled outside its doors, along with the priest. I searched for Matthew and found him standing at the top of the short flight of stairs. Through the transparent veil, I could feel his regard. Like sun and moon, we were unconcerned at this moment with time, distance, and difference. All that mattered was our position relative to each other.

I gathered my skirts and went to him. The brief climb felt endless. Did time misbehave this way for all brides, I wondered, or only for witches?

The priest beamed at me from the door but made no effort to admit us to the church. He was clutching a book in his hands but didn't open it. I frowned in confusion.

"All right, *mon coeur*?" Matthew murmured.

"Aren't we going inside?"

"Marriages take place at the church door to avoid bloody disputes later over whether or not the ceremony took place as reported. We can thank God there isn't a blizzard."

"*Commencez!*" the priest commanded, nodding at Matthew.

My entire role in the ceremony was to utter eleven words. Matthew was charged with fifteen. Philippe had informed the priest that we would then repeat our vows, in English, because it was important that the bride fully understand what she was promising. This brought the total number of words necessary to make us husband and wife to fifty-two.

"*Maintenant!*" The priest was shivering and wanted his supper.

"*Je, Matthew, donne mon corps à toi, Diana, en loyal mariage.*" Matthew took my hands in his. "I, Matthew, give my body to you, Diana, in faithful matrimony."

"*Et je le reçois,*" I replied. "And I receive it."

We were halfway through. I took a deep breath and kept going.

"*Je, Diana, donne mon corps à toi, Matthew.*" The hard part over, I quickly said my final line. "I, Diana, give my body to you, Matthew."

"*Et je le reçois, avec joie.*" Matthew drew the veil over my head. "And I receive it, with joy."

"Those aren't the right words," I said fiercely. I had memorized the vows, and there was no "*avec joie*" anywhere in them.

"They are," Matthew insisted, lowering his head.

We'd been married by vampire custom when we mated and again by common law when Matthew had put Ysabeau's ring on my finger in Madison. Now we were married a third time.

What happened afterward was a blur. There were torches and a long walk up the hill surrounded by well-wishers. Chef's feast was already laid out, and people tucked into it with enthusiasm. Matthew and I sat alone at the family table, while Philippe strolled about serving wine and making sure the children got their fair share of spit-roasted hare and cheese fritters. Occasionally he cast a proud look in our direction, as if we'd slain dragons that afternoon.

"I never thought I would see this day," Philippe told Matthew as he placed a slice of custard tart before us.

The feast seemed to be winding down when the men started shoving the tables to the sides of the hall. Pipes and drums sounded from the minstrels' gallery above.

"By tradition the first dance belongs to the bride's father," Philippe said with a bow to me. He led me to the floor. Philippe was a good dancer, but even so I got us tangled.

"May I?" Matthew tapped on his father's shoulder.

"Please. Your wife is trying to break my foot." Philippe's wink took the sting out of his words, and he withdrew, leaving me with my husband.

Others were still dancing, but they drew away and left us in the center of the room. The music deliberately slowed as a musician plucked on the strings of his lute, and the sweet tones of a wind instrument piped an accompaniment. As we parted and came together, once, twice, again, the distractions of the room faded.

"You're a far better dancer than Philippe, no matter what your mother says," I told him, breathless even though the dance was measured.

"That's because you're following my lead," he teased. "You fought Philippe every step of the way."

When the dance brought us together once more, he took me by the elbows, pulled me tight against his body, and kissed me. "Now that we're married, will you keep forgiving my sins?" he asked, swinging back into the regular steps.

"That depends," I said warily. "What have you done now?"

"I've crushed your ruff beyond redemption."

I laughed, and Matthew kissed me again, briefly but emphatically. The drummer took it as a cue, and the music's tempo increased. Other couples whirled and hopped their way across the floor. Matthew drew us into relative safety near the fireplace before we were trampled. Philippe was there a moment later.

"Take your wife to bed and finish this," Philippe murmured.

"But the guests . . ." Matthew protested.

"Take your wife to bed, my son," Philippe repeated. "Steal away now, before the others decide to accompany you upstairs and make sure you do your duty. Leave everything to me." He turned, kissing me formally on both cheeks before murmuring something in Greek and sending us to Matthew's tower.

Though I knew this part of the château in my own time, I had yet to see it in its sixteenth-century splendor. The order of Matthew's apartments had changed. I expected to see books in the room off the first landing, but instead there was a large canopied bed. Catrine and Jehanne brought out a carved box for my new jewels, filled up the basin, and bustled around with fresh linens. Matthew sat before the fire and pulled off his boots, taking up a glass of wine when he was through.

"Your hair, *madame?*" Jehanne asked, eyeing my husband speculatively.

"I'll take care of it," Matthew said gruffly, his eyes on the fire.

"Wait," I said, pulling the moon-shaped jewels free from my hair and putting them in Jehanne's upturned palm. She and Catrine removed the veil and departed, leaving me standing near the bed and Matthew lounging fireside with his feet on one of the clothing chests.

When the door closed, Matthew put down his glass of wine and came to me, twining his fingers in my hair and tugging gently to dislodge in moments what it had taken the girls nearly thirty minutes to achieve. He tossed the rope of pearls aside. My hair tumbled over my shoulders, and Matthew's nostrils flared as he took in my scent. Wordlessly he pulled my body against his and bent to fit his mouth to mine.

But there were questions that needed to be asked and answered first. I drew away.

"Matthew, are you sure . . . ?"

Cool fingers slid underneath my ruff, finding the ties that connected it to my bodice.

*Snap. Snap. Snap.*

The stiffened linen came free from my neck and fell to the floor. Matthew loosened the buttons that kept my high neckline clasped tight. He bent his head and kissed my throat. I clutched at his doublet.

"Matthew," I repeated. "Is this about—"

He silenced me with another kiss while he lifted the heavy chain from my shoulders. We broke off momentarily so Matthew could get it over my head. Then his hands breached the crenellated line of *pickadils* where sleeves met bodice. His fingers slid among the gaps, searching out a weak point in the garment's defenses.

"There it is," he murmured, hooking his index fingers around the edges and giving a decided yank. One sleeve, then the other, slid down each arm and onto the floor. Matthew seemed entirely unconcerned, but it was my wedding gown and not easily replaced.

"My gown," I said, squirming in his arms.

"Diana." Matthew drew his head back and rested his hands on my waist.

"Yes?" I said breathlessly. I tried to reach the sleeve with the toe of my slipper and push it where it was less likely to be crushed.

"The priest blessed our marriage. The entire village wished us well. There was food, and dancing. I did think we might draw the night to a close by making love. Yet you seem more interested in your wardrobe." He had located still another set of laces that fastened my skirts to the bottom of the pointed bodice, about three inches below my belly button. Lightly, Matthew swept his thumbs between edge of the bodice and my pubic bone.

"I don't want our first time together to be about satisfying your father." In spite of my protests, my hips arched toward him in silent invitation while he kept up that maddening movement of his thumbs, like the beating of an angel's wings. He made a soft sound of satisfaction and untied the bow hidden there.

*Tug. Rasp. Tug. Rasp. Tug. Rasp.*

Matthew's nimble fingers pulled on each crossing of the laces, drawing them through the concealed holes. There were twelve in all, and my body bowed and straightened with the force of his attentions.

"At last," he said with satisfaction. Then he groaned. "Christ. There are more."

"Oh, you're nowhere near through. I'm trussed up like a Christmas goose," I said as he lifted the bodice away from the skirts, revealing the corset below. "Or, more accurately, an Advent goose."

But Matthew wasn't paying any attention to me. Instead my husband was focused on the place where my nearly transparent high-necked smock disappeared into the heavy reinforced fabric of the corset. He pressed his lips against the swell. Bowing his head in a reverential pose, he took in a jagged breath.

So did I. It was surprisingly erotic, the brush of his lips somehow magnified by the fine lawn boundary. Not knowing what made him stop his previously single-minded efforts to get me unclothed, I cradled his head in my hands and waited for him to make his next move.

At last Matthew took my hands and wrapped them around the carved post that held up the corner of the canopy. "Hold on," he said.

*Tug. Rasp. Tug. Rasp.* Before he was finished, Matthew took a moment to slide his hands inside the stays. They swooped around my rib cage and found my breasts. I moaned softly as he trapped my smock between the warm, pebbled skin of my nipples and his cool fingers. He pulled me back against him.

"Do I seem like a man interested in pleasing anyone but you?" he murmured into my ear. When I didn't immediately answer, one hand snaked down my stomach to press me closer. The other remained where it was, cupping my breast.

"No." My head tilted back into his shoulder, exposing my neck.

"Then no more talk about my father. And I'll buy you twenty identical gowns tomorrow if you will stop worrying about your sleeves now." Matthew was busily ruching up my smock so that the hem skirted the tops of my legs. I loosed my grip on the bedpost, grabbed at his hand, and placed it at the juncture of my thighs.

"No more talking," I agreed, gasping when his fingers parted my flesh.

Matthew quieted me further with a kiss. The slow movements of his hands were causing an entirely different reaction as the tension in my body rose.

"Too many clothes," I said breathlessly. His agreement was unstated, but evident in the haste with which he slid the corset down my arms. The laces were loose enough now that I could push it over my hips and step out of it. I unfastened his breeches while Matthew unbuttoned his doublet. These two items had been joined at his hips by just as many crossed laces as my bodice and skirt.

When we were both wearing nothing more than hose, I my smock, and Matthew his shirt, we paused, awkwardness returning.

"Will you let me love you, Diana?" Matthew said, sweeping away my anxiety with that simple, courteous question.

"I will," I whispered. He knelt and carefully untied the ribbons that held up my stockings. They were blue, which Catrine said was the color of fidelity. Matthew rolled the hose down my legs, a press of lips on knees and ankles marking their passage. He removed his own hose so quickly that I never had an opportunity to note the color of his garters.

Matthew lifted me slightly so that my toes were barely gripping the floor and he could fit himself into the notch between my legs.

"We may not make it to the bed," I said, grabbing onto his shoulders. I wanted him inside me, quickly.

But we did make it to that soft, shadowed place, ridding ourselves of our linen along the way. Once there, my body welcomed him into the moon of my thighs while my arms reached to draw him down to me. Even so I gasped in surprise when our two bodies became one—warm and cold, light and dark, female and male, witch and vampire, a conjunction of opposites.

Matthew's expression went from reverential to wondering when he began to move within me, and it became intent after he angled his body and I reacted with a pleased cry. He slipped his arm under the small of my back and lifted me into his hips while my hands gripped his shoulders.

We fell into the rhythm unique to lovers, pleasing each other with soft touches of mouth and hands as we rocked together, together until all we had left to give were our hearts and souls. Looking deep into each other's eyes, we exchanged our final vows with flesh and spirit, trembling like newborns.

"Let me love you forever," Matthew murmured against my damp forehead, his lips trailing a cold path across my brow as we lay twined together.

"I will," I promised once more, tucking my body even closer against him.

**13**

"I like being married," I said drowsily. Since surviving the day-after feast and the receiving of gifts—most of them mooing or clucking—we'd done nothing for days but make love, talk, sleep, and read. Occasionally Chef sent up a tray of food and drink to sustain us. Otherwise we were left alone. Not even Philippe interrupted our time together.

"You seem to be taking to it well," Matthew said, nuzzling the tip of his cold nose behind my ear. I was lying, facedown and legs sprawled, in a room used to store spare weaponry above the smithy. Matthew was on top of me, shielding me from the draft coming through the gaps in the wooden door. Though I was unsure of how much of my own body would be exposed if someone walked in, Matthew's posterior and bare legs were certainly on view. He moved against me suggestively.

"You can't possibly want to do that again." I laughed happily when he repeated the movement. I wondered if this sexual stamina was a vampire thing or a Matthew thing.

"Are you criticizing my creativity already?" He turned me over and settled between my thighs. "Besides, I was thinking of this instead." He lowered his mouth to mine and slid gently inside me.

"We came out here to work on my shooting," I said sometime later. "Is this what you meant by target practice?"

Matthew rumbled with laughter. "There are hundreds of Auvergnat euphemisms for making love, but I don't believe that's one of them. I'll ask Chef if he's familiar with it."

"You will not."

"Are you being prim, Dr. Bishop?" he asked with mock surprise, picking a piece of straw from the hair tangled at the small of my back. "Don't bother. No one is under any illusions about how we're spending our time."

"I see your point," I said, pulling the hose that were formerly his over my knees. "Now that you've lured me here, you might as well try to figure out what I'm doing wrong."

"You're a novice and can't expect to hit the mark every time," he said, getting to his feet and rummaging for his own hose. One leg was still attached to his breeches, which were lying close by, but the other was nowhere to be seen. I reached underneath my shoulder and handed him the wadded-up ball they'd become.

"With good coaching I could become an expert." I'd now seen Matthew shoot, and he was a born archer with his long arms and fine, strong fingers. I picked up the curved bow, a burnished crescent of horn and wood propped up against a nearby pile of hay. The twisted leather bowstring swung free.

"Then you should be spending time with Philippe, not with me. His handling of the bow is legendary."

"Your father told me Ysabeau is a better shot." I was using her bow, but so far her skills had not rubbed off on me.

"That's because *Maman* is the only creature who has ever landed an arrow in his side." He beckoned at the bow. "Let me string it for you."

There was already a pink stripe across my cheek from the first time I'd tried to attach the bowstring to its ring. It required enormous strength and dexterity to bend back the upper and lower limbs of the bow into proper alignment. Matthew braced the lower limb against his thigh, bent the upper limb back with one hand, and used the other to tie off the bowstring.

"You make that look easy." It had looked easy when he'd twisted the cork from a bottle of champagne back in modern Oxford, too.

"It is—if you're a vampire and have had roughly a thousand years of practice." Matthew handed me the bow with a smile. "Remember, keep your shoulders in a straight line, don't think too long about the shot, and make the release soft and smooth."

He made it *sound* easy, too. I turned to face the target. Matthew had used a few daggers to pin a soft cap, a doublet, and a skirt to a pile of hay. At first I thought the goal was to hit something: the hat, the doublet, the skirt. Matthew explained that the goal was to hit what I was aiming for. He demonstrated his point by shooting a single arrow into a haystack, encircling it clockwise with five other arrows, then splitting the center shaft down the middle with a sixth.

I drew an arrow out of the quiver, nocked it, looked down the line of sight provided by my left arm, and pulled the bowstring back. I hesitated. The bow was already misaligned.

"Shoot," Matthew said sharply.

When I released the string, the arrow whizzed by the hay and fell flat on the ground.

"Let me try again," I said, reaching for the quiver by my feet.

"I've seen you shoot witchfire at a vampire and blow a hole straight through her chest," Matthew said quietly.

"I don't want to talk about Juliette." I tried to set the arrow in place, but my hands shook. I lowered the bow. "Or Champier. Or the fact that my powers seem to have totally disappeared. Or how I can make fruit wither and see colors and lights around people. Can't we just leave it—for one week?" Once again, my magic (or lack thereof) was a regular topic of conversation.

"The archery was supposed to help jostle your witchfire into action," Matthew pointed out. "Talking about Juliette may help."

"Why can't this just be about me getting some exercise?" I asked impatiently.

"Because we need to understand why your power is changing," Matthew said calmly. "Raise the bow, pull the arrow back, and let it fly."

"At least I hit the hay this time," I said after the arrow landed in the upper right corner of the haystack.

"Too bad you were aiming lower."

"You're taking all the fun out of this."

Matthew's expression turned serious. "There's nothing lighthearted about survival. This time nock the arrow but close your eyes before you aim."

"You want me to use my instincts." My laugh was shaky as I placed the arrow in the bow. The target was in front of me, but rather than focus on it I closed my eyes as Matthew suggested. As soon as I did, the weight of the air distracted me. It pressed on my arms, my thighs, and settled like a heavy cloak on my shoulders. The air held the tip of the arrow up, too. I adjusted my stance, shoulders widening as they pushed the air aside. A breeze, a caress of movement, pulled a few strands of hair away from my ear in response.

*What do you want?* I asked the breeze crossly.

*Your trust,* it whispered in reply.

My lips parted in astonishment, my mind's eye opened, and I saw the tip of the arrow burning gold with the heat and pressure that had been beaten into it at the forge. The fire that was trapped there wanted to fly free again, but it would stay where it was unless I let go of my fear. I puffed out a soft exhalation, making room for faith. My breath passed along the arrow's shaft, and I released the bowstring. Held aloft on my breath, the arrow flew.

"I hit it." My eyes remained closed, but I didn't need to see to know that my arrow had reached its target.

"You did. The question is how." Matthew took the bow from my fingers before it could fall.

"Fire was trapped in the arrow, and the weight of the air was wrapped around the shaft and the tip." I opened my eyes.

"You felt the elements just as you did the water under Sarah's orchard in Madison and the sunlight in the quince at the Old Lodge." Matthew sounded thoughtful.

"Sometimes it seems like the world is full of invisible potential that is just beyond my grasp. Maybe if I were like Thetis and could shift my shape at will, I would know what to do with it all." I reached for the bow and another arrow. So long as I kept my eyes closed, I hit the target. As soon as I peeked at my surroundings, however, my shots went wide or fell short.

"That's enough for today," Matthew said, working on a knot that was forming next to my right shoulder blade. "Chef expects rain later this week. Maybe we should go riding while we can." Chef was not only a dab hand with pastry but a decent meteorologist, too. He usually sent up a forecast with the breakfast tray.

We rode out into the countryside and spotted several bonfires burning in the fields on our way home, and Sept-Tours blazed with torches. Tonight was Saturnalia, the official beginning of the holiday season at the château. The ecumenical Philippe wanted no one to feel left out and so gave equal time to Roman and Christian traditions. There was even a strand of Norse Yule running through the mix, which I felt sure could be traced to the absent Gallowglass.

"You two can't be tired of each other's company so soon!" Philippe boomed from the minstrels' gallery when we returned. He was wearing a splendid set of antlers atop his head, making him look like a bizarre combination of lion and stag. "We didn't expect to see you for another fortnight. But now that you're here, you can make yourself useful. Take some stars and moons and hang them wherever there is an empty spot."

The great hall was draped in so much greenery that it looked and smelled like the forest. Several wine barrels stood unattended so that revelers could have a cup whenever the spirit moved them. Cheers greeted our return. The decorating crew wanted Matthew to climb up the chimneypiece and affix a large tree limb to one of the beams. He scampered up the stone with an agility that suggested it was not his first time.

It was impossible to resist the holiday spirit, and when supper rolled around, the two of us volunteered to serve the meal to the guests in a ritual of topsy-turvy that made the servants into lords and the lords their servants. My champion Thomas drew the long straw and presided over the celebrations as the Lord of Misrule. He was seated in Philippe's place on a stack of cushions, wearing the priceless gold-and-ruby crown from upstairs as though it were a stage prop. Whatever harebrained request Thomas made was granted by Philippe in his role as court fool. His favors this night included a romantic dance with Alain (Matthew's father opted to take the part of the woman), driving the dogs into a frenzy by playing a whistling flute, and making shadow dragons climb up the wall accompanied by the screams of the children.

Philippe didn't forget the adults, setting up elaborate games of chance to occupy them while he entertained his smallest subjects. He gave each grown-up a bag of beans to make wagers and promised a sack of money to the person with the most at the end of the evening. The enterprising Catrine made a killing by exchanging kisses for beans, and had I been given any tokens, I would have bet them all on her taking the final prize.

Throughout the evening I would look up and see Matthew and Philippe standing side by side, exchanging a few words or sharing a joke. As they bent their heads together, one dark and one bright, the difference in their appearances was striking. But in so many other ways, they were alike. With every passing day, his father's unquenchable high spirits wore down some of Matthew's sharp edges. Hamish had been right: Matthew was not the same man here. He was even finer. And in spite of my fears at Mont Saint-Michel, he was still mine.

Matthew felt my gaze and looked at me quizzically. I smiled and blew him a kiss across the hall. He dipped his head, shyly pleased.

Around five minutes before midnight, Philippe whisked the cover off an item standing by the fireplace.

"Christ. Philippe swore he'd have that clock up and running again, but I didn't believe him." Matthew joined me as the children and adults squealed in delight.

The clock was unlike any I'd ever seen before. A carved and gilded cabinet surrounded a water barrel. A long copper pipe stretched up from the barrel and dropped water into the hull of a splendid model ship suspended by a rope wound around a cylinder. As the ship grew incrementally heavier from the weight of the water, the cylinder turned and moved a single hand around a dial on the face of the clock, indicating the time. The whole structure was nearly as tall as I was.

"What happens at midnight?" I asked.

"No doubt whatever it is involves the gunpowder he asked for yesterday," Matthew said grimly.

Having displayed the clock with suitable ceremony, Philippe began a tribute to friends past and present and family new and old, as befitted a festival honoring the ancient god. He named every creature the community had lost over the past year, including (when prompted by the Lord of Misrule) Thomas's kitten, Prunelle, who had died tragically by misadventure. The hand continued to inch toward twelve.

At midnight precisely, the ship detonated with a deafening explosion. The clock shuddered to a stop in its splintered wooden case.

"*Skata.*" Philippe looked sadly at his ruined clock.

"Monsieur Finé, God rest his soul, would not be pleased with your improvements to his design." Matthew waved the smoke from his eyes as he bent to take a closer look. "Every year Philippe tries something new: jets of water, chiming bells, a mechanical owl to hoot the hours. He's been tinkering with it ever since King François lost it to him in a card game."

"The cannon were supposed to fire little sparks and give a puff of smoke. It would have amused the children," said Philippe indignantly. "Something was amiss with your gunpowder, *Matthaios.*"

Matthew laughed. "Evidently not, judging by the wreckage."

"*C'est dommage,*" Thomas said with a sympathetic shake of the head. He was crouched next to Philippe, his crown askew and a look of adult concern on his face.

"*Pas de problème.* Next year we will do better," Philippe assured Thomas breezily.

Shortly thereafter we left the people of Saint-Lucien to their gambling and revelry. Upstairs, I lingered by the fireside until Matthew doused the candles and got into bed. When I joined him, I hitched up my night rail and straddled his hips.

"What are you doing?" Matthew was surprised to find himself flat on his back in his own bed, his wife looking down at him.

"Misrule wasn't just for men," I said, running my nails down his chest. "I read an article about it in graduate school, called 'Women on Top.'"

"Accustomed as you are to being in charge, I cannot imagine you learned much from it, *mon coeur.*" Matthew's eyes smoldered as I shifted my weight to trap him more securely between my thighs.

"Flatterer." My fingertips traveled from his trim hips up and over the ridges in his abdomen and across the muscles in his shoulders. I leaned over him and pinned his arms to the bed, giving him an excellent view of my body through the night rail's open neckline. He groaned.

"Welcome to the world turned upside down." I released him long enough to remove my night rail, then grasped his hands and lowered myself onto his chest so that the tips of my bare breasts brushed his skin.

"Christ. You're going to kill me."

"Don't you dare die now, vampire," I said, guiding him inside me, rocking gently, holding out the promise of more. Matthew reacted with a low moan. "You like that," I said softly.

He urged me toward a harder, faster rhythm. But I kept my movements slow and steady, reveling in the way our bodies fit. Matthew was a cool presence at my core, a delicious source of friction that heated my blood. I was staring deep into his eyes when he climaxed, and the raw vulnerability there sent me hurtling after him. I collapsed onto his torso, and when I moved to climb off, his arms tightened around me.

"Stay there," he whispered.

I did stay, until Matthew woke me hours later. He made love to me again in the quiet before the dawn and held me as I underwent the metamorphosis from fire to water to air and returned once more to dreams.

Friday marked the shortest day of the year and the celebration of Yule. The village was still recovering from Saturnalia and had Christmas yet before them, but Philippe was undeterred.

"Chef butchered a hog," he said. "How could I disappoint him?"

During a break in the weather, Matthew went to the village to help repair a roof that had collapsed under the weight of the latest snowfall. I left him there, throwing hammers down a ridgepole to another carpenter and delighted at the prospect of a morning of grueling physical labor in freezing temperatures.

I closeted myself in the library with a few of the family's finer alchemical books and some blank sheets of paper. One was partially covered with doodles and diagrams that would have made sense to no one but me. With all that was happening in the château, I'd abandoned my attempts to make spirit of wine. Thomas and Étienne wanted to be running around with their friends and sticking their fingers into Chef's latest cake batter, not helping me with a science experiment.

"Diana." Philippe was moving at great speed and was halfway into the room before he noticed me. "I thought you were with Matthew."

"I couldn't bear to see him up there," I confessed. He nodded in understanding.

"What are you doing?" he asked, looking over my shoulder.

"Trying to figure out what Matthew and I have to do with alchemy." My brain felt fuzzy with disuse and lack of sleep.

Philippe dropped a handful of small paper triangles, scrolls, and squares onto the table and pulled up a chair. He pointed to one of my sketches. "This is Matthew's seal."

"It is. It's also the symbols for silver and gold, the moon and the sun." The hall had been decorated with spangled versions of these heavenly bodies for Saturnalia. "I've been thinking about it since Monday night. I understand why a witch might be symbolized by the crescent moon and silver—they're both linked to the goddess. But why would anyone use a sun or gold to denote a vampire?" It went against every bit of popular lore.

"Because we are unchanging. Our lives do not wax or wane, and, like gold, our bodies resist corruption from death or disease."

"I should have thought of that." I made some notes.

"You have had a few other things on your mind." Philippe smiled. "Matthew is very happy."

"Not only because of me," I said, meeting my father-in-law's gaze. "Matthew is happy to be with you again."

Shadows scudded through Philippe's eyes. "Ysabeau and I like it when our children come home. They have their own lives, but it doesn't make their absence any easier to bear."

"And today you are missing Gallowglass, too," I said. Philippe seemed uncharacteristically subdued.

"I am." He stirred the folded papers with his fingers. "It was Hugh, my eldest, who brought him into the family. Hugh always made wise decisions when it came to sharing his blood, and Gallowglass was no exception. He is a fierce warrior with his father's sense of honor. It comforts me to know that my grandson is in England with Matthew."

"Matthew seldom mentions Hugh."

"He was closer to Hugh than to any of his other brothers. When Hugh died with the last of the Templars at the hands of the church and the king, it shook Matthew's loyalties. It was some time before he was able to free himself of his blood rage and come back to us."

"And Gallowglass?"

"Gallowglass is not yet ready to leave his grief behind, and until he does so, he will not set foot in France. My grandson exacted retribution from the men who betrayed Hugh's trust, as did Matthew, but revenge is never an adequate remedy for loss. One day my grandson will return. I am sure of it." For a moment Philippe looked old, no longer the vigorous ruler of his people but a father who had suffered the misfortune to outlive his sons.

"Thank you, Philippe." I hesitated before covering his hand with mine. He clasped it briefly and stood. Then he took up one of the alchemy books. It was Godfrey's beautifully illustrated copy of the *Aurora Consurgens,* the text that had first lured me to Sept-Tours.

"Such a curious subject, alchemy," Philippe murmured, flipping through the pages. He found the picture of the Sun King and the Moon Queen jousting on the back of a lion and a griffin, and he smiled broadly. "Yes, this will do." He tucked one of his paper shapes between the pages.

"What are you doing?" I was overcome with curiosity.

"It is a game that Ysabeau and I play. When one of us is away, we leave messages hidden in the pages of books. So much happens in a day, it is impossible to remember everything when we see each other again. This way we can come upon little memories like this one when we least expect it, and share them."

Philippe went to the shelves and picked out a volume in a worn leather binding. "This is one of our favorite stories, *The Song of Armouris.* Ysabeau and I have simple tastes and enjoy stories of adventure. We are always hiding messages in this." He stuffed a scroll of paper down the spine between the binding and the gatherings of vellum. A folded rectangle fell out of the bottom as he worked it into the tight space.

"Ysabeau has taken to using a knife so that her messages are harder to find. She is full of tricks, that one. Let's see what she says." Philippe opened up the paper and read it silently. He looked up with a twinkle in his eyes and cheeks that were redder than usual.

I laughed and rose. "I think you might need more privacy to compose your reply!"

"*Sieur.*" Alain shifted in the doorway, his face serious. "Messengers have arrived. One from Scotland. Another from England. A third from Lyon."

Philippe sighed and cursed under his breath. "They might have waited until after the Christian feast."

My mouth soured.

"It cannot be good news," Philippe said, catching my expression. "What did the messenger from Lyon report?"

"Champier took precautions before he left and told others that he had been called here. Now that he has not returned home, his friends are asking questions. A group of witches is preparing to leave the city in search of him, and they are headed in this direction," Alain explained.

"When?" I whispered. It was too soon.

"The snow will slow them, and they will find travel difficult over the holy days. A few more days, perhaps a week."

"And the other messengers?" I asked Alain.

"They are in the village, looking for *milord*."

"To call him back to England, no doubt," I said.

"If so, Christmas Day will be the best time to set out. Few will be on the roads, and the moon will be dark. These are ideal travel conditions for *manjasang*, but not for warmbloods," Philippe said matter-of-factly. "There are horses and lodgings ready for you as far as Calais. A boat waits to take you to Dover. I sent word to Gallowglass and Raleigh to prepare for your return."

"You've been expecting this," I said, shaken at the prospect of leaving. "But I'm not ready. People still know I'm different."

"You blend in better than you think. You've been conversing with me in perfectly good French and Latin all morning, for instance." My mouth opened in disbelief. Philippe laughed. "It is true. I switched back and forth twice, but you didn't notice." His face grew serious. "Shall I go down and tell Matthew about my arrangements?"

"No," I said, my hand on his arm. "I'll do it."

Matthew was sitting on the ridgepole, a letter in each hand and a frown on his face. When he spotted me, he slid down the slope of an eave and landed on the ground with the grace of a cat. His happiness and light-hearted banter of this morning were nothing more than a memory. Matthew removed his doublet from a rusted torch bracket. Once he'd shrugged it over his shoulders, the carpenter was gone and the prince had returned.

"Agnes Sampson confessed to fifty-three indictments of witchcraft."

Matthew swore. "Scottish officials have yet to learn that heaping on charges makes every single one look less convincing. According to this account, the devil reported to Sampson that King James was his greatest enemy. Elizabeth must be delighted not to find herself in first place."

"Witches don't believe in the devil," I told him. Of all the bizarre things humans said about witches, this was the most incomprehensible.

"Most creatures will believe in anything that promises to bring an end to their immediate misery if they've been starved, tortured, and frightened for weeks on end." Matthew ran his fingers through his hair. "Agnes Sampson's confession—unreliable as it is—provides proof that the witches are meddling in politics, just as King James contends."

"Thereby breaking the covenant," I said, understanding why Agnes had been so vigorously pursued by the Scottish king.

"Yes. Gallowglass wants to know what to do."

"What did you do when you were here . . . before?"

"I let Agnes Sampson's death pass unchallenged, a proper civil punishment for a crime that was outside the bounds of Congregation protection." His eyes met mine. Witch and historian struggled with the impossible choice before me.

"Then you have to keep silent again," I said, the historian winning the contest.

"My silence will mean her death."

"And your speaking out will change the past, perhaps with unimaginable consequences for the present. I don't want the witch to die any more than you do, Matthew. But if we start changing things, where will we stop?" I shook my head.

"So I will watch the whole gruesome business in Scotland unfold, again. This time it looks so different, though," he said reluctantly. "William Cecil has directed me to return home so that I can gather intelligence on the Scottish situation for the queen. I have to obey his orders, Diana. I don't have a choice."

"We'd have to go to England even without Cecil's summons. Champier's friends have noticed he's missing. And we can leave immediately. Philippe's been making arrangements for a speedy departure, just in case."

"That's my father," Matthew said with a humorless laugh.

"I'm sorry we have to leave so soon," I whispered.

Matthew hooked me into his side. "If not for you, my last memories of my father would be of a broken shell of a man. We must take the bitter with the sweet."

Over the next several days, Matthew and his father went through a ritual of farewell that must have been familiar, given all the good-byes the two had exchanged. But this time was unique. It would be a different Matthew who would next come to Sept-Tours, one with no knowledge of me or of Philippe's future.

"The people of Saint-Lucien have long known the company of *manjasang*," Philippe assured me when I worried how Thomas and Étienne would be able to keep it all secret. "We come, we go. They ask no questions, and we offer no explanations. It has always been this way."

Even so, Matthew made sure his own plans were clear. I overheard him talking with Philippe in the hay barn after a morning of sparring.

"The last thing I will do before we return to our own time is to send you a message. Be ready to order me to Scotland to secure the family's alliance with King James. From there I should go to Amsterdam. The Dutch will be opening up trade routes with the East."

"I can manage, Matthew," Philippe said mildly. "Until then I expect regular updates from England and news of how you and Diana are faring."

"Gallowglass will keep you abreast of our adventures," Matthew promised.

"It is not the same thing as hearing it from you," Philippe said. "It will be very difficult not to gloat over what I know of your future when you get pompous, Matthew. Somehow I will manage that, too."

Time played tricks on us during our last days at Sept-Tours, first dragging, then accelerating without warning. On Christmas Eve, Matthew went down to the church for Mass along with most of the household. I remained in the château and found Philippe in his office on the other side of the great hall. He was, as ever, writing letters.

I knocked on the door. It was a formality, since he had no doubt been tracking my approach since I'd left Matthew's tower, but it didn't seem right to barge in uninvited.

*"Introite."* It was the same command he'd issued when I'd first arrived, but it sounded so much less forbidding now that I knew him better.

"I'm sorry to disturb you, Philippe."

"Come in, Diana," he said, rubbing his eyes. "Did Catrine find my boxes?"

"Yes, and the cup and pen case, too." He insisted that I take his handsome traveling set on the journey. Each item was made of stiffened leather and could withstand the perils of snow, rain, and rough handling. "I wanted to be sure to thank you before we left—and not just for the wedding. You fixed something in Matthew that was broken."

Philippe pushed his stool back and studied me. "It is I who should be thanking you, Diana. The family has been trying to mend Matthew's spirit for more than a thousand years. If I'm remembering correctly, it took you less than forty days."

"Matthew wasn't like this," I said with a shake of the head, "not until he was here, with you. There was a darkness in him that I couldn't reach."

"A man like Matthew never frees himself of the shadows completely. But perhaps it is necessary to embrace the darkness in order to love him," Philippe continued.

"*Do not refuse me because I am dark and shadowed,*" I murmured.

"I do not recognize the verse," Philippe said with a frown.

"It's from that alchemical book I showed you earlier—the *Aurora Consurgens*. The passage reminded me of Matthew, but I still don't understand why. I will, though."

"You are very like that ring, you know," Philippe said, tapping his finger on the table. "It was another of Ysabeau's clever messages."

"She wanted you to know she approved of the marriage," I said, my thumb reaching for the comforting weight.

"No. Ysabeau wanted me to know she approved of *you*. Like the gold from which it is made, you are steadfast. You hide many secrets within you, just as the bands of the ring hide the poesies from view. But it is the stone that best captures who you are: bright on the surface, fiery within, and impossible to break."

"Oh, I'm breakable," I said ruefully. "You can shatter a diamond by hitting it with an ordinary hammer, after all."

"I've seen the scars Matthew left on you. I suspect there are others, too, though less visible. If you did not fall to pieces then, you will not now." Philippe rounded the table. He kissed me tenderly on each cheek, and my eyes filled.

"I should go. We're setting out early tomorrow." I turned to leave, then whirled around and flung my arms around Philippe's massive shoulders. How could such a man ever be broken?

"What is it?" Philippe murmured, taken aback.

"You will not be alone either, Philippe de Clermont," I whispered fiercely. "I'll find a way to be with you in the darkness, I promise. And when you think the whole world has abandoned you, I'll be there, holding your hand."

"How could it be otherwise," Philippe said gently, "when you are in my heart?"

The next morning only a few creatures were gathered in the courtyard to send us on our way. Chef had tucked all sorts of snacks for me into Pierre's saddlebags, and Alain had stuffed the rest of the available space with letters for Gallowglass, Walter, and scores of other recipients. Catrine stood by, eyes puffy with crying. She had wanted to go with us, but Philippe wouldn't allow it.

And there was Philippe, who gathered me up in a bear hug before letting me go. He and Matthew spoke quietly for a few moments. Matthew nodded.

"I am proud of you, *Matthaios*," said Philippe, clasping him briefly on the shoulder. Matthew moved slightly toward his father when Philippe released him, reluctant to break the connection.

When Matthew turned to me, his face was resolute. He helped me into the saddle before swinging effortlessly onto the back of his horse.

"*Khaire*, Father," Matthew said, eyes gleaming.

"*Khairete, Matthaios kai Diana,*" Philippe replied.

For Matthew there was no turning for a last glimpse of his father and no softening of the stiffness in his back. He kept his eyes on the road ahead, facing the future rather than the past.

I turned once, when a flash of movement caught my eye. It was Philippe, riding along a neighboring ridge, determined not to let go of his son until it was necessary.

"Good-bye, Philippe," I whispered into the wind, hoping that he would hear.

"Ysabeau? Are you all right?"

"Of course." Ysabeau was bending back the covers on a priceless old book and shaking it upside down.

Emily Mather looked at Ysabeau doubtfully. The library was in a state of utter chaos. The rest of the château was neat as a pin, but this room looked as if a tornado had blown through it. Books were strewn everywhere. Someone had pulled them off the shelves and flung them onto every other available surface.

"It must be here. He would have known that the children were together." Ysabeau flung the book aside and reached for another. It pained Emily to her librarian's soul to see books mistreated like this.

"I don't understand. What are you looking for?" She picked up the discarded volume and closed it gently.

"Matthew and Diana were going to 1590. I was not at home then, but in Trier. Philippe would have known about Matthew's new wife. He would have left me word." Ysabeau's hair hung down around her face and flowed nearly to her waist. Impatiently she took it in her hands and twisted it out of her way. After examining the spine and pages of her latest victim, she sliced open the end paper with the sharp nail of her index finger. Finding nothing hidden there, she growled with frustration.

"But these are books, not letters," Emily said carefully. She didn't know Ysabeau well, but Emily was well acquainted with the more gruesome legends about Matthew's mother and what she had done in Trier and other places. The matriarch of the de Clermont family was no friend to witches, and even though Diana trusted the woman, Emily was still not sure.

"I am not looking for a letter. We hid little notes to each other in the pages of books. I searched through every volume in the library when he died, wanting to have every last piece of him. But I must have missed something."

"Maybe it wasn't there to be found—not then." A dry voice spoke from the shadows by the door. Sarah Bishop's red hair was wild and her face white with worry and lack of sleep. "Marthe is going to have a fit when she sees this. And it's a good thing Diana isn't around. She'd give you a lecture on book preservation that would bore you stupid." Tabitha, who accompanied Sarah everywhere, shot from between the witch's legs.

It was Ysabeau's turn to be confused. "What do you mean, Sarah?"

"Time is tricky. Even if everything went according to plan and Diana took Matthew back to the first day of November in 1590, it may still be too soon to look for a message from your husband. And you wouldn't have found a message before, because Philippe hadn't met my niece yet." Sarah paused. "I think Tabitha's eating that book."

Tabitha, delighted to be in a house with an ample supply of mice and plenty of dark corners for hiding, had recently taken to climbing the furniture and the drapes. She was perched on one of the library shelves, gnawing on the corner of a leather-bound volume.

*"Kakó gati!"* Ysabeau cried, rushing over to the shelves. "That is one of Diana's favorites."

Tabitha, who had never backed down from a confrontation with another predator with the exception of Miriam, swiped at the book so that it fell to the floor. She jumped down after it, hovering over her prize like a lion guarding a particularly desirable treat.

"It's one of those alchemy books with pictures in it," Sarah said, liberating the book from her cat and flipping through the pages. She gave the cover a sniff. "Well, no wonder Tabitha wants to chew on it. It smells of mint and leather, just like her favorite toy."

A square of paper, folded and folded and folded again, fluttered to the floor. Deprived of the book, Tabitha picked up the paper between her sharp teeth and stalked toward the door.

Ysabeau was waiting for her. She picked Tabitha up by the scruff of the neck and pried the paper from the cat's mouth. Then she kissed the surprised feline on the nose. "Clever cat. You will have fish for supper."

"Is that what you were looking for?" Emily eyed the scrap. It didn't seem worth tearing the room apart.

Ysabeau's answer was clear from the way she handled it. She carefully unfolded it to reveal a five-inch square of thick paper, both sides covered in tiny characters.

"That's written in some kind of code," said Sarah. She swung her zebra-striped reading glasses onto her nose from the cord around her neck to get a better look.

"Not a code—Greek." Ysabeau's hands trembled as she smoothed the paper flat.

"What does it say?" Sarah asked.

"Sarah!" Emily scolded. "It's private."

"It's from Philippe. He saw them," Ysabeau breathed, her eyes racing across the text. Her hand went to her mouth, relief vying with disbelief.

Sarah waited for the vampire to finish reading. It took two minutes, which was ninety seconds longer than she would have given anyone else. "Well?"

"They were with him for the holidays. '*On the morning of the Christians' holy celebration, I said farewell to your son. He is happy at last, mated to a woman who walks in the footsteps of the goddess and is worthy of his love,*'" Ysabeau read aloud.

"Are you sure he means Matthew and Diana?" Emily found the phrasing oddly formal and vague for an exchange between husband and wife.

"Yes. Matthew was always the child we worried over, though his brothers and sisters got into far worse predicaments. My one wish was to see Matthew happy."

"And the reference to the 'woman who walks in the footsteps of the goddess' is pretty clear," Sarah agreed. "He couldn't very well give her name and identify Diana as a witch. What if someone else had found it?"

"There is more," Ysabeau continued. "*Fate still has the power to surprise us, bright one. I fear there are difficult times ahead for all of us. I will do what I can, in what time remains to me, to ensure your safety and that of our children and grandchildren, those whose blessings we already enjoy and those as yet unborn.*'"

Sarah swore. "Unborn, not unmade?"

"Yes," Ysabeau whispered. "Philippe always chose his words carefully."

"So he was trying to tell us something about Diana and Matthew," Sarah said.

Ysabeau sank onto the sofa. "A long, long time ago, there were rumors about creatures who were different—immortal but powerful, too. Around the time the covenant was first signed, some claimed that a witch gave birth to a baby who wept tears of blood like a vampire. Whenever the child did so, fierce winds blew in from the sea."

"I've never heard that before," Emily said, frowning.

"It was dismissed as a myth—a story created to engender fear among creatures. Few among us now would remember, and even fewer would believe it possible." Ysabeau touched the paper in her lap. "But Philippe knew it was true. He held the child, you see, and knew it for what it was."

"Which was what?" Sarah said, stunned.

"A *manjasang* born of a witch. The poor child was starving. The witch's family took the baby boy from her and refused to feed him blood on the grounds that if he was forced to take only milk, it would keep him from turning into one of us."

"Surely Matthew knows this story," Emily said. "You would have told him for his research, if not for Diana's sake."

Ysabeau shook her head. "It was not my tale to tell."

"You and your secrets," Sarah said bitterly.

"And what of *your* secrets, Sarah?" Ysabeau cried. "Do you really believe that the witches—creatures like Satu and Peter Knox—know nothing about this *manjasang* child and its mother?"

"Stop it, both of you," Emily said sharply. "If the story is true, and other creatures know it, then Diana is in grave danger. Sophie too."

"Her parents were both witches, but she is a daemon," Sarah said, thinking of the young couple who had appeared on her doorstep in New York days before Halloween. No one understood how the two daemons fit into this mystery.

"So is Sophie's husband, but their daughter will be a witch. She and Nathaniel are further proof that we don't understand how witches, daemons, and vampires reproduce and pass their abilities on to their children," Emily said, worried.

"Sophie and Nathaniel aren't the only creatures who need to stay clear of the Congregation. It's a good thing Matthew and Diana are safely in 1590 and not here." Sarah was grim.

"But the longer those two stay in the past, the more likely it is they'll change the present," Emily observed. "Sooner or later, Diana and Matthew will give themselves away."

"What do you mean, Emily?" asked Ysabeau.

"Time has to adjust—and not in the melodramatic way people think, with wars averted and presidential elections changed. It will be little things, like this note, that pop up here and there."

"Anomalies," Ysabeau murmured. "Philippe was always looking for anomalies in the world. It is why I still read all the newspapers. It became our habit to look through them each morning." Her eyes closed against the memory. "He loved the sports section, of course, and read the education columns as well. Philippe was worried about what children would learn in the future. He established fellowships for the study of Greek and philosophy, and he endowed colleges for women. I always thought it strange."

"He was looking for Diana," Emily said with the certainty of someone blessed with second sight.

"Perhaps. Once I asked him why he was so preoccupied with current events and what he hoped to discover in the papers. Philippe said he would know it when he saw it," Ysabeau replied. She smiled sadly. "He loved his mysteries and said if it were possible, he would like to be a detective, like Sherlock Holmes."

"We need to make sure we notice any of these little time bumps before the Congregation does," said Sarah.

"I will tell Marcus," Ysabeau agreed with a nod.

"You should have told Matthew about that mixed-species baby." Sarah was unable to keep the note of recrimination from her voice.

"My son loves Diana, and if he had known about that child, Matthew would have turned his back on her rather than put her—and the baby—in danger."

"Bishops aren't so easily cowed, Ysabeau. If Diana wanted your son, she would have found a way to have him."

"Well, Diana did want him, and they have each other now," Emily pointed out. "But we're not going to have to share this news only with Marcus. Sophie and Nathaniel have to know, too."

Sarah and Emily left the library. They were staying in Louisa de Clermont's old room, down the hall from Ysabeau. Sarah thought there were times of day when it smelled a bit like Diana.

Ysabeau remained after they'd gone, gathering up books and reshelving them. When the room was orderly once again, she returned to the sofa and picked up the message from her husband. There was more to it than she had revealed to the witches. She reread the final lines.

"*But enough of these dark matters. You must keep yourself safe, too, so that you can enjoy the future with them. It has been two days since I reminded you that you hold my heart. I wish that I could do so every moment, so that you do not forget it, or the name of the man who will cherish yours forevermore. Philipos.*"

In the last days of his life, there had been moments when Philippe couldn't remember his own name, let alone hers.

"Thank you, Diana," Ysabeau whispered into the night, "for giving him back to me."

Several hours later, Sarah heard a strange sound overhead—like music, but more than music. She stumbled out of the room to find Marthe in the hall, wrapped in an old chenille bathrobe with a frog embroidered on the pocket, a bittersweet expression on her face.

"What is that?" Sarah asked, looking up. Nothing human could hope to produce a sound that beautiful and poignant. There must be an angel on the roof.

"Ysabeau is singing again," Marthe answered. "She has only done so once since Philippe died—when your niece was in danger and needed to be pulled back into this world."

"Is she all right?" There was so much grief and loss in every note that Sarah's heart constricted. There weren't words to describe the sound.

Marthe nodded. "The music is a good thing, a sign that her mourning may at last be coming to an end. Only then will Ysabeau begin to live again."

Two women, vampire and witch, listened until the final notes of Ysabeau's song faded into silence.

# PART III

# London:
# The Blackfriars

15

"It looks like a demented hedgehog," I observed. The London skyline was filled with needlelike spires that stuck up from the huddle of buildings that surrounded them. "What is that?" I gasped, pointing to a vast expanse of stone pierced by tall windows. High above the wooden roof was a charred, stout stump that made the building's proportions look all wrong.

"St. Paul's," Matthew explained. This was not Christopher Wren's graceful white-domed masterpiece, its bulk concealed until the last moment by modern office blocks. Old St. Paul's, perched on London's highest hill, was seen all at once.

"Lightning struck the spire, and the wood of the roof caught fire. The English believe it was a miracle the entire cathedral didn't burn to the ground," he continued.

"The French, not surprisingly, believe that the hand of the Lord was evident somewhat earlier in the event," commented Gallowglass. He had met us at Dover, commandeered a boat in Southwark, and was now rowing us all upstream. "No matter when God showed His true colors, He hasn't provided money for its repair."

"Nor has the queen." Matthew devoted his attention to the wharves on the shoreline, and his right hand rested on the hilt of his sword.

I had never imagined that Old St. Paul's would be so big. I gave myself another pinch. I had been administering them since spotting the Tower (it, too, looked enormous without skyscrapers all around) and London Bridge (which functioned as a suspended shopping mall). Many sights and sounds had impressed me since our arrival in the past, but nothing had taken my breath away like my first glimpses of London.

"Are you sure you don't want to dock in town first?" Gallowglass had been dropping hints about the wisdom of this course of action since we'd climbed into the boat.

"We're going to the Blackfriars," Matthew said firmly. "Everything else can wait."

Gallowglass looked dubious, but he kept rowing until we reached the westernmost reaches of the old, walled city. There we docked at a steep set of stone stairs. The bottom treads were submerged in the river, and from the look of the walls the tide would continue to rise until the rest were underwater, too. Gallowglass tossed a line to a brawny man who thanked him profusely for returning his property in one piece.

"You seem only to travel in other people's boats, Gallowglass. Maybe Matthew should give you your own for Christmas," I said drily. Our return to England—and the old calendar—meant we were celebrating the holiday twice this year.

"And deprive me of one of my few pleasures?" Gallowglass's teeth showed in his beard. Matthew's nephew thanked the boatman and tossed him a coin the size and weight of which reduced the poor fellow's previous anxiety to a hazy glow of appreciation.

We passed from the landing through an archway and onto Water Lane, a narrow, twisting artery crowded with houses and shops. With every rising floor, the houses jutted farther over the street, like a clothes chest with the upper drawers pulled out. This effect was heightened by the linens, carpets, and other items hanging out the windows. Everyone was taking advantage of the unusually fine weather to air out lodgings and garments.

Matthew retained a firm grip on my hand, and Gallowglass walked to my right. Sights and sounds came at us from every direction. Fabrics in saturated red, green, brown, and gray swung from hips and shoulders as skirts and cloaks were twitched away from wagon wheels and caught on the packages and weapons carried by passersby. The ring of hammers, the neighing of horses, the distant lowing of a cow, and the sound of metal rolling on stone competed for attention. Dozens of signs bearing angels, skulls, tools, brightly colored shapes, and mythological figures swayed and squeaked in the wind that blew up from the water. Above my head a wooden sign swung on its metal rod. It was decorated with a white deer, its delicate antlers circled with a golden band.

"Here we are," Matthew said. "The Hart and Crown."

The building was half-timbered, like most on the street. A vaulted passage spanned two arrays of windows. A shoemaker was busy at work on one side of the arch, while the woman opposite kept track of several children, customers, and a large account book. She gave Matthew a brisk nod.

"Robert Hawley's wife rules over his apprentices and customers with an iron fist. Nothing happens in the Hart and Crown without Margaret's knowledge," explained Matthew. I made a mental note to befriend the woman at the earliest opportunity.

The passage emptied out into the building's interior courtyard—a luxury in a city as densely packed as London. The courtyard boasted another rare amenity: a well that provided clean water to the residents of the complex. Someone had taken advantage of the courtyard's southern exposure by tearing up the old paving stones to plant a garden, and now its neat, empty beds patiently awaited spring. A group of washerwomen conducted business out of an old shed next to a shared privy.

To the left, a twisting set of stairs rose to our rooms on the first floor, where Françoise was waiting to welcome us on the wide landing. She'd flung open the stout door into the apartments, crowding a cupboard with pierced sides. A goose, denuded of feathers and with its neck broken, was tied to one of the cupboard's knobs.

"At last." Henry Percy appeared, beaming. "We've been waiting for hours. My good lady mother sent you a goose. She heard reports that no fowl are to be had in the city and became alarmed that you would go hungry."

"It is good to see you, Hal," Matthew said with a laugh and a shake of his head at the goose. "How is your mother?"

"Always a termagant at Christmas, thank you. Most of the family found excuses to be elsewhere, but I am detained here at the queen's pleasure. Her Majesty shouted across the audience chamber that I could not be trusted even so far as P-P-Petworth." Henry stammered and looked ill at the recollection.

"You are more than welcome to spend Christmas with us, Henry," I said, taking off my cloak and stepping inside, where the scent of spices and freshly cut fir filled the air.

"It is good of you to invite me, Diana, but my sister Eleanor and brother George are in town and they shouldn't have to brave her on their own."

"Stay with us this evening at least," Matthew urged, steering him to the right, where warmth and firelight beckoned, "and tell us what has happened while we were away."

"All is quiet here," Henry reported cheerfully.

"Quiet?" Gallowglass stomped up the stairs, looking frostily at the earl. "Marlowe's at the Cardinal's Hat, drunk as a fiddler, trading verses with that impoverished scrivener from Stratford who trails after him in hopes of becoming a playwright. For now Shakespeare seems content with learning how to forge your signature, Matthew. According to the innkeeper's records, you promised to pay Kit's room and board charges last week."

"I left them only an hour ago," Henry protested. "Kit knew that Matthew and Diana were due to arrive this afternoon. He and Will promised to be on their best behavior."

"That explains it, then," Gallowglass muttered sarcastically.

"Is this your doing, Henry?" I looked from the entrance hall into our main living quarters. Someone had tucked holly, ivy, and fir around the fireplace and the window frames and mounded them in the center of an oak table. The fireplace was loaded with logs, and a cheerful fire hissed and crackled.

"Françoise and I wanted your first Christmas to be festive," Henry said, turning pink.

The Hart and Crown represented urban living at its sixteenth-century best. The parlor was a good size but felt snug and comfortable. Its western wall was filled with a multipaned window that overlooked Water Lane. It was perfectly situated for people-watching, with a cushioned seat built into the base. Carved wainscoting warmed the walls, each panel covered with twisting flowers and vines.

The room's furnishings were spare but well made. A wide settle and two deep chairs waited by the fireplace. The oak table in the center of the room was unusually fine, less than three feet across but quite long, its legs decorated with the delicate faces of caryatids and herms. A beam set with candles hung over the table. It could be raised and lowered by use of the smooth rope-and-pulley system suspended from the ceiling. Carved lions' heads snarled from the front band of a monstrous cupboard that held a wide array of beakers, pitchers, cups, and goblets—though very few plates, as befitted a vampire household.

Before we settled down to our dinner of roast goose, Matthew showed me our bedroom and his private office. Both were across the entrance hall opposite the parlor. Gabled windows overlooked the courtyard, making both rooms feel light and surprisingly airy. The bedroom had only three pieces of furniture: a four-poster bed with a carved headboard and heavy wooden tester, a tall linen press with paneled sides and door, and a long, low chest under the windows. The last was locked, and Matthew explained that it held his suit of armor and several spare weapons. Henry and Françoise had been in here, too. Ivy crawled up the bedposts, and they'd tied sprigs of holly to the headboard.

Whereas the bedroom looked barely occupied, Matthew's office was clearly well used. Here there were baskets of paper, bags and tankards full of quills, pots of ink, enough wax to make several dozen candles, balls of twine, and so much waiting mail that my heart sank just thinking about it.

A comfortable-looking chair with a sloping back and curved arms sat before a table with extendable leaves. Except for the heavy table legs with their bulbous, cup-shaped carvings, everything was plain and practical.

Though I had blanched at the piles of work that awaited him, Matthew was unconcerned. "It can all wait. Not even spies conduct business on Christmas Eve," he told me.

Over dinner we talked more about Walter's latest exploits and the shocking state of traffic in London, and we steered clear of more sober subjects, like Kit's latest drinking binge and the enterprising William Shakespeare. After the plates were cleared, Matthew pulled a small game table away from the wall. He removed a deck of cards from the compartment under the tabletop and proceeded to teach me how to gamble, Elizabethan style. Henry had just persuaded Matthew and Gallowglass to play flapdragon—an alarming game that involved setting raisins alight in a dish of brandy and betting on who could swallow the greatest number—when the sound of carolers rose from the street outside the windows. They were not all singing in the same key, and those who didn't know the words were inserting scandalous details about the personal lives of Joseph and Mary.

"Here, *milord*," Pierre said, thrusting a bag of coins at Matthew.

"Do we have cakes?" Matthew asked Françoise.

She looked at him as if he'd lost his mind. "Of course we have cakes. They are in the new food cupboard on the landing, where the smell will not disturb anyone," Françoise said, pointing in the direction of the stairs. "Last year you gave them wine, but I do not believe they require it tonight."

"I'll go with you, Matt," Henry volunteered. "I like a good song on Christmas Eve."

The appearance of Matthew and Henry downstairs was marked by a definite uptick in the choir's volume. When the carolers came to a rather uneven finish, Matthew thanked them and passed out coins. Henry distributed the cakes, which led to many bows and a hushed "Thank you, my lord" as the news passed that this was the Earl of Northumberland. The carolers moved off to another house, following some mysterious order of precedence that they hoped would ensure them the best refreshments and payments.

Soon I could no longer smother my yawns, and Henry and Gallowglass began to gather up their gloves and cloaks. Both were smiling like satisfied matchmakers when they headed for the door. Matthew joined me in bed, holding me until I fell asleep, humming carols and naming the city's many bells as they sounded the hour.

"There is St. Mary-le-Bow," he said, listening to the sounds of the city. "And St. Katherine Cree."

"Is that St. Paul's?" I asked as a prolonged clarion sounded.

"No. The lightning that took off the steeple destroyed the bells, too," he said. "That's St. Saviour's. We passed it on our way into town." The rest of London's churches caught up with Southwark's cathedral. Finally a straggler finished with a discordant clang, the last sound I heard before sleep overtook me.

In the middle of the night, I was awakened by conversation coming from Matthew's study. I felt the bed, but he was no longer with me. The leather straps that held up the mattress squeaked and stretched as I jumped to the cold floor. I shivered and threw on a shawl before leaving the room.

Judging by the pools of wax in the shallow candlestands, Matthew had been working for hours. Pierre was with him, standing next to the shelves built into a recess by the fireplace. He looked as though he'd been dragged backward through the Thames mud at low tide.

"I've been all over the city with Gallowglass and his Irish friends," Pierre murmured. "If the Scots know anything more about the schoolmaster, they will not divulge it, *milord.*"

"What schoolmaster?" I stepped into the room. It was then I spotted the narrow door hidden in the wooden paneling.

"I am sorry, *madame.* I did not mean to wake you." Pierre's dismay showed through the filth, and the stench that accompanied him made my eyes water.

"It's all right, Pierre. Go. I'll find you later." Matthew waited while his servant fled, shoes squelching. Matthew's eyes drifted to the shadows by the fireplace.

"The room that lies beyond that door wasn't on your welcome tour," I pointed out, going to his side. "What's happened now?"

"More news from Scotland. A jury sentenced a wizard named John Fian—a schoolmaster from Prestonpans—to death. While I was away, Gallowglass tried to find out what truth, if any, lies behind the wild accusations: worshipping Satan, dismembering dead bodies in a graveyard, transforming moles' feet into pieces of silver so he was never without money, going to sea in a ship with the devil and Agnes Sampson to thwart the king's policies." Matthew tossed a paper onto the table in front of him. "So far as I can tell, Fian is one of what we used to call the *tempestarii,* and nothing more."

"A windwitch, or possibly a waterwitch," I said, translating the unfamiliar term.

"Yes," Matthew agreed with a nod. "Fian augmented his teacher's salary by causing thunderstorms during dry spells and early thaws when it looked as if the Scottish winter would never end. His fellow villagers adored him, by all accounts. Even Fian's pupils had nothing but praise. Fian might have been a bit of a seer—he's credited with foretelling people's deaths, but that could have been something Kit cooked up to embellish the story for an English audience. He's obsessed with a witch's second sight, as you'll remember."

"Witches are vulnerable to the shifting moods of our neighbors, Matthew. One minute we're friends, the next we're run out of town—or worse."

"What happened to Fian was definitely worse," Matthew said grimly.

"I can imagine," I said with a shudder. If Fian had been tortured as Agnes Sampson had, he must have welcomed death. "What's in that room?"

Matthew considered telling me that it was a secret but wisely refrained. He stood. "It would be better if I showed you. Stay by me. It's not yet dawn, and we can't take a candle into the room for fear that someone will see it from outside. I don't want you to trip." I nodded mutely and took his hand.

We stepped across the threshold into a long room with a row of windows barely larger than arrow slits tucked under the eaves. After a few moments, my eyes adjusted and gray shapes began to emerge from the gloom. A pair of old garden chairs woven from willow twigs stood across from each other, their backs curved forward. Low, battered benches were set out in two rows down the center of the room. Each bore a strange assortment of objects: books, papers, letters, hats, and clothes. From the right came a gleam of metal: swords, hilts up and points down. A pile of daggers rested on the floor nearby. There was a scratching sound, too, and a scurry of feet.

"Rats." Matthew's voice was matter-of-fact, but I couldn't help drawing my night rail tight against my legs. "Pierre and I do what we can, but it's impossible to get rid of them entirely. They find all this paper irresistible." He gestured up, and I noticed for the first time the bizarre festoons on the walls.

I crept closer and peered at the garlands. Each one hung from a thin, twisted cord affixed to the plaster with a square-headed nail. The cord had then been threaded through the upper-left-hand corner of a series of documents. The knot in the end of the cord was slung back up and looped around the same nail, creating a wreath of paper.

"One of the world's first file cabinets. You say I keep too many secrets," he said softly, reaching out and snagging one of the garlands. "You can add these to your reckoning."

"But there are thousands of them." Surely not even a fifteen-hundred-year-old vampire could possess so many.

"There are," Matthew agreed. He watched as my eyes swept the room, taking in the archive he guarded. "We remember what other creatures want to forget, and that makes it possible for the Knights of Lazarus to protect those in our care. Some of the secrets go back to the reign of the queen's grandfather. Most of the older files have already been moved to Sept-Tours for safekeeping."

"So many trails of paper," I murmured, "and all of them ultimately lead back to you and the de Clermonts." The room faded until I saw only the loops and swirls of the words unwinding into long, intertwined filaments. They formed a map of connections that linked subjects, authors, dates. There was something I needed to understand about these crisscrossing lines. . . .

"I've been going through these papers since you fell asleep, looking for references to Fian. I thought that there might be mention of him here," Matthew said, leading me back into his study, "something that might explain why his neighbors turned on him. There must be a pattern that will tell us why the humans are behaving this way."

"If you find it, my fellow historians will be eager to know. But understanding Fian's case doesn't guarantee you can prevent the same thing from happening to me." The ticking muscle in Matthew's jaw told me that my words found their target. "And I'm quite sure you didn't delve into the matter this closely before."

"I'm no longer that man who turned a blind eye to all this suffering—and I don't want to become him again." Matthew pulled out his chair and dropped heavily into it. "There must be something I can do."

I gathered him in my arms. Even seated, Matthew was so tall that the top of his head hit my rib cage. He burrowed into me. He stilled, then drew slowly away, his eyes fixed on my abdomen.

"Diana. You're—" He stopped.

"Pregnant. I thought so," I said matter-of-factly. "My period's been irregular ever since Juliette, so I wasn't sure. I was sick on the way from Calais to Dover, but the seas were rough and that fish I had before we left was definitely dodgy."

He continued to stare at my belly. I rattled on nervously.

"My high-school health teacher was right: You really can get pregnant the first time you have sex with a guy." I'd done the math and was pretty sure conception had occurred during our wedding weekend.

Still he was silent.

"Say something, Matthew."

"It's impossible." He looked stunned.

"Everything about us is impossible." I lowered a trembling hand to my stomach.

Matthew twined his fingers through mine and finally looked me in the eye. I was surprised by what I saw there: awe, pride, and a hint of panic. Then he smiled. It was an expression of complete joy.

"What if I'm no good at being a parent?" I asked uncertainly. "You've been a father—you know what to do."

"You're going to be a wonderful mother" was his prompt response. "All that children need is love, a grown-up to take responsibility for them, and a soft place to land." Matthew moved our clasped hands over my belly in a gentle caress. "We'll tackle the first two together. The last will be up to you. How are you feeling?"

"A bit tired and queasy, physically. Emotionally, I don't know where to begin." I drew a shaky breath. "Is it normal to be frightened and fierce and tender all at once?"

"Yes—and thrilled and anxious and sick with dread, too," he said softly.

"I know it's ridiculous, but I keep worrying that my magic might hurt the baby, even though thousands of witches give birth every year." *But they aren't married to vampires.*

"This isn't a normal conception," Matthew said, reading my mind. "Still, I don't think you need to concern yourself." A shadow moved through his eyes. I could practically see him adding one more worry to his list.

"I don't want to tell anyone. Not yet." I thought of the room next door. "Can your life include one more secret—at least for a little while?"

"Of course," Matthew said promptly. "Your pregnancy won't show for months. But Françoise and Pierre will know soon from your scent, if they don't already, and so will Hancock and Gallowglass. Happily, vampires don't usually ask personal questions."

I laughed softly. "It figures that I'll be the one to give the secret away. You can't possibly be any more protective, so no one is going to guess what we're hiding based on your behavior."

"Don't be too sure of that," he said, smiling broadly. Matthew flexed his fingers over mine. It was a distinctly protective gesture.

"If you keep touching me that way, people are going to figure it out pretty quickly," I agreed drily, running my fingers along his shoulder. He shivered. "You're not supposed to shiver when you feel something warm."

"That's not why I'm trembling." Matthew stood, blocking out the light from the candles.

My heart caught at the sight of him. He smiled, hearing the slight irregularity, and drew me toward the bed. We shed our clothes, tossing them to the floor, where they lay in two white pools that caught the silvery light from the windows.

Matthew's touches were feather-light while he tracked the minute changes already taking place in my body. He lingered over each centimeter of tender flesh, but his cool attention increased the ache rather than soothing it. Every kiss was as knotted and complex as our feelings about sharing a child. At the same time, the words he whispered in the darkness encouraged me to focus solely on him. When I could bear waiting no longer, Matthew seated himself within me, his movements unhurried and gentle, like his kiss.

I arched my back in an effort to increase the contact between us, and Matthew stilled. With my spine bowed, he was poised at the entrance to my womb. And in that brief, forever moment, father, mother, and child were as close as any three creatures could be.

"My whole heart, my whole life," he promised, moving within me.

I cried out, and Matthew held me close until the trembling stopped. He then kissed his way down the length of my body, starting with my witch's third eye and continuing on to my lips, throat, breastbone, solar plexus, navel, and, at last, my abdomen.

He stared down at me, shook his head, and gave me a boyish grin. "We made a child," he said, dumbfounded.

"We did," I agreed with an answering smile.

Matthew slid his shoulders between my thighs, pushing them wide. With one arm wrapped around my knee, and the other twined around the opposite hip so his hand could rest on the pulse there, he lowered his head onto my belly as though it were a pillow and let out a contented sigh. Utterly quiet, he listened for the soft whooshing of the blood that now sustained our child. When he heard it, he tilted his head so our eyes met. He smiled, bright and true, and returned to his vigil.

In the candlelit darkness of Christmas morning, I felt the quiet power that came from sharing our love with another creature. No longer a solitary meteor moving through space and time, I was now part of a complicated planetary system. I needed to learn how to keep my own center of gravity while being pulled this way and that by bodies larger and more powerful than I was. Otherwise Matthew, the de Clermonts, our child—and the Congregation—might pull me off course.

My time with my mother had been too short, but in seven years she had taught me plenty. I remembered her unconditional love, the hugs that seemed to encompass days, and how she was always right where I needed her to be. It was as Matthew said: Children needed love, a reliable source of comfort, and an adult willing to take responsibility for them.

It was time to stop treating our sojourn here as an advanced seminar in Shakespeare's England and recognize it instead as my last, best chance to figure out who I was, so that I could help my child understand his place in the world.

But first I needed to find a witch.

**16**

We passed the weekend quietly, reveling in our secret and indulging in the speculations of all parents-to-be. Would the newest member of the de Clermont clan have black hair like his father but my blue eyes? Would he like science or history? Would he be skilled with his hands like Matthew or all thumbs like me? As for the sex, we had different opinions. I was convinced it was a boy, and Matthew was equally sure it was a girl.

Exhausted and exhilarated, we took a break from thoughts of the future to view sixteenth-century London from the warmth of our rooms. We started at the windows overlooking Water Lane, where I spied the distant towers of Westminster Abbey, and finished in chairs pulled up to the bedroom windows, where we could see the Thames. Neither the cold nor the fact that it was the Christian day of rest kept the watermen from their business making deliveries and ferrying passengers. At the bottom of our street, a group of rowers-for-hire huddled on the stairs that led down to the waterside, their empty boats bobbing up and down on the swells.

Matthew shared his memories of the city during the course of the afternoon as the tide rose and fell. He told me about the time in the fifteenth century when the Thames froze for more than three months—so long that temporary shops were built on the ice to cater to the foot traffic. He also reminisced about his unproductive years at Thavies Inn, where he had gone through the motions of studying the law for the fourth and final time.

"I'm glad you got to see it before we leave," he said, squeezing my hand. One by one, people were illuminating their lamps, hanging them from the prows of boats and setting them in the windows of houses and inns. "We'll even try to fit in a visit to the Royal Exchange."

"We're going back to Woodstock?" I asked, confused.

"For a short time, perhaps. Then we'll be going back to our present."

I stared at him, too startled to speak.

"We don't know what to expect during the gestation period, and for your safety—and the child's—we need to monitor the baby. There are tests to run, and it would be a good idea to have a baseline ultrasound. Besides, you'll want to be with Sarah and Emily."

"But, Matthew," I protested, "we can't go home yet. I don't know how."

His head swung around.

"Em explained it clearly before we left. To travel *back* in time, you need three objects to take you where you want to go. To travel *forward* you need witchcraft, but I can't do spells. It's why we came."

"You can't possibly carry the baby to term here," Matthew said, shooting out of his chair.

"Women do have babies in the sixteenth century," I said mildly. "Besides, I don't feel any different. I can't be more than a few weeks pregnant."

"Will you be powerful enough to carry both her and me back to the future? No, we need to leave as soon as possible, and well before she's born." Matthew drew to a halt. "What if timewalking damages the fetus in some way? Magic is one thing, but this—" He sat down abruptly.

"Nothing has changed," I said soothingly. "The baby can't be much bigger than a grain of rice. Now that we're in London, it shouldn't be difficult to find someone to help me with my magic—not to mention one who understands timewalking better than Sarah and Em."

"She's the size of a lentil." Matthew stopped. He thought for a few moments and came to a decision. "By six weeks all the most critical fetal developments will have taken place. That should give you plenty of time." He sounded like a doctor, not a father. I was beginning to prefer Matthew's premodern rages to his modern objectivity.

"That gives me only a few weeks, What if I need seven?" Had Sarah been in the room, she would have warned him that my reasonableness was not a good sign.

"Seven weeks would be fine," Matthew said, lost in his own thoughts.

"Oh, well, that's good. I'd hate to feel rushed when it comes to something as important as figuring out who I am." I strode toward him.

"Diana, that's not—"

We were standing nose to nose now. "I don't have a chance of being a good mother without knowing more about the power in my blood."

"This isn't good—"

"Don't you dare say this isn't good for the baby. I'm not some *vessel*." My temper was at full boil now. "First it was my blood you wanted for your scientific experiments, and now it's this baby."

Matthew, damn him, stood quietly by, arms crossed and gray eyes hard.

"Well?" I demanded.

"Well what? Apparently my participation in this conversation isn't required. You're already finishing my sentences. You might as well start them, too."

"This has nothing to do with my hormones," I said. Belatedly it occurred to me that this statement alone was probably evidence to the contrary.

"That hadn't occurred to me until you mentioned it."

"That's not what it sounded like."

His eyebrow rose.

"I'm the same person I was three days ago. Pregnancy isn't a pathological condition, and it doesn't eliminate our reasons for being here. We haven't even had a proper chance to look for Ashmole 782."

"Ashmole 782?" Matthew made an impatient sound. "Everything has changed, and you are *not* the same person. We can't keep this pregnancy a secret indefinitely. In a matter of days, every vampire will be able to smell the changes in your body. Kit will figure it out soon after, and he'll be asking about the father—because it can't be me, can it? A pregnant witch living with a *wearh* will raise the animosity of every creature in this city, even the ones who don't care much for the covenant. Someone could complain to the Congregation. My father will demand we go back to Sept-Tours for your safety, and I can't endure saying good-bye to him one more time." His voice rose steadily with each problem.

"I didn't think—"

"No," Matthew interrupted, "you didn't. You couldn't have. Christ, Diana. Before, you and I were in a forbidden marriage. That's hardly unique. Now you're carrying my child. That's not only unique—other creatures believe it's impossible. Three more weeks, Diana. Not a moment more." He was implacable.

"You might not be able to find a witch willing to help by then," I persisted. "Not with what's happening in Scotland."

"Who said anything about willingness?" Matthew's smile chilled me.

"I'm going to the parlor to read." I turned toward the bedroom, wanting to be as far from him as possible. He was waiting for me in the doorway, his arm barring my passage.

"I will not lose you, Diana," he said, emphatic but quiet. "Not to look for an alchemical manuscript and not for the sake of an unborn child."

"And I will not lose myself," I retorted. "Not to satisfy your need for control. Not before I find out who I am."

* * *

On Monday, I was again sitting in the parlor, picking through *The Faerie Queene* and going out of my mind with boredom when the door opened. *Visitors.* I clapped the book shut eagerly.

"I don't think I'll ever be warm again." Walter stood dripping in the doorway. George and Henry were with him, both looking equally wretched.

"Hello, Diana." Henry sneezed, then greeted me with a formal bow before heading to the fireplace and extending his fingers toward the flames with a groan.

"Where is Matthew?" I asked, motioning George toward a seat.

"With Kit. We left them at a bookseller." Walter gestured in the direction of St. Paul's. "I'm famished. The stew Kit ordered for dinner was inedible. Matt said Françoise should make us something to eat." Raleigh's mischievous grin betrayed his lie.

The lads were on their second plates of food and their third helping of wine when Matthew came home with Kit, an armful of books, and a full complement of facial hair courtesy of one of these wizard barbers I kept hearing about. My husband's trim new mustache suited the width of his mouth, and his beard was fashionably small and well shaped. Pierre followed behind, bearing a linen sack of paper rectangles and squares.

"Thank God," Walter said, nodding approvingly at the beard. "Now you look like yourself."

"Hello, my heart," Matthew said, kissing me on the cheek. "Do you recognize me?"

"Yes—even though you look like a pirate," I said with a laugh.

"It is true, Diana. He and Walter look like brothers now," admitted Henry.

"Why do you persist in calling Matthew's wife by her first name, Henry? Has Mistress Roydon become your ward? Is she your sister now? The only other explanation is that you are planning a seduction," Marlowe grumbled, plunking himself down in a chair.

"Stop poking at the hornet's nest, Kit," Walter chided.

"I have belated Christmas presents," Matthew said, sliding his stack in my direction.

"Books." It was disconcerting to feel their obvious newness—the creak of the tight bindings as they protested being opened for the first time, the smell of paper and the tang of ink. I was used to seeing volumes like these in a worn condition within library reading rooms, not resting on the table where we ate our meals. The top volume was a blank book to replace the one still in Oxford. The next was a book of prayers, beautifully bound. The ornate title page was adorned with a reclining figure of the biblical patriarch Jesse. A sprawling tree emerged from his stomach. My forehead creased. Why had Matthew bought me a prayer book?

"Turn the page," he urged, his hands heavy and quiet against the small of my back.

On the reverse was a woodcut of Queen Elizabeth kneeling in prayer. Skeletons, biblical figures, and classical virtues decorated each page. The book was a combination of text and imagery, just like the alchemical treatises I studied.

"It's exactly the kind of book a respectable married lady would own," Matthew said with a grin. He lowered his voice conspiratorially. "That should satisfy your desire to keep up appearances. But don't worry. The next one isn't respectable at all."

I put the prayer book aside and took the thick volume Matthew offered. Its pages were sewn together and slipped inside a protective wrapper of thick vellum. The treatise promised to explain the symptoms and cures of every disease known to afflict mankind.

"Religious books are popular gifts, and easy to sell. Books about medicine have a smaller audience and are too costly to bind without a commission," Matthew explained as I fingered the limp covering. He handed me yet another volume. "Luckily, I had already ordered a bound copy of this one. It's hot off the presses and destined to be a bestseller."

The item in question was covered in simple black leather, with some silver stamps for ornamentation. Inside was a first edition of Philip Sidney's *Arcadia*. I laughed, remembering how much I'd hated reading it in college.

"A witch cannot live by prayer and physic alone." Matthew's eyes twinkled with mischief. His mustache tickled when he moved to kiss me.

"Your new face is going to take some getting used to," I said, laughing and rubbing my lips at the unexpected sensation.

The Earl of Northumberland eyed me as he would a piece of horseflesh in need of a training regimen. "These few titles will not keep Diana occupied for long. She is used to more varied activity."

"As you say. But she can hardly roam the city and offer classes on alchemy." Matthew's mouth tightened with amusement. Hour by hour, his accent and choice of words molded to the time. He leaned over me, sniffed the wine jug, and grimaced. "Is there something to drink that hasn't been dosed with cloves and pepper? It smells dreadful."

"Diana might enjoy Mary's company," Henry suggested, not having heard Matthew's query.

Matthew stared at Henry. "Mary?"

"They are of a similar age and temperament, I think, and both are paragons of learning."

"The countess is not only learned but also has a propensity for setting things alight," Kit observed, pouring himself another generous beaker of wine. He stuck his nose in it and breathed deeply. It smelled rather like Matthew. "Stay away from her stills and furnaces, Mistress Roydon, unless you want fashionably frizzled hair."

"Furnaces?" I wondered who this could be.

"Ah, yes. The Countess of Pembroke," George said, eyes gleaming at the prospect of patronage.

"Absolutely not." Between Raleigh, Chapman, and Marlowe, I'd met enough literary legends to last me a lifetime. The countess was the foremost woman of letters in the country, and Sir Philip Sidney's sister. "I'm not ready for Mary Sidney."

"Nor is Mary Sidney ready for you, Mistress Roydon, but I suspect that Henry is right. You will soon grow tired of Matthew's friends and need to seek your own. Without them you will be prone to idleness and melancholy." Walter nodded to Matthew. "You should invite Mary here to share supper."

"The Blackfriars would come to a complete standstill if the Countess of Pembroke appeared on Water Lane. It would be far better to send Mistress Roydon to Baynard's Castle. It's just over the wall," Marlowe said, eager to be rid of me.

"Diana would have to walk into the city," Matthew said pointedly.

Marlowe gave a dismissive snort. "It's the week between Christmas and New Year. Nobody will pay attention if two married women share a cup of wine and some gossip."

"I'd be happy to take her," Walter volunteered. "Perhaps Mary will want to know more about my venture in the New World."

"You'll have to ask the countess to invest in Virginia another time. If Diana goes, I'll be with her." Matthew's eyes sharpened. "I wonder if Mary knows any witches?"

"She's a woman, isn't she? Of course she knows witches," Marlowe said.

"Shall I write to her, then, Matt?" Henry inquired.

"Thank you, Hal." Matthew was clearly unconvinced of the merits of the plan. Then he sighed. "It's been too long since I've seen her. Tell Mary we'll call on her tomorrow."

My initial reluctance to meet Mary Sidney faded as our rendezvous approached. The more I remembered—and discovered—about the Countess of Pembroke, the more excited I became.

Françoise was in a state of high anxiety about the visit, and she fussed over my clothes for hours. She fixed a particularly frothy ruff around the high neckline of a black velvet jacket that Maria had fashioned for me in France. She also cleaned and pressed my flattering russet gown with its bands of black velvet. It went well with the jacket and provided a jolt of color. Once I was dressed, Françoise pronounced me passable, though too severe and German-looking for her tastes.

I bolted down some stew filled with chunks of rabbit and barley at midday in an effort to speed our departure. Matthew took an interminable time sipping his wine and questioning me in Latin about my morning. His expression was devilish.

"If you're trying to infuriate me, you're succeeding!" I told him after a particularly convoluted question.

*"Refero mihi in latine, quaeso,"* Matthew said in a professorial tone. When I threw a hunk of bread at him, he laughed and ducked.

Henry Percy arrived just in time to catch the bread neatly with one hand. He returned it to the table without comment, smiled serenely, and asked if we were ready to depart.

Pierre materialized without a sound from the shadows near the entrance to the shoe shop and began walking up the street with a diffident air, his right hand firmly around the hilt of his dagger. When Matthew turned us toward the city, I looked up. There was St. Paul's.

"I'm not likely to get lost with that in the neighborhood," I murmured.

As we made our slow progress toward the cathedral, my senses grew accustomed to the chaos and it was possible to pick out individual sounds, smells, and sights. Bread baking. Coal fires. Wood smoke. Fermentation. Freshly washed garbage, courtesy of yesterday's rains. Wet wool. I breathed deeply, making a mental note to stop telling my students that if you went back in time, you would be knocked over instantly by the foul smell. Apparently that wasn't true, at least not in late December.

Men and women looked up from their work and out their windows with unabashed curiosity as we passed, bobbing their heads respectfully when they recognized Matthew and Henry. We stepped by a printing establishment, passed another where a barber was cutting a man's hair, and skirted a busy workshop where hammers and heat indicated that someone was working in fine metals.

As the strangeness wore off, I was able to focus on what people were saying, the texture of their clothes, the expressions on their faces. Matthew had told me our neighborhood was full of foreigners, but it sounded like Babel. I turned my head. "What language is she speaking?" I whispered with a glance at a plump woman wearing a deep blue-green jacket trimmed with fur. It was, I noted, cut rather like my own.

"Some dialect of German," said Matthew, lowering his head to mine so that I could hear him over the noise in the street.

We passed through the arch of an old gatehouse. The lane widened into a street that had managed against all odds to retain most of its paving. A sprawling, multistoried building to our right buzzed with activity.

"The Dominican priory," Matthew explained. "When King Henry expelled the priests, it became a ruin, then a tenement. There's no telling how many people are crammed in there now." He glanced across the courtyard, where a listing stone-and-timber wall spanned the distance between the tenement and the back of another house. A sorry excuse for a door hung from a single set of hinges.

Matthew looked up at St. Paul's and then down at me. His face softened. "To hell with caution. Come on."

He steered me through an opening between a section of the old city wall and a house that looked as though it were about to tip its third story onto passersby. It was possible to make progress along the slim thoroughfare only because everyone was moving in the same direction: up, north, out. We were carried by the wave of humanity into another street, this one much wider than Water Lane. The noise increased, along with the crowds.

"You said the city was deserted because of the holidays," I remarked.

"It is," Matthew replied. After a few steps, we were pitched into an even greater maelstrom. I stopped in my tracks.

St. Paul's windows glimmered in the pale afternoon light. The churchyard around it was a solid mass of people—men, women, children, apprentices, servants, clergymen, soldiers. Those who weren't shouting were listening to those who were, and everywhere you looked, there was paper. It was hung up on strings outside bookstalls, nailed to any solid surface, made into books, and waved in the faces of onlookers. A group of young men huddled around one post covered with flapping announcements, listening to someone slowly sound out job advertisements. Every now and then, one would break free from the rest, hands slapping him on the back as he pulled his cap down and set off in search of employment.

"Oh, Matthew." It was all I could manage.

People continued to swarm around us, carefully avoiding the tips of the long swords my escorts wore at their waists. A breeze caught at my hood. I felt a tingle, followed by a faint pressure. Somewhere in the busy church-yard, a witch and a daemon had sensed our presence. Three creatures and a nobleman traveling together were hard to ignore.

"We've caught someone's attention," I said. Matthew didn't seem overly concerned as he scanned the nearby faces. "Someone like me. Someone like Kit. No one like you."

"Not yet," he said under his breath. "You aren't to come here by your-self, Diana—ever. Stay in the Blackfriars, with Françoise. If you go any farther than that passageway"—Matthew nodded behind us—"Pierre or I must be with you." When he was satisfied that I had taken his warning se-riously, he drew me away. "Let's go see Mary."

We turned south again, toward the river, and the wind flattened my skirts against my legs. Though we were walking downhill, every step was a struggle. A low whistle sounded as we passed by one of London's many churches, and Pierre disappeared into an alley. He popped out of another just as I spotted a familiar-looking building behind a wall.

"That's our house!"

Matthew nodded and directed my attention down the street. "And that is Baynard's Castle."

It was the largest building I had seen yet except for the Tower, St. Paul's, and the distant prospect of Westminster Abbey. Three crenellated towers faced the river, linked by walls that were easily twice the height of any nearby houses.

"Baynard's Castle was built to be approached from the river, Diana," Henry said in an apologetic tone as we traveled down another winding lane. "This is the back entrance, and not how visitors are supposed to ar-rive—but it is a great deal warmer on a day like this."

We ducked into an imposing gatehouse. Two men wearing charcoal gray uniforms with maroon, black, and gold badges strolled up to identify the visitors. One recognized Henry and grabbed at his companion's sleeve before he could question us.

"Lord Northumberland!"

"We're here to see the countess." Henry swung his cloak in the direction of the guard. "See if you can get that dry. And find Master Roydon's man something hot to drink, if you would." The earl cracked his fingers inside his leather gloves and grimaced.

"Of course, my lord," the gatekeeper said, eyeing Pierre with suspicion.

The castle was arranged around two enormous hollow squares, the central spaces filled with leafless trees and the vestiges of summer flowers. We climbed a wide set of stairs and met up with more liveried servants, one of whom led us to the countess's solar: an inviting room with large, south-facing windows overlooking the river. They provided a view of the same stretch of the Thames that was visible from the Blackfriars.

Despite the similarity of the view, there was no mistaking this lofty, bright space for our house. Though our rooms were large and comfortably furnished, Baynard's Castle was the home of aristocracy, and it showed. Wide, cushioned settles flanked the fireplace, along with chairs so deep that a woman could curl up in one with all her skirts tucked around her. Tapestries enlivened the stone walls with splashes of bright color and scenes from classical mythology. There were signs, too, of a scholar's mind at work. Books, bits of ancient statuary, natural objects, pictures, maps, and other curiosities covered the tables.

"Master Roydon?" A man with a pointed beard and dark hair peppered with gray stood. He held a small board in one hand and a tiny brush in the other.

"Hilliard!" Matthew said, his delight evident. "What brings you here?"

"A commission for Lady Pembroke," the man said, waving his palette. "I must put the finishing touches on this miniature. She wishes to have it for a gift at the New Year." His bright brown eyes studied me.

"I forget, you have not met my wife. Diana, this is Nicholas Hilliard, the limner."

"I am honored," I said, dipping into a curtsy. London had well over a hundred thousand residents. Why did Matthew have to know everyone that historians would one day find significant? "I know and admire your work."

"She has seen the portrait of Sir Walter that you painted for me last year," Matthew said smoothly, covering up my too-effusive greeting.

"One of his best pieces, I agree," Henry said, looking over the artist's shoulder. "This seems destined to rival it, though. What an excellent likeness of Mary, Hilliard. You've captured the intensity of her gaze." Hilliard looked pleased.

A servant appeared with wine, and Henry, Matthew, and Hilliard conversed in low voices while I examined an ostrich egg set in gold and a nautilus shell in a silver stand, both of which sat on a table along with several priceless mathematical instruments that I didn't dare touch.

"Matt!" The Countess of Pembroke stood in the doorway wiping ink-stained fingers on a handkerchief hastily supplied by her maid. I wondered why anyone would bother, since her mistress's dove-gray gown was already splotched and even singed in places. The countess peeled the simple garment from her body, revealing a far more splendid velvet and taffeta outfit in a rich shade of plum. As she passed the early-modern equivalent of a lab coat to her servant, I smelled a distinct whiff of gunpowder. The countess tucked up a tight curl of blond hair that had drifted down by her right ear. She was tall and willowy, with creamy skin and deep-set brown eyes.

She stretched out her hands in welcome. "My dear friend. I have not seen you for years, not since my brother Philip's funeral."

"Mary," Matthew said, bowing over her hand. "You are looking well."

"London does not agree with me, as you know, but it has become a tradition that we travel here for the queen's anniversary celebrations, and I stayed on. I am working on Philip's psalms and a few other fancies and do not mind it so much. And there are consolations, like seeing old friends." Mary's voice was airy, but it still conveyed her sharp intelligence.

"You are indeed flourishing," Henry said, adding his welcome to Matthew's and looking at the countess approvingly.

Mary's brown eyes fixed on me. "And who is this?"

"My happiness at seeing you has pushed my manners aside. Lady Pembroke, this is my wife, Diana. We are recently wed."

"My lady." I dropped the countess a deep curtsy. Mary's shoes were encrusted with fantastic gold and silver embroidery that suggested Eden, covered as they were with snakes, apples, and insects. They must have cost a fortune.

"Mistress Roydon," she said, her eyes snapping with amusement. "Now that that's over with, let us be plain Mary and Diana. Henry tells me that you are a student of alchemy."

"A *reader* of alchemy, my lady," I corrected, "that is all. Lord Northumberland is too generous."

Matthew took my hand in his. "And you are too modest. She knows a vast amount, Mary. As Diana is new to London, Hal thought you might help her find her way in the city."

"With pleasure," the Countess of Pembroke said. "Come, we shall sit by the window. Master Hilliard requires strong light for his work. While he finishes my portrait, you will tell me all the news. Little happens in the kingdom that is beyond Matthew's notice and understanding, Diana, and I have been at home in Wiltshire for months."

Once we were settled, her servant returned with a plate of preserved fruit.

"Ooh," Henry said, happily wiggling his fingers over the yellow, green, and orange confections. "Comfits. You make them like no one else."

"And I shall share my secret with Diana," Mary said, looking pleased. "Of course, once she has the receipt, I may never have the pleasure of Henry's company again."

"Now, Mary, you go too far," he protested around a mouthful of candied orange peel.

"Is your husband with you, Mary, or does the queen's business keep him in Wales?" Matthew inquired.

"The Earl of Pembroke left Milford Haven several days ago but will go to court rather than come here. I have William and Philip with me for company, and we will not linger much longer in the city but go on to Ramsbury. The air is healthier there." A sad look crossed her face.

Mary's words reminded me of the statue of William Herbert in the Bodleian Library quadrangle. The man I passed on the way to Duke Humfrey's every day, and one of the library's greatest benefactors, was this woman's young son. "How old are your children?" I asked, hoping that the question was not too personal.

The countess's face softened. "William is ten, and Philip is just six. My daughter, Anne, is seven but she was ill this past month, and my husband felt she should remain at Wilton."

"Nothing serious?" Matthew frowned.

More shadows scudded across the countess's face. "Any sickness that afflicts my children is serious," she said softly.

"Forgive me, Mary. I spoke without thinking. My intention was only to offer what assistance I can." My husband's voice deepened with regret. The conversation was touching on a shared history unknown to me.

"You have kept those I love from harm on more than one occasion. I haven't forgotten it, Matthew, nor would I fail to call on you again if necessary. But Anne suffered from a child's ague, nothing more. The physicians assure me she will recover." Mary turned to me. "Do you have children, Diana?"

"Not yet," I said, shaking my head. Matthew's gray glance settled on me for a moment, then flitted away. I tugged nervously at the bottom of my jacket.

"Diana has not been married before," Matthew said.

"Never?" The Countess of Pembroke was fascinated by this piece of information and opened her mouth to question me further. Matthew cut her off.

"Her father and mother died when she was young. There was no one to arrange it."

Mary's sympathy increased. "A young girl's life is sadly dependent upon the whims of her guardians."

"Indeed." Matthew arched an eyebrow at me. I could imagine what he was thinking: I was lamentably independent, and Sarah and Em were the least whimsical creatures on earth.

The conversation moved on to politics and current events. I listened attentively for a while, trying to reconcile hazy recollections of a long-ago history class with the complicated gossip that the other three exchanged. There was talk of war, a possible Spanish invasion, Catholic sympathizers, and the religious tension in France, but the names and places were often unfamiliar. As I relaxed into the warmth of Mary's solar, and comforted by the constant chatter, my mind drifted.

"I am done here, Lady Pembroke. My servant Isaac will deliver the miniature by week's end," Hilliard announced, packing up his equipment.

"Thank you, Master Hilliard." The countess extended her hand, sparkling with the jewels from her many rings. He kissed it, nodded to Henry and Matthew, and departed.

"Such a talented man," Mary said, shifting in her chair. "He has grown so popular I was fortunate to secure his services." Her feet twinkled in the firelight, the silver embroidery on her richly colored slippers picking up hints of red, orange, and gold. I wondered idly who had designed the intricate pattern for the embroidery. Had I been closer, I would have asked to touch the stitches. Champier had been able to read my flesh with his fingers. Could an inanimate object provide similar information?

Though my fingers were nowhere near the countess's shoes, I saw the face of a young woman. She was peering at a sheet of paper with the design for Mary's shoes on it. Tiny holes along the lines of the drawing solved the mystery of how its intricacies had been transferred to leather. Focusing on the drawing, my mind's eye took several steps backward in time. Now I saw Mary sitting with a stern, stubborn-jawed man, a table full of insect and plant specimens before them. Both were talking with great animation about a grasshopper, and when the man began to describe it in detail, Mary took up her pen and sketched its outlines.

*So Mary is interested in plants and insects, as well as alchemy,* I thought, searching her shoes for the grasshopper. There it was, on the heel. So lifelike. And the bee on her right toe looked as though it might fly away at any moment.

A faint buzzing filled my ears as the silver-and-black bee detached itself from the Countess of Pembroke's shoe and took to the air.

"Oh, no," I gasped.

"What a strange bee," Henry commented, swatting at it as it flew past.

But I was looking instead at the snake that was slithering off Mary's foot and into the rushes. "Matthew!"

He shot forward and lifted the snake by the tail. It extended its forked tongue and hissed indignantly at the rough treatment. With a flick of his wrist, he tossed the snake into the fire, where it sizzled for a moment before catching light.

"I didn't mean . . ." I trailed off.

"It's all right, *mon coeur*. You cannot help it." Matthew touched my cheek before he looked at the countess, who was staring down at her mismatching slippers. "We need a witch, Mary. There is some urgency."

"I know no witches," was the Countess of Pembroke's swift reply.

Matthew's eyebrows rose.

"None to whom I would introduce your wife. You know I don't like to speak of such matters, Matthew. When he returned safe from Paris, Philip told me what you were. I was a child then and understood it as a fable. That is how I wish to keep it."

"And yet you practice alchemy," Matthew observed. "Is that a fable, too?"

"I practice alchemy to understand God's miracle of creation!" Mary cried. "There is no . . . witchcraft . . . in alchemy!"

"The word you were searching for is 'evil.'" The vampire's eyes were dark and the set of his mouth forbidding. The countess instinctively recoiled. "You are so sure of yourself and your God that you claim to know His mind?"

Mary felt the rebuke but was not ready to give up the fight. "My God and your God are not the same, Matthew." My husband's eyes narrowed, and Henry picked at his hose nervously. The countess's chin rose. "Philip told me about that, too. You still adhere to the pope and the Mass. He saw past the errors of your faith to the man underneath, and I have done the same in the hope that one day you will perceive the truth and follow it."

"Why, when you see the truth about creatures like Diana and me every day and still deny it?" Matthew sounded weary. He stood. "We will not trouble you again, Mary. Diana will find a witch some other way."

"Why can we not go on as we have before and speak no more about this?" The countess looked at me and bit her lip, uncertainty in her eyes.

"Because I love my wife and want to see her safe."

Mary studied him for a moment, gauging his sincerity. It must have satisfied her. "Diana need not fear me, Matt. But no one else in London should be trusted with the knowledge of her. What is happening in Scotland is making people fearful, and quick to blame others for their misfortunes."

"I'm so sorry about your shoes," I said awkwardly. They would never be the same.

"We will not mention it," Mary said firmly, rising to say her good-byes.

None of us said a word as we left Baynard's Castle. Pierre sauntered out of the gatehouse behind us, jamming his cap on his head.

"That went very well, I think," Henry said, breaking the silence.

We turned on him in disbelief.

"There were a few difficulties, to be sure," he said hastily, "but there was no mistaking Mary's interest in Diana or her continued devotion to you, Matthew. You must give her a chance. She was not raised to trust easily. It's why matters of faith trouble her so." He drew his cloak around him. The wind had not diminished, and it was getting dark. "Alas, I must leave you here. My mother is in Aldersgate and expects me for supper."

"Has she recovered from her indisposition?" Matthew asked. The dowager countess had complained about shortness of breath over Christmas, and Matthew was concerned it might be her heart.

"My mother is a Neville. She will, therefore, live forever and cause trouble at every opportunity!" Henry kissed me on the cheek. "Do not worry about Mary, or about that . . . er, other matter." He wiggled his eyebrows meaningfully and departed.

Matthew and I watched him go before turning toward the Blackfriars. "What happened?" he asked quietly.

"Before, it was my emotions that set off the magic. Now an idle question is enough to make me see beneath the surface of things. But I have no idea how I animated that bee."

"Thank God you were thinking about Mary's shoes. If you'd been examining her tapestries, we would have found ourselves in the midst of a war between the gods on Mount Olympus," he said drily.

We passed quickly through St. Paul's Churchyard and back into the relative quiet of the Blackfriars. The day's earlier frenetic activity had slowed to a more leisurely pace. Craftsmen congregated in doorways to share notes on business, leaving their apprentices to finish up the day's tasks.

"Do you want takeout?" Matthew pointed at a bake shop. "It's not pizza, alas, but Kit and Walter are devoted to Prior's meat pies." My mouth watered at the scent coming from inside, and I nodded.

Master Prior was shocked when Matthew entered his premises and nonplussed when questioned in detail about the sources and relative freshness of his meat. Finally I settled on a savory pie filled with duck. I wasn't having venison, no matter how recently it had been killed.

Matthew paid Prior for the food while the baker's assistants wrapped it. Every few seconds they gave us furtive glances. I was reminded that a witch and a vampire drew human suspicion like a candle drew moths.

Dinner was comfortable and cozy, though Matthew seemed a bit preoccupied. Soon after I'd finished my pie, footsteps sounded on the wooden stairs. *Not Kit,* I thought, crossing my fingers, *not tonight.*

When Françoise opened the door, two men in familiar charcoal livery were waiting. Matthew frowned and stood. "Is the countess unwell? Or one of the boys?"

"All are well, sir." One of them held out a carefully folded piece of paper. On top was an irregular blob of red wax bearing the impression of an arrowhead. "From the Countess of Pembroke," he explained with a bow, "for Mistress Roydon."

It was strange to see the formal address on the reverse: *"Mistress Diana Roydon, at the sign of the Hart and Crown, the Blackfriars."* My wandering fingers easily summoned up an image of Mary Sidney's intelligent face. I carried the letter over to the fire, slid my finger under the seal, and sat down to read. The paper was thick and crackled as I spread it out. A smaller slip of paper fluttered onto my lap.

"What does Mary say?" Matthew asked after dismissing the messengers. He stood behind me and rested his hands on my shoulders.

"She wants me to come to Baynard's Castle on Thursday. Mary has an alchemical experiment under way that she thinks might interest me." I couldn't keep the incredulity out of my voice.

"That's Mary for you. She's cautious but loyal," Matthew said, dropping a kiss on my head. "And she always did have amazing recuperative powers. What's on the other paper?"

I picked it up and read aloud the first lines of the enclosed verses.

> *"Yea, when all me so misdeemed,*
> *I to most a monster seemed,*
> *Yet in thee my hope was strong."*

"Well, well, well," Matthew interrupted with a chuckle. "My wife has arrived." I looked at him in confusion. "Mary's most treasured project is not alchemical but a new rendition of the Psalms for English Protestants. Her brother Philip began it and died before it was complete. Mary's twice the poet he was. Sometimes she suspects as much, though she'll never admit it. That's the beginning of Psalm Seventy-one. She sent it to you to show the world that you're part of her circle—a trusted confidante and friend." His voice dropped to a mischievous whisper. "Even if you did ruin her shoes." With a final chuckle, Matthew withdrew to his study, dogged by Pierre.

I'd taken over one end of the heavy-legged table in the parlor for a desk. Like every work surface I'd ever occupied, it was now littered with both trash and treasures. I rooted around and found my last sheets of blank paper, selected a fresh quill, and swept a spot clear.

It took five minutes to write a brief response to the countess. There were two embarrassing blotches on it, but my Italic hand was reasonably good, and I'd remembered to spell some of the words phonetically so that they wouldn't look too modern. When in doubt I doubled a consonant or added a final *e*. I shook sand on the sheet and waited until it absorbed the excess ink before blowing it into the rushes. Once the letter was folded, I realized that I had no wax or signet to close it. *That will have to be fixed.*

I set my note aside for Pierre and returned to the slip of paper. Mary had sent me all three stanzas of Psalm 71. I took up the new blank book that Matthew had bought for me and opened it to the first page. After dipping the quill into the nearby pot of ink, I moved the sharp point carefully across the sheet.

> *They by whom my life is hated*
> *With their spies have now debated*
> *Of their talk, and, lo, the sum:*
> *God, they say, hath him forsaken.*
> *Now pursue, he must be taken;*
> *None will to his rescue come.*

When the ink was dry, I closed my book and slid it underneath Philip Sidney's *Arcadia*.

There was more to this gift from Mary than a simple offer of friendship, of that I was certain. While the lines I'd read aloud to Matthew were an acknowledgment of his service to her family and a declaration that she would not turn away from him now, the final lines held a message for me: We were being watched. Someone suspected that all was not as it seemed on Water Lane, and Matthew's enemies were betting that even his allies would turn against him once they discovered the truth.

Matthew, a vampire as well as the queen's servant and a member of the Congregation, couldn't be involved with finding a witch to serve as my magical tutor. And with a baby on the way, finding one quickly had taken on a new significance.

I pulled a sheet of paper toward me and began to make a list.

*Sealing Waxe*
*A Signet*

London was a big city. And I was going to do some shopping.

**17**

"**I**'m going out."

Françoise looked up from her sewing. Thirty seconds later Pierre was climbing the stairs. Had Matthew been at home, he would no doubt have appeared as well, but he was out conducting some mysterious business in the city. I'd woken to the sight of his damp suit still drying by the fireplace. He'd been called away in the night and returned, only to leave once more.

"Indeed?" Françoise's eyes narrowed. She had suspected I was up to no good ever since I'd gotten dressed. Instead of grumbling about the number of petticoats she pulled over my head, today I'd added another made out of warm gray flannel. Then we argued about which gown I should wear. I preferred the comfortable clothes I'd brought from France over Louisa de Clermont's more splendid garments. Matthew's sister, with her dark hair and porcelain skin, could pull off a gown of vivid turquoise velvet ("Verdigris," Françoise had corrected me) or a sickly gray-green taffeta (appropriately called "Dying Spaniard"), but they looked ghastly with my faint freckles and reddish-blond curls, and they were too grand to wear around town.

"Perhaps *madame* should wait until Master Roydon returns," Pierre suggested. He shifted nervously from one foot to the other.

"No, I think not. I've made a list of things I need, and I want to go shopping for them myself." I scooped up the leather bag of coins given to me by Philippe. "Is it all right to carry a bag, or am I supposed to stick the money into my bodice and fish the coins out when necessary?" This aspect of historical fiction had always fascinated me—women stuffing things into their dresses—and I was looking forward to discovering whether the items were as easy to remove in public as the novelists suggested. Sex was certainly not as easy to arrange in the sixteenth century as it was made out to be in some romances. There were too many clothes in the way, for a start.

"*Madame* will not carry money at all!" Françoise pointed to Pierre, who loosened the strings of a bag tied around his waist. It was apparently bottomless and held a considerable stash of pointy implements, including pins, needles, something that looked like a set of picklocks, and a dagger. Once my leather bag was included, it jingled at his slightest movement.

Out on Water Lane, I strode with as much determination as my pattens (those helpful wooden wedges that slipped over my shoes and kept me from the muck) would allow in the direction of St. Paul's. The fur-lined cloak billowed around my feet, its thick fabric a barrier to the clinging fog. We were enjoying a temporary reprieve from the recent downpours, but the weather was by no means dry.

Our first stop was at Master Prior's bakery for some buns studded with currants and candied fruit. I was often hungry in the late afternoons and would want something sweet. My next visit was near the alley that linked the Blackfriars to the rest of London, at a busy printing shop marked with the sign of an anchor.

"Good morning, Mistress Roydon," the proprietor said the moment I crossed the threshold. Apparently my neighbors knew me without introduction. "You are here to pick up your husband's book?"

I nodded confidently in spite of not knowing which book he was talking about, and he pulled at a slim volume that was resting on a high shelf. A flip through the pages revealed that it dealt with military affairs and ballistics.

"I am sorry there was no bound copy of your physic book," he said as he wrapped Matthew's purchase. "When you can part with it, I will have it bound to suit you."

So this was where my compendium of illnesses and cures had come from. "I thank you, Master . . ." I trailed off.

"Field," he supplied.

"Master Field," I repeated. A bright-eyed young woman with a baby on her hip came out of the office at the back of the shop, a toddler clinging to her skirts. Her fingers were rough and ingrained with ink.

"Mistress Roydon, this is my wife, Jacqueline."

"Ah. Madame Roydon." The woman's accent was softly French and reminded me of Ysabeau. "Your husband told us you are a great reader, and Margaret Hawley reports that you study alchemy."

Jacqueline and her husband knew a great deal about my business. No doubt they also were apprised of my shoe size and the type of meat pie I preferred. It struck me as even odder, therefore, that no one in the Blackfriars seemed to have noticed I was a witch.

"Yes," I said, straightening the seams of my gloves. "Do you sell unbound paper, Master Field?"

"Of course," Field said with a confused frown. "Have you filled your book with commonplaces already?" Ah. He was the source of my notebook, too.

"I require paper for correspondence," I explained. "And sealing wax. And a signet. Can I purchase them here?" The Yale bookstore had all kinds of stationery, pens, and sticks of brightly colored, entirely pointless wax along with cheap brass seals made in the shape of letters. Field and his wife exchanged glances.

"I will send more paper this afternoon," he said. "But you'll want a goldsmith for the signet so it can be made into a ring. All I have here are worn letters from the printing press that are waiting to be melted down and recast."

"Or you could see Nicholas Vallin," Jacqueline suggested. "He is expert with metals, Mistress Roydon, and also makes fine clocks."

"Just down the lane?" I said, pointing over my shoulder.

"He is not a goldsmith," Field protested. "We do not want to cause Monsieur Vallin trouble."

Jacqueline was unperturbed. "There are benefits to living in the Blackfriars, Richard. Working outside the regulations of the guilds is one of them. Besides, the Goldsmiths Company will not bother anyone here for something as insignificant as a woman's ring. If you want sealing wax, Mistress Roydon, you will need to go to the apothecary."

Soap was on my list of purchases, too. And apothecaries used distillation apparatus. Even though my focus was necessarily shifting from alchemy to magic, there was no need to forgo an opportunity to learn something more useful.

"Where is the nearest apothecary?"

Pierre coughed. "Perhaps you should consult with Master Roydon."

Matthew would have all sorts of opinions, most of which would involve sending Françoise or Pierre to fetch what I required. The Fields awaited my reply with interest.

"Perhaps," I said, staring at Pierre indignantly. "But I would like Mistress Field's recommendation all the same."

"John Hester is highly regarded," Jacqueline said with a touch of mischief, pulling the toddler free of her skirts. "He provided a tincture for my son's ear that cured its aching." John Hester, if memory served, was interested in alchemy, too. Perhaps he knew a witch. Even better, he might *be* a witch, which would suit my real intentions admirably. I was not simply out shopping today. I was out to be seen. Witches were a curious bunch. If I offered myself up as bait, one would bite.

"It is said that even the Countess of Pembroke seeks his advice for the young lord's *megraines*," her husband added. So the entire neighborhood knew I'd been to Baynard's Castle, too. Mary was right: We were being watched. "Master Hester's shop is near Paul's Wharf, marked with the sign of a still."

"Thank you, Mistress Field." Paul's Wharf must be near St. Paul's Churchyard, and I could go there that afternoon. I redrew my mental map of today's excursion.

After we said our farewells, Françoise and Pierre turned down the lane toward home.

"I'm going on to the cathedral," I said, heading in the other direction.

Impossibly, Pierre was standing before me. "*Milord* will not be pleased."

"*Milord* is not here. Matthew left strict instructions that I wasn't to go there without you. He didn't say I was a prisoner in my own house." I thrust the book and the buns at Françoise. "If Matthew returns before I do, tell him where we are and that I'll be back soon."

Françoise took the parcels, exchanged a long look with Pierre, and proceeded down Water Lane.

"*Prenez garde, madame,*" Pierre murmured as I passed him.

"I'm always careful," I said calmly, stepping straight into a puddle.

Two coaches had collided and were jammed in the street leading to St. Paul's. The lumbering vehicles resembled enclosed wagons and were nothing like the dashing carriages in Jane Austen films. I skirted them with Pierre on my heels, dodging the irritated horses and the no-less-irritated occupants, who stood in the middle of the street and shouted about who was to blame. Only the coachmen seemed unconcerned, chatting to each other quietly from their perches above the fray.

"Does this happen often?" I asked Pierre, pulling back my hood so that I could see him.

"These new conveyances are a nuisance," he said sourly. "It was much better when people walked or rode horses. But it is no matter. They will never catch on."

*That's what they told Henry Ford,* I thought.

"How far is Paul's Wharf?"

"*Milord* does not like John Hester."

"That's not what I asked, Pierre."

"What does *madame* wish to purchase in the churchyard?" Pierre's distraction technique was familiar to me from years in the classroom. But I had no intention of telling anyone the real reason we were picking our way across London.

"Books," I said shortly.

We entered the precincts of St. Paul's, where every inch not taken up by paper was occupied by someone selling a good or service. A kindly middle-aged man sat on a stool, inside a lean-to affixed to a shed, which was itself built up against one of the cathedral walls. This was by no means an unusual office environment for the place. A huddle of people gathered around his stall. If I were lucky, there would be a witch among them.

I made my way through the crowd. They all seemed to be human. What a disappointment.

The man looked up, startled, from a document he was carefully transcribing for a waiting customer. A scrivener. *Please, let this not be William Shakespeare,* I prayed.

"Can I help you, Mistress Roydon?" he said in a French accent. *Not Shakespeare.* But how did he know my identity?

"Do you have sealing wax? And red ink?"

"I am not an apothecary, Mistress Roydon, but a poor teacher." His customers began to mutter about the scandalous profits enjoyed by grocers, apothecaries, and other extortionists.

"Mistress Field tells me that John Hester makes excellent sealing wax." Heads turned in my direction.

"Rather expensive, though. So is his ink, which he makes from iris flowers." The man's assessment was confirmed by murmurs from the crowd.

"Can you point me in the direction of his shop?"

Pierre grabbed my elbow. "*Non,*" he hissed in my ear. As this only earned us more human attention, he quickly dropped it again.

The scrivener's hand rose and pointed east. "You will find him at Paul's Wharf. Go to the Bishop's Head and then turn south. But Monsieur Cornu knows the way."

I glanced back at Pierre, who was staring fixedly at a spot somewhere above my head. "Does he? Thank you."

"That's Matthew Roydon's *wife?*" someone said with a chuckle as we stepped out of the throng. *"Mon dieu.* No wonder he looks exhausted."

I didn't move immediately in the direction of the apothecary. Instead, with my eyes fixed on the cathedral, I began a slow circumnavigation of its enormous bulk. It was surprisingly graceful given its size, but that unfortunate lightning strike had ruined its appearance forever.

"This is not the fastest way to the Bishop's Head." Pierre was one step behind me instead of his usual three and therefore ran into me when I stopped to look up.

"How tall was the spire?"

"Almost as tall as the building is long. *Milord* was always fascinated by how they managed to build it so high." The missing spire would have made the whole building soar, with the slender pinnacle echoing the delicate lines of the buttresses and the tall Gothic windows.

I felt a surge of energy that reminded me of the temple to the goddess near Sept-Tours. Deep under the cathedral, something sensed my presence. It responded with a whisper, a slight stirring beneath my feet, a sigh of acknowledgment—and then it was gone. There was power here—the kind that was irresistible to witches.

Pushing my hood from my face, I slowly surveyed the buyers and sellers in St. Paul's Churchyard. Daemons, witches, and vampires sent flickers of attention my way, but there was too much activity for me to stand out. I needed a more intimate situation.

I continued past the north side of the cathedral and rounded its eastern end. The noise increased. Here all attention was focused on a man in a raised, open-air pulpit covered by a cross-topped roof. In the absence of an electric public-address system, the man kept his audience engaged by shouting, making dramatic gestures, and conjuring up images of fire and brimstone.

There was no way that one witch could compete with so much hell and damnation. Unless I did something dangerously conspicuous, any witch who spotted me would think I was nothing more than a fellow creature out shopping. I smothered a sigh of frustration. My plan had seemed infallible in its simplicity. In the Blackfriars there were no witches. But here in St. Paul's, there were too many. And Pierre's presence would deter any curious creature who might approach me.

"Stay here and don't move," I ordered, giving him a stern look. My chances of catching the eye of a friendly witch might increase if he weren't standing by radiating vampire disapproval. Pierre leaned against the upright support of a bookstall and fixed his eyes on me without comment.

I waded into the crowd at the foot of Paul's Cross, looking from left to right as if to locate a lost friend. I waited for a witch's tingle. They were here. I could feel them.

"Mistress Roydon?" a familiar voice called. "What brings you here?"

George Chapman's ruddy face poked out between the shoulders of two dour-looking gentlemen who were listening to the preacher blame the ills of the world on an unholy cabal of Catholics and merchant adventurers.

There was no witch to be found, but the members of the School of Night were, as usual, everywhere.

"I'm looking for ink. And sealing wax." The more I repeated this, the more inane it sounded.

"You'll need an apothecary, then. Come, I'll take you to my own man." George held out his elbow. "He is quite reasonable, as well as skilled."

"It is getting late, Master Chapman," Pierre said, materializing from nowhere.

"Mistress Roydon should take the air while she has the opportunity. The watermen say the rain will return soon, and they are seldom wrong. Besides, John Chandler's shop is just outside the walls, on Red Cross Street. It's not half a mile."

Meeting up with George now seemed fortuitous rather than exasperating. Surely we would pass a witch on our stroll.

"Matthew would not object to my walking with Master Chapman— especially not with you accompanying me, too," I told Pierre, taking George's arm. "Is your apothecary anywhere near Paul's Wharf?"

"Quite the opposite," George said. "But you don't want to shop on Paul's Wharf. John Hester is the only apothecary there, and his prices are beyond the bounds of good sense. Master Chandler will do you a better service, at half the cost."

I put John Hester on my to-do list for another day and took George's arm. We strolled out of St. Paul's Churchyard to the north, passing grand houses and gardens.

"That's where Henry's mother lives," George said, gesturing at a particularly imposing set of buildings to our left. "He hates the place and lived around the corner from Matt until Mary convinced him that his lodgings were beneath an earl's dignity. Now he's moved into a house on the Strand.

Mary is pleased, but Henry finds it gloomy, and the damp disagrees with his bones."

The city walls were just beyond the Percy family house. Built by the Romans to defend Londinium from invaders, they still marked its official boundaries. Once we'd passed through Aldersgate and over a low bridge, there were open fields and houses clustered around churches. My gloved hand rose to my nose at the smell that accompanied this pastoral view.

"The city ditch," George said apologetically, gesturing at a river of sludge beneath our feet. "It is, alas, the most direct route. We will be in better air soon." I wiped at my watering eyes and sincerely hoped so.

George steered me along the street, which was broad enough to accommodate passing coaches, wagons full of food, and even a team of oxen. While we walked, he chatted about his visit with his publisher, William Ponsonby. Chapman was crushed that I didn't recognize the name. I knew little about the nuances of the Elizabethan book trade and so drew him out about the subject. George was happy to gossip about the many playwrights Ponsonby snubbed, including Kit. Ponsonby preferred to work with the serious literary set, and his stable of authors was illustrious indeed: Edmund Spenser, the Countess of Pembroke, Philip Sidney.

"Ponsonby would publish Matt's poetry as well, but he has refused." George shook his head, perplexed.

"His poetry?" That brought me to a sudden halt. I knew that Matthew admired poetry, but not that he wrote it.

"Yes. Matt insists his verses are fit only for the eyes of friends. We are all fond of his elegy for Mary's brother, Philip Sidney. *'But eies and eares and ev'ry thought / Were with his sweete perfections caught.'*" George smiled. "It is marvelous work. But Matthew has little use for the press and complains that it has only resulted in discord and ill-considered opinions."

In spite of his modern laboratory, Matthew was an old fuddy-duddy with his fondness for antique watches and vintage automobiles. I pressed my lips together to keep from smiling at this latest evidence of his traditionalism. "What are his poems about?"

"Love and friendship for the most part, though recently he and Walter have been exchanging verses about . . . darker subjects. They seem to think out of a single mind these days."

"Darker?" I frowned.

"He and Walter do not always approve of what happens around them," George said in a low voice, his eyes darting over the faces of passersby.

"They can be prone to impatience—Walter especially—and often give the lie to those in positions of power. It is a dangerous tendency."

"Give the lie," I said slowly. There was a famous poem called "*The Lie.*" It was anonymous, but attributed to Walter Raleigh. "*'Say to the court, it glows / And shines like rotten wood'?*"

"So Matt has shared his verses with you." George sighed once more. "He manages to convey in a few words a full range of feeling and meaning. It is a talent I envy."

Though the poem was familiar, Matthew's relationship to it was not. But there would be plenty of time in the evenings ahead to pursue my husband's literary efforts. I dropped the subject and listened while George offered his opinions on whether writers were now required to publish too much in order to survive, and the need for decent copy editors to keep errors from creeping into printed books.

"There is Chandler's shop," George said, pointing to the intersection where an off-kilter cross sat on a raised platform. A gang of boys was busy chipping one of the rough cobbles out of the base. It didn't take a witch to foresee that the stone might soon be launched through a shop window.

The closer we got to the apothecary's place of business, the colder the air felt. Just as at St. Paul's, there was another surge of power, but an oppressive atmosphere of poverty and desperation hung over the neighborhood. An ancient tower crumbled on the northern side of the street, and the houses around it looked as though a gust of wind might carry them away. Two youths shuffled closer, eyeing us with interest, until a low hiss from Pierre stopped them in their tracks.

John Chandler's shop suited the neighborhood's Gothic atmosphere perfectly. It was dark, pungent, and unsettling. A stuffed owl hung from the ceiling, and the toothy jaws of some unfortunate creature were tacked above a diagram of a body with severed and broken limbs, pierced through with weapons. A carpenter's awl entered the poor fellow's left eye at a jaunty angle.

A stooped man emerged from behind a curtain, wiping his hands on the sleeves of his rusty black bombazine coat. It bore a resemblance to the academic gowns worn by Oxford and Cambridge undergraduates and was just as rumpled. Bright hazel eyes met mine without a trace of hesitation, and my skin tingled with recognition. Chandler was a witch. After crossing most of London, I'd finally located one of my own people.

"The streets around you grow more dangerous with every passing week, Master Chandler." George peered out the door at the gang hovering nearby.

"That pack of boys runs wild," Chandler said. "What can I do for you today, Master Chapman? Are you in need of more tonic? Have your headaches returned?"

George made a detailed accounting of his many aches and pains. Chandler murmured sympathetically every now and then and drew a ledger closer. The men pored over it, giving me a chance to examine my surroundings.

Elizabethan apothecary shops were evidently the general stores of the period, and the small space was stuffed to the rafters with merchandise. There were piles of vividly illustrated broadsides, like the one of the wounded man tacked up on the wall, and jars of candied fruit. Used books sat on one table, along with a few newer titles. A set of pottery crocks offered a splash of brightness in the otherwise dim room, all of them labeled with the names of medicinal spices and herbs. Specimens from the animal kingdom on display included not only the stuffed owl and jawbone but also some wizened rodents tied up by their tails. I spotted pots of ink, quill pens, and spools of string, too.

The shop was organized in loose thematic groupings. The ink was near the quills and the used books, under the wise old owl. The mice hung above a crock labeled *"Ratbane,"* which sat next to a book promising not only to help you catch fish but to build *"sundrie Engines and trappes to take Polcats, Buzzards, rattes, mice, and all other kindes of Vermin and beasts."* I had been wondering how to get rid of the unwanted guests in Matthew's attic. The detailed plans in the pamphlet exceeded my handywoman skills, but I'd find someone who could execute them. If the brace of mice in Chandler's shop was any indication, the traps certainly worked.

"Excuse me, mistress," Chandler murmured, reaching past me. Fascinated, I watched as he took the mice to his workbench and sliced the ears off with delicate precision.

"What are they for?" I asked George.

"Powdered mouse ears are effective against warts," he explained earnestly while Chandler wielded his pestle.

Relieved that I did not suffer from this particular complaint, I drifted over to the owl guarding the stationery department. I found a pot of red ink, deep and rich.

*Your* wearh *friend will not appreciate having to carry that bottle home, mistress. It is made from hawk's blood and is used for writing out love spells.*

So Chandler had the power of silent speech. I returned the ink to its place and picked up a dog-eared pamphlet. The images on the first sheet showed a wolf attacking a small child and a man being horribly tortured and then executed. It reminded me of the tabloids at the cash registers in modern grocery stores. When I flipped the page over, I was startled to read about someone named Stubbe Peter, who appeared in the shape of a wolf and fed off the blood of men, women, and children until they were dead. It was not only Scottish witches who were in the public eye. So were vampires.

My eyes raced across the page. I noted with relief that Stubbe lived in far-off Germany. The anxiety returned when I saw that the uncle of one of his victims ran the brewery between our house and Baynard's Castle. I was aghast at the gruesome details of the killings, as well as the lengths humans would go to in order to cope with the creatures in their midst. Here Stubbe Peter was depicted as a witch, and his strange behavior was attributed to a pact with the devil that made it possible for him to change shape and satisfy his unnatural taste for blood. But it was far more likely that the man was a vampire. I slid the pamphlet underneath my other book and made my way to the counter.

"Mistress Roydon requires some supplies," George explained to the apothecary as I drew near.

Chandler's mind went carefully blank at the mention of my name.

"Yes," I said slowly. "Red ink, if you have it. And some scented soap, for washing."

"Aye." The wizard searched through some small pewter vessels. When he found the right one, he put it on the counter. "And do you require sealing wax to match the ink?"

"Whatever you have will be fine, Master Chandler."

"I see you have one of Master Hester's books," George said, picking up a nearby volume. "I told Mistress Roydon that your ink is as good as Hester's and half the price."

The apothecary smiled weakly at George's compliment and put several sticks of carnation-colored wax and two balls of sweet-smelling soap on the table next to my ink. I dropped the pest-control manual and the pamphlet about the German vampire onto the surface. Chandler's eyes rose to mine. They were wary.

"Yes," Chandler said, "the printer across the way left a few copies with me, as it dealt with a medical subject."

"That will be of interest to Mistress Roydon, too," George said, plunking it onto my pile. I wondered, not for the first time, how humans could be so oblivious to what happened around them.

"But I am not sure this treatise is appropriate for a lady. . . ." Chandler trailed off, looking meaningfully at my wedding ring.

George's quick response drowned out my own silent retort. "Oh, her husband will not mind. She is a student of alchemy."

"I'll take it," I said decidedly.

As Chandler wrapped our purchases, George asked him if he could recommend a spectacle maker.

"My publisher, Master Ponsonby, is worried my eyes will fail me before my translation of Homer is complete," he explained self-importantly. "I have a receipt from my mother's servant, but it has not resulted in a cure."

The apothecary shrugged. "These old wives' remedies sometimes help, but mine is more reliable. I will send around a poultice made from egg whites and rose water. Soak flax pads in it and apply them to the eyes."

While George and Chandler bargained over the price of the medicine and made arrangements for its delivery, Pierre gathered the packages and stood by the door.

"Farewell, Mistress Roydon," Chandler said with a bow.

"Thank you for your assistance, Master Chandler," I replied. *I am new in town and looking for a witch to help me.*

"You are welcome," he said smoothly, "though there are excellent apothecaries in the Blackfriars." *London is a dangerous place. Have care from whom you request assistance.*

Before I could ask the apothecary how he knew where I lived, George was shepherding me out onto the street with a cheerful good-bye. Pierre was so close behind that I could feel his occasional cool breaths.

The touch of eyes was unmistakable as we made our progress back to town. An alert had been issued while I was in Chandler's shop, and word that a strange witch was near had spread throughout the neighborhood. At last I had achieved my objective for the afternoon. Two witches came out onto their front step, arms linked at the elbows, and scrutinized me with tingling hostility. They were so similar in face and body that I wondered if they were twins.

*"Wearh,"* one mumbled, spitting at Pierre and forking her fingers in a sign against the devil.

"Come, mistress. It is late," Pierre said, his fingers gripping my forearm.

Pierre's desire to get me away from St. Giles as quickly as possible and George's desire for a cup of wine made our return to the Blackfriars far quicker than the journey out. Once we were safely back in the Hart and Crown, there was still no sign of Matthew, and Pierre disappeared in search of him. Soon thereafter Françoise made pointed remarks about the lateness of the hour and my need for rest. Chapman took the hint and said his farewells.

Françoise sat by the fireplace, her sewing at her side, and watched the door. I tried out my new ink by ticking items off my shopping list and adding *"rat trappe."* I turned next to John Hester's book. The blank sheet of paper folded discreetly around it masked the salacious contents. It enumerated cures for venereal diseases, most of them involving toxic concentrations of mercury. No wonder Chandler had objected to selling a copy to a married woman. I had just started the second fascinating chapter when I heard murmurs coming from Matthew's study. Françoise's mouth tightened, and she shook her head.

"He will need more wine tonight than we have in the house," she observed, heading for the stairs with one of the empty jugs that sat by the door.

I followed the sound of my husband's voice. Matthew was still in his study, peeling his clothes off and flinging them into the fire.

"He is an evil man, *milord*," Pierre said grimly, unbuckling Matthew's sword.

"'Evil' doesn't do that fiend justice. The word that does hasn't been coined yet. After today I'd swear before judges he is the devil himself." Matthew's long fingers loosened the ties of his close-fitting breeches. They dropped to the floor, and he bent to catch them up. They flew through the air and into the fire, but not fast enough to hide the spots of blood. A musty smell of wet stone, age, and filth evoked in me sudden memories of being held captive at La Pierre. The gorge rose in my throat. Matthew spun around.

"Diana." He took in my distress with one deep breath and ripped the shirt above his head before stepping over his discarded boots and coming to my side in nothing but a pair of linen drawers. The firelight played off his shoulders, and one of his many scars—this one long and deep, just over his shoulder joint—winked in and out of sight.

"Are you hurt?" I struggled to get the words out of my constricted throat, and my eyes were glued to the clothes burning in the fireplace. Matthew followed my gaze and swore softly.

"That isn't my blood." That Matthew had someone else's blood on him was not much comfort. "The queen ordered me to be present when a prisoner was . . . questioned." His slight hesitation told me that "tortured" was the word he was avoiding. "Let me wash, and I'll join you for supper." Matthew's words were warm, but he looked tired and angry. And he was careful not to touch me.

"You've been underground." There was no mistaking the smell.

"I've been at the Tower."

"And your prisoner—is he dead?"

"Yes." His hand passed over his face. "I'd hoped to arrive early enough to stop it—this time—but I miscalculated the tides. All I could do, once again, was insist that his suffering end."

Matthew had been through the man's death once before. Today he could have remained at home and not concerned himself with a lost soul in the Tower. A lesser creature would have. I reached out to touch him, but he stepped away.

"The queen will have my hide when she discovers that the man died before revealing his secrets, but I no longer care. Like most humans, Elizabeth finds it easy to turn a blind eye when it suits her," he said.

"Who was he?"

"A witch," Matthew said flatly. "His neighbors reported him for having a poppet with red hair. They feared that it was an image of the queen. And the queen feared that the behavior of the Scottish witches, Agnes Sampson and John Fian, was encouraging English witches to act against her. No, Diana." Matthew gestured for me to stay where I was when I stepped forward to comfort him. "That's as close as you will ever be to the Tower and what happens there. Go to the parlor. I'll join you shortly."

It was difficult to leave him, but honoring his request was all I could do for him now. The wine, bread, and cheese waiting on the table were unappetizing, but I took a piece of one of the buns I'd purchased that morning and slowly reduced it to crumbs.

"Your appetite is off." Matthew slipped into the room, silent as a cat, and poured himself some wine. He drank it down in one long draft and replenished the cup.

"So is yours," I said. "You're not feeding regularly." Gallowglass and

Hancock kept inviting him to join them on their nocturnal hunts, but Matthew always refused.

"I don't want to talk about that. Tell me about your day instead." *Help me to forget.* Matthew's unspoken words whispered around the room.

"We went shopping. I picked up the book you'd ordered from Richard Field and met his wife, Jacqueline."

"Ah." Matthew's smile widened, and a bit of stress lifted from his mouth. "The new Mrs. Field. She outlived her first husband and is now leading her second husband in a merry dance. The two of you will be fast friends by the end of next week. Did you see Shakespeare? He's staying with the Fields."

"No." I added more crumbs to the growing pile on the table. "I went to the cathedral." Matthew pitched slightly forward. "Pierre was with me," I said hastily, dropping the bun on the table. "And I ran into George."

"He was no doubt hanging around the Bishop's Head waiting for William Ponsonby to say something nice to him." Matthew's shoulders lowered as he chuckled.

"I never reached the Bishop's Head," I confessed. "George was at Paul's Cross, listening to a sermon."

"The crowds that gather to hear the preachers can be unpredictable," he said softly. "Pierre knows better than to let you linger there." As if by magic, his servant appeared.

"We didn't stay long. George took me to his apothecary. I bought a few more books and some supplies. Soap. Sealing wax. Red ink." I pressed my lips together.

"George's apothecary lives in Cripplegate." Matthew's voice went flat. He looked up at Pierre. "When Londoners complain about crime, the sheriff goes there and picks up everyone who looks idle or peculiar. He has an easy time of it."

"If the sheriff targets Cripplegate, why are there so many creatures by the Barbican Cross and so few here in the Blackfriars?" The question took Matthew by surprise.

"The Blackfriars was once Christian holy ground. Daemons, witches, and vampires got into the habit of living elsewhere long ago and haven't yet moved back. The Barbican Cross, however, was put up on land where the Jewish cemetery was hundreds of years ago. After the Jews were expelled from England, city officials used the unconsecrated graveyard for criminals, traitors, and excommunicates instead. Humans consider it haunted and avoid the place."

"So it was the unhappiness of the dead I felt, not just the living." The words slipped out before I could stop them. Matthew's eyes narrowed.

Our conversation was not improving his frayed temper, and my uneasiness grew by the minute. "Jacqueline recommended John Hester when I asked after an apothecary, but George said his man was just as good and less expensive. I didn't ask about the neighborhood."

"The fact that John Chandler isn't pushing opiates on his customers like Hester does is rather more important to me than his reasonable rates. Still, I don't want you in Cripplegate. Next time you need writing supplies, send Pierre or Françoise to fetch them. Better yet, visit the apothecary three doors up on the other side of Water Lane."

"Mistress Field did not tell *madame* that there was an apothecary in the Blackfriars. A few months ago, Monsieur de Laune and Jacqueline disagreed about the best treatment for her eldest son's putrid throat," Pierre murmured by way of explanation.

"I don't care if Jacqueline and de Laune pulled swords on each other in the nave of St. Paul's at the stroke of noon. Diana isn't to go traipsing across the city."

"It's not just Cripplegate that's dangerous," I said, pushing the pamphlet about the German vampire across the table. "I bought Hester's treatise on syphilis from Chandler, and a book about trapping animals. This was for sale, too."

"You bought what?" Matthew choked on his wine, his attention fixed on the wrong book.

"Forget about Hester. This pamphlet tells the story of a man in league with the devil who changes into a wolf and drinks blood. One of the men involved in its publication is our neighbor, the brewer by Baynard's Castle." I tapped my finger on the pamphlet for emphasis.

Matthew drew the loosely bound sheets of paper toward him. His breath hitched when he reached the significant part. He handed it to Pierre, who made a similarly quick study of it.

"Stubbe is a vampire, isn't he?"

"Yes. I didn't know that news of his death had traveled this far. Kit is supposed to tell me about the gossip in the broadsides and popular press so we can cover it up if necessary. Somehow he missed this." Matthew shot a grim look at Pierre. "Make sure someone else is assigned to the job, and don't let Kit know." Pierre tilted his head in acknowledgment.

"So these legends about werewolves are just more pitiful human attempts to deny knowledge of vampires." I shook my head.

"Don't be too hard on them, Diana. They're focused on witches at the moment. It will be the daemons' turn in another hundred years or so, thanks to the reform of the asylums. After that, humans will get around to vampires, and witches will be nothing more than a wicked fairy tale to frighten children." Matthew looked worried, in spite of his words.

"Our next-door neighbor is preoccupied with werewolves, not witches. And if you could be mistaken for one, I want you to stop worrying about me and start taking care of yourself. Besides, it shouldn't be long now before a witch knocks on our door." I clung to the certainty that it would be dangerous for Matthew to look any further for a witch. My husband's eyes flashed a warning, but his mouth remained closed until his anger was under control.

"I know you're itching for independence, but the next time you decide to take matters into your own hands, promise you'll discuss it with me first." His response was far milder than I expected.

"Only if you promise to listen. You're being watched, Matthew. I'm sure of it, and so is Mary Sidney. You take care of the queen's business and the problem in Scotland, and let me take care of this."

When he opened his mouth to negotiate further, I shook my head.

"*Listen to me.* A witch will come. I promise."

18

Matthew was waiting for me in Mary's airy solar at Baynard's Castle the next afternoon, staring out at the Thames with an amused expression. He turned at my approach, grinning at the Elizabethan version of a lab coat that covered my golden brown bodice and skirts. The underlying white sleeves that stuck out from my shoulders were ridiculously padded, but the ruff around my neck was small and unobtrusive, making it one of my more comfortable outfits.

"Mary can't leave her experiment. She said we should come in time for dinner on Monday." I flung my arms around his neck and kissed him soundly. He reared back.

"Why do you smell of vinegar?"

"Mary washes in it. It cleans your hands better than soap."

"You left my house covered with the sweet scent of bread and honey, and the Countess of Pembroke returns you to me smelling like a pickle." Matthew's nose went to the patch of skin behind my ear. He gave a satisfied sigh. "I knew I could find some place the vinegar hadn't reached."

"Matthew," I murmured. The countess's maid, Joan, was standing right behind us.

"You're behaving like a prim Victorian rather than a bawdy Elizabethan," Matthew said, laughing. He straightened with one last caress of my neck. "How was your afternoon?"

"Have you seen Mary's laboratory?" I exchanged the shapeless gray coat for my cloak before sending Joan away to tend to her other duties. "She's taken over one of the castle's towers and painted the walls with images of the philosopher's stone. It's like working inside a Ripley scroll! I've seen the Beinecke's copy at Yale, but it's only twenty feet long. Mary's murals are twice as big. It made it hard to focus on the work."

"What was your experiment?"

"We hunted the green lion," I replied proudly, referring to a stage of the alchemical process that combined two acidic solutions and produced startling color transformations. "We almost caught it, too. But then something went wrong and the flask exploded. It was fantastic!"

"I'm glad you don't work in my lab. Generally speaking, explosions are to be avoided when working with nitric acid. You two might do something a bit less volatile next time, like distilling rose water." Matthew's eyes narrowed. "You weren't working with mercury?"

"Don't worry. I wouldn't do anything that might harm the baby," I said defensively.

"Every time I say something about your well-being, you assume my concern lies elsewhere." His brows drew together in a scowl. Thanks to his dark beard and mustache—which I was still getting used to—Matthew looked even more forbidding. But I didn't want to argue with him.

"Sorry," I said quickly before changing the subject. "Next week we're going to mix up a fresh batch of *prima materia*. That has mercury in it, but I promise not to touch it. Mary wants to see if it will putrefy into the alchemical toad by the end of January."

"That sounds like a festive start to the New Year," Matthew said, settling the cloak over my shoulders.

"What were you looking at?" I peered out the windows.

"Someone's building a bonfire across the river for New Year's Eve. Every time they send the wagon for fresh wood, the local residents filch what's already there. The pile gets smaller by the hour. It's like watching Penelope ply her needle."

"Mary said no one will be working tomorrow. Oh, and to be sure to tell Françoise to buy extra manchet—that's bread, right?—and to soak it in milk and honey to make it soft again for Saturday's breakfast." It was Elizabethan French toast in all but name. "I think Mary's worried I might go hungry in a house run by vampires."

"Lady Pembroke has a don't-ask, don't-tell policy when it comes to creatures and their habits," Matthew observed.

"She certainly never mentioned what happened to her shoes," I said thoughtfully.

"Mary Sidney survives as her mother did: by turning a blind eye to every inconvenient truth. The women in the Dudley family have had to do so."

"Dudley?" I frowned. That was a family of notorious troublemakers—nothing at all like the mild-mannered Mary.

"Lady Pembroke's mother was Mary Dudley, a friend of Her Majesty and sister to the queen's favorite, Robert." Matthew's mouth twisted. "She was brilliant, just like her daughter. Mary Dudley filled her head with ideas so there was no room in it for knowledge of her father's treason, or her brothers' missteps. When she caught smallpox from our blessed sovereign, Mary Dudley never acknowledged that both the queen and her own husband thereafter preferred the company of others rather than face her disfigurement."

I stopped, shocked. "What happened to her?"

"She died alone and embittered, like most Dudley women before her. Her greatest triumph was marrying off her fifteen-year-old namesake to the forty-year-old Earl of Pembroke."

"Mary Sidney was a bride at fifteen?" The shrewd, vibrant woman ran an enormous household, reared a pack of energetic children, and was devoted to her alchemical experiments, all with no apparent effort. Now I understood how. Lady Pembroke was younger than me by a few years, but by the age of thirty she'd been juggling these responsibilities for half her life.

"Yes. But Mary's mother provided her all the tools necessary for her survival: iron discipline, a deep sense of duty, the best schooling money could buy, a love of poetry, and her passion for alchemy."

I touched my bodice, thinking of the life growing within me. What tools would he need to survive in the world?

We talked about chemistry on our way home. Matthew explained that the crystals that Mary brooded over like a hen were oxidized iron ore and that she would later distill them in a flask to make sulfuric acid. I'd always been more interested in the symbolism of alchemy than in its practical aspects, but my afternoon with the Countess of Pembroke had shown me how intriguing the links between the two might be.

Soon we were safely inside the Hart and Crown and I was sipping a warm tisane made from mint and lemon balm. It turned out the Elizabethans did have teas, but they were all herbal. I was chattering on about Mary when I noticed Matthew's smile.

"What's so funny?"

"I haven't seen you like this before," he commented.

"Like what?"

"So animated—full of questions and reports of what you've been doing and all the plans you and Mary have for next week."

"I like being a student again," I confessed. "It was difficult at first, not to have all the answers. Over the years I've forgotten how much fun it is to have nothing but questions."

"And you feel free here, in a way that you didn't in Oxford. Secrets are a lonely business." Matthew's eyes were sympathetic as his fingers moved along my jaw.

"I was never lonely."

"Yes you were. I think you still are," he said softly.

Before I could shape a response, Matthew had me out of my seat and was backing us toward the wall by the fireplace. Pierre, who was nowhere to be seen only moments before, appeared at the threshold.

Then a knock sounded. Matthew's shoulder muscles bunched, and a dagger flashed at his thigh. When he nodded, Pierre stepped out onto the landing and flung open the door.

"We have a message from Father Hubbard." Two male vampires stood there, both dressed in expensive clothes that were beyond the reach of most messengers. Neither was more than fifteen. I'd never seen a teenage vampire and had always imagined there must be prohibitions against it.

"Master Roydon." The taller of the two vampires tugged at the tip of his nose and studied Matthew with eyes the color of indigo. Those eyes moved from Matthew to me, and my skin smarted from the cold. "Mistress." Matthew's hand tightened on his dagger, and Pierre moved to stand more squarely between us and the door.

"Father Hubbard wants to see you," the smaller vampire said, looking with contempt at the weapon in Matthew's hand. "Come when the clocks toll seven."

"Tell Hubbard I'll be there when it's convenient," said Matthew with a touch of venom.

"Not just you," the taller boy said.

"I haven't seen Kit," Matthew said with a touch of impatience. "If he's in trouble, your master has a better idea where to look for him than I do, Corner." It was an apt name for the boy. His adolescent frame was all angles and points.

"Marlowe's been with Father Hubbard all day." Corner's tone dripped with boredom.

"Has he?" Matthew said, eyes sharp.

"Yes. Father Hubbard wants the witch," Corner's companion said.

"I see." Matthew's voice went flat. There was a blur of black and silver, and his polished dagger was quivering, point first, in the doorjamb near Corner's eye. Matthew strolled in their direction. Both vampires took an involuntary step back. "Thank you for the message, Leonard." He nudged the door closed with his foot.

Pierre and Matthew exchanged a long, silent look while adolescent vampire feet racketed down the stairs.

"Hancock and Gallowglass," ordered Matthew.

"At once." Pierre whirled out of the room, narrowly avoiding Françoise. She pulled the dagger from the doorframe.

"We had visitors," Matthew explained before she could complain about the state of the woodwork.

"What is this about, Matthew?" I asked.

"You and I are going to meet an old friend." His voice remained ominously even.

I eyed the dagger, which was now lying on the table. "Is this old friend a vampire?"

"Wine, Françoise." Matthew grabbed at a few sheets of paper, disordering my carefully arranged piles. I muffled a protest as he picked up one of my quills and wrote with furious speed. He hadn't looked at me since the knock on the door.

"There is fresh blood from the butcher. Perhaps you should . . ."

Matthew looked up, his mouth compressed into a thin line. Françoise poured him a large goblet of wine without further protest. When she was finished, he handed her two letters.

"Take this to the Earl of Northumberland at Russell House. The other goes to Raleigh. He'll be at Whitehall." Françoise went immediately, and Matthew strode to the window, staring up the street. His hair was tangled in his high linen collar, and I had a sudden urge to put it to rights for him. But the set of his shoulders warned me that he wouldn't welcome such a proprietary gesture.

"Father Hubbard?" I reminded him. But Matthew's mind was elsewhere.

"You're going to get yourself killed," he said roughly, his back still turned. "Ysabeau warned me you have no instinct for self-preservation. How many times does something like this have to happen before you develop one?"

"What have I done now?"

"You wanted to be seen, Diana," he said harshly. "Well, you were."

"Stop looking out the window. I'm tired of talking to the back of your head." I spoke quietly, though I wanted to throttle him. "Who is Father Hubbard?"

"Andrew Hubbard is a vampire. He rules London."

"What do you mean, he rules London? Do all the vampires in the city obey him?" In the twenty-first century, London's vampires were renowned for their strong allegiance to the pack, their nocturnal habits, and their loyalty—or so I'd heard from other witches. Not as flamboyant as the vampires in Paris, Venice, or Istanbul, nor as bloodthirsty as those in Moscow, New York, and Beijing, London vampires were a well-organized bunch.

"Not just the vampires. Witches and daemons, too." Matthew turned on me, his eyes cold. "Andrew Hubbard is a former priest, one with a poor education and enough grasp of theology to cause trouble. He became a vampire when the plague first came to London. It had killed nearly half the city by 1349. Hubbard survived the first wave of the epidemic, caring for the sick and burying the dead, but in time he succumbed."

"And someone saved him by making him a vampire."

"Yes, though I've never been able to find out who it was. There are plenty of legends, though, most about his supposedly divine resurrection. When he was certain he was going to die, people say he dug a grave for himself in the churchyard and climbed into it to wait for God. Hours later Hubbard rose and walked out among the living." Matthew paused. "I don't believe he's been entirely sane since.

"Hubbard gathers up lost souls," Matthew continued. "There were too many to count in those days. He took them in—orphans, widows, men who had lost entire families in a single week. Those who fell ill he made into vampires, rebaptizing them and ensuring they had homes, food, and jobs. Hubbard considers them his children."

"Even the witches and daemons?"

"Yes," said Matthew tersely. "He takes them through a ritual of adoption, but it's nothing at all like the one Philippe performed. Hubbard tastes their blood. He claims it reveals the content of their souls and provides proof that God has entrusted them to his care."

"It reveals their secrets to him, too," I said slowly.

Matthew nodded. No wonder he wanted me to stay far away from this Father Hubbard. If a vampire tasted my blood, he would know about the baby—and who his father was.

"Philippe and Hubbard reached an agreement that exempted the de Clermonts from his family rituals and obligations. I probably should have told him you were my wife before we entered the city."

"But you chose not to," I said carefully, hands clenching. Now I knew why Gallowglass had requested that we dock somewhere other than at the foot of Water Lane. Philippe was right. There were times when Matthew behaved like an idiot—or the most arrogant man alive.

"Hubbard stays out of my way, and I stay out of his. As soon as he knows you're a de Clermont, he'll leave you alone, too." Matthew spotted something in the street below. "Thank God." Heavy footsteps sounded on the stairs, and a minute later Gallowglass and Hancock stood in our parlor. "It took you two long enough."

"And hello to you, Matthew," Gallowglass said. "So Hubbard's demanded an audience at last. And before you suggest it, don't even think about tweaking his nose by leaving Auntie here. Whatever the plan, she's going, too."

Uncharacteristically, Matthew ran his hand through his hair from back to front.

"Shit," Hancock said, watching the progress of Matthew's fingers. Making his hair stand up like a cockscomb was apparently another of Matthew's tells—one that meant his creative well of evasion and half-truths had run dry. "Your only plan was to avoid Hubbard. You don't have another. We've never been certain if you were a brave man or a fool, de Clermont, but I think this might decide the question—and not in your favor."

"I planned to take Diana to Hubbard on Monday."

"After she'd been in the city for ten days," Gallowglass observed.

"There was no need for haste. Diana is a de Clermont. Besides, we aren't in the city," Matthew said quickly. At my look of confusion, he continued. "The Blackfriars isn't really part of London."

"I'm not going into Hubbard's den and arguing the geography of the city with him again," Gallowglass said, slapping his gloves against his thigh. "He didn't agree when you made this argument so you could station the brotherhood in the Tower after we arrived to help the Lancastrians in 1485, and he's not going to agree to it now."

"Let's not keep him waiting," said Hancock.

"We have plenty of time." Matthew's tone was dismissive.

"You never have understood the tides, Matthew. I assume we're going by water, since you think the Thames isn't really part of the city either. If so, we may already be too late. Let's move." Gallowglass jerked his thumb in the direction of the front door.

Pierre was waiting for us there, tugging black leather over his hands. He'd swapped his usual brown cloak for a black one that was far too long to be fashionable. A silver device covered his right arm: a snake circling a cross with a crescent moon tucked into the upper quadrant. This was Philippe's crest, distinct from Matthew's only by the absence of the star and fleur-de-lis.

Once Gallowglass and Pierre were similarly outfitted, Françoise settled a matching cloak on Matthew's shoulders. Its heavy folds swept the floor, making him look taller and even more imposing. When the four of them stood together, it was an intimidating sight, one that provided a plausible inspiration for every human account of darkly cloaked vampires ever written.

At the bottom of Water Lane, Gallowglass surveyed the available vessels. "That one might hold us all," he said, pointing to a long rowboat and letting out an ear-piercing whistle. When the man standing by it asked where we were headed, the vampire embarked on a complicated set of instructions regarding our route, which of the city's many docks we were going to put in to, and who would be rowing. After Gallowglass growled at him, the poor man huddled near the lamp in the bow of his boat and looked nervously over his shoulder every now and again.

"Frightening every boatman we meet is not going to improve relations with our neighbors," I commented as Matthew boarded, looking pointedly at the brewery next door. Hancock picked me up without ceremony and handed me off to my husband. Matthew's arm tightened around me as the boat shot out into the river. Even the waterman gasped at the speed.

"There's no need to draw attention to ourselves, Gallowglass," Matthew said sharply.

"Do you want to row and I'll keep your wife warm?" When Matthew didn't reply, Gallowglass shook his head. "Thought not."

The soft glow of lamps from London Bridge penetrated the gloom ahead of us, and the crashing sound of fast-moving water became louder with each stroke that Gallowglass took. Matthew eyed the shoreline. "Put in at the Old Swan Stairs. I want to be back in this boat and headed upstream before the tide turns."

"Quiet." Hancock's whisper had a sharp edge. "We're supposed to be sneaking up on Hubbard. We might as well have proceeded down Cheapside with trumpets and banners for all the noise you're making."

Gallowglass turned back toward the stern and gave two powerful pulls with his left hand. A few more pulls put us at the landing—nothing more than a rickety set of steps, really, attached to some listing pylons—where several men waited. The boatman waved them off with a few terse words, hopping out of the boat as soon as he was able.

We climbed to street level and wended through twisting lanes in silence, darting between houses and across small gardens. The vampires moved with the stealth of cats. I moved less surely, stumbling on loose stones and stepping into waterlogged potholes. At last we turned in to a broad street. Laughter came from the far end, and light spilled into the street from wide windows. I rubbed my hands together, drawn to the warmth. Perhaps that was our destination. Perhaps this would be simple, and we could meet Andrew Hubbard, show him my wedding ring, and return home.

Matthew led us across the street instead and into a desolate churchyard whose gravestones tipped toward each other as if the dead sought comfort from one another. Pierre had a solid metal ring full of keys, and Gallowglass fitted one into the lock of the door next to the bell tower. We walked through the ramshackle nave and passed through a wooden door to the left of the altar. Narrow stone stairs plunged down into the darkness. With my limited warm-blooded sight, there was no way to keep my bearings as we twisted and turned through narrow passageways and crossed expanses that smelled of wine, must, and human decay. The experience was straight out of the tales that humans told to discourage people from lingering in church basements and graveyards.

We moved deeper into a warren of tunnels and subterranean rooms and entered a dimly lit crypt. Hollow eyes stared out from the heaped skulls in a small ossuary. A vibration in the stone floor and the muffled sound of bells indicated that somewhere above us the clocks were striking seven. Matthew hurried us along into another tunnel that showed a soft glow in the distance.

At the end we stepped into a cellar used to store wine unloaded from ships on the Thames. A few barrels stood by the walls, and the fresher scent of sawdust competed with the smell of old wine. I spied the source of the former aromas: neatly stacked coffins, arranged by size from long boxes capable of holding Gallowglass to minuscule caskets for infants. Shadows moved and flickered in the deep corners, and in the center of the room a ritual of some kind was taking place amid a throng of creatures.

"My blood is yours, Father Hubbard." The man who spoke was frightened. "I give it willingly, that you might know my heart and number me among your family." There was silence, a cry of pain. Then the air filled with a taut sense of expectation.

"I accept your gift, James, and promise to protect you as my child," a rough voice answered. "In exchange you will honor me as your father. Greet your brothers and sisters."

Amid the hubbub of welcome, my skin registered a sensation of ice.

"You're late." The rumble of sound cut through the chatter and set the hair on my neck prickling. "And traveling with a full retinue, I see."

"That's impossible, since we had no appointment." Matthew gripped my elbow as dozens of glances nudged, tingled, and chilled my skin.

Soft steps approached, circled. A tall, thin man appeared directly before me. I met his stare without flinching, knowing better than to show fear to a vampire. Hubbard's eyes were deep-set under a heavy brow bone with veins of blue, green, and brown radiating through the slate-colored iris.

The vampire's eyes were the only colorful thing about him. Otherwise he was preternaturally pale, with white-blond hair cropped close to his skull, nearly invisible eyebrows and lashes, and a wide horizontal slash of lips set in a clean-shaven face. His long black coat, which looked like a cross between a scholar's gown and a cleric's cassock, accentuated his ca- daverous build. There was no mistaking the strength in his broad, slightly stooped shoulders, but the rest of him was practically skeletal.

There was a blur of motion as blunt, powerful fingers took my chin and jerked my head to the side. In the same instant, Matthew's hand wrapped around the vampire's wrist.

Hubbard's cold glance touched my neck, taking in the scar there. For once I wished Françoise had outfitted me with the largest ruff she could find. He exhaled in an icy gust smelling of cinnabar and fir before his wide mouth tightened, the edges of his lips turning from pale peach to white.

"We have a problem, Master Roydon," said Hubbard.

"We have several, Father Hubbard. The first is that you have your hands on something that belongs to me. If you don't remove them, I'll tear this den to pieces before sunrise. What happens afterward will make every crea- ture in the city—daemon, human, *wearh,* and witch—think the end of days is upon us." Matthew's voice vibrated with fury.

Creatures emerged from the shadows. I saw John Chandler, the apoth- ecary from Cripplegate, who met my eyes defiantly. Kit was there, too, standing next to another daemon. When his friend's arm slid through the crook in his elbow, Kit pulled away slightly.

"Hello, Kit," Matthew said, his voice dead. "I thought you would have run off and hidden by now."

Hubbard held my chin for a few moments longer, pulling my head back until I faced him once more. My anger at Kit and the witch who had betrayed us must have shown, and he shook his head in warning.

"*'Thou shalt not hate thy brother in thy heart,'*" he murmured, releasing me. Hubbard's eyes swept the room. "Leave us."

Matthew's hands cupped my face, and his fingers smoothed the skin of my chin to erase Hubbard's scent. "Go with Gallowglass. I'll see you shortly."

"She stays," Hubbard said.

Matthew's muscles twitched. He wasn't used to being countermanded. After a considerable pause, he ordered his friends and family to wait outside. Hancock was the only one not to obey immediately.

"Your father says a wise man can see more from the bottom of a well than a fool can from a mountaintop. Let's hope he's right," Hancock muttered, "because this is one hell of a hole you've put us in tonight." With one last look, he followed Gallowglass and Pierre through a break in the far wall. A heavy door closed, and there was silence.

The three of us stood so close that I could hear the next soft expulsion of air from Matthew's lungs. As for Hubbard, I wondered if the plague had done more than drive him mad. His skin was waxy rather than porcelain, as though he still suffered the lingering effect of illness.

"May I remind you, Monsieur de Clermont, you are here under my sufferance." Hubbard sat in the chamber's grand, solitary chair. "Even though you represent the Congregation, I permit your presence in London because your father demands it. But you have flouted our customs and allowed your wife to enter the city without introducing her to me and to my flock. And then there is the matter of your knights."

"Most of the knights who accompanied me have lived in this city longer than you have, Andrew. When you insisted they join your 'flock' or leave the city boundaries, they resettled outside the walls. You and my father agreed that the de Clermonts would not bring *more* of the brotherhood into the city. I haven't."

"And you think my children care about these subtleties? I saw the rings they wore and the devices on their cloaks." Hubbard leaned forward, his eyes menacing. "I was led to believe you were halfway to Scotland. Why are you still here?"

"Perhaps you don't pay your informants enough," Matthew suggested. "Kit's very short on funds these days."

"I don't buy love and loyalty, nor do I resort to intimidation and torment to have my way. Christopher willingly does what I ask, like all godly children do when they love their father."

"Kit has too many masters to be faithful to any one of them."

"Couldn't the same be said of you?" After delivering his challenge to Matthew, Hubbard turned to me and deliberately drank in my scent. He made a soft, sorrowful sound. "But let us speak of your marriage. Some of my children believe that relationships between a witch and a *wearh* are abhorrent. But the Congregation and its covenant are no more welcome in my city than are your father's vengeful knights. Both interfere with God's wish that we live as one family. Also, your wife is a time spinner," Hubbard said. "I do not approve of time spinners, for they tempt men and women with ideas that do not belong here."

"Ideas like choice and freedom of thought?" I interjected. "What are you afraid—"

"Next," Hubbard interrupted, his focus still on Matthew as though I were invisible, "there is the matter of your feeding on her." His eyes moved to the scar that Matthew had left on my neck. "When the witches discover it, they will demand an inquiry. If your wife is found guilty of willingly offering her blood to a vampire, she will be shunned and cast out of London. If you are found guilty of taking it without her consent, you will be put to death."

"So much for family sentiment," I muttered.

"Diana," Matthew warned.

Hubbard tented his fingers and studied Matthew once more. "And finally, she is breeding. Will the child's father come looking for her?"

That brought my responses to a halt. Hubbard had not yet ferreted out our biggest secret: that Matthew was the father of my child. I fought down the panic. *Think—and stay alive.* Maybe Philippe's advice would get us out of this predicament.

"No," Matthew said shortly.

"So the father is dead—from natural causes or by your hand," Hubbard said, casting a long look at Matthew. "In that case the witch's child will be brought into my flock when it is born. His mother will become one of my children now."

"No," Matthew repeated, "she will not."

"How long do you imagine the two of you will survive outside London when the rest of the Congregation hears of these offenses?" Hubbard shook his head. "Your wife will be safe here so long as she is a member of my family and there is no more sharing of blood between you."

"You will not put Diana through that perverted ceremony. Tell your 'children' that she belongs to you if you must, but you will not take her blood or that of her child."

"I will not lie to the souls in my care. Why is it, my son, that secrets and war are the only responses you have when God puts a challenge before you? They only lead to destruction." Hubbard's throat worked with emotion. "God reserves salvation for those who believe in something greater than themselves."

Before Matthew could shoot back a reply, I put my hand on his arm to quiet him.

"Excuse me, Father Hubbard," I said. "If I understand correctly, the de Clermonts are exempt from your governance?"

"That is correct, Mistress Roydon. But *you* are not a de Clermont. You are merely married to one."

"Wrong," I retorted, keeping my husband's sleeve in a tight grip. "I am Philippe de Clermont's blood-sworn daughter, as well as Matthew's wife. I'm a de Clermont twice over, and neither I nor my child will ever call you father."

Andrew Hubbard looked stunned. As I heaped silent blessings on Philippe for always staying three steps ahead of the rest of us, Matthew's shoulders finally relaxed. Though far away in France, his father had ensured our safety once more.

"Check if you like. Philippe marked my forehead here," I said, touching the spot between my brows where my witch's third eye was located. It was slumbering at the moment, unconcerned with vampires.

"I believe you, Mistress Roydon," Hubbard said finally. "No one would have the temerity to lie about such a thing in a house of God."

"Perhaps you can help me, then. I'm in London to seek help with some finer points of magic and witchcraft. Who among your children would you recommend for the task?" My request erased Matthew's grin.

"Diana," he growled.

"My father would be very pleased if you could assist me," I said, calmly ignoring him.

"And what form would this pleasure take?" Andrew Hubbard was a Renaissance prince, too, and interested in gaining whatever strategic advantage he could.

"First, my father would be pleased to hear about our quiet hours at home on the eve of the New Year," I said, meeting his eyes. "Everything else I tell him in my next letter will depend on the witch you send to the Hart and Crown."

Hubbard considered my request. "I will discuss your needs with my children and decide who might best serve you."

"Whoever he sends will be a spy," Matthew warned.

"You're a spy, too," I pointed out. "I'm tired. I want to go home."

"Our business here is done, Hubbard. I trust that Diana, like all de Clermonts, is in London with your approval." Matthew turned to leave without waiting for an answer.

"Even de Clermonts must be careful in the city," Hubbard called after us. "See that you remember it, Mistress Roydon."

Matthew and Gallowglass spoke in low voices on our row home, but I was silent. I refused help getting out of the boat and began the climb up Water Lane without waiting for them. Even so, Pierre was ahead of me by the time I reached the passage into the Hart and Crown, and Matthew was at my elbow. Inside, Walter and Henry were waiting for us. They shot to their feet.

"Thank God," Walter said.

"We came as soon as we heard that you were in need. George is sick abed, and neither Kit nor Tom could be found," Henry explained, eyes darting anxiously between me and Matthew.

"I'm sorry to have called you. My alarm was premature," Matthew said, his cloak swirling around his feet as he took it from his shoulders.

"If it concerns the order—" Walter began, eyeing the cloak.

"It doesn't," Matthew assured him.

"It concerns *me*," I said. "And before you come up with some other disastrous scheme, understand this: The witches are my concern. Matthew is being watched, and not just by Andrew Hubbard."

"He's used to it," Gallowglass said gruffly. "Pay the gawpers no mind, Auntie."

"I need to find my own teacher, Matthew," I said. My hand fluttered down to where the point of my bodice covered the top of my belly. "No witch is going to part with her secrets so long as any of you are involved. Everyone who enters this house is either a *wearh*, a philosopher, or a spy. Which means, in the eyes of my people, that any one of you could turn us in to the authorities. Berwick may seem far away, but the panic is spreading."

Matthew's gaze was frosty, but at least he was listening.

"If you order a witch here, one will come. Matthew Roydon always gets his way. But instead of help, I'll get another performance like the one Widow Beaton gave. That's not what I need."

"You need Hubbard's help even less," Hancock said sourly.

"We don't have much time," I reminded Matthew. Hubbard didn't know that the baby was Matthew's, and Hancock and Gallowglass hadn't perceived the changes to my scent—yet. But this evening's events had driven home our precarious position.

"All right, Diana. We'll leave the witches to you. But no lies," Matthew said, "and no secrets either. One of the people in this room has to know where you are at all times."

"Matthew, you cannot—" Walter protested.

"I trust my wife's judgment," Matthew said firmly.

"That's what Philippe says about Granny," Gallowglass muttered under his breath. "Just before all hell breaks loose."

**19**

"If this is what hell looks like," Matthew murmured the week after our encounter with Hubbard, "Gallowglass is going to be sadly disappointed."

There was, in truth, very little fire and brimstone about the fourteen-year-old witch standing before us in the parlor.

"Hush," I said, mindful of how sensitive a child that age could be. "Did Father Hubbard explain why you are here, Annie?"

"Yes, mistress," Annie replied miserably. It was difficult to tell if the girl's pallor was due to her natural coloring or some combination of fear and poor nutrition. "I'm to serve you and accompany you about the city on your business."

"No, that wasn't our agreement," Matthew said impatiently, his booted feet landing heavily on the wooden floor. Annie flinched. "Do you have any power or knowledge to speak of, or is Hubbard playing some joke?"

"I have a little skill," Annie stammered, her pale blue eyes contrasting with her white skin. "But I need a place, and Father Hubbard said—"

"Oh, I can imagine what Father Hubbard said," Matthew snorted contemptuously. The look I gave him held sufficient warning that he blinked and was quiet.

"Allow her a chance to explain," I told him sharply before giving the girl an encouraging smile. "Go on, Annie."

"As well as serving you, Father Hubbard said I'm to take you to my aunt when she returns to London. She is at a lying-in at present and refused to leave while the woman still had need of her."

"Your aunt is a midwife as well as a witch?" I asked gently.

"Yes, mistress. A fine midwife and a powerful witch," Annie said proudly, straightening her spine. When she did so, her too-short skirts exposed her skinny ankles to the cold. Andrew Hubbard outfitted his sons in warm, well-fitting clothes, but his daughters received no such consideration. I smothered my irritation. Françoise would have to get her needles out.

"And how did you come to be part of Father Hubbard's family?"

"My mother was not a virtuous woman," Annie murmured, twisting her hands in her thin cloak. "Father Hubbard found me in the undercroft of St. Anne's Church near Aldersgate, my mother dead beside me. My aunt was newly married and soon had babes of her own. I was six years old. Her husband did not want me raised among his sons for fear I would corrupt them with my sinfulness."

So Annie, now a teenager, had been with Hubbard for more than half her life. The thought was chilling, and the idea that a six-year-old could corrupt anyone was beyond comprehension, but this story explained both her abject look and the girl's peculiar name: Annie Undercroft.

"While Françoise gets you something to eat, I can show you where you will sleep." I'd been up to the third floor that morning to inspect the small bed, three-legged stool, and worn chest set aside to hold the witch's belongings. "I'll help carry your things."

"Mistress?" Annie said, confused.

"She brought nothing," Françoise said, casting disapproving looks at the newest member of the household.

"Never mind. She'll have belongings soon enough." I smiled at Annie, who looked uncertain.

Françoise and I spent the weekend making sure that Annie was clean as a whistle, clothed and shod properly, and that she knew enough basic math to make small purchases for me. To test her I sent her to the nearby apothecary for a penny's worth of quill pens and half a pound of sealing wax (Philippe was right: Matthew went through office supplies at an alarming pace), and she came back promptly with change to spare.

"He wanted a shilling!" Annie complained. "That wax isn't even good for candles, is it?"

Pierre took a shine to the girl and made it his business to elicit a rare, sweet smile from Annie whenever he could. He taught her how to play cat's cradle and volunteered to walk with her on Sunday when Matthew dropped broad hints that he would like us to be alone for a few hours.

"He won't . . . take advantage of her?" I asked Matthew as he unbuttoned my favorite item of clothing: a sleeveless boy's jerkin made of fine black wool. I wore it with a set of skirts and a smock when we were at home.

"Pierre? Good Christ no." Matthew looked amused.

"It's a fair question." Mary Sidney had not been much older when she was married off to the highest bidder.

"And I gave you a truthful answer. Pierre doesn't bed young girls." His hands stilled after he freed the last button. "This is a pleasant surprise. You're not wearing a corset."

"It's uncomfortable, and I'm blaming it on the baby."

He lifted the jerkin away from my body with an appreciative sound.

"And he'll keep other men from bothering her?"

"Can this conversation possibly wait until later?" Matthew said, his exasperation showing. "Given the cold, they won't be gone for long."

"You're very impatient in the bedroom," I observed, sliding my hands into the neck of his shirt.

"Really?" Matthew arched his aristocratic brows in mock disbelief. "And here I thought the problem was my admirable restraint."

He spent the next few hours showing me just how limitless his patience could be in an empty house on a Sunday. By the time everybody returned, we were both pleasantly exhausted and in a considerably better frame of mind.

Everything returned to normal on Monday, however. Matthew was distracted and irritable as soon as the first letters arrived at dawn, and he sent his apologies to the Countess of Pembroke when it became clear that the obligations of his many jobs wouldn't allow him to accompany me to our midday meal.

Mary listened without surprise as I explained the reason for Matthew's absence, blinked at Annie like a mildly curious owl, and sent her off to the kitchens in the care of Joan. We shared a delicious lunch, during which Mary offered detailed accounts of the private lives of everyone within shouting distance of the Blackfriars. Afterward, we withdrew to her laboratory with Joan and Annie to assist us.

"And how is your husband, Diana?" the countess asked, rolling up her sleeves, her eyes fixed on the book before her.

"In good health," I said. This, I had learned, was the Elizabethan equivalent of "Fine."

"That is welcome news." Mary turned and stirred something that looked noxious and smelled worse. "Much depends on it, I fear. The queen relies on him more than on any other man in the kingdom except Lord Burghley."

"I wish his good humor was more reliable. Matthew is mercurial these days. He's possessive one moment and ignores me as if I were a piece of furniture the next."

"Men treat their property that way." She picked up a jug of water.

"I am not his property," I said flatly.

"What you and I know, what the law says, and how Matthew himself feels are three entirely separate issues."

"They shouldn't be," I said quickly, ready to argue the point. Mary silenced me with a gentle, resigned smile.

"You and I have an easier time with our husbands than other women do, Diana. We have our books and the leisure to indulge our passions, thank God. Most do not." Mary gave everything in her beaker a final stir and decanted the contents into another glass vessel.

I thought of Annie: a mother who'd died alone in a church cellar, an aunt who couldn't take her in because of her husband's prejudices, a life that promised little in the way of comfort or hope. "Do you teach your female servants how to read?"

"Certainly," Mary responded promptly. "They learn to write and reckon, too. Such skills will make them more valuable to a good husband—one who likes to earn money as well as spend it." She beckoned to Joan, who helped her move the fragile glass bubble full of chemicals to the fire.

"Then Annie shall learn as well," I said, giving the girl a nod. She clung to the shadows, looking ghostly with her pale face and silver-blond hair. Education would increase her confidence. She'd had a definite lilt in her step ever since haggling with Monsieur de Laune over the price of sealing wax.

"She will have reason in future to thank you for it," said Mary. Her face was serious. "We women own nothing absolutely, save what lies between our ears. Our virtue belongs first to our father and then to our husband. We dedicate our duty to our family. As soon as we share our thoughts with another, put pen to paper or thread a needle, all that we do and make belongs to someone else. So long as she has words and ideas, Annie will always possess something that is hers alone."

"If only you were a man, Mary," I said with a shake of my head. The Countess of Pembroke could run rings around most creatures, regardless of their sex.

"Were I a man, I would be on my estates now, or paying court to Her Majesty like Henry, or seeing to matters of state like Matthew. Instead I am here in my laboratory with you. Weighing it all in the balance, I believe we are the better off—even if we are sometimes put on a pedestal or mistaken for a kitchen stool." Mary's round eyes twinkled.

I laughed. "You may be right."

"Had you ever been to court, you would have no doubts on this score. Come," Mary said, turning to her experiment. "Now we wait while the *prima materia* is exposed to the heat. If we have done well, this is what will generate the philosopher's stone. Let us review the next steps of the process in hopes that the experiment will succeed."

I always lost track of time while there were alchemical manuscripts around, and I looked up, dazed, when Matthew and Henry walked in to the laboratory. Mary and I had been deep in conversation about the images in a collection of alchemical texts known as the *Pretiosa Margarita Novella*—the *New Pearl of Great Price*. Was it already late afternoon?

"It can't be time to go. Not yet," I protested. "Mary has this manuscript—"

"Matthew knows the book, for his brother gave it to me. Now that Matthew has a learned wife, he may regret having done so," Mary said with a laugh. "There are refreshments waiting in the solar. I had hoped to see you both today." At this, Henry gave Mary a conspiratorial wink.

"That is kind, Mary," Matthew said, kissing me on the cheek in greeting. "Apparently you two haven't reached the vinegar stage yet. You still smell of vitriol and magnesia."

I put down the book reluctantly and washed while Mary finished making notes of the day's work. Once we were settled in the solar, Henry could no longer curb his excitement.

"Is it time now, Mary?" he asked the countess, shifting in his chair.

"You have the same enthusiasm for giving presents as young William does," she replied with a laugh. "Henry and I have a gift in honor of the New Year and your marriage."

But we had nothing to give them in return. I looked at Matthew, uncomfortable with this one-way exchange.

"I wish you luck, Diana, if you hope to stay ahead of Mary and Henry when it comes to gifts," he said ruefully.

"Nonsense," Mary replied. "Matthew saved my brother Philip's life and Henry's estates. No gifts can repay such debts. Do not ruin our pleasure with such talk. It is a tradition to give gifts to those newly wed, and it is New Year. What did you give the queen, Matthew?"

"After she sent poor King James another clock to remind him to bide his time quietly, I considered giving her a crystal hourglass. I thought it might be a useful reminder of her relative mortality," he said drily.

Henry looked at him with horror. "No. Not really."

"It was an idle thought in a moment of frustration," Matthew reassured him. "I gave her a covered cup, of course, like everyone else."

"Don't forget our gift, Henry," said Mary, now equally impatient.

Henry drew out a velvet pouch and presented it to me. I fumbled with the strings and finally drew out a heavy gold locket on an equally weighty chain. Its face was golden filigree studded with rubies and diamonds, Matthew's moon and star in its center. I flipped the locket over, gasping at the brilliant enamelwork with its flowers and scrolling vines. Carefully I opened the clasp at the bottom, and a miniature rendering of Matthew looked up at me.

"Master Hilliard made the preliminary sketches when he was here. With the holidays he was so busy that his assistant, Isaac, had to help with the painting," Mary explained.

I cupped the miniature in my hand, tilting it this way and that. Matthew was painted as he looked at home when he was working late at night in his study off the bedroom. His shirt open at the neck and trimmed with lace, he met the viewer's gaze with a lift of his right eyebrow in a familiar combination of seriousness and mocking humor. Black hair was swept back from his forehead in its typically disordered fashion, and the long fingers of his left hand held a locket. It was a surprisingly frank and erotic image for the time.

"Is it to your liking?" Henry asked.

"I love it," I said, unable to stop staring at my new treasure.

"Isaac is rather more . . . daring in his composition than his master is, but when I told him it was a wedding gift, he convinced me that such a locket would remain a wife's special secret and could reveal the private man rather than the public." Mary looked over my shoulder. "It is a good likeness, but I do wish Master Hilliard would learn how to better capture a person's chin."

"It's perfect, and I will treasure it always."

"This one is for you," Henry said, handing Matthew an identical bag. "Hilliard felt you might show it to others and wear it at court, so it is somewhat more . . . er, circumspect."

"Is that the locket Matthew is holding in my miniature?" I said, pointing to the distinctive milky stone set in a simple gold frame.

"I believe so," Matthew said softly. "Is it a moonstone, Henry?"

"An ancient specimen," Henry said proudly. "It was among my curiosities, and I wanted you to have it. The intaglio is of the goddess Diana, you see."

The miniature within was more respectable, but startling nonetheless in its informality. I was wearing the russet gown trimmed with black velvet. A delicate ruff framed my face without covering the shining pearls at my throat. But it was the arrangement of my hair that signaled that this was an intimate gift appropriate for a new husband. It flowed freely over my shoulders and down my back in a wild riot of red-gold curls.

"The blue background emphasizes Diana's eyes. And the set of her mouth is so true to life." Matthew, too, was overwhelmed by the gift.

"I had a frame made," Mary said, gesturing at Joan, "to display them when they are not being worn." It was more a shallow box, with two oval niches lined in black velvet. The two miniatures fit perfectly inside and gave the effect of a pair of portraits.

"It was thoughtful of Mary and Henry to give us such a gift," Matthew said later, when we were back at the Hart and Crown. He slid his arms around me from behind and laced his hands over my belly. "I haven't even had time to take your picture. I never imagined my first likeness of you would be by Nicholas Hilliard."

"The portraits are beautiful," I said, covering his hands with mine.

"But . . . ?" Matthew drew back and tilted his head.

"Miniatures by Nicholas Hilliard are sought after, Matthew. These won't disappear when we do. And they're so exquisite I couldn't bear to destroy them before we go." Time was like my ruff: It started out as a smooth, flat, tightly woven fabric. Then it was twisted and cut and made to double back on itself. "We keep touching the past in ways that are bound to leave smudges on the present."

"Maybe that's what we're supposed to be doing," Matthew suggested. "Perhaps the future depends on it."

"I don't see how."

"Not now. But it is possible that we'll look back one day and discover that it was the miniatures that made all the difference." He smiled.

"Imagine what finding Ashmole 782 would do, then." I looked up at him. Seeing Mary's illuminated alchemical books had brought the mysterious volume and our frustrated search for it vividly back to mind. "George had no luck finding it in Oxford, but it must be somewhere in England. Ashmole acquired our manuscript from somebody. Rather than looking for the manuscript, we should look for the person who sold it to him."

"These days there's a steady traffic in manuscripts. Ashmole 782 could be anywhere."

"Or it could be right here," I insisted.

"You may be right," Matthew agreed. But I could tell that his mind was on more immediate concerns than our elusive tome. "I'll send George out to make inquiries among the booksellers."

All thoughts of Ashmole 782 fled the next morning, however, when a note arrived from Annie's aunt, the prosperous midwife. She was back in London.

"The witch will not come to the house of a notorious *wearh* and spy," Matthew reported after he had read its contents. "Her husband objects to the plan, for fear it will ruin his reputation. We are to go to her house near St. James's Church on Garlic Hill." When I didn't react, Matthew scowled and continued. "It's on the other side of town, within spitting distance of Andrew Hubbard's den."

"You are a vampire," I reminded him. "She is a witch. We aren't supposed to mix. This witch's husband is right to be cautious."

Matthew insisted on accompanying Annie and me across town anyway. The area surrounding St. James's Church was far more prosperous than the Blackfriars, with spacious, well-kept streets, large houses, busy shops, and a tidy churchyard. Annie led us into an alley across from the church. Though dark, it was as neat as a pin.

"There, Master Roydon," the girl said. She directed Matthew's attention to the sign with a windmill on it before darting ahead with Pierre to alert the household to our arrival.

"You don't have to stay," I told Matthew. This visit was nerve-racking enough without him hovering and glowering.

"I'm not going anywhere," he replied grimly.

We were met at the door by a round-faced woman with a snub nose, a gentle chin, and rich brown hair and eyes. Her face was serene, although her eyes snapped with irritation. She had stopped Pierre in his tracks. Only Annie had been admitted to the house and stood to one side in the doorway looking dismayed at the impasse.

I also stopped in my tracks, my mouth open in surprise. Annie's aunt was the spitting image of Sophie Norman, the young daemon to whom we'd waved good-bye at the Bishop house in Madison.

"*Dieu,*" Matthew murmured, looking down at me in amazement.

"My aunt, Susanna Norman," Annie whispered. Our reaction had unsettled her. "She says—"

"Susanna *Norman?*" I asked, unable to take my eyes from her face. Her name and strong resemblance to Sophie couldn't be a coincidence.

"As my niece said. You appear to be out of your element, Mistress Roydon," Mistress Norman said. "And you are not welcome here, *wearh.*"

"Mistress Norman," Matthew said with a bow.

"Did you not get my letter? My husband wants nothing to do with you." Two boys shot out of the door. "Jeffrey! John!"

"Is this him?" the elder said. He studied Matthew with interest, then turned his attention on me. The child had power. Though he was still on the brink of adolescence, his abilities could already be felt in the crackle of undisciplined magic that surrounded him.

"Use the talents God gave you, Jeffrey, and don't ask idle questions." The witch looked at me appraisingly. "You certainly made Father Hubbard sit up and take notice. Very well, come inside." When we moved to do so, Susanna held up her hand. "Not you, *wearh.* My business is with your wife. The Golden Gosling has decent wine, if you are determined to remain nearby. But it would be better for all concerned if you were to let your man see Mistress Roydon home."

"Thank you for the advice, mistress. I'm sure I'll find something satisfactory at the inn. Pierre will wait in the courtyard. He doesn't mind the cold." Matthew gave her a wolfish smile.

Susanna looked sour and turned smartly. "Come along, Jeffrey," she called over her shoulder. Jeffrey commandeered his younger brother, cast one more interested glance at Matthew, and followed. "When you are ready, Mistress Roydon."

"I can't believe it," I whispered as soon as the Normans were out of sight. "She has to be Sophie's great-grandmother many times over."

"Sophie must be descended through either Jeffrey or John." Matthew pulled thoughtfully on his chin. "One of those boys is the missing link in our chain of circumstances that leads from Kit and the silver chess piece to the Norman family and on to North Carolina."

"The future really is taking care of itself," I said.

"I thought it would. As for the present, Pierre will be right here and I'll be close by." The fine lines around his eyes deepened. He didn't want to be more than six inches away from me at the best of times.

"I'm not sure how long this will take," I said, squeezing his arm.

"It doesn't matter," Matthew assured me, brushing my lips with his. "Stay as long as you need."

Inside, Annie hastily took my cloak and returned to the fire, where she had been stooped over something on the hearth.

"Have a care, Annie," Susanna said, sounding harassed. Annie was carefully lifting a shallow saucepan from a metal stand set over the embers of the fire. "Widow Hackett's daughter requires that draft to help her sleep, and the ingredients are costly."

"I can't figure her out, Mama," Jeffrey said, looking at me. His eyes were disconcertingly wise for one so young.

"Nor I, Jeffrey, nor I. But that's probably why she's here. Take your brother into the other room. And be quiet. Your father is sleeping, and he needs to remain so."

"Yes, Mama." Jeffrey scooped up two wooden soldiers and a ship from the table. "This time I'll let you be Walter Raleigh so you can win the battle," he promised his brother.

Susanna and Annie stared at me in the silence that followed. Annie's faint pulses of power were already familiar. But I was not prepared for the steady current of inquiry that Susanna turned my way. My third eye opened. Finally someone had roused my witch's curiosity.

"That's uncomfortable," I said, turning my head to break the intensity of Susanna's gaze.

"It should be," she said calmly. "Why do you require my help, mistress?"

"I was spellbound. It's not what you think," I said when Annie took an immediate step away from me. "Both of my parents were witches, but neither one understood the nature of my talents. They didn't want me to come to any harm, so they bound me. The bindings have loosened, however, and strange things are happening."

"Such as?" Susanna said, pointing Annie to a chair.

"I've summoned witchwater a few times, though not recently. Sometimes I see colors surrounding people, but not always. And I touched a quince and it shriveled." I was careful not to mention my more spectacular outbreaks of magic. Nor did I mention the odd threads of blue and amber in the corners or the way handwriting had started to escape from Matthew's books and reptiles flee from Mary Sidney's shoes.

"Was your mother or father a waterwitch?" Susanna asked, trying to make sense of my story.

"I don't know," I said honestly. "They died when I was young."

"Perhaps you are better suited to the craft, then. Though many wish to possess the rough magics of water and fire, they are not easy to come by," said Susanna with a touch of pity. My Aunt Sarah thought witches who relied on elemental magic were dilettantes. Susanna, on the other hand, was inclined to see spells as a lesser form of magical knowledge. I smothered a sigh at these bizarre prejudices. Weren't we all witches?

"My aunt was not able to teach me many spells. Sometimes I can light a candle. I have been able to call objects to me."

"But you are a grown woman!" Susanna said, her hands settling on her hips. "Even Annie has more skills than that, and she is but fourteen. Can you concoct philters from plants?"

"No." Sarah had wanted me to learn how to make potions, but I had declined.

"Are you a healer?"

"No." I was beginning to understand Annie's browbeaten expression.

Susanna sighed. "Why Andrew Hubbard requires my assistance, I do not know. I have quite enough to do with my patients, an infirm husband, and two growing sons." She took a chipped bowl from the shelf and a brown egg from a rack by the window. She placed both on the table before me and pulled out a chair. "Sit, and tuck your hands beneath your legs."

Mystified, I did as she requested.

"Annie and I are going to Widow Hackett's house. While we're gone, you are to get the contents of that egg into the bowl without using your hands. It requires two spells: a motion spell and a simple opening charm. My son John is eight, and he can already do it without thinking."

"But—"

"If the egg isn't in the bowl when I return, no one can help you, Mistress Roydon. Your parents may have been right to bind you if your power is so weak that you cannot even crack an egg."

Annie gave me an apologetic look as she lifted the pan into her arms. Susanna clapped a lid on it. "Come, Annie."

Sitting alone in the Normans' gathering room, I considered the egg and the bowl.

"What a nightmare," I whispered, hoping the boys were too far away to hear.

I took a deep breath and gathered my energy. I knew the words to both spells, and I wanted the egg to move—wanted it badly. Magic was nothing more than desire made real, I reminded myself.

I focused my desires on the egg. It hopped on the table, once, then subsided. Silently I repeated the spell. And again. And again.

Minutes later the only result of my efforts was a thin skim of perspiration on my forehead. All I had to do was lift the egg and crack it. And I had failed.

"Sorry," I murmured to my flat stomach. "With any luck you'll take after your father." My stomach flopped over. Nerves and rapidly changing hormones were hell on the digestion.

Did chickens get morning sickness? I tilted my head and looked at the egg. Some poor hen had been robbed of her unhatched chick to feed the Norman family. My nausea increased. Perhaps I should consider vegetarianism, at least during the pregnancy.

But maybe there was no chick at all, I comforted myself. Not every egg was fertilized. My third eye peered under the surface of the shell, through the thickening layers of albumen to the yolk. Traces of life ran in thin streaks of red across the yolk's surface.

"Fertile," I said with a sigh. I shifted on my hands. Em and Sarah had kept hens for a while. It took a hen only three weeks to hatch an egg. Three weeks of warmth and care, and there was a baby chicken. It didn't seem fair that I had to wait months before our child saw the light of day.

Care and warmth. Such simple things, yet they ensured life. What had Matthew said? *All that children need is love, a grown-up to take responsibility for them, and a soft place to land.* The same was true for chicks. I imagined what it would feel like to be surrounded in a mother hen's feathery warmth, safely cocooned from bumps and bruises. Would our child feel like that, floating in the depths of my womb? If not, was there a spell for it? One woven from responsibility, that would wrap the baby in care and warmth and love yet be gentle enough to give him both safety and freedom?

"That's my real desire," I whispered.

*Peep.*

I looked around. Many households had a few chickens pecking around the hearth.

*Peep.* It was coming from the egg on the table. There was a crack, then a beak. A bewildered set of black eyes blinked at me from a feathered head slicked down with moisture.

Someone behind me gasped. I turned. Annie's hand was clapped over her mouth, and she was staring at the chick on the table.

"Aunt Susanna," Annie said, dropping her hand. "Is that . . . ?" She trailed off and pointed wordlessly at me.

"Yes. That's the *glaem* left over from Mistress Roydon's new spell. Go. Fetch Goody Alsop." Susanna spun her niece around and sent her back the way she came.

"I didn't get the egg into the bowl, Mistress Norman," I apologized. "The spells didn't work."

The still-wet chick set up a protest, one indignant *peep* after another.

"Didn't work? I am beginning to think you know nothing about being a witch," said Susanna incredulously.

I was beginning to think she was right.

## 20

Phoebe found the quiet at Sotheby's Bond Street offices unsettling this Tuesday night. Though she'd been working at the London auction house for two weeks, she was still not accustomed to the building. Every sound—the buzzing of the overhead lights, the security guard pulling on the doors to make sure they were locked, the distant sound of recorded laughter on a television—made her jump.

As the junior person in the department, it had fallen on Phoebe to wait behind a locked door for Dr. Whitmore to arrive. Sylvia, her supervisor, had been adamant that someone needed to see the man after hours. Phoebe suspected that this request was highly irregular but was too new in the job to make more than a weak protest.

"Of course you will stay. He'll be here by seven o'clock," Sylvia had said smoothly, fingering her strand of pearls before picking up her ballet tickets from the desk. "Besides, you don't have anywhere else to be, do you?"

Sylvia was right. Phoebe had nowhere else to be.

"But who is he?" Phoebe asked. It was a perfectly legitimate question, but Sylvia had looked affronted.

"He's from Oxford and an important client of this firm. That's all you need to know," Sylvia replied. "Sotheby's values confidentiality, or did you miss that part of your training?"

And so Phoebe was still at her desk. She waited well beyond the promised hour of seven. To pass the time, she went through the files to find out more about the man. She didn't like meeting people without knowing as much about their background as possible. Sylvia might think all she needed was his name and a vague sense of his credentials, but Phoebe knew different. Her mother had taught her what a valuable weapon such personal information could be when wielded against guests at cocktail parties and formal dinners. Phoebe hadn't been able to find any Whitmores in the Sotheby archives, however, and his customer number led to a simple card in a locked file cabinet that said *de Clermont Family—inquire with the president.*

At five minutes to nine, she heard someone outside the door. The man's voice was gruff yet strangely musical.

"This is the third wild-goose chase you've sent me on in as many days, Ysabeau. Please try to remember that I have things to do. Send Alain next time. There was a brief pause. "You think I'm not busy? I'll call you after I see them." The man made a muffled oath. "Tell your intuition to take a break, for God's sake."

The man sounded strange: half American and half British, with blurred edges to his accent suggesting that these weren't the only languages he knew. Phoebe's father had been in the queen's diplomatic service, and his voice was similarly ambiguous, as though he hailed from everywhere and nowhere.

The bell rang, another shrill sound that made her flinch, despite the fact that Phoebe was expecting it. She pushed away from her desk and strode across the room. She was wearing her black heels, which had cost a fortune but made her look taller and, Phoebe told herself, more authoritative. It was a trick she'd learned from Sylvia at her first interview, when she had worn flats. Afterward she'd vowed never to appear "adorably petite" again.

She looked through the peephole to see a smooth forehead, scruffy blond hair, and a pair of brilliant blue eyes. Surely this wasn't Dr. Whitmore.

A sudden rap on the door startled her. Whoever this man was, he had no manners. Irritated, Phoebe punched the button on the intercom. "Yes?" she said impatiently.

"Marcus Whitmore here to see Ms. Thorpe."

Phoebe looked through the peephole once more. Impossible. No one this young would warrant Sylvia's attention. "Might I see some identification?" she said crisply.

"Where is Sylvia?" The blue eyes narrowed.

"At the ballet. *Coppélia*, I believe." Sylvia's tickets were the best in the house, the extravagance claimed as a business expense. The man on the other side of the door slapped an identification card flat against the peephole. Phoebe reared back. "If you would be so kind as to step away? I can't see anything at that distance." The card moved a few inches from the door.

"Really, Miss . . . ?"

"Taylor."

"Miss Taylor, I am in a hurry." The card disappeared, replaced by those twin blue beacons. Phoebe drew back again in surprise, but not before she'd made out the name on the card and his affiliation with a scientific research project in Oxford.

It was Dr. Whitmore. What business did a scientist have with Sotheby's? Phoebe pushed the release for the door.

As soon as the click sounded, Whitmore pushed his way through. He was dressed for a club in Soho, with his black jeans, vintage gray U2 T-shirt, and a ridiculous pair of high-top Converse trainers (also gray). A leather cord circled his neck, and a handful of ornaments of dubious provenance and little worth hung down from it. Phoebe straightened the hem of her impeccably clean white blouse and looked at him with annoyance.

"Thank you," Whitmore said, standing far closer to her than was normal in polite society. "Sylvia left a package for me."

"If you would be seated, Dr. Whitmore." She gestured to the chair in front of her desk.

Whitmore's blue eyes moved from the chair to her. "Must I? This won't take long. I'm only here to confirm that my grandmother isn't seeing zebras where there are only horses."

"Excuse me?" Phoebe inched toward her desk. There was a security alarm under the desk's surface, next to the drawer. If the man continued to misbehave, she would use it.

"The package." Whitmore kept his gaze directed at her. There was a spark of interest there. Phoebe recognized it and crossed her arms in an effort to deflect it. He pointed to the padded box on the desk without looking at it. "I'm guessing that's it."

"Please sit down, Dr. Whitmore. It's long past closing time, I'm tired, and there is paperwork to be filled out before I can let you examine whatever it is that Sylvia set aside." Phoebe reached up and rubbed at the back of her neck. It was cricked from looking up at him. Whitmore's nostrils flared, and his eyelids drifted down. Phoebe noticed that his eyelashes were darker than his blond hair, and longer and thicker than hers. Any woman would kill for lashes like those.

"I really think you had better give me the box and let me be on my way, Miss Taylor." The gruff voice smoothed out, deepened into a warning, though Phoebe couldn't understand why. What was he going to do, steal the box? Again she considered sounding the alarm but thought better of it. Sylvia would be furious if she offended a client by calling the guards.

Instead Phoebe stepped to the desk, picked up a paper and a pen, and returned to thrust them at the visitor. "Fine. I'm happy to do this standing up if you prefer, Dr. Whitmore, though it's a great deal less comfortable."

"That's the best offer I've had in some time." Whitmore's mouth twitched. "If we're going to proceed according to Hoyle, though, I think you should call me Marcus."

"Hoyle?" Phoebe flushed and drew herself up to her full height. Whitmore wasn't taking her seriously. "I don't think he works here."

"I certainly hope not." He scrawled a signature. "Edmond Hoyle's been dead since 1769."

"I'm fairly new at Sotheby's. You'll have to forgive me for not understanding the reference." Phoebe sniffed. Once again she was too far from the hidden button underneath her desk to use it. Whitmore might not be a thief, but she was beginning to think he was mad.

"Here's your pen," Marcus said politely, "and your form. See?" He leaned closer. "I did exactly what you asked me to. I'm really very well behaved. My father made sure of it."

Phoebe took the pen and paper from him. As she did, her fingers brushed against the back of Whitmore's hand. Its coldness made her shiver. There was a heavy gold signet on his pinkie finger, she noticed. It looked medieval, but no one walked around London with such a rare and valuable ring on his finger. It must be a fake—though a good one.

She inspected the form as she returned to the desk. It all seemed to be in order, and if this man turned out to be some kind of criminal—which wouldn't surprise her a bit—at least she wouldn't be guilty of breaking the rules. Phoebe lifted the lid of the box, prepared to surrender it to the odd Dr. Whitmore for his examination. She hoped that then she could go home.

"Oh." Her voice caught in surprise. She'd expected to see a fabulous diamond necklace or a Victorian set of emeralds in fussy gold filigree—something her own grandmother would like.

Instead the box contained two oval miniatures, set into niches that had been formed to adhere perfectly to their edges and protect them from damage. One was of a woman with long golden hair tinged with red. An open-necked ruff framed her heart-shaped face. Her pale eyes looked out at the viewer with calm assurance, and her mouth curved in a gentle smile. The background was the vivid blue common to the work of the Elizabethan limner Nicholas Hilliard. The other miniature depicted a man with a shock of black hair brushed back from his forehead. A straggling beard and mustache made him look younger than his black eyes suggested, and his white linen shirt was also open at the neck, showing flesh that was milkier than the cloth. Long fingers held a jewel suspended from a thick chain. Behind the man, golden flames burned and twisted, a symbol of passion.

A soft breath tickled her ear. "Holy Christ." Whitmore looked like he'd seen a ghost.

"They're beautiful, aren't they? This must be the set of miniatures that just arrived. An old couple in Shropshire found them hidden in the back of their silver chest when they were looking for a place to store some new pieces. Sylvia reckons they'll fetch a good price."

"Oh, there's no doubt about that." Marcus pushed a button on his phone.

*"Oui?"* said an imperious French voice at the other end of the line. This was the problem with cell phones, Phoebe thought. Everybody shouted on them, and you could hear private conversations.

"You were right about the miniatures, *Grand-mère.*"

A self-satisfied sound drifted out of the phone. "Do I have your complete attention now, Marcus?"

"No. And thank God for it. My complete attention isn't good for anybody." Whitmore eyed Phoebe and smiled. The man was charming, Phoebe reluctantly admitted. "But give me a few days before you send me on another errand. Just how much are you willing to pay for them, or shouldn't I ask?"

*"N'importe quel prix."*

*The price doesn't matter.* These were words that made auction houses happy. Phoebe stared down at the miniatures. They really were extraordinary.

Whitmore and his grandmother concluded their conversation, and the man's fingers immediately flew across his phone, transmitting another message.

"Hilliard believed that his portrait miniatures were best viewed in private," Phoebe mused aloud. "He felt that the art of limning put too many of his subjects' secrets on display. You can see why. These two look like they kept all kinds of secrets."

"You're right there," Marcus murmured. His face was very close, giving Phoebe an opportunity to examine his eyes more closely. They were bluer than she had first realized, bluer even than the azurite- and ultramarine-enriched pigments Hilliard used.

The phone rang. When Phoebe reached to answer it, she thought his hand drifted down, just for a moment, to her waist.

"Give the man his miniatures, Phoebe." It was Sylvia.

"I don't understand," she said numbly. "I'm not authorized—"

"He's purchased them outright. Our obligation was to get the highest possible price for their pieces. We've done that. The Taverners will be able to spend their autumn years in Monte Carlo if they choose. And you can tell Marcus that if I've missed the *danse de fête*, I'll be enjoying his family's box seats for next season's performances." Sylvia disconnected the line.

The room was silent. Marcus Whitmore's finger rested gently on the gold case that circled the miniature of the man. It looked like a gesture of longing, an attempt to connect to someone long dead and anonymous.

"I almost believe that, were I to speak, he might hear me," Marcus said wistfully.

Something was off. Phoebe couldn't identify what it was, but there was more at stake here than the acquisition of two sixteenth-century miniatures.

"Your grandmother must have a very healthy bank account, Dr. Whitmore, to pay so handsomely for two unidentifiable Elizabethan portraits. As you are also a Sotheby's client, I feel I should tell you that you surely overpaid for them. A portrait of Queen Elizabeth I from this period might go for six figures with the right buyers in the room, but not these." The identity of the sitter was crucial to such valuations. "We'll never know who these two were. Not after so many centuries of obscurity. Names are important."

"That's what my grandmother says."

"Then she is aware that without a definite attribution the value of these miniatures will probably not increase."

"To be honest," Marcus said, "my grandmother doesn't need to make a return on her investment. And Ysabeau would prefer it if no one else knows who they are."

Phoebe frowned at the odd phrasing. Did his grandmother think she *did* know?

"It's a pleasure doing business with you, Phoebe, even if we did do it standing up. This time." Marcus paused, smiled his charming smile. "You don't mind my calling you Phoebe?"

Phoebe *did* mind. She rubbed at her neck in exasperation, pushing aside her black, collar-length hair. Marcus's eyes lingered on the curve of her

shoulders. When she made no reply, he closed the box, tucked the miniatures under his arm, and backed away.

"I'd like to take you to dinner," he said mildly, seemingly unaware of
Phoebe's clear signals of uninterest. "We can celebrate the Taverners' good
fortune, as well as the sizable commission that you will be splitting with
Sylvia."

Sylvia? Split a commission? Phoebe's mouth gaped in disbelief. The
chances that her boss might do such a thing were less than nil. Marcus's
expression darkened.

"It was a condition of the deal. My grandmother wouldn't have it any
other way." His voice was gruff. "Dinner?"

"I don't go out with strange men after dark."

"Then I'll ask you out to dinner tomorrow, after we've had lunch. Once
you've spent two hours in my company, I won't be 'strange' any longer."

"Oh, you'll still be strange," Phoebe muttered, "and I don't take lunch.
I eat at my desk." She looked away in confusion. Had she said the first part
aloud?

"I'll pick you up at one," said Marcus, his smile widening. Phoebe's
heart sank. She *had* said it aloud. "And don't worry, we won't go far."

"Why not?" Did he think she was afraid of him or couldn't keep up
with his strides? God, she hated being short.

"I just wanted you to know that you could wear those shoes again without fearing you'd break your neck," Marcus said innocently. His eyes traveled slowly from her toes over her black leather pumps, lingered on her
ankles, and then crawled up the curve of her calf. "I like them."

Who did this man think he was? He was behaving like an eighteenth-
century rake. Phoebe took decisive steps toward the door, her heels making
satisfyingly sharp clicks. She pushed the button to release the lock and
held the door open. Marcus made an appreciative sound as he strolled
toward her.

"I shouldn't be so forward. My grandmother disapproves of that almost
as much as she disapproves of being cut out of a business deal. But here's
the thing, Phoebe." Whitmore lowered his mouth until it was inches from
her ear and dropped his voice to a whisper. "Unlike the men who have
taken you out to dinner and perhaps gone back to your flat for something
afterward, your propriety and fine manners don't frighten me off. Quite
the contrary. And I can't help imagining what you're like when that icy
control melts."

Phoebe gasped.

Marcus took her hand. His lips pressed against her flesh as he stared into her eyes "Until tomorrow. And make sure the door locks behind me. You're in enough trouble." Dr. Whitmore walked backward out of the room, gave her another bright smile, turned, and whistled his way out of sight.

Phoebe's hand was trembling. That man—that strange man with no grasp of proper etiquette and startling blue eyes—had kissed her. At her place of work. Without her permission.

And she hadn't slapped him, which is what well-bred daughters of diplomats were taught to do as a last resort against unwanted advances at home and abroad.

She was indeed in trouble.

**21**

"Was I right to call you, Goody Alsop?" Susanna twisted her hands in her apron and looked at me anxiously. "I nearly sent her home," she said weakly. "If I had . . ."

"But you didn't, Susanna." Goody Alsop was so old and thin that her skin clung to the bones of her hands and wrists. The witch's voice was strangely hearty for someone so frail, however, and intelligence snapped in her eyes. The woman might be an octogenarian, but no one would dare call her infirm.

Now that Goody Alsop had arrived, the main room in the Norman apartments was full to bursting. With some reluctance Susanna allowed Matthew and Pierre to stand just inside the door, provided they didn't touch anything. Jeffrey and John divided their attention between the vampires and the chick, now safely nestled inside John's cap by the fire. Its feathers were beginning to fluff in the warm air, and it had, mercifully, stopped peeping. I sat on a stool by the fire next to Goody Alsop, who occupied the room's only chair.

"Let me have a look at you, Diana." When Goody Alsop reached her fingers toward my face, just as Widow Beaton and Champier had, I flinched. The witch stopped and frowned. "What is it, child?"

"A witch in France tried to read my skin. It felt like knives," I explained in a whisper.

"It will not be entirely comfortable—what examination is?—but it should not hurt." Her fingers explored my features. Her hands were cool and dry, the veins standing out against mottled skin and crawling over bent joints. I felt a slight digging sensation, but it was nothing like the pain I'd experienced at Champier's hands.

"Ah," she breathed when she reached the smooth skin of my forehead. My witch's eye, which had lapsed into its typical frustrating inactivity the moment Susanna and Annie found me with the chick, opened fully. Goody Alsop was a witch worth knowing.

Looking into Goody Alsop's third eye, I was plunged into a world of color. Try as I might, the brightly woven threads refused to resolve into something recognizable, though I felt once more the tantalizing prospect that they could be put to some use. Goody Alsop's touch tingled as she probed my body and mind with her second sight, energy pulsing around her in a purple-tinged orange. In my limited experience, no one had ever manifested that particular combination of colors. She tutted here and there, made an approving sound or two.

"She's a strange one, isn't she?" Jeffrey whispered, peering over Goody Alsop's shoulder.

"Jeffrey!" Susanna gasped, embarrassed at her son's behavior. "Mistress Roydon, if you please."

"Very well. Mistress Roydon's a strange one," said Jeffrey, unrepentant. He shifted his hands to his knees and bent closer.

"What do you see, young Jeffrey?" Goody Alsop asked.

"She—Mistress Roydon—is all the colors of a rainbow. Her witch's eye is blue, even though the rest of her is green and silver, like the goddess. And why is there a rim of red and black there?" Jeffrey pointed to my forehead.

"That's a *wearh*'s mark," Goody Alsop said, smoothing it with her fingers. "It tells us she belongs to Master Roydon's family. Whenever you see this, Jeffrey—and it is quite rare—you must heed it as a warning. The *wearh* who made it will not take it kindly if you meddle with the warmblood he has claimed."

"Does it hurt?" the child wondered.

"Jeffrey!" Susanna cried again. "You know better than to pester Goody Alsop with questions."

"We face a dark future if children stop asking questions, Susanna," Goody Alsop remarked.

"A *wearh*'s blood can heal, but it doesn't harm," I told the boy before Goody Alsop could answer. There was no need for another witch to grow up fearing what he didn't understand. My eyes shifted to Matthew, whose claim on me went far deeper than his father's blood oath. Matthew was willing to let Goody Alsop's examination continue—for now—but his eyes never left the woman. I mustered a smile, and his mouth tightened a fraction in response.

"Oh." Jeffrey sounded mildly interested at this piece of intelligence. "Can you make the *glaem* again, Mistress Roydon?" To their chagrin, the boys had missed that manifestation of magical energy.

Goody Alsop rested a gnarled finger in the indentation over Jeffrey's lip, effectively silencing the boy. "I need to talk to Annie now. After we're through, Master Roydon's man is going to take all three of you to the river. When you get back, you can ask me whatever you'd like."

Matthew inclined his head toward the door, and Pierre rounded up his two young charges and, after a wary look at the old woman, took them downstairs to wait. Like Jeffrey, Pierre needed to overcome his fear of other creatures.

"Where is the girl?" Goody Alsop asked, turning her head.

Annie crept forward. "Here, Goody."

"Tell us true, Annie," Goody Alsop said in a firm tone. "What have you promised Andrew Hubbard?"

"N-nothing," Annie stammered, her eyes shifting to mine.

"Don't lie, Annie. 'Tis a sin," Goody Alsop chided. "Out with it."

"I'm to send word if Master Roydon plans to leave London again. And Father Hubbard sends one of his men when the mistress and master are still abed to question me about what goes on in the house." Annie's words tumbled out. When through, she clapped her hands over her mouth as though she couldn't believe she'd revealed so much.

"We must abide by the letter of Annie's agreement with Hubbard, if not its spirit." Goody Alsop thought for a moment. "If Mistress Roydon leaves the city for any reason, Annie will send word to me first. Wait an hour before you let Hubbard know, Annie. And if you speak a word to anyone of what happens here, I'll clap a binding spell on your tongue that thirteen witches won't be able to break." Annie looked justifiably terrified at the prospect. "Go and join the boys, but open all the doors and windows before you leave. I will send for you when it is time to return."

Annie's expression while she opened the shutters and doors was full of apology and dread, and I gave her an encouraging nod. The poor child was in no position to stand up to Hubbard and had done what she had to in order to survive. With one more frightened look at Matthew, whose attitude toward her was distinctly chilly, she left.

At last, the house quiet and drafts swirling around my ankles and shoulders, Matthew spoke. He was still propped up against the door, his black clothes absorbing what little light there was in the room.

"Can you help us, Goody Alsop?" His courteous tone bore no resemblance to his high-handed treatment of Widow Beaton.

"I believe so, Master Roydon," Goody Alsop replied.

"Please take your ease," Susanna said, gesturing Matthew toward a nearby stool. There was, alas, little chance of a man of Matthew's size being comfortable on a small three-legged stool, but he straddled it without complaint. "My husband is sleeping in the next room. He mustn't overhear the *wearh*, or our conversation."

Goody Alsop plucked at the gray wool and pearly linen that covered her neck and drew her fingers away, pulling something insubstantial with them. The witch stretched out her hand and flicked her wrist, releasing a shadowy figure into the room. Her exact replica walked off into Susanna's bedchamber.

"What was that?" I asked, hardly daring to breathe.

"My fetch. She will watch over Master Norman and make sure we are not disturbed." Goody Alsop's lips moved, and the drafts stopped. "Now that the doors and windows are sealed, we will not be overheard either. You can rest easy on that score, Susanna."

Here were two spells that might prove useful in a spy's household. I opened my mouth to ask Goody Alsop how she'd managed them, but before I could utter a word, she held up her hand and chuckled.

"You are very curious for a grown woman. I fear you'll try Susanna's patience even more than Jeffrey does." She sat back and regarded me with a pleased expression. "I have waited a long time for you, Diana."

"Me?" I said doubtfully.

"Without question. It has been many years since the first auguries foretold your arrival, and with the passing of time some among us gave up hope. But when our sisters told us of the portents in the north, I knew to expect you." Goody Alsop was referring to Berwick and the strange occurrences in Scotland. I sat forward, ready to question her further, but Matthew shook his head slightly. He still wasn't sure the witch could be trusted. Goody Alsop saw my husband's silent request and chuckled again.

"So I was right, then," Susanna said, relieved.

"Yes, child. Diana is indeed a weaver." Goody Alsop's words reverberated in the room, potent as any spell.

"What's that?" I whispered.

"There is much we don't understand about our present situation, Goody Alsop." Matthew took my hand. "Perhaps you should treat us both like Jeffrey and explain it as you would to a child."

"Diana is a maker of spells," Goody Alsop said. "We weavers are rare creatures. That is why the goddess sent you to me."

"No, Goody Alsop. You're mistaken," I protested with a shake of my head. "I'm terrible with spells. My Aunt Sarah has great skill, but not even she has been able to teach me the craft of the witch."

"Of course you cannot perform the spells of other witches. You must devise your own." Goody Alsop's pronouncement went against everything I'd been taught. I looked at her in amazement.

"Witches learn spells. We don't invent them." Spells were passed from generation to generation, within families and among coven members. We jealously guarded that knowledge, recording words and procedures in grimoires along with the names of the witches who mastered their accompanying magic. More experienced witches trained the younger members of the coven to follow in their footsteps, mindful of the nuances of each spell and every witch's past experience with it.

"Weavers do," Goody Alsop replied.

"I've never heard of a weaver," Matthew said carefully.

"Few have. We are a secret, Master Roydon, one that few witches discover, let alone *wearhs*. You are familiar with secrets and how to keep them, I think." Her eyes twinkled with mischief.

"I've lived many years, Goody Alsop. I find it hard to believe that witches could keep the existence of weavers from other creatures all that time." He scowled. "Is this another of Hubbard's games?"

"I am too old for games, Monsieur de Clermont. Oh, yes, I know who you really are and what position you occupy in our world," Goody Alsop said when Matthew looked surprised. "Perhaps you cannot hide the truth from witches as well as you think."

"Perhaps not," Matthew purred in warning. His growling further amused the old woman.

"That trick might frighten children like Jeffrey and John and moon-touched daemons like your friend Christopher, but it does not scare me." Her voice turned serious. "Weavers hide because once we were sought out and murdered, just like your father's knights. Not everyone approved of our power. As you well know, it can be easier to survive when your enemies think you are already dead."

"But who would do such a thing, and why?" I hoped that the answer wouldn't lead us back to the long-standing enmity between vampires and witches.

"It wasn't the *wearhs* or the daemons who hunted us down, but other witches," Goody Alsop said calmly. "They fear us because we are different. Fear breeds contempt, then hate. It is a familiar story. Once witches destroyed whole families lest the babes grew to be weavers, too. The few weavers who survived sent their own children into hiding. A parent's love for a child is powerful, as you will both soon discover."

"You know about the baby," I said, my hands moving protectively over my belly.

"Yes." Goody Alsop nodded gravely. "You are already making a powerful weaving, Diana. You will not be able to keep it hidden from other witches for long."

"A child?" Susanna's eyes were huge. "Conceived between a witch and a *wearh*?"

"Not just any witch. Only weavers can work such magic. There is a reason the goddess chose you for this task, Susanna, just as there is a reason she called me. You are a midwife, and all your skills will be needed in the days ahead."

"I have no experience that will help Mistress Roydon," Susanna protested.

"You have been assisting women in childbirth for years," Goody Alsop observed.

"Warmblooded women, Goody, with warmblooded babes!" Susanna said indignantly. "Not creatures like—"

"*Wearhs* have arms and legs, just like the rest of us," Goody Alsop interrupted. "I cannot imagine this child will be any different."

"Just because it has ten fingers and ten toes does not mean it has a soul," Susanna said, eyeing Matthew with suspicion.

"I'm surprised at you, Susanna. Master Roydon's soul is as clear to me as your own. Have you been listening to your husband again, and his prattle about the evil in *wearhs* and daemons?"

Susanna's mouth tightened. "What if I have, Goody?"

"Then you are a fool. Witches see the truth plainly—even if their husbands are full of nonsense."

"It is not such an easy matter as you make it out to be," Susanna muttered.

"Nor does it need to be so difficult. The long-awaited weaver is among us, and we must make plans."

"Thank you, Goody Alsop," Matthew said. He was relieved that someone agreed with him at last. "You are right. Diana must learn what she needs to know quickly. She cannot have the child here."

"That isn't entirely your decision, Master Roydon. If the child is meant to be born in London, then that is where it will be born."

"Diana doesn't belong here," Matthew said, adding quickly, "in London."

"Bless us, that is clear enough. But as she is a time spinner, merely moving her to another place will not help. Diana would be no less conspicuous in Canterbury or York."

"So you know another of our secrets." Matthew gave the old woman a cold stare. "As you know so much, you must have also divined that Diana will not be returning to her own time alone. The child and I will be going with her. You will teach her what she needs in order to do it." Matthew was taking charge, which meant that things were about to take their usual turn for the worse.

"Your wife's education is my business now, Master Roydon—unless you think you know more about what it means to be a weaver than I do," Goody Alsop said mildly.

"He knows that this is a matter between witches," I told Goody Alsop, putting a restraining hand on his arm. "Matthew won't interfere."

"Everything about my wife is my business, Goody Alsop," said Matthew. He turned to me. "And this is not a matter solely between witches. Not if the witches here might turn against my mate and my child."

"So it was a witch and not a *wearh* who injured you," Goody Alsop said softly. "I felt the pain and knew that a witch was part of it but hoped that was because the witch was healing the damage done to you rather than causing it. What has the world come to that one witch would do such a thing to another?"

Matthew fixed his attention on Goody Alsop. "Maybe the witch also realized that Diana was a weaver."

It hadn't occurred to me that Satu might have known. Given what Goody Alsop had told me about my fellow witches' attitude toward weavers, the idea that Peter Knox and his cronies in the Congregation might suspect me of harboring such a secret sent my blood racing. Matthew sought my hand, taking it between both of his.

"It is possible, but I cannot say for certain," Goody Alsop told us regretfully. "Nevertheless we must do what we can in the time the goddess provides to prepare Diana for her future."

"Stop," I said, slapping my palm on the table. Ysabeau's ring chimed against the hard wood. "You're all talking as though this weaving business makes sense. But I can't even light a candle. My talents are magical. I have wind, water—even fire—in my blood."

"If I can see your husband's soul, Diana, you will not be surprised that I have also seen your power. But you are not a firewitch or a waterwitch, no matter what you believe. You cannot command these elements. If you were foolish enough to attempt it, you would be destroyed."

"But I nearly drowned in my own tears," I said stubbornly. "And to save Matthew I killed a *wearh* with an arrow of witchfire. My aunt recognized the smell."

"A firewitch has no need of arrows. The fire leaves her and arrives at its target in an instant." Goody Alsop shook her head. "These were but simple weavings, my child, fashioned from grief and love. The goddess has given you her blessing to borrow the powers you need but not to command any of them absolutely."

"Borrow them." I thought over the frustrating events of the past months and the glimmers of magic that would never behave as they were supposed to do. "So that's why these abilities come and go. They were never really mine."

"No witch could hold so much power within her without upsetting the balance of the worlds. A weaver selects carefully from the magic around her and uses it to shape something new."

"But there must be thousands of spells in existence—not to mention charms and potions. Nothing I make could possibly be original." I drew my hand across my forehead, and the spot where Philippe had made his blood oath seemed cold to the touch.

"All spells came from somewhere, Diana: a moment of need, a longing, a challenge that could not be met any other way. And they came from someone, too."

"The first witch," I whispered. Some creatures believed that Ashmole 782 was the first grimoire, a book that contained the original enchantments and charms devised by our people. Here was another connection between me and the mysterious manuscript. I looked at Matthew.

"The first weaver," Goody Alsop corrected gently, "as well as those who followed. Weavers are not simply witches, Diana. Susanna is a great witch, with more knowledge about the magic of the earth and its lore than any of her sisters in London. For all her gifts, though, she cannot weave a new spell. You can."

"I can't even imagine how to begin," I said.

"You hatched that chick," Goody Alsop said, pointing to the sleepy yellow ball of fluff.

"But I was trying to crack an egg!" I protested. Now that I understood marksmanship, I was aware this was a problem. My magic, like my arrows, had missed its target.

"Obviously not. If you were trying simply to crack an egg, we would be enjoying some of Susanna's excellent custard. You had something else in mind." The chick concurred, emitting a particularly loud and clear peep.

She was right. I had indeed had other things on my mind: our child, whether we could nurture him properly, how we might keep him safe.

Goody Alsop nodded. "I thought so."

"I spoke no words, performed no ritual, concocted nothing." I was clinging to what Sarah had taught me about the craft. "All I did was ask some questions. They weren't even particularly good questions."

"Magic begins with desire. The words come much, much later," Goody Alsop explained. "Even then a weaver cannot always reduce a spell to a few lines for another witch to use. Some weavings resist, no matter how hard we try. They are for our use alone. It is why we are feared."

"*It begins with absence and desire,*" I murmured. Past and present clashed again as I repeated the first line of the verse that had accompanied the single page of Ashmole 782 someone once sent to my parents. On this occasion, when the corners lit up and illuminated the dust motes in shades of blue and gold, I didn't look away. Neither did Goody Alsop. Matthew's and Susanna's eyes followed ours, but neither saw anything out of the ordinary.

"Exactly. See there, how time feels your absence and wants you back to weave yourself into your former life." She beamed, clapping her hands together as though I'd made her a particularly fine crayon drawing of a house and she planned to display it on her refrigerator door. "Of course, time is not ready for you now. If it were, the blue would be much brighter."

"You make it sound as though it's possible to combine magic and the craft, but they're separate," I said, still confused. "Witchcraft uses spells, and magic is an inherited power over an element, like air or fire."

"Who taught you such nonsense?" Goody Alsop snorted, and Susanna looked appalled. "Magic and witchcraft are but two paths that cross in the wood. A weaver is able to stand at the crossroads with one foot placed on each path. She can occupy the place between, where the powers are the greatest."

Time protested this revelation with a loud cry.

*"A child between, a witch apart,"* I murmured in wonder. The ghost of Bridget Bishop had warned me of the dangers associated with such a vulnerable position. "Before we came here, the ghost of one of my ancestors—Bridget Bishop—told me that was my fate. She must have known I was a weaver."

"So did your parents," Goody Alsop said. "I can see the last remaining threads of their binding. Your father was a weaver, too. He knew you would follow his path."

"Her father?" Matthew asked.

"Weavers are seldom men, Goody Alsop," Susanna cautioned.

"Diana's father was a weaver of great talent but no training. His spell was pieced together rather than properly woven. Still, it was made with love and served its purpose for a time, rather like the chain that binds you to your *wearh*, Diana." The chain was my secret weapon, providing the comforting sensation that I was anchored to Matthew in my darkest moments.

"Bridget told me something else that same night: *'There is no path forward that does not have him in it.'* She must have known about Matthew, too," I confessed.

"You never told me about this conversation, *mon coeur*," Matthew said, sounding more curious than annoyed.

"Crossroads and paths and vague prophecies didn't seem important then. With everything that happened afterward, I forgot." I looked at Goody Alsop. "Besides, how could I have been making spells without knowing it?"

"Weavers are surrounded by mystery," Goody Alsop told me. "We haven't the time to seek answers to all your questions now but must focus instead on teaching you to manage the magic as it moves through you."

"My powers have been misbehaving," I admitted, thinking of the shriveled quinces and Mary's ruined shoes. "I never know what's going to happen next."

"That's not unusual for a weaver first coming into her power. But your brightness can be seen and felt, even by humans." Goody Alsop sat back in her chair and studied me. "If witches see your *glaem* like young Annie did, they might use the knowledge for their own purposes. We will not let you or the child fall into Hubbard's clutches. I trust you can manage the Congregation?" she said, looking at Matthew. Goody Alsop construed Matthew's silence as consent.

"Very well, then. Come to me on Mondays and Thursdays, Diana. Mistress Norman will see to you on Tuesdays. I shall send for Marjorie Cooper on Wednesdays and Elizabeth Jackson and Catherine Streeter on Fridays. Diana will need their help to reconcile the fire and water in her blood, or she will never produce more than a vapor."

"Perhaps it is not wise to make all those witches privy to this particular secret, Goody," Matthew said.

"Master Roydon is right. There are already too many whispers about the witch. John Chandler has been spreading news of her to ingratiate himself with Father Hubbard. Surely we can teach her ourselves," said Susanna.

"And when did you become a firewitch?" Goody Alsop retorted. "The child's blood is full of flame. My talents are dominated by witchwind, and yours are grounded in the earth's power. We are not sufficient to the task."

"Our gathering will draw too much attention if we proceed with your plan. We are but thirteen witches, yet you propose to involve five of us in this business. Let some other gathering take on the problem of Mistress Roydon—the one in Moorgate, perhaps, or Aldgate."

"The Aldgate gathering has grown too large, Susanna. It cannot govern its own affairs, never mind take on the education of a weaver. Besides, it is too far for me to travel, and the bad air by the city ditch worsens my rheumatism. We will train her in this parish, as the goddess intended."

"I cannot—" Susanna began.

"I am your elder, Susanna. If you wish to protest further, you will need to seek a ruling from the Rede." The air thickened uncomfortably.

"Very well, Goody. I will send my request to Queenhithe." Susanna seemed startled by her own announcement.

"Who is Queen Hithe?" I asked Matthew, my voice low.

"Queenhithe is a place, not a person," he murmured. "But what is this about a reed?"

"I have no idea," I confessed.

"Stop whispering," Goody Alsop said, shaking her head in annoyance. "With the charm on the windows and the doors, your muttering stirs the air and hurts my ears."

Once the air quieted, Goody Alsop continued. "Susanna has challenged my authority in this matter. As I am the leader of the Garlickhythe gathering—and the Vintry's ward elder as well—Mistress Norman must present her case to the other ward elders in London. They will decide on our course of action, as they do whenever there are disagreements between witches. There are twenty-six elders, and together we are known as the Rede."

"So this is just politics?" I said.

"Politics and prudence. Without a way to settle our own disputes, Father Hubbard would have his *wearh* fingers in even more of our affairs," said Goody Alsop. "I am sorry if I offend you, Master Roydon."

"No offense taken, Goody Alsop. But if you take this matter to your elders, Diana's identity will be known across London." Matthew stood. "I can't allow that."

"Every witch in the city has already heard about your wife. News travels quickly here, no small thanks to your friend Christopher Marlowe," Goody Alsop said, craning her neck to meet his eyes. "Sit down, Master Roydon. My old bones no longer bend that way." To my surprise, Matthew sat.

"The witches of London still do not know you are a weaver, Diana, and that is the important thing," Goody Alsop continued. "The Rede will have to be told, of course. When other witches hear that you've been called before the elders, they will assume you are being disciplined for your relationship with Master Roydon, or that you are being bound in some fashion to keep him from gaining access to your blood and power."

"Whatever they decide, will you still be my teacher?" I was used to being the object of other witches' scorn and knew better than to hope that the witches of London would approve of my relationship with Matthew. It mattered little to me whether Marjorie Cooper, Elizabeth Jackson, and Catherine Streeter (whoever they were) participated in Goody Alsop's educational regimen. But Goody Alsop was different. This was one witch whose friendship and help I wanted to have.

"I am the last of our kind in London and one of only three known weavers in this part of the world. The Scottish weaver Agnes Sampson lies in a prison in Edinburgh. No one has seen or heard from the Irish weaver for years. The Rede has no choice but to let me guide you," Goody Alsop assured me.

"When will the witches meet?" I asked.

"As soon as it can be arranged," Goody Alsop promised.

"We will be ready for them," Matthew assured her.

"There are some things that your wife must do for herself, Master Roydon. Carrying the babe and seeing the Rede are among them," Goody Alsop replied. "Trust is not an easy business for a *wearh*, I know, but you must try for her sake."

"I trust my wife. You felt what witches have done to her, so you will not be surprised that I don't trust any of your kind with her," Matthew said.

"You must try," Goody Alsop repeated. "You cannot offend the Rede. If you do, Hubbard will have to intervene. The Rede will not suffer that additional insult and will insist on the Congregation's involvement. No matter our other disagreements, no one in this room wants the Congregation's attention focused on London, Master Roydon."

Matthew took Goody Alsop's measure. Finally he nodded. "Very well, Goody."

I was a weaver.

Soon I would be a mother.

*A child between, a witch apart,* whispered the ghostly voice of Bridget Bishop.

Matthew's sharp inhalation told me that he had detected some change in my scent. "Diana is tired and needs to go home."

"She is not tired but fearful. The time for that has passed, Diana. You must face who you truly are," Goody Alsop said with mild regret.

But my anxiety continued to rise even after we were safely back in the Hart and Crown. Once there, Matthew took off his quilted jacket. He wrapped it around my shoulders, trying to ward off the chilly air. The fabric retained his smell of cloves and cinnamon, along with traces of smoke from Susanna's fire and the damp air of London.

"I'm a weaver." Perhaps if I kept saying it, this fact would begin to make sense. "But I don't know what that means or who I am anymore."

"You are Diana Bishop—a historian, a witch." He took me by the shoulders. "No matter what else you have been before or might one day be, this is who you are. And you are my life."

"Your wife," I corrected him.

"My life," he repeated. "You are not just my heart but its beating. Before I was only a shadow, like Goody Alsop's fetch." His accent was stronger, his voice rough with emotion.

"I should be relieved to have the truth at last," I said through chattering teeth as I climbed into bed. The cold seemed to have taken root in the marrow of my bones. "All my life I wondered why I was different. Now I know, but it doesn't help."

"One day it will," Matthew promised, joining me under the coverlet. He folded his arms around me. We twined our legs like the roots of a tree, each clinging to the other for support as we worked our bodies closer. Deep within me the chain that I had somehow forged out of love and longing for someone I had yet to meet flexed between us and became fluid. It was thick and unbreakable, filled with a life-giving sap that flowed continuously from witch to vampire and back to witch. Soon I no longer felt between but blissfully, completely centered. I took a deep breath, then another. When I tried to draw away, Matthew refused.

"I'm not ready to let you go yet," he said, pulling me closer.

"You must have work to do—for the Congregation, Philippe, Elizabeth. I'm fine, Matthew," I insisted, though I wanted to stay exactly where I was for as long as possible.

"Vampires reckon time differently than warmbloods do," he said, still unwilling to release me.

"How long is a vampire minute, then?" I asked, snuggling under his chin.

"It's hard to say," Matthew murmured. "Some length of time between an ordinary minute and forever."

22

Assembling the twenty-six most powerful witches in London was no small feat. The Rede did not take place as I had imagined—in a single, court-room-style meeting with witches arrayed in neat rows and me standing before them. Instead it unfolded over several days in shops, taverns, and parlors all over the city. There were no formal introductions, and no time was wasted on other social niceties. I saw so many unfamiliar witches that soon they all blurred together.

Some aspects of the experience stood out, however. For the first time I felt the unquestionable power of a firewitch. Goody Alsop hadn't misled me—there was no mistaking the burning intensity of the redheaded witch's gaze or touch. Though the flames in my blood leaped and danced when she was near, I was clearly no firewitch. This was confirmed when I met two more firewitches in a private room at the Mitre, a tavern in Bishopsgate.

"She'll be a challenge," one observed after she'd finished reading my skin.

"A time-spinning weaver with plenty of water and fire in her," the other agreed. "Not a combination I thought to see in my lifetime."

The Rede's windwitches convened at Goody Alsop's house, which was more spacious than its modest exterior suggested. Two ghosts wandered the rooms, as did Goody Alsop's fetch, who met visitors at the door and glided about silently making sure that everyone was comfortable.

The windwitches were a less fearsome lot than the firewitches, their touches light and dry as they quietly assessed my strengths and shortcomings.

"A stormy one," murmured a silver-haired witch of fifty or so. She was petite and lithe and moved with a speed that suggested gravity did not have the same hold on her as on the rest of us.

"Too much direction," another said, frowning. "She needs to let matters take their own course, or every draft she makes is likely to become a full-blown gale."

Goody Alsop accepted their comments with thanks, but when they all left, she seemed relieved.

"I will rest now, child," she said weakly, rising from her chair and moving toward the rear of the house. Her fetch trailed after her like a shadow.

"Are there any men among the Rede, Goody Alsop?" I asked, taking her elbow.

"Only a handful remain. All the young wizards have gone off to university to study natural philosophy," she said with a sigh. "These are strange times, Diana. Everyone is in such a rush for something new, and witches think books will teach them better than experience. I'll take my leave of you now. My ears are ringing from all that talking."

A solitary waterwitch came to the Hart and Crown on Thursday morning. I was lying down, exhausted from traipsing all over town the previous day. Tall and supple, the waterwitch did not so much step as flow into the house. She met a solid obstacle, however, in the wall of vampires in the entrance hall.

"It's all right, Matthew," I said from the door of our bedchamber, beckoning her forward.

When we were alone, the waterwitch surveyed me from head to toe. Her glance tingled like salt water on my skin, as bracing as a dip in the ocean on a summer day.

"Goody Alsop was right," she said in a low, musical voice. "There is too much water in your blood. We cannot meet with you in groups for fear of causing a deluge. You must see us one at a time. It will take all day, I'm afraid."

So instead of my going to the waterwitches, the waterwitches came to me. They trickled in and out of the house, driving Matthew and Françoise mad. But there was no denying my affinity with them, or the undertow that I felt in a waterwitch's presence.

"The water did not lie," one waterwitch murmured after sliding her fingertips over my forehead and shoulders. She turned my hands over to examine the palms. She was scarcely older than me, with striking coloring: white skin, black hair, and eyes the color of the Caribbean.

"What water?" I asked as she traced the tributaries leading away from my lifeline.

"Every waterwitch in London collected rainwater from midsummer to Mabon, then poured it into the Rede's scrying bowl. It revealed that the long-awaited weaver would have water in her veins." The waterwitch let out a sigh of relief and released my hands. "We are in need of new spells after helping turn back the Spanish fleet. Goody Alsop has been able to replenish the windwitches' supply, but the Scottish weaver was gifted with earth, so she could not help us—even if she had wished to. You are a true daughter of the moon, though, and will serve us well."

On Friday morning a messenger came to the house with an address on Bread Street and instructions for me to go there at eleven o'clock to meet the last remaining members of the Rede: the two earthwitches. Most witches had some degree of earth magic within them. It was the foundation for the craft, and in modern covens earthwitches had no special distinction. I was curious to see if the Elizabethan earthwitches were any different.

Matthew and Annie went with me, as Pierre was occupied on an errand for Matthew and Françoise was out shopping. We were just clearing St. Paul's Churchyard when Matthew turned on an urchin with a filthy face and painfully thin legs. Matthew's blade was at the child's ear in a flash.

"Move that finger so much as a hair, lad, and I'll take your ear off," he said softly.

I looked down with surprise to see the child's fingers brushing against the bag I wore at my waist.

There was always a hint of potential violence about Matthew, even in my own time, but in Elizabeth's London it was much closer to the surface. Still, there was no need for him to turn his venom on one so small.

"Matthew," I warned, noting the terror on the child's face, "stop it."

"Another man would have your ear or haul you before the bailiffs." Matthew narrowed his eyes, and the child blanched further.

"Enough," I said shortly. I touched the child's shoulder, and he flinched. In a flash my witch's eye saw a man's heavy hand striking the child and driving him into a wall. Beneath my fingers, concealed by a rough shirt that was all the boy had to keep out the cold, blood suffused his skin in an ugly bruise. "What's your name?"

"Jack, my lady," the boy whispered. Matthew's knife was still pressed to his ear, and we were beginning to attract attention.

"Put the dagger away, Matthew. This child is no danger to either of us."

Matthew withdrew his knife with a hiss.

"Where are your parents?"

Jack shrugged. "Haven't any, my lady."

"Take the boy home, Annie, and have Françoise get him some food and clothes. Introduce him to warm water, if you can, and put him in Pierre's bed. He looks tired."

"You cannot adopt every stray in London, Diana." Matthew drove his dagger into its sheath for emphasis.

"Françoise could use someone to run errands for her." I smoothed the boy's hair back from his forehead. "Will you work for me, Jack?"

"Aye, mistress." Jack's stomach gave an audible gurgle, and his wary eyes held a trace of hope. My witch's third eye opened wide, seeing into his cavernous stomach and hollow, trembling legs. I drew a few coins from my purse.

"Buy him a slice of pie from Master Prior on the way, Annie. He's ready to drop from hunger, but that should hold him until Françoise can make him a proper meal."

"Yes, Mistress," Annie said. She gripped Jack around the arm and towed him in the direction of the Blackfriars.

Matthew frowned at their departing backs and then at me. "You're doing that child no favors. This Jack—if that's his real name, which I sincerely doubt—won't live out the year if he continues to steal."

"The child won't live out the week unless an adult takes responsibility for him. What is that you said? Love, a grown-up to care for them, and a soft place to land?"

"Don't turn my words against me, Diana. That was about our child, not some homeless waif." Matthew, who had met more witches in the past few days than most vampires did in a lifetime, was spoiling for a fight.

"I was a homeless waif once."

My husband drew back as if I'd slapped him.

"Not so easy to turn him away now, is it?" I didn't wait for him to respond. "If Jack doesn't come with us, we might as well take him straight to Andrew Hubbard. There he'll either be fitted for a coffin or had for supper. Either way he'll be looked after better than he would be out here on the streets."

"We have servants enough," Matthew said coolly.

"And you have money to spare. If you can't afford it, I'll pay his wages out of my own funds."

"You'd better come up with a fairy tale to tuck him into bed with while you're at it." Matthew gripped my elbow. "Do you think he won't notice he's living with three *wearhs* and two witches? Human children always see more clearly into the world of creatures than adults do."

"Do you think Jack will care what we are if he has a roof over his head, food in his belly, and a bed where he can sleep the night in safety?" A woman stared at us in confusion from across the street. A vampire and a witch shouldn't be having such a heated discussion in public. I pulled the hood closer around my face.

"The more creatures we let into our lives here, the trickier this all becomes," Matthew said. He noticed the woman watching us and released my arm. "And that goes double for the humans."

After visiting the two solid, grave earthwitches, Matthew and I retreated to opposite ends of the Hart and Crown until our tempers cooled. Matthew attacked his mail, bellowing for Pierre and letting out a voluble stream of curses against Her Majesty's government, his father's whims, and the folly of King James of Scotland. I spent the time talking to Jack about his duties. While the boy had a fine skill set when it came to picking locks, pockets, and country bumpkins who could be fleeced of all their possessions in confidence games, he could not read, write, cook, sew, or do anything else that might assist Françoise and Annie. Pierre, however, took a serious interest in the boy, especially after he recovered his lucky charm from the inner pocket of the boy's secondhand doublet.

"Come with me, Jack," Pierre said, holding open the door and jerking his head toward the stairs. He was on his way out to collect the latest missives from Matthew's informants, and he clearly planned on taking advantage of our young charge's familiarity with London's underworld.

"Yes, sir," Jack said, his voice eager. He already looked better after just one meal.

"Nothing dangerous," I warned Pierre.

"Of course not, *madame*," the vampire said innocently.

"I mean it," I retorted. "And have him back before dark."

I was sorting through papers on my desk when Matthew came out from his study. Françoise and Annie had gone to Smithfield to see the butchers for meat and blood, and we had the house to ourselves.

"I'm sorry, *mon coeur*," Matthew said, sliding his hands around my waist from behind. He dropped a kiss on my neck. "Between the Rede and the queen, it's been a long week."

"I'm sorry, too. I understand why you don't want Jack here, Matthew, but I couldn't ignore him. He was hurt and hungry."

"I know," Matthew said, drawing me in tightly so that my back fit against his chest.

"Would your reaction have been different if we'd found the boy in modern Oxford?" I asked, staring into the fire rather than meeting his eyes.

Ever since the incident with Jack, I had been preoccupied with the question of whether Matthew's behavior was rooted in vampire genetics or Elizabethan morals.

"Probably not. It's not easy for vampires to live among warmbloods, Diana. Without an emotional bond, warmbloods are nothing more than a source of nourishment. No vampire, however civilized and well mannered, can remain in close proximity to one without feeling the urge to feed on them." His breath was cool against my neck, tickling the sensitive spot where Miriam had used her blood to heal the wound Matthew had made there.

"You don't seem to want to feed on me." There had been no indication that Matthew wrestled with such an urge, and he had flatly refused his father's suggestions that he take my blood.

"I can manage my cravings far better than when we first met. Now my desire for your blood is not so much about nourishment as control. To feed from you would primarily be an assertion of dominance now that we're mated."

"And we have sex for that," I said matter-of-factly. Matthew was a generous and creative lover, but he definitely considered the bedroom his domain.

"Excuse me?" he said, his eyebrows drawn into a scowl.

"Sex and dominance. It's what modern humans think vampire relationships are all about," I said. "Their stories are full of crazed alpha-male vampires throwing women over their shoulders before dragging them off for dinner and a date."

"Dinner and a date?" Matthew was aghast. "Do you mean . . . ?"

"Uh-huh. You should see what Sarah's friends in the Madison coven read. Vampire meets girl, vampire bites girl, girl is shocked to find out there really are vampires. The sex, blood, and overprotective behavior all come quickly thereafter. Some of it is pretty explicit." I paused. "There's no time for bundling, that's for sure. I don't remember much poetry or dancing either."

Matthew swore. "No wonder your aunt wanted to know if I was hungry."

"You really should read this stuff, if only to see what humans think. It's a public-relations nightmare. Far worse than what witches have to overcome." I turned around to face him. "You'd be surprised how many women seem to want a vampire boyfriend anyway, though."

"What if their vampire boyfriends were to behave like callous bastards in the street and threaten starving orphans?"

"Most fictional vampires have hearts of gold, barring the occasional jealous rage and consequent dismemberment." I smoothed the hair away from his eyes.

"I can't believe we're having this conversation," Matthew said.

"Why? Vampires read books about witches. The fact that Kit's *Doctor Faustus* is pure fantasy doesn't stop you from enjoying a good supernatural yarn."

"Yes, but all that manhandling and then making love . . ." Matthew shook his head.

"You've manhandled me, as you so charmingly put it. I seem to recall being hoisted into your arms at Sept-Tours on more than one occasion," I pointed out.

"Only when you were injured!" Matthew said indignantly. "Or tired."

"Or when you wanted me in one spot and I was in another. Or when the horse was too tall, or the bed was too high, or the seas were too rough. Honestly, Matthew. You have a very selective memory when it suits you. As for making love, it's not always the tender act that you describe. Not in the books I've seen. Sometimes it's just a good, hard—"

Before I could finish my sentence, a tall, handsome vampire flung me over his shoulder.

"We will continue this conversation in private."

"Help! I think my husband is a vampire!" I laughed and pounded on the backs of his thighs.

"Be quiet," he growled. "Or you'll have Mistress Hawley to contend with."

"If I were a human woman and not a witch, that growly sound you just made would make me swoon. I'd be all yours, and you could have your way with me." I giggled.

"You're already all mine," Matthew reminded me, depositing me on the bed. "I'm changing this ridiculous plot, by the way. In the interests of originality—not to mention verisimilitude—we're skipping dinner and moving right on to the date."

"Readers would love a vampire who said that!" I said.

Matthew seemed not to care about my editorial contributions. He was too busy lifting my skirts. We were going to make love fully clothed. How deliciously Elizabethan.

"Wait a minute. At least let me take off my bum roll." Annie had informed me that this was the proper name for the doughnut-shaped thing that kept my skirts respectably full and flouncy.

But Matthew was not inclined to wait.

"To hell with the bum roll." He loosened the front ties on his breeches, grabbed my hands, and pinned them over my head. With one thrust he was inside me.

"I had no idea that talking about popular fiction would have this effect on you," I said breathlessly as he started to move. "Remind me to discuss it with you more often."

We were just sitting down to supper when I was called to Goody Alsop's house.

The Rede had made its ruling.

When Annie and I arrived with our two vampire escorts and Jack trailing behind, we found her in the front parlor with Susanna and three unfamiliar witches. Goody Alsop sent the men to the Golden Gosling and steered me toward the group by the fire.

"Come, Diana, and meet your teachers." Goody Alsop's fetch pointed me to an empty chair and withdrew into her mistress's shadow. All five witches studied me. They looked like a bunch of prosperous city matrons, with their thick woolen gowns in dark, wintry colors. Only their tingling glances gave them away as witches.

"So the Rede agreed with your initial plan," I said slowly, trying to meet their eyes. It was never good to show a teacher fear.

"They did," Susanna said with resignation. "You will forgive me, Mistress Roydon. I have two boys to think of, and a husband too ill to provide for us. A neighbor's goodwill can be lost overnight."

"Let me introduce you to the others," Goody Alsop said, turning slightly toward the woman to her right. She was around sixty, short in stature, round of face, and, if her smile was any indication, generous of spirit. "This is Marjorie Cooper."

"Diana," Marjorie said with a nod that set her small ruff rustling. "Welcome to our gathering."

While meeting the Rede, I'd learned that Elizabethan witches used the term "gathering" much as modern witches used the word "coven" to indicate a recognized community of witches. Like everything else in London, the city's gatherings coincided with parish boundaries. Though it was strange to think of witches' covens and Christian churches fitting so neatly together, it made sound organizational sense and provided an extra measure of safety, since it kept the witches' affairs among close neighbors.

There were, therefore, more than a hundred gatherings in London proper and a further two dozen in the suburbs. Like the parishes, the gatherings were organized into larger districts known as wards. Each ward sent one of its elders to the Rede, which oversaw all of the witches' affairs in the city.

With panics and witch-hunts brewing, the Rede was worried that the old system of governance was breaking down. London was bursting with creatures already, and more poured in every day. I had heard muttering about the size of the Aldgate gathering—which included more than sixty witches instead of the normal thirteen to twenty—as well as the large gatherings in Cripplegate and Southwark. To avoid the notice of humans, some gatherings had started "hiving off" and splitting into different septs. But new gatherings with inexperienced leaders were proving problematic in these difficult times. Witches in the Rede who were gifted with second sight foresaw troubles ahead.

"Marjorie is gifted with the magic of earth, like Susanna. Her specialty is remembering," Goody Alsop explained.

"I have no need of grimoires or these new almanacs all the booksellers are peddling," Marjorie said proudly.

"Marjorie perfectly remembers every spell she has ever mastered and can recall the exact configuration of the stars for every year she has been alive—and for many years when she was not yet born."

"Goody Alsop feared you would not be able to write down all you learn here and take it with you. Not only will I help you find the right words so that another witch might use the spells you devise, but I'll teach you how to be at one with those words so that none can ever take them from you." Marjorie's eyes sparkled, and her voice lowered conspiratorially. "And my husband is a vintner. He can get you much better wine than you are drinking now. I understand wine is important to *wearhs*."

I laughed aloud at this, and the other witches joined in. "Thank you, Mistress Cooper. I will pass your offer on to my husband."

"Marjorie. We are sisters here." For once I didn't cringe at being called another witch's sister.

"I am Elizabeth Jackson," said the elderly woman on the other side of Goody Alsop. She was somewhere between Marjorie and Goody Alsop in age.

"You're a waterwitch." I felt the affinity as soon as she spoke.

"I am." Elizabeth had steely gray hair and eyes and was as tall and straight as Marjorie was short and round. While many of the waterwitches in the Rede had been sinuous and flowing, Elizabeth had the brisk clarity of a mountain stream. I sensed she would always tell me the truth, even when I didn't want to hear it.

"Elizabeth is a gifted seer. She will teach you the art of scrying."

"My mother was known for her second sight," I said hesitantly. "I would like to follow in her footsteps."

"But she had no fire," Elizabeth said decidedly, beginning her truth-telling immediately. "You may not be able to follow your mother in every-thing, Diana. Fire and water are a potent mix, provided they don't extinguish each other."

"We will see to it that doesn't happen," the last witch promised, turning her eyes to me. Until then she'd been studiously avoiding my gaze. Now I could see why: There were golden sparks in her brown eyes, and my third eye shot open in alarm. With that extra sight, I could see the nimbus of light that surrounded her. This must be Catherine Streeter.

"You're even . . . even more powerful than the firewitches in the Rede," I stammered.

"Catherine is a special witch," Goody Alsop admitted, "a firewitch born of two firewitches. It happens rarely, as though nature herself knows that such a light cannot be hidden."

When my third eye closed, dazzled by the sight of the thrice-blessed firewitch, Catherine seemed to fade. Her brown hair dulled, her eyes dimmed, and her face was handsome but unmemorable. Her magic sprang to life again, however, as soon as she spoke.

"You have more fire than I expected," she said thoughtfully.

"'Tis a pity she was not here when the Armada came," Elizabeth said.

"So it's true? The famous 'English wind' that blew the Spanish ships away from England's shores was raised by witches?" I asked. It was part of witches' lore, but I'd always dismissed it as a myth.

"Goody Alsop was most useful to Her Majesty," Elizabeth said proudly. "Had you been here, I think we might have been able to make burning water—or fiery rain at the very least."

"Let us not get ahead of ourselves," Goody Alsop said, holding up one hand. "Diana has not yet made her weaver's forspell."

"Forspell?" I asked. Like gatherings and the Rede, this was not a term I knew.

"A forspell reveals the shape of a weaver's talents. Together we will form a blessed circle. There we will temporarily turn your powers loose to find their own way, unencumbered by words or desires," Goody Alsop replied. "It will tell us much about your talents and what we must do to train them, as well as reveal your familiar."

"Witches don't have familiars." This was another human conceit, like worshipping the devil.

"Weavers do," Goody Alsop said serenely, motioning toward her fetch. "This is mine. Like all familiars, she is an extension of my talents."

"I'm not sure having a familiar is such a good idea in my case," I said, thinking about the blackened quinces, Mary's shoes, and the chick. "I have enough to worry about."

"That is the reason you cast a forspell—to face your deepest fears so that you can work your magic freely. Still, it can be a harrowing experience. There have been weavers who entered the circle with hair the color of a raven's wing and left it with tresses as white as snow," Goody Alsop admitted.

"But it will not be as heartbreaking as the night the *wearh* left Diana and the waters rose in her," Elizabeth said softly.

"Or as lonely as the night she was closed in the earth," Susanna said with a shiver. Marjorie nodded sympathetically.

"Or as frightening as the time the firewitch tried to open you," Catherine assured me, her fingers turning orange with fury.

"The moon will be full dark on Friday. Candlemas is but a few weeks away. And we are entering a period that is propitious for spells inclining children toward study," Marjorie remarked, her face creased with concentration as she recalled the relevant information from her astonishing memory.

"I thought this was the week for snakebite charms?" Susanna said, drawing a small almanac out of her pocket.

While Marjorie and Susanna discussed the magical intricacies of the schedule, Goody Alsop, Elizabeth, and Catherine stared at me intently.

"I wonder . . ." Goody Alsop looked at me with open speculation and tapped a finger against her lips.

"Surely not," Elizabeth said, voice hushed.

"We are not getting ahead of ourselves, remember?" Catherine said.

"The goddess has blessed us enough." As she said it, her brown eyes sparked green, gold, red, and black in rapid succession. "But perhaps . . ."

"Susanna's almanac is all wrong. But we have decided it will be more auspicious if Diana weaves her forspell next Thursday, under the waxing crescent moon," Marjorie said, clapping her hands with delight.

"Oof," Goody Alsop said, poking her finger in her ear to shield it from the disturbance in the air. "Gently, Marjorie, gently."

With my new obligations to the St. James Garlickhythe gathering and my ongoing interest in Mary's alchemical experiments, I found myself spending more time outside the house while the Hart and Crown continued to serve as a center for the School of Night and the hub for Matthew's work. Messengers came and went with reports and mail, George often stopped by for a free meal and to tell us about his latest futile efforts to find Ashmole 782, and Hancock and Gallowglass dropped off their laundry downstairs and whiled away the hours by my fire, scantily clad, until it was returned to them. Kit and Matthew had reached an uneasy truce after the business with Hubbard and John Chandler, which meant that I often found the playwright in the front parlor, staring moodily into the distance and then writing furiously. The fact that he helped himself to my supply of paper was an additional source of annoyance.

Then there were Annie and Jack. Integrating two children into the household was a full-time business. Jack, whom I supposed to be about seven or eight (he had no idea of his actual age), delighted in deviling the teenage girl. He followed her around and mimicked her speech. Annie would burst into tears and pelt upstairs to fling herself on her bed. When I chastised Jack for his behavior, he sulked. Desperate for a few quiet hours, I found a schoolmaster willing to teach them reading, writing, and reckoning, but the two of them quickly drove the recent Cambridge graduate away with their blank stares and studied innocence. Both preferred shopping with Françoise and running around London with Pierre to sitting quietly and doing their sums.

"If our child behaves like this, I'll drown him," I told Matthew, seeking a moment of respite in his study.

"She *will* behave like this, you can be certain of it. And you won't drown her," Matthew said, putting down his pen. We still disagreed about the baby's sex.

"I've tried everything. I've reasoned, cajoled, pleaded—hell, I even bribed them." Master Prior's buns had only ratcheted up Jack's energy level.

"Every parent makes those mistakes," he said with a laugh. "You're trying to be their friend. Treat Jack and Annie like pups. The occasional sharp nip on the nose will establish your authority better than a mince pie will."

"Are you giving me parenting tips from the animal kingdom?" I was thinking of his early research into wolves.

"As a matter of fact, I am. If this racket continues, they'll have me to contend with, and I don't nip. I bite." Matthew glowered at the door as a particularly loud crash echoed through our rooms, followed by an abject "Sorry, mistress."

"Thanks, but I'm not desperate enough to resort to obedience training. Yet," I said, backing out of the room.

Two days of using my teacher voice and administering time-outs instilled some degree of order, but the children required a great deal of activity to keep their exuberance in check. I abandoned my books and papers and took them on long walks down Cheapside and into the suburbs to the west. We went to the markets with Françoise and watched the boats unloading their cargo at the docks in the Vintry. There we imagined where the goods came from and speculated about the origins of the crews.

Somewhere along the way, I stopped feeling like a tourist and started feeling as though Elizabethan London was my home.

We were shopping Saturday morning at the Leadenhall Market, London's premier emporium for fine groceries, when I saw a one-legged beggar. I was fishing a penny out of my bag for him when the children disappeared into a hatmaker's shop. They could wreak havoc—expensive havoc—in such a place.

"Annie! Jack!" I called, dropping the penny in the man's palm. "Keep your hands to yourselves!"

"You are far from home, Mistress Roydon," a deep voice said. The skin on my back registered an icy stare, and I turned to find Andrew Hubbard.

"Father Hubbard," I said. The beggar inched away.

Hubbard looked around. "Where is your woman?"

"If you are referring to Françoise, she is in the market," I said tartly. "Annie is with me, too. I haven't had a chance to thank you for sending her to us. She is a great help."

"I understand you have met with Goody Alsop."

I made no reply to this blatant fishing expedition.

"Since the Spanish came, she does not stir from her house unless there is good reason."

Still I was silent. Hubbard smiled.

"I am not your enemy, mistress."

"I didn't say you were, Father Hubbard. But who I see and why is not your concern."

"Yes. Your father-in-law—or do you think of him as your father?—made that quite clear in his letter. Philippe thanked me for assisting you, of course. With the head of the de Clermont family, the thanks always precede the threats. It is a refreshing change from your husband's usual behavior."

My eyes narrowed. "What is it that you want, Father Hubbard?"

"I suffer the presence of the de Clermonts because I must. But I am under no obligation to continue doing so if there is trouble." Hubbard leaned toward me, his breath frosty. "And you are causing trouble. I can smell it. Taste it. Since you've come, the witches have been . . . difficult."

"That's an unfortunate coincidence," I said, "but I'm not to blame. I'm so unschooled in the arts of magic that I can't even crack an egg into a bowl." Françoise came out of the market. I dropped Hubbard a curtsy and moved to step past him. His hand shot out and grabbed me around the wrist. I looked down at his cold fingers.

"It's not just creatures who emit a scent, Mistress Roydon. Did you know that secrets have their own distinct odor?"

"No," I said, drawing my wrist from his grasp.

"Witches can tell when someone lies. *Wearhs* can smell a secret like a hound can scent a deer. I will run your secret to ground, Mistress Roydon, no matter how you try to conceal it."

"Are you ready, *madame*?" Françoise asked, frowning as she drew closer. Annie and Jack were with her, and when the girl spotted Hubbard, she blanched.

"Yes, Françoise," I said, finally looking away from Hubbard's uncanny, striated eyes. "Thank you for your counsel, Father Hubbard, and the information."

"If the boy is too much for you, I would be happy to take care of him," Hubbard murmured as I walked by. I turned and strode back to him.

"Keep your hands off what's mine." Our eyes locked, and this time it was Hubbard who looked away first. I returned to my huddle of vampire, witch, and human. Jack looked anxious and was now shifting from one foot to the other as if considering bolting. "Let's go home and have some gingerbread," I said, taking hold of his arm.

"Who is that man?" he whispered.

"That's Father Hubbard" was Annie's hushed reply.

"The one in the songs?" Jack said, looking over his shoulder. Annie nodded.

"Yes, and when he—"

"Enough, Annie. What did you see in the hat shop?" I asked, gripping Jack more tightly. I extended my hand toward the overflowing basket of groceries. "Let me take that, Françoise."

"It will not help, *madame*," Françoise said, though she handed me the basket. "*Milord* will know you have been with that fiend. Not even the cabbage's scent will hide it." Jack's head turned in interest at this morsel of information, and I gave Françoise a warning look.

"Let's not borrow trouble," I said as we turned toward home.

Back at the Hart and Crown, I divested myself of basket, cloak, gloves, and children and took a cup of wine in to Matthew. He was at his desk, bent over a sheaf of paper. My heart lightened at the now-familiar sight.

"Still at it?" I asked, reaching over his shoulder to put the wine before him. I frowned. His paper was covered with diagrams, X's and O's, and what looked like modern scientific formulas. I doubted that it had anything to do with espionage or the Congregation, unless he was devising a code. "What are you doing?"

"Just trying to figure something out," Matthew said, sliding the paper away.

"Something genetic?" The X's and O's reminded me of biology and Gregor Mendel's peas. I drew the paper back. There weren't just X's and O's on the page. I recognized initials belonging to members of Matthew's family: YC, PC, MC, MW. Others belonged to my own: DB, RB, SB, SP. Matthew had drawn arrows between individuals, and lines crisscrossed from generation to generation.

"Not strictly speaking," Matthew said, interrupting my examination. It was a classic Matthew nonanswer.

"I suppose you'd need equipment for that." At the bottom of the page, a circle surrounded two letters: B and C—*Bishop and Clairmont.* Our child. This had something to do with the baby.

"In order to draw any conclusions, certainly." Matthew picked up the wine and carried it toward his lips.

"What's your hypothesis, then?" I asked. "If it involves the baby, I want to know what it is."

Matthew froze, his nostrils flaring. He put the wine carefully on the table and took my hand, pressing his lips to my wrist in a seeming gesture of affection. His eyes went black.

"You saw Hubbard," he said accusingly.

"Not because I sought him out." I pulled away. That was a mistake.

"Don't," Matthew rasped, his fingers tightening. He drew another shuddering breath. "Hubbard touched you on the wrist. Only the wrist. Do you know why?"

"Because he was trying to get my attention," I said.

"No. He was trying to capture mine. Your pulse is here," Matthew said, his thumb sweeping over the vein. I shivered. "The blood is so close to the surface that I can see it as well as smell it. Its heat magnifies any foreign scent placed there." His fingers circled my wrist like a bracelet. "Where was Françoise?"

"In Leadenhall Market. I had Jack and Annie with me. There was a beggar, and—" I felt a brief, sharp pain. When I looked down, my wrist was torn and blood welled from a set of shallow, curved nicks. *Teeth marks.*

"That's how fast Hubbard could have taken your blood and known everything about you." Matthew's thumb pressed firmly into the wound.

"But I didn't see you move," I said numbly.

His black eyes gleamed. "Nor would you have seen Hubbard, if he'd wanted to strike."

Perhaps Matthew wasn't as overprotective as I thought.

"Don't let him get close enough to touch you again. Are we clear?"

I nodded, and Matthew began the slow business of managing his anger. Only when he was in control of it did he answer my initial question.

"I'm trying to determine the likelihood of passing my blood rage to our child," he said, a tinge of bitterness in his tone. "Benjamin has the affliction. Marcus doesn't. I hate the fact that I could curse an innocent child with it."

"Do you know why Marcus and your brother Louis were resistant, when you, Louisa, and Benjamin were not?" I carefully avoided assuming that this accounted for all his children. Matthew would tell me more when—if—he was able.

His shoulders lost their sharp edge. "Louisa died long before it was possible to run proper tests. I don't have enough data to draw any reliable conclusions."

"You have a theory, though," I said, thinking of his diagrams.

"I've always thought of blood rage as a kind of infection and supposed Marcus and Louis had a natural resistance to it. But when Goody Alsop told us that only a weaver could bear a *wearh* child, it made me wonder if I've been looking at this the wrong way. Perhaps it's not something in Marcus that's resistant but something in me that's receptive, just as a weaver is receptive to a *wearh*'s seed, unlike any other warmblooded woman."

"A genetic predisposition?" I asked, trying to follow his reasoning.

"Perhaps. Possibly something recessive that seldom shows up in the population unless both parents carry the gene. I keep thinking of your friend Catherine Streeter and your description of her as 'thrice-blessed,' as though her genetic whole is somehow greater than the sum of its parts."

Matthew was quickly lost in the intricacies of his intellectual puzzle. "Then I started wondering whether the fact that you are a weaver is sufficient to explain your ability to conceive. What if it's a combination of recessive genetic traits—not only yours but mine as well?" When his hands drove through his hair in frustration, I took it as a sign that the last of the blood rage was gone and heaved a silent sigh of relief.

"When we get back to your lab, you'll be able to test your theory." I dropped my voice. "And once Sarah and Em hear they're going to be aunts, you'll have no problem getting them to give you a blood sample—or to babysit. They both have bad cases of granny lust and have been borrowing the neighbors' children for years to satisfy it."

That conjured a smile at last.

"Granny lust? What a rude expression." Matthew approached me. "Ysabeau's probably developed a dire case of it, too, over the centuries."

"It doesn't bear thinking about," I said with a mock shudder.

It was in these moments—when we talked about the reactions of others to our news rather than analyzing our own responses to it—that I felt truly pregnant. My body had barely registered the new life it was carrying, and in the day-to-day busyness at the Hart and Crown it was easy to forget that we would soon be parents. I could go for days without thinking about it, only to be reminded of my condition when Matthew came to me, deep in the night, to rest his hands on my belly in silent communion while he listened for the signs of new life.

"Nor can I bear to think of you in harm's way." Matthew took me in his arms. "Be careful, *ma lionne*," he whispered against my hair.

"I will. I promise."

"You wouldn't recognize danger if it came to you with an engraved invitation." He drew away so that he could look into my eyes. "Just remember: Vampires are not like warmbloods. Don't underestimate how lethal we can be."

Matthew's warning echoed long after he delivered it. I found myself watching the other vampires in the household for the small signs that they were thinking of moving or that they were hungry or tired, restless or bored. The signs were subtle and easy to miss. When Annie walked past Gallowglass, his lids dropped to shutter the avid expression in his eyes, but it was over so quickly I might have imagined it, just as I might have imagined the flaring of Hancock's nostrils when a group of warmbloods passed by on the street below.

I was not imagining the extra laundry charges to clean the blood from their linen, however. Gallowglass and Hancock were hunting and feeding in the city, though Matthew did not join them. He confined himself to what Françoise could procure from the butchers.

When Annie and I went to Mary's on Monday afternoon, as was our custom, I remained more alert to my surroundings than I had been since our arrival. This time it wasn't to absorb the details of Elizabethan life but to make sure we weren't being watched or followed. I kept Annie safely within arm's reach, and Pierre retained a firm grip on Jack. We had learned the hard way that it was the only hope we had of keeping the boy from "magpie-ing," as Hancock called it. In spite of our efforts, Jack still managed to commit numerous acts of petty theft. Matthew instituted a new household ritual in an effort to combat it. Jack had to empty his pockets every night and confess how he'd come by his extraordinary assortment of shiny objects. So far it hadn't put a damper on his activities.

Given his light fingers, Jack could not yet be trusted in the Countess of Pembroke's well-appointed home. Annie and I took our leave of Pierre and Jack, and the girl's expression brightened considerably at the prospect of a long gossip with Mary's maid, Joan, and a few hours of freedom from Jack's unwanted attentions.

"Diana!" Mary cried when I crossed the threshold of her laboratory. No matter how many times I entered, it never failed to take my breath away, with its vivid murals illustrating the making of the philosopher's stone. "Come, I have something to show you."

"Is this your surprise?" Mary had been hinting that she would soon delight me with a display of her alchemical proficiency.

"Yes," Mary replied, drawing her notebook from the table. "See here, it is now the eighteenth of January, and I began the work on the ninth of December. It has taken exactly forty days, just as the sages promised."

Forty was a significant number in alchemical work, and Mary could have been conducting any number of experiments. I looked through her laboratory entries in an effort to figure out what she'd been doing. Over the past two weeks, I'd learned Mary's shorthand and the symbols she used for the various metals and substances. If I understood correctly, she began this process with an ounce of silver dissolved in aqua fortis—the "strong water" of the alchemists, known in my own time as nitric acid. To this, Mary added distilled water.

"Is this your mark for mercury?" I asked, pointing to an unfamiliar glyph.

"Yes—but only the mercury I obtain from the finest source in Germany." Mary spared no expense when it came to her laboratory, chemicals, or equipment. She drew me toward another example of her commitment to quality at any price: a large glass flask. It was free of imperfections and clear as crystal, which meant it had come from Venice. The English glass made in Sussex was marred with tiny bubbles and faint shadows. The Countess of Pembroke preferred the Venetian stuff—and could afford it.

When I saw what was inside, a premonitory finger brushed against my shoulders.

A silver tree grew from a small seed in the bottom of the flask. Branches had sprouted from the trunk, forking out and filling the top of the vessel with glittering strands. Tiny beads at the ends of the branches suggested fruit, as though the tree were ripe and ready for harvesting.

"The *arbor Dianæ*," Mary said proudly. "It is as though God inspired me to make it so that it would be here to welcome you. I have tried to grow the tree before, but it has never taken root. No one could see such a thing and doubt the truth and power of the alchemical art."

Diana's tree was a sight to behold. It gleamed and grew before my eyes, sending out new shoots to fill the remaining space in the vessel. Knowing that it was nothing more than a dendritic amalgam of crystallized silver did little to diminish my wonder at seeing a lump of metal go through what looked like a vegetative process.

On the wall opposite, a dragon sat over a vessel similar to the one Mary had used to house the *arbor Dianæ*. The dragon held his tail in his mouth, and drops of his blood fell into the silvery liquid below. I sought out the next image in the series: the bird of Hermes who flew toward the chemical marriage. The bird reminded me of the illustration of the wedding from Ashmole 782.

"I think it might be possible to devise a quicker method to achieve the same result," Mary said, drawing back my attention. She pulled a quill from her upswept hair, leaving a black smudge over her ear. "What do you imagine would happen if we filed the silver before dissolving it in the aqua fortis?"

We spent a pleasant afternoon discussing new ways to make the *arbor Dianæ,* but it was over all too soon.

"Will I see you Thursday?" Mary asked.

"I'm afraid I have another obligation," I said. I was expected at Goody Alsop's before sunset.

Mary's face fell. "Friday, then?"

"Friday," I agreed.

"Diana," Mary said hesitantly, "are you well?"

"Yes," I said in surprise. "Do I seem ill?"

"You are pale and look tired," she admitted. "Like most mothers I am prone to— Oh." Mary stopped abruptly and turned bright pink. Her eyes dropped to my stomach, then flew back to my face. "You are with child."

"I will have many questions for you in the weeks ahead," I said, taking her hand and giving it a squeeze.

"How far along are you?" she asked.

"Not far," I said, keeping my answer deliberately vague.

"But the child cannot be Matthew's. A *wearh* is not able to father a child." Mary said, her hand rising to her cheek in wonder. "Matthew welcomes the babe, even though it is not his?"

Though Matthew had warned me that everybody would assume the child belonged to another man, we hadn't discussed how to respond. I would have to punt.

"He considers it his own blood," I said firmly. My answer only seemed to increase her concern.

"You are fortunate that Matthew is so selfless when it comes to protecting those who are in need. And you—can *you* love the child, though you were taken against your will?"

Mary thought I'd been raped—and perhaps that Matthew had married me only to shield me from the stigma of being pregnant and single.

"The child is innocent. I cannot refuse it love." I was careful neither to deny nor confirm Mary's suspicions. Happily, she was satisfied with my response, and, characteristically, she probed no further. "As you can imagine," I added, "we are eager to keep this news quiet for as long as possible."

"Of course," Mary agreed. "I will have Joan make you a soft custard that fortifies the blood yet is very soothing to the stomach if taken at night before you sleep. It was a great help to me in my last pregnancy and seemed to lessen my sickness in the morning."

"I have been blessedly free of that complaint so far," I said, drawing on my gloves. "Matthew promises me it will come any day now."

"Hmm," Mary mused, a shadow crossing her face. I frowned, wondering what was worrying her now. She saw my expression and smiled brightly. "You should guard against fatigue. When you are here on Friday, you must not stand so long but take your ease on a stool while we work." Mary fussed over the arrangement of my cloak. "Stay out of drafts. And have Françoise make a poultice for your feet if they start to swell. I will send a receipt for it with the custard. Shall I have my boatman take you to Water Lane?"

"It's only a five-minute walk!" I protested with a laugh. Finally Mary let me leave on foot, but only after I assured her that I would avoid not only drafts but also cold water and loud noises.

That night I dreamed I slept under the limbs of a tree that grew from my womb. Its branches shielded me from the moonlight while, high above, a dragon flew through the night. When it reached the moon, the dragon's tail curled around it and the silver orb turned red.

I awoke to an empty bed and blood-soaked sheets.

"Françoise!" I cried, feeling a sudden, sharp cramp.

Matthew came running instead. The devastated look on his face when he reached my side confirmed my fears.

## 23

"We have all lost babes, Diana," Goody Alsop said sadly. "It is a pain most women know."

"All?" I looked around Goody Alsop's keeping room at the witches of the Garlickhythe gathering.

The stories tumbled out, of babies lost in childbirth and others who died at six months or six years. I didn't know any women who had miscarried— or I didn't think I did. Had one of my friends suffered such a loss, without my knowing it?

"You are young and strong," Susanna said. "There is no reason to think you cannot conceive another child."

No reason at all, except for the fact that my husband wouldn't touch me again until we were back in the land of birth control and fetal monitors.

"Maybe," I said with a noncommittal shrug.

"Where is Master Roydon?" Goody Alsop said quietly. Her fetch drifted around the parlor as if she thought she might find him in the window-seat cushions or sitting atop the cupboard.

"Out on business," I said, drawing my borrowed shawl tighter. It was Susanna's, and it smelled like burned sugar and chamomile, just as she did.

"I heard he was at the Middle Temple Hall with Christopher Marlowe last night. Watching a play, by all accounts." Catherine passed the box of comfits she'd brought to Goody Alsop.

"Ordinary men can pine terribly for a lost child. I am not surprised that a *wearh* would find it especially difficult. They are possessive, after all." Goody Alsop reached for something red and gelatinous. "Thank you, Catherine."

The women waited in silence, hoping I'd take Goody Alsop and Catherine up on their circumspect invitation to tell them how Matthew and I were faring.

"He'll be fine," I said tightly.

"He should be here," Elizabeth said sharply. "I can see no reason why his loss should be more painful than yours!"

"Because Matthew has endured a thousand years of heartbreak and I've only endured thirty-three," I said, my tone equally sharp. "He is a *wearh*, Elizabeth. Do I wish he were here rather than out with Kit? Of course. Will I beg him to stay at the Hart and Crown for my sake? Absolutely not." My voice was rising as my hurt and frustration spilled over. Matthew had been unfailingly sweet and tender with me. He'd comforted me as I faced the hundreds of fragile dreams for the future that had been destroyed when I miscarried our child.

It was the hours he was spending elsewhere that had me concerned.

"My head tells me Matthew must have a chance to grieve in his own way," I said. "My heart tells me he loves me even though he prefers to be with his friends now. I just wish he could touch me without regret." I could feel it whenever he looked at me, held me, took my hand. It was unbearable.

"I am sorry, Diana," Elizabeth said, her face contrite.

"It's all right," I assured her.

But it wasn't all right. The whole world felt discordant and wrong, with colors that were too bright and sounds so loud they made me jump. My body felt hollow, and no matter what I tried to read, the words failed to keep my attention.

"We will see you tomorrow, as planned," Goody Alsop said briskly as the witches departed.

"Tomorrow?" I frowned. "I'm in no mood to make magic, Goody Alsop."

"I'm in no mood to go to my grave without seeing you weave your first spell, so I shall expect you when the bells ring six."

That night I stared into the fire as the bells rang six, and seven, and eight, and nine, and ten. When the bells rang three, I heard a sound on the stairs. Thinking it was Matthew, I went to the door. The staircase was empty, but a clutch of objects sat on the stairs: an infant's sock, a sprig of holly, a twist of paper with a man's name written on it. I gathered them all up in my lap as I sank onto one of the worn treads, clutching my shawl tight around me.

I was still trying to figure out what the offerings meant and how they had gotten there when Matthew shot up the stairs in a soundless blur. He stopped abruptly.

"Diana." He drew the back of his hand across his mouth, his eyes green and glassy.

"At least you'll feed when you're with Kit," I said, getting to my feet.

"It's nice to know that your friendship includes more than poetry and chess."

Matthew put his boot on the tread next to my feet. He used his knee to press me toward the wall, effectively trapping me. His breath was sweet and slightly metallic.

"You're going to hate yourself in the morning," I said calmly, turning my head away. I knew better than to run when the tang of blood was still on his lips. "Kit should have kept you with him until the drugs were out of your system. Does all the blood in London have opiates in it?" It was the second night in a row Matthew had gone out with Kit and come home high as a kite.

"Not all," Matthew purred, "but it is the easiest to come by."

"What are these?" I held up the sock, the holly, and the scroll.

"They're for you," Matthew said. "More arrive every night. Pierre and I collect them before you are awake."

"When did this start?" I didn't trust myself to say more.

"The week before— The week you met with the Rede. Most are requests for help. Since you— Since Monday there have been gifts for you, too." Matthew held out his hand. "I'll take care of them."

I drew my hand closer to my heart. "Where are the rest?"

Matthew's mouth tightened, but he showed me where he was keeping them—in a box in the attic, shoved under one of the benches. I picked through the contents, which were somewhat similar to what Jack pulled out of his pockets each night: buttons, bits of ribbon, a piece of broken crockery. There were locks of hair, too, and dozens of pieces of paper inscribed with names. Though they were invisible to most eyes, I could see the jagged threads that hung from every treasure, all waiting to be tied off, joined up, or otherwise mended.

"These are requests for magic." I looked up at Matthew. "You shouldn't have kept this from me."

"I don't want you performing spells for every creature in the city of London," Matthew said, his eyes darkening.

"Well, I don't want you to eat out every night before going drinking with your friends! But you're a vampire, so sometimes that's what you need to do," I retorted. "I'm a witch, Matthew. Requests like this have to be handled carefully. My safety depends on my relations with our neighbors. I can't go stealing boats like Gallowglass or growling at people."

"*Milord.*" Pierre stood at the far end of the attics, where a narrow stair twirled down to a hidden exit behind the laundresses' giant washtubs.

"What?" Matthew said impatiently.

"Agnes Sampson is dead." Pierre looked frightened. "They took her to Castlehill in Edinburgh on Saturday, garroted her, and then burned the body."

"Christ." Matthew paled.

"Hancock said she was fully dead before the wood was lit. She wouldn't have felt anything," Pierre went on. It was a small mercy, one not always afforded to a convicted witch. "They refused to read your letter, *milord*. Hancock was told to leave Scottish politics to the Scottish king or they'd put the screws to him the next time he showed his face in Edinburgh."

"Why can't I fix this?" Matthew exploded.

"So it's not just the loss of the baby that's driven you toward Kit's darkness. You're hiding from the events in Scotland, too."

"No matter how hard I try to set things right, I cannot seem to break this cursed pattern," Matthew said. "Before, as the queen's spy, I delighted in the trouble in Scotland. As a member of the Congregation, I considered Sampson's death an acceptable price to pay to maintain the status quo. But now . . ."

"Now you're married to a witch," I said. "And everything looks different."

"Yes. I'm caught between what I once believed and what I now hold most dear, what I once proudly defended as gospel truth and the magnitude of what I no longer know."

"I will go back into the city," Pierre said, turning toward the door. "There may be more to discover."

I studied Matthew's tired face. "You can't expect to understand all of life's tragedies, Matthew. I wish we still had the baby, too. And I know it seems hopeless right now, but that doesn't mean there isn't a future to look forward to—one in which our children and family are safe."

"A miscarriage this early in pregnancy is almost always a sign of a genetic anomaly that makes the fetus nonviable. If that happened once . . ." His voice trailed off.

"There are genetic anomalies that don't compromise the baby," I pointed out. "Take me, for instance." I was a chimera, with mismatching DNA.

"I can't bear losing another child, Diana. I just . . . can't."

"I know." I was bone weary and wanted the blessed oblivion of sleep as much as he did. I had never known my child as he had known Lucas, and the pain was still unbearable. "I have to be at Goody Alsop's house at six tonight." I looked up at him. "Will you be out with Kit?"

"No," Matthew said softly. He pressed his lips to mine—briefly, regretfully. "I'll be with you."

Matthew was true to his word, and escorted me to Goody Alsop's before going to the Golden Gosling with Pierre. In the most courteous way possible, the witches explained that *wearhs* were not welcome. Taking a weaver safely through her forspell required a considerable mobilization of supernatural and magical energy. *Wearhs* would only get in the way.

My Aunt Sarah would have paid close attention to how Susanna and Marjorie readied the sacred circle. Some of the substances and equipment they used were familiar—like the salt they sprinkled on the floorboards to purify the space—but others were not. Sarah's witch's kit consisted of two knives (one with a black handle and one with a white), the Bishop grimoire, and various herbs and plants. Elizabethan witches required a greater variety of objects to work their magic, including brooms. I'd never seen a witch with a broom except on Halloween when they were de rigueur, along with pointed hats.

Each of the witches of the Garlickhythe gathering brought a unique broom with her to Goody Alsop's house. Marjorie's was fashioned from a cherry branch. At the top of the staff, someone had carved glyphs and symbols. Instead of the usual bristles, Marjorie had tied dried herbs and twigs to the bottom where the central limb forked into thinner branches. She told me that the herbs were important to her magic—agrimony to break enchantments, lacy feverfew with the white-and-yellow flowers still attached for protection, the sturdy stems of rosemary with their glaucous leaves for purification and clarity. Susanna's broom was made from elm, which was symbolic of the phases of life from birth to death and related to her profession as a midwife. So, too, were the plants tied to the staff: the fleshy green leaves of adder's tongue for healing, boneset's frothy white flower heads for protection, the spiky leaves of groundsel for good health.

Marjorie and Susanna carefully swept the salt in a clockwise direction until the fine grains had traveled over every inch of the floor. The salt would not only cleanse the space, Marjorie explained, but also ground it so that my power wouldn't spill over into the world once it was fully unbound.

Goody Alsop stopped up the windows, the doors—even the chimney. The house ghosts were given the option of staying out of the way amid the roof beams or finding temporary refuge with the family who lived downstairs. Not wishing to miss anything, and slightly jealous of the fetch who had no choice but to stay by her mistress, the ghosts flitted among the rafters and gossiped about whether any of the residents of Newgate Street would get a moment's peace now that the specters of medieval Queen Isabella and a murderess named Lady Agnes Hungerford had resumed their squabbling.

Elizabeth and Catherine settled my nerves—and drowned out the gruesome details of Lady Agnes's terrible deeds and death—by sharing some of their early magical adventures and drawing me out about my own. Elizabeth was impressed by how I'd channeled the water from under Sarah's orchard, pulling it into my palms drop by drop. And Catherine crowed with delight when I shared how a bow and arrow rested heavy in my hands just before the witchfire flew.

"The moon has risen," Marjorie said, her round face pink with anticipation. The shutters were closed, but none of the other witches questioned her.

"It is time, then," Elizabeth said briskly, all business.

Each witch went from one corner of the room to the next, breaking off a twig from her broom and placing it there. But these were not random piles. They'd arranged the twigs so as to overlap and form a pentacle, the witch's five-pointed star.

Goody Alsop and I took up our positions at the center of the circle. Though its boundaries were invisible, that would change when the other witches took their appointed places. Once they had, Catherine murmured a spell and a curved line of fire traveled from witch to witch, binding the circle.

Power surged in its center. Goody Alsop had warned me that what we were doing this night invoked ancient magics. Soon the buffeting wave of energy was replaced by something that tingled and snapped like a thousand witchy glances.

"Look around you with your witch's sight," Goody Alsop said, "and tell me what you see."

When my third eye opened, I half expected to find that the air itself had come to life, every particle charged with possibility. Instead the room was filled with filaments of magic.

"Threads," I said, "as though the world is nothing more than a tapestry."

Goody Alsop nodded. "To be a weaver is to be tied to the world around you and see it in strands and hues. While some ties fetter your magic, others yoke the power in your blood to the four elements and the great mysteries that lie beyond them. Weavers learn how to release the ties that bind and use the rest."

"But I don't know how to tell them apart." Hundreds of strands brushed against my skirts and bodice.

"Soon you will test them, like a bird tests its wings, to discover what secrets they hold for you. Now, we will simply cut them all away, so that they can return to you unbound. As I snip the threads, you must resist the temptation to grab at the power around you. Because you are a weaver, you will want to mend what is broken. Leave your thoughts free and your mind empty. Let the power do as it will."

Goody Alsop released my arm and began to weave her spell with sounds that bore no resemblance to speech but were strangely familiar. With each utterance I saw the filaments fall away from me, coiling and twisting. A roaring filled my ears. My arms heeded the sound as if it were a command, rising up and stretching out until I was standing in the same T-shaped position that Matthew had placed me in at the Bishop house when I drew the water from underneath Sarah's old orchard.

The strands of magic—all those threads of power that I could borrow but not hold—crept back toward me as if they were made of iron filings and I were a magnet. As they came to rest in my hands, I struggled against the urge to close my fists around them. The desire to do so was strong, as Goody Alsop predicted it would be, but I let them slide over my skin like the satin ribbons in the stories my mother told me when I was a child.

So far everything had happened as Goody Alsop had told me it would. But no one could predict what might occur when my powers took shape, and the witches around the circle braced themselves to meet the unknown. Goody Alsop had warned me that not all weavers shaped a familiar in their forspell, so I shouldn't expect one to appear. But my life these past months had taught me that the unexpected was more likely than not when I was around.

The roaring intensified, and the air stirred. A swirling ball of energy hung directly over my head. It drew power from the room but kept collapsing into its own center like a black hole. My witch's eye closed tightly against the dizzying, roiling sight.

Something pulsed in the midst of the storm. It pulled free and took on a shadowy form. As soon as it did so, Goody Alsop fell silent. She gave me one final, long look before she left me, alone, in the center of the circle.

There was a beating of wings, the lash of a barbed tail. A hot, moist breath licked across my cheek. A transparent creature with the reptilian head of a dragon hovered in the air, bright wings striking the rafters and sending the ghosts scuttling for cover. It had only two legs, and the curved talons on its feet looked as deadly as the points along its long tail.

"How many legs does it have?" Marjorie called, unable to see clearly from her position. "Is it just a dragon?"

*Just a dragon?*

"It's a firedrake," Catherine said in wonder. She raised her arms, ready to cast a warding spell if it decided to strike. Elizabeth Jackson's arms moved, too.

"Wait!" Goody Alsop cried, interrupting their magic. "Diana has not yet completed her weaving. Perhaps she will find a way to tame her."

*Tame her?* I looked at Goody Alsop incredulously. I wasn't even sure if the creature before me was substance or spirit. She seemed real, but I could see right through her.

"I don't know what to do," I said, beginning to panic. Every flap of the creature's wings sent a shower of sparks and drops of fire into the room.

"Some spells begin with an idea, others with a question. There are many ways to think about what comes next: tying a knot, twisting a rope, even forging a chain like the one that you made between you and your *wearh*," Goody Alsop said, her tone low and soothing. "Let the power move through you."

The firedrake roared in impatience, her feet extending toward me. What did she want? A chance to pick me up and carry me from the house? A comfortable place to perch and rest her wings?

The floor underneath me creaked.

"Step aside!" Marjorie cried.

I moved just in time. A moment later a tree sprouted from the place where my feet had recently been planted. The trunk rose up, divided into two stout limbs, and branched out further. Shoots grew into green leaves at the tips, and then came white blossoms, and finally red berries. In a matter of seconds, I was standing beneath a full-grown tree, one that was flowering and fruiting at the same time.

The firedrake's feet gripped at the tree's uppermost branches. For a moment she seemed to rest there. A branch creaked and cracked. The firedrake lifted back into the air, a gnarled piece of the tree clutched in her talons. The firedrake's tongue flicked out in a lash of fire, and the tree burst into flame. There were far too many flammable objects in the room—the wooden floors and furniture, the fabric that clothed the witches. All I could think was that I must stop the fire from spreading. I needed water—and lots of it.

There was a heavy weight in my right hand. I looked down, expecting to see a bucket. Instead I was holding an arrow. Witchfire. But what good was more fire?

"No, Diana! Don't try to shape the spell!" Goody Alsop warned.

I shook myself free of thoughts of rain and rivers. As soon as I did, instinct took over and my two arms rose in front of me, my right hand drew back, and once my fingers unfurled, the arrow flew into the heart of the tree. The flames shot up high and fast, blinding me. The heat died down, and when my sight returned, I found myself atop a mountain under a vast, starry sky. A huge crescent moon hung low in the heavens.

"I've been waiting for you." The goddess's voice was little more than a breath of wind. She was wearing soft robes, her hair cascading down her back. There was no sign of her usual weapons, but a large dog padded along at her side. He was so big and black he might have been a wolf.

"You." A sense of dread squeezed around my heart. I had been expecting to see the goddess since I lost the baby. "Did you take my child in exchange for saving Matthew's life?" My question came out part fury, part despair.

"No. That debt is settled. I have already taken another. A dead child is of no use to me." The huntress's eyes were green as the first shoots of willow in spring.

My blood ran cold. "Whose life have you taken?"

"Yours."

"Mine?" I said numbly. "Am I . . . dead?"

"Of course not. The dead belong to another. It is the living I seek." The huntress's voice was now as piercing and bright as a moonbeam. "You promised I could take anyone—anything—in exchange for the life of the one you love. I chose you. And I am not done with you yet."

The goddess took a step backward. "You gave your life to me, Diana Bishop. It is now time to make use of it."

A cry overhead alerted me to the presence of the firedrake. I looked up, trying to make her out against the moon. When I blinked, her outline was perfectly visible against Goody Alsop's ceiling. I was back in the witch's house, no longer on a barren hilltop with the goddess. The tree was gone, reduced to a heap of ash. I blinked again.

The firedrake blinked back at me. Her eyes were sad and familiar—black, with silver irises rather than white. With another harsh cry, she released her talons. The branch of the tree fell into my arms. It felt like the arrow's shaft, heavier and more substantial than its size would suggest. The firedrake bobbed her head, smoke coming in wisps from her nostrils. I was tempted to reach up and touch her, wondering if her skin would be warm and soft like a snake, but something told me she wouldn't welcome it. And I didn't want to startle her. She might rear back and poke her head through the roof. I was already worried about the condition of Goody Alsop's house after the tree and the fire.

"Thank you," I whispered.

The firedrake replied with a quiet moan of fire and song. Her silver-and-black eyes were ancient and wise as she studied me, her tail flicking back and forth pensively. She stretched her wings to their full extent before tightening them around her body and dematerializing.

All that was left of the firedrake was a tingling sensation in my ribs that told me somehow she was inside me, waiting until I needed her. With the weight of this beast heavily inside me, I fell to my knees, and the branch clattered to the floor. The witches rushed forward.

Goody Alsop reached me first, her thin arms reaching around to gather me close. "You did well, child, you did well," she whispered. Elizabeth cupped her hand and with a few words transformed it into a shallow silver dipper full of water. I drank from it, and when the cup was empty, it went back to being nothing more than a hand.

"This is a great day, Goody Alsop," Catherine said, her face wreathed in smiles.

"Aye, and a hard one for such a young witch," Goody Alsop said. "You do nothing by halves, Diana Roydon. First you are no ordinary witch but a weaver. And then you weave a forspell that called forth a rowan tree simply to tame a firedrake. Had I foreseen this, I would not have believed it."

"I saw the goddess," I explained as they helped me to my feet, "and a dragon."

"That was no dragon," Elizabeth said.

"It had but two legs," Marjorie explained. "That makes her not only a creature of fire but one of water, too, capable of moving between the elements. The firedrake is a union of opposites."

"What is true of the firedrake is true of the rowan tree as well," Goody Alsop said with a proud smile. "It is not every day that a rowan tree pushes its branches into one world while leaving its roots in another."

In spite of the happy chatter of the women who surrounded me, I found myself thinking of Matthew. He was waiting at the Golden Gosling for news. My third eye opened, seeking out a twisted thread of black and red that led from my heart, across the room, through the keyhole, and into the darkness beyond. I gave it a tug, and the chain inside me responded with a sympathetic chime.

"If I'm not very much mistaken, Master Roydon will be around shortly to collect his wife," Goody Alsop said drily. "Let's get you on your feet, or he'll think we cannot be trusted with you."

"Matthew can be protective," I said apologetically. "Even more so since . . ."

"I've never known a *wearh* who wasn't. It's their nature," Goody Alsop said, helping me up. The air had gone particulate again, brushing softly against my skin as I moved.

"Master Roydon need not fear in this case," Elizabeth said. "We will make sure you can find your way back from the darkness, just like your firedrake."

"What darkness?"

The witches went silent.

"What darkness?" I repeated, pushing my fatigue aside.

Goody Alsop sighed. "There are witches—a very few witches—who can move between this world and the next."

"Time spinners," I said with a nod. "Yes, I know. I'm one of them."

"Not between this *time* and the next, Diana, but between this *world* and the next." Marjorie gestured at the branch by my feet. "Life—and death. You can be in both worlds. That is why the rowan chose you, not the alder or the birch."

"We did wonder if this might be the case. You were able to conceive a *wearh*'s child, after all." Goody Alsop looked at me intently. The blood had drained from my face. "What is it, Diana?"

"The quinces. And the flowers." My knees weakened again but I remained standing. "Mary Sidney's shoe. And the oak tree in Madison."

"And the *wearh*," Goody Alsop said softly, understanding without my telling her. "So many signs pointing to the truth."

A muffled thumping rose from outdoors.

"He mustn't know," I said urgently, grabbing at Goody Alsop's hand. "Not now. It's too soon after the baby, and Matthew doesn't want me meddling with matters of life and death."

"It is a bit late for that," she said sadly.

"Diana!" Matthew's fist pounded on the door.

"The *wearh* will split the wood in two," Marjorie observed. "Master Roydon won't be able to break the binding spell and enter, but the door will make a fearsome crash when it gives way. Think of your neighbors, Goody Alsop."

Goody Alsop gestured with her hand. The air thickened, then relaxed.

Matthew was standing before me in the space of a heartbeat. His gray eyes raked over me. "What happened here?"

"If Diana wants you to know, she will tell you," said Goody Alsop. She turned to me. "In light of what happened tonight, I think you should spend time with Catherine and Elizabeth tomorrow."

"Thank you, Goody," I murmured, grateful that she had not revealed my secrets.

"Wait." Catherine went to the branch from the rowan tree and snapped off a thin twig. "Take this. You should have a piece with you at all times for a talisman." Catherine dropped the bit of wood into my palm.

Not only Pierre but Gallowglass and Hancock were waiting for us in the street. They hustled me into a boat that waited at the bottom of Garlic Hill. After we arrived back at Water Lane Matthew sent everyone away, and we were left in the blissful quiet of our bedchamber.

"I don't need to know what happened," Matthew said roughly, closing the door behind him. "I just need to know that you're truly all right."

"I'm truly fine." I turned my back to him so that he could loosen the laces on my bodice.

"You're afraid of something. I can smell it." Matthew spun me around to face him.

"I'm afraid of what I might find out about myself." I met his eyes squarely.

"You'll find your truth." He sounded so sure, so unconcerned. But he didn't know about the dragon and the rowan and what they meant for a weaver. Matthew didn't know that my life belonged to the goddess either, nor that it was because of the bargain I'd made to save him.

"What if I become someone else and you don't like her?"

"Not possible," he assured me, drawing me closer.

"Even if we find out that the powers of life and death are in my blood?" Matthew pulled away.

"Saving you in Madison wasn't a fluke, Matthew. I breathed life into Mary's shoes, too—just as I sucked the life out of the oak tree at Sarah's and the quinces here."

"Life and death are big responsibilities." Matthew's gray-green eyes were somber. "But I will love you regardless. You forget, I have power over life and death, too. What is it you told me that night I went hunting in Oxford? You said there was no difference between us. *'Occasionally I eat partridge. Occasionally you feed on deer.'*

"We are more similar, you and I, than either of us imagined," Matthew continued. "But if you can believe good of me, knowing what you do of my past deeds, then you must allow me to believe the same of you."

Suddenly I wanted to share my secrets. "There was a firedrake and a tree—"

"And the only thing that matters is that you are safely home," he said, quieting me with a kiss.

Matthew held me so long and so tightly that for a few blissful moments I—almost—believed him.

The next day I went to Goody Alsop's house to meet with Elizabeth Jackson and Catherine Streeter as promised. Annie accompanied me, but she was sent over to Susanna's house to wait until my lesson was done.

The rowan branch was propped up in the corner. Otherwise the room looked perfectly ordinary and not at all like the kind of place where witches drew sacred circles or summoned firedrakes. Still, I expected some more visible signs that magic was about to be performed—a cauldron, perhaps, or colored candles to signify the elements.

Goody Alsop gestured to the table, where four chairs were arranged.

"Come, Diana, and sit. We thought we might begin at the beginning. Tell us about your family. Much is revealed by following a witch's bloodline."

"But I thought you would teach me how to weave spells with fire and water."

"What is blood, if not fire and water?" Elizabeth said.

Three hours later I was talked out and exhausted from dredging up memories of my childhood—the feeling of being watched, Peter Knox's visit to the house, my parents' death. But the three witches didn't stop there. I relived every moment of high school and college, too: the daemons who followed me, the few spells I could perform without too much trouble, the strange occurrences that began only after I met Matthew. If there was a pattern to any of it, I failed to see it, but Goody Alsop sent me off with assurances that they would soon have a plan.

I dragged myself to Baynard's Castle. Mary tucked me into a chair and refused my help, insisting I rest while she figured out what was wrong with our batch of *prima materia*. It had gone all black and sludgy, with a thin film of greenish goo on top.

My thoughts drifted while Mary worked. The day was sunny, and a beam of light sliced through the smoky air and fell on the mural depicting the alchemical dragon. I sat forward in my chair.

"No," I said. "It can't be."

But it was. The dragon was not a dragon for it had only two legs. It was a firedrake and carried its barbed tail in its mouth, like the ouroboros on the de Clermont banner. The firedrake's head was tilted to the sky, and it held a crescent moon in its jaws. A multipointed star rose above it. *Matthew's emblem*. How had I not noticed before?

"What is it, Diana?" asked a frowning Mary.

"Would you do something for me, Mary, even if the request is strange?" I was already untying the silk cord at my wrists in anticipation of her answer.

"Of course. What is it you need?"

The firedrake dripped squiggly blobs of blood into the alchemical vessel below its wings. There the blood swam in a sea of mercury and silver.

"I want you to take my blood and put it in a solution of aqua fortis, silver, and mercury," I said. Mary's glance moved from me to the firedrake and back. "For what is blood but fire and water, a conjunction of opposites, and a chemical wedding?"

"Very well, Diana," Mary agreed, sounding mystified. But she asked no more questions.

I flicked my finger confidently over the scar on my inner arm. I had no need for a knife this time. The skin parted, as I knew it would, and the blood welled up simply because I had need of it. Joan rushed forward with a small bowl to catch the red liquid. On the wall above, the silver and black eyes of the firedrake followed the drops as they fell.

"*It begins with absence and desire, it begins with blood and fear,*" I whispered.

"*It began with a discovery of witches,*" time responded, in a primeval echo that set alight the blue and amber threads that flickered against the room's stone walls.

24

"Is it going to keep doing that?" I stood, frowning, hands on my hips, and stared up at Susanna's ceiling.

"'She,' Diana. Your firedrake is female," Catherine said. She was also looking at the ceiling, her expression bemused.

"She. It. That." I pointed up. I had been trying to weave a spell when my dragon escaped confinement within my rib cage. Again. She was now plastered to the ceiling, breathing out gusts of smoke and chattering her teeth in agitation. "I can't have it—her—flying around the room whenever she feels the urge." The repercussions would be serious should she become loose at Yale among the students.

"That your firedrake broke free is merely a symptom of a much more serious problem." Goody Alsop extended a bunch of brightly colored silken strands, knotted together at the top. The ends flowed free like the ribbons on a maypole and numbered nine in all, in shades of red, white, black, silver, gold, green, brown, blue, and yellow. "You are a weaver and must learn to control your power."

"I am well aware of that, Goody Alsop, but I still don't see how this—embroidery floss—will help," I said stubbornly. The dragon squawked in agreement, waxing more substantial with the sound and then waning into her typical smoky outlines.

"And what do you know about being a weaver?" Goody Alsop asked sharply.

"Not much," I confessed.

"Diana should sip this first." Susanna approached me with a steaming cup. The scents of chamomile and mint filled the air. My dragon cocked her head in interest. "It is a calming draft and may soothe her beast."

"I am not so concerned with the firedrake," Catherine said dismissively. "Getting one to obey is always difficult—like trying to curb a daemon who is intent on making mischief." It was, I thought, easy for her to say. She didn't have to persuade the beast to climb back inside her.

"What plants went into the tisane?" I asked, taking a sip of Susanna's brew. After Marthe's tea I was a bit suspicious of herbal concoctions. No sooner was the question out of my mouth than the cup began to bloom with sprigs of mint, the straw-scented flowers of chamomile, foamy Angelica, and some stiff, glossy leaves that I couldn't identify. I swore.

"You see!" Catherine said, pointing to the cup. "It's as I said. When Diana asks a question, the goddess answers it."

Susanna looked at her beaker with alarm as it cracked under the pressure of the swelling roots. "I think you are right, Catherine. But if she is to weave rather than break things, she will need to ask better questions."

Goody Alsop and Catherine had figured out the secret to my power: It was inconveniently tied to my curiosity. Now certain events made better sense: my white table and its brightly colored puzzle pieces that came to my rescue whenever I faced a problem, the butter flying out of Sarah's refrigerator in Madison when I wondered if there was more. Even the strange appearance of Ashmole 782 at the Bodleian Library could be explained: When I filled out the call slip, I'd wondered what might be in the volume. Earlier today my simple musings about who might have written one of the spells in Susanna's grimoire had caused the ink to unspool from the page and re-form on the table next to it in an exact likeness of her dead grandmother.

I promised Susanna to put the words back as soon as I figured out how.

And so I discovered that the practice of magic was not unlike the practice of history. The trick to both wasn't finding the correct answers but formulating better questions.

"Tell us again about calling witchwater, Diana, and the bow and arrow that appear when someone you love is in trouble," Susanna suggested. "Perhaps that will provide some method we can follow."

I rehearsed the events of the night Matthew had left me at Sept-Tours when the water had come out of me in a flood and the morning in Sarah's orchard when I'd seen the veins of water underground. And I carefully accounted for every time the bow had appeared—even when there was no arrow or when there was but I didn't shoot it. When I finished, Catherine drew a satisfied sigh.

"I see the problem now. Diana is not fully present unless she is protecting someone or when forced to face her fears," Catherine observed. "She is always puzzling over the past or wondering about the future. A witch must be entirely in the here and now to work magic." My firedrake flapped her wings in agreement, sending warm gusts of air around the room.

"Matthew always thought there was a connection between my emotions, my needs, and my magic," I told them.

"Sometimes I wonder if that *wearh* is not part witch," Catherine said. The others laughed at the ridiculous notion of Ysabeau de Clermont's son having even a drop of witch's blood.

"I think it's safe to leave the firedrake to her own devices for the time being and return to the matter of Diana's disguising spell," Goody Alsop said, referring to my need to shield the surfeit of energy that was released whenever I used magic. "Are you making any progress?"

"I felt wisps of smoke form around me," I said hesitantly.

"You need to focus on your knots," Goody Alsop said, looking pointedly at the cords in my lap. Each shade could be found in the threads that bound the worlds, and manipulating the cords—twisting and tying them—worked a sympathetic magic. But first I needed to know which strands to use. I took hold of the colorful cords by the topknot. Goody Alsop had taught me how to blow gently on the strands while focusing my intentions. That was supposed to loosen the appropriate cords for whatever spell I was trying to weave.

I blew into the strands so that they shimmered and danced. The yellow and brown cords worked themselves loose and dropped into my lap, along with the red, blue, silver, and white. I ran my fingers down the nine-inch lengths of twisted silk. Six strands meant six different knots, each one more complex than the last.

My knot-making skills were still clumsy, but I found this part of weaving oddly soothing. When I practiced the elaborate twistings and crossings with ordinary string, the result was something reminiscent of ancient Celtic knotwork. There was a hierarchical order to the knots. The first two were single and double slipknots. Sarah used them sometimes, when she was making a love spell or some other binding. But only weavers could make the intricate knots that involved as many as nine distinct crossings and ended with the two free ends of the cord magically fused to make an unbreakable weaving.

I took a deep breath and refocused my intentions. A disguise was a form of protection, and purple was its color. But there was no purple cord.

Without delay the blue and red cords rose up and spun together so tightly that the final result looked exactly like the mottled purple candles that my mother used to set in the windows on the nights when the moon was dark.

"With knot of one, the spell's begun," I murmured, looping the purple cord into the simple slipknot. The firedrake crooned an imitation of my words.

I looked up at her and was struck once again by the firedrake's changeable appearance. When she breathed out, she faded into a blurred smudge of smoke. When she breathed in, her outlines sharpened. She was a perfect balance of substance and spirit, neither one nor the other. Would I ever feel that coherent?

"With knot of two, the spell be true." I made a double knot along the same purple cord. Wondering if there was a way I could fade into gray obscurity whenever I wished, the way the firedrake did, I ran the yellow cord through my fingers. The third knot was the first true weaver's knot I had to make. Though it involved only three crossings, it was still a challenge.

"With knot of three, the spell is free." I looped and twisted the cord into a trefoil shape, then drew the ends together. They fused to form the weaver's unbreakable knot.

Sighing with relief, I dropped it into my lap, and from my mouth came a gray mist finer than smoke. It hung around me like a shroud. I gasped in surprise, letting out more of the eerie, transparent fog. I looked up. Where had the firedrake gone? The brown cord leaped into my fingers.

"With knot of four, the power is stored." I loved the pretzel-like shape of the fourth knot, with its sinuous bends and twists.

"Very good, Diana," Goody Alsop said. This was the moment in my spells when everything tended to go wrong. "Now, remain in the moment and bid the dragon to stay with you. If she is so inclined, she will hide you from curious eyes."

The firedrake's cooperation seemed too much to hope for, but I made the pentacle-shaped knot anyway, using the white cord. "With knot of five, the spell will thrive."

The firedrake swooped down and nestled her wings against my ribs.

*Will you stay with me?* I silently asked her.

The firedrake wrapped me in a fine gray cocoon. It dulled the black of my skirts and jacket, turning them a deep charcoal. Ysabeau's ring glittered less brightly, the fire at the heart of the diamond dimmed. Even the silver cord in my lap looked tarnished. I smiled at the firedrake's silent answer.

"With knot of six, this spell I fix," I said. My final knot was not as symmetrical as it should have been, but it held nonetheless.

"You are indeed a weaver, child," Goody Alsop said, letting out her breath.

I felt marvelously inconspicuous on my walk home, wrapped in my firedrake muffler, but came to life again when my feet crossed over the threshold of the Hart and Crown. A package waited for me there, along with Kit. Matthew was still spending too much time with the mercurial daemon. Marlowe and I exchanged cool greetings, and I had started unpicking the package's protective wrappings when Matthew let out a mighty roar.

"Good Christ!" Where moments before there was empty space, there was now Matthew, staring at a piece of paper in disbelief.

"What does the Old Fox want now?" Kit asked sourly, jamming his pen into a pot of ink.

"I just received a bill from Nicholas Vallin, the goldsmith up the lane," Matthew said, scowling. I looked at him innocently. "He charged me fifteen pounds for a mousetrap." Now that I better understood the purchasing power of a pound—and that Mary's servant Joan earned only five pounds a year—I could see why Matthew was shocked.

"Oh. That." I returned my attention to the package. "I asked him to make it."

"You had one of the finest goldsmiths in London make you a mousetrap?" Kit was incredulous. "If you have any more funds to spare, Mistress Roydon, I hope you will allow me to undertake an alchemical experiment for you. I will transmute your silver and gold into wine at the Cardinal's Hat!"

"It's a rat trap, not a mousetrap," I muttered.

"Might I see this rat trap?" Matthew's tone was ominously even.

I removed the last of the wrappings and held out the article in question.

"Silver gilt. And engraved, too," Matthew said, turning it over in his hand. After looking more closely at it, he swore. *"'Ars longa, vita brevis.' Art is long, but life is short.* Indeed."

"It's supposed to be very effective." Monsieur Vallin's cunning design resembled a watchful feline, with a pair of finely worked ears on the hinge, a wide set of eyes carved into the cross brace. The edges of the trap resembled a mouth, complete with lethal teeth. It reminded me a bit of Sarah's cat, Tabitha. Vallin had provided an added bit of whimsy by perching a silver mouse on the cat's nose. The tiny creature bore no resemblance to the long-toothed monsters that prowled around our attics. The mere thought of them munching their way through Matthew's papers while we slept made me shudder.

"Look. He's engraved the bottom of it, too," Kit said, following the romping mice around the base of the trap. "It bears the rest of Hippocrates' aphorism—and in Latin, no less. *'Occasio præceps, experimentum periculosum, iudicium difficile.'*"

"It may be an excessively sentimental inscription, given the instrument's purpose," I admitted.

"Sentimental?" Matthew's eyebrow shot up. "From the viewpoint of the rat, it sounds quite realistic: *Opportunity is fleeting, experiment dangerous, and judgment difficult.*" His mouth twitched.

"Vallin took advantage of you, Mistress Roydon," Kit pronounced. "You should refuse payment, Matt, and send the trap back."

"No!" I protested. "It's not his fault. We were talking about clocks, and Monsieur Vallin showed me some beautiful examples. I shared my pamphlet from John Chandler's shop in Cripplegate—the one with the instructions on how to catch vermin—and told Monsieur Vallin about our rat problem. One thing led to another." I looked down at the trap. It really was an extraordinary piece of craftsmanship, with its tiny gears and springs.

"All of London has a rat problem," Matthew said, struggling for control. "Yet I know of no one who requires a silver-gilt toy to resolve it. A few affordable cats normally suffice."

"I'll pay him, Matthew." Doing so would probably empty out my purse, and I would be forced to ask Walter for more funds, but it couldn't be helped. Experience was always valuable. Sometimes it was costly, too. I held out my hand for the trap.

"Did Vallin design it to strike the hours? If so, and it is the world's only combined timepiece and pest-control device, perhaps the price is fair after all." Matthew was trying to frown, but his face broke into a grin. Instead of giving me the trap, he took my hand, brought it to his mouth, and kissed it. "I'll pay the bill, *mon coeur,* if only to have the right to tease you about it for the next sixty years."

At that moment George hurried into the front hall. A blast of cold air entered with him.

"I have news!" He flung his cloak aside and struck a proud pose.

Kit groaned and put his head in his hands. "Don't tell me. That idiot Ponsonby is pleased with your translation of Homer and wants to publish it without further corrections."

"Not even you will dim my pleasure in today's achievements, Kit." George looked around expectantly. "Well? Are none of you the least bit curious?"

"What is your news, George?" Matthew said absently, tossing the trap into the air and catching it again.

"I found Mistress Roydon's manuscript."

Matthew's grip on the rat trap tightened. The mechanism sprang open. When he released his fingers, it fell to the table with a clatter as it snapped shut again. "Where?"

George took an instinctive step backward. I'd been on the receiving end of my husband's questions and understood how disconcerting a full blast of vampiric attention could be.

"I knew you were the man to find it," I told George warmly, putting my hand on Matthew's sleeve to slow him down. George was predictably mollified by this remark and returned to the table, where he pulled out a chair and sat.

"Your confidence means a great deal to me, Mistress Roydon," George said, taking off his gloves. He sniffed. "Not everyone shares it."

"Where. Is. It?" Matthew asked slowly, his jaw clenched.

"It is in the most obvious place imaginable, hiding in plain sight. I am rather surprised we did not think of it straightaway." He paused once more to make sure he had everyone's full attention. Matthew emitted a barely audible growl of frustration.

"George," Kit warned. "Matthew has been known to bite."

"Dr. Dee has it," George blurted out when Matthew shifted his weight.

"The queen's astrologer," I said. George was right: We should have thought of the man long before this. Dee was an alchemist, too—and had the largest library in England. "But he's in Europe."

"Dr. Dee returned from Europe over a year ago. He's living outside London now."

"Please tell me he isn't a witch, daemon, or vampire," I entreated.

"He's just a human—and an utter fraud," Marlowe said. "I wouldn't trust a thing he says, Matt. He used poor Edward abominably, forcing him to peer into crystal stones and talk to angels about alchemy day and night. Then Dee took all the credit!"

"'Poor Edward'?" Walter scoffed, opening the door without invitation or ceremony and stepping inside. Henry Percy was with him. No member of the School of Night could be within a mile of the Hart and Crown and not be drawn irresistibly to our hearth. "Your daemon friend led him by the nose for years. Dr. Dee is well rid of him, if you ask me." Walter picked up the rat trap. "What's this?"

"The goddess of the hunt has turned her attention to smaller prey," Kit said with a smirk.

"Why, that's a mousetrap. But no one would be foolish enough to make a mousetrap out of silver gilt," Henry said, looking over Walter's shoulder. "It looks like Nicholas Vallin's work. He made Essex a handsome watch when he became a Knight of the Garter. Is it a child's toy of some sort?"

A vampire's fist crashed onto my table, splitting the wood.

"George," Matthew ground out, "do tell us about Dr. Dee."

"Ah. Yes. Of course. There is not much to tell. I did w-what you asked," George stammered. "I visited the bookstalls, but there was no information to be had. There was talk of a volume of Greek poetry for sale that sounded most promising for my translation—but I digress." George stopped and gulped. "Widow Jugge suggested I talk to John Hester, the apothecary at Paul's Wharf. Hester sent me to Hugh Plat—you know, the vintner who lives in St. James Garlickhythe." I followed this complicated intellectual pilgrimage closely, hoping I might reconstruct George's route when I next visited Susanna. Perhaps she and Plat were neighbors.

"Plat is as bad as Will," Walter said under his breath, "forever writing things down that are none of his concern. The fellow asked after my mother's method for making pastry."

"Master Plat said that Dr. Dee has a book from the emperor's library. No man can read it, and there are strange pictures in it, too," George explained. "Plat saw it when he went to Dr. Dee for alchemical guidance."

Matthew and I exchanged looks.

"It's possible, Matthew," I said in a low voice. "Elias Ashmole tracked down what was left of Dee's library after his death, and he was particularly interested in the alchemical books."

"Dee's death. And how did the good doctor meet his end, Mistress Roydon?" Marlowe asked softly, his brown eyes nudging me. Henry, who hadn't heard Kit's question, spoke before I could answer.

"I will ask to see it," Henry said, nodding decidedly. "It will be easy enough to arrange on my way back to Richmond and the queen."

"You might not recognize it, Hal," Matthew said, prepared to ignore Kit as well, even though he had heard him. "I'll go with you."

"You didn't see it either." I shook my head, hoping to loosen Marlowe's prodding stare. "Besides, if there's a visit being paid to John Dee, I'm going."

"You needn't give me that fierce look, *ma lionne*. I know perfectly well that nothing will convince you to leave this to me. Not if there are books and an alchemist involved." Matthew held up an admonishing finger. "But no questions. Understood?" He had seen the magical mayhem that could result.

I nodded, but my fingers were crossed in the fold of my skirt in that age-old charm to ward off the evil consequences that came from knotting up the truth.

"No questions from Mistress Roydon?" Walter muttered. "I wish you luck with that, Matt."

Mortlake was a small hamlet on the Thames located between London and the queen's palace at Richmond. We made the trip in the Earl of Northumberland's barge, a splendid vessel with eight oarsmen, padded seats, and curtains to keep out the drafts. It was a far more comfortable—not to mention more sedate—journey than I was accustomed to when Gallowglass wielded the oars.

We'd sent a letter ahead warning Dee of our intention to visit him. Mrs. Dee, Henry explained with great delicacy, did not appreciate guests who dropped in unannounced. Though I could sympathize, it was unusual at a time when open-door hospitality was the rule.

"The household is somewhat . . . er, irregular because of Dr. Dee's pursuits," Henry explained, turning slightly pink. "And they have a prodigious number of children. It is often rather . . . chaotic."

"So much so that the servants have been known to throw themselves down the well," Matthew observed pointedly.

"Yes. That was unfortunate. I doubt any such thing will happen during our visit," Henry muttered.

I didn't care what state the household was in. We were on the brink of being able to answer so many questions: why this book was so sought after, if it could tell us more about how we creatures had come into being. And of course Matthew believed that it might shed light on why we otherworldly creatures were going extinct in our modern times.

Whether for propriety's sake or to avoid his disorderly brood, Dr. Dee was strolling in his brick-walled garden as if it were high summer and not the end of January. He was wearing the black robes of a scholar, and a tight-fitting hood covered his head and extended down his neck, topped with a flat cap. A long white beard jutted from his chin, and his arms were clasped behind his back as he made his slow progress around the barren garden.

"Dr. Dee?" Henry called over the wall.

"Lord Northumberland! I trust you are in good health?" Dee's voice was quiet and raspy, though he took care (as most did) to alter it slightly for Henry's benefit. He removed his cap and swept a bow.

"Passable for the time of year, Dr. Dee. We are not here about my health, though. I have friends with me, as I explained in my letter. Let me introduce you."

"Dr. Dee and I are already acquainted." Matthew gave Dee a wolfish smile and a low bow. He knew every other strange creature of the time. Why not Dee?

"Master Roydon," Dee said warily.

"This is my wife, Diana," Matthew said, inclining his head in my direction. "She is a friend to the Countess of Pembroke and joins her ladyship in alchemical pursuits."

"The Countess of Pembroke and I have corresponded on alchemical matters." Dee forgot all about me and focused instead on his own close connection to a peer of the realm. "Your message indicated you wanted to see one of my books, Lord Northumberland. Are you here on Lady Pembroke's behalf?"

Before Henry could respond, a sharp-faced, ample-hipped woman came out of the house in a dark brown gown trimmed with fur that had seen better days. She looked irritated, then spotted the Earl of Northumberland and plastered a welcoming look over her face.

"And here is my own dear wife," Dee said uneasily. "The Earl of Northumberland and Master Roydon are arrived, Jane," he called out.

"Why haven't you asked them inside?" Jane scolded, wringing her hands in distress. "They will think we are not prepared to receive guests, which of course we are, at all times. Many seek out my husband's counsel, my lord."

"Yes. That is what brings us here, too. You are in good health I see, Mistress Dee. And I understand from Master Roydon that the queen recently graced your house with a visit."

Jane preened. "Indeed. John has seen Her Majesty three times since November. The last two times she happened upon us at our far gate, as she rode along the Richmond road."

"Her Majesty was generous to us this Christmas," Dee said. He twisted the cap in his hands. Jane looked at him sourly. "We had thought . . . but it is no matter."

"Delightful, delightful," Henry said quickly, rescuing Dee from any potential awkwardness. "But enough small talk. There is a particular book we wished to see—"

"My husband's library is esteemed more than he is!" Jane said sullenly. "Our expenses while visiting the emperor were extreme, and we have many mouths to feed. The queen said she would help us. She did give us a small reward but promised more."

"No doubt the queen was distracted by more pressing concerns." Matthew had a small, heavy pouch in his hands. "I have the balance of her gift here. And I value your husband, Mistress Dee, not just his books. I've added to Her Majesty's purse for his pains on our behalf."

"I . . . I thank you, Master Roydon," Dee stammered, exchanging glances with his wife. "It is kind of you to see to the queen's business. Matters of state must always take precedence over our difficulties, of course."

"Her Majesty does not forget those who have given her good service," Matthew said. It was a blatant untruth, as everyone standing in the snowy garden knew, but it went unchallenged.

"You must all take your ease inside by the fire," Jane said, her interest in hospitality sharply increased. "I will bring wine and see that you are not disturbed." She dropped a curtsy to Henry, an even lower one to Matthew, then bustled back in the direction of the door. "Come, John. They'll turn to ice if you keep them out here any longer."

Twenty minutes spent inside the Dees' house proved that its master and mistress were representatives of that peculiar breed of married people who bickered incessantly over perceived slights and unkindnesses, all the while remaining devoted. They exchanged barbed comments while we admired the new tapestries (a gift from Lady Walsingham), the new wine ewer (a gift from Sir Christopher Hatton), and the new silver salt (a gift from the Marchioness of Northampton). The ostentatious gifts and invective having run their course, we were—at long last—ushered into the library.

"I'm going to have a hell of a time getting you out of here," Matthew whispered, grinning at the expression of wonder on my face.

John Dee's library was nothing like what I had expected. I'd imagined it would look much like a spacious private library belonging to a well-heeled gentleman of the nineteenth century—for reasons that now struck me as completely indefensible. This was no genteel space for smoking pipes and reading by the fire. With only candles for illumination, the room was surprisingly dark on this winter day. A few chairs and a long table awaited readers by a south-facing bay of windows. The walls of the room were hung with maps, celestial charts, anatomical diagrams, and the broadside almanac sheets that could be had at every apothecary and bookshop in London for pennies. Decades of them were on display, presumably maintained as a reference collection for when Dee was drawing up a horoscope or making other heavenly calculations.

Dee owned more books than any of the Oxford or Cambridge colleges, and he required a working library—not one for show. Not surprisingly, the most precious commodity was not light or seating but shelf space. To maximize what was available, Dee's bookshelves were freestanding and set perpendicular to the walls. The simple oak bookshelves were double-faced, with the shelves set at varied heights to hold the different sizes of Elizabethan books. Two sloped reading surfaces topped the shelves, making it possible to study a text and then accurately return it.

"My God," I murmured. Dee turned in consternation at my oath.

"My wife is overwhelmed, Master Dee," Matthew explained. "She has never been in such a grand library."

"There are many libraries that are far more spacious and boast more treasures than mine, Mistress Roydon."

Jane Dee arrived on cue, just when it was possible to divert the conversation to the poverty of the household.

"The Emperor Rudolf's library is very fine," Jane said, heading past us with a tray holding wine and sweetmeats. "Even so, he was not above stealing one of John's best books. The emperor took advantage of my husband's generosity, and we have little hope of compensation."

"Now, Jane," John chided, "His Majesty did give us a book in return."

"Which book was that?" Matthew said carefully.

"A rare text," Dee said unhappily, watching his wife's retreating form as she headed for the table.

"Nothing but gibberish!" Jane retorted.

It was Ashmole 782. It had to be.

"Master Plat told us about just such a book. It is why we are here. Perhaps we might enjoy your wife's hospitality first and then see the emperor's book?" Matthew suggested, smooth as a cat's whisker. He held out his arm to me, and I took it with a squeeze.

While Jane fussed and poured and complained about the cost of nuts over the holiday season and how she had been brought to near bankruptcy by the grocer, Dee went in search of Ashmole 782. He scanned the shelves of one bookcase and pulled a volume free.

"That's not it," I murmured to Matthew. It was too small.

Dee plunked the book on the table in front of Matthew and lifted the limp vellum cover.

"See. There is naught in it but meaningless words and lewd pictures of women in their bath." Jane harrumphed out of the room, muttering and shaking her head.

This was not Ashmole 782, but it was nonetheless a book I knew: the Voynich manuscript, otherwise known as Yale University's Beinecke MS 408. The manuscript's contents were a mystery. No code breaker or linguist had yet figured out what the text said, and botanists hadn't been able to identify the plants. Theories abounded to explain its mysteries, including one suggesting that it had been written by aliens. I let out a disappointed sound.

"No?" Matthew asked. I shook my head and bit my lip in frustration. Dee mistook my expression for annoyance with Jane, and he rushed to explain.

"Please forgive my wife. Jane finds this book most distressing, for it was she who discovered it among our boxes when we returned from the emperor's lands. I had taken another book with me on the journey—a treasured book of alchemy that once belonged to the great English magician Roger Bacon. It was larger than this, and contained many mysteries."

I pitched forward in my seat.

"My assistant, Edward, could understand the text with divine assistance, though I could not," Dee continued. "Before we left Prague, Emperor Rudolf expressed an interest in the work. Edward had told him some of the secrets contained therein—about the generation of metals and a secret method for obtaining immortality."

So Dee had once possessed Ashmole 782 after all. And his daemonic helper, Edward Kelley, could read the text. My hands were shaking with excitement, and I concealed them in the folds of my skirt.

"Edward helped Jane pack up my books when we were ordered home. Jane believes that Edward stole the book away, replacing it with this item from His Majesty's collection." Dee hesitated, looked sorrowful. "I do not like to think ill of Edward, for he was my trusted companion and we spent much time together. He and Jane were never on good terms, and at first I dismissed her theory."

"But now you think it has merit," Matthew observed.

"I go over the events of our last days, Master Roydon, trying to recall a detail that might exonerate my friend. But everything I remember only points the finger of blame more decidedly in his direction." Dee sighed. "Still, this text may yet prove to contain secrets of worth."

Matthew flipped through the pages. "These are chimeras," he said, studying the images of plants. "The leaves and stems and flowers don't match but have been assembled from different plants."

"What do you make of these?" I said, turning to the astrological roundels that followed. I peered at the writing in the center. Funny. I'd seen the manuscript many times before and never paid any attention to the notes.

"These inscriptions are written in the tongue of ancient Occitania," Matthew said quietly. "I knew someone once with handwriting very like this. Did you happen to meet a gentleman from Aurillac while you were at the emperor's court?"

Did he mean *Gerbert*? My excitement turned to anxiety. Had Gerbert mistaken the Voynich manuscript for the mysterious book of origins? At my question the handwriting in the center of the astrological diagram began to quiver. I clapped the book shut to keep it from dancing off the page.

"No, Master Roydon," Dee said with a frown. "Had I done so, I would have asked him about the famed magician from that place who became pope. There are many truths hidden in old tales told around the fire."

"Yes," Matthew agreed, "if only we are wise enough to recognize them."

"That is why I so regret the loss of my book. It was once owned by Roger Bacon, and I was told by the old woman who sold it to me that he prized it for holding divine truths. Bacon called it the *Verum Secretum Secretorum*." Dee looked wistfully at the Voynich manuscript. "It is my dearest wish to have it returned."

"Perhaps I can be of some use," Matthew said.

"You, Master Roydon?"

"If you would permit me to take this book, I could try to have it put back where it belongs—and have your book restored to its rightful owner." Matthew pulled the manuscript toward him.

"I would be forever in your debt, sir," Dee said, agreeing to the deal without further negotiation.

The minute we pulled away from the public landing in Mortlake, I started peppering Matthew with questions.

"What are you thinking, Matthew? You can't just pack up the Voynich manuscript and send it to Rudolf with a note accusing him of double-dealing. You'll have to find someone crazy enough to risk his life by breaking into Rudolf's library and stealing Ashmole 782."

"If Rudolf has Ashmole 782, it won't be in his library. It will be in his cabinet of curiosities," Matthew said absently, staring at the water.

"So this . . . Voynich was not the book you were seeking?" Henry had been following our exchange with polite interest. "George will be so disappointed not to have solved your mystery."

"George may not have solved it, Hal, but he's shed considerable light on the situation," Matthew said. "Between my father's agents and my own, we'll get Dee's lost book."

We'd caught the tide back to town, which sped our return. The torches were lit on the Water Lane landing in anticipation of our arrival, but two men in the Countess of Pembroke's livery waved us off.

"Baynard's Castle, if you please, Master Roydon!" one called across the water.

"Something must be wrong," Matthew said, standing in the prow of the barge. Henry directed the oarsmen to proceed the extra distance down the river, where the countess's landing was similarly ablaze with beacons and lanterns.

"Is it one of the boys?" I asked Mary when she rushed down the hall to meet us.

"No. They are well. Come to the laboratory. At once," she called over her shoulder, already heading back in the direction of the tower.

The sight that greeted us there was enough to make both Matthew and me gasp.

"It is an altogether unexpected *arbor Dianæ*," Mary said, crouching down so that she was at eye level with the bulbous chamber at the alembic's base that held the roots of a black tree. It wasn't like the first *arbor Dianæ*, which was entirely silver and far more delicate in its structure. This one, with its stout, dark trunk and bare limbs, reminded me of the oak tree in Madison that had sheltered us after Juliette's attack. I'd pulled the vitality out of that tree to save Matthew's life.

"Why isn't it silver?" Matthew asked, wrapping his hands around the countess's fragile glass alembic.

"I used Diana's blood," Mary replied. Matthew straightened and gave me an incredulous look.

"Look at the wall," I said, pointing at the bleeding firedrake.

"It's the green dragon—the symbol for aqua regia or aqua fortis," he said after giving it a cursory glance.

"No, Matthew. *Look* at it. Forget what you think it depicts and try to see it as if it were the first time."

"*Dieu.*" Matthew sounded shocked. "Is that my insignia?"

"Yes. And did you notice that the dragon has its tail in its mouth? And that it's not a dragon at all? Dragons have four legs. That's a firedrake."

"A firedrake. Like . . ." Matthew swore again.

"There have been dozens of different theories about what ordinary substance was the crucial first ingredient required to make the philosopher's stone. Roger Bacon—who owned Dr. Dee's missing manuscript—believed it was blood." I was confident this piece of information would get Matthew's attention. I crouched down to look at the tree.

"And you saw the mural and followed your instincts." After a momentary pause, Matthew ran his thumb along the vessel's wax seal, cracking the wax. Mary gasped in horror as he ruined her experiment.

"What are you doing?" I asked, shocked.

"Following a hunch of my own and adding something to the alembic." Matthew lifted his wrist to his mouth, bit down on it, and held it over the narrow opening. His dark, thick blood dripped into the solution and fell into the bottom of the vessel. We stared into the depths.

Just when I thought nothing was going to happen, thin streaks of red began to work their way up the tree's skeletal trunk. Then golden leaves sprouted from the branches.

"Look at that," I said, amazed.

Matthew smiled at me. It was a smile still tinged with regret, but there was some hope in it, too.

Red fruits appeared among the leaves, sparkling like tiny rubies. Mary began to murmur a prayer, her eyes wide.

"My blood made the structure of the tree, and your blood made it bear fruit," I said slowly. My hand went to my hollow belly.

"Yes. But why?" Matthew replied.

If anything could tell us about the mysterious transformation that occurred when witch and *wearh* combined their blood, it would be Ashmole 782's strange pictures and mysterious text.

"How long did you say it would take you to get Dee's book back?" I asked Matthew.

"Oh, I don't imagine it will take very long," he murmured. "Not once I put my mind to it."

"The sooner the better," I said mildly, twining my fingers through his as we watched the ongoing miracle that our blood had wrought.

25

The strange tree continued to grow and develop the next day and the next: Its fruit ripened and fell among the tree's roots in the mercury and *prima materia*. New buds formed, blossomed, and flowered. Once a day the leaves turned from gold to green and back to gold. Sometimes the tree put out new branches or a new root stretched out to seek sustenance. "I have yet to find a good explanation for it," Mary said, gesturing at the piles of books that Joan had pulled down from the shelves. "It is as if we have created something entirely new."

In spite of the alchemical distractions, I hadn't forgotten my witchier concerns. I wove and rewove my invisible gray cloak, and each time I did it faster and the results were finer and more effective. Marjorie promised me that I would soon be able to put my weaving to words so other witches could perform the spell.

After walking back home from St. James Garlickhythe a few days later, I climbed the stairs to our rooms at the Hart and Crown, shedding my disguising spell as I did so. Annie was across the courtyard fetching the clean linen from the washerwomen. Jack was with Pierre and Matthew. I wondered what Françoise had procured for dinner. I was famished.

"If someone doesn't feed me in the next five minutes, I'm going to start screaming." My announcement as I crossed the threshold was punctuated by the sound of pins scattering on the wooden floorboards as I pulled free the stiff, embroidered panel on the front of my dress. I tossed the stomacher onto the table. My fingers reached for the laces that held my bodice together.

A gentle cough came from the direction of the fireplace.

I whirled around, my fingers clutching at the fabric covering my breasts.

"Screaming will do little good, I fear." A voice as raspy as sand swirling in a glass came from the depths of the chair that was drawn up to the fireplace. "I sent your servant for wine, and my old limbs do not move fast enough to meet your needs."

Slowly I came around the bulk of the chair. The stranger in my house lifted one gray eyebrow, and his gaze flickered over the site of my immodesty. I frowned at his bold glance.

"Who are you?" The man was not daemon, witch, or vampire but merely a wrinkled human.

"I believe that your husband and his friends call me the Old Fox. I am also, for my sins, the lord high treasurer." The shrewdest man in England, and certainly one of its most ruthless, allowed his words to sink in. His kindly expression did nothing to diminish the sharpness of his gaze.

*William Cecil was sitting in my parlor.* Too stunned to dip into the appropriately deep curtsy, I gawped at him instead.

"I am somewhat familiar to you, then. I am surprised my reputation has reached so far, for it is clear to me and many others that you are a stranger here." When I opened my mouth to reply, Cecil's hand came up. "It is wise policy, madam, not to share overmuch with me."

"What can I do for you, Sir William?" I felt like a schoolgirl sent to the principal's office.

"My reputation precedes me, but not my title. *'Vanitatis vanitatum, omnis vanitas,'*" Cecil said drily. "I am called Lord Burghley now, Mistress Roydon. The queen is a generous mistress."

I swore silently. I'd never taken any interest in the dates when members of the aristocracy were elevated to even higher levels of rank and privilege. When I needed to know, I looked it up in the *Dictionary of National Biography.* Now I'd insulted Matthew's boss. I would atone by flattering him in Latin.

"*'Honor virtutis praemium,'*" I murmured, gathering my wits about me. *Esteem is the reward of virtue.* One of my neighbors at Oxford was a graduate of the Arnold School. He played rugby and celebrated New College victories by shouting this phrase at the top of his lungs in the Turf, to the delight of his teammates.

"Ah, the Shirley motto. Are you a member of that family?" Lord Burghley tented his fingers before him and looked at me with greater interest. "They are known for their propensity to wander."

"No," I said. "I'm a Bishop . . . not an actual bishop." Lord Burghley inclined his head in silent acknowledgment of my obvious statement. I felt an absurd desire to bare my soul to the man—that or run as far and fast in the opposite direction as possible.

"Her Majesty accepts a married clergy, but female bishops are, thanks be to God, outside the scope of her imagination."

"Yes. No. Is there something I can do for you, my lord?" I repeated, a deplorable note of desperation creeping into my tone. I gritted my teeth.

"I think not, Mistress Roydon. But perhaps I can do something for you. I advise you to return to Woodstock. Without delay."

"Why, my lord?" I felt a flicker of fear.

"Because it is winter and the queen is insufficiently occupied at present." Burghley looked at my left hand. "And you are married to Master Roydon. Her Majesty is generous, but she doesn't approve when one of her favorites marries without her permission."

"Matthew isn't the queen's favorite—he's her spy." I clapped my hand over my mouth, but it was too late to recall the words.

"Favorites and spies are not mutually exclusive—except where Walsingham was concerned. The queen found his strict morality maddening and his sour expression unendurable. But Her Majesty is fond of Matthew Roydon. Some would say dangerously so. And your husband has many secrets." Cecil hauled himself to his feet, using a staff for leverage. He groaned. "Go back to Woodstock, mistress. It is best for all concerned."

"I won't leave my husband." Elizabeth might eat courtiers for breakfast, as Matthew had warned, but she was not going to run me out of town. Not when I was finally getting settled, finding friends, and learning magic. And certainly not when Matthew dragged himself home every day looking as if he'd been pulled backward through a knothole, only to spend all night answering correspondence sent to him by the queen's informants, his father, and the Congregation.

"Tell Matthew that I called." Lord Burghley made his slow way to the door. There he met Françoise, who was carrying a large jug of wine and looking disgruntled. At the sight of me, her eyes widened. She was not pleased to find me home, entertaining, with my bodice undone. "Thank you for the conversation, Mistress Roydon. It was most illuminating."

The lord high treasurer of England crept down the stairs. He was too old to be traveling about in the late afternoon, alone, in January. I followed him to the landing, watching his progress with concern.

"Go with him, Françoise," I urged her, "and make sure Lord Burghley finds his own servants." They were probably at the Cardinal's Hat getting inebriated with Kit and Will, or waiting in the crush of coaches at the top of Water Lane. I didn't want to be the last person to see Queen Elizabeth's chief adviser alive.

"No need, no need," Burghley said over his shoulder. "I am an old man with a stick. The thieves will ignore me in favor of someone with an earring and a slashed doublet. The beggars I can beat off, if need be. And my men are not far from here. Remember my advice, mistress."

With that he disappeared into the dusk.

"*Dieu.*" Françoise crossed herself, then forked her fingers against the evil eye for good measure. "He is an old soul. I do not like the way he looked at you. It is a good thing *milord* is not yet home. He would not have liked it either."

"William Cecil is old enough to be my grandfather, Françoise," I retorted, returning to the warmth of the parlor and, finally, loosening my laces. I groaned as the constriction lessened.

"Lord Burghley did not look at you as though he wanted to bed you." Françoise glanced pointedly at my bodice.

"No? How *did* he look at me, then?" I poured myself some wine and plopped down in my chair. The day was taking a decided turn for the worse.

"Like you were a lamb ready for slaughter and he was weighing the price you would bring."

"Who is threatening to eat Diana for dinner?" Matthew had arrived with the stealth of a cat and was taking off his gloves.

"Your visitor. You just missed him." I took a sip of wine. As soon as I swallowed, Matthew was there to lift it from my hands. I made an exasperated sound. "Can you wave or something to let me know you're about to move? It's disconcerting when you just appear before me like that."

"As you've divined that looking out the window is one of my tells, I feel honor bound to share that changing the subject is one of yours." Matthew took a sip of wine and set the cup on the table. He rubbed tiredly at his face. "What visitor?"

"William Cecil was waiting by the fire when I came home."

Matthew went eerily still.

"He's the scariest grandfatherly person I've ever met," I continued, reaching for the wine again. "Burghley may look like Father Christmas, with his gray hair and beard, but I wouldn't turn my back on him."

"That's very wise," Matthew said quietly. He regarded Françoise. "What did he want?"

She shrugged. "I do not know. He was here when I came home with *madame*'s pork pie. Lord Burghley asked for wine. That daemon drank everything in the house earlier today. I went out for more."

Matthew disappeared. He returned at a more sedate pace, looking relieved. I shot to my feet. *The attics—and all the secrets hidden there.*

"Did he—"

"No," Matthew interrupted. "Everything is exactly as I left it. Did William say why he was here?"

"Lord Burghley told me to tell you he called." I hesitated. "And he told
me to leave the city."

Annie entered the room, along with a chattering Jack and a grinning
Pierre, but after one look at Matthew's face, Pierre's smile dissolved. I took
the linens from Annie.

"Why don't you take the children to the Cardinal's Hat, Françoise?" I
said. "Pierre will go, too."

"Huzzah!" Jack shouted, delighted at the prospect of a night out. "Master Shakespeare is teaching me to juggle."

"So long as he doesn't try to improve your penmanship, I have no objection," I said, catching Jack's hat as he tossed it in the air. The last thing we
needed was the boy adding forgery to his list of skills. "Go and have your
supper. And try to remember what your handkerchief is for."

"I will," Jack said, wiping his nose with his sleeve.

"Why did Lord Burghley come all the way to the Blackfriars to see
you?" I asked when we were alone.

"Because I received intelligence from Scotland today."

"What now?" I said, my throat closing. It was not the first time the Berwick witches had been discussed in my presence, but somehow Burghley's
presence made it seem as though the evil was creeping over our threshold.

"King James continues to question the witches. William wanted to discuss what—if anything—the queen should do in response." He frowned at
the change in my scent as the fear took hold. "You shouldn't trouble yourself with what's happening in Scotland."

"Not knowing doesn't keep it from happening."

"No," Matthew said, his fingers gentle on my neck as he tried to rub the
tension away. "Neither does knowing."

The next day I came home from Goody Alsop's carrying a small wooden
spell box—a place to let my written spells incubate until they were ready
for another witch to use. Finding a way to put my magic to words was the
next step in my evolution as a weaver. Right now the box held only my

weaver's cords. Marjorie didn't think my disguising spell was quite ready for other witches yet.

A wizard on Thames Street made the box from the limb from the rowan that the firedrake gave me the night I made my forspell. He'd carved a tree on its surface, the roots and branches weirdly intertwined so that you couldn't tell them apart. Not a single nail held the box together. Instead there were nearly invisible joints. The wizard was proud of his work, and I couldn't wait to show it to Matthew.

The Hart and Crown was oddly quiet. Neither the fire nor the candles in the parlor were lit. Matthew was in his study, alone. Three wine jugs stood on the table before him. Two of them were, presumably, empty. Matthew didn't normally drink so heavily.

"What's wrong?"

He picked up a sheet of paper. Thick red wax clung to its folds. The seal was cracked across the middle. "We are called to court."

I sank into the chair opposite. "When?"

"Her Majesty has graciously permitted us to wait until tomorrow." Matthew snorted. "Her father was not half so forgiving. When Henry wanted people to attend him, he sent for them even if they were in their bed and a gale was blowing."

I had been eager to meet the queen of England—when I was back in Madison. After meeting the shrewdest man in the kingdom, I no longer had any desire to meet the canniest woman. "Must we go?" I asked, half hoping Matthew would dismiss the royal command.

"In her letter the queen took pains to remind me of her statute against conjurations, enchantments, and witchcrafts." Matthew tossed the paper onto the table. "It would seem Mr. Danforth wrote a letter to his bishop. Burghley buried the complaint, but it resurfaced." Matthew swore.

"Then why are we going to court?" I clutched at my spell box. The cords inside were slithering around, eager to help answer my question.

"Because if we are not in the audience chamber at Richmond Palace by two in the afternoon tomorrow, Elizabeth will arrest us both." Matthew's eyes looked like chips of sea glass. "It won't take long for the Congregation to learn the truth about us then."

The household was thrown into an uproar at our news. Their anticipation was shared by the neighborhood the next morning when the Countess of Pembroke arrived shortly after dawn with enough garments to outfit the parish. She traveled by river, having taken her barge to the Blackfriars—although the actual distance was no more than a few hundred feet. Her appearance on the Water Lane landing was treated as a public spectacle of enormous importance, and for a few moments a hush fell over our normally raucous street.

Mary looked serene and unperturbed when she finally stepped into the parlor, allowing Joan and a line of lesser servants to file in behind her.

"Henry tells me you are expected at court this afternoon. You have nothing suitable to wear." With an imperious finger, Mary directed still more of her crew in the direction of our bedchamber.

"I was going to wear the gown I was married in," I protested.

"But it is French!" Mary said, aghast. "You cannot wear that!"

Embroidered satins, luscious velvets, sparkling silks interwoven with real gold and silver thread, and piles of diaphanous material of unknown purpose passed by my nose.

"This is too much, Mary. Whatever are you thinking?" I said, narrowly avoiding collision with still one more servant.

"No one goes into battle without proper armor," Mary said with her characteristic blend of airiness and tartness. "And Her Majesty, may God preserve her, is a formidable opponent. You will require all the protection my wardrobe can afford."

Together we picked through the options. How we were going to make the necessary alterations so that Mary's clothes would fit me was a mystery, but I knew better than to inquire. I was Cinderella, and the birds of the forest and the fairies of the wood would be called upon if the Countess of Pembroke felt it necessary.

We finally settled on a black gown thickly embroidered with silver fleurs-de-lis and roses. It was a design from last year, Mary said, and lacked the large cartwheel-shaped skirts now in vogue. Elizabeth would be pleased by my frugal disregard for the whims of fashion.

"And silver and black are the queen's colors. That's why Walter is always wearing them," Mary explained, smoothing the puffed sleeves.

But my favorite garment by far was the white satin petticoat that would be visible at the front of the divided skirts. It was embroidered, too, with mainly flora and fauna, accompanied by bits of classical architecture, scientific instruments, and female personifications of the arts and sciences. I recognized the same hand at work as that of the genius who'd created Mary's shoes. I avoided touching the embroidery to make sure, not wanting Lady Alchemy to walk off the petticoat before I'd had the opportunity to wear it.

It took four women two hours to get me dressed. First I was laced into my clothes, which were padded and puffed to ridiculous proportions, with thick quilting and a wide farthingale that was just as unwieldy as I had imagined. My ruff was suitably large and ostentatious, though not, Mary assured me, as large as the queen's would be. Mary clipped an ostrich fan to my waist. It hung down like a pendulum and swayed when I walked. With its feathery plumes and ruby- and pearl-studded handle, the accessory was easily worth ten times what my mousetrap cost, and I was glad that it was literally attached to me at the hip.

The subject of jewelry proved controversial. Mary had her coffer with her and pulled out one priceless item after another. But I insisted on wearing Ysabeau's earrings rather than the ornate diamond drops that Mary suggested. They went surprisingly well with the rope of pearls Joan slung over my shoulder. To my horror, Mary dismembered the chain of broom blossoms that Philippe had given me for my wedding and pinned one of the floral links to the center of my bodice. She caught the pearls up with a red bow and tied it to the pin. After a long discussion, Mary and Françoise settled on a simple pearl choker to fill my open neckline. Annie affixed my gold arrow to my ruff with another jeweled pin, and Françoise dressed my hair so that it framed my face in a puffed-out heart shape. For the final touch, Mary settled a pearl-studded coif on the back of my head, covering the braided knots that Françoise piled there.

Matthew, who had been in an increasingly foul mood as the hour of doom approached, managed to smile and look suitably impressed.

"I feel like I'm in a stage costume," I said ruefully.

"You look lovely—formidably so," he assured me. He looked splendid, too, in his solid black velvet suit of clothes with tiny touches of white at the wrists and collar. And he was wearing my portrait miniature around his neck. The long chain was looped up on a button so that the moon faced outward and my image was close to his heart.

My first glimpse of Richmond Palace was the top of a creamy stone tower, the royal standard snapping in the breeze. More towers soon appeared, sparkling in the crisp winter air like those of a castle out of a fairy story. Then the vast sprawl of the palace complex came into view: the strange rectangular arcade to the southeast, the three-storied main building to the southwest, surrounded by a wide moat, and the walled orchard beyond.

Behind the main building were still more towers and peaks, including a pair of buildings that reminded me of Eton College. An enormous crane rose up into the air beyond the orchard, and swarms of men unloaded boxes and parcels for the palace's kitchens and storerooms. Baynard's Castle, which had always seemed very grand to me, appeared in retrospect a slightly down-at-the-heels former royal residence.

The oarsmen directed the barge to a landing. Matthew ignored the stares and questions, preferring to let Pierre or Gallowglass respond for him. To the casual observer, Matthew looked slightly bored. But I was close enough to see him scanning the riverbank, alert and on guard.

I looked across the moat to the two-storied arcade. The ground floor's arches were open to the air, but the upper floor was glazed with leaded windows. Eager faces peered out, hoping to catch a glimpse of the new arrivals and obtain a morsel of gossip. Matthew quickly put his bulk between the barge and the curious courtiers, obscuring me from easy view.

Liveried servants, each one bearing a sword or a pike, led us through a simple guard chamber and into the main part of the palace. The warren of ground-floor rooms was as hectic and bustling as any modern office building, with servants and court officers rushing to meet requests and obey orders. Matthew turned to the right; our guards politely blocked his way.

"She'll not see you in private before you've been draped over tenterhooks in public," Gallowglass muttered under his breath. Matthew swore.

We obediently followed our escorts to a grand staircase. It was thronged with people, and the clash of human, floral, and herbal scents was dizzying. Everybody was wearing perfume in an effort to ward off unpleasant odors, but I had to wonder if the result was worse. When the crowd spotted Matthew, there were whispers as the sea of people parted. He was taller than most and gave off the same brutal air as most of the other male aristocrats I'd met. The difference was that Matthew really was lethal—and on some level the warmbloods recognized it.

After passing through a series of three antechambers, each filled to bursting with padded, scented, and jeweled courtiers of both sexes and all ages, we finally arrived at a closed door. There we waited. The whispers around us rose to murmurs. A man shared a joke, and his companions tittered. Matthew's jaw clenched.

"Why are we waiting?" I said, my voice pitched so that only Matthew and Gallowglass could hear.

"To amuse the queen—and to show the court that I am no more than a servant."

When at last we were admitted to the royal presence, I was surprised to find that this room, too, was full of people. "Private" was a relative term in the court of Elizabeth. I searched for the queen, but she was nowhere in sight. Fearing that we were going to have to wait again, my heart sank.

"Why is it that for every year I grow older, Matthew Roydon seems to look two years younger?" said a surprisingly jovial voice from the direction of the fireplace. The most lavishly dressed, heavily scented, and thickly painted creatures in the room turned slightly to study us. Their movement revealed Elizabeth, the queen bee seated at the center of the hive. My heart skipped a beat. Here was a legend brought to life.

"I see no great change in you, Your Majesty," Matthew said, inclining slightly at the waist. "*'Semper eadem,'* as the saying goes." The same words were painted in the banner under the royal crest that ornamented the fireplace. *Always the same.*

"Even my lord treasurer can manage a deeper bow than that, sir, and he suffers from a rheum." Black eyes glittered from a mask of powder and rouge. Beneath her sharply hooked nose, the queen compressed her thin lips into a hard line. "And I prefer a different motto these days: *Video et taceo.*"

*I see and am silent.* We were in trouble.

Matthew seemed not to notice and straightened as though he were a prince of the realm and not the queen's spy. With his shoulders thrown back and his head erect, he was easily the tallest man in the room. There were only two people remotely close to him in height: Henry Percy, who was standing against the wall looking miserable, and a long-legged man of about the earl's age with a mop of curly hair and an insolent expression, who stood at the queen's elbow.

"Careful," Burghley murmured as he passed by Matthew, camouflaging his admonishment with regular thumps of his staff. "You called for me, Your Majesty?"

"Spirit and Shadow in the same place. Tell me, Raleigh, does that not violate some dark principle of philosophy?" the queen's companion drawled out. His friends pointed at Lord Burghley and Matthew and laughed.

"If you had gone to Oxford and not Cambridge, Essex, you would know the answer and be spared the ignominy of having to ask." Raleigh casually shifted his weight and placed his hand conveniently near the hilt of his sword.

"Now, Robin," the queen said with an indulgent pat on his elbow. "You know that I do not like it when others use my pet names. Lord Burghley and Master Roydon will forgive you for doing so this time."

"I take it the lady is your wife, Roydon." The Earl of Essex turned his brown eyes on me. "We did not know you were wed."

"Who is this 'we'?" the queen retorted, giving him a smack this time. "It is no business of yours, my Lord Essex."

"At least Matt isn't afraid to be seen around town with her." Walter stroked his chin. "You're recently married, too, my lord. Where is your wife on this fine winter's day?" *Here we go,* I thought as Walter and Essex jockeyed for position.

"Lady Essex is on Hart Street, in her mother's house, with the earl's newborn heir at her side," Matthew replied on Essex's behalf. "Congratulations, my lord. When I called on the countess, she told me he was to be named after you."

"Yes. Robert was baptized yesterday," Essex said stiffly. He looked a bit alarmed at the thought that Matthew had been around his wife and child.

"He was, my lord." Matthew gave the earl a truly terrifying smile. "Strange. I did not see you at the ceremony."

"Enough squabbling!" Elizabeth shouted, angry that the conversation was no longer under her control. She tapped her long fingers on the upholstered arm of her chair. "I gave neither of you permission to wed. You are both ungrateful, grasping wretches. Bring the girl to me."

Nervous, I smoothed my skirts and took Matthew's arm. The dozen steps between the queen and me seemed to stretch on to infinity. When at last I reached her side, Walter looked sharply at the floor. I sank into a curtsy and remained there.

"She has manners at least," Elizabeth conceded. "Raise her up."

When I met her eyes, I learned that the queen was extremely nearsighted. Even though I was no more than three feet from her, she squinted as though she couldn't make out my features.

"Hmph," Elizabeth pronounced when her inspection was through. "Her face is coarse."

"If you think so, then it is fortunate that you are not wed to her," Matthew said shortly.

Elizabeth peered at me some more. "There is ink on her fingers."

I hid the offending digits behind my borrowed fan. The stains from the oak-gall ink were impossible to remove.

"And what fortune am I paying you, Shadow, that your wife can afford such a fan?" Elizabeth's voice had turned petulant.

"If we are going to discuss Crown finances, perhaps the others might take their leave," Lord Burghley suggested.

"Oh, very well," Elizabeth said crossly. "You shall stay, William, and Walter, too."

"And me," Essex said.

"Not you, Robin. You must see to the banquet. I wish to be entertained this evening. I am tired of sermonizing and history lessons, as though I were a schoolgirl. No more tales of King John or adventures of a lovelorn shepherdess pining for her shepherd. I want Symons to tumble. If there must be a play, let it be the one with the necromancer and the brass head that divines the future." Elizabeth rapped her knuckles on the table. "*Time is, time was, time is past.*' I do love that line."

Matthew and I exchanged looks.

"I believe the play is called *Friar Bacon and Friar Bungay,* Your Majesty," a young woman whispered into her mistress's ear.

"That's the one, Bess. See to it, Robin, and you shall sit by me." The queen was quite an actress herself. She could go from furious to petulant to wheedling without missing a beat.

Somewhat mollified, the Earl of Essex withdrew, but not before shooting Walter a withering stare. Everyone flurried after him. Essex was now the most important person in their proximity, and, like moths to a flame, the other courtiers were eager to share his light. Only Henry seemed reluctant to depart, but he was given no choice. The door closed firmly behind them.

"Did you enjoy your visit to Dr. Dee, Mistress Roydon?" The queen's voice was sharp. There wasn't a cajoling note in it now. She was all business.

"We did, Your Majesty," Matthew replied.

"I know full well your wife can speak for herself, Master Roydon. Let her do so."

Matthew glowered but remained quiet.

"It was most enjoyable, Your Majesty." I had just spoken to Queen Elizabeth I. Pushing aside my disbelief, I continued. "I am a student of alchemy and interested in books and learning."

"I know what you are."

Danger flashed all around me, a firestorm of black threads snapping and crying.

"I am your servant, Your Majesty, like my husband." My eyes remained resolutely focused on the queen of England's slippers. Happily, they weren't particularly interesting and remained inanimate.

"I have courtiers and fools enough, Mistress Roydon. You will not earn a place among them with that remark." Her eyes glittered ominously. "Not all of my intelligencers report to your husband. Tell me, Shadow, what business did you have with Dr. Dee?"

"It was a private matter," Matthew said, keeping his temper with difficulty.

"There is no such thing—not in my kingdom." Elizabeth studied Matthew's face. "You told me not to trust my secrets to those whose allegiance you had not already tested for me," she continued quietly. "Surely my own loyalty is not in question."

"It was a private matter, between Dr. Dee and myself, madam," Matthew said, sticking to his story.

"Very well, Master Roydon. Since you are determined to keep your secret, I will tell you *my* business with Dr. Dee and see if it loosens your tongue. I want Edward Kelley back in England."

"I believe he is Sir Edward now, Your Majesty," Burghley corrected her.

"Where did you hear that?" Elizabeth demanded.

"From me," Matthew said mildly. "It is, after all, my job to know these things. Why do you need Kelley?"

"He knows how to make the philosopher's stone. And I will not have it in Hapsburg hands."

"Is that what you're afraid of?" Matthew sounded relieved.

"I am afraid of dying and leaving my kingdom to be fought over like a scrap of meat between dogs from Spain and France and Scotland," Elizabeth said, rising and advancing on him. The closer she came, the greater their differences in size and strength appeared. She was such a small woman to have survived against impossible odds for so many years. "I am afraid of what will become of my people when I am gone. Every day I pray for God's help in saving England from certain disaster."

"Amen," Burghley intoned.

"Edward Kelley is not God's answer, I promise you that."

"Any ruler who possesses the philosopher's stone will have an inexhaustible supply of riches." Elizabeth's eyes glittered. "Had I more gold at my disposal, I could destroy the Spanish."

"And if wishes were thrushes, beggars would eat birds," Matthew replied.

"Mind your tongue, Roydon," Burghley warned.

"Her Majesty is proposing to paddle in dangerous waters, my lord. It is my job to warn her of that, too." Matthew was carefully formal. "Edward Kelley is a daemon. His alchemical work lies perilously close to magic, as Walter can attest. The Congregation is desperate to keep Rudolf II's fascination for the occult from taking a dangerous turn as it did with King James."

"James had every right to arrest those witches!" Elizabeth said hotly. "Just as I have every right to claim the benefit should one of my subjects make the stone."

"Did you strike such a hard bargain with Walter when he went to the New World?" Matthew inquired. "Had he found gold in Virginia, would you have demanded it all be handed over to you?"

"I believe that's exactly what our arrangement stipulated," Walter said drily, adding a hasty, "though I would, of course, have been delighted for Her Majesty to have it."

"I knew you could not be trusted, Shadow. You are in England to serve me—yet you argue for this Congregation of yours as though their wishes were more important."

"I have the same desire that you do, Your Majesty: to save England from disaster. If you go the way of King James and start persecuting the daemons, witches, and *wearhs* among your subjects, you will suffer for it, and so will the realm."

"What do you propose I do instead?" Elizabeth asked.

"I propose we make an agreement—one not far different from the bargain you struck with Raleigh. I will see to it that Edward Kelley returns to England so that you can lock him in the Tower and force him to deliver up the philosopher's stone—if he can."

"And in return?" Elizabeth was her father's daughter, after all, and understood that nothing in this life was free.

"In return you will harbor as many of the Berwick witches as I can get out of Edinburgh until King James's madness has run its course."

"Absolutely not!" Burghley said. "Think, madam, what might happen to your relationship with our neighbors to the north if you were to invite scores of Scottish witches over the border!"

"There are not so many witches left in Scotland," Matthew said grimly, "since you refused my earlier pleas."

"I did think, Shadow, that one of your occupations while in England was to make sure your people did not meddle in our politics. What if these private machinations are found out? How will you explain your actions?" The queen scrutinized him.

"I will say that misery acquaints every man with strange bedfellows, Your Majesty."

Elizabeth made a soft sound of amusement. "That is doubly true for women," she said drily. "Very well. We are agreed. You will go to Prague and get Kelley. Mistress Roydon may attend upon me, here at court, to ensure your speedy return."

"My wife is not part of our bargain, and there is no need to send me to Bohemia in January. You are determined to have Kelley back. I will see to it that he is delivered."

"You are not king here!" Elizabeth jabbed at his chest with her finger. "You go where I send you, Master Roydon. If you do not, I will have you and your witch of a wife in the Tower for treason. And worse," she said, her eyes sparking.

Someone scratched at the door.

"Enter!" Elizabeth bellowed.

"The Countess of Pembroke requests an audience, Your Majesty," a guard said apologetically.

"God's teeth," the queen swore. "Am I never to know a moment's peace? Show her in."

Mary Sidney sailed into the room, her veils and ruffs billowing as she moved from the chilly antechamber to the overheated room the queen occupied. She dropped a graceful curtsy midway, floated further into the room, and dropped another perfect curtsy. "Your Majesty," she said, head bowed.

"What brings you to court, Lady Pembroke?"

"You once granted me a boon, Your Majesty—a guard against future need."

"Yes, yes," Elizabeth said testily. "What has your husband done now?"

"Nothing at all." Mary got to her feet. "I have come to ask for permission to send Mistress Roydon on an important errand."

"I cannot imagine why," Elizabeth retorted. "She seems neither useful nor resourceful."

"I have need of special glasses for my experiments that can only be acquired from Emperor Rudolf's workshops. My brother's wife—forgive me, for since Philip's death she is now remarried and the Countess of Essex—tells me that Master Roydon is being sent to Prague. Mistress Roydon will go with him, with your blessing, and fetch what I require."

"That vain, foolish boy! The Earl of Essex cannot resist sharing every scrap of intelligence he has with the world." Elizabeth whirled away in a flurry of silver and gold. "I'll have the popinjay's head for this!"

"You did promise me, Your Majesty, when my brother died defending your kingdom, that you would grant me a favor one day." Mary smiled serenely at Matthew and me.

"And you want to waste such a precious gift on these two?" Elizabeth looked skeptical.

"Once Matthew saved Philip's life. He is like a brother to me." Mary blinked at the queen with owlish innocence.

"You can be as smooth as ivory, Lady Pembroke. I wish we saw more of you at court." Elizabeth threw up her hands. "Very well. I will keep my word. But I want Edward Kelley in my presence by midsummer—and I don't want this bungled, or for all of Europe to know my business. Do you understand me, Master Roydon?"

"Yes, Your Majesty," Matthew said through gritted teeth.

"Get yourself to Prague, then. And take your wife with you, to please Lady Pembroke."

"Thank you, Majesty." Matthew looked rather alarmingly as if he wished to rip Elizabeth Tudor's bewigged head from her body.

"Out of my sight, all of you, before I change my mind." Elizabeth returned to her chair and slumped against its carved back.

Lord Burghley indicated with a jerk of his head that we were to follow the queen's instructions. But Matthew couldn't leave matters where they stood.

"A word of caution, Your Majesty. Do not place your trust in the Earl of Essex."

"You do not like him, Master Roydon. Nor does William or Walter. But he makes me feel young again." Elizabeth turned her black eyes on him. "Once you performed that service for me and reminded me of happier times. Now you have found another and I am abandoned."

"'*My care is like my shadow in the sun / Follows me flying, flies when I pursue it, / Stands and lies by me, doth what I have done,*'" Matthew said softly. "I am your Shadow, Majesty, and have no choice but to go where you lead."

"And I am tired," Elizabeth said, turning her head away, "and have no stomach for poetry. Leave me."

"We're not going to Prague," Matthew said once we were back in Henry's barge and headed toward London. "We must go home."

"The queen will not leave you in peace just because you flee to Woodstock, Matthew," Mary said reasonably, burrowing into a fur blanket.

"He doesn't mean Woodstock, Mary," I explained. "Matthew means somewhere . . . farther."

"Ah." Mary's brow furrowed. "Oh." Her face went carefully blank.

"But we're so close to getting what we wanted," I said. "We know where the manuscript is, and it may answer all our questions."

"And it may be nonsense, just like the manuscript at Dr. Dee's house," Matthew said impatiently. "We'll get it another way."

But later Walter persuaded Matthew that the queen was serious and would have us both in the Tower if we refused her. When I told Goody Alsop, she was as opposed to Prague as Matthew was.

"You should be going to your own time, not traveling to far-off Prague. Even if you were to stay here, it will take weeks to ready a spell that might get you home. Magic has guiding rules and principles that you have yet to master, Diana. All you have now is a wayward firedrake, a *glaem* that is near to blinding, and a tendency to ask questions that have mischievous answers. You do not have enough knowledge of the craft to succeed with your plan."

"I will continue to study in Prague, I promise." I took her hands in mine. "Matthew made a bargain with the queen that might protect dozens of witches. We cannot be separated. It's too dangerous. I won't let him go to the emperor's court without me."

"No," she said with a sad smile. "Not while there is breath in your body. Very well. Go with your *wearh*. But know this, Diana Roydon: You are setting a new course. And I cannot foresee where it might lead."

"The ghost of Bridget Bishop told me '*There is no path forward that does not have him in it.*' When I feel our lives spinning into the unknown, I take comfort from those words," I said, trying to comfort her. "So long as Matthew and I are together, Goody Alsop, our direction does not matter."

Three days later on the feast of St. Brigid, we set sail on our long journey to see the Holy Roman Emperor, find a treacherous English daemon, and, at long last, catch a glimpse of Ashmole 782.

# 26

Verin de Clermont sat in her Berlin home and stared down at the newspaper in disbelief.

**The Independent**
*1 February 2010*

A SURREY WOMAN has discovered a manuscript belonging to Mary Sidney, famed Elizabethan poetess and sister to Sir Philip Sidney.

"It was in my mother's airing cupboard at the top of the stairs," Henrietta Barber, 62, told the Independent. Mrs. Barber was clearing out her mother's belongings before she went into care. "It looked like a tatty old bunch of paper to me."

The manuscript, experts believe, represents a working alchemical notebook kept by the Countess of Pembroke during the winter of 1590/91. The countess's scientific papers were thought to have been destroyed in a fire at Wilton House in the seventeenth century. It is not clear how the item came to be in the possession of the Barber family.

"We remember Mary Sidney primarily as a poet," commented a representative of Sotheby's Auction House, who will put the item up for bid in May, "but in her own time she was known as a great practitioner of alchemy."

The manuscript is of particular interest as it shows that the countess was assisted in her laboratory. In one experiment, labeled "the making of the arbor Dianæ," she identifies her assistant by the initials DR. "We might never be able to identify the man who helped the Countess of Pembroke," explained historian Nigel Warminster of Cambridge University, "but this manuscript will nevertheless tell us an enormous amount about the growth of experimentation in the Scientific Revolution."

"What is it, *Schatz*?" Ernst Neumann put a glass of wine in front of his wife. She looked far too serious for a Monday night. This was Verin's Friday face.

"Nothing," she murmured, her eyes still fixed on the lines of print before her. "A piece of unfinished family business."

"Is Baldwin involved? Did he lose a million euros today?" His brother-in-law was an acquired taste, and Ernst didn't entirely trust him. Baldwin had trained him in the intricacies of international commerce when Ernst was still a young man. Ernst was nearly sixty now, and the envy of his friends with his young wife. Their wedding photos, which showed Verin looking exactly as she did today and a twenty-five-year-old version of himself, were safely hidden from view.

"Baldwin's never lost a million of anything in his life." Verin hadn't actually answered his question, Ernst noticed.

He pulled the English newspaper toward him and read what was printed there. "Why are you interested in an old book?"

"Let me make a phone call first," she replied cagily. Her hands were steady on the phone, but Ernst recognized the expression in her unusual silver eyes. She was angry, and frightened, and thinking of the past. He'd seen that same look moments before Verin saved his life, wrenching him away from her stepmother.

"Are you calling Mélisande?"

"Ysabeau," Verin said automatically, punching in numbers.

"Ysabeau, yes," Ernst said. Understandably, he found it hard to think of Verin's stepmother by any other name than the one used by the de Clermont family matriarch when she'd killed Ernst's father after the war.

Verin's call took an inordinately long time to connect. Ernst could hear strange clicks, almost as though the call were being forwarded again and again. Finally it went through. The phone rang.

"Who is this?" a young voice asked. He sounded American—or English, maybe, but with his accent nearly gone.

Verin hung up immediately. She dropped the phone to the table and buried her face in her hands. "Oh, God. It's really happening, just as my father said it would."

"You're frightening me, *Schatz*," Ernst said. He'd seen many horrors in his life, but none so vivid as those that tormented Verin on those rare occasions when she actually slept. The nightmares about Philippe were enough to unravel his normally composed wife. "Who was that on the phone?"

"It wasn't who it was supposed to be," Verin replied, her voice muffled. Gray eyes rose to meet his. "Matthew should have answered, but he can't. Because he's not here. He's there." She looked at the paper.

"Verin, you are not making any sense," Ernst said sternly. He'd never met this troublesome stepbrother, the family intellectual and black sheep.

But she was already dialing the phone again. This time the call went straight through.

"You've read today's papers, Auntie Verin. I've been expecting your call for hours."

"Where are you, Gallowglass?" Her nephew was a drifter. In the past he'd sent postcards with nothing but a phone number on them from whatever stretch of road he was traveling at the moment: the autobahn in Germany, Route 66 in the States, Trollstigen in Norway, the Guoliang Tunnel Road in China. She'd received fewer of these terse announcements since the age of international cell phones. With GPS and the Internet, she could locate Gallowglass anywhere. Verin rather missed the postcards, though.

"Somewhere outside Warrnambool," Gallowglass said vaguely.

"Where the hell is Warrnambool?" Verin demanded.

"Australia," Ernst and Gallowglass said at the same moment.

"Is that a German accent I hear? Have you found a new boyfriend?" Gallowglass teased.

"Watch yourself, pup," Verin snapped. "You may be family, but I can still rip your throat out. That's my husband, Ernst."

Ernst sat forward in his chair and shook his head in warning. He didn't like it when his wife took on a male vampire—even though she was stronger than most. Verin waved off his concern.

Gallowglass chuckled, and Ernst decided that this unfamiliar vampire might be all right. "There's my scary Auntie Verin. It's good to hear your voice after all these years. And don't pretend you're any more surprised to see that story than I was to get your call."

"Part of me hoped he was raving," Verin confessed, remembering the night when she and Gallowglass had sat by Philippe's bed and listened to his ramblings.

"Did you imagine it was contagious and that I was raving, too?" Gallowglass snorted. He sounded very much like Philippe these days, Verin noticed.

"I hoped that was the case, as a matter of fact." It had been easier to believe than the alternative: that her father's impossible tale of a time-spinning witch was true.

"Will you be keeping your promise anyway?" Gallowglass said softly.

Verin hesitated. It was only a moment, but Ernst saw it. Verin always kept her promises. When he'd been a terrified, cowering boy, Verin had promised him that he would grow to be a man. Ernst had clung to that assurance when he was six, just as he clung to the promises Verin had made since.

"You haven't seen Matthew with her. Once you do—"

"I'll think my stepbrother is even more of a problem? Not possible."

"Give her a chance, Verin. She's Philippe's daughter, too. And he had excellent taste in women."

"The witch isn't his real daughter," Verin said quickly.

On a road somewhere near Warrnambool, Gallowglass pressed his lips together and refused to reply. Verin might know more about Diana and Matthew than anyone else in the family, but she didn't know as much as he did. There would be endless opportunities to discuss vampires and children once the couple was back. There was no need to argue about it now.

"Besides, Matthew isn't here," Verin said, looking at the paper. "I called the number. Someone else answered, and it wasn't Baldwin." That's why she had disconnected so quickly. If Matthew wasn't leading the brotherhood, the telephone number should have been passed on to Philippe's only surviving full-blooded son. "The number" had been generated in the earliest years of the telephone. Philippe had picked it: 917, for Ysabeau's birthday in September. With each new technology and every successive change in the national and international telephone system, the number referred seamlessly on to another, more modern iteration.

"You reached Marcus." Gallowglass had called the number, too.

"Marcus?" Verin was aghast. "The future of the de Clermonts depends upon *Marcus*?"

"Give him a chance, too, Auntie Verin. He's a good lad." Gallowglass paused. "As for the family's future, that depends on all of us. Philippe knew that, or he wouldn't have made us promise to return to Sept-Tours."

Philippe de Clermont had been very specific with his daughter and grandson. They were to watch for signs: stories of a young American witch with great power, the name Bishop, alchemy, and then a rash of anomalous historical discoveries.

Then, and only then, were Gallowglass and Verin to return to the de Clermont family seat. Philippe hadn't been willing to divulge why it was so important that the family come together, but Gallowglass knew.

For decades Gallowglass had waited. Then he heard stories of a witch from Massachusetts named Rebecca, one of the last descendants of Salem's Bridget Bishop. Reports of her power spread far and wide, as did news of her tragic death. Gallowglass tracked her surviving daughter to upstate New York. He'd checked on the girl periodically, watching as Diana Bishop played on the monkey bars at the playground, went to birthday parties, and graduated from college. Gallowglass had been as proud as any parent to see her pass her Oxford viva. And he often stood beneath the carillon in Harkness Tower at Yale, the power of the bells' sound reverberating through his body, while the young professor walked across campus. Her clothing was different, but there was no mistaking Diana's determined gait or the set of her shoulders, whether she was wearing a farthingale and ruff or a pair of trousers and an unflattering man's jacket.

Gallowglass tried to keep his distance, but sometimes he had to interfere—like the day her energy drew a daemon to her side and the creature began to follow her. Still, Gallowglass prided himself on the hundreds of other times he'd refrained from rushing down the stairs of Yale's bell tower, throwing his arms around Professor Bishop, and telling her how glad he was to see her after so many years.

When Gallowglass learned that Baldwin had been called to Sept-Tours at Ysabeau's behest for some unspecified emergency involving Matthew, the Gael knew it was only a matter of time before the historical anomalies appeared. Gallowglass had seen the announcement about the discovery of a pair of previously unknown Elizabethan miniatures. By the time he'd managed to reach Sotheby's, they had already been purchased. Gallowglass had panicked, thinking they might have fallen into the wrong hands. But he'd underestimated Ysabeau. When he talked to Marcus this morning, Matthew's son confirmed that they were sitting safely on Ysabeau's desk at Sept-Tours. It had been more than four hundred years since Gallowglass had secreted the pictures away in a house in Shropshire. It would be good to see them—and the two creatures they depicted—once more.

Meanwhile he was preparing for the gathering storm as he always did: by traveling as far and fast as he could. Once it had been the seas and then the rails, but now Gallowglass took to the roads, motorcycling around as many hairpin turns and mountainsides as he could. With the wind streaming through his shaggy hair and his leather jacket fastened tight around his neck to hide the fact that his skin never showed any hint of tan, Gallowglass readied himself for the call of duty to fulfill his long-ago promise to defend the de Clermonts no matter what the cost.

"Gallowglass? Are you still there?" Verin's voice crackled through the phone, pulling her nephew from his reveries.

"Still here, Auntie."

"When are you going?" Verin sighed and rested her head in her hand. She couldn't bring herself to look at Ernst yet. Poor Ernst, who had knowingly married a vampire and, in doing so, had unwittingly involved himself in a tangled tale of blood and desire that looped and swirled through the centuries. But she'd promised her father, and even though Philippe was dead, Verin had no intention of disappointing him now, and for the first time.

"I told Marcus to expect me the day after tomorrow." Gallowglass would no more admit he was relieved by his aunt's decision than Verin would admit that she'd had to consider whether to stand by her oath.

"We'll see you there." That would give Verin some time to break the news to Ernst that he was going to have to share her stepmother's roof. He wasn't going to be pleased.

"Travel safe, Auntie Verin," Gallowglass managed to get out before she hung up.

Gallowglass put the phone in his pocket and stared out to sea. He'd been shipwrecked once on this stretch of Australia's coast. He was fond of the sites where he'd been washed ashore, a merman coming aground in a tempest to find he could live on solid ground after all. He reached for his cigarettes. Like riding a motorcycle without a helmet, smoking was a way of thumbing his nose at the universe that had given him immortality with one hand but with the other taken away everyone he loved.

"And you'll take these from me, too, won't you?" he asked the wind. It sighed out a reply. Matthew and Marcus had very decided opinions about secondhand smoke. Just because it wouldn't kill them, they argued, that didn't mean they should go about exterminating everybody else.

"If we kill them all, what will we eat?" Marcus had pointed out with infallible logic. It was a curious notion for a vampire, but Marcus was known for them, and Matthew wasn't much better. Gallowglass attributed this tendency to too much education.

He finished his cigarette and reached back into his pocket for a small leather pouch. It contained twenty-four disks an inch across and a quarter of an inch thick. They were cut from a branch he'd pulled from an ash tree that grew near his ancestral home. Each one had a mark burned into the surface, an alphabet for a language that no one spoke anymore.

He had always possessed a healthy respect for magic, even before he met Diana Bishop. There were powers abroad on the earth and the seas that no creature understood, and Gallowglass knew well enough to look the other way when they approached. But he couldn't resist the runes. They helped him to navigate the treacherous waters of his fate.

He sifted his fingers through the smooth wooden circles, letting them fall through his hand like water. He wanted to know which way the tide was running—with the de Clermonts or against them?

When his fingers stilled, he drew out the rune that would tell him where matters stood now. *Nyd,* the rune for absence and desire. Gallowglass dipped his hand into the bag again to better understand what he wanted the future to hold. *Odal,* the glyph for home, family, and inheritance. He drew out the final rune, the one that would show him how to fulfill his gnawing wish to belong.

*Rad.* It was a confusing rune, one that stood for both an arrival and a departure, a journey's beginning and its ending, a first meeting as well as a long-awaited reunion. Gallowglass's hand closed around the bit of wood. This time its meaning was clear.

"You travel safely, too, Auntie Diana. And bring that uncle of mine with you," Gallowglass said to the sea and the sky before he climbed back onto his bike and headed into a future he could no longer imagine nor postpone.

# PART IV

# The Empire: Prague

## 27

"Where are my red hose?" Matthew clomped downstairs and scowled at the boxes scattered all over the ground floor. His mood had taken a decided turn for the worse halfway through our four-week journey when we parted ways with Pierre, the children, and our luggage in Hamburg. We'd lost ten additional days by virtue of traveling from England into a Catholic country that reckoned time by a different calendar. In Prague, it was now the eleventh of March and the children and Pierre had yet to arrive.

"I'll never find them in this mess!" Matthew said, taking out his frustration on one of my petticoats.

After we'd lived out of saddlebags and a single shared trunk for weeks, our belongings had arrived three days after we did at the tall, narrow house perched on the steep avenue leading to Prague Castle known as Sporren-gasse. Our German neighbors presumably dubbed it Spur Street because that was the only way you could persuade a horse to make the climb.

"I didn't know you owned red hose," I said, straightening up.

"I do." Matthew started rooting around in a box that contained my linen.

"Well, they won't be in there," I said, pointing out the obvious.

The vampire ground his teeth. "I've looked everywhere else."

"I'll find them." I eyed his perfectly respectable black leggings. "Why red?"

"Because I am trying to catch the Holy Roman Emperor's attention!" Matthew dove into another pile of my clothes.

Bloodred stockings would do more than capture a wandering eye, given that the man who proposed to wear them was a six-foot-three vampire, and most of his height was leg. Matthew's commitment to the plan was unwavering, however. I focused my mind, asked for the hose to show themselves, and followed the red threads. The ability to keep track of people and objects was an unforeseen fringe benefit of being a weaver, and one I'd had several opportunities to use on the trip.

"Has my father's messenger arrived?" Matthew contributed another petticoat to the snowy mountain growing between us and resumed digging.

"Yes. It's over by the door—whatever it is." I fished through contents of an overlooked chest: chain-mail gauntlets, a shield with a double-headed eagle on it, and an elaborately chased cup-and-stick gizmo. Triumphant, I brandished the long red tubes. "Found them!"

Matthew had forgotten the hosiery crisis. His father's package now held his complete attention. I looked to see what had him so amazed.

"Is that . . . a Bosch?" I knew Hieronymus Bosch's work because of his bizarre use of alchemical equipment and symbolism. He covered his panels with flying fish, insects, enormous household implements, and eroticized fruit. Long before psychedelic was stylish, Bosch saw the world in bright colors and unsettling combinations.

Like Matthew's Holbeins at the Old Lodge, however, this work was unfamiliar. It was a triptych, assembled from three hinged wooden panels. Designed to sit on an altar, triptychs were kept closed except for special religious celebrations. In modern museums the exteriors were seldom on display. I wondered what other stunning images I'd been missing.

The artist had covered the outside panels with a velvety black pigment. A wizened tree shimmering in the moonlight spanned the two front panels. A tiny wolf crouched in its roots, and an owl perched in the upper branches. Both animals gazed at the viewer knowingly. A dozen other eyes shone out from the dark ground around the tree, disembodied and staring. Behind the dead oak, a stand of deceptively normal trees with pale trunks and iridescent green branches shed more light on the scene. Only when I took a closer look did I see the ears growing out of them, as though they were listening to the sounds of the night.

"What does it mean?" I asked, staring at Bosch's work in wonder.

Matthew's fingers fiddled with the fastenings on his doublet. "It represents an old Flemish proverb: '*The forest has eyes, and the woods have ears; therefore I will see, be silent, and hear.*'" The words perfectly captured the secretive life Matthew led and reminded me of Elizabeth's current choice of motto.

The triptych's interior showed three interrelated scenes: One panel showed the fallen angels, painted against the same velvety black background. At first glance they looked more like dragonflies with their shimmering double wings, but they had human bodies, with heads and legs that twisted in torment as the angels fell through the heavens. On the opposite panel, the dead rose for the Last Judgment in a scene far more gruesome than the frescoes at Sept-Tours. The gaping jaws of fish and wolves provided entrances to hell, sucking in the damned and consigning them to an eternity of pain and agony.

The center, however, showed a very different image of death: the resurrected Lazarus calmly climbing out of his coffin. With his long legs, dark hair, and serious expression, he looked rather like Matthew. All around the borders of the center panel, lifeless vines produced strange fruits and flowers. Some dripped blood. Others gave birth to people and animals. And no Jesus was in sight.

"Lazarus resembles you. No wonder you don't want Rudolf to have it." I handed Matthew his hose. "Bosch must have known you were a vampire, too."

"Jeroen—or Hieronymus as you know him—saw something he shouldn't have," Matthew said darkly. "I didn't know that Jeroen had witnessed me feeding until I saw the sketches he made of me with a warmblood. From that day on, he believed all creatures had a dual nature, part human and part animal."

"And sometimes part vegetable," I said, studying a naked woman with a strawberry for a head and cherries for hands running away from a pitchfork-wielding devil wearing a stork as a hat. Matthew made a soft sound of amusement. "Does Rudolf know you're a vampire, as Elizabeth does and Bosch did?" I was increasingly concerned by the number of people who were in on the secret.

"Yes. The emperor knows I'm a member of the Congregation, too." He twisted his bright red hose into a knot. "Thank you for finding these."

"Tell me now if you have a habit of losing your car keys, because I'm not putting up with this kind of panic every morning when you get ready for work." I slid my arms around his waist and rested my cheek on his heart. That slow, steady beat always calmed me.

"What are you going to do, divorce me?" Matthew returned the embrace, resting his head on mine so that we fit together perfectly.

"You promised me vampires don't do divorce." I gave him a squeeze. "You're going to look like a cartoon character if you put those red socks on. I'd stick to the black if I were you. You'll stand out regardless."

"Witch," Matthew said, releasing me with a kiss.

He went up the hill to the castle, wearing sober black hose and carrying a long, convoluted message (partially in verse) offering Rudolf a marvelous book for his collections. He came back down four hours later empty-handed, having delivered the note to an imperial flunky. There had been no audience with the emperor. Instead Matthew had been kept waiting along with all the other ambassadors seeking audience.

"It was like being stuck in a cattle truck with all those warm bodies cooped up together. I tried to go somewhere with clear air to breathe, but the nearby rooms were full of witches."

"Witches?" I climbed down from the table I was using to put Matthew's sword safely on top of the linen cupboard in preparation for Jack's arrival.

"Dozens of them," Matthew said. "They were complaining about what's happening in Germany. Where's Gallowglass?"

"Your nephew is buying eggs and securing the services of a housekeeper and a cook." Françoise had flatly refused to join our expedition to Central Europe, which she viewed as a godless land of Lutherans. She was now back at the Old Lodge, spoiling Charles. Gallowglass was serving as my page and general dogsbody until the others arrived. He had excellent German and Spanish, which made him indispensable when it came to provisioning our household. "Tell me more about the witches."

"The city is a safe haven for every creature in Central Europe who fears for his safety—daemon, vampire, or witch. But the witches are especially welcome in Rudolf's court, because he covets their knowledge. And their power."

"Interesting," I said. No sooner had I started wondering about their identities than a series of faces appeared to my third eye. "Who is the wizard with the red beard? And the witch with one blue and one green eye?"

"We aren't going to be here long enough for their identities to matter," Matthew said ominously on his way out the door. Having concluded the day's business for Elizabeth, he was headed across the river to Prague's Old Town on behalf of the Congregation. "I'll see you before dark. Stay here until Gallowglass returns. I don't want you getting lost." More to the point, he didn't want me stumbling upon any witches.

Gallowglass returned to Sporrengasse with two vampires and a pretzel. He handed the latter to me and introduced me to my new servants.

Karolína (the cook) and Tereza (the housekeeper) were members of a sprawling clan of Bohemian vampires dedicated to serving the aristocracy and important foreign visitors. Like the de Clermont retainers, they earned their reputation—and an unusually large salary—because of their preternatural longevity and wolfish loyalty. For the right price, we were also able to buy assurances of secrecy from the clan's elder, who had removed the women from the household of the papal ambassador. The ambassador graciously consented out of deference to the de Clermonts. They had, after all, been instrumental in rigging the last papal election, and he knew who buttered his bread. I cared only that Karolína knew how to make omelets.

Our household established, Matthew loped up the hill each morning to the castle while I unpacked, met my neighbors in the neighborhood below the castle walls called Malá Strana, and watched for the absent members of the household. I missed Annie's cheerfulness and wide-eyed approach to the world, as well as Jack's unfailing ability to get himself into trouble. Our winding street was packed with children of all ages and nationalities, since most of the ambassadors lived there. It turned out that Matthew was not the only foreigner in Prague to be kept at arm's length by the emperor. Every person I met regaled Gallowglass with tales of how Rudolf had snubbed some important personage only to spend hours with a bookish antiquarian from Italy or a humble miner from Saxony.

It was late afternoon on the first day of spring, and the house was filling with the homely scents of pork and dumplings when a scrappy eight-year-old tackled me.

"Mistress Roydon!" Jack crowed, his face buried in my bodice and his arms wrapped tightly around me. "Did you know that Prague is really four towns in one? London is only one town. And there is a castle, too, and a river. Pierre will show me the watermill tomorrow."

"Hello, Jack," I said, stroking his hair. Even on the grueling, freezing journey to Prague, he had managed to shoot up in height. Pierre must have been shoveling food into him. I looked up and smiled at Annie and Pierre. "Matthew will be so glad that you've all arrived. He's missed you."

"We've missed him, too," Jack said, tilting his head back to look at me. He had dark circles under his eyes, and in spite of his growth spurt he looked wan.

"Have you been ill?" I asked, feeling his forehead. Colds could turn deadly in this harsh climate, and there was talk of a nasty epidemic in the Old Town that Matthew thought was a strain of flu.

"He's been having trouble sleeping," Pierre said quietly. I could tell from his serious tone that there was more to the story, but it could wait.

"Well, you'll sleep tonight. There is an enormous featherbed in your room. Go with Tereza, Jack. She'll show you where your things are and get you washed up before supper." In the interests of vampire propriety, the warmbloods would be sleeping with Matthew and me on the second floor, since the house's narrow layout permitted only a keeping room and kitchen on the ground floor. That meant that the first floor was dedicated to formal rooms for receiving guests. The rest of the household's vampires had staked their claim on the lofty third floor, with its expansive views and windows that could be flung open to the elements.

"Master Roydon!" Jack shrieked, hurling himself at the door and flinging it open before Tereza could stop him. How he detected Matthew was a mystery, given the growing darkness and Matthew's head-to-toe adoption of slate-colored wool.

"Easy," Matthew said, catching Jack before he hurt himself running into a pair of solid vampire legs. Gallowglass snatched at Jack's cap as he went by, ruffling the boy's hair.

"We almost froze. In the river. And the sled turned over once, but the dog was not hurt. I ate roasted boar. And Annie caught her skirt in the wagon wheel and almost tumbled out." Jack couldn't get the details of their journey out of his mouth fast enough. "I saw a blazing star. It was not very big, but Pierre told me I must share it with Master Harriot when we return home. I drew a picture of it for him." Jack's hand slid inside his grimy doublet and pulled out an equally grimy slip of paper. He presented this to Matthew with the reverence normally accorded to a holy relic.

"This is quite good," Matthew said, studying the drawing with appropriate care. "I like how you've shown the curve of the tail. And you put the other stars around it. That was wise, Jack. Master Harriot will be pleased at your powers of observation."

Jack flushed. "That was my last piece of paper. Do they sell paper in Prague?" Back in London, Matthew had taken to supplying Jack with a pocketful of paper scraps every morning. How Jack went through them was a matter of some speculation.

"The city is awash in the stuff," Matthew said. "Pierre will take you to the shop in Malá Strana tomorrow."

After that exciting promise, it was hard to get the children upstairs, but Tereza proved to possess the precise mix of gentleness and resolve to accomplish the task. That gave the four grown-ups a chance to talk freely.

"Has Jack been sick?" Matthew asked Pierre with a frown.

"No, *milord*. Since we left you, his sleep has been troubled." Pierre hesitated. "I think the evils in his past haunt him."

Matthew's forehead smoothed out, but he still looked concerned. "And otherwise the journey was as you expected?" This was his cagey way of asking whether they had been set upon by bandits or plagued by supernatural or preternatural beings.

"It was long and cold," Pierre said matter-of-factly, "and the children were always hungry."

Gallowglass bellowed with laughter. "Well, that sounds about right."

"And you, *milord?*" Pierre shot a veiled glance at Matthew. "Is Prague as you expected?"

"Rudolf hasn't seen me. Rumor has it that Kelley is in the uppermost reaches of the Powder Tower blowing up alembics and God-knows-what-else," Matthew reported.

"And the Old Town?" Pierre asked delicately.

"It is much as it ever was." Matthew's tone was breezy and light—a dead giveaway that he was concerned about something.

"So long as you ignore the gossip coming from the Jewish quarter. One of their witches has made a creature from clay who prowls the streets at night." Gallowglass turned innocent eyes on his uncle. "Saving that, it is practically unchanged from the last time we were here to help Emperor Ferdinand secure the city in 1547."

"Thank you, Gallowglass," Matthew said. His tone was as chilly as the wind off the river.

Surely it would require more than an ordinary spell to construct a creature from mud and set it in motion. Such a rumor could mean only one thing: Somewhere in Prague was a weaver like me, one who could move between the world of the living and the world of the dead. But I didn't have to call Matthew on his secret. His nephew beat me to it.

"You didn't think you could keep news of the clay creature from Auntie?" Gallowglass shook his head in amazement. "You don't spend enough time at the market. The women of Malá Strana know everything, including what the emperor is having for breakfast and that he's refused to see you."

Matthew ran his fingers over the painted wooden surface of the triptych and sighed. "You'll have to take this up to the palace, Pierre."

"But that is the altarpiece from Sept-Tours," Pierre protested. "The emperor is known for his caution. Surely it is only a matter of time before he admits you."

"Time is the one commodity we lack—and the de Clermonts have altarpieces aplenty," Matthew said ruefully. "Let me write a note to the emperor, and you can be on your way."

Matthew dispatched Pierre and the painting shortly thereafter. His servant returned just as empty-handed as Matthew had, with no assurances of a future meeting.

All around me the threads that bound the worlds were tightening and shifting in a weaving whose pattern was too large for me to perceive or understand. But something was brewing in Prague. I could feel it.

That night I awoke to the sound of soft voices in the room adjoining our bedchamber. Matthew was not next to me, reading, as he had been when I'd dropped off to sleep. I padded to the door to see who was with him.

"Tell me what happens when I shade the side of the monster's face." Matthew's hand moved swiftly over the large sheet of foolscap before him.

"It makes him seem farther away!" Jack whispered, awestruck by the transformation.

"You try it," Matthew said, handing Jack his pen. Jack gripped it with great concentration, his tongue stuck slightly out. Matthew rubbed the boy's back with his hand, relaxing the taut muscles wrapped around his rangy frame. Jack was not quite sitting on his knee but leaning into the vampire's comforting bulk for support. "So many monsters," Matthew murmured, meeting my eyes.

"Do you want to draw yours?" Jack inched the paper in Matthew's direction. "Then you could sleep, too."

"Your monsters have frightened mine away," Matthew said, returning his attention to Jack, his face grave. My heart hurt for the boy and all he had endured in his brief, hard life.

Matthew met my eyes again and indicated with a slight shift of his head that he had everything under control. I blew him a kiss and returned to the warm, feathery nest of our bed.

The next day we received a note from the emperor. It was sealed with thick wax and ribbons.

"The painting worked, *milord*," Pierre said apologetically.

"It figures. I loved that altarpiece. Now I'll have a hell of a time getting my hands on it again," Matthew said, sitting back in his chair. The wood creaked in protest. Matthew reached out for the letter. The penmanship was elaborate, with so many swirls and curlicues that the letters were practically unrecognizable.

"Why is the handwriting so ornate?" I wondered.

the Hoefnagels have arrived from Vienna and have nothing to occupy their time. The fancier the handwriting, the better, as far as His Majesty is concerned," Pierre replied cryptically.

"I'm to go to Rudolf this afternoon," Matthew said with a satisfied smile, folding up the message. "My father will be pleased. He sent some money and jewels, too, but it would appear that the de Clermonts got off lightly this time."

Pierre held out another, smaller letter, addressed in a plainer style. "The emperor added a postscript. In his own hand."

I looked over Matthew's shoulder as he read it.

*"Bringen das Buch. Und die Hexe."* The emperor's swirling signature, with its elaborate *R,* looping *d* and *l,* and double *f*'s, was at the bottom.

My German was rusty, but the message was clear: *Bring the book. And the witch.*

"I spoke too soon," Matthew muttered.

"I told you to hook him with Titian's great canvas of Venus that Grandfather took off King Philip's hands when his wife objected to it," Gallowglass observed. "Like his uncle, Rudolf has always been unduly fond of redheads. And saucy pictures."

"And witches," my husband said under his breath. He threw the letter on the table. "It wasn't the painting that baited him, but Diana. Maybe I should refuse his invitation."

"That was a command, Uncle." Gallowglass's brow lowered.

"And Rudolf has Ashmole 782," I said. "It's not going to simply appear in front of the Three Ravens on Sporrengasse. We're going to have to find it."

"Are you calling us ravens, Auntie?" Gallowglass said with mock offense.

"I'm talking about the sign on the house, you great oaf." Like every other residence on the street, ours had a symbol over the door rather than a house number. After the neighborhood caught fire in the middle of the century, the emperor's grandfather had insisted on having some way to tell houses apart besides the popular sgraffito decorations scratched into the plaster.

Gallowglass grinned. "I knew very well what you were talking about. But I do love seeing you go all shiny like that when your *glaem*'s raised."

I pulled my disguising spell around me with a harrumph, dimming my shininess to more acceptable, human levels.

"Besides," Gallowglass continued. "Among my people it's a great compliment to be likened to a raven. I'll be Muninn, and Matthew we'll call Huginn. Your name will be Göndul, Auntie. You'll make a fine Valkyrie."

"What is he talking about?" I asked Matthew blankly.

"Odin's ravens. And his daughters."

"Oh. Thank you, Gallowglass," I said awkwardly. It couldn't be a bad thing to be likened to a god's daughter.

"Even if this book of Rudolf's is Ashmole 782, we're not sure it contains answers to our questions." Our experience with the Voynich manuscript still worried Matthew.

"Historians never know if a text will provide answers. If it doesn't, though, we'll still have better questions as a result," I replied.

"Point taken." Matthew's lips quirked. "As I can't get in to see the emperor or his library without you, and you won't leave Prague without the book, there is nothing for it. We'll both go to the palace."

"You've been hoist by your own petard, Uncle," Gallowglass said cheerfully. He gave me a broad wink.

When compared to our visit to Richmond, the trip up the street to see the emperor seemed almost like popping next door to borrow a cup of sugar from a neighbor—though it required a more formal costume. The papal ambassador's mistress was much my size, and her wardrobe had provided me with a suitably luxurious and circumspect garment for the wife of an English dignitary—or a de Clermont, she quickly added. I loved the style of clothing worn by well-heeled women in Prague: simple gowns with high necks, bell-shaped skirts, embroidered coats with hanging sleeves trimmed in fur. The small ruffs they wore served as another welcome barrier between the elements and me.

Matthew had happily abandoned his dreams of red hose in favor of his usual gray and black, accented with a deep green that was the most attractive color I had ever seen him wear. This afternoon it provided flashes of color peeking through the slashes on his bulbous britches and the lining peeking around the open collar of his jacket.

"You look splendid," I said after inspecting him.

"And you look like a proper Bohemian aristocrat," he replied, kissing me on the cheek.

"Can we go now?" Jack said, dancing with impatience. Someone had found him a suit of black-and-silver livery and put a cross and crescent moon on the sleeve.

"So we are going as de Clermonts, not as Roydons," I said slowly.

"No. We are Matthew and Diana Roydon," Matthew replied. "We're just traveling with the de Clermont family servants."

"That should confuse everybody," I commented as we left the house.

"Exactly," Matthew said with a smile.

Had we been going as ordinary citizens, we would have climbed the new palace steps, which clung to the ramparts and provided a safe way for pedestrians. Instead we wended our way up Sporrengasse on horseback as befitted a representative of the queen of England, which gave me a chance to fully take in the houses with their canted foundations, colorful sgraffito, and painted signs. We passed the house of the Red Lion, the Golden Star, the Swan, and the Two Suns. At the top of the hill, we took a sharp turn into a neighborhood filled with the mansions of aristocrats and court appointees, called Hradčany.

It was not my first glimpse of the castle, for I'd seen it looming over its surroundings when we came into Prague and could look up to its ramparts from our windows. But this was the closest I'd yet been to it. The castle was even larger and more sprawling at close range than it had appeared at a distance, like an entirely separate city full of trade and industry. Ahead were the Gothic pinnacles of St. Vitus Cathedral, with round towers punctuating the walls. Though built for defense, the towers now housed workshops for the hundreds of artisans who made their home at Rudolf's court.

The palace guard admitted us through the west gate and into an enclosed courtyard. After Pierre and Jack took charge of the horses, our armed escorts headed for a range of buildings tucked against the castle walls. They had been built relatively recently, and the stone was crisp-edged and gleaming. These looked like office buildings, but beyond them I could see high roofs and medieval stonework.

"What's happened now?" I whispered to Matthew. "Why aren't we going to the palace?"

"Because there's nobody there of any importance," said Gallowglass. He held the Voynich manuscript in his arms, safely wrapped in leather and bound with straps to keep the pages from warping in the damp weather.

"Rudolf found the old Royal Palace drafty and dark," Matthew explained, helping me over the slick cobbles. "His new palace faces south and overlooks a private garden. Here he's farther away from the cathedral—and the priests."

The halls of the residence were busy, with people rushing to and fro shouting in German, Czech, Spanish, and Latin depending on which part of Rudolf's empire they came from. The closer we got to the emperor, the more frenetic the activity became. We passed a room filled with people arguing over architectural drawings. Another room housed a lively debate about the merits of an elaborate gold-and-stone bowl fashioned to look like a seashell. Finally the guards left us in a comfortable salon with heavy chairs, a tiled stove that pumped out a significant amount of heat, and two men in deep conversation. They turned toward us.

"Good day, old friend," a kindly man of around sixty said in English. He beamed at Matthew.

"Tadeáš." Matthew gripped his arm warmly. "You are looking well."

"And you are looking young." The man's eyes twinkled. His glance caused no tell-tale reaction on my skin. "And here is the woman everyone is talking about. I am Tadeáš Hájek." The human bowed, and I curtsied in response.

A slender gentleman with an olive complexion and hair nearly as dark as Matthew's strolled over to us. "Master Strada," Matthew said with a bow. He was not as pleased to see this man as he was the first.

"Is she truly a witch?" Strada surveyed me with interest. "If so, my sister Katharina would like to meet her. She is with child, and the pregnancy troubles her."

"Surely Tadeáš—the royal physician—is better suited to seeing after the birth of the emperor's child," Matthew said, "or have matters with your sister changed?"

"The emperor still treasures my sister," Strada said frostily. "For that reason alone, her whims should be indulged."

"Have you seen Joris? He has been talking about nothing but your altarpiece since His Majesty opened it," Tadeáš asked, changing the subject.

"Not yet, no." Matthew's eyes went to the door. "Is the emperor in?"

"Yes. He is looking at a new painting by Master Spranger. It is very large and . . . ah, detailed."

"Another picture of Venus," Strada said with a sniff.

"This Venus looks rather like your sister, sir." Hájek smiled.

*"Ist das Matthäus höre ich?"* said a nasal voice from the far end of the room. Everyone turned and swept into deep bows. I curtsied automatically. It was going to be a challenge to follow the conversation. I had expected Rudolf to speak Latin, not German. *"Und Sie das Buch und die Hexe gebracht, ich verstehe. Und die norwegische Wolf."*

Rudolf was a small man with a disproportionately long chin and a pronounced underbite. The full, fleshy lips of the Hapsburg family exaggerated the prominence of the lower half of his face, although this was somewhat balanced by his pale, protruding eyes and thick, flattened nose. Years of good living and fine drink had given him a portly profile, but his legs remained thin and spindly. He tottered toward us on high-heeled red shoes ornamented with gold stamps.

"I brought my wife, Your Majesty, as you commanded," Matthew said, placing a slight emphasis on the word "wife." Gallowglass translated Matthew's English into flawless German, as if my husband didn't know the language—which I knew he did, after traveling with him from Hamburg to Wittenberg to Prague by sled.

*"Y su talento para los juegos también,"* Rudolf said, switching effortlessly into Spanish as though that might convince Matthew to converse with him directly. He studied me slowly, lingering over the curves of my body with a thoroughness that made me long for a shower. *"Es una lástima que se casó en absoluto, pero aún más lamentable que ella está casada con usted."*

"Very regrettable, Majesty," Matthew said sharply, sticking resolutely to English. "But I assure you we are thoroughly wed. My father insisted upon it. So did the lady." This remark only made Rudolf scrutinize me with greater interest.

Gallowglass took mercy on me and thumped the book onto the table. *"Das Buch."*

That got their attention. Strada unwrapped it while Hájek and Rudolf speculated on just how wonderful this new addition to the imperial library might prove to be. When it was exposed to view, however, the air in the room thickened with disappointment.

"What joke is this?" Rudolf snapped in German.

"I am not sure I take Your Majesty's meaning," Matthew replied. He waited for Gallowglass to translate.

"I mean that I already know this book," Rudolf sputtered.

"That doesn't surprise me, Your Majesty, since you gave it to John Dee—by mistake, I am told." Matthew bowed.

"The emperor does not make mistakes!" Strada said, pushing the book away in disgust.

"We all make mistakes, Signor Strada," Hájek said gently. "I am sure, though, that there is some other explanation as to why this book has been returned to the emperor. Perhaps Dr. Dee uncovered its secrets."

"It is nothing but childish pictures," retorted Strada.

"Is that why this picture book found its way into Dr. Dee's baggage? Did you hope he would be able to understand what you could not?" Matthew's words were having an adverse effect on Strada, who turned purple. "Perhaps you borrowed Dee's book, Signor Strada, the one with alchemical pictures from Roger Bacon's library, in hope that it would help you decipher this one. That is a far more pleasant prospect than imagining you would have tricked poor Dr. Dee out of his treasure. Of course his Majesty could not have known of such an evil business." Matthew's smile was chilling.

"And is this book that you say I have the only treasure of mine you wish to take back to England?" Rudolf asked sharply. "Or does your avarice extend to my laboratories?"

"If you mean Edward Kelley, the queen needs some assurance that he is here of his own free will. Nothing more," Matthew lied. He then took the conversation in a less trying direction. "Do you like your new altarpiece, Your Majesty?"

Matthew had provided the emperor just enough room to regroup—and save face. "The Bosch is exceptional. My uncle will be most aggrieved to learn that I have acquired it." Rudolf looked around. "Alas, this room is not suitable for its display. I wanted to show it to the Spanish ambassador, but here you cannot get far enough from the painting to view it properly. It is a work that you must come upon slowly, allowing the details to emerge naturally. Come. See where I have put it."

Matthew and Gallowglass arranged themselves so that Rudolf couldn't get too close to me as we trooped through the door and into a room that looked like the storeroom for an overstuffed and understaffed museum. Shelves and cabinets held so many shells, books, and fossils that they threatened to topple over. Huge canvases—including the new painting of Venus, which was not simply detailed but openly erotic—were propped up against bronze statues. This must be Rudolf's famed curiosity cabinet, his room of wonders and marvels.

"Your Majesty needs more space—or fewer specimens," Matthew commented, grabbing a piece of porcelain to keep it from smashing to the floor.

"I will always find a place for new treasures." The emperor's gaze settled on me once more. "I am building four new rooms to hold them all. You can see them working." He pointed out the window to two towers and the long building that was beginning to connect them to the emperor's apartments and another new piece of construction opposite. "Until then Ottavio and Tadeáš are cataloging my collection and instructing the architects on what I require. I do not want to move everything into the new *Kunstkammer* only to outgrow it again."

Rudolf led us through a warren of additional storerooms until we finally arrived at a long gallery with windows on both sides. It was full of light, and after the gloom and dust of the preceding chambers, entering it felt like taking in a lungful of clean air.

The sight in the center of the room brought me up short. Matthew's altarpiece sat open on a long table covered with thick green felt. The emperor was right: You couldn't fully appreciate the colors when you stood close to the work.

"It is beautiful, Dona Diana." Rudolf took advantage of my surprise to grasp my hand. "Notice how what you perceive changes with each step. Only vulgar objects can be seen at once, for they have no mysteries to reveal."

Strada looked at me with open animosity, Hájek with pity. Matthew was not looking at me at all, but at the emperor.

"Speaking of which, Majesty, might I see Dee's book?" Matthew's expression was guileless, but no one in the room was fooled for an instant. The wolf was on the prowl.

"Who knows where it is?" Rudolf had to drop my hand in order to wave vaguely at the rooms we had just left.

"Signor Strada must be neglecting his duties, if such a precious manuscript cannot be found when the emperor requires it," Matthew said softly.

"Ottavio is very busy at present, with matters of importance!" Rudolf glared at Matthew. "And I do not trust Dr. Dee. Your queen should beware his false promises."

"But you trust Kelley. Perhaps he knows its whereabouts?"

At this the emperor looked distinctly uneasy. "I do not want Edward disturbed. He is at a very delicate stage in the alchemical work."

"Prague has many charms, and Diana has been commissioned to purchase some alchemical glassware for the Countess of Pembroke. We will occupy ourselves with that task until Sir Edward is able to receive visitors. Perhaps Signor Strada will be able to find your missing book by then."

"This Countess of Pembroke is the sister of the queen's hero, Sir Philip Sidney?" Rudolf asked, his interest caught. When Matthew opened his mouth to answer, Rudolf stopped him with a raised hand. "It is Dona Diana's business. We will let her answer."

"Yes, Your Majesty," I responded in Spanish. My pronunciation was atrocious. I hoped that would diminish his interest.

"Charming," Rudolf murmured. *Damn.* "Very well then, Dona Diana must visit my workshops. I enjoy fulfilling a lady's wishes."

It was not clear which lady he meant.

"As for Kelley and the book, we shall see. We shall see." Rudolf turned back to the triptych. "*I will see, be silent, and hear.*' Isn't that the proverb?"

**28**

"**D**id you see the werewolf, Frau Roydon? He is the emperor's game-keeper, and my neighbor Frau Habermel has heard him howling at night. They say he feeds on the imperial deer running in the Stag Moat." Frau Huber picked up a cabbage in her gloved hand and gave it a suspicious sniff. Herr Huber had been a merchant at London's Steelyard, and though she bore no love for the city, she spoke English fluently.

"Pah. There is no werewolf," Signorina Rossi said, turning her long neck and tutting over the price of the onions. "My Stefano tells me there are many daemons in the palace, however. The bishops at the cathedral wish to exorcise them, but the emperor refuses." Like Frau Huber, Rossi had spent time in London. Then she had been mistress to an Italian artist who wanted to bring mannerism to the English. Now she was mistress to another Italian artist who wanted to introduce the art of glass cutting to Prague.

"I saw no werewolves or daemons," I confessed. The women's faces fell. "But I did see one of the emperor's new paintings." I dropped my voice. "It showed Venus. Rising from her bath." I gave them both significant looks.

In the absence of otherworldly gossip, the perversions of royalty would suffice. Frau Huber drew herself straight.

"Emperor Rudolf needs a wife. A good Austrian woman, who will cook for him." She condescended to buy a cabbage from the grateful vegetable seller, who had been putting up with her criticisms of his produce for nearly thirty minutes. "Tell us again about the unicorn's horn. It is supposed to have miraculous curative powers."

It was the fourth time in two days I'd been asked to account for the marvels among the emperor's curiosities. News of our admittance to Rudolf's private apartments preceded our return to the Three Ravens, and the ladies of Malá Strana were lying in wait the next morning, eager for my impressions.

Since then the appearance of imperial messengers at the house, as well as the liveried servants of dozens of Bohemian aristocrats and foreign dignitaries, had roused their curiosity further. Now that Matthew had been received at court, his star was sufficiently secure in the imperial heavens that his old friends were willing to acknowledge his arrival—and ask for his help. Pierre pulled out the ledgers, and soon the Prague branch of the de Clermont bank was open for business, though I saw precious little money received and a steady stream of funds flow out to settle overdue accounts with the merchants of Prague's Old Town.

"You received a package from the emperor," Matthew told me when I returned from the market. He pointed with his quill at a lumpy sack. "If you open it, Rudolf will expect you to express your thanks personally."

"What could it be?" I felt the outlines of the object inside. It wasn't a book.

"Something we'll regret receiving, I warrant." Matthew jammed the quill in the inkpot, causing a minor eruption of thick black liquid onto the surface of the desk. "Rudolf is a collector, Diana. And he's not simply interested in narwhal horns and bezoar stones. He covets people as well as objects and is just as unlikely to part with them once they're in his possession."

"Like Kelley," I said, loosening the parcel's strings. "But I'm not for sale."

"We are all for sale." Matthew's eyes widened. "Good Christ."

A two-foot-tall, gold-and-silver statue of the goddess Diana sat between us, naked except for her quiver, riding sidesaddle on the back of a stag with her ankles demurely crossed. A pair of hunting dogs sat at her feet.

Gallowglass whistled. "Well, I'd say the emperor has made his desires known in this case."

But I was too busy studying the statue to pay much attention. A small key was embedded in the base. I gave it a turn, and the stag took off across the floor. "Look, Matthew. Did you see that?"

"You're in no danger of losing Uncle's attention," Gallowglass assured me.

It was true: Matthew was staring angrily at the statue.

"Whoa, young Jack." Gallowglass caught Jack by the collar as the boy sped into the room. But Jack was a professional thief, and such delaying tactics were of little use when he smelled something of value. He slid to the floor in a boneless heap, leaving Gallowglass holding the jacket, and sprang after the deer.

"Is it a toy? Is it for me? Why is that lady not wearing any clothes? Isn't she cold?" The questions poured out of Jack in an unbroken torrent. Tereza, who was as interested in spectacle as any of the other women in Malá

Strana, came to see what the fuss was about. She gasped at the naked woman in her employer's office and clapped her hand over Jack's eyes.

Gallowglass peered at the statue's breasts. "Aye, Jack. I'd say she's cold." This earned him a cuff on the head from Tereza, who still retained a firm grip on the squirming child.

"It's an automaton, Jack," Matthew said, picking the thing up. When he did, the stag's head sprang open, revealing the hollow chamber within. "This one is meant to run down the emperor's dinner table. When it stops, the person closest must drink from the stag's neck. Why don't you go show Annie what it does?" He snapped the head back in place and handed the priceless object to Gallowglass. Then he gave me a serious look. "We need to talk."

Gallowglass propelled Jack and Tereza out of the room with promises of pretzels and skating.

"You're in dangerous territory, my love." Matthew ran his fingers through his hair, which never failed to make him look more handsome. "I've told the Congregation that your status as my wife is a convenient fiction to protect you from charges of witchcraft and to keep the Berwick witch hunts confined to Scotland."

"But our friends and your fellow vampires know it's more than that," I said. A vampire's sense of smell didn't lie, and Matthew's unique scent covered me. "And the witches know there's something more to our relationship than meets even their third eye."

"Perhaps, but Rudolf is neither a vampire nor a witch. The emperor will have been assured by his own contacts within the Congregation that there is no relationship between us. Therefore there is nothing to preclude his chasing after you." Matthew's fingers found my cheek. "I don't share, Diana. And if Rudolf were to go too far . . ."

"You'd keep your temper in check." I covered his hand with mine. "You know that I'm not going to let the Holy Roman Emperor—or anybody else, for that matter—seduce me. We need Ashmole 782. Who cares if Rudolf stares at my breasts?"

"Staring I can handle." Matthew kissed me. "There's something else you should know before you go off to thank the emperor. The Congregation has fed Rudolf's appetites for women and curiosities for some time as a way to win his cooperation. If the emperor wishes to have you and takes the matter to the other eight members, their judgment won't be in our favor. The Congregation will turn you over to him because they cannot afford to have Prague fall into the hands of men like the archbishop of Trier and his Jesuit friends. And they don't want Rudolf to become another King James, out for creatures' blood. Prague may appear to be an oasis for the otherworldly. But like all oases, its refuge is a mirage."

"I understand," I said. Why did everything touching Matthew have to be so snarled? Our lives reminded me of the knotted cords in my spell box. No matter how many times I picked them apart, they soon tangled again.

Matthew released me. "When you go to the palace, take Gallowglass with you."

"You're not coming?" Given his concerns, I was shocked that Matthew was going to let me out of his sight.

"No. The more Rudolf sees us together, the more active his imagination and his acquisitiveness will become. And Gallowglass just may be able to wheedle his way in to Kelley's laboratory. My nephew is far more charming than I am." Matthew grinned, but the expression did nothing to alleviate the darkness in his eyes.

Gallowglass insisted he had a plan, one that would keep me from having to speak to Rudolf privately yet would display my gratitude publicly. It wasn't until I heard the bells ringing the hour of three that I caught my first glimmer of what his plan might entail. The crush of people trying to enter St. Vitus Cathedral through the pointed arches of the side entrance confirmed it.

"There goes Sigismund," Gallowglass said, bending close to my ear. The noise from the bells was deafening, and I could barely hear him. When I looked at him in confusion, he pointed up, to a golden grille on the adjacent steeple. "Sigismund. The big bell. That's how you know you're in Prague."

St. Vitus Cathedral was textbook Gothic with its flying buttresses and needlelike pinnacles. On a dark winter afternoon, it was even more so. The candles inside were blazing, but in the vast expanse of the cathedral they provided nothing more than pinpricks of yellow in the gloom. Outside, the light had faded so much that the colorful stained glass and vivid frescoes were of minimal help in lifting the oppressively heavy atmosphere. Gallowglass carefully stationed us under a brace of torches.

"Give your disguising spell a good shake," he suggested. "It's so dark in here that Rudolf might miss you."

"Are you telling me to get shiny?" I gave him my most repressive schoolmarm expression. His only reply was a grin.

We waited for Mass to begin with an interesting assortment of humble palace staff, royal officials, and aristocrats. Some of the artisans still bore the stains and singes associated with their work, and most of them looked exhausted. Once I'd surveyed the crowd, I looked up to take in the size and style of the cathedral.

"That's a whole lot of vaulting," I murmured. The ribbing was far more complicated than in most Gothic churches in England.

"That's what happens when Matthew gets an idea in his head," Gallowglass commented.

"Matthew?" I gaped.

"He was passing through Prague long ago, and Peter Parler, the new architect, was too green for such an important commission. The first outbreak of the plague had killed most of the master masons, however, so Parler was left in charge. Matthew took him under his wing, and the two of them went a bit mad. Can't say I ever understood what he and young Peter were trying to accomplish, but it's eye-catching. Wait until you see what they did to the Great Hall."

I had my mouth open to ask another question when a hush fell over the assembled crowd. Rudolf had arrived. I craned my neck in an effort to see.

"There he is," Gallowglass murmured, jerking his head up and to the right. Rudolf had entered St. Vitus on the second floor, from the enclosed walkway that I'd spotted spanning the courtyard between the palace and the cathedral. He was standing on a balcony decorated with colorful heraldic shields celebrating his many titles and honors. Like the ceiling, the balcony was held up by unusually ornate vaulting, though in this case it resembled the gnarled branches of a tree. Based on the breathtaking purity of the cathedral's other architectural supports, I didn't think this was Matthew's work.

Rudolf took his seat overlooking the central nave while the crowd bowed and curtsied in the direction of the royal box. For his part, Rudolf looked uncomfortable at having been noticed. In his private chambers, he was at ease with his courtiers, but here he seemed shy and reserved. He turned to listen to a whispering attendant and caught sight of me. He inclined his head graciously and smiled. The crowd swung around to see whom the emperor had singled out for his benediction.

"Curtsy," Gallowglass hissed. I dropped down again.

We managed to get through the actual Mass without incident. I was relieved to find that no one, not even the emperor, was expected to take the sacrament, and the whole ceremony was over quickly. At some point Rudolf quietly slipped away to his private apartments, no doubt to pore over his treasures.

With the emperor and priests gone, the nave turned into a cheerful gathering place as friends exchanged news and gossip. I spotted Ottavio Strada in the distance, deep in conversation with a florid gentleman in expensive woolen robes. Dr. Hájek was here, too, laughing and talking to a young couple who were obviously in love. I smiled at him, and he made a small bow in my direction. Strada I could do without, but I liked the emperor's physician.

"Gallowglass? Shouldn't you be hibernating, like the rest of the bears?" A slight man with deep-set eyes approached, his mouth twisted into a wry smile. He was wearing simple, expensive clothes, and the gold ring on his fingers spoke of his prosperity.

"We should all be hibernating in this weather. It is good to see you in such health, Joris." Gallowglass clasped his hand and struck him on the back. The man's eyes popped at the force of the blow.

"I would say the same about you, but since you are always healthy, I will spare us both the empty courtesy." The man turned to me. "And here is La Diosa."

"Diana," I said, bobbing a greeting.

"That is not your name here. Rudolf calls you 'La Diosa de la Caza.' It is Spanish for the goddess of the chase. The emperor has commanded poor Master Spranger to abandon his latest sketches of Venus in her bath in favor of a new subject: Diana interrupted at her toilette. We all wait eagerly to see if Spranger is capable of making such an enormous change on such short notice." The man bowed. "Joris Hoefnagel."

"The calligrapher," I said, thinking back to Pierre's remark about the ornate penmanship on Matthew's official summons to Rudolf's court. But that name was familiar. . . .

"The artist," Gallowglass corrected gently.

"La Diosa." A gaunt man swept his hat off with scarred hands. "I am Erasmus Habermel. Would you be so kind as to visit my workshop as soon as you are able? His Majesty would like you to have an astronomical compendium so as to better note the changes in the fickle moon, but it must be exactly to your liking."

Habermel was a familiar name, too. . . .

"She is coming to me tomorrow." A portly man in his thirties pushed his way through the growing crowd. His accent was distinctly Italian. "La Diosa is to sit for a portrait. His Majesty wishes to have her likeness engraved in stone as a symbol of her permanence in his affections." Perspiration broke out on his upper lip.

"Signor Miseroni!" another Italian said, clasping his hands melodramatically to his heaving chest. "I thought we understood each other. La Diosa must practice her dance if she is to take part in the entertainment next week as the emperor wishes." He bowed in my direction. "I am Alfonso Pasetti, La Diosa, His Majesty's dancing master."

"But my wife does not like to dance," said a cool voice behind me. A long arm snaked around and took my hand, which was fiddling with the edge of my bodice. "Do you, *mon coeur*?" This last endearment was accompanied by a kiss on the knuckles and a warning nip of teeth.

"Matthew is right on cue, as always," Joris said with a hearty laugh. "How are you?"

"Disappointed not to find Diana at home," Matthew said in a slightly aggrieved tone. "But even a devoted husband must yield to God in his wife's affections."

Hoefnagel watched Matthew closely, gauging every change of expression. I suddenly realized who this was: the great artist who was such an acute observer of nature that his illustrations of flora and fauna seemed as though they, like the creatures on Mary's shoes, could come to life.

"Well, God is done with her for today. I think you are free to take your wife home," Hoefnagel said mildly. "You promise to enliven what would otherwise be a very dull spring, La Diosa. For that we are all grateful."

The men dispersed after getting assurances from Gallowglass that he would keep track of my varied, conflicting appointments. Hoefnagel was the last to leave.

"I will keep an eye out for your wife, *Schaduw*. Perhaps you should, too."

"My attention is always on my wife, where it belongs. How else did I know to be here?"

"Of course. Forgive my meddling. *The forest has ears, and the fields have eyes.*" Hoefnagel bowed. "I will see you at court, La Diosa."

"Her name is Diana," Matthew said tightly. "Madame de Clermont will also serve."

"And here I was led to understand it was Roydon. My mistake." Hoefnagel took a few steps backward. "Good evening, Matthew." His footsteps echoed on the stone floors and faded into silence.

"*Schaduw?*" I asked. "Does that mean what it sounds like?"

"It's Dutch for 'Shadow.' Elizabeth isn't the only person to call me by that name." Matthew looked to Gallowglass. "What is this entertainment Signor Pasetti mentioned?"

"Oh, nothing out of the ordinary. It will no doubt be mythological in theme, with terrible music and even worse dancing. Having had too much to drink, the courtiers will all stumble into the wrong bedchambers at the end of the night. Nine months later there will be a flock of noble babes of uncertain parentage. The usual."

"'*Sic transit gloria mundi,*'" Matthew murmured. He bowed to me. "Shall we go home, La Diosa?" The nickname made me uncomfortable when strangers used it, but when it came out of Matthew's mouth, it was almost unbearable. "Jack tells me that tonight's stew is particularly appetizing."

Matthew was distant all evening, watching me with heavy eyes as I heard about the children's day and Pierre brought him up to date on various happenings in Prague. The names were unfamiliar and the narrative so confusing that I gave up trying to follow it and went to bed.

Jack's cries woke me, and I rushed to him only to discover that Matthew had already reached the boy. He was wild, thrashing and crying out for help.

"My bones are flying apart!" he kept saying. "It hurts! It hurts!"

Matthew bundled him up tight against his chest so that he couldn't move. "Shh. I've got you now." He continued to hold Jack until only faint tremors radiated through the child's slender limbs.

"All the monsters looked like ordinary men tonight, Master Roydon," Jack told him, snuggling deeper into my husband's arms. He sounded exhausted, and there were blue smudges under his eyes that made him look far older than his years.

"They often do, Jack," Matthew said. "They often do."

The next few weeks were a whirlwind of appointments—with the emperor's jeweler, the emperor's instrument maker, and the emperor's dancing master. Each encounter took me deeper into the heart of the huddle of buildings that composed the imperial palace, to workshops and residences that were reserved for Rudolf's prize artists and intellectuals.

Between engagements Gallowglass took me to parts of the palace that I had not yet seen. To the menagerie, where Rudolf kept his leopards and lions much as he kept his limners and musicians on the narrow streets east of the cathedral. To the Stag Moat, which had been altered so that Rudolf could enjoy better sport. To the sgraffito-covered games hall, where courtiers could take their exercise. To the new greenhouses built to protect the emperor's precious fig trees from the harsh Bohemian winter.

But there was one place where not even Gallowglass could gain admission: the Powder Tower, where Edward Kelley worked over his alembics and crucibles in an attempt to make the philosopher's stone. We stood outside it and tried to talk our way past the guards stationed at the entrance. Gallowglass even resorted to bellowing a hearty greeting. It brought the neighbors running to see if there was a fire but didn't elicit a reaction from Dr. Dee's erstwhile assistant.

"It's as if he's a prisoner," I told Matthew after the supper dishes were cleared and Jack and Annie were safely tucked into their beds. They'd enjoyed another exhausting round of skating, sledding, and pretzels. We'd given up the pretense that they were our servants. I hoped the opportunity to behave like a normal eight-year-old boy would help to end Jack's nightmares. But the palace was no place for them. I was terrified they might wander off and get lost forever, unable to speak the language or tell people to whom they belonged.

"Kelley *is* a prisoner," Matthew said, toying with the stem of his goblet. It was heavy silver and glinted in the firelight.

"They say he goes home occasionally, usually in the middle of the night when there is no one around to see. At least he gets some relief from the emperor's constant demands."

"You haven't met Mistress Kelley," Matthew said drily.

I hadn't, which struck me as odd the more I considered it. Perhaps I was taking the wrong route to meet the alchemist. I'd allowed myself to be swept into court life with the hope of knocking on Kelley's laboratory door and walking straight in to demand Ashmole 782. But given my new familiarity with courtly life, such a direct approach was unlikely to succeed.

The next morning I made it a point to go with Tereza to do the shopping. It was absolutely frigid outside, and the wind was fierce, but we trudged to the market nonetheless.

"Do you know my countrywoman Mistress Kelley?" I asked Frau Huber as we waited for the baker to wrap our purchases. The housewives of

Malá Strana collected the bizarre and unusual as avidly as Rudolf did. "Her husband is one of the emperor's servants."

"One of the emperor's caged alchemists, you mean," Frau Huber said with a snort. "There are always odd things happening in that household. And it was worse when the Dees were here. Herr Kelley was always looking at Frau Dee with lust."

"And Mistress Kelley?" I prompted her.

"She does not go out much. Her cook does the shopping." Frau Huber did not approve of this delegation of housewifely responsibility. It opened the door to all sorts of disorder, including (she contended) Anabaptism and a thriving black market in purloined kitchen staples. She had made her feelings on this point clear at our first meeting, and it was one of the chief reasons I went out in all weathers to buy cabbage.

"Are we discussing the alchemist's wife?" Signorina Rossi said, tripping across the frozen stones and narrowly avoiding a wheelbarrow full of coal. "She is English and therefore very strange. And her wine bills are much larger than they should be."

"How do you two know so much?" I asked when I'd finished laughing.

"We share the same laundress," Frau Huber said, surprised.

"None of us have any secrets from our laundresses," Signorina Rossi agreed. "She did the washing for the Dees, too. Until Signora Dee fired her for charging so much to clean the napkins."

"A difficult woman, Jane Dee, but you could not fault her thrift," Frau Huber admitted with a sigh.

"Why do you need to see Mistress Kelley?" Signorina Rossi inquired, stowing a braided loaf of bread in her basket.

"I want to meet her husband. I am interested in alchemy and have some questions."

"Will you pay?" Frau Huber asked, rubbing her fingers together in a universal and apparently timeless gesture.

"For what?" I said, confused.

"His answers, of course."

"Yes," I agreed, wondering what devious plan she was concocting.

"Leave it to me," Frau Huber said. "I am hungry for schnitzel, and the Austrian who owns the tavern near your house, Frau Roydon, knows what schnitzel should be."

The Austrian schnitzel wizard's teenage daughter, it turned out, shared a tutor with Kelley's ten-year-old stepdaughter, Elisabeth. And his cook was married to the laundress's aunt, whose sister-in-law helped out around the Kelleys' house.

It was thanks to this occult chain of relationships forged by women, and not Gallowglass's court connections, that Matthew and I found ourselves in the Kelleys' second-floor parlor at midnight, waiting for the great man to arrive.

"He should be here at any moment," Joanna Kelley assured us. Her eyes were red-rimmed and bleary, though whether this resulted from too much wine or from the cold that seemed to afflict the entire household was not clear.

"Do not trouble yourself on our account, Mistress Kelley. We keep late hours," Matthew said smoothly, giving her a dazzling smile. "And how do you like your new house?"

After much espionage and investigation among the Austrian and Italian communities, we discovered that the Kelleys had recently purchased a house around the corner from the Three Ravens in a complex known for its inventive street sign. Someone had taken a few leftover wooden figures from a nativity scene, sawed them in half, and arranged them on a board. They had, in the process, removed the infant Jesus from his crèche and replaced it with the head of Mary's donkey.

"The Donkey and Cradle meets our needs at present, Master Roydon." Mistress Kelley issued forth an awe-inspiring sneeze and took a swig of wine. "We had thought the emperor would set aside a house for us in the palace itself, given Edward's work, but this will do." A regular thumping sounded on the winding stairs. "Here is Edward."

A walking staff appeared first, then a stained hand, followed by an equally stained sleeve. The rest of Edward Kelley looked just as disreputable. His long beard was unkempt and stuck out from a dark skullcap that hid his ears. If he'd had a hat, it was gone now. And he was fond of his dinners, gauging by his Falstaffian proportions. Kelley limped into the room whistling, then froze at the sight of Matthew.

"Edward." Matthew rewarded the man with another of those dazzling smiles, but Kelley didn't seem nearly as pleased to receive it as his wife had. "Imagine us meeting again so far from home."

"How did you . . . ?" Edward said hoarsely. He looked around the room, and his eyes fell on me with a nudging glance that was as insidious as any I'd felt from a daemon. But there was more: disturbances in the threads that surrounded him, irregularities in the weaving that suggested he was not just daemonic—he was unstable. His lips curled. "The witch."

"The emperor has elevated her rank, just as he did yours. She is La Diosa—the goddess—now," Matthew said. "Do sit down and rest your leg. It troubles you in the cold, as I remember."

"What business do you have with me, Roydon?" Edward Kelley gripped his staff tighter.

"He is here on behalf of the queen, Edward. I was in my bed," Joanna said plaintively. "I get so little rest. And because of this dreadful ague, I have not yet met our neighbors. You did not tell me there were English people living so close. Why, I can see Mistress Roydon's house from the tower window. You are at the castle. I am alone, longing to speak my native tongue, and yet—"

"Go back to bed, my dear," Kelley said, dismissing Joanna. "Take your wine with you."

Mrs. Kelley sniffled off obligingly, her expression miserable. To be an Englishwoman in Prague without friends or family was difficult, but to have your husband welcomed in places where you were forbidden to go must make it doubly so. When she was gone, Kelley clumped over to the table and sat down in his wife's chair. With a grimace he lifted his leg into place. Then he pinned his dark, hostile eyes on Matthew.

"Tell me what I must do to get rid of you," he said bluntly. Kelley might have Kit's cunning, but he had none of his charm.

"The queen wants you," Matthew said, equally blunt. "We want Dee's book."

"Which book?" Edward's reply was quick—too quick.

"For a charlatan you are an abominable liar, Kelley. How do you manage to take them all in?" Matthew swung his long, booted legs onto the table. Kelley cringed when the heels struck the surface.

"If Dr. Dee is accusing me of theft," Kelley blustered, "then I must insist on discussing this matter in the emperor's presence. He would not want me treated thus, my honor impugned in my own house."

"Where is it, Kelley? In your laboratory? In Rudolf's bedchamber? I will find it with or without your help. But if you were to tell me your secret, I might be inclined to let the other matter rest." Matthew picked at a speck on his britches. "The Congregation is not pleased with your recent behavior." Kelley's staff clattered to the floor. Matthew obligingly picked it up. He touched the worn end to Kelley's neck. "Is this where you touched the tapster at the inn, when you threatened his life? That was careless, Edward.

All this pomp and privilege has gone to your head." The staff dropped down to Kelley's considerable belly and rested there.

"I cannot help you." Kelley winced as Matthew increased the pressure on the stick. "It is the truth! The emperor took the book from me when . . ." Kelley trailed off, rubbing his hand across his face as if to erase the vampire sitting across from him.

"When what?" I said, leaning forward. When I touched Ashmole 782 in the Bodleian, I'd immediately known it was different.

"You must know more about this book than I do," Kelley spit at me, his eyes blazing. "You witches were not surprised to hear of its existence, though it took a daemon to recognize it!"

"I am losing my patience, Edward." The wooden staff cracked in Matthew's hands. "My wife asked you a question. Answer it."

Kelley gave Matthew a slow, triumphant look and pushed at the end of the staff, dislodging it from his abdomen. "You hate witches—or so everyone believes. But I see now that you share Gerbert's weakness for the creatures. You are in love with this one, just as I told Rudolf."

"Gerbert." Matthew's tone was flat.

Kelley nodded. "He came when Dee was still in Prague, asking questions about the book and nosing about in my business. Rudolf let him enjoy one of the witches from the Old Town—a seventeen-year-old girl and very pretty, with rosy hair and blue eyes just like your wife. No one has seen her since. But there was a very fine fire that Walpurgis Night. Gerbert was given the honor of lighting it." Kelley shifted his eyes to me. "I wonder if we will have a fire again this year?"

The mention of the ancient tradition of burning a witch to celebrate spring was the final straw for Matthew. He had Kelley half out the window by the time I realized what was happening.

"Look down, Edward. It is not a steep fall. You would survive it, I fear, though you might break a bone or two. I would collect you and take you up to your bedchamber. That has a window, too, no doubt. Eventually I will find a place that is high enough to snap your sorry carcass in two. By then every bone in your body will be in pieces and you will have told me what I want to know." Matthew turned black eyes on me when I rose. "Sit. Down." He took a deep breath. "Please." I did.

"Dee's book shimmered with power. I could smell it the moment he pulled it off the shelf at Mortlake. He was oblivious to its significance, but

I knew." Kelley couldn't talk fast enough now. When he paused to take a breath, Matthew shook him. "The witch Roger Bacon owned it and valued it for a great treasure. His name is on the title page, along with the inscription *'Verum Secretum Secretorum.'*"

"But it's nothing like the *Secretum*," I said, thinking of the popular medieval work. "That's an encyclopedia. This has alchemical illustrations."

"The illustrations are nothing but a screen against the truth," Kelley said, wheezing. "That is why Bacon called it *The True Secret of Secrets*."

"What does it say?" I asked, rising with excitement. This time Matthew didn't warn me off. He also dragged Kelley back inside. "Were you able to read the words?"

"Perhaps," Kelley said, straightening his robe.

"He couldn't read the book either." Matthew released Kelley with disgust. "I can smell the duplicity through his fear."

"It's written in a foreign tongue. Not even Rabbi Loew could decipher it."

"The Maharal has seen the book?" Matthew had that still, alert look that he got just before he pounced.

"Apparently you didn't ask Rabbi Loew about it when you were in the Jewish Town to seek out the witch who made this clay creature they call the golem. Nor could you find the culprit and his creation." Kelley looked contemptuous. "So much for your famous power and influence. You couldn't even frighten the Jews."

"I don't think the words are Hebrew," I said, remembering the fast-moving symbols I'd glimpsed in the palimpsest.

"They aren't. The emperor had Rabbi Loew come to the palace just to be sure." Kelley had revealed more than he'd intended. His eyes shifted to his staff, and the threads around him warped and twisted. An image came to me of Kelley lifting his staff to strike someone. What was he up to?

Then I realized: He was planning on striking *me*. An unintelligible sound broke free from my mouth, and when I held out my hand, Kelley's staff flew straight into it. My arm transformed into a branch for a moment before returning to its normal outlines. I prayed that it had all happened too fast for Kelley to perceive the change. The look on his face told me my hopes were in vain.

"Don't let the emperor see you do that," Kelley smirked, "or he'll have you locked away, yet another curiosity for him to savor. I've told you what you wanted to know, Roydon. Call off the Congregation's dogs."

"I don't think I can," Matthew said, taking the staff from me. "You are not harmless, no matter what Gerbert thinks. But I'll leave you alone—for now. Don't do anything more to warrant my attention and you just may see the summer." He tossed the staff into the corner.

"Good night, Master Kelley." I gathered up my cloak, wanting to be as far away from the daemon as fast as possible.

"Enjoy your moment in the sun, witch. They pass quickly in Prague." Kelley remained where he was while Matthew and I started to descend the stairs.

I could still feel his nudging glances in the street. And when I looked back toward the Donkey and Cradle, the crooked and broken threads that bound Kelley to the world shimmered with malevolence.

After days of careful negotiation, Matthew was able to arrange a visit to Rabbi Judah Loew. To make room for it, Gallowglass had to cancel my upcoming appointments at court, citing illness.

Unfortunately, this announcement caught the emperor's attention, and the house was flooded with medicines: terra sigillata, the clay with marvelous healing properties; bezoar stones harvested from the gallbladders of goats to ward off poison; a cup made of unicorn horn with one of the emperor's family recipes for an electuary. The latter involved roasting an egg with saffron before beating it into a powder with mustard seed, angelica, juniper berries, camphor, and several other mysterious substances, then turning it into a paste with treacle and lemon syrup. Rudolf sent Dr. Hájek along to administer it. But I had no intention of swallowing this unappetizing concoction, as I informed the imperial physician.

"I will assure the emperor that you will recover," he said drily. "Happily, His Majesty is too concerned with his own health to risk traveling down Sporrengasse to confirm my prognosis."

We thanked him profusely for his discretion and sent him home with one of the roasted chickens that had been delivered from the royal kitchens to tempt my appetite. I threw the note that accompanied it into the fire—"*Ich verspreche Sie werden nicht hungern. Ich halte euch zufrieden. Rudolff*"—after Matthew explained that the wording left some doubt as to whether Rudolf was referring to the chicken when he promised to satisfy my hunger.

On our way across the Moldau River to Prague's Old Town, I had my first opportunity to experience the hustle and bustle of the city center. There, affluent merchants conducted business in arcades nestled beneath the three- and four-story houses that lined the twisting streets. When we turned north, the city's character changed: The houses were smaller, the residents more shabbily dressed, the businesses less prosperous. Then we crossed over a wide street and passed through a gate into the Jewish Town. More than five thousand Jews lived in this small enclave smashed between the industrial riverbank, the Old Town's main square, and a convent. The

Jewish quarter was crowded—inconceivably so, even by London standards—with houses that were not so much constructed as grown, each structure evolving organically from the walls of another like the chambers in a snail's shell.

We found Rabbi Loew via a serpentine route that made me long for a bag of bread crumbs to be sure we could find our way back. The residents slid cautious glances in our direction, but few dared to greet us. Those who did called Matthew "Gabriel." It was one of his many names, and the use of it here signaled that I'd slipped down one of Matthew's rabbit holes and was about to meet another of his past selves.

When I stood before the kindly gentleman known as the Maharal, I understood why Matthew spoke of him in hushed tones. Rabbi Loew radiated the same quiet sense of power that I'd seen in Philippe. His dignity made Rudolf's grandiose gestures and Elizabeth's petulance seem laughable in comparison. And it was all the more striking in this age, when brute force was the usual method of imposing one's will on others. The Maharal's reputation was based on scholarship and learning, not physical prowess.

"The Maharal is one of the finest men who has ever lived," Matthew said simply when I asked him to tell me more about Judah Loew. Considering how long Matthew had roamed the earth, this was a considerable accolade.

"I did think, Gabriel, that we had concluded our business," Rabbi Loew said sternly in Latin. He looked and sounded very much like a headmaster. "I would not share the name of the witch who made the golem before, and I will not do so now." Rabbi Loew turned to me. "I am sorry, Frau Roydon. My impatience with your husband made me forget my manners. It is a pleasure to meet you."

"I haven't come about the golem," Matthew replied. "My business today is private. It concerns a book."

"What book is that?" Though the Maharal did not blink, a disturbance in the air around me suggested some subtle reaction on his part. Since meeting Kelley, I realized that my magic had been tingling as though plugged into an invisible current. My firedrake was stirring. And the threads surrounding me kept bursting into color, highlighting an object, a person, a path through the streets as if trying to tell me something.

"It is a volume my wife found at a university far away from here," Matthew said. I was surprised that he was being this truthful. So was Rabbi Loew.

"Ah. I see we are to be honest with each other this afternoon. We should do so where it is quiet enough for me to enjoy the experience. Come into my study."

He led us into one of the small rooms tucked into the warren of a ground floor. It was comfortingly familiar, with its scarred desk and piles of books. I recognized the smell of ink and something that reminded me of the rosin box in my childhood dance studio. An iron pot by the door held what looked like small brown apples, bobbing up and down in an equally brown liquid. Its appearance was witchworthy, conjuring up concerns about what else might be lurking in the cauldron's unsavory depths.

"Is this batch of ink more satisfactory?" Matthew said, poking at one of the floating balls.

"It is. You have done me a service by telling me to add those nails to the pot. It does not require so much soot to make it black, and the consistency is better." Rabbi Loew gestured toward a chair. "Please sit." He waited until I was settled and then took the only other seat: a three-legged stool. "Gabriel will stand. He is not young, but his legs are strong."

"I'm young enough to sit at your feet like one of your pupils, Maharal." Matthew grinned and folded himself gracefully into a cross-legged position.

"My students have better sense than to take to the floor in this weather." Rabbi Loew studied me. "Now. To business. Why has the wife of Gabriel ben Ariel come so far to look for a book?" I had a disconcerting sense that he wasn't talking about my trip across the river, or even across Europe. How could he possibly know that I wasn't from this time?

As soon as my mind formed the question, a man's face swam in the air over Rabbi Loew's shoulder. The face, though young, already showed worry creases around deep-set gray eyes, and the dark brown beard was graying in the center of his chin.

"Another witch told you about me," I said softly.

Rabbi Loew nodded. "Prague is a wonderful city for news. Alas, half of what is said is untrue." He waited for a moment. "The book?" Rabbi Loew reminded me.

"We think it might tell us about how creatures like Matthew and me came to be," I explained.

"This is not a mystery. God made you, just as he made me and Emperor Rudolf," the Maharal replied, settling more deeply into his chair. It was a typical posture for a teacher, one that developed naturally after years spent giving students the space to wrestle with new ideas. I felt a familiar sense of anticipation and dread as I prepared my response. I didn't want to disappoint Rabbi Loew.

"Perhaps, but God has given some of us additional talents. You cannot make the dead live again, Rabbi Loew," I said, responding to him as if he were a tutor at Oxford. "Nor do strange faces appear before you when you pose a simple question."

"True. But you do not rule Bohemia, and your husband's German is better than mine even though I have conversed in the language since a child. Each of us is uniquely gifted, Frau Roydon. In the world's apparent chaos, there is still evidence of God's plan."

"You speak of God's plan with such confidence because you know your origins from the Torah," I replied. "*Bereishit*—'In the beginning'—is what you call the book the Christians know as Genesis. Isn't that right, Rabbi Loew?"

"It seems I have been discussing theology with the wrong member of Ariel's family," Rabbi Loew said drily, though his eyes twinkled with mischief.

"Who is Ariel?" I asked.

"My father is known as Ariel among Rabbi Loew's people," Matthew explained.

"The angel of wrath?" I frowned. That didn't sound like the Philippe I knew.

"The lord with dominion over the earth. Some call him the Lion of Jerusalem. Recently my people have had reason to be grateful to the Lion, though the Jews have not—and will never—forget his many past wrongs. But Ariel makes an effort to atone. And judgment belongs to God." Rabbi Loew considered his options and came to a decision. "The emperor did show me such a book. Alas, his Majesty did not give me much time to study it."

"Anything you could tell us about it would be useful," Matthew said, his excitement visible. He leaned forward and hugged his knees to his chest, just as Jack did when he was listening intently to one of Pierre's stories. For a few moments, I was able to see my husband as he must have looked as a child learning the carpenter's craft.

"Emperor Rudolf called me to his palace in hope that I would be able to read the text. The alchemist, the one they call Meshuggener Edward, had it from the library of his master, the Englishman John Dee." Rabbi Loew sighed and shook his head. "It is difficult to understand why God chose to make Dee learned but foolish and Edward ignorant yet cunning.

"Meshuggener Edward told the emperor that this ancient book contained the secrets of immortality," Loew continued. "To live forever is every powerful man's dream. But the text was written in a language no one understood, except for the alchemist."

"Rudolf called upon you, thinking it was an ancient form of Hebrew," I said, nodding.

"It may well be ancient, but it is not Hebrew. There were pictures, too. I did not understand the meaning, but Edward said they were alchemical in nature. Perhaps the words explain those images."

"When you saw it, Rabbi Loew, were the words moving?" I asked, thinking back to the lines I'd seen lurking under the alchemical illustrations.

"How could they be moving?" Loew frowned. "They were just symbols, written in ink on the page."

"Then it isn't broken—not yet," I said, relieved. "Someone removed several pages from it before I saw it in Oxford. It was impossible to figure out the text's meaning because the words were racing around looking for their lost brothers and sisters."

"You make it sound as though this book is alive," Rabbi Loew said.

"I think it is," I confessed. Matthew looked surprised. "It sounds unbelievable, I know. But when I think back to that night, and what happened when I touched the book, that's the only way to describe it. The book recognized me. It was . . . hurting somehow, as though it had lost something essential."

"There are stories among my people of books written in living flame, with words that move and twist so that only those chosen by God can read them." Rabbi Loew was testing me again. I recognized the signs of a teacher quizzing his students.

"I've heard those stories," I replied slowly. "And the stories about other lost books, too—the tablets Moses destroyed, Adam's book in which he recorded the true names of every part of creation."

"If your book is as significant as they are, perhaps it is God's will that it remain hidden." Rabbi Loew sat back once more and waited.

"But it's not hidden," I said. "Rudolf knows where it is, even if he cannot read it. Who would you rather had the custody of such a powerful object: Matthew or the emperor?"

"I know many wise men who would say that to choose between Gabriel ben Ariel and His Majesty would only determine the lesser of two evils." Rabbi Loew's attention shifted to Matthew. "Happily, I do not count myself among them. Still, I cannot help you further. I have seen this book— but I do not know its present location."

"The book is in Rudolf's possession—or at least it was. Until you confirmed that, we only had Dr. Dee's suspicions and the assurances of the aptly named Crazy Edward," Matthew said grimly.

"Madmen can be dangerous," observed Rabbi Loew. "You should be more careful who you hang out of windows, Gabriel."

"You heard about that?" Matthew looked sheepish.

"The town is buzzing with reports that Meshuggener Edward was flying around Malá Strana with the devil. Naturally, I assumed you were involved." This time Rabbi Loew's tone held a note of gentle reproof. "Gabriel, Gabriel. What will your father say?"

"That I should have dropped him, no doubt. My father has little patience with creatures like Edward Kelley."

"You mean madmen."

"I meant what I said, Maharal," Matthew said evenly.

"The man you talk so easily about killing is, alas, the only person who can help you find your wife's book." Rabbi Loew stopped, considered his words. "But do you truly want to know its secrets? Life and death are great responsibilities."

"Given what I am, you will not be surprised that I am familiar with their particular burdens." Matthew's smile was humorless.

"Perhaps. But can your wife also carry them? You may not always be with her, Gabriel. Some who would share their knowledge with a witch will not do so with you."

"So there *is* a maker of spells in the Jewish Town," I said. "I wondered when I heard about the golem."

"He has been waiting for you to seek him out. Alas, he will see only a fellow witch. My friend fears Gabriel's Congregation, and with good reason," Rabbi Loew explained.

"I would like to meet him, Rabbi Loew." There were precious few weavers in the world. I couldn't miss the opportunity to know this one.

Matthew stirred, a protest rising to his lips.

"This is important, Matthew." I rested my hand on his arm. "I promised Goody Alsop not to ignore this part of me while we are here."

"One should find wholeness in marriage, Gabriel, but it should not be a prison for either party," said Rabbi Loew.

"This isn't about our marriage or the fact that you're a witch." Matthew rose, his large frame filling the room. "It can be dangerous for a Christian woman to be seen with a Jewish man." When I opened my mouth to protest, Matthew shook his head. "Not for you. For him. You must do what Rabbi Loew tells you to do. I don't want him or anyone else in the Jewish Town to come to harm—not on our account."

"I won't do anything to bring attention to myself—or to Rabbi Loew," I promised.

"Then go and see this weaver. I'll be in the Ungelt, waiting." Matthew brushed his lips against my cheek and was gone before he could have second thoughts. Rabbi Loew blinked.

"Gabriel is remarkably quick for one so large," the rabbi said, getting to his feet. "He reminds me of the emperor's tiger."

"Cats do recognize Matthew as one of their kind," I said, thinking of Sarah's cat, Tabitha.

"The notion that you have married an animal does not distress you. Gabriel is fortunate in his choice of wife." Rabbi Loew picked up a dark robe and called to his servant that we were leaving.

We departed in what I supposed was a different direction, but I couldn't be sure, since all my attention was focused on the freshly paved streets, the first I'd seen since arriving in the past. I asked Rabbi Loew who had provided such an unusual convenience.

"Herr Maisel paid for them, along with a bathhouse for the women. He helps the emperor with small financial matters—like his holy war against the Turks." Rabbi Loew picked his way around a puddle. It was then that I saw the golden ring stitched onto the fabric over his heart.

"What is that?" I said, nodding at the badge.

"It warns unsuspecting Christians that I am a Jew." Rabbi Loew's expression was wry. "I have long believed that even the dullest would eventually discover it, with or without the badge. But the authorities insist that there can be no doubt." Rabbi Loew's voice dropped. "And it is far preferable to the hat the Jews were once required to wear. Bright yellow and shaped like a chess piece. Just try to ignore *that* in the market."

"That's what humans would do to me and Matthew if they knew we were living among them." I shivered. "Sometimes it's better to hide."

"Is that what Gabriel's Congregation does? It keeps you hidden?"

"If so, then they're doing a poor job of it," I said with a laugh. "Frau Huber thinks there's a werewolf prowling around the Stag Moat. Your neighbors in Prague believe that Edward Kelley can fly. Humans are hunting for witches in Germany and Scotland. And Elizabeth of England and Rudolf of Austria know all about us. I suppose we should be thankful that some kings and queens tolerate us."

"Toleration is not always enough. The Jews are tolerated in Prague—for the moment—but the situation can change in a heartbeat. Then we would find ourselves out in the countryside, starving in the snow." Rabbi Loew turned in to a narrow alley and entered a house identical to most other houses in most of the other alleys we passed through. Inside, two men sat at a table covered with mathematical instruments, books, candles, and paper.

"Astronomy will provide a common ground with Christians!" one of the men exclaimed in German, pushing a piece of paper toward his companion. He was around fifty, with a thick gray beard and heavy brow bones that shielded his eyes. His shoulders had the chronic stoop of most scholars.

"Enough, David!" the other exploded. "Maybe common ground is not the promised land we hope for."

"Abraham, this lady wishes to speak with you," Rabbi Loew said, interrupting their debate.

"All the women in Prague are eager to meet Abraham." David, the scholar, stood. "Whose daughter wants a love spell this time?"

"It is not her father that should interest you but her husband. This is Frau Roydon, the Englishman's wife."

"The one the emperor calls La Diosa?" David laughed and clasped Abraham's shoulder. "Your luck has turned, my friend. You are caught between a king, a goddess, and a *nachzehrer*." My limited German suggested this unfamiliar word meant "devourer of the dead."

Abraham said something rude in Hebrew, if Rabbi Loew's disapproving expression was any indication, and turned to face me at last. He and I looked at each other, witch to witch, but neither of us could bear it for long. I twisted away with a gasp, and he winced and pressed his eyelids with his fingers. My skin was tingling all over, not just where his eyes had fallen. And the air between us was a mass of different, bright hues.

"Is she the one you were waiting for, Abraham ben Elijah?" Rabbi Loew asked.

"She is," Abraham said. He turned away from me and rested his fists on the table. "My dreams did not tell me that she was the wife of an *alukah,* however."

*"Alukah?"* I looked to Rabbi Loew for an explanation. If the word was German, I couldn't decipher it.

"A leech. It is what we Jews call creatures like your husband," he replied. "For what it is worth, Abraham, Gabriel consented to the meeting."

"You think I trust the word of the monster who judges my people from his seat on the Qahal while turning a blind eye to those who murder them?" Abraham cried.

I wanted to protest that this was not the same Gabriel—the same Matthew—but stopped. Something I said might get everyone in this room killed in another six months when the sixteenth-century Matthew was back in his rightful place.

"I am not here for my husband or the Congregation," I said, stepping forward. "I am here for myself."

"Why?" Abraham demanded.

"Because I, too, am a maker of spells. And there aren't many of us left."

"There were more, before the Qahal—the Congregation—set up their rules." Abraham said, a challenge in his tone. "God willing, we will live to see children born with these gifts."

"Speaking of children, where is your golem?" I asked.

David guffawed. "Mother Abraham. What would your family in Chelm say?"

"They would say I had befriended an ass with nothing in his head but stars and idle fancies, David Gans!" Abraham said, turning red.

My firedrake, which had been restive for days, roared to life with all this merriment. Before I could stop her, she was free. Rabbi Loew and his friends gaped at the sight.

"She does this sometimes. It's nothing to worry about." My tone went from apologetic to brisk as I reprimanded my unruly familiar. "Come down from there!"

My firedrake tightened her grip on the wall and shrieked at me. The old plaster was not up to the task of supporting a creature with a ten-foot wingspan. A large chunk fell free, and she chattered in alarm. Her tail lashed out to the side and anchored itself into the adjacent wall for added security. The firedrake hooted triumphantly.

"If you don't stop that, I'm going to have Gallowglass give you a really evil name," I muttered. "Does anyone see her leash? It looks like a gauzy chain." I searched along the skirting boards and found it behind the kindling basket, still connected to me. "Can one of you hold the slack for a minute while I rein her in?" I turned, my hands full of translucent links.

The men were gone.

"Typical," I muttered. "Three grown men and a woman, and guess who gets stuck with the dragon?"

Heavy feet clomped across the wooden floors. I angled my body so that I could see around the door. A small, reddish gray creature wearing dark clothes and a black cap on his bald head was staring at my firedrake.

"No, Yosef." Abraham stood between me and the creature, his hands raised as if he were trying to reason with it. But the golem—for this must be the legendary creature fashioned from the mud of the Moldau and animated with a spell—kept moving his feet in the firedrake's direction.

"Yosef is fascinated by the witch's dragon," said David.

"I believe the golem shares his maker's fondness for pretty girls," Rabbi Loew said. "My reading suggests that a witch's familiar often has some of his maker's characteristics."

"The golem is Abraham's familiar?" I was shocked.

"Yes. He didn't appear when I made my first spell. I was beginning to think I didn't have a familiar." Abraham waved his hands at Yosef, but the golem stared unblinking at the firedrake sprawled against the wall. As if she knew she had an admirer, the firedrake stretched her wings so that the webbing caught the light.

I held up my chain. "Didn't he come with something like this?"

"That chain doesn't seem to be helping *you* much," Abraham observed.

"I have a lot to learn!" I said indignantly. "The firedrake appeared when I wove my first spell. How did you make Yosef?"

Abraham pulled a rough set of cords from his pocket. "With ropes like these."

"I have cords, too." I reached into the purse hidden in my skirt pocket for my silks.

"Do the colors help you to separate out the world's threads and use them more effectively?" Abraham stepped toward me, interested in this variation of weaving.

"Yes. Each color has a meaning, and to make a new spell I use the cords to focus on a particular question." I looked at the golem in confusion. He was still staring at the firedrake. "But how did you go from cords to a creature?"

"A woman came to me to ask for a new spell to help her conceive. I started making knots in the rope while I considered her request and ended up with something that looked like the skeleton of a man." Abraham went to the desk, took up a piece of David's paper, and, in spite of his friend's protests, sketched out what he meant.

"It's like a poppet," I said, looking at his drawing. Nine knots were connected by straight lines of rope: a knot for its head, one for its heart, two knots for hands, another knot for the pelvis, two more for knees, and a final two for the feet.

"I mixed clay with some of my own blood and put it on the rope like flesh. The next morning Yosef was sitting by the fireplace."

"You brought the clay to life," I said, looking at the enraptured golem.

Abraham nodded. "A spell with the secret name of God is in his mouth. So long as it remains there, Yosef walks and obeys my instructions. Most of the time."

"Yosef is incapable of making his own decisions," Rabbi Loew explained. "Breathing life into clay and blood does not give a creature a soul, after all. So Abraham cannot let the golem out of his sight for fear Yosef will make mischief."

"I forgot to take the spell out of his mouth one Friday when it was time for prayers," Abraham admitted sheepishly. "Without someone to tell him what to do, Yosef wandered out of the Jewish Town and frightened our Christian neighbors. Now the Jews think Yosef's purpose is to protect us."

"A mother's work is never done," I murmured with a smile. "Speaking of which . . ." My firedrake had fallen asleep and was gently snoring, her cheek pillowed against the plaster. Gently, so as not to irritate her, I drew on the chain until she released her grip on the wall. She flapped her wings sleepily, became as transparent as smoke, and slowly dissolved into nothingness as she was absorbed back into my body.

"I wish Yosef could do that," Abraham said enviously.

"And I wish I could keep her quiet by removing a piece of paper from under her tongue!" I retorted.

Seconds later I felt the sense of ice on my back.

"Who is this?" said a low voice.

The new arrival was not large or physically intimidating—but he was a vampire, one with dark blue eyes set into a long, pale face under dusky hair. There was something commanding about the look he gave me, and I took an instinctive step away from him.

"It is nothing that concerns you, Herr Fuchs," Abraham said curtly.

"There is no need for bad manners, Abraham." Rabbi Loew's attention turned to the vampire. "This is Frau Roydon, Herr Fuchs. She has come from Malá Strana to visit the Jewish Town."

The vampire fixed his eyes on me, and his nostrils flared just as Matthew's did when he was picking up a new scent. His eyelids drifted closed. I took another step away.

"Why are you here, Herr Fuchs? I told you I would meet you outside the synagogue," Abraham said, clearly rattled.

"You were late." Herr Fuchs's blue eyes snapped open, and he smiled at me. "But now that I know why you were detained, I no longer mind."

"Herr Fuchs is visiting from Poland, where he and Abraham knew each other," Rabbi Loew said, finishing his introductions.

Someone on the street called out in greeting. "Here is Herr Maisel," Abraham said. He sounded as relieved as I felt.

Herr Maisel, provider of paved streets and fulfiller of imperial defense budgets, broadcast his prosperity from his immaculately cut woolen suit, his fur-lined cape, and the bright yellow circle that proclaimed him a Jew. This last was affixed to the cape with golden thread, which made it look like a nobleman's insignia rather than a mark of difference.

"There you are, Herr Fuchs." Herr Maisel handed a pouch to the vampire. "I have your jewel." Maisel bowed to Rabbi Loew and to me. "Frau Roydon."

The vampire took the pouch and removed a heavy chain and pendant. I couldn't see the design clearly, though the red and green enamel were plain. The vampire bared his teeth.

"Thank you, Herr Maisel." Fuchs held up the jewel, and the colors caught the light. "The chain signifies my oath to slay dragons, no matter where they are found. I have missed wearing it. The city is full of dangerous creatures these days."

Herr Maisel snorted. "No more than usual. And leave the city's politics alone, Herr Fuchs. It will be better for all of us if you do so. Are you ready to meet your husband, Frau Roydon? He is not the most patient of men."

"Herr Maisel will see you safely to the Ungelt," Rabbi Loew promised. He leveled a long look at Herr Fuchs. "See Diana to the street, Abraham. You will stay with me, Herr Fuchs, and tell me about Poland."

"Thank you, Rabbi Loew." I curtsied in farewell.

"It was a pleasure, Frau Roydon." Rabbi Loew paused. "And if you have time, you might reflect on what I said earlier. None of us can hide forever."

"No." Given the horrors the Jews of Prague would see over the next centuries, I wished he were wrong. With a final nod to Herr Fuchs, I left the house with Herr Maisel and Abraham.

"A moment, Herr Maisel," Abraham said when we were out of earshot of the house.

"Make it quick, Abraham," Herr Maisel said, withdrawing a few feet.

"I understand you are looking for something in Prague, Frau Roydon. A book."

"How do you know that?" I felt a whisper of alarm.

"Most of the witches in the city know it, but I can see how you are connected to it. The book is closely guarded, and force will not work to free it." Abraham's face was serious. "The book must come to you, or you will lose it forever."

"It's a book, Abraham. Unless it sprouts legs, we are going to have to go into Rudolf's palace and fetch it."

"I know what I see," Abraham said stubbornly. "The book will come to you, if only you ask for it. Don't forget."

"I won't," I promised. Herr Maisel looked pointedly in our direction. "I have to go. Thank you for meeting me and introducing me to Yosef."

"May God keep you safe, Diana Roydon," Abraham said solemnly, his face grave.

Herr Maisel escorted me the short distance from the Jewish Town to the Old Town. Its spacious square was thronged with people. The twin towers of Our Lady of Tyn rose to our left, while the stolid outlines of the Town Hall crouched to our right.

"If we didn't have to meet Herr Roydon, we would stop and see the clock strike the hours," Herr Maisel said apologetically. "You must ask him to take you past it on your way to the bridge. Every visitor to Prague should see it."

At the Ungelt, where the foreign merchants traded under the watchful eyes of the customs officer, the merchants looked at Maisel with open hostility.

"Here is your wife, Herr Roydon. I made sure she noticed all the best shops on her way to meet you. She will have no problem finding the finest craftsmen in Prague to see to her needs and those of your household." Maisel beamed at Matthew.

"Thank you, Herr Maisel. I am grateful for your assistance and will be sure to let His Majesty know of your kindness."

"It is my job, Herr Roydon, to see to the prosperity of His Majesty's people. And it was a pleasure, too, of course," he said. "I took the liberty of hiring horses for your journey back. They are waiting for you near the town clock." Maisel touched the side of his nose and winked conspiratorially.

"You think of everything, Herr Maisel," Matthew murmured.

"Someone has to, Herr Roydon," responded Maisel.

Back at the Three Ravens, I was still taking my cloak off when an eight-year-old boy and a flying mop practically knocked me off my feet. The mop was attached to a lively pink tongue and a cold black nose.

"What is this?" Matthew bellowed, steadying me so that I could locate the mop's handle.

"His name is Lobero. Gallowglass says he will grow into a great beast and that he might as well have a saddle fitted for him as a leash. Annie loves him, too. She says he will sleep with her, but I think we should share. What do you think?" Jack said, dancing with excitement.

"The wee mop came with a note," Gallowglass said. He pushed himself away from the doorframe and strolled over to Matthew to deliver it.

"Need I ask who sent the creature?" Matthew said, snatching at the paper.

"Oh, I don't think so," Gallowglass said. His eyes narrowed. "Did something happen while you were out, Auntie? You look done in."

"Just tired," I said with a breezy wave of my hand. The mop had teeth as well as a tongue, and he bit down on my fingers as they passed by his as-yet-undiscovered mouth. "Ouch!"

"This has to stop." Matthew crushed the note in his fingers and flung it to the floor. The mop pounced on it with a delighted bark.

"What did the note say?" I was pretty sure I knew who had sent the puppy.

"'*Ich bin Lobero. Ich will euch aus den Schatten der Nacht zu schützen,*'" Matthew said flatly.

I made an impatient sound. "Why does he keep writing to me in German? Rudolf knows I have a hard time understanding it."

"His Majesty delights in knowing I will have to translate his professions of love."

"Oh." I paused. "What did this note say?"

"'I am Lobero. I will protect you from the shadow of night.'"

"And what does 'Lobero' mean?" Once, many moons ago, Ysabeau had taught me that names were important.

"It means 'Wolf Hunter' in Spanish, Auntie." Gallowglass picked up the mop. "This bit of fluff is a Hungarian guard dog. Lobero will grow so big he'll be able to take down a bear. They're fiercely protective—and nocturnal."

"A bear! When we bring him back to London, I will tie a ribbon around his neck and take him to the bearbaitings so that he can learn how to fight," Jack said with the gruesome delight of a child. "Lobero is a brave name, don't you think? Master Shakespeare will want to use it in his next play." Jack wriggled his fingers in the puppy's direction, and Gallowglass obligingly deposited the squirming mass of white fur in the boy's arms. "Annie! I will feed Lobero next!" Jack pelted up the stairs, holding the dog in a death grip.

"Shall I take them away for a few hours?" Gallowglass asked after getting a good look at Matthew's stormy face.

"Is Baldwin's house empty?"

"There are no tenants in it, if that's what you mean."

"Take everybody." Matthew lifted my cloak from my shoulders.

"Even Lobero?"

"Especially Lobero."

Jack chattered like a magpie throughout supper, picking fights with Annie and managing to send a fair bit of food Lobero's way through a variety of occult methods. Between the children and the dog, it was almost possible to ignore the fact that Matthew was reconsidering his plans for the evening. On the one hand, he was a pack animal and something in him enjoyed having so many lives to take care of. On the other hand, he was a predator and I had an uneasy feeling that I was tonight's prey. The predator won. Not even Tereza and Karolína were allowed to stay.

"Why did you send them all away?" We were still by the fire in the house's main, first-floor room, where the comforting smells of dinner still filled the air.

"What happened this afternoon?" he asked.

"Answer my question first."

"Don't push me. Not tonight," Matthew warned.

"You think *my* day has been easy?" The air between us was crackling with blue and black threads. It looked ominous and felt worse.

"No." Matthew slid his chair back. "But you're keeping something from me, Diana. What happened with the witch?"

I stared at him.

"I'm waiting."

"You can wait until hell freezes over, Matthew, because I'm not your servant. I asked you a question." The threads went purple, beginning to twist and distort.

"I sent them away so that they wouldn't witness this conversation. Now, what happened?" The smell of cloves was choking.

"I met the golem. And his maker, a Jewish weaver named Abraham. He has the power of animation, too."

"I've told you I don't like it when you play with life and death." Matthew poured himself more wine.

"You play with them all the time, and I accept that as part of who you are. You're going to have to accept it's part of me, too."

"And this Abraham. Who is he?" Matthew demanded.

"God, Matthew. You cannot be jealous because I met another weaver."

"Jealous? I am long past that warmblooded emotion." He took a mouthful of wine.

"Why was this afternoon different from every other day we spend apart while you're out working for the Congregation and your father?"

"It's different because I can smell every single person you've been in contact with today. It's bad enough that you always carry the scent of Annie and Jack. Gallowglass and Pierre try not to touch you, but they can't help it—they're around you too much. Then we add the scents of the Maharal, and Herr Maisel, and at least two other men. The only scent I can bear to have mixed with yours is my own, but I cannot keep you in a cage, and so I endure it the best I can." Matthew put down his cup and shot to his feet in an attempt to put some distance between us.

"That sounds like jealousy to me."

"It's not. I could manage jealousy," he said, furious. "What I am feeling now—this terrible gnawing sense of loss and rage because I cannot get a clear impression of *you* in the chaos of our life—is beyond my control." His pupils were large and getting larger.

"That's because you are a vampire. You're possessive. It's who you are," I said flatly, approaching him in spite of his anger. "And I am a witch. You promised to accept me as I am—light and dark, woman and witch, my own person as well as your wife." What if he had changed his mind? What if he wasn't willing to have this kind of unpredictability in his life?

"I do accept you." Matthew reached out a gentle finger and touched my cheek.

"No, Matthew. You tolerate me, because you think that one day I'll beat my magic into submission. Rabbi Loew warned me that tolerance can be withdrawn, and then you're out in the cold. My magic isn't something to manage. It's *me*. And I'm not going to hide myself from you. That's not what love is."

"All right. No more hiding."

"Good." I sighed with relief, but it was short-lived.

Matthew had me out of the chair and up against the wall in one clean move, his thigh pressed between mine. He pulled a curl free so that it trailed down my neck and onto my breast. Without releasing me, he bent his head and pressed his lips to the edge of my bodice. I shivered. It had been some time since he'd kissed me there, and our sex life had been practically nonexistent since the miscarriage. Matthew's lips brushed along my jaw and over the veins of my neck.

I grabbed his hair and pulled his head away. "Don't. Not unless you plan on finishing what you start. I've had enough bundling and regretful kisses to last a lifetime."

With a few blindingly fast vampire moves, Matthew had loosened the fastenings on his britches, rucked my skirts around my waist, and plunged inside me. It wasn't the first time I'd been taken against the wall by someone trying to forget his troubles for a few precious moments. On several occasions I'd even been the aggressor.

"This is about you and me—nothing else. Not the children. Not the damn book. Not the emperor and his gifts. Tonight the only scents in this house will be ours."

Matthew's hands gripped my buttocks, and his fingers were all that was saving me from being bruised as his thrusts carried my body toward the wall. I wrapped my hands in the collar of his shirt and pulled his face toward mine, ravenous for the taste of him. But Matthew was no more willing to let me control the kiss than he was our lovemaking. His lips were hard and demanding, and when I persisted in my attempts to get the upper hand, he gave me a warning nip on the lower lip.

"Oh, God," I said breathlessly as his steady rhythm set my nerves rushing toward a release. "Oh—"

"Tonight I won't even share you with Him." Matthew kissed the rest of my exclamation away. One hand retained its grip on my buttock, the other dipped between my legs.

"Who has your heart, Diana?" Matthew asked, a stroke of his thumb threatening to take me over the edge of sanity. He moved, moved again. Waited for my answer. "Say it," he growled.

"You know the answer," I said. "You have my heart."

"Only me," he said, moving once more so that the coiled tension in both of us finally found release.

"Only . . . forever . . . you," I gasped, my legs shaking around his hips. I slid my feet to the floor.

Matthew was breathing heavily, his forehead pressed to mine. His eyes showed a flash of regret as he lowered my skirts. He kissed me gently, almost chastely.

Our lovemaking, no matter how intense, had not satisfied whatever was driving Matthew to keep pursuing me in spite of the fact that I was indisputably his. I was beginning to worry that nothing could.

My frustration burbled over, taking shape in a concussive wave of air that carried him away from me and into the opposite wall. Matthew's eyes went black at his change of position.

"And how was that for you, my heart?" I asked softly. His face registered surprise. I snapped my fingers, releasing the air's hold on him. His muscles flexed as he regained his mobility. He opened his mouth to speak. "Don't you dare apologize," I said fiercely. "If you'd touched me in a way I didn't like, I would have said no."

Matthew's mouth tightened.

"I can't help thinking about your friend Giordano Bruno: *'Desire urges me on, as fear bridles me.'* I'm not afraid of your power, or your strength, or anything else about you," I said. "What are *you* afraid of, Matthew?"

Regretful lips brushed over mine. That, and a whisper of breeze against my skirts, told me he had fled rather than answer.

30

"Master Habermel stopped by. Your compendium is on the table." Matthew didn't look up from the plans to Prague Castle that he'd somehow procured from the emperor's architects. In the past few days, he'd given me wide berth and taken to channeling his energy into unearthing the secrets of the palace guard so that he could breach Rudolf's security. In spite of Abraham's advice, which I'd duly conveyed, Matthew preferred a proactive strategy. He wanted us out of Prague. Now.

I approached his side, and he looked up with restless, hungry eyes.

"It's just a gift." I put down my gloves and kissed him deeply. "My heart is yours, remember?"

"It isn't just a gift. It came with an invitation to go hunting tomorrow." Matthew wrapped his hands around my hips. "Gallowglass informed me that we will be accepting it. He's found a way into the emperor's apartments by seducing some poor maid into showing him Rudolf's erotic-picture collection. The palace guard will either be hunting with us or napping. Gallowglass figures it's as good a chance as we're going to get to look for the book."

I glanced over at Matthew's desk, where another small parcel lay. "Do you know what that is, too?"

He nodded and reached over and picked it up. "You're always receiving gifts from other men. This one is from me. Hold out your hand." Intrigued, I did what he asked.

He pressed something round and smooth into my palm. It was the size of a small egg.

A stream of cool, heavy metal flowed around the mysterious egg as tiny salamanders filled my hand. They were made of silver and gold, with diamonds set into their backs. I lifted one of the creatures, and up came a chain made entirely of paired salamanders, their heads joined at the mouth and their tails entwined. Still nestled in my palm was a ruby. A very large, very red ruby.

"It's beautiful!" I looked up at Matthew. "When did you have time to buy this?" It wasn't the kind of chain that goldsmiths stocked for drop-in customers.

"I've had it for a while," Matthew confessed. "My father sent it with the altarpiece. I wasn't sure you'd like it."

"Of course I like it. Salamanders are alchemical, you know," I said, giving him another kiss. "Besides, what woman would object to two feet of silver, gold, and diamond salamanders and a ruby big enough to fill an eggcup?"

"These particular salamanders were a gift from the king when I returned to France late in 1541. King Francis chose the salamander in flames for his emblem, and his motto was '*I nourish and extinguish*.'" Matthew laughed. "Kit enjoyed the conceit so much he adapted it for his own use: '*What nourishes me destroys me*.'"

"Kit is definitely a glass-half-empty daemon," I said, joining in his laughter. I poked at one of the salamanders, and it caught the light from the candles. I started to speak, then stopped.

"What?" Matthew said.

"Have you given this to someone . . . before?" After the other night, my own sudden insecurity was embarrassing.

"No," Matthew said, taking my hand and its treasure between his.

"I'm sorry. It's ridiculous, I know, especially considering Rudolf's behavior. I'd rather not wonder, that's all. If you give me something you once gave to a former lover, just tell me."

"I wouldn't give you something I'd first given to someone else, *mon coeur*." Matthew waited until I met his eyes. "Your firedrake reminded me of Francis's gift, so I asked my father to fish it out of its hidey-hole. I wore it once. Since then it's been sitting in a box."

"It's not exactly everyday wear," I said, trying to laugh. But it didn't quite work. "I don't know what's wrong with me."

Matthew pulled me down into a kiss. "My heart belongs to you no less than yours belongs to me. Never doubt it."

"I won't."

"Good. Because Rudolf is doing everything he can to wear us both down. We need to keep our heads. And then we need to get the hell out of Prague."

Matthew's words came back to haunt me the next afternoon, when we joined Rudolf's closest companions at court for an afternoon of sport. The

plan had been to ride out to the emperor's hunting lodge at White Mountain to shoot deer, but the heavy gray skies kept us closer to the palace. It
was the second week of April, but spring came slowly to Prague, and snow
was still possible.

Rudolf called Matthew over to his side, leaving me to the mercy of the
women of the court. They were openly curious and entirely at a loss about
what to do with me.

The emperor and his companions drank freely from the wine that the
servants passed. Given the high speeds of the impending chase, I wished
there were regulations about drinking and riding. Not that I had much to
worry about in Matthew's case. For one thing, he was being rather abstemi-
ous. And there was little chance of him dying, even if his horse did crash
into a tree.

Two men arrived, a long pole resting on their shoulders to provide a
perch for the splendid assortment of falcons that would be bringing down
the birds this afternoon. Two more men followed bearing a single, hooded
bird with a lethal curved beak and brown feathered legs that gave the effect
of boots. It was huge.

"Ah!" Rudolf said, rubbing his hands together with delight. "Here is my
eagle, Augusta. I wanted La Diosa to see her, even though we cannot fly her
here. She requires more room to hunt than the Stag Moat provides."

Augusta was a fitting name for such a proud creature. The eagle was
nearly three feet tall and, though hooded, held her head at a haughty angle.

"She can sense that we are watching her," I murmured.

Someone translated this for the emperor, and he smiled at me approvingly. "One huntress understands another. Take her hood off. Let Augusta
and La Diosa get acquainted."

A wizened old man with bowed legs and a cautious expression approached the eagle. He pulled on the leather strings that tightened the
hood around Augusta's head and gently drew it away from the bird. The
golden feathers around her neck and head ruffled in the breeze, highlighting their texture. Augusta, sensing freedom and danger both, spread her
wings in a gesture that could be read either as the promise of imminent
flight or as a warning.

But I was not the one Augusta wanted to meet. With unerring instinct
her head turned to the only predator in the company more dangerous than
she was. Matthew stared back at her gravely, his eyes sad. Augusta cried out
in acknowledgment of his sympathy.

"I did not bring Augusta out to amuse Herr Roydon but to meet La Diosa," Rudolf grumbled.

"And I thank you for the introduction, Your Majesty," I said, wanting to capture the moody monarch's attention.

"Augusta has taken down two wolves, you know," Rudolf said with a pointed look at Matthew. The emperor's feathers were far more ruffled than those of his prize bird. "They were both bloody struggles."

"Were I the wolf, I would simply lie down and let the lady have her way," Matthew said lazily. He was every inch the courtier this afternoon in a green-and-gray ensemble, his black hair pushed under a rakish cap that provided little protection from the elements but did provide an opportunity to display a silver badge on its crown—the de Clermont family's ouroboros—lest Rudolf forgot with whom he was dealing.

The other courtiers smirked and tittered at his daring remark. Rudolf, once he had made sure the laughter was not directed at him, joined in. "It is another thing we have in common, Herr Roydon," he said, pounding on Matthew's shoulder. He surveyed me. "Neither of us fears a strong woman."

The tension broken, the falconer returned Augusta to her perch with some relief and asked the emperor which bird he wished to use this afternoon to take down the royal grouse. Rudolf fussed over his selection. Once the emperor chose a large gyrfalcon, the Austrian archdukes and German princes fought over the remaining birds until only a single animal was left. It was small and shivering in the cold. Matthew reached for it.

"That is a woman's bird," Rudolf said with a snort, settling into his saddle. "I had it sent for La Diosa."

"In spite of her name, Diana doesn't like hunting. But it's no matter. I will fly the merlin," Matthew said. He ran the jesses through his fingers, put out his hand, and the bird stepped onto his gloved wrist. "Hello, beauty," he murmured while the bird adjusted her feet. With every small step, her bells jingled.

"Her name is Šárka," the gamekeeper whispered with a smile.

"Is she as clever as her namesake?" Matthew asked him.

"More so," the old man answered with a grin.

Matthew leaned toward the bird and took one of the strings that held her hood in his teeth. His mouth was so close to Šárka, and the gesture so intimate, that it could have been mistaken for a kiss. Matthew drew the string back. Once that was done, it was easy for him to remove the hood with his other hand and slip the decorated leather blindfold into a pocket.

Šárka blinked as the world came into view. She blinked again, studying me and then the man who held her.

"Can I touch her?" There was something irresistible about the soft layers of brown-and-white feathers.

"I wouldn't. She's hungry. I don't think she gets her fair share of kills," Matthew said. He looked sad again, even wistful. Šárka made low, chortling sounds and kept her eyes on Matthew.

"She likes you." It was no wonder. They were both hunters by instinct, both fettered so that they couldn't give in to the urge to track and kill.

We rode on a twisting path down into the river gorge that had once served as the palace moat. The river was gone and the gorge fenced in to keep the emperor's game from roaming the city. Red deer, roe deer, and boar all prowled the grounds. So, too, did the lions and other big cats from the menagerie on those days when Rudolf decided to hunt down his prey with them rather than birds.

I expected utter chaos, but hunting was as precisely choreographed as any ballet. As soon as Rudolf released his gyrfalcon into the air, the birds resting in the trees rose up in a cloud, taking flight to avoid becoming a snack. The gyrfalcon swooped down and flew over the brush, the wind whistling through the bells on his feet. Startled grouse erupted from cover, running and flapping in all directions before taking to the air. The gyrfalcon banked, selected a target, harried it into position, and shot forward to hit it with talons and beak. The grouse fell from the sky, the falcon pursuing it relentlessly to the ground, where the grouse, startled and injured, was finally killed. The gamekeepers released the dogs and ran with them across the snowy ground. The horses thundered after, the men's cries of triumph drowned out by the baying of the hounds.

When the horses and riders caught up, we found the falcon standing by its prey, its wings curved to shield the grouse from rival claimants. Matthew had adopted a similar stance at the Bodleian Library, and I felt his eyes fall on me to make sure that I was nearby.

Now that the emperor had the first kill, the others were free to join in the hunt. Together they caught more than a hundred birds, enough to feed a fair number of courtiers. There was only one altercation. Not surprisingly, it occurred between Rudolf's magnificent silver gyrfalcon and Matthew's small brown-and-white merlin.

Matthew had been hanging back from the rest of the male pack. He released his bird well after the others and was unhurried in claiming the grouse that she brought down. Though none of the other men got off their mounts, Matthew did, coaxing Šárka away from her prey with a murmured word and a bit of meat that he'd pulled off a previous kill.

Once, however, Šárka failed to connect with the grouse she was pursuing. It eluded her, flying straight into the path of Rudolf's gyrfalcon. But Šárka refused to yield. Though the gyrfalcon was larger, Šárka was scrappier and more agile. To reach her grouse, the merlin flew past my head so closely that I felt the changing pressure in the air. She was such a little thing—smaller even than the grouse, and definitely outsized by the emperor's bird. The grouse flew higher, but there was no escape. Šárka quickly reversed direction and sank her curved talons into her prey, her weight carrying them both down. The indignant gyrfalcon screamed in frustration, and Rudolf added his own loud protest.

"Your bird interfered with mine," Rudolf said furiously as Matthew kicked his horse forward to fetch the merlin.

"She isn't my bird, Your Majesty," Matthew said. Šárka, who had puffed herself up and stretched out her wings to look as large and menacing as possible, let out a shrill peep as he approached. Matthew murmured something that sounded vaguely familiar and more than a little amorous, and the bird's feathers smoothed. "Šárka belongs to you. And today she has proved to be a worthy namesake of a great Bohemian warrior."

Matthew picked up the merlin, grouse and all, and held it up for the court to see. Šárka's jesses swung freely, and her bells tinkled with sound as he circled her around. Unsure what their response should be, the courtiers waited for Rudolf to do something. I intervened instead.

"Was this a female warrior, husband?"

Matthew stopped in his rotation and grinned. "Why, yes, wife. The real Šárka was small and feisty, just like the emperor's bird, and knew that a warrior's greatest weapon lies between the ears." He tapped his head to make sure everyone received the message. Rudolf not only received it, he looked nonplussed.

"She sounds rather like the ladies of Malá Strana," I said drily. "And what did Šárka do with her intelligence?" Before Matthew could answer, an unfamiliar young woman spoke.

"Šárka took down a troop of soldiers," she explained in fluid Latin with a heavy Czech accent. A white-bearded man I took to be her father looked at her approvingly, and she blushed.

"Really?" I said, interested. "How?"

"By pretending she needed rescuing and then inviting the soldiers to celebrate her freedom with too much wine." Another woman, this one elderly with a beak of a nose to rival Augusta's, snorted in disgust. "Men fall for that every time."

I burst out laughing. To her evident surprise, so did the beaky, aristocratic old lady.

"I fear, Emperor, that the ladies will not have their heroine blamed for the faults of others." Matthew reached into his pocket for the hood and gently set it over the crown of Šárka's proud head. He leaned in and tightened the cord with his teeth. The gamekeeper took the merlin to a smattering of approving applause.

We adjourned to a red-and-white-roofed Italianate house set at the edge of the palace grounds for wine and refreshments, though I would have preferred to linger in the gardens where the emperor's narcissi and tulips were blooming. Other members of the court joined us, including the sour-faced Strada, Master Hoefnagel, and the instrument maker Erasmus Habermel, whom I thanked for my compendium.

"What we need to lift our boredom is a spring feast now that Lent is almost over," said one young male courtier in a loud voice. "Don't you think so, Your Majesty?"

"A masque?" Rudolf took a sip of his wine and stared at me. "If so, the theme should be Diana and Actaeon."

"That theme is so common, Your Majesty, and rather English," Matthew said sadly. Rudolf flushed. "Perhaps we might do Demeter and Persephone instead. It is more fitting for the season."

"Or the story of Odysseus," Strada suggested, shooting me a nasty look. "Frau Roydon could play Circe and turn us into piglets."

"Interesting, Ottavio," Rudolf said, tapping his full lower lip with his index finger. "I might enjoy playing Odysseus."

*Not on your life,* I thought. Not with the requisite bedroom scene and Odysseus making Circe promise not to forcibly take his manhood.

"If I might offer a suggestion," I said, eager to stave off disaster.

"Of course, of course," Rudolf said earnestly, taking my hand and giving it a solicitous pat.

"The story I have in mind requires someone to take the role of Zeus, the king of the gods," I told the emperor, drawing my hand gently away.

"I would be a convincing Zeus," he said eagerly, a smile lighting his face. "And you will play Callisto?" *Absolutely not.* I was not going to let Rudolf pretend to ravage and impregnate me.

"No, Your Majesty. If you insist that I take part in the entertainment, I will play the goddess of the moon." I slid my hand into the bend of Matthew's arm. "And to atone for his earlier remark, Matthew will play Endymion."

"Endymion?" Rudolf's smile wavered.

"Poor Rudolf. Outfoxed again," Matthew murmured for only me to hear. "Endymion, Your Majesty," he said, this time in a voice pitched to carry, "the beautiful youth who is cast into enchanted sleep so as to preserve his immortality and Diana's chastity."

"I know the legend, Herr Roydon!" Rudolf warned.

"Apologies, Your Majesty," Matthew said with a graceful, albeit shallow, bow. "Diana will look splendid, arriving in her chariot so that she can gaze wistfully upon the man she loves."

Rudolf was imperial purple by this point. We were waved out of the royal presence and left the palace to make the brief, downhill trip to the Three Ravens.

"I have only one request," Matthew said as we entered our front door. "I may be a vampire, but April is a cold month in Prague. In deference to the temperature, the costumes you design for Diana and Endymion should be more substantial than a lunar crescent for your hair and a dishcloth to drape around my hips."

"I've only just cast you in this role and you're already making artistic demands!" I flung up one hand in mock indignation. "Actors!"

"That's what you deserve for working with amateurs," Matthew said with a smile. "I know just how the masque should begin: *'And lo! from opening clouds, I saw emerge / The loveliest moon, that ever silver'd o'er / A shell for Neptune's goblet.'*"

"You cannot use Keats!" I laughed. "He's a Romantic poet—it's three hundred years too soon."

*"'She did soar / So passionately bright, my dazzled soul / Commingling with her argent spheres did roll / Through clear and cloudy, even when she went / At last into a dark and vapoury tent,'"* he exclaimed dramatically, pulling me into his arms.

"And I suppose you'll want *me* to find you a tent," Gallowglass said, thundering down the stairs.

"And some sheep. Or maybe an astrolabe. Endymion can be either a shepherd or an astronomer," Matthew said, weighing his options.

"Rudolf's gamekeeper will never part with one of his strange sheep," Gallowglass said dourly.

"Matthew is welcome to use my compendium." I looked around. It was supposed to be on the mantelpiece, out of Jack's reach. "Where has it gone?"

"Annie and Jack are showing it to Mop. They think it's enchanted."

Until then I hadn't noticed the threads running straight up the stairs from the fireplace—silver, gold, and gray. In my rush to reach the children and find out what was going on with the compendium, I stepped on the hem of my skirt. By the time I reached Annie and Jack, I'd managed to give the bottom a new, scalloped edge.

Annie and Jack had the little brass-and-silver compendium opened up like a book, its inner wings folded out to their full extent. Rudolf's desire had been to give me something to track the movements of the heavens, and Habermel had outdone himself. The compendium contained a sundial, a compass, a device to compute the length of the hours at different seasons of the year, an intricate lunar volvelle—whose gears could be set to tell the date, time, ruling sign of the zodiac, and phase of the moon—and a latitude chart that included (at my request) the cities of Roanoke, London, Lyon, Prague, and Jerusalem. One of the wings had a spine into which I could fit one of the hottest new technologies: the erasable tablet, which was made of specially treated paper that one could write on and then carefully wipe off to make fresh notes.

"Look, Jack, it's doing it again," Annie said, peering down at the instrument. Mop (no one in the house called him Lobero anymore, except for Jack) started barking, wagging his tail with excitement as the lunar volvelle began to spin of its own accord.

"I bet you a penny that the full moon will be in the window when the spinning stops," Jack said, spitting in his hand and holding it out to Annie.

"No betting," I said automatically, crouching down next to Jack.

"When did this start, Jack?" Matthew asked, fending off Mop.

Jack shrugged.

"It's been happening since Herr Habermel sent it," Annie confessed.

"Does it spin like this all day or only at certain times?" I asked.

"Only once or twice. And the compass just spins once." Annie looked miserable. "I should have told you. I knew it was magical from the way it feels."

"It's all right." I smiled at her. "No harm done." With that I put my finger in the center of the volvelle and commanded the thing to stop. It did. As soon as the revolutions ceased, the silver and gold threads around the compendium slowly dissolved, leaving only the gray thread behind. It was quickly lost among the many colorful strands that filled our house.

"What does it mean?" Matthew asked later, when the house was quiet and I had my first opportunity to put the compendium out of the children's reach. I'd decided to leave it atop the flat canopy over our bed. "By the way, everybody hides things on top of the tester. It will be the first place Jack searches for it."

"Somebody is looking for us." I pulled the compendium back down and sought out a new place to conceal it.

"In Prague?" Matthew held out his hand for the small instrument, and when I handed it to him, he slipped it into his doublet.

"No. In time."

Matthew sat down on the bed with a thunk and swore.

"It's my fault." I looked at him sheepishly. "I tried to weave a spell so that the compendium would warn me if somebody was thinking of stealing it. The spell was supposed to keep Jack out of trouble. I guess I need to go back to the drawing board."

"What makes you think it's someone in another time?" Matthew asked.

"Because the lunar volvelle is a perpetual calendar. The gears were spinning as though it were trying to input information beyond its technical specifications. It reminds me of the words racing around in Ashmole 782."

"Maybe the whirring of the compass indicates that whoever is looking for us is in a different place, too. Like the lunar volvelle, the compass can't find true north because it's being asked to compute two sets of directions: one for us in Prague and one for someone else."

"Do you think it's Ysabeau or Sarah, and they need our help?" It was Ysabeau who had sent Matthew the copy of *Doctor Faustus* to help us reach 1590. She knew where we were headed.

"No," Matthew said, his voice sure. "They wouldn't give us away. It's someone else." His gray-green eyes settled on me. The restless, regretful look was back.

"You're looking at me as though I've betrayed you somehow." I sat next to him on the bed. "If you don't want me to do the masque, I won't."

"It's not that." Matthew got up and walked away. "You're still keeping something from me."

"We all keep things to ourselves, Matthew," I said. "Little things that don't matter. Sometimes big things, say, like being on the Congregation." His accusations rankled, given all that I still did not know about him.

Matthew's hands were suddenly on my shoulders, lifting me up. "You will never forgive me for that." His eyes looked black, and his fingers dug into my arms.

"You promised me you would tolerate my secrets," I said. "Rabbi Loew is right. Tolerance isn't enough."

Matthew released me with a curse. I heard Gallowglass on the steps, Jack's sleepy murmurs down the hall.

"I'm taking Jack and Annie to Baldwin's house," Gallowglass said from the door. "Tereza and Karolína have already gone. Pierre will come with me, and so will the dog." His voice dropped. "You frighten the boy when you argue, and he's known enough fear in his short life. Sort yourselves out or I'll take them back to London and leave the two of you here to shift for yourselves." Gallowglass's blue eyes were fierce.

Matthew sat silently by the fire, a cup of wine in his hands and a dark expression on his face as he stared into the flames. As soon as the group departed, he was on his feet and headed to the door.

Without thinking or planning, I released my firedrake. *Stop him,* I commanded. She covered him in a gray mist as she flew over and around him, took solid form by the door, and dug the spiked edges of her wings onto either side of its frame. When Matthew got too close, a tongue of fire shot out of her mouth in warning.

"You're not going anywhere," I said. It took enormous effort to keep my voice from rising. Matthew might be able to overpower me, but I doubted he could successfully wrestle with my familiar. "My firedrake is a bit like Šárka: small but scrappy. I wouldn't piss her off."

Matthew turned, his eyes cold.

"If you're angry with me, say it. If I've done something you don't like, tell me. If you want to end this marriage, have the courage to end it cleanly so that I might—might—be able to recover from it. Because if you keep looking at me as though you wish we weren't married, you're going to destroy me."

"I have no desire to end this marriage," he said tightly.

"Then be my husband." I advanced on him. "Do you know what I thought watching those beautiful birds fly today? 'That's what Matthew would look like, if only he were free to be himself.' And when I saw you put on Šárka's hood, blinding her so that she couldn't hunt as her instincts tell her to do, I saw the same look of regret in her eyes that I have seen in yours every day since I lost the baby."

"This isn't about the baby." His eyes held a warning now.

"No. It's about me. And you. And something so terrifying you can't acknowledge it: that in spite of your so-called powers over life and death, you don't control everything and can't keep me, or anyone else you love, from harm."

"And you think it's losing the baby that brought that fact home?"

"What else could it be? Your guilt over Blanca and Lucas nearly destroyed you."

"You're wrong." Matthew's hands were wrapped in my hair, pulling down the knot of braids and releasing the scent of chamomile and mint from the soap I used. His pupils looked inky and huge. He drank in the scent of me, and some of the green returned.

"Tell me what it is, then."

"This." He reached for the edge of my bodice and rent it in two. Then he loosened the cord that kept the wide neckline of my smock from sliding off my shoulders so that it exposed the tops of my breasts. His finger traced the blue vein that surfaced there and continued beneath the folds of linen.

"Every day of my life is a battle for control. I fight my anger and the sickness that follows in its wake. I struggle with hunger and thirst, because I don't believe it is right for me to take blood from other creatures—not even the animals, though I can bear that better than taking it from someone I might see again on the street." His eyes rose to mine. "And I am at war with myself over this unspeakable urge to possess you body and soul in ways that no warmblood can fathom."

"You want my blood," I whispered in sudden understanding. "You lied to me."

"I lied to myself."

"I told you—repeatedly—that you can have it," I said. I grabbed at the smock and tore it further, bending my head to the side and exposing my jugular. "Take it. I don't care. I just want you back." I bit back a sob.

"You're my mate. I would never voluntarily take blood from your neck." Matthew's fingers were cool on my flesh as he drew the smock back into place. "When I did so in Madison, it was because I was too weak to stop myself."

"What's wrong with my neck?" I said, confused.

"Vampires only bite strangers and subordinates on the neck. Not lovers. Certainly not mates."

"Dominance," I said, thinking back to our previous conversations about vampires, blood, and sex, "and feeding. So it's mostly humans who get bitten there. There's the kernel of truth in that vampire legend."

"Vampires bite their mates here," Matthew said, "near the heart." His lips pressed against the bare flesh above the edge of my smock. It was where he had kissed me on our wedding night, when his emotions had overwhelmed him.

"I thought your wanting to kiss me there was just ordinary lust," I said.

"There is nothing ordinary about a vampire's desire to take blood from this vein." He moved his mouth a centimeter lower along the blue line and pressed his lips again.

"But if it's not about feeding or dominance, what is it about?"

"Honesty." When Matthew met my eyes, they were still more black than green. "Vampires keep too many secrets to ever be completely honest. We could never share them all verbally, and most are too complex to make sense, even when you try. And there are prohibitions against sharing secrets in my world."

"'It's not your tale to tell,'" I said. "I've heard that a few times."

"To drink from your lover is to know that nothing is hidden." Matthew stared down at my breast, touched the vein again with his fingertip. "We call this the heart vein. The blood tastes sweeter here. There is a sense of complete possession and belonging—but it requires complete control, too, not to be swept up in the strong emotions that result." His voice was sad.

"And you don't trust your control because of the blood rage."

"You've seen me in its grip. It's sparked by protectiveness. And who poses a greater danger to you than I do?"

I shrugged the smock off my shoulders, pulling my arms out of the sleeves until I was bare from the waist up. I felt for the lacings on my skirt and yanked them free.

"Don't." Matthew's eyes had blackened further. "There is no one here in case—"

"You drain me?" I stepped out of my skirt. "If you couldn't trust yourself to do this when Philippe was within earshot, you're not likely to do it with Gallowglass and Pierre standing by to help."

"This isn't a matter for jokes."

"No." I took his hands in mine. "It's a matter for husbands and wives.

It's a matter of honesty and trust. I have nothing to hide from you. If taking blood from my vein is going to put an end to your incessant need to hunt down what you imagine to be my secrets, then that is what you're going to do."

"It isn't something a vampire does just once," Matthew warned, trying to pull away.

"I didn't think it was." I threaded my fingers into the hair at the nape of his neck. "Take my blood. Take my secrets. Do what your instincts are screaming for you to do. There are no hoods or jesses here. In my arms you should be free, even if nowhere else."

I drew his mouth to mine. He responded tentatively at first, his fingers wrapped around my wrists as if he hoped to break away at the earliest opportunity. But his instincts were strong and his yearning palpable. The threads that bound the world shifted and adjusted around me as if to make room for such powerful feelings. I drew gently away, my breasts lifting with each breath.

He looked so frightened that it hurt my heart. But there was desire, too. *Fear and desire.* No wonder they'd featured in his All Souls essay back when he'd won his fellowship. Who could understand the war between them better than a vampire?

"I love you," I whispered, dropping my hands so that they hung by my sides. He had to do this himself. I couldn't play any role in bringing his mouth to my vein.

The wait was excruciating, but at last he lowered his head. My heart was beating fast, and I heard him draw in a deep, long breath.

"Honey. You always smell like honey," he murmured in amazement, just before his sharp teeth broke the skin.

When he'd taken my blood before, Matthew had been careful to anesthetize the site with a touch of his own blood so that I felt no pain. Not so this time, but soon the skin went numb from the pressure of Matthew's mouth on my flesh. His hands cradled me as he angled me back toward the surface of the bed. I hung in midair waiting for him to be satisfied that there was nothing between us but love.

About thirty seconds after he started, Matthew stopped. He looked up at me in surprise, as if he'd discovered something unexpected. His eyes went full black, and for one fleeting moment I though that the blood rage was surfacing.

"It's all right, my love," I whispered.

Matthew lowered his head, drinking in more until he discovered what he needed. It took little more than a minute. He kissed the place over my heart with the same expression of gentle reverence he had worn on our wedding night at Sept-Tours and looked up at me shyly.

"And what did you find?" I asked.

"You. Only you," Matthew murmured.

His shyness quickly turned to hunger as he kissed me, and before long we were twined together. Except for our brief encounter standing against the wall, we had not made love for weeks, and our rhythm was awkward at first as we remembered how to move together. My body coiled tighter and tighter. Another fast glide, a deep kiss, was all it would take to set me flying.

Matthew slowed instead. Our eyes met and locked. I had never seen him look the way he did at that moment—vulnerable, hopeful, beautiful, free. There were no secrets between us now, no emotions guarded in case disaster struck and we were swept along into the dark places where hope couldn't survive.

"Can you feel me?" Matthew was now a point of stillness at my core. I nodded again. He smiled and moved with deliberate care. "I'm inside you, Diana, giving you life."

I'd said the same words to him as he drank my blood and pulled himself from the edge of death back into the world. I didn't think he'd been aware of them at the time.

He moved within me again, repeating the words like an incantation. It was the simplest, purest form of magic in the world. Matthew was already woven into my soul. He was now woven into my body, just as I was woven into his. My heart, which had broken and broken again in the past months with every sad touch and regretful look, began to knit together once more.

When the sun crept over the horizon, I reached up and touched him between the eyes.

"I wonder if I could read your thoughts, too."

"You already have," Matthew said, lowering my fingers and kissing their tips. "Back in Oxford, when you received the picture of your parents. You weren't conscious of what you were doing. But you kept answering questions I wasn't able to ask aloud."

"Can I try again?" I asked, half expecting him to say no.

"Of course. If you were a vampire I would already have offered my blood." He lay back on the pillow.

I hesitated for a moment, stilled my thoughts, and focused on a simple question. *How can I know Matthew's heart?*

A single silver thread shimmered between my own heart and the spot on his forehead where his third eye would be if he were a witch. The thread shortened, drawing me closer until my lips pressed against his skin.

An explosion of sights and sounds burst in my head like fireworks. I saw Jack and Annie, Philippe and Ysabeau. I saw Gallowglass and men I didn't recognize who occupied important places in Matthew's memories. I saw Eleanor and Lucas. There was a feeling of triumph as he conquered some scientific mystery, a shout of joy as he rode out in the forest to hunt and kill as he was made to do. I saw myself, smiling up at him.

Then I saw the face of Herr Fuchs, the vampire I'd met in the Jewish town, and heard quite distinctly the words *My son, Benjamin.*

I sat back on my heels abruptly, my fingers touching my trembling lips.

"What is it?" Matthew said, sitting up and frowning.

"Herr Fuchs!" I looked at him in horror, afraid he had thought the worst. "I didn't realize he was your son, that he was Benjamin." There hadn't been a hint of blood rage about the creature.

"It's not your fault. You're not a vampire, and Benjamin only reveals what he chooses." Matthew's voice was soothing. "I must have sensed his presence around you—a trace of scent, some inkling that he was near. That's what made me think you were keeping something from me. I was wrong. I'm sorry for doubting you, *mon coeur.*"

"But Benjamin must have known who I was. Your scent would have been all over me."

"Of course he knew," Matthew said dispassionately. "I will look for him tomorrow, but if Benjamin doesn't want to be found, there will be nothing to do but warn Gallowglass and Philippe. They'll let the rest of the family know that Benjamin has reappeared."

"Warn them?" My skin pricked with fear at his nod.

"The only thing more frightening than Benjamin in the grip of blood rage is Benjamin when he is lucid, as he was when you were with Rabbi Loew. It is as Jack said," Matthew replied. "The most terrifying monsters always look just like ordinary men."

## 31

That night marked the true beginning of our marriage. Matthew was more centered than I had ever seen him. Gone were the sharp retorts, abrupt changes of direction, and impulsive decisions that had characterized our time together thus far. Instead Matthew was methodical, measured—but no less deadly. He fed more regularly, hunting in the city and the villages nearby. As his muscles gained in weight and strength, I came to see what Philippe had already observed: Unlikely though it might seem given his size, his son had been wasting away for want of proper nourishment.

I was left with a silvery moon on my breast marking the place where he drank. It was unlike any other scar on my body, lacking the tough buildup of protective tissue that formed over most wounds. Matthew told me that this was due to a property in his saliva, which sealed the bite without letting it heal completely.

Matthew's ritual taking of his mate's blood from a vein near the heart and my new ritual of the witch's kiss that gave me access to his thoughts provided us with a deeper intimacy. We didn't make love every time he joined me in bed, but when we did, it was always preceded and followed by those two searing moments of absolute honesty that removed not only Matthew's greatest worry but mine: that our secrets would somehow destroy us. And even when we didn't make love, we talked in the open, easy way that lovers dream of doing.

The next morning, Matthew told Gallowglass and Pierre about Benjamin. Gallowglass's fury was shorter-lived than Pierre's fear, which rose to the surface whenever someone knocked on the door or approached me in the market. The vampires searched for him day and night, with Matthew planning the expeditions.

But Benjamin could not be found. He had simply vanished.

Easter came and went, and our plans for Rudolf's spring festival the following Saturday reached their final stages. Master Hoefnagel and I transformed the palace's Great Hall into a blooming garden with pots of tulips.

I was in awe of the place, with its graceful curved vaults supporting the arched roof like the branches of a willow tree.

"We'll move the emperor's orange trees here as well," Hoefnagel said, his eyes gleaming with possibilities. "And the peacocks."

On the day of the performance, servants dragged every spare candelabrum in the palace and cathedral into the echoing expanse of stone to provide the illusion of a starry night sky and spread fresh rushes on the floor. For the stage we used the base of the stairs leading up to the royal chapel. It was Master Hoefnagel's idea, since then I could appear at the top of the staircase, like the moon, while Matthew charted my changing position with one of Master Habermel's astrolabes.

"You don't think we're being too philosophical?" I wondered aloud, worrying at my lip with my fingers.

"This is the court of Rudolf II," Hoefnagel said drily. "There is no such thing as too philosophical."

When the court filed in for the banquet, they gasped in amazement at the scene we'd set.

"They like it," I whispered to Matthew from behind the curtain that concealed us from the crowd. Our grand entrance was scheduled for the dessert course, and we were holed up in the Knights' Staircase off the hall until then. Matthew had been keeping me occupied with tales of olden times, when he had ridden his horse up the wide stone steps for a joust. When I'd questioned the room's suitability for this particular purpose, he quirked an eyebrow at me.

"Why do you think we made the room so big and the ceiling so high? Prague winters can be damn long, and bored young men with weapons are dangerous. Far better to have them run at each other at high speed than start wars with neighboring kingdoms."

With the free pouring of wine and the liberal serving of food, the din in the room was soon deafening. When the desserts went by, Matthew and I slipped into our places. Master Hoefnagel had painted some lovely pastoral scenery for Matthew and grudgingly allotted him one of the orange trees to sit beneath on his felt-covered stool meant to look like a rock. I would wait for my cue and then come out of the chapel and stand behind an old wooden door turned on its side and painted to resemble a chariot.

"Don't you dare make me laugh," I warned Matthew when he kissed me on the cheek for luck.

"I do love a challenge," he whispered back.

As strains of music filled through the room, the courtiers gradually hushed. When the room was fully quiet, Matthew lifted his astrolabe to the heavens and the masque began.

I had decided that our best approach to the production involved minimal dialogue and maximum dancing. For one thing, who wanted to sit around after a big dinner and listen to speeches? I'd been to enough academic events to know that wasn't a good idea. Signor Pasetti was delighted to teach some of the court ladies a "dance of the wandering stars," which would provide Matthew something heavenly to observe while he waited for his beloved moon to appear. With famous court beauties given a role in the entertainment and wearing fabulously spangled and jeweled costumes, the masque quickly took on the tone of a school play, complete with admiring parents. Matthew made agonized faces as though he weren't sure he could endure the spectacle for one more moment.

When the dance ended, the musicians cued my entrance with a crash of drums and blare of trumpets. Master Hoefnagel had rigged up a curtain over the chapel doors, so that all I had to do was push my way through them with a goddess's éclat (and without spearing my moon headdress on the fabric as I had done in rehearsal) and stare wistfully down at Matthew. He, goddess willing, would stare raptly at me without crossing his eyes or looking suggestively at my breasts.

I took a moment to get in character, drew in a deep breath, and pushed confidently through the curtains, trying to glide and float like the moon.

The court gasped in wonder.

Pleased that I had made such a convincing entrance, I looked down at Matthew. His eyes were round as saucers.

*Oh, no.* I felt with my toe for the floor, but as I suspected, I was already a few inches above it—and rising. I reached out a hand to anchor myself to the edge of my chariot and saw that a distinctively pearly gleam was emanating from my skin. Matthew jerked his head up in the direction of my tiara and its little silver crescent moon. Without a mirror I had no idea what it was doing, but I feared the worst.

"La Diosa!" Rudolf said, standing up and applauding. "Wonderful! A wonderful effect!"

Uncertainly, the court joined in. A few of them crossed themselves first.

Holding the room's complete attention, I clasped my hands to my bosom and batted my eyes at Matthew, who returned my admiring looks with a grim smile. I concentrated on lowering myself to the floor so that I could make my way to Rudolf's throne. As Zeus, he occupied the most splendid carved piece of furniture we could find in the palace attics. It was unbelievably ugly, but it suited the occasion.

Happily, I was not glowing so much anymore as I approached the emperor, and the audience had stopped looking at my head as if it were a Roman candle. I sank into a curtsy.

"Greetings, La Diosa," Rudolf boomed in what was meant to be a godlike tone but was only a classic example of overacting.

"I am in love with the beautiful Endymion," I said, rising and gesturing back to the staircase, where Matthew had sunk into a downy nest of feather beds and was feigning sleep. I had written the lines myself. (Matthew suggested I say, "If you do not agree to leave me in peace, Endymion will tear your throat out." I vetoed that, along with the Keats.) "He looks so peaceful. And though I am a goddess and will never age, fair Endymion will soon grow old and die. I beg of you, make him immortal so that he can stay with me always."

"On one condition!" Rudolf shouted, abandoning all pretense of godlike sonorousness in favor of simple volume. "He must sleep for the rest of time, never waking. Only then will he remain young."

"Thank you, mighty Zeus," I said, trying not to sound too much like a member of a British comedy troupe. "Now I can gaze upon my beloved forevermore."

Rudolf scowled. It was a good thing he hadn't been granted script approval.

I withdrew to my chariot and walked slowly backward through the curtains while the court ladies performed their final dance. When it was over, Rudolf led the court in a round of loud stomping and clapping that almost brought the roof down. What it did not do was rouse Endymion.

"Get up!" I hissed as I went past to thank the emperor for providing us an opportunity to entertain his royal self. All I got in response was a theatrical snore.

And so I curtsied alone in front of Rudolf and made speeches in praise of Master Habermel's astrolabe, Master Hoefnagel's sets and special effects, and the quality of the music.

"I was greatly entertained, La Diosa—much more than I expected to be. You may ask Zeus for a reward," Rudolf said, his eyes drifting over my shoulder and down to the swell of my breasts. "Whatever you wish. Name it and it shall be yours."

The room's idle chatter stopped. In the silence I heard Abraham's words: *The book will come to you, if only you ask for it.* Could it really be that simple?

Endymion stirred in his downy bed. Not wanting him to interfere, I flapped my hands behind my back to encourage him to return to his dreams. The court held its breath, waiting for me to name a prestigious title, a piece of land, a fortune in gold.

"I would like to see Roger Bacon's alchemical book, Your Majesty."

"You have balls of iron, Auntie," Gallowglass said in a tone of hushed admiration on the way home. "Not to mention a way with words."

"Why, thank you," I said, pleased. "By the way, what was my head doing during the masque? People were staring at it."

"Wee stars rose out of the moon and then faded away. I wouldn't worry. It looked so real that everybody will assume it was an illusion. Most of Rudolf's aristocrats are human, after all."

Matthew's response was more guarded. "Don't be too pleased yet, *mon coeur*. Rudolf may have had no other choice than to agree, given the situation, but he hasn't produced the manuscript. This is a very complicated dance you're doing. And you can be sure the emperor will want something from you in return for a glimpse of his book."

"Then we will have to be long gone before he can insist upon it," I said.

But it turned out that Matthew was right to be cautious. I had imagined that he and I would be invited to view the treasure the next day, in private. Yet no such invitation arrived. Days passed before we received a formal summons to dine at the palace with some up-and-coming Catholic theologians. Afterward, the note promised, a select group would be invited back to Rudolf's rooms to see items of particular mystical and religious import from the emperor's collections. Among the visitors was one Johannes Pistorius, who had grown up Lutheran, converted to Calvinism, and was about to become a Catholic priest.

"We're being set up," Matthew said, fingers running back and forth through his hair. "Pistorius is a dangerous man, a ruthless adversary, and a witch. He will be back here in ten years to serve as Rudolf's confessor."

"Is it true he's being groomed for the Congregation?" Gallowglass asked quietly.

"Yes. He's just the kind of intellectual thug that the witches want representing them. No offense meant, Diana. It is a difficult time for witches," he conceded.

"None taken," I said mildly. "But he's not a member of the Congregation yet. You are. What are the chances he'll want to cause trouble with you watching him, if he has those aspirations?"

"Excellent—or Rudolf wouldn't have asked him to dine with us. The emperor is drawing his battle lines and rallying his troops."

"What, exactly, is he planning to fight over?"

"The manuscript—and you. He won't give up either."

"I told you before that I wasn't for sale. I'm not war booty either."

"No, but you're unclaimed territory so far as Rudolf's concerned. Rudolf is an Austrian archduke, king of Hungary, Croatia, and Bohemia, margrave of Moravia, and Holy Roman Emperor. He is also Philip of Spain's nephew. The Hapsburgs are an acquisitive and competitive family and will stop at nothing to get what they want."

"Matthew's not coddling you, Auntie," Gallowglass said somberly when I started to protest. "If you were my wife, you'd have been out of Prague the day the first gift arrived."

Because of the delicacy of the situation, Pierre and Gallowglass accompanied us to the palace. Three vampires and a witch caused the expected ripples of interest as we went toward the Great Hall, which, once upon a time, Matthew had helped to design.

Rudolf seated me near him, and Gallowglass took up a position behind my chair like a well-mannered servant. Matthew was placed at the opposite end of the banqueting table with an attentive Pierre. To a casual observer, Matthew was having a grand time among a raucous group of ladies and young men who were eager to find a role model with more dash than the emperor. Gales of laughter occasionally drifted in our direction from Matthew's rival court, which did nothing to brighten His Majesty's dour mood.

"But why does there have to be so much bloodshed, Father Johannes?" Rudolf complained to the fleshy, middle-aged physician sitting to his left. Pistorius's ordination was still several months away, but, with the zeal typical of the convert, he made no objection to his premature elevation to the priesthood.

"Because heresy and unorthodoxies must be rooted out completely, Your Majesty. Otherwise they find fresh soil in which to grow." Pistorius's heavy-lidded eyes fell on me, his glance probing. My witch's third eye opened, indignant at his rude attempts to capture my attention, which was strikingly similar to Champier's method for ferreting out my secrets. I was beginning to dislike university-educated wizards. I put down my knife and returned his stare. He was the first to break it.

"My father believed that tolerance was a wiser policy," Rudolf replied. "And you have studied the Jewish wisdom of the kabbalah. There are men of God who would call that heresy."

Matthew's keen hearing allowed him to zero in on my conversation as intensely as Šárka had pursued her grouse. He frowned.

"My husband tells me you are a physician, Herr Pistorius." It was not a smooth conversational segue, but it did the job.

"I am, Frau Roydon. Or I was, before I turned my attention from the preservation of bodies to the salvation of souls."

"Father Johannes's reputation is based on his cures for the plague," Rudolf said.

"I was merely a vehicle for God's will. He is the only true healer," Pistorius said modestly. "Out of love for us, He created many natural remedies that can effect miraculous results in our imperfect bodies."

"Ah, yes. I remember your advocacy of bezoars as panaceas against illness. I sent La Diosa one of my stones when she was lately ill." Rudolf smiled at him approvingly.

Pistorius studied me. "Your cure evidently worked, Your Majesty."

"Yes. La Diosa is fully recovered. She looks very well," Rudolf said, his lower lip jutting out even further as he examined me. I wore a simple black gown embroidered in white covered with a black velvet robe. A gauzy ruff winged away from my face, and the red ruby of Matthew's salamander necklace was arranged to hang in the notch of my throat, providing the only splash of color in my otherwise somber outfit. Rudolf's attention fixed on the beautiful piece of jewelry. He frowned and motioned to a servant.

"It's hard to say whether the bezoar stone or Emperor Maximilian's electuary was the more beneficial," I said, looking to Dr. Hájek for assistance while Rudolf held his whispered conversation. He was tucking into the third game course, and after a startled cough to free the bit of venison he had just swallowed, Hájek rose to the occasion.

"I believe it was the electuary, Dr. Pistorius," Hájek admitted. "I prepared it in a cup made from the unicorn's horn. Emperor Rudolf believed this would increase its efficacy."

"La Diosa took the electuary from a horn spoon, too," Rudolf said, his eyes lingering on my lips now, "for additional surety."

"Will this cup and spoon be among the specimens we see tonight in your cabinet of wonders, Your Majesty?" Pistorius asked. The air between me and the other witch came to sudden, crackling life. Threads surrounding the physician-priest exploded in violent red and orange hues, warning me of the danger. Then he smiled. *I do not trust you, witch,* he whispered into my mind. *Nor does your would-be lover, Emperor Rudolf.*

The wild boar that I was chewing—a delicious dish flavored with rosemary and black pepper that, according to the emperor, was supposed to heat the blood—turned to dust in my mouth. Instead of its achieving its desired effect, my blood ran cold.

"Is something wrong?" Gallowglass murmured, bending low over my shoulder. He handed me a shawl, which I hadn't asked for and didn't know he was carrying.

"Pistorius has been invited upstairs to see the book," I said, turning my head toward him and speaking in rapid English to reduce the risk of being understood. Gallowglass smelled of sea salt and mint, a bracing and reassuring combination. My nerves steadied.

"Leave it to me," he replied, giving my shoulder a squeeze. "By the way, you're a bit shiny, Auntie. It would be best if no one saw stars tonight."

Having delivered his warning shot across the bow, Pistorius turned the conversation to other topics and engaged Dr. Hájek in a lively debate about the medical benefits of theriac. Rudolf divided his time between sneaking melancholic looks at me and glaring at Matthew. The closer we got to seeing Ashmole 782, the less appetite I had, so I made small talk with the noblewoman next to me. It was only after five more courses—including a parade of gilded peacocks and a tableau of roast pork and suckling pigs—that the banquet finally concluded.

"You look pale," Matthew said, whisking me away from the table.

"Pistorius suspects me." The man reminded me of Peter Knox and Champier, and for similar reasons. "Intellectual thug" was the perfect description for both of them. "Gallowglass said he would take care of it."

"No wonder Pierre followed on his heels, then."

"What is Pierre going to do?"

"Make sure Pistorius gets out of here alive," Matthew said cheerfully. "Left to his own devices, Gallowglass would strangle the man and throw him into the Stag's Moat for the lions' midnight snack. My nephew is almost as protective of you as I am."

Rudolf's invited guests accompanied him to his inner sanctum: the private gallery where Matthew and I viewed the Bosch altarpiece. Ottavio Strada met us there to guide us through the collection and answer our questions.

When we entered the room, Matthew's altarpiece still sat in the center of the green-covered table. Rudolf had scattered other objects around it for our viewing pleasure. While the guests oohed and aahed over Bosch's work, I scanned the room. There were some stunning cups made out of semiprecious stones, an enameled chain of office, a long horn reputedly from a unicorn, some statuary, and a carved Seychelles nut—a nice mix of the expensive, the medicinal, and the exotic. But no alchemical manuscript.

"Where is it?" I hissed to Matthew. Before he could respond, I felt the touch of a warm hand on my arm. Matthew stiffened.

"I have a gift for you, *querida diosa.*" Rudolf's breath smelled of onions and red wine, and my stomach flopped over in protest. I turned, expecting to see Ashmole 782. Instead the emperor was holding up the enameled chain. Before I could protest, he draped it over my head and settled it on my shoulders. I looked down and saw a green ouroboros hanging from a circle of red crosses, thickly encrusted with emeralds, rubies, diamonds, and pearls. The color scheme reminded me of the jewel Herr Maisel gave to Benjamin.

"That is a strange gift to give my wife, Your Majesty," Matthew said softly. He was standing right behind the emperor and looking at the necklace with distaste. This was my third such chain, and I knew there must be a meaning behind the symbolism. I lifted the ouroboros so that I could study the enameling. It wasn't an ouroboros, exactly, because it had feet. It looked more like a lizard or a salamander than a snake. A bloody red cross emerged from the lizard's flayed back. Most important, the tail was not held in the creature's mouth but wrapped around the lizard's throat, strangling it.

"It is a mark of respect, Herr Roydon." Rudolf placed a subtle emphasis on the name. "This once belonged to King Vladislaus and was passed on to my grandmother. The insignia belongs to a brave company of Hungarian knights known as the Order of the Defeated Dragon."

"Dragon?" I said faintly, looking at Matthew. With its stumpy legs, this might well be a dragon. But it was otherwise strikingly similar to the de

Clermont family's emblem—except this ouroboros was dying a slow, painful death. I remembered Herr Fuchs's oath—Benjamin's oath—to slay dragons wherever he found them.

"The dragon symbolizes our enemies, especially those who might wish to interfere with our royal prerogatives." Rudolf said it in a civilized tone, but it was a virtual declaration of war on the whole de Clermont clan. "It would please me if you would wear it next time you come to court." Rudolf's finger touched the dragon at my breast lightly and lingered there. "Then you can leave your little French salamanders at home."

Matthew's eyes, which were glued to the dragon and the imperial finger, went black when Rudolf made his insulting remark about French salamanders. I tried to think like Mary Sidney and come up with a response that was appropriate for the period and likely to calm the vampire. I'd deal with my outraged sense of feminism later.

"Whether or not I wear your gift will be up to my husband, Your Majesty," I said coolly, forcing myself not to step away from Rudolf's finger. I heard gasps, a few hushed whispers. But the only reaction I cared about was Matthew's.

"I see no reason you should not wear it for the rest of the evening, *mon coeur*," Matthew said agreeably. He was no longer concerned that the queen of England's ambassador sounded like a French aristocrat. "Salamanders and dragons are kin, after all. Both will endure the flames to protect those they love. And the emperor is being kind enough to show you his book." Matthew looked around. "Though it seems Signor Strada's incompetency continues, for the book is not here." Another bridge burned behind us.

"Not yet, not yet," Rudolf said testily. "I have something else to present to La Diosa first. Go see my carved nut from the Maldives. It is the only one of its kind." Everybody but Matthew trooped off obediently in the direction of Strada's pointing finger. "You, too, Herr Roydon."

"Of course," Matthew murmured, imitating his mother's tone perfectly. He slowly trailed after the crowd.

"Here is something I requested especially. Father Johannes helped to procure the treasure." Rudolf looked around the room but failed to locate Pistorius. He frowned. "Where has he gone, Signor Strada?"

"I have not seen him since we left the Great Hall, Your Majesty," Strada replied.

"You!" Rudolf pointed to a servant. "Go and find him!" The man left immediately, and at a run. The emperor gathered his composure and returned his attention to the strange object in front of us. It looked like a crude carving of a naked man. "This, La Diosa, is a fabled root from Eppendorf. A century ago a woman stole a consecrated host from the church and planted it by the light of the full moon to increase her garden's fertility. The next morning they discovered an enormous cabbage."

"Growing out of the host?" Surely something was being lost in translation, unless I very much misunderstood the nature of the Christian Eucharist. An *arbor Dianæ* was one thing. An *arbor brassicæ* was quite another.

"Yes. It was a miracle. And when the cabbage was dug up, its root resembled the body of Christ." Rudolf held out the item to me. It was crowned with a golden diadem studded with pearls. Presumably that had been added later.

"Fascinating," I said, trying to look and sound interested.

"I wanted you to see it in part because it resembles a picture in the book you requested. Fetch Edward, Ottavio."

Edward Kelley entered, clutching a leather-bound volume to his chest.

As soon as I saw it, I knew. My entire body was tingling while the book was still across the room. Its power was palpable—far more so than it had been at the Bodleian on that September night when my whole life changed.

Here was the missing Ashmole manuscript—before it belonged to Elias Ashmole and before it went missing.

"You will sit here, with me, and we will look at the book together." Rudolf gestured toward a table and two chairs that were set up in an intimate tête-à-tête. "Give me the book, Edward." Rudolf held out his hand, and Kelley reluctantly placed the book in it.

I shot Matthew a questioning look. What if the manuscript started to glow as it had in the Bodleian or behaved strangely in some other way? And what if I weren't able to stop my mind from wondering about the book or its secrets? An eruption of magic at this point would be disastrous.

*This is why we're here,* said his confident nod.

I sat down next to the emperor, and Strada ushered the courtiers around the room to the unicorn's horn. Matthew drifted still closer. I stared at the book in front of me, hardly daring to believe that the moment had come when I would at last see Ashmole 782 whole and complete.

"Well?" Rudolf demanded. "Are you going to open it?"

"Of course," I said, pulling the book closer. No iridescence escaped from the pages. For purposes of comparison, I rested my hand on the cover for just a moment, as I had when I'd retrieved Ashmole 782 from the stacks.

Then it had sighed in recognition, as though it had been waiting for me to show up. This time the book lay still.

I flipped open the hide-bound wooden board of the front cover, revealing a blank sheet of parchment. My mind raced back over what I'd seen months ago. This was the sheet on which Ashmole and my father would one day write the book's title.

I turned the page and felt the same sense of uncanny heaviness. When the page fell open, I gasped.

The first, missing page of Ashmole 782 was a glorious illumination of a tree. The tree's trunk was knotted and gnarled, thick and yet sinuous. Branches sprang from the top, twisting and turning their way across the page and ending in a defiant combination of leaves, bright red fruit, and flowers. It was like the *arbor Dianæ* that Mary had made using blood drawn from Matthew and me.

When I bent closer, my breath caught in my throat. The tree's trunk was not made of wood, sap, and bark. It was made of hundreds of bodies— some writhing and thrashing in pain, some serenely entwined, others alone and frightened.

At the bottom of the page, written in a late-thirteenth-century hand, was the title Roger Bacon had given it: *The True Secret of Secrets.*

Matthew's nostrils flared, as though he were trying to identify a scent. The book did have a strange odor—the same musty smell that I had noticed at Oxford.

I turned the page. Here was the image sent to my parents, the one the Bishop house had saved for so many years: the phoenix enfolding the chemical wedding in her wings, while mythical and alchemical beasts witnessed the union of Sol and Luna.

Matthew looked shocked, and he was now staring at the book. I frowned. He was still too far away to see it clearly. What had surprised him?

Quickly, I flipped over the image of the alchemical wedding. The third missing page turned out to be two alchemical dragons, their tails intertwined and their bodies locked in either a battle or an embrace—it was impossible to tell which. A rain of blood fell from their wounds, pooling in a basin from which sprang dozens of naked, pale figures. I'd never seen an alchemical image like it.

Matthew stood over the emperor's shoulder, and I expected his shock to turn to excitement at seeing these new images and getting closer to solving the book's mysteries. But he looked as if he'd seen a ghost. A white hand covered his mouth and nose. When I frowned with concern, Matthew nodded to me, a sign that I should keep going.

I took a deep breath and turned to what should be the first of the strange alchemical images I'd seen in Oxford. Here, as expected, was the baby girl with the two roses. What was unexpected was that every inch of space around her was covered in text. It was an odd mix of symbols and a few scattered letters. In the Bodleian this text had been hidden by a spell that transformed the book into a magical palimpsest. Now, with the book intact, the secret text was on full view. Though I could see it, I still couldn't read it.

My fingers traced the lines of text. My touch unmade the words, transforming them into a face, a silhouette, a name. It was as though the text were trying to tell a story involving thousands of creatures.

"I would have given you anything you asked for," Rudolf said, his breath hot against my cheek. Once again I smelled onions and wine. It was so unlike Matthew's clean, spicy scent. And Rudolf's warmth was off-putting now that I was used to a vampire's cool temperature. "Why did you choose this? It cannot be understood, though Edward believes it contains a great secret."

A long arm reached between us and gently touched the page. "Why, this is as meaningless as the manuscript you foisted off on poor Dr. Dee." Matthew's face belied his words. Rudolf might not have seen the muscle ticking in Matthew's jaw or known how the fine lines around his eyes deepened when he concentrated.

"Not necessarily," I said hastily. "Alchemical texts require study and contemplation if you wish to understand them fully. Perhaps if I spent more time with it . . ."

"Even then one must have God's special blessing," Rudolf said, scowling at Matthew. "Edward is touched by God in ways you are not, Herr Roydon."

"Oh, he's touched all right," Matthew said, looking over at Kelley. The English alchemist was acting strange now that the book was not in his possession. There were threads connecting him and the book. But why was Kelley bound to Ashmole 782?

As the question went through my mind, the fine yellow and white threads tying Kelley to Ashmole 782 took on a new appearance. Instead of the normal tight twist of two colors or a weave of horizontal and vertical threads, these spooled loosely around an invisible center, like the curling ribbons on a birthday present. Short, horizontal threads kept the curls from touching. It looked like—

*A double helix.* My hand rose to my mouth, and I stared down at the manuscript. Now that I'd touched the book, its musty smell was on my fingers. It was strong, gamy, like—

*Flesh and blood.* I looked to Matthew, knowing that the expression on my face mirrored the shocked look I had seen on his.

"You don't look well, *mon coeur*," he said solicitously, helping me to my feet. "Let me take you home." Edward Kelley chose this moment to lose control.

"I hear their voices. They speak in tongues I cannot understand. Can you hear them?"

He moaned in distress, his hands clapped over his ears.

"What are you chattering about?" Rudolf said. "Dr. Hájek, something is wrong with Edward."

"You will find your name in it, too," Edward told me, his voice getting louder, as if he were trying to drown out some other sound. "I knew it the moment I saw you."

I looked down. Curling threads bound me to the book, too—only mine were white and lavender. Matthew was bound to it by curling strands of red and white.

Gallowglass appeared, unannounced and uninvited. A burly guard followed him, clutching at his own limp arm.

"The horses are ready," Gallowglass informed us, gesturing toward the exit.

"You do not have permission to be here!" Rudolf shouted, his fury mounting as his careful arrangements disintegrated. "And you, La Diosa, do not have permission to leave."

Matthew paid absolutely no attention to Rudolf. He simply took my arm and strode in the direction of the door. I could feel the manuscript pulling on me, the threads stretching to bring me back to its side.

"We can't leave the book. It's—"

"I know what it is," Matthew said grimly.

"Stop them!" Rudolf screamed.

But the guard with the broken arm had already tangled with one angry vampire tonight. He wasn't going to tempt fate by interfering with Matthew. Instead his eyes rolled up into his head and he dropped to the floor in a faint.

Gallowglass threw my cloak over my shoulders as we pelted down the stairs. Two more guards—both unconscious—lay at the bottom.

"Go back and get the book!" I ordered Gallowglass, breathless from my constrictive corset and the speed at which we were moving across the court-yard. "We can't let Rudolf have it now that we know what it is."

Matthew stopped, his fingers digging into my arm. "We won't leave Prague without the manuscript. I'll go back and get it, I promise. But first we are going home. You must have the children ready to leave the moment I get back."

"We've burned our bridges, Auntie," Gallowglass said grimly. "Pistorius is locked up in the White Tower. I killed one guard and injured three more. Rudolf touched you most improperly, and I have a strong desire to see him dead, too."

"You don't understand, Gallowglass. That book may be the answer to *everything*," I managed to squeak out before Matthew had me in motion again.

"Oh, I understand more than you think I do." Gallowglass's voice floated in the breeze next to me. "I picked up the scent of it downstairs when I knocked out the guards. There are dead *wearhs* in that book. Witches and daemons, too, I warrant. Whoever could have imagined that the lost Book of Life would stink to high heaven of death?"

"Who would make such a thing?" Twenty minutes later I was shivering by the fireplace in our main first-floor room, clutching a beaker of herbal tea. "It's gruesome."

Like most manuscripts, Ashmole 782 was made of vellum—specially prepared skin that had been soaked in lime to remove the hair, scraped to take away the subcutaneous layers of flesh and fat, then soaked again before being stretched on a frame and scraped some more.

The difference here was that the creatures used to make the vellum were not sheep, calves, or goats but daemons, vampires, and witches.

"It must have been kept as a record." Matthew was still trying to come to terms with what we had seen.

"But it has hundreds of pages," I said in disbelief. The thought of someone flaying so many daemons, vampires, and witches and making vellum from their skins was incomprehensible. I wasn't sure I would ever sleep through the night again.

"Which means the book contains hundreds of distinct pieces of DNA." Matthew had run his fingers through his hair so many times he was starting to resemble a porcupine.

"The threads twisting between us and Ashmole 782 looked like double helices," I said. We'd had to explain modern genetics to Gallowglass, who, without the intervening four and a half centuries of biology and chemistry, was doing his best to follow it.

"So D-N-A is like a family tree, but its branches cover more than just one family?" Gallowglass sounded out "DNA" slowly, with a break between each letter.

"Yes," Matthew said. "That's about it."

"Did you see the tree on the first page?" I asked Matthew. "The trunk was made of bodies, and the tree was flowering, fruiting, and leafing out just like the *arbor Dianæ* we made in Mary's laboratory."

"No, but I saw the creature with its tail in its mouth," Matthew said.

I tried feverishly to recall what I'd seen, but my photographic memory failed me when I needed it most. There was too much new information to absorb.

"The picture showed two creatures fighting—or embracing, I couldn't tell which. I didn't have a chance to count their legs. Their falling blood was generating hundreds of creatures. Although if one of them was not a four-legged dragon but a snake . . ."

"And one was a two-legged firedrake, then those alchemical dragons could symbolize you and me." Matthew swore, briefly but with feeling.

Gallowglass listened patiently until we were through, then went back to his original topic. "And this D-N-A, it lives in our skin?"

"Not just your skin, but your blood, bones, hair, nails—it's throughout your entire body," Matthew explained.

"Huh." Gallowglass rubbed his chin. "And what question is it you have in mind, exactly, when you say this book might have all the answers?"

"Why we're different from the humans," Matthew said simply. "And why a witch like Diana might carry a *wearh*'s child."

Gallowglass gave us a radiant smile. "You mean your child, Matthew. I knew full well Auntie was capable of that back in London. She never smelled like anyone but herself—and you. Did Philippe know?"

"Few people knew," I said quickly.

"Hancock did. So did Françoise and Pierre. My guess is Philippe was told all about it." Gallowglass stood. "I'll just go fetch Auntie's book, then. If it has to do with de Clermont babes, we must have it."

"Rudolf will have locked it up tight or tucked it into bed with him," Matthew predicted. "It's not going to be easy to take it from the palace, especially not if they've found Pistorius and he's out casting spells and making mischief."

"Speaking of Emperor Rudolf, can we get that necklace off Auntie's shoulders? I hate that bloody insignia."

"Gladly," I said, plucking at the chain and tossing the garish object onto the table. "What, exactly, does the Order of the Defeated Dragon have to do with the de Clermonts? I assume that they must not be friends with the Knights of Lazarus, given the fact that the poor ouroboros has been partially skinned and is strangling itself."

"They hate us and wish us dead," Matthew said flatly. "The Drăculeşti disapprove of my father's broad-minded views on Islam and the Ottomans and have vowed to bring us all down. That way they can fulfill their political aspirations unchecked."

"And they want the de Clermont money," Gallowglass observed.

"The Drăculeşti?" My voice was faint. "But Dracula is a human myth—one meant to spread fear about vampires." It was *the* human myth about vampires.

"That would come as some surprise to the patriarch of the clan, Vlad the Dragon," Gallowglass commented, "though he would be pleased to know he will go on terrifying people."

"The humans' Dracula—the Dragon's son known as the Impaler—was only one of Vlad's brood," Matthew explained.

"The Impaler was a nasty bastard. Happily, he's dead now, and all we have to worry about are his father, his brothers, and their Báthory allies." Gallowglass looked somewhat cheered.

"According to human accounts, Dracula lived on for centuries—he may still be living. Are you sure he's really dead?" I asked.

"I watched Baldwin rip his head off and bury it thirty miles away from the rest of his body. He was really dead then, and he's really dead now." Gallowglass looked at me reprovingly. "You should know better than to believe these human stories, Auntie. They've never got more than a speck of truth in them."

"I think Benjamin had one of these dragon emblems. Herr Maisel gave it to him. I noticed the similarity in colors when the emperor first held it out."

"You told me Benjamin left Hungary," Matthew said accusingly to his nephew.

"He did. I swear it. Baldwin ordered him to leave or face the same fate as the Impaler. You should have seen Baldwin's face. The devil himself wouldn't have disobeyed your brother."

"I want us all as far from Prague as possible by the time the sun rises," Matthew said grimly. "Something is very wrong. I can smell it."

"That may not be such a good idea. Do you not know what night it is?" Gallowglass asked. Matthew shook his head. "Walpurgisnacht. They are lighting bonfires all around the city and burning effigies of witches—unless they can find a real one, of course."

"Christ." Matthew drove his fingers through his hair, giving it a good shake as he did. "At least the fires will provide some distraction. We have to figure out how to circumvent Rudolf's guards, get into his private chambers, and find the book. Then, fires or no fires, we are getting out of the city."

"We're *wearhs*, Matthew. If anyone can steal it, we can," Gallowglass said confidently.

"It's not going to be as easy as you think. We may get in, but will we get out?"

"I can help, Master Roydon." Jack's voice sounded like a flute compared to Gallowglass's rumbling bass and Matthew's baritone. Matthew turned and scowled at him.

"No, Jack," he said firmly. "You aren't to steal anything, remember? Besides, you've only been to the palace stables. You wouldn't have any idea where to look."

"Er . . . that's not strictly true." Gallowglass looked uncomfortable. "I took him to the cathedral. And the Great Hall to see the cartoons you once drew on the walls of the Knights' Staircase. And he's been to the kitchens. Oh," Gallowglass said as an afterthought, "Jack went to the menagerie, too, of course. It would have been cruel not to let him see the animals."

"He has been to the castle with me as well," Pierre said from the doorway. "I didn't want him to go adventuring one day and get lost."

"And where did *you* take him, Pierre?" Matthew's tone was icy. "The throne room, so he could jump up and down on the royal seat?"

"No, *milord*. I took him to the blacksmith's shop and to meet Master Hoefnagel." Pierre drew himself up to his full, relatively diminutive height and stared his employer down. "I thought he should show his drawings to someone with real skill in these matters. Master Hoefnagel was most impressed and drew a pen-and-ink portrait of him on the spot for a reward."

"Pierre also took me to the guards' chamber," Jack said in a small voice. "That's where I got these." He held up a ring of keys. "I only wanted to see the unicorn, for I couldn't imagine how a unicorn climbed the stairs and thought they must have wings. Then Master Gallowglass showed me the Knights' Staircase—I like your drawing of the running deer very much, Master Roydon. The guards were talking. I couldn't understand everything, but the word *einhorn* stuck out, and I thought maybe they knew where it was, and—"

Matthew took Jack by the shoulders and crouched down so that their eyes met. "Do you know what they would have done if they'd caught you?" My husband looked as fearful as the child did.

Jack nodded.

"And seeing a unicorn was worth being beaten?"

"I've been beaten before. But I've never seen a magical beast. Except for the lion in the emperor's menagerie. And Mistress Roydon's dragon." Jack looked horrified and clapped his hand over his mouth.

"So you've seen that, too? Prague has been an eye-opening experience for all concerned, then." Matthew stood and held out his hand. "Give me the keys." Jack did so, reluctantly. Matthew bowed to the boy. "I am in your debt, Jack."

"But I was bad," Jack whispered. He rubbed his backside, as if he had already felt the punishment Matthew was bound to dole out.

"I'm bad all the time," Matthew confessed. "Sometimes good comes of it."

"Yes, but nobody beats *you*," Jack said, still trying to understand this strange world where grown men were in debt to little boys and his hero was not perfect after all.

"Matthew's father beat him with a sword once. I saw it." The firedrake's wings fluttered softly within my rib cage in silent agreement. "Then he knocked him over and stood on him."

"He must be as big as the emperor's bear Sixtus," Jack said, awed at the thought of anyone conquering Matthew.

"He is," Matthew said, growling like the bear in question. "Back to bed. Now."

"But I'm nimble—and quick," Jack protested. "I can get Mistress Roydon's book without anyone seeing me."

"So can I, Jack," Matthew promised.

Matthew and Gallowglass returned from the palace covered with blood, dirt, and soot—and bearing Ashmole 782.

"You got it!" I cried. Annie and I were waiting on the first floor. We had small bags packed with traveling essentials.

Matthew opened the cover. "The first three pages are gone."

The book that had been whole just hours before was now broken, the text racing across the page. I'd planned on running my fingers over the letters and symbols once it was in our possession to determine its meaning. Now that was impossible. As soon as my fingertips touched the page, the words skittered in every direction.

"We found Kelley with the book. He was bent over it and crooning like a madman." Matthew paused. "The book was talking back."

"He tells you true, Auntie. I heard the words, though I couldn't make them out."

"Then the book really is alive," I murmured.

"And really dead, too," Gallowglass said, touching the binding. "It's an evil thing as well as a powerful one."

"When Kelley spotted us, he screamed at the top of his lungs and started ripping pages from the book. Before I could reach him, the guards were there. I had to choose between the book and Kelley." Matthew hesitated. "Did I do the right thing?"

"I think so," I said. "When I found the book in England, it was broken. And it may be easier to find the fugitive pages in the future than it would be now." Modern search engines and library catalogs would be enormously helpful since I knew what I was seeking.

"Provided the pages weren't destroyed," Matthew said. "If that's the case . . ."

"Then we'll never know all of the book's secrets. Even so, your modern laboratory might reveal more about what's left than we imagined when we set out on this quest."

"So you're ready to go back?" Matthew asked. There was a spark of something in his eye. He smothered it quickly. Was it excitement? Dread?

I nodded. "It's time."

We fled Prague by the light of the bonfires. Our fellow creatures were in hiding on Walpurgisnacht, not wanting to be seen by the revelers in case they found themselves flung onto the pyre.

The frigid waters of the North Sea were just navigable, and the spring thaw had broken up the ice in the harbors. Boats were leaving the ports for England, and we were able to catch one without delay. Even so, the weather was stormy when we pulled away from the European shore.

In our cabin belowdecks, I found Matthew studying the book. He had discovered that it was sewn together with long strands of hair.

*"Dieu,"* he murmured, "how much more genetic information might this thing contain?" Before I could stop him, he touched the tip of his pinkie to his tongue and then to the drops of blood showering down from the baby's hair on the first extant page.

"Matthew!" I said, horrified.

"Just as I thought. The inks contain blood. And if that's the case, my guess is that the gold and silver leaf on these illustrations is applied to a glue base made from bones. Creature bones."

The boat lurched leeward, and my stomach went along with it. When I was through being sick, Matthew held me in his arms. The book lay between us, slightly open, the lines of text searching to find their place in the order of things.

"What have we done?" I whispered.

"We've found the Tree of Life and the Book of Life, all wrapped up in one." Matthew rested his cheek on my hair.

"When Peter Knox told me the book held all the witches' original spells, I told him he was mad. I couldn't imagine anyone being so foolish as to put so much knowledge in one place." I touched the book. "But this book contains so much more—and we still don't know what the words say. If this were to fall into the wrong hands in our own time—"

"It could be used to destroy us all," Matthew finished.

I craned my head to look at him. "What are we going to do with it, then? Take it back with us to the future or leave it here?"

"I don't know, *mon coeur.*" He gathered me closer, muffling the sound of the storm as it lashed against the hull.

"But this book may well hold the key to all your questions." I was surprised that Matthew could part with it now that he knew what it contained.

"Not all," he said. "There's one only you can answer."

"What's that?" I asked with a frown.

"Are you seasick or are you with child?" Matthew's eyes were as heavy and stormy as the sky, with glints of bright lightning.

"You would know better than I." We had made love only a few days ago, soon after I realized that my period was late.

"I didn't see the child in your blood or hear its heart—not yet. It's the change in your scent that I noticed. I remember it from last time. You can't be more than a few weeks pregnant."

"I would have thought my being pregnant would make you more eager than ever to keep the book with you."

"Maybe my questions don't need answers as urgently as I thought they did." To prove his point, Matthew put the book on the floor, out of sight. "I thought it would tell me who I am and why I'm here. Perhaps I already know."

I waited for him to explain.

"After all my searching, I discover that I am who I always was: Matthew de Clermont. Husband. Father. Vampire. And I am here for only one reason: To make a difference."

## 33

Peter Knox dodged the puddles in the courtyard of the Strahov Monastery in Prague. He was on his annual spring circuit of libraries in central and Eastern Europe. When the tourists and scholars were at their lowest ebb, Knox went from one old repository to another, making sure that nothing untoward had turned up in the past twelve months that might cause the Congregation—or him—trouble. In each library he had a trusted informant, a member of staff who was of sufficiently high standing to have free access to the books and manuscripts, but not so elevated that he might later be required to take a principled stand against library treasures simply . . . disappearing.

Knox had been making regular visits like this since he'd finished his doctorate and begun working for the Congregation. Much had changed since World War II, and the Congregation's administrative structure had adjusted to the times. With the transportation revolution of the nineteenth century, trains and roads allowed a new style of governance, with each species policing its own kind rather than overseeing a geographic location. It meant a lot of traveling and letter writing, both possible in the Age of Steam. Philippe de Clermont had been instrumental in modernizing the Congregation's operations, though Knox had long suspected he did it more to protect vampire secrets than to promote progress.

Then the world wars disrupted communications and transportation networks, and the Congregation reverted to its old ways. It was more sensible to break up the globe into slices than to crisscross it tracking down a specific individual accused of wrongdoing. No one would have dared to suggest such a radical change when Philippe was alive. Happily, the former head of the de Clermont family was no longer around to resist. The Internet and e-mail threatened to make such trips unnecessary, but Knox liked tradition.

Knox's mole at the Strahov Library was a middle-aged man named Pavel Skovajsa. He was brown all over, like foxed paper, and wore a pair of Communist-era glasses that he refused to replace, though it was unclear whether his reluctance was for historical or sentimental reasons. Usually the two men met in the monastery brewery, which had gleaming copper tanks and served an excellent amber beer named after St. Norbert, whose earthly remains rested nearby.

But this year Skovajsa had actually found something.

"It is a letter. In Hebrew," Skovajsa had whispered down the phone line. He was suspicious of new technology, didn't have a cell phone, and detested e-mail. That's why he was employed in the conservation department, where his idiosyncratic approach to knowledge wouldn't slow the library's steady march toward modernity.

"Why are you whispering, Pavel?" Knox had asked in irritation. The only problem with Skovajsa was that he liked to think of himself as a spy hewn from the ice of the Cold War. As a result he was a tad paranoid.

"Because I took a book apart to get at it. Someone hid it underneath the endpapers of a copy of Johannes Reuchlin's *De Arte Cabalistica*," Skovajsa explained, his excitement mounting. Knox looked at his watch. It was so early that he hadn't had his coffee yet. "You must come, at once. It mentions alchemy and that Englishman who worked for Rudolf II. It may be important."

Knox was on the next flight out of Berlin. And now Skovajsa had spirited him away to a dingy room in the basement of the library illuminated by a single bare lightbulb.

"Isn't there somewhere more comfortable for us to conduct business?" Knox said, eyeing the metal table (also Communist-era) with suspicion. "Is that goulash?" He pointed to a sticky spot on its surface.

"The walls have ears, and the floors have eyes." Skovajsa wiped at the spot with the hem of his brown sweater. "We are safer here. Sit. Let me bring you the letter."

"And the book," Knox said sharply. Skovajsa turned, surprised at his tone.

"Yes, of course. The book, too."

"That isn't *On the Art of Kabbalah*," Knox said when Skovajsa returned, growing more irritated with each passing moment. Johannes Reuchlin's book was slim and elegant. This monstrosity had to be nearly eight hundred pages long. When it hit the table, the impact reverberated across the top and down the metal legs.

"Not exactly," Skovajsa said defensively. "It's Galatino's *De Arcanis Catholicae Veritatis*. But the Reuchlin is in it." A cavalier approach to precise bibliographic details was one of Knox's bêtes noires.

"The title page has inscriptions in Hebrew, Latin, and French." Skovajsa flung open the cover. Since there was nothing to support the spine of the large tome, Knox was not surprised to hear an ominous crack. He looked at Skovajsa in alarm. "Don't worry," the conservationist reassured him, "it isn't cataloged. I only discovered it because it was shelved next to our other copy, which was due to go out for rebinding. It probably came here by mistake when our books were returned in 1989."

Knox dutifully examined the title page and its inscriptions.

Genesis 49:27 בנימין זאב יטרף בבקר יאכל עד ולערב יחלק שלל
*Beniamin lupus rapax mane comedet praedam et vespere dividet spolia.*
*Benjamin est un loup qui déchire; au matin il dévore la proie, et sur le soir il partage le butin.*

"It is an old hand, is it not? And the owner was clearly well educated," Skovajsa said.

"*Benjamin shall raven as a wolf: in the morning he shall devour the prey, and at night he shall divide the spoil,*'" Knox mused. He couldn't imagine what these verses had to do with *De Arcanis.* Galatino's work contributed a single shot in the Catholic Church's war against Jewish mysticism—the same war that had led to book burnings, inquisitorial proceedings, and witch hunts in the sixteenth century. Galatino's position on these matters was given away by his title: *Concerning Secrets of the Universal Truth.* In a nifty bit of intellectual acrobatics, Galatino argued that the Jews had anticipated Christian doctrines and that the study of kabbalah could help Catholic efforts to convert the Jews to the true faith.

"Perhaps the owner's name was Benjamin?" Skovajsa looked over his shoulder and passed Knox a file. Knox was happy to see that it was not stamped TOP SECRET in red letters. "And here is the letter. I do not know Hebrew, but the name Edwardus Kellaeus and alchemy—*alchymia*—are in Latin."

Knox turned the page. He was dreaming. He had to be. The letter was dated from the second day of Elul 5369—1 September 1609 in the Christian calendar. And it was signed Yehuda ben Bezalel, a man most knew as Rabbi Judah Loew.

"You know Hebrew, yes?" Skovajsa said.

"Yes." This time it was Knox who was whispering. "Yes," he said more strongly. He stared at the letter.

"Well?" Skovajsa said after nearly a minute of silence had passed. "What does it say?"

"It seems that a Jew from Prague met Edward Kelley and was writing to a friend to tell him so." It was true—in a way.

"Long life and peace to you, Benjamin son of Gabriel, cherished friend," Rabbi Loew wrote.

*I received your letter from my birth city with great joy. Poznań is a better place for you than Hungary, where nothing awaits you but misery. Though I am an old man, your letter brought back clearly the strange events that occurred in the spring of 5351 when Edwardus Kellaeus, student of alchymia and beloved of the emperor, came to me. He raved about a man he had killed and that the emperor's guards would soon arrest him for murder and treason. He foresaw his own death, crying out, "I will fall like the angels into hell." He also spoke of this book you seek, which was stolen from Emperor Rudolf, as you know. Kellaeus sometimes called it the Book of Creation and sometimes the Book of Life. Kellaeus wept, saying that the end of the world was upon us. He kept repeating omens, such as "It begins with absence and desire," "It begins with blood and fear," "It begins with a discovery of witches," and so forth.*

*In his madness Kellaeus had removed three pages from this Book of Life even before it was taken from the emperor. He gave one leaf to me. Kellaeus would not tell me to whom he had given the other pages, speaking in riddles about the angel of death and the angel of life. Alas, I do not know the book's present whereabouts. I no longer have my leaf from it, having given it to Abraham ben Elijah for safekeeping. He died of the pestilence, and the page may be forever lost. The only one who might be able to shed light on the mystery is your maker. May your interest in healing this broken book extend to healing your broken lineage so that you might find peace with the Father who gave you life and breath. The Lord guard your spirit, from your loving friend Yehuda of the holy city of Prague, son of Bezalel, 2nd of the month Elul 5369*

"That's all?" Skovajsa said after another long pause. "It's just about a meeting?"

"In essence." Knox made rapid calculations on the back of the folder. Loew died in 1609. Kelley visited him eighteen years before that. *Spring 1591.* He dug in his pocket for his phone and looked at the display in disgust. "Don't you get a signal up here?"

"We're underground," Skovajsa said, shrugging as he pointed to the thick walls. "So was I right to tell you about this?" He licked his lips in anticipation.

"You did well, Pavel. I'm taking the letter. And the book." They were the only items Knox had ever removed from the Strahov Library.

"Good. I thought it was worth your time, what with the mention of alchemy." Pavel grinned.

What happened next was regrettable. Skovajsa had the misfortune, after years of rooting about without success, of finding something precious to Knox. With a few words and a small gesture, Knox made sure Pavel would never be able to share what he had seen with another creature. For sentimental and ethical reasons, Knox didn't kill him. That would have been a vampire's response, as he knew from finding Gillian Chamberlain propped up against his door at the Randolph Hotel last autumn. Being a witch, he simply freed the clot already lurking in Skovajsa's thigh so it could travel up to his brain. Once there, it caused a massive stroke. It would be hours before someone found him, and too late for any good to come of it.

Knox found his way back to his rental car with the biblically proportioned book and the letter safely tucked under his arm. Once he was far enough from the Strahov complex, he pulled over to the side of the road and took out the letter, his hands shaking.

Everything the Congregation knew about the mysterious book of origins—Ashmole 782—was based on fragments such as this. Any new discovery dramatically increased their knowledge. And this letter contained more than just a brief description of the book and some veiled hints as to its significance. There were names and dates and the startling revelation that the book Diana Bishop had seen in Oxford was missing three pages.

Knox looked over the letter again. He wanted to know more—to squeeze every potentially useful bit of information from it. This time certain words and phrases stood out: *your broken lineage; the Father who gave you life and breath; your maker.* On the first reading, Knox assumed that

Loew was talking about God. Upon the second he came to a very different conclusion. Knox picked up his phone and punched in a single number.

"*Oui.*"

"Who is Benjamin ben Gabriel?" Knox demanded.

There was a moment of complete silence.

"Hello, Peter," said Gerbert of Aurillac. Knox's free hand curled into a fist at the bland response. This was so typical of the vampires on the Congregation. They talked about honesty and cooperation, but they had lived too long and knew too much. And, like all predators, they weren't eager to share their spoils.

"'*Benjamin shall raven like a wolf.*' I know Benjamin ben Gabriel is a vampire. Who is he?"

"No one of importance."

"Do you know what happened in Prague in 1591?" Knox asked tightly.

"A great many things. You cannot expect me to rehearse every event for you, like a grammar-school history teacher."

Knox heard a faint tremble in Gerbert's voice, something that only someone who knew the man well would catch. Gerbert, the venerable vampire who was never at a loss for words, was nervous.

"Dr. Dee's assistant, Edward Kelley, was in the city in 1591."

"We've been over this before. It's true, the Congregation once believed that Ashmole 782 might have been in Dee's library. But I met with Edward Kelley in Prague when those suspicions first surfaced in the spring of 1586. Dr. Dee had a book full of pictures. It wasn't ours. Since then we've tracked down every item from Dee's library just to be sure. Elias Ashmole didn't come into possession of the manuscript through Dee or Kelley."

"You're wrong. Kelley had the book in May 1591." Knox paused. "And he took it apart. The book Diana Bishop saw in Oxford was missing three pages."

"What do you know, Peter?" Gerbert said sharply.

"What do *you* know, Gerbert?" Knox didn't like the vampire, but they had been allies for years. Both men understood that cataclysmic change was coming to their world. In the aftermath there would be winners and losers. Neither man had any intention of being on the losing side.

"Benjamin ben Gabriel is Matthew Clairmont's son," Gerbert said reluctantly.

"His son?" Knox repeated numbly. Benjamin de Clermont was on none of the elaborate vampire genealogies the Congregation kept.

"Yes. But Benjamin disowned his bloodline. It is not something that a vampire does lightly, for the rest of the family is likely to kill him to protect their secrets. Matthew forbade any de Clermont to take his son's life. And no one has caught a glimpse of Benjamin since the nineteenth century, when he disappeared in Jerusalem."

The bottom dropped out of Knox's world. Matthew Clairmont couldn't be allowed to have Ashmole 782. Not if it held the witches' most cherished lore.

"Well, we're going to have to find him," Knox said grimly, "because according to this letter Edward Kelley scattered the three pages. One he gave to Rabbi Loew, who passed it on to someone called Abraham ben Elijah of Chelm."

"Abraham ben Elijah was once known as a very powerful witch. Do you creatures know anything about your own history?"

"We know not to trust vampires. I'd always dismissed that prejudice as histrionics, not history, but now I'm not so sure." Knox paused. "Loew told Benjamin to ask his father for help. I knew that de Clermont was hiding something. We have to find Benjamin de Clermont and make him tell us what he—and his father—know about Ashmole 782."

"Benjamin de Clermont is a volatile young man. He was afflicted with the same illness that plagued Matthew's sister Louisa." The vampires called it blood rage, and the Congregation wondered if the disease was not somehow related to the new illness afflicting vampires—the one that was resulting in so many warmblooded deaths after failed attempts to make new vampires. "If there really are three lost sheets from Ashmole 782, we will find them without his help. It will be better that way."

"No. It's time for the vampires to yield their secrets." Knox knew that the success or failure of their plans might well depend on this unstable branch of the de Clermont family tree. He looked at the letter once more. Loew was clear that he had wanted Benjamin to heal not only the book but his relationship with his family. Matthew Clairmont might know more about this business than any of them suspected.

"I suppose you'll be wanting to timewalk to Rudolphine Prague now to look for Edward Kelley," Gerbert grumbled, trying to stifle an impatient sigh. Witches could be so impulsive.

"On the contrary. I'm going to Sept-Tours."

Gerbert snorted. Storming the de Clermont family château was an even more ridiculous idea than going back to the past.

"Tempting though that might be, it isn't wise. Baldwin turns a blind eye only because of the rift between him and Matthew." It was Philippe's only strategic failure, so far as Gerbert could remember, to hand over the Knights of Lazarus to Matthew rather than to the elder son who had always thought he was entitled to the position. "Besides, Benjamin no longer considers himself a de Clermont—and the de Clermonts certainly don't believe he's one of theirs. The last place we would find him is Sept-Tours."

"For all we know, Matthew de Clermont has had one of the missing pages in his possession for centuries. The book is of no use to us if it's incomplete. Besides, it's time that vampire pays for his sins—and those of his mother and father, too." Together they had been responsible for the deaths of thousands of witches. Let the vampires worry about placating Baldwin. Knox had justice on his side.

"Don't forget the sins of his lover," Gerbert said, his voice vicious. "I miss my Juliette. Diana Bishop owes me a life for the one she took."

"I have your support, then?" Knox didn't care one way or the other. He'd be leading a raiding party of witches against the de Clermont stronghold before the week's end, with or without Gerbert's help.

"You do," Gerbert agreed reluctantly. "They are all gathering there, you know. The witches. The vampires. There are even a few daemons inside. They are calling themselves the Conventicle. Marcus sent a message to the vampires on the Congregation demanding that the covenant be repealed."

"But that would mean—"

"The end of our world," Gerbert finished.

# PART V

# London:
# The Blackfriars

34

"You failed me!"

A red damask shoe sailed through the air. Matthew tilted his head just before it struck. The shoe continued past his ear, knocked a bejeweled armillary sphere off the table, and came to rest on the floor. The interlocking rings of the sphere spun around in their fixed orbits in impotent frustration.

"I wanted Kelley, you fool. Instead I got the emperor's ambassador, who told me of your many indiscretions. When he demanded to see me, it was not yet eight o'clock and the sun had barely risen." Elizabeth Tudor was afflicted with a toothache, which didn't improve her disposition. She sucked in one cheek to cushion the infected molar and grimaced. "And where were you? Creeping back into my presence with no concern for my suffering."

A blue-eyed beauty stepped forward and handed Her Majesty a cloth saturated with clove oil. With Matthew seething next to me, the spiciness in the room was already overpowering. Elizabeth placed the cloth delicately between her cheek and gums, and the woman stepped away, her green gown swishing around her ankles. It was an optimistic hue for this cloudy day in May, as if she hoped to speed summer's arrival. The fourth-floor tower room in Greenwich Palace afforded a sweeping view of the gray river, muddy ground, and England's stormy skies. In spite of the many windows, the silvery morning light did little to dispel the heaviness of the room, which was resolutely masculine and early Tudor in its furnishings. The carved initials on the ceiling—an intertwined *H* and *A* for Henry VIII and Anne Boleyn—indicated that the room had been decorated around the time of Elizabeth's birth and seldom used since.

"Perhaps we should hear Master Roydon out before you throw the inkwell," William Cecil suggested mildly. Elizabeth's arm stopped, but she didn't put down the weighty metal object.

"We do have news of Kelley," I began, hoping to help.

"We did not seek your opinion, Mistress Roydon," the queen of England said sharply. "Like too many women at my court, you are utterly without governance or decorum. If you wish to remain at Greenwich with your husband rather than being sent back to Woodstock where you belong, you would be wise to take Mistress Throckmorton as your model. She does not speak unless directed to do so."

Mistress Throckmorton glanced at Walter, who was standing next to Matthew. We had met him on the back stairs to the queen's private chambers, and though Matthew dismissed it as unnecessary, Walter had insisted on accompanying us into the lion's den.

Bess's lips compressed as she held back her amusement, but her eyes danced. The fact that the queen's attractive young ward and her dashing, saturnine pirate were intimate was apparent to everyone save Elizabeth. Cupid had managed to ensnare Sir Walter Raleigh, just as Matthew promised. The man was utterly besotted.

Walter's mouth softened at his lover's challenging stare, and the frank appraisal he gave her in return promised that the subject of her decorum would be addressed in a more private venue.

"As you do not require Diana's presence, perhaps you will let my wife go home and take her rest as I requested," Matthew said evenly, though his eyes were as black and angry as the queen's. "She has been traveling for some weeks." The royal barge had intercepted us before we'd even set foot at the Blackfriars.

"Rest! I have had nothing but sleepless nights since hearing of your adventures in Prague. She will rest when I am through with you!" Elizabeth shrieked, the inkwell following in the path of the royal footwear. When it veered toward me like a late-breaking curveball, Matthew reached out and caught it. Wordlessly he passed it to Raleigh, who tossed it to the groom already in possession of the queen's shoe.

"Master Roydon would be far more difficult to replace than that astronomical toy, Majesty." Cecil held out an embroidered cushion. "Perhaps you would consider this if you are in need of further ammunition."

"Do not think to direct me, Lord Burghley!" the queen fumed. She turned with fury on Matthew. "Sebastian St. Clair did not treat my father thus. He would not have dared to provoke the Tudor lion."

Bess Throckmorton blinked at the unfamiliar name. Her golden head turned from Walter to the queen like a spring daffodil seeking out the sun. Cecil coughed gently at the young woman's evident confusion.

"Let us reminisce about your blessed father at some other time, when we can devote proper attention to his memory. Did you not have questions for Master Roydon?" The queen's secretary looked at Matthew apologetically. *Which devil would you prefer?* his expression seemed to say.

"You are right, William. It is not in the nature of lions to dally with mice and other insignificant creatures." The queen's disdain somehow managed to diminish Matthew to the size of a small boy. Once he looked suitably contrite—though the muscle ticking in his jaw made me wonder how sincere his remorse really was—she took a moment to steady herself, her hands retaining a white-knuckled grip on the chair's arms.

"I wish to know how my Shadow bungled matters so badly." Her voice turned plaintive. "The emperor has alchemists aplenty. He does not need mine."

Walter's shoulders lowered a fraction, and Cecil smothered a sigh of relief. If the queen was calling Matthew by his nickname, then her anger was already softening.

"Edward Kelley cannot be plucked from the emperor's court like a stray weed, no matter how many roses grow there," Matthew said. "Rudolf values him too highly."

"So Kelley has succeeded at last. The philosopher's stone *is* in his possession," Elizabeth said with a sharp intake of breath. She clutched at the side of her face as the air hit her sore tooth.

"No, he hasn't succeeded—and that's the heart of the matter. So long as Kelley promises more than he is able to produce, Rudolf will never part with him. The emperor behaves like an inexperienced youth rather than a seasoned monarch, fascinated by what he cannot have. His Majesty loves the chase. It fills his days and occupies his dreams," Matthew said impassively.

The sodden fields and swollen rivers of Europe had put us at a considerable distance from Rudolf II, but there were moments when I could still feel his unwelcome touch and acquisitive glances. In spite of the May warmth and the fire blazing in the hearth, I shivered.

"The new French ambassador writes to me that Kelley has turned copper into gold."

"Philippe de Mornay is no more trustworthy than your former ambassador—who, as I recall, attempted to assassinate you." Matthew's tone was perfectly poised between obsequiousness and irritation. Elizabeth did a double take.

"Are you baiting me, Master Roydon?"

"I would never bait a lion—or even the lion's cub," Matthew drawled.

Walter closed his eyes as if he couldn't bear to witness the inevitable devastation Matthew's words would cause. "I was badly scarred after one such encounter and have no desire to mar my beauty further for fear that you could no longer abide the sight of me."

There was a shocked silence, broken at last by an unladylike bellow of laughter. Walter's eyes popped open.

"You got what you deserved, sneaking up on a young maid when she was sewing," Elizabeth said with something that sounded very much like indulgence. I shook my head slightly, sure I was hearing things.

"I shall keep that in mind, Majesty, should I happen upon another young lioness with a sharp pair of shears."

Walter and I were now as confused as Bess. Only Matthew, Elizabeth, and Cecil seemed to understand what was being said—and what was not.

"Even then you were my Shadow." The look Elizabeth gave Matthew made her appear to be a girl again and not a woman fast approaching sixty. Then I blinked, and she was an aging, tired monarch once more. "Leave us."

"Your . . . M-majesty?" Bess stammered.

"I wish to speak to Master Roydon privately. I don't suppose he will permit his loose-tongued wife out of his sight, so she may stay, too. Wait for me in my privy chamber, Walter. Take Bess with you. We shall join you presently."

"But—" Bess protested. She looked about nervously. Staying near the queen was her job, and without protocol to guide her she was at sea.

"You shall have to help me instead, Mistress Throckmorton." Cecil took several painful steps away from the queen, aided by his heavy stick. As he passed by Matthew, Cecil gave him a hard look. "We will leave Master Roydon to see to Her Majesty's welfare."

When the queen waved the grooms out of the room, the three of us were left alone.

"*Jesu,*" Elizabeth said with a groan. "My head feels like a rotten apple about to split. Could you not have chosen a more opportune time to cause a diplomatic incident?"

"Let me examine you," Matthew requested.

"You think to provide me care that my surgeon cannot, Master Roydon?" said the queen with wary hope.

"I believe I can spare you some pain, if God wills it."

"Even unto his death, my father spoke of you with longing." Elizabeth's hands twitched against the folds of her skirt. "He likened you to a tonic, whose benefits he had failed to appreciate."

"How so?" Matthew made no effort to hide his curiosity. This was not a story he had heard before.

"He said you could rid him of an evil humor faster than any man he had ever known—though, like most physic, you could be difficult to swallow." Elizabeth smiled at Matthew's booming laughter, and then her smile faltered. "He was a great and terrible man—and a fool."

"All men are fools, Your Majesty," Matthew said swiftly.

"No. Let us speak plainly to each other again, as though I were not queen of England and you were not a *wearh*."

"Only if you let me look at your tooth," Matthew said, crossing his arms over his chest.

"Once an invitation to share intimacies with me would have been sufficient inducement, and you would not have attached further conditions to my proposal." Elizabeth sighed. "I am losing more than my teeth. Very well, Master Roydon." She opened her mouth obediently. Even though I was a few feet away, I could smell the decay. Matthew took her head in his hands so that he could see the problem more clearly.

"It is a miracle you have any teeth at all," he said sternly. Elizabeth turned pink with irritation and struggled to reply. "You may shout at me when I am done. By then you will have good reason to do so, as I will have confiscated your candied violets and sweet wine. That will leave you with nothing more damaging to drink than peppermint water and nothing to suck on but a clove rub for your gums. They are badly abscessed."

Matthew drew his finger along her teeth. Several of them wiggled alarmingly, and Elizabeth's eyes bulged. He made a sound of displeasure.

"You may be queen of England, Lizzie, but that doesn't give you a knowledge of physic and surgery. It would have been wiser to heed the surgeon's advice. Now, hold still."

While I tried to regain my composure after hearing my husband call the queen of England "Lizzie," Matthew withdrew his index finger, rubbed it against his own sharp eyetooth so that it drew a bead of blood, and returned it to Elizabeth's mouth. Though he was careful, the queen winced. Then her shoulders lowered in relief.

"'Ank 'ewe," she mumbled around his fingers.

"Don't thank me yet. There won't be a comfit or sweetmeat for five miles when I'm through. And the pain will return, I'm afraid." Matthew drew his fingers away, and the queen felt around her mouth with her tongue.

"Aye, but for now it is gone," she said gratefully. Elizabeth gestured at the nearby chairs. "I fear there is nothing left but to settle accounts. Sit down and tell me about Prague."

After spending weeks at the emperor's court, I knew it was an extraordinary privilege to be invited to sit in the presence of any ruler, but I was doubly grateful for the chance to do so now. The voyage had exacerbated the normal fatigue of the first weeks of pregnancy. Matthew pulled out one of the chairs for me, and I lowered myself into it. I pressed the small of my back against the carving, using its knobs and bumps to give the aching joints a massage. Matthew's hand automatically reached for the same area, pushing and kneading to relieve the soreness. Envy flashed across the queen's features.

"You are in pain, too, Mistress Roydon?" the queen inquired solicitously. She was being too nice. When Rudolf treated a courtier like this, something sinister was usually afoot.

"Yes, Your Majesty. Alas, it is nothing peppermint water will solve," I said ruefully.

"Nor will it smooth the emperor's ruffled feathers. His ambassador tells me that you have stolen one of Rudolf's books."

"Which book?" Matthew asked. "Rudolf has so many." As most vampires had not been acquainted with the state of innocence for some time, his performance of it rang hollow.

"We are not playing games, Sebastian," the queen said quietly, confirming my suspicion that Matthew had gone by the name of Sebastian St. Clair when he was at Henry's court.

"You are always playing games," he shot back. "In this you are no different from the emperor, or Henry of France."

"Mistress Throckmorton told me that you and Walter have been exchanging verses about the fickleness of power. But I am not one of those vain potentates, fit for nothing save scorn and ridicule. I was raised by hard schoolmasters," the queen retorted. "Those around me—mother, aunts, stepmothers, uncles, cousins—are gone. I survived. So do not give me the lie and think to get away with it. I ask you again, what of the book?"

"We don't have it," I interjected.

Matthew looked at me in shock.

"The book is not in our possession. At present." It was doubtless already at the Hart and Crown, safely tucked into Matthew's attic archive. I'd passed the book to Gallowglass, wrapped in protective oilskin and leather, when the royal barge had pulled alongside us on our way up the Thames.

"Well, well." Elizabeth's mouth slowly widened, showing her blackened teeth. "You surprise me. And your husband too, it seems."

"I am nothing but surprises, Your Majesty. Or so I am told." No matter how many times Matthew referred to her as Lizzie or she called him Sebastian, I was careful to address her formally.

"The emperor seems to be in the grip of some illusion, then. How do you account for it?"

"There is nothing remarkable about that," Matthew said with a snort. "I fear the madness that has afflicted his family is now touching Rudolf. Even now his brother Matthias plots his downfall and positions himself to seize power when the emperor can no longer rule."

"No wonder the emperor is so eager to keep Kelley. The philosopher's stone will cure him and make the issue of his successor moot." The queen's expression soured. "He will live on forever, without fear."

"Come, Lizzie. You know better than that. Kelley cannot make the stone. He cannot save you or anyone else. Even queens and emperors must one day die."

"We are friends, Sebastian, but do not forget yourself." Elizabeth's eyes glittered.

"When you were seven and asked me if your father planned to kill his new wife, I told you the truth. I was honest with you then, and I will be honest with you now, however much it angers you. Nothing will bring your youth back, Lizzie, or resurrect those you have lost," Matthew said implacably.

"Nothing?" Elizabeth slowly studied him. "I see no lines or gray hairs on you. You look exactly as you did fifty years ago at Hampton Court when I took my shears to you."

"If you are asking me to use my blood to make you a *wearh,* Your Majesty, the answer must be no. The covenant forbids meddling in human politics—and that certainly includes altering the English succession by placing a creature on the throne." Matthew's expression was forbidding.

"And would that be your answer if Rudolf made this request?" Elizabeth asked, black eyes glittering.

"Yes. It would lead to chaos—and worse." The prospect was chilling.

"Your realm is safe," Matthew assured her. "The emperor is behaving like a spoiled child denied a treat. That is all."

"Even now his uncle, Philip of Spain, is building ships. He plans another invasion!"

"And it will come to nothing," Matthew promised.

"You sound very sure."

"I am."

Lion and wolf regarded each other across the table. When at last Elizabeth was satisfied, she looked away with a sigh.

"Very well. You don't have the emperor's book, and I do not have Kelley or the stone. We must all learn to live with disappointment. Still, I must give the emperor's ambassador something to sweeten his mood."

"What about this?" I drew my purse from my skirts. Apart from Ashmole 782 and the ring on my finger, it contained my most treasured possessions—the silken cords that Goody Alsop had given me to weave my spells, a smooth pebble of glass Jack had found in the sands of the Elbe and taken for a jewel, a fragment of precious bezoar stone for Susanna to use in her medicines, Matthew's salamanders. And one hideously ornate collar with a dying dragon hanging from it that had been given to me by the Holy Roman Emperor. I placed the last on the table between the queen and me.

"That is a bauble for a queen, not a gentleman's wife." Elizabeth reached out to touch the sparkling dragon. "What did you give to Rudolf that he would bestow this upon you?"

"It is as Matthew said, Your Majesty. The emperor covets what he can never have. He thought this might win my affections. It did not," I said with a shake of my head.

"Perhaps Rudolf cannot bear to have others know that he let something so valuable slip away," Matthew suggested.

"Do you mean your wife or this jewel?"

"My wife," Matthew said shortly.

"The jewel might be useful anyway. Perhaps he meant to give the necklace to me," Elizabeth mused, "but you took it upon yourself to carry it here for its greater safety."

"Diana's German is not very good," Matthew agreed with a wry smile. "When Rudolf put it over her shoulders, he might have been doing so only to better imagine how it would look on you."

"Oh, I doubt that," Elizabeth said drily.

"If the emperor intended this necklace for the queen of England, he would have wished to give it to her with appropriate ceremony. If we give the ambassador the credit he is due . . ." I suggested.

"There's a pretty solution. It will satisfy no one, of course, but it will give my courtiers something to cut their teeth on until some new curiosity emerges." Elizabeth tapped the table pensively. "But there's still the matter of this book."

"Would you believe me if I told you it wasn't important?" Matthew asked.

Elizabeth shook her head. "No."

"I thought not. What of the opposite—that the future may depend upon it?" Matthew asked.

"That is even more far-fetched. But since I have no desire for Rudolf or any of his kin to hold the future in their grasp, I will leave the matter of returning it to you—should it ever come into your possession again, of course."

"Thank you, Your Majesty," I said, relieved that the matter had been resolved with relatively few lies.

"I did not do it for you," Elizabeth reminded me sharply. "Come, Sebastian. Hang the jewel around my neck. Then you can transform yourself back into Master Roydon and we will go down to the presence chamber and put on a show of gratitude to amaze them all."

Matthew did as he was bid, his fingers lingering on the queen's shoulders longer than was necessary. She patted his hand.

"Is my wig straight?" Elizabeth asked me as she rose to her feet.

"Yes, Your Majesty." In truth it was slightly askew after Matthew's ministrations.

Elizabeth reached up and gave her wig a tug. "Teach your wife how to tell a convincing lie, Master Roydon. She will need to be better schooled in the arts of deceit, or she will not survive long at court."

"The world needs honesty more than it needs another courtier," commented Matthew, taking her elbow. "Diana will remain as she is."

"A husband who values honesty in his own wife." Elizabeth shook her head. "This is the best evidence I have yet seen that the world is coming to an end as Dr. Dee foretold."

When Matthew and the queen appeared in the doorway to the privy chamber, a hush fell over the crowd. The room was packed to the rafters, and wary glances darted from the queen to a youth the age of an undergraduate I took to be the imperial ambassador, to William Cecil and back.

Matthew released the queen's hand, which was held aloft on his bent arm. My firedrake's wings beat with alarm inside my ribs.

I put my hand on my diaphragm to soothe the beast. *Here be the real dragons,* I silently warned.

"I thank the emperor for his gift, Your Excellency," Elizabeth said, walking straight toward the teenager with her hand extended for him to kiss. The young man stared at her blankly. *"Gratias tibi ago."*

"They get younger all the time," Matthew murmured as he drew me next to him.

"That's what I say about my students," I whispered back. "Who is he?"

"Vilém Slavata. You must have seen his father in Prague."

I studied young Vilém and tried to imagine what he might look like in twenty years. "Was his father the round one with the dimpled chin?"

"One of them. You've described most of Rudolf's officials," Matthew pointed out when I shot him an exasperated glance.

"Stop whispering, Master Roydon!" Elizabeth turned a withering glance on my husband, who bowed apologetically. Her Majesty continued, rattling on in Latin. *"Decet eum qui dat, non meminisse beneficii: eum vero, qui accipit, intueri non tam munus quam dantis animum."* The queen of England had set the ambassador a language examination to see if he was worthy of her.

Slavata blanched. The poor boy was going to fail it.

*It becomes him who gives not to remember the favor: but it becomes she who receives not to look upon the gift as much as the soul of the giver.* I coughed to hide my chortle once I'd sorted out the translation.

"Your Majesty?" Vilém stammered in heavily accented English.

"Gift. From the emperor." Elizabeth pointed imperiously at the collar of enameled crosses draped over her slim shoulders. The dragon hung down further on Her Majesty than it had on me. She sighed with exaggerated exasperation. "Tell him what I said in his own language, Master Roydon. I do not have the patience for Latin lessons. Does the emperor not educate his servants?"

"His Excellency knows Latin, Your Majesty. Ambassador Slavata attended university at Wittenberg and went on to study law at Basel, if my memory serves. It is not the language that confuses him but your message."

"Then let us be right clear so that he—and his master—receive it. And not for my sake," Elizabeth said darkly. "Proceed." With a shrug, Matthew repeated Her Majesty's message in Slavata's native tongue.

"I understood what she said," young Slavata responded, dazed. "But what does she mean?"

"You are confused," Matthew continued sympathetically in Czech. "It is common among new ambassadors. Don't worry about it. Tell the queen that Rudolf is delighted to give her this jewel. Then we can have dinner."

"Will you tell her for me?" Slavata was completely out of his depth.

"I do hope you have not caused another misunderstanding between Emperor Rudolf and me, Master Roydon," Elizabeth said, plainly irritated that her command of seven languages did not extend to Czech.

"His Excellency reports that the emperor wishes Your Majesty health and happiness. And Ambassador Slavata is delighted that the necklace is where it belongs and not missing, as the emperor feared." Matthew looked at his mistress benignly. She started to say something, closed her mouth with a snap, and glared at him. Slavata, eager to learn, wanted to know how Matthew had managed to silence the queen of England. When the ambassador made a gesture to encourage Matthew to translate, Cecil took the young man in hand.

"Delightful news, Excellency. I think you've had lessons enough for one day. Come, dine with me," Cecil said, steering him to a nearby table. The queen, upstaged now by both her spy and her chief adviser, harrumphed as she climbed the dais, helped up the three low stairs by Bess Throckmorton and Raleigh.

"What happens now?" I whispered. The show was over, and the room's occupants were displaying signs of restlessness.

"I will wish to talk further, Master Roydon," Elizabeth called while her cushions were being arranged to her satisfaction. "Do not go far."

"Pierre will be in the presence chamber next door. He'll show you to my room, where there's a bed and some peace and quiet. You can rest until Her Majesty frees me. It shouldn't take long. She only wants a full report on Kelley." Matthew brought my hand to his lips and gave it a formal kiss.

Knowing Elizabeth's fondness for her male attendants, it could well take hours.

Even though I was braced for the clamor of the presence chamber, it knocked me back a step. Courtiers not sufficiently important to warrant dining in the privy chamber jostled me as they passed, eager to get to their own dinner before the food was gone. My stomach flipped over at the scent of roasted venison. I would never get used to it, and the baby didn't like it either.

Pierre and Annie were standing by the wall with the other servants. They both looked relieved as I came into view.

"Where is *milord*?" Pierre asked, pulling me out of the crush of bodies.

"Waiting on the queen," I said. "I'm too tired to stand up—or eat. Can you take me to Matthew's room?"

Pierre cast a worried look at the entrance to the privy chamber. "Of course."

"I know the way, Mistress Roydon," Annie said. Newly returned from Prague and well into her second visit to the court of Elizabeth, Annie was affecting an attitude of studied nonchalance.

"I showed her *milord*'s room when you were led away to see Her Majesty," Pierre assured me. "It is just downstairs, below the apartments once used by the king's wife."

"And now used by the queen's favorites, I suppose," I said under my breath. No doubt that's where Walter was sleeping—or not sleeping, as the case may be. "Wait here for Matthew, Pierre. Annie and I can find our way."

"Thank you, *madame*." Pierre looked at me gratefully. "I do not like to leave him too long with the queen."

The members of the queen's staff were tucking into their dinner in the far-less-splendid surrounds of the guard chamber. They regarded Annie and me with idle curiosity as we walked through.

"There must be a more direct route," I said, biting my lip and looking down the long flight of stairs. The Great Hall would be even more crowded.

"I'm sorry, mistress, but there isn't," Annie said apologetically.

"Let's face the mob, then," I said with a sigh.

The Great Hall was thronged with petitioners for the queen's attention. A rustle of excitement greeted my appearance from the direction of the royal apartments, followed by murmurs of disappointment when I proved to be no one of consequence. After Rudolf's court I was more accustomed to being an object of attention, but it was still uncomfortable to feel the heavy gaze of the humans, the few nudges from daemons, the tingling glance of a solitary witch. When the cold stare of a vampire settled on my back, though, I looked around in alarm.

"Mistress?" Annie inquired.

My eyes scanned the crowd, but I was unable to locate the source.

"Nothing, Annie," I murmured, uneasy. "It's just my imagination playing tricks."

"You are in need of rest," she chided, sounding very like Susanna.

But no rest awaited me in Matthew's spacious ground-floor rooms overlooking the queen's private gardens. Instead I found England's premier playwright. I sent Annie to extract Jack from whatever mess he'd gotten himself into and steeled myself to face Christopher Marlowe.

"Hello, Kit," I said. The daemon looked up from Matthew's desk, pages of verse scattered around him. "All alone?"

"Walter and Henry are dining with the queen. Why are you not with them?" Kit looked pale, thin, and distracted. He rose and began to gather his papers, glancing anxiously at the door as though he expected someone to walk in and interrupt us.

"Too tired." I yawned. "But there's no need for you to go. Stay and wait for Matthew. He will be glad to see you. What are you writing?"

"A poem." After this abrupt reply, Kit sat. Something was off. The daemon seemed positively twitchy.

The tapestry on the wall behind him showed a golden-haired maiden standing in a tower overlooking the sea. She held up a lantern and peered into the distance. *That explains it.*

"You're writing about Hero and Leander." It was not phrased as a question. Kit had probably been pining for Matthew and working on the epic love poem since we'd boarded ship at Gravesend back in January. He didn't respond.

After a few moments I recited the relevant lines.

> "*Some swore he was a maid in mans attire,*
> *For in his lookes were all that men desire,*
> *A pleasant smiling cheeke, a speaking eye,*
> *A brow for Love to banquet roiallye,*
> *And such as knew he was a man would say,*
> *Leander, thou art made for amorous play:*
> *Why art thou not in love and lov'd of all?*"

Kit exploded from his seat. "What witch's mischief is this? You know what I am doing as soon as I do it."

"No mischief, Kit. Who would understand how you feel better than I?" I said carefully.

Kit seemed to gather his control, though his hands were shaking as he stood. "I must go. I am to meet someone in the tiltyard. There is talk of a special pageant next month before the queen sets off for her summer travels. I've been asked to assist." Every year Elizabeth progressed around the country with a wagon train of attendants and courtiers, sponging off her nobles and leaving behind enormous debts and empty larders.

"I'll be sure to tell Matthew you were here. He'll be sorry he missed you."

A bright gleam entered Marlowe's eyes. "Perhaps you would like to come with me, Mistress Roydon. It is a fine day, and you have not seen Greenwich."

"Thank you, Kit." I was puzzled by his rapid change of mood, but he was, after all, a daemon. And he was mooning over Matthew. Though I'd hoped to rest, and Kit's overtures were stilted, I should make an effort in the interests of harmony. "Is it far? I'm somewhat tired after the journey."

"Not far at all." Kit bowed. "After you."

The tiltyard at Greenwich resembled a grand track-and-field stadium, with roped-off areas for athletes, stands for spectators, and scattered equipment. Two sets of barricades stretched down the center of the compacted surface.

"Is that where the jousting takes place?" I could imagine the sound of hooves pounding the earth as knights sped toward each other, their lances angled across the necks of their mounts so they could strike their opponent's shield and unseat him.

"Yes. Would you like to take a closer look?" Kit asked.

The place was deserted. Lances were stuck in the ground here and there. I saw something that looked alarmingly similar to a gibbet, with its upright pole and long arm. Rather than a body, however, a bag of sand swung at the end. It had been run through, and sand trickled out in a thin stream.

"A quintain," Marlowe explained, gesturing at the device. "Riders aim their lances at the sandbag." He reached up and gave the arm a push to show me. It swung around, providing a moving target to hone the knight's skill. Marlowe's eyes scanned the tiltyard.

"Is the man you're meeting here?" I looked around, too. But the only person I could see was a tall, dark-haired woman wearing a lavish red dress. She was far in the distance, no doubt having some romantic assignation before dinner.

"Have you seen the other quintain?" Kit pointed in the opposite direction, where a mannequin made of straw and rough burlap was tied to a post. This, too, looked more like a form of execution than a piece of sporting equipment.

I felt a cold, focused glance. Before I could turn around, a vampire caught me with arms that had the familiar sense of being more steel than flesh. But these arms did not belong to Matthew.

"Why, she is even more delicious than I'd hoped," a woman said, her cold breath snaking around my throat.

*Roses. Civet.* I registered the scents, tried to remember where I'd smelled the combination before.

*Sept-Tours. Louisa de Clermont's room.*

"Something in her blood is irresistible to *wearhs*," Kit said roughly. "I do not understand what it is, but even Father Hubbard seems to be in her thrall."

Sharp teeth rasped against my neck, though they did not break the skin. "It will be amusing to play with her."

"Our plan was to kill her," Kit complained. He was even twitchier and more restless now that Louisa was here. I remained silent, trying desperately to figure out what game they were playing. "Then everything will be as it was before."

"Patience." Louisa drank in my scent. "Can you smell her fear? It always sharpens my appetite."

Kit inched closer, fascinated.

"But you are pale, Christopher. Do you need more physic?" Louisa modified her grasp on me so that she could reach into her purse. She handed Kit a sticky brown lozenge. He took it from her eagerly, thrusting the ball into his mouth. "They are miraculous, are they not? The warmbloods in Germany call them 'Stones of Immortality,' for the ingredients somehow make even pitiful humans feel that they are divine. And they have made you feel strong again."

"It is the witch who weakens me, just as she weakened your brother." Kit's eyes turned glassy, and there was a sickeningly sweet tang to his breath. *Opiates.* No wonder he was behaving so strangely.

"Is that true, witch? Kit says you bound my brother against his will." Louisa swung me around. Her beautiful face embodied every warmblood's nightmare of a vampire: porcelain-pale skin, dusky black hair, and dark eyes that were as fogged with opium as Kit's. Malevolence rolled off her, and her perfectly bowed red lips were not only sensual but cruel. This was a creature who would hunt and kill without a hint of remorse.

"I did not bind your brother. I chose him—and he chose me, Louisa."

"You know who I am?" Louisa's dark eyebrows rose.

"Matthew doesn't keep secrets from me. We are mates. Husband and wife, too. Your father presided over our marriage." *Thank you, Philippe.*

"Liar!" Louisa screamed. Her pupils engulfed the iris as her control snapped. It was not just drugs that I would have to contend with but blood rage, too.

"Trust nothing she says," Kit warned. He pulled a dagger from his doublet and grabbed my hair. I cried out at the pain as he wrenched my head back. Kit's dagger orbited my right eye. "I am going to pluck out her eyes so that she can no longer use them for enchantments or to see my fate. She knows my death. I am sure of it. Without her witch's sight, she will have no hold on us—or on Matthew."

"The witch does not deserve such a swift death," Louisa said bitterly.

Kit pressed the point into my flesh just under the brow bone, and a drop of blood rolled down my cheek. "That wasn't our agreement, Louisa. To break her spell, I must have her eyes. Then I want her dead and gone. So long as the witch lives, Matthew will not forget her."

"Shh, Christopher. Do I not love you? Are we not allies?" Louisa reached for Kit and kissed him deeply. She moved her mouth along his jaw and down to where the blood pounded in his veins. Her lips brushed against the skin, and I saw the smear of blood that accompanied her movement. Kit drew a shuddering breath and closed his eyes.

Louisa drank hungrily from the daemon's neck. While she did, we stood in a tight knot, locked together in the vampire's strong arms. I tried to squirm away, but her grip on me only tightened as her teeth and lips battened on Kit.

"Sweet Christopher," she murmured when she had drunk her fill, licking at the wound. The mark on Kit's neck was silvery and soft, just like the scar on my breast. Louisa must have fed from him before. "I can taste the immortality in your blood and see the beautiful words that dance through your thoughts. Matthew is a fool not to want to share them with you."

"He wants only the witch." Kit touched his neck, imagining that it was Matthew, and not his sister, who had drunk from his veins. "I want her dead."

"As do I." Louisa turned her bottomless black eyes on me. "And so we will compete for her. Whoever wins may do with her as she—or he—will to make her atone for the wrongs she has done my brother. Do you agree, my darling boy?"

The two of them were high as kites now that Louisa had shared Kit's opiate-laden blood. I started to panic, then recalled Philippe's instructions at Sept-Tours.

*Think. Stay alive.*

Then I remembered the baby, and my panic returned. I couldn't endanger our child.

Kit nodded. "I will do anything to have Matthew's regard once more."

"I thought so." Louisa smiled and kissed him deeply again. "Shall we choose our colors?"

## 35

"You are making a terrible mistake, Louisa," I warned, struggling against my bonds. She and Kit had removed the shapeless straw-and-burlap mannequin and tied me to the post in its place. Then Kit had blindfolded me with a strip of dark blue silk taken from the tip of one of the waiting lances, so that I could not enchant them with my gaze. The two stood nearby, arguing over who would use the black-and-silver lance and who the green-and-gold.

"You'll find Matthew with the queen. He'll explain everything." I tried to keep my voice steady, but it trembled. Matthew had told me about his sister in modern Oxford, while we drank tea by his fireplace at the Old Lodge. She was as vicious as she was beautiful.

"You dare to utter his name?" Kit was wild with anger.

"Do not speak again, witch, or I will let Christopher remove your tongue after all." Louisa's voice was venomous, and I didn't need to see her eyes to know that poppy and blood rage were not a good mix. The point of Ysabeau's diamond scratched lightly against my cheek, drawing blood. Louisa had broken my finger wrenching it off and was now wearing it herself.

"I am Matthew's wife, his mate. What do you imagine his reaction will be when he finds out what you've done?"

"You are a monster—a beast. If I win the challenge, I will strip you of your false humanity and expose what lies underneath." Louisa's words trickled into my ears like poison. "Once I have, Matthew will see what you truly are, and he will share in our pleasure at your death."

When their conversation faded into the distance, I had no way of knowing where they were or from which direction they might return. I was utterly alone.

*Think. Stay alive.*

Something fluttered in my chest. But it wasn't panic. It was my firedrake. I wasn't alone. And I was a witch. I didn't need my eyes to see the world around me.

*What do you see?* I asked the earth and the air.

It was my firedrake who answered. She chirped and chattered, her wings stirring in the space between my belly and lungs as she assessed the situation.

*Where are they?* I wondered.

My third eye opened wide, revealing the shimmering colors of late spring in all their blue and green glory. One darker green thread was twisted with white and tangled with something black. I followed it to Louisa, who was climbing onto the back of an agitated horse. It wouldn't stand still for the vampire and kept shying away. Louisa bit it on the neck, which made the horse stand stock-still but did nothing to alleviate its terror.

I followed another set of threads, these crimson and white, thinking they might lead to Matthew. Instead I saw a bewildering whirl of shapes and colors. I fell—far, far until I landed on a cold pillow. *Snow.* I drew the cold winter air into my lungs. I was no longer tied to a stake on a late-May afternoon at Greenwich Palace. I was four or five, lying on my back in the small yard behind our house in Cambridge.

And I remembered.

*My father and I had been playing after a heavy snowfall. My mittens were Harvard crimson against the white. We were making angels, our arms and legs sweeping up and down. I was fascinated by how, if I moved my arms quickly enough, the white wings seemed to take on a red tinge.*

*"It's like the dragon with the fiery wings," I whispered to my father. His arms stilled.*

*"When did you see a dragon, Diana?" His voice was serious. I knew the difference between that tone and his usual teasing one. It meant he expected an answer—and a truthful one.*

*"Lots of times. Mostly at night." My arms beat faster and faster. The snow underneath their span was changing color, shimmering with green and gold, red and black, silver and blue.*

*"And where was it?" he whispered, staring at the snowdrifts. They were mounting up around me, heaving and rumbling as though alive. One grew tall and stretched itself into a slender dragon's head. The drift stretched wide into a pair of wings. The dragon shook flakes of snow from its white scales. When it turned and looked at my father, he murmured something and patted its nose as though he and the dragon had already met. The dragon breathed warm vapor into the frigid air.*

*"Mostly it's inside me—here." I sat up to show my father what I meant. My*

mittened hands went to the curved bones of my ribs. They were warm through the skin, through my jacket, through the chunky knit of the mittens. "But when she needs to fly, I have to let her out. There's not enough room for her wings otherwise."

A pair of shining wings rested on the snow behind me.

"You left your own wings behind," my father said gravely.

The dragon wormed her way out of the snowdrift. Her silver-and-black eyes blinked as she pulled free, rose into the air, and disappeared over the apple tree, becoming more insubstantial with every flap of her wings. Mine were already fading on the snow behind me.

"The dragon won't take me with her. And she never stays around for very long," I said with a sigh. "Why is that, Daddy?"

"Maybe she has somewhere else to be."

I considered this possibility. "Like when you and Mommy go to school?" It was perplexing to think of parents going to school. All the children on the block thought so, even though most of their parents spent all day at school, too.

"Just like that." My father was still sitting in the snow, his arms wrapped around his knees. He smiled. "I love the witch in you, Diana."

"She scares Mommy."

"Nah." My father shook his head. "Mommy is just scared of change."

"I tried to keep the dragon a secret, but I think she knows anyway," I said glumly.

"Mommies usually do," my father said. He looked down at the snow. My wings were entirely gone now. "But she knows when you want hot chocolate, too. If we go inside, my guess is she'll have it ready." My father got to his feet and held out his hand.

I slipped mine, still wearing crimson mittens, into his warm grip.

"Will you always be here to hold my hand when it gets dark?" I asked. Night was falling, and I was suddenly afraid of the shadows. Monsters lurked in the gloom, strange creatures who watched me as I played.

"Nope," my father said with a shake of his head. My lip trembled. That wasn't the answer I wanted. "But don't worry." His voice dropped to a whisper. "You'll always have your dragon."

A drop of blood fell from the pierced skin around my eye to the ground by my feet. Even though I was blindfolded, I could see its leisurely movement and the way it landed with a wet splat. A black shoot emerged from the spot.

Hooves thundered toward me. Someone gave a high, keening cry that conjured up images of ancient battles. The sound made the firedrake even more restless. I needed to free myself. Fast.

Instead of trying to see the threads that led to Kit and Louisa, I focused on the ones wrapped in the fibers that bound my wrists and ankles. I was starting to make progress loosening them when something sharp and heavy splintered against my ribs. The impact knocked the breath from my body.

"A hit!" Kit cried. "The witch is mine!"

"A glancing blow," Louisa corrected. "You must seat the lance in her body to claim her as your prize."

Sadly, I didn't know the rules—neither of jousting nor of magic, either. Goody Alsop had made that plain before we left for Prague. *All you have now is a wayward firedrake, a glaem that is near to blinding, and a tendency to ask questions that have mischievous answers,* she'd said. I'd been neglecting my weaving in favor of court intrigue and stopped pursuing my magic to hunt for Ashmole 782. Perhaps if I'd stayed in London, I would have known how to get myself out of this mess. Instead I was bound to a thick log like a witch about to be set alight.

*Think. Stay alive.*

"We must try again," Louisa said. Her words faded as she wheeled her horse around and rode away.

"Don't do this, Kit," I said. "Think what it will do to Matthew. If you want me gone, I'll go. I promise."

"Your promises are nothing, witch. You will cross your fingers and find a way to wriggle out of your assurances. I can see the *glaem* about you even now as you try to work your magic against me."

*A glaem near to blinding. Questions that elicit mischievous answers. And a wayward firedrake.*

Everything went still.

*What should we do?* I asked the firedrake.

Her response was to snap her wings, extending them fully. They slid between my ribs, through the flesh, and emerged on either side of my spine. The firedrake stayed where she was, her tail wrapped protectively around my womb. She peeked out from behind my sternum, her silver-and-black eyes bright, and flapped her wings again.

*Stay alive,* she whispered in reply, her words sending a pall of gray mist into the air around me.

The force of her wings snapped the thick wooden pole at my back, and the barbs on their scalloped edges sliced through the rope that bound my wrists. Something sharp and clawlike cut through the bindings around my ankles, too. I rose twenty feet up into the air as Kit and Louisa entered the firedrake's disorienting gray cloud. They were moving too quickly to stop or change direction. Their lances crossed, tangled, and the force of the clash sent them both flying from their saddles onto the hard earth below.

I ripped the blindfold from my eyes with my undamaged hand just as Annie appeared at the edge of the tiltyard.

"Mistress!" she cried. But I didn't want her here, not around Louisa de Clermont.

"Go!" I hissed. My words emerged in fire and smoke as I circled above Kit and Louisa.

Blood trickled from my wrists and feet. Wherever the red beads fell, a black shoot grew. Soon a palisade of slender black trunks surrounded the dazed daemon and vampire. Louisa tried to pull them from the ground, but my magic held.

"Shall I tell you your futures?" I asked harshly. Both stared up at me from their pen with avid, fearful eyes. "You will never get your heart's desire, Kit, because sometimes what we want most, we cannot have. And you will never fill the hollow places inside you, Louisa—neither with blood nor with anger. And both of you will die, because death comes for all of us sooner or later. But your deaths will not be gentle. I promise you that."

A whirlwind approached. It stilled, became recognizable as Hancock.

"Davy!" Louisa's pearly fingers gripped the black stakes that surrounded her. "Help us. The witch used her magic to bring us down. Take her eyes and you will take her power, too."

"Matthew is already on his way, Louisa," Hancock answered. "You are safer in that stockade under Diana's protection than you would be running from his anger."

"None of us is safe. She will fulfill the ancient prophecy, the one that Gerbert shared with *Maman* all those years ago. She will bring down the de Clermonts!"

"There's no truth in it," Hancock said with pity.

"There is!" Louisa insisted. "*'Beware the witch with the blood of the lion and the wolf, for with it she shall destroy the children of night.'* This is the witch of the prophecy! Don't you see?"

"You're not well, Louisa. I can see that plainly."

Louisa drew herself up, indignant. "I am a *manjasang* and in perfect health, Hancock."

Henry and Jack arrived next, their sides heaving with exertion. Henry scanned the tiltyard.

"Where is she?" he shouted at Hancock, spinning around.

"Up there," Hancock said, jerking his thumb in the air. "Just like Annie said."

"Diana." Henry sighed with relief.

A dark cyclone of gray and black whipped across the tiltyard and came to rest at a broken stake that marked the spot where I had been bound. Matthew needed no one to tell him where I was now. His eyes unerringly found me.

Walter and Pierre were the last to arrive. Pierre was carrying Annie piggyback, her thin arms wrapped tight around his neck. When he stopped, she slid from his back.

"Walter!" Kit cried, joining Louisa at the barrier. "She must be stopped. Let us out. I know what to do now. I spoke with a witch in Newgate, and—"

An arm punched through the black railings, and long, white fingers grabbed Kit around the throat. Marlowe gurgled to silence.

"Not. One. Word." Matthew's eyes swept over Louisa.

"*Matthieu.*" Blood and drugs further slurred Louisa's French pronunciation of his name. "Thank God you are here. I am glad to see you."

"You shouldn't be." Matthew flung Kit away.

I lowered down behind him, the newly sprouted wings withdrawing back inside my ribs. My firedrake remained alert, however, her tail tightly coiled. Matthew sensed me there and hooked me into his arm, though he never took his eyes off my captives. His fingers brushed against the spot where the lance had gone through bodice, corset, and skin only to be stopped by the bony cage of my ribs. It was damp where the blood had soaked through.

Matthew spun me around and fell to his knees, tearing the fabric from the wound. He swore. One hand settled on my abdomen, and his eyes searched mine.

"I'm fine. We're fine," I assured him.

He stood, his eyes black and the vein in his temple throbbing.

"Master Roydon?" Jack sidled closer to Matthew. His chin was trembling. Matthew's hand shot out and grabbed him by the collar, stopping him before he could get too close to me. Jack didn't flinch. "Are you having a nightmare?"

Matthew's hand dropped, releasing the boy. "Yes, Jack. A terrible nightmare."

Jack slid his hand into Matthew's. "I will wait by your side until it passes." My eyes pricked with tears. It was what Matthew said to him deep in the night, when Jack's terrors threatened to engulf him.

Matthew's hand tightened on Jack's in silent acknowledgment. The two of them stood—one tall and broad and filled with preternatural health, the other slight and awkward and only now shedding the shadows of neglect. Matthew's rage began to ebb.

"When Annie told me a female *wearh* had you, I never imagined—" He couldn't continue.

"It was Christopher!" Louisa cried, distancing herself from the wild daemon at her side. "He said you were enchanted. But I can smell her blood on you. You are not under her spell, but feeding from her."

"She is my mate," Matthew explained, his tone deadly. "And she is with child."

Marlowe's breath came out in a hiss. His eyes nudged my belly. My broken hand moved to protect our child from the daemon's gaze.

"'Tis impossible. Matthew cannot . . ." Kit's confusion turned to fury. "Even now she has bewitched him. How could you betray him thus? Who fathered your child, Mistress Roydon?"

Mary Sidney had assumed I had been raped. Gallowglass had first attributed the baby to a deceased lover or husband, either of which would have roused Matthew's protective instincts and explained our swift romance. For Kit the only possible answer was that I had cuckolded the man he loved.

"Take her, Hancock!" Louisa begged. "We cannot allow a witch to introduce her bastard into the de Clermont family."

Hancock shook his head at Louisa and crossed his arms.

"You tried to run my mate down. You drew her blood," Matthew said. "And the child is no bastard. It's mine."

"It is not possible," Louisa said, but she sounded uncertain.

"The child is *mine*," her brother repeated fiercely. "My flesh. My blood."

"She carries the blood of the wolf," Louisa whispered. "The witch *is* the one the prophecy foretold. If the baby lives, it will destroy us all!"

"Get them out of my sight." Matthew's voice was dead with rage. "Before I tear them into pieces and feed them to the dogs." He kicked down the palisade and grabbed his friend and his sister.

"I'm not going—" Louisa began. She looked down to find Hancock's hand wrapped around her arm.

"Oh, you'll go where I take you," he said softly. Hancock worked Ysabeau's ring from her finger and tossed it to Matthew. "I believe that belongs to your wife."

"And Kit?" Walter asked, eyeing Matthew warily.

"As they're so fond of each other, lock him up with Louisà." Matthew thrust the daemon at Raleigh.

"But she'll—" Walter began.

"Feed on him?" Matthew looked sour. "She has already. The only way a vampire feels the effects of wine or physic is from a warmblood's vein."

Walter gauged Matthew's mood and nodded. "Very well, Matthew. We will follow your wishes. Take Diana and the children to the Blackfriars. Leave everything else to Hancock and me."

"I told him there was nothing to worry about. The baby is fine." I lowered my smock. We'd come straight home, but Matthew had sent Pierre to fetch Susanna and Goody Alsop anyway. Now the house was full to bursting with angry vampires and witches. "Maybe you can convince him of it."

Susanna rinsed her hands in the basin of hot, soapy water. "If your husband will not believe his own eyes, nothing I can do or say will persuade him." She called for Matthew. Gallowglass came with him, the two of them filling the doorway.

"Are you all right, in truth?" Gallowglass's face was ashen.

"I had a broken finger and a cracked rib. I could have gotten them falling on the stairs. Thanks to Susanna, my finger is completely healed." I stretched my hand. It was still swollen, and I had to wear Ysabeau's ring on my other hand, but I could move the fingers without pain. The gash in my side would take more time. Matthew had refused to use vampire blood to heal it, so Susanna had resorted to a few magical stitches and a poultice instead.

"There are many good reasons to hate Louisa at this moment," Matthew said grimly, "but here is something to be thankful for: She did not wish to kill you. Louisa's aim is impeccable. Had she wanted to put her lance through your heart, you would be dead."

"Louisa was too preoccupied with the prophecy that Gerbert shared with Ysabeau."

Gallowglass and Matthew exchanged looks.

"It's nothing," Matthew said dismissively, "just some idiotic thing he dreamed up to excite *Maman.*"

"It was Meridiana's prophecy, wasn't it?" I had known it in my bones ever since Louisa mentioned it. The words brought back memories of Gerbert's touch at La Pierre. And they had made the air around Louisa snap with electricity, as though she were Pandora and had taken the lid off a trove of long-forgotten magic.

"Meridiana wanted to frighten Gerbert about the future. She did." Matthew shook his head. "It's got nothing to do with you."

"Your father is the lion. You are the wolf." Ice pooled in the pit of my stomach. It told me something was wrong with me, inside where the light could never quite reach. I looked at my husband, one of the children of the night mentioned in the prophecy. Our first child had already died. I shuttered my thoughts, not wanting to hold them in my heart or my head long enough to make an impression. But it did no good. There was too much honesty between us now to hide from Matthew—or myself.

"You have nothing to fear," Matthew said, brushing his lips over mine. "You are too full of life to be a harbinger of destruction."

I let him reassure me, but my sixth sense ignored him. Somehow, somewhere, a dangerous and deadly force had been unleashed. Even now I could feel its threads tightening, drawing me toward the darkness.

I was waiting under the sign of the Golden Gosling for Annie to pick up some stew for tonight's supper when the steady regard of a vampire drove the hint of summer from the air.

"Father Hubbard," I said, turning in the direction of the coldness.

The vampire's eyes flickered over my rib cage. "I am surprised your husband allows you to walk about the city unaccompanied, given what happened at Greenwich—and that you are carrying his child."

My firedrake, who had become fiercely protective since the incident in the tiltyard, coiled her tail around my hips.

"Everybody knows that *wearhs* can't father children on warmblooded women," I said dismissively.

"It seems that the impossible holds little sway with a witch such as you." Hubbard's grim countenance tightened further. "Most creatures believe that Matthew's contempt for witches is unchangeable, for example. Few would entertain the notion that it was he who made it possible for Barbara Napier to escape the pyre in Scotland." The events in Berwick continued to occupy Matthew's time as well as creature and human gossip in London.

"Matthew was nowhere near Scotland at the time."

"He didn't need to be. Hancock was in Edinburgh, posing as one of Napier's 'friends.' It was he who brought the matter of her pregnancy to the court's attention." Hubbard's breath was cold and smelled of the forest.

"The witch was innocent of the charges against her," I said brusquely, drawing my shawl around my shoulders. "The jury acquitted her."

"Of a single charge." Hubbard held my gaze. "She was found guilty of many more. And, given your recent return, perhaps you have not heard: King James found a way to reverse the jury's decision in Napier's case."

"Reverse it? How?"

"The king of Scots is not greatly enamored of the Congregation these days, no small thanks to your husband. Matthew's slippery sense of the covenant and his interference in Scottish politics have inspired His Majesty to find his own legal loopholes. James is putting the jurors who acquitted the witch on trial. They are charged with miscarrying the king's justice. Intimidating the jurors will better ensure the outcome of future trials."

"That wasn't Matthew's plan," I said, my mind reeling.

"It sounds sufficiently devious for Matthew de Clermont. Napier and her babe may live, but dozens more innocent creatures will die because of it." Hubbard's expression was deadly. "Isn't that what the de Clermonts want?"

"How dare you!"

"I have the—" Annie stepped out onto the street and nearly dropped her pot. I reached out and hooked her into my arm.

"Thank you, Annie."

"Do you know where your husband is this fine May morning, Mistress Roydon?"

"He is out on business." Matthew had made sure I ate my breakfast, kissed me, and left the house with Pierre. Jack had been inconsolable when Matthew told him he must stay behind with Harriot. I felt a flicker of unease. It wasn't like Matthew to refuse Jack a trip into town.

"No," Hubbard said softly, "he is in Bedlam with his sister and Christopher Marlowe."

Bedlam was an oubliette in all but name—a place for forgetting, where the insane were locked up with those interred by their own families on some trumped-up charge simply to be rid of them. With nothing but straw for bedding, no regular supply of food, not a shred of kindness from the jailers, and no treatment of any sort, most inmates never escaped. If they did, they rarely recovered from the experience.

"Not content with altering the judgment in Scotland, Matthew now seeks to mete out his own justice here in London," Hubbard continued. "He went to question them this morning. I understand he is still there."

It was past noon.

"I have seen Matthew de Clermont kill quickly, when he is enraged. It is terrible to behold. To see him do so slowly, painstakingly, would make the most resolute atheist believe in the devil."

*Kit.* Louisa was a vampire and shared Ysabeau's blood. She could fend for herself. But a daemon . . .

"Go to Goody Alsop, Annie. Tell her I've gone to Bedlam to look after Master Marlowe and Master Roydon's sister." I turned the girl in the proper direction and released her, putting my own body squarely between her and the vampire.

"I must stay with you," Annie said, her eyes huge. "Master Roydon made me promise!"

"Someone must know where I've gone, Annie. Tell Goody Alsop what you heard here. I can find my way to Bedlam." In truth I had only a vague notion of the notorious asylum's location, but I had other means of discovering Matthew's whereabouts. I wrapped imaginary fingers around the chain within me and got ready to pull it.

"Wait." Hubbard's hand closed around my wrist. I jumped. He called to someone in the shadows. It was the angular young man Matthew referred to by the strangely fitting name Amen Corner. "My son will take you."

"Matthew will know I've been with you now." I looked down at Hubbard's hand. It was still wrapped around my wrist, transferring his telltale scent to my warm skin. "He'll take it out on the boy."

Hubbard's grip tightened, and I let out a soft sound of understanding.

"If you wanted to accompany me to Bedlam as well, Father Hubbard, all you needed to do was ask."

Hubbard knew every shortcut and back alley between St. James Garlickhythe and Bishopsgate. We passed beyond the city limits and into one of London's squalid suburbs. Like Cripplegate, the area around Bedlam was poverty-stricken and desperately crowded. But the true horrors were yet to come.

The keeper met us at the gate and led us into what had once been known as the Hospital of St. Mary of Bethlehem. Master Sleford was well acquainted with Father Hubbard and could not bow and scrape enough as he led us to one of the stout doors across the pitted courtyard. Even with the thick wood and stone of the old medieval priory between us, the inmates' screams were piercing. Most of the windows were unglazed and open to the elements. The stench of rot, filth, and age was overwhelming.

"Don't," I said, refusing Hubbard's proffered hand as we entered the dank, close confines. There was something obscene about taking his help when I was free and the inmates were offered no assistance at all.

Inside, I was bombarded by the ghosts of past inmates and the jagged threads that twisted around the hospital's current tormented inhabitants. I dealt with the horror by engaging in macabre mathematical exercises, dividing the men and women I saw into smaller groups only to lump them together in a new way.

I counted twenty inmates during our walk down the corridor. Fourteen were daemons. A half dozen of the twenty were completely unclothed, and ten more were dressed only in rags. A woman wearing a filthy though expensive man's suit stared at us with open hostility. She was one of the three humans in the place. There were two witches and one vampire as well. Fifteen of the poor souls were manacled to the wall, chained to the floor, or both. Four of the other five were unable to stand and crouched by the walls chattering and scraping at the stone. One of the patients was free. He danced, naked, down the corridor ahead of us.

One room had a door. Something told me that Louisa and Kit were behind it.

The keeper unlocked the door and knocked sharply. When he didn't get an immediate response, he pounded.

"I heard you the first time, Master Sleford." Gallowglass looked decidedly the worse for wear, with fresh scratches down his cheek and blood on his doublet. When he saw me standing behind Sleford, he did a double take. "Auntie."

"Let me in."

"That's not such a good—" Gallowglass took another look at my expression and stepped aside. "Louisa's lost a fair bit of blood. She's hungry. Stay away from her, unless you're of a mind to be bitten or clawed. I've trimmed her nails, but there's not much I can do about her teeth."

Although nothing stood in my way, I remained rooted to the threshold. The beautiful, cruel Louisa was chained to an iron ring set into the stone floor. Her dress was in tatters, and blood from deep gashes in her neck covered her. Someone had been asserting his dominance over Louisa—someone stronger and angrier than she was.

I searched the shadows until I found a dark figure crouched over a lump on the floor. Matthew's head swung up, his face ghostly pale and his eyes black as night. Not a speck of blood was on him. Like Hubbard's offer of help, his cleanliness was somehow obscene.

"You should be at home, Diana." Matthew stood.

"I am exactly where I need to be, thank you." I moved in my husband's direction. "Blood rage and poppy don't mix, Matthew. How much of their blood have you taken?" The lump on the floor stirred.

"I am here, Christopher," Hubbard called. "You will come to no more harm."

Marlowe wept with relief, his body racked with sobs.

"Bedlam isn't in London, Hubbard," Matthew said coldly. "You're out of your bailiwick, and Kit is beyond your protection."

"Christ, here we go again." Gallowglass closed the door in Sleford's stunned face. "Lock it!" he barked through the wood, punctuating his command with a thud of his fist.

Louisa sprang to her feet when the metal mechanism ground shut, the chains rattling around her ankles and wrists. One of them snapped, and I jumped as the broken links chimed against the floor. A sympathetic banging of chains sounded along the corridor.

"Notmybloodnotmybloodnotmyblood," Louisa chanted. She was as flat as possible against the far wall. When I met her eyes, she whimpered and turned away. "Begone, *fantôme*. I have already died once and have nothing to fear from ghosts like you."

"Be quiet." Matthew's voice was low, but it cracked through the room with enough force that we all jumped.

"Thirsty," Louisa croaked. "Please, Matthew."

There was a regular splat of wetness against stone. With each splash Louisa's body jerked. Someone had suspended a stag's head by the antlers, its eyes empty and staring. Blood fell, one drop at a time, from its severed neck and onto the floor just beyond the reach of Louisa's chains.

"Stop torturing her!" I stepped forward, but Gallowglass's hand held me back.

"I can't let you interfere, Auntie," he said firmly. "Matthew's right: You don't belong in the middle of this."

"Gallowglass." Matthew shook his head in warning. Gallowglass released my arm and watched his uncle warily.

"Very well, then. Let me answer your earlier question, Auntie. Matthew has had just enough of Kit's blood to keep his blood rage burning. You may need this if you want to talk to him." Gallowglass tossed me a knife. I made no move to catch it, and the blade clattered to the stones.

"You are more than this disease, Matthew." I stepped over the blade and made my way to his side. We stood so close that my skirts brushed against his boots. "Let Father Hubbard see to Kit."

"No." Matthew's expression was unyielding.

"What would Jack think if he saw you this way?" I was willing to use guilt rather than steel to bring Matthew to his senses. "You're his hero. Heroes do not torment their friends or family."

"They tried to kill you!" Matthew's roar reverberated through the small room.

"They were out of their minds with opiates and alcohol. Neither of them knew what they were doing," I retorted. "Nor, may I add, do you in your present state."

"Don't fool yourself. Both of them knew exactly what they were doing. Kit was ridding himself of an obstacle to his happiness without a care for anyone else. Louisa was succumbing to the same cruel urges she's indulged since the day she was made." Matthew ran his fingers through his hair. "I know what I'm doing, too."

"Yes—you're punishing yourself. You are convinced that biology is destiny, at least so far as your own blood rage is concerned. As a result you think you're just like Louisa and Kit. Just another madman. I asked you to stop denying your instincts, Matthew, not to become a slave to them."

This time, when I took a step toward Matthew's sister, she sprang at me, spitting and snarling.

"And there's your greatest fear for the future: that you will be reduced to an animal, chained up and waiting for the next punishment because it's what you deserve." I went back to him, gripping his shoulders. "You are not this man, Matthew. You never were."

"I've told you before not to romanticize me," he said shortly. He dragged his eyes away from mine, but not before I'd seen the desperation there.

"So this is for my benefit, too? You're still trying to prove that you're not worth loving?" His hands were clenched at his sides. I reached for them and forced them open, pulling them flat against my belly. "Hold our child, look me in the eye, and tell us that there's no hope for a different ending to this story."

As on the night I'd waited for him to take my vein, time stretched out to infinity while Matthew wrestled with himself. Now, as then, I could do nothing to speed the process or help him choose life over death. He had to grab hope's fragile thread without any help from me.

"I don't know," he finally admitted. "Once I knew that love between a vampire and a witch was wrong. I was sure the four species were distinct. I accepted the deaths of witches if it meant that vampires and daemons survived." Though his pupils still eclipsed his eyes, a bright sliver of green appeared. "I told myself that the madness among daemons and the weaknesses among vampires were relatively recent developments, but now that I see Louisa and Kit . . ."

"You don't know." I lowered my voice. "None of us do. It's a frightening prospect. But we have to hope in the future, Matthew. I don't want our children to be born under this same shadow, hating and fearing who they are."

I waited for him to fight me further, but he remained silent.

"Let Gallowglass take responsibility for your sister. Allow Hubbard to tend to Kit. And try to forgive them."

"*Wearhs* do not forgive as easily as warmbloods do," Gallowglass said gruffly. "You cannot ask that of him."

"Matthew asked it of you," I pointed out.

"Aye, and I told him the best he could hope for was that I might, in time, forget. Don't demand more from Matthew than he can give, Auntie. He is his own worst rack master, and he needs no assistance from you." Gallowglass's voice held a warning.

"I would like to forget, witch," Louisa said primly, as if she were making a simple choice of fabric for a new gown. She waved her hand in the air. "All of this. Use your magic and make these horrible dreams go away."

It was in my power to do it. I could see the threads binding her to Bedlam, to Matthew, and to me. But though I didn't want to torture Louisa, I was not so forgiving as to grant her peace.

"No, Louisa," I said. "You will remember Greenwich for the rest of your days, and me, and even how you hurt Matthew. Let that be your prison, and not this place." I turned to Gallowglass. "Make sure she isn't a danger to herself or anyone else, before you set her free."

"Oh, she won't enjoy any freedom," Gallowglass promised. "She'll go from here to wherever Philippe sends her. After what she's done, my grandfather will never let her roam again."

"Tell them, Matthew!" Louisa pleaded. "You understand what it is to have these . . . things crawling in your skull. I cannot bear them!" She pulled at her hair with a manacled hand.

"And Kit?" Gallowglass asked. "You are sure you want him in Hubbard's custody, Matthew? I know that Hancock would be delighted to dispatch him."

"He is Hubbard's creature, not mine." Matthew's tone was absolute. "I care not what happens to him."

"What I did was out of love—" Kit began.

"You did it out of spite," Matthew said, turning his back on his best friend.

"Father Hubbard," I called as he rushed to collect his charge. "Kit's actions at Greenwich will be forgotten, provided that what happened here stays within these walls."

"You promise this, on behalf of all the de Clermonts?" Hubbard's pale eyebrows lifted. "Your husband must give me this assurance, not you."

"My word is going to have to be enough," I said, standing my ground.

"Very well, Madame de Clermont." It was the first time that Hubbard had used the title. "You are indeed Philippe's daughter. I accept your family's terms."

Even after we left Bedlam, I could feel its darkness clinging to us. Matthew did, too. It followed us everywhere we went in London, accompanied us to dinner, visited with our friends. There was only one way to rid ourselves of it.

We had to return to our present.

Without discussion or conscious plans, we both began putting our affairs in order, snipping the threads that bound us to the past we now shared. Françoise had been planning to rejoin us in London, but we sent word for her to remain at the Old Lodge. Matthew had long and complicated conversations with Gallowglass about the lies his nephew would have to tell so as not to reveal to the sixteenth-century Matthew that he'd been temporarily replaced by his future self. The sixteenth-century Matthew could not be allowed to see Kit or Louisa, for neither could be trusted. Walter and Henry would make up some story to explain any discontinuities in behavior. Matthew sent Hancock to Scotland to prepare for a new life there. I worked with Goody Alsop, perfecting the knots I would use to weave the spell that would carry us into the future.

Matthew met me in St. James Garlickhythe after one of my lessons and suggested we stroll through St. Paul's Churchyard on our way home. It was two weeks from midsummer, and the days were sunny and bright in spite of Bedlam's persistent pall.

Though Matthew still looked drawn after his experience with Louisa and Kit, it felt almost like old times when we stopped at the booksellers to see the latest titles and news. I was reading a fresh volley in the war of words between two spatting Cambridge graduates when Matthew stiffened.

"Chamomile. Oak leaves. And coffee." His head swung around at the unfamiliar scent.

"Coffee?" I asked, wondering how something that had not yet come to England could possibly be scenting the air around St. Paul's. But Matthew was no longer beside me to answer. Instead he was pushing his way through the crowd, his sword in one hand.

I sighed. Matthew couldn't stop himself from going after every thief in the market. At times I wished his eyesight were not so keen, his moral compass less absolute.

This time he was pursuing a man about five inches shorter than he was, with thick brown curls peppered with gray. The man was slender and slightly stooped at the shoulders, as though he spent too much time hunched over books. Something about the combination tugged at my memory.

The man sensed the danger approaching and turned. Alas, he carried a pitifully small dagger no bigger than a penknife. That wasn't going to be much use against Matthew. Hoping to avoid a bloodbath, I hurried after my husband.

Matthew grabbed the poor man's hand so tightly that his inadequate weapon fell to the ground. With one knee the vampire pressed his prey against the bookstall, the flat of his sword against the man's neck. I did a double take.

"Daddy?" I whispered. It couldn't be. I stared at him incredulously, my heart hammering with excitement and shock.

"Hello, Miss Bishop," my father replied, glancing up from Matthew's sharp-edged blade. "Fancy meeting you here."

## 37

My father looked calm as he faced an unfamiliar, armed vampire and his own grown daughter. Only the slight tremor in his voice and his white-knuckled grip on the stall gave him away.

"Dr. Proctor, I presume." Matthew stepped away and sheathed his weapon.

My father straightened his serviceable brown jacket. It was all wrong. Someone—probably my mother—had tried to modify a Nehru jacket into something resembling a cleric's cassock. And his britches were too long, more like something Ben Franklin would wear than Walter Raleigh. But his familiar voice, which I hadn't heard for twenty-six years, was exactly right.

"You've grown in the past three days," he said shakily.

"You look just as I remember," I said numbly, still stunned by the fact that he was standing before me. Mindful that two witches and a *wearh* might be too much for the St. Paul's Churchyard crowd, and unsure what to do in this novel situation, I fell back on social convention. "Do you want to come back to our house for a drink?" I suggested awkwardly.

"Sure, honey. That would be great," he said with a tentative nod.

My father and I couldn't stop looking at each other—not on our way home nor when we reached the safety of the Hart and Crown, which was, miraculously, empty. There he caught me up in a fierce hug.

"It's really you. You sound just like your mom," he said, holding me at arm's length to study my features. "You look like her, too."

"People tell me I have your eyes," I said, studying him in turn. When you're seven, you don't notice such things. You only think to look for them afterward, when it's too late.

"So you do." Stephen laughed.

"Diana has your ears, too. And your scents are somewhat similar. It's how I recognized you at St. Paul's." Matthew ran his hand nervously over his cropped hair, then stuck it out to my father. "I'm Matthew."

My father eyed the offered hand. "No last name? Are you some sort of celebrity, like Halston or Cher?" I had a sudden, vivid image of what I'd missed by not having my father around when I was a teenager, making an ass out of himself when he met the boys I dated. My eyes filled.

"Matthew has plenty of last names. It's just . . . complicated," I said, sniffing back the tears. My father looked alarmed at the sudden welling up of emotion.

"Matthew Roydon will do for now," Matthew said, capturing my father's attention. He and my father shook hands.

"So you're the vampire," my father said. "Rebecca is worried sick about the practicalities of your relationship with my daughter, and Diana can't even ride a bicycle yet."

"Oh, Dad." The minute the words were out of my mouth I blushed. I sounded as if I were twelve. Matthew smiled as he moved to the table.

"Won't you sit down and have some wine, Stephen?" Matthew handed him a cup and then pulled out a chair for me. "Seeing Diana must be something of a shock."

"You could say so. I'd love some." My father sat, took a sip of wine, and nodded approvingly before making a visible effort to take charge. "So," he said briskly, "we've said hello, you've invited me back to your house, and now I've had a drink. These are the essential Western greeting rituals. Now we can get down to it. What are you doing here, Diana?"

"Me? What are *you* doing here? And where is Mom?" I pushed away the wine that Matthew poured for me.

"Your mother is at home taking care of you." My father shook his head, amazed. "I can't believe it. You can't be more than ten years younger than I am."

"I always forget you're so much older than Mom."

"You're with a vampire and you have something against our May-December romance?" My father's whimsical expression invited me to laugh.

I did, while quickly doing the math. "So you've come from around 1980?"

"Yep. I finally got my grades turned in and headed out to do some exploring." Stephen studied us. "Is this when and where you two met?"

"No. We met in September 2009 at Oxford. In the Bodleian Library." I looked at Matthew, who gave me an encouraging smile. I turned back to my father and took a deep breath. "I can timewalk like you. I brought Matthew with me."

"I know you can timewalk, peanut. You scared the hell out of your mother last August when you disappeared on your third birthday. A time-walking toddler is a mother's worst nightmare." He looked at me shrewdly. "So you've got my eyes, ears, scent, and timewalking ability. Anything else?"

I nodded. "I can make up spells."

"Oh. We hoped you would be inclined toward fire like your mom, but no such luck." My father looked uncomfortable and dropped his voice. "You probably shouldn't mention your talent in the company of other witches. And when they try to teach you their spells, just let them go in one ear and out the other. Don't even attempt to learn them."

"I wish you'd told me that before. It would have helped me with Sarah," I said.

"Good old Sarah." My father's laugh was warm and infectious.

There was a thunder of feet on the stairs, and then a four-legged mop and a boy hurtled across the threshold, banging the door into the wall with the force of their enthusiastic entrance.

"Master Harriot said I may go out with him again and look at the stars, and he promises not to forget me this time. Master Shakespeare gave me this." Jack waved a slip of paper in the air. "He says it is a letter of credit. And Annie kept staring at a boy in the Cardinal's Hat while she ate her pie. Who is that?" The last was said with one grimy finger pointed in my father's direction.

"That's Master Proctor," Matthew said, catching Jack around the waist. "Did you feed Mop on your way in?" There had been no way to separate boy and dog in Prague, so Mop had come to London, where his strange appearance made him something of a local curiosity.

"Of course I fed Mop. He eats my shoes if I forget, and Pierre said he would pay for one new pair without telling you about it, but not a second." Jack clapped his hand over his mouth.

"I am sorry, Mistress Roydon. He ran down the street and I couldn't catch him." A frowning Annie rushed into the room, then stopped short, the color draining from her face as she stared at my father.

"It's all right, Annie," I said gently. She had been afraid of unfamiliar creatures ever since Greenwich. "This is Master Proctor. He's a friend."

"I have marbles. Do you know how to play ring taw?" Jack was eyeing my father with open speculation as he tried to determine whether the new arrival would be a useful person to have around.

"Master Proctor is here to speak with Mistress Roydon, Jack." Matthew spun him around. "We need water, wine, and bread. You and Annie divide up the chores, and when Pierre gets back, he'll take you to Moorfields."

With some grumbling Jack accompanied Annie back out into the street. I met my father's eyes at last. He had been watching Matthew and me without speaking, and the air was thick with his questions.

"Why are you here, honey?" my father repeated quietly when the children were gone.

"We thought we might find someone to help me out with some questions about magic and alchemy." For some reason I didn't want my father to know the details. "My teacher is called Goody Alsop. She and her coven have taken me in."

"Nice try, Diana. I'm a witch, too, so I know when you're skirting the truth." My father sat back in his chair. "You'll have to tell me eventually. I just thought this would save some time."

"Why are *you* here, Stephen?" Matthew asked.

"Just hanging out. I'm an anthropologist. It's what I do. What do you do?"

"I'm a scientist—a biochemist, based in Oxford."

"You're not just 'hanging out' in Elizabethan London, Dad. You have the page from Ashmole 782 already." I suddenly understood why he was here. "You're looking for the rest of the manuscript." I lowered the wooden candle beam. Master Habermel's astronomical compendium was nestled between two candles. We had to move it every day, because Jack found it every day.

"What page?" my father asked, sounding suspiciously innocent.

"The page with the picture of the alchemical wedding on it. It came from a Bodleian Library manuscript." I opened the compendium. It was completely still, just as I expected. "Look, Matthew."

"Cool," my father said with a whistle.

"You should see her mousetrap," Matthew said under his breath.

"What does it do?" My father reached for the compendium to take a closer look.

"It's a mathematical instrument for telling time and tracking astronomical events like the phases of the moon. It started to move on its own when we were in Prague. I thought it meant someone was looking for Matthew and me, but now I wonder if it wasn't picking up on you, looking for the manuscript." It still acted up periodically, its wheels spinning without warning. Everybody in the house called it the "witch clock."

"Maybe I should go get the book," Matthew said, rising.

"It's all right," my father replied, motioning for him to sit. "There's no rush. Rebecca isn't expecting me for a few days."

"So you'll be here—in London?"

My father's face softened. He nodded.

"Where are you staying?" Matthew asked.

"Here!" I said indignantly. "He's staying here." After so many years without him, letting him out of my sight was unthinkable.

"Your daughter has very definite opinions about her family checking into hotels," Matthew told my father with a wry smile, remembering how I'd reacted when he'd tried to put Marcus and Miriam up in an inn in Cazenovia. "You're welcome to stay with us, of course."

"I've got rooms on the other side of town," my father said hesitantly.

"Stay." I pressed my lips together and blinked to keep back the tears. "Please." I had so much I wanted to ask him, so many questions only he could answer. My father and husband exchanged a long look.

"All right," my father said finally. "It would be great to hang out with you for a little while."

I tried to give him our room, since Matthew wouldn't be able to sleep with a strange person in the house and I could easily fit on the window seat, but my father refused. Pierre gave up his bed instead. I stood on the landing and listened enviously while Jack and my father chattered away like old friends.

"I think Stephen has everything he needs," Matthew said, sliding his arms around me.

"Is he disappointed in me?" I wondered aloud.

"Your father?" Matthew sounded incredulous. "Of course not!"

"He seems a little uncomfortable."

"When Stephen kissed you good-bye a few days ago, you were a toddler. He's overwhelmed, that's all."

"Does he know what's going to happen to him and Mom?" I whispered.

"I don't know, *mon coeur,* but I think so." Matthew drew me toward our bedchamber. "Come to bed. Everything will look different in the morning."

Matthew was right: My father was a bit more relaxed the next day, though he didn't look as if he'd slept much. Neither did Jack.

"Does the kid always have such bad nightmares?" my father asked.

"I'm sorry he kept you up," I apologized. "Change makes him anxious. Matthew usually takes care of him."

"I know. I saw him," my father said, sipping at the herbal tisane that Annie prepared.

That was the problem with my father: He saw everything. His watchfulness put vampires to shame. Though I had hundreds of questions—about my mother and her magic, about the page from Ashmole 782—they all seemed to dry up under his quiet regard. Occasionally he asked me about something trivial. Could I throw a baseball? Did I think Bob Dylan was a genius? Had I been taught how to pitch a tent? He asked no questions about Matthew and me, or where I went to school, or even what I did for a living. Without any expression of interest on his part, I felt awkward volunteering the information. By the end of our first day together, I was practically in tears.

"Why won't he talk to me?" I demanded as Matthew unlaced my corset.

"Because he's too busy listening. He's an anthropologist—a professional watcher. You're the historian in the family. Questions are your forte, not his."

"I get tongue-tied around him and don't know where to start. And when he does talk to me, it's always about strange topics, like whether allowing designated hitters has ruined baseball."

"That's what a father would talk to his daughter about when he started taking her to baseball games. So Stephen does know he won't see you grow up. He just doesn't know how much time he has left with you."

I sank onto the edge of the bed. "He was a huge Red Sox fan. I remember Mom saying that between getting her pregnant and Carlton Fisk hitting a home run in the sixth game of the World Series, 1975 was the best fall semester of his life, even if Cincinnati did beat Boston in the end."

Matthew laughed softly. "I'm sure the fall semester of 1976 topped it."

"Did the Sox actually win that year?"

"No. Your father did." Matthew kissed me and blew out the candle.

When I came home from running errands the next day, I found my father sitting in the parlor of our empty apartments with Ashmole 782 open in front of him.

"Where did you find that?" I asked, putting my parcels on the table. "Matthew was supposed to hide it." I had a hard enough time keeping the children away from that blasted compendium.

"Jack gave it to me. He calls it 'Mistress Roydon's book of monsters.'

I was understandably eager to see it once I heard that." My father turned the page. His fingers were shorter than Matthew's, and blunt and forceful rather than tapered and dexterous. "Is this the book the picture of the wedding came from?"

"Yes. There were two other pictures in it as well: one of a tree, another of two dragons shedding their blood." I stopped. "I'm not sure how much more I should tell you, Dad. I know things about your relationship to this book that you don't know—things that haven't even happened yet."

"Then tell me what happened to you after you discovered it in Oxford. And I want the truth, Diana. I can see the damaged threads between you and the book, all twisted and snarled. And someone harmed you physically."

Silence lay heavily in the room, and there was nowhere to hide from my father's scrutiny. When I couldn't stand it any longer, I met his eyes.

"It was witches. Matthew fell asleep, and I went outside to get some air. It was supposed to be safe. A witch captured me." I shifted in my seat. "End of story. Let's talk about something else. Don't you want to know where I went to school? I'm a historian. I have tenure. At Yale." I would talk about anything with my father—except the chain of events that started with the delivery of an old photo to my rooms at New College and ended with the death of Juliette.

"Later. Now I need to know why another witch wanted this book so badly she was willing to kill you for it. Oh, yes," he said at my incredulous look, "I figured that out on my own. A witch used an opening spell on your back and left a terrible scar. I can feel the wound. Matthew's eyes linger there, and your dragon—I know about her, too—shields it with her wings."

"Satu—the witch who captured me—isn't the only creature who wants the book. So does Peter Knox. He's a member of the Congregation."

"Peter Knox," my father said softly. "Well, well, well."

"Have you two met?"

"Unfortunately, yes. He's always had a thing for your mother. Happily, she loathes him." My father looked grim and turned another page. "I sure as hell hope Peter doesn't know about the dead witches in this. There's some dark magic hanging around this book, and Peter has always been interested in that aspect of the craft. I know why he might want it, but why do you and Matthew need it so badly?"

"Creatures are disappearing, Dad. The daemons are getting wilder. Vampire blood is sometimes incapable of transforming a human. And witches aren't producing as many offspring. We're dying out. Matthew believes that this book might help us understand why," I explained. "There's a lot of genetic information in the book—skin, hair, even blood and bones."

"You've married the creature equivalent of Charles Darwin. And is he interested in origins as well as extinction?"

"Yes. He's been trying for a long time to figure out how daemons, witches, and vampires are related to one another and to humans. This manuscript—if we could put it back together and understand its contents—might provide important clues."

My father's hazel eyes met mine. "And these are simply theoretical concerns for your vampire?"

"Not anymore. I'm pregnant, Dad." My hand settled lightly on my abdomen. It had been doing so a lot lately, without my thinking about it.

"I know." He smiled. "I figured that out, too, but it's good to hear you say it."

"You've only been here for forty-eight hours. I don't like to rush things any more than you do," I said, feeling shy. My father got up and took me in his arms. He held me tight. "Besides, you should be surprised. Witches and vampires aren't supposed to fall in love. And they're definitely not supposed to have babies together."

"Your mother warned me about it—she's seen it all with that uncanny sight of hers." He laughed. "What a worrywart. If it's not you she's fussing over, it's the vampire. Congratulations, honey. A child is a wonderful gift."

"I just hope we can handle it. Who knows what our child will be like?"

"You can handle more than you think." My father kissed me on the cheek. "Come on, let's take a walk. You can show me your favorite places in the city. I'd love to meet Shakespeare. One of my idiot colleagues actually thinks Queen Elizabeth wrote *Hamlet*. And speaking of colleagues: How, after years of buying you Harvard bibs and mittens, did I end up with a daughter who teaches at Yale?"

"I'm curious about something," my father said, staring into his wine.

The two of us had enjoyed a lovely walk, we'd all finished a leisurely supper, the children had been sent to bed, and Mop was snoring by the fireplace. Thus far, it had been a perfect day.

"What's that, Stephen?" Matthew asked, looking up from his own cup with a smile.

"How long do you two think you can keep this crazy life you're leading under control?"

Matthew's smile dissolved. "I'm not sure I understand your question," he said stiffly.

"The two of you hold on to everything so damn tightly." My father took a sip of his wine and stared pointedly at Matthew's clenched fist over the rim of his cup. "You might inadvertently destroy what you most love with that grip, Matthew."

"I'll keep that in mind." Matthew was controlling his temper—barely. I opened my mouth to smooth things over.

"Stop trying to fix things, honey," my father said before I could utter a word.

"I'm not," I protested.

"Yes, you are," Stephen said. "Your mother does it all the time, and I recognize the signs. This is my one chance to talk to you as an adult, Diana, and I'm not going to mince words because they make you—or him—uncomfortable."

My father stuck his hand in his jacket and drew out a pamphlet. "You've been trying to fix things, too, Matthew."

*"Newes from Scotland,"* read the small print above the larger type of the headline: DECLARING THE DAMNABLE LIFE OF DOCTOR FIAN A NOTABLE SORCERER, WHO WAS BURNED IN EDENBROUGH IN JANUARIE LAST.

"The whole town is talking about the witches in Scotland," my father said, pushing the pages toward Matthew. "But the creatures are telling a different tale than the warmbloods are. They say that the great and terrible Matthew Roydon, enemy to witches, has been defying the Congregation's wishes and saving the accused."

Matthew's fingers stopped the pages' progress. "You shouldn't believe everything you hear, Stephen. Londoners are fond of idle gossip."

"For two control freaks, you certainly are stirring up a world of trouble. And the trouble won't end here. It will follow you home, too."

"The only thing that is going to follow us home from 1591 is Ashmole 782," I said.

"You can't take the book." My father was emphatic. "It belongs here. You've twisted time enough, staying as long as you have."

"We've been very careful, Dad." I was stung by his criticism.

"Careful? You've been here for seven months. You've conceived a child. The longest I've ever spent in the past is two weeks. You aren't timewalkers anymore. You've succumbed to one of the most basic transgressions of anthropological fieldwork: You've gone native."

"I was here before, Stephen," Matthew said mildly, though his fingers drummed on his thigh. That was never a good sign.

"I'm aware of that, Matthew," my father shot back. "But you've introduced far too many variables for the past to remain as it was."

"The past has changed us," I said, facing down my father's angry stare. "It stands to reason that *we've* changed *it,* too."

"And that's okay? Timewalking is a serious business, Diana. Even for a brief visit, you need a plan—one that includes leaving everything behind as you found it."

I shifted in my seat. "We weren't supposed to be here this long. One thing led to another, and now—"

"Now you're going to leave a mess. You'll probably find one when you get home, too." My father looked at us somberly.

"I get it, Dad. We screwed up."

"You did," he said gently. "You two might want to think about that while I go to the Cardinal's Hat. Someone named Gallowglass introduced himself in the courtyard. He says he's Matthew's relative and promised to help me meet Shakespeare, since my own daughter refused." My father gave me a peck on the cheek. There was disappointment in it, as well as forgiveness. "Don't wait up for me."

Matthew and I sat in silence while the sound of my father's footsteps faded. I took a shaky breath.

"Did we screw up, Matthew?" I reviewed the past months: meeting Philippe, breaking through Matthew's defenses, getting to know Goody Alsop and the other witches, finding out I was a weaver, befriending Mary and the ladies of Malá Strana, taking Jack and Annie into our home and our hearts, recovering Ashmole 782, and, yes, conceiving a child. My hand dropped to my belly in a protective gesture. There wasn't a single thing I would change, if given the choice.

"It's hard to know, *mon coeur,*" Matthew said somberly. "Time will tell."

"I thought we could go see Goody Alsop. She's helping me with my spell to return to the future." I stood before my father, my spell box clutched in my hands. I was still uneasy around him after the lecture he'd given Matthew and me last night.

"It's about time," my father said, reaching for his jacket. He still wore it like a modern man, taking it off the minute he was indoors and rolling up his shirtsleeves. "I didn't think any of my hints were getting through to you. I can't wait to meet an experienced weaver. And are you finally going to show me what's in the box?"

"If you were curious about it, why didn't you ask?"

"You'd covered it so carefully with that wispy thing of yours that I figured you didn't want anybody to mention it," he said as we descended the stairs.

When we arrived in the parish of St. James Garlickhythe, Goody Alsop's fetch opened the door.

"Come in, come in," the witch said, beckoning us toward her seat by the fire. Her eyes were bright and snapping with excitement. "We've been waiting for you."

The whole coven was there, sitting on the edge of their seats.

"Goody Alsop, this is my father, Stephen Proctor."

"The weaver." Goody Alsop beamed with satisfaction. "You're a watery one, like your daughter." My father hung back as he always did, watching everybody and saying as little as possible while I made the introductions. All the women smiled and nodded, though Catherine had to repeat everything to Elizabeth Jackson because my father's accent was so strange.

"But we are being rude. Would you care to share your creature's name?" Goody Alsop peered at my father's shoulders, where the faint outlines of a heron could be seen. I'd never noticed it before.

"You can see Bennu?" my father said, surprised.

"Of course. He perches, open-winged, across your shoulders. My familiar spirit does not have wings, even though I am strongly tied to the air. She was easier to tame for that reason, I suspect. When I was a girl, a weaver came to London with a harpy for a familiar. Ella was her name, and she was very difficult to train."

Goody Alsop's fetch wafted around my father, crooning softly to the bird as it became more visible.

"Perhaps your Bennu can coax Diana's firedrake to give up her name. It would make it much easier for your daughter to return to her own time, I think. We don't want any trace of her familiar left here, dragging Diana back to London."

"Wow." My father was struggling to take it all in—the gathering of witches, Goody Alsop's fetch, the fact that his secrets were on display.

"Who?" Elizabeth Jackson asked politely, assuming she'd misunderstood.

My father drew back and studied Elizabeth carefully. "Have we met?"

"No. It is the water in my veins that you recognize. We are happy to have you among us, Master Proctor. London has not had three weavers within her walls in some time. The city is abuzz."

Goody Alsop motioned to the chair beside her. "Do sit."

My father took the place of honor. "Nobody at home knows about this weaving business."

"Not even Mom?" I was aghast. "Dad, you've got to tell her."

"Oh, she knows. But I didn't have to tell her. I showed her." My father's fingers curled and released in an instinctive gesture of command.

The world lit up in shades of blue, gray, lavender, and green as he plucked at all the hidden watery threads in the room: the willow branches in a jug by the window, the silver candlestick that Goody Alsop used for her spells, the fish that was waiting to be roasted for supper. Everyone and everything in the room was cast into those same watery hues. Bennu took flight, his silver-tipped wings stirring the air into waves. Goody Alsop's fetch was blown this way and that in the currents, her shape shifting into a long-stemmed lily, then returning to human form and sprouting wings. It was as if the two familiars were playing. At the prospect of recreation, my firedrake flicked her tail and beat her own wings against my ribs.

"Not now," I told her tightly, gripping at my bodice. The last thing we needed was a cavorting firedrake. My control over the past might have slipped, but I knew better than to let go of a dragon in Elizabethan London.

"Let her out, Diana," my father urged. "Ben will take care of her."

But I couldn't bring myself to do it. My father called to Bennu, who faded into his shoulders. The watery magic around me faded, too.

"Why are you so afraid?" my father asked quietly.

"I'm afraid because of this!" I waved my cords in the air. "And this!" I hit my ribs, jostling my firedrake. She belched in response. My hand slid down to where our child was growing. "And this. It's too much. I don't need to use showy elemental magic the way you just did. I'm happy as I am."

"You can weave spells, command a firedrake, and bend the rules that govern life and death. You're as volatile as creation itself, Diana. These are powers any self-respecting witch would kill for."

I looked at him in horror. He'd brought the one thing I couldn't face into the room: Witches had already killed for these powers. They'd killed my father, and my mother, too.

"Putting your magic into neat little boxes and keeping it separate from your craft isn't going to keep Mom and me from our fates," my father continued sadly.

"That's not what I'm trying to do."

"Really?" His eyebrows lifted. "You want to try that again, Diana?"

"Sarah says elemental magic and the craft are separate. She says—"

"Forget what Sarah says!" My father took me by the shoulders. "You aren't Sarah. You aren't like any other witch who has ever lived. And you don't have to choose between spells and the power that's right at your fingertips. We're weavers, right?"

I nodded.

"Then think of elemental magic as the warp—the strong fibers that make up the world—and spells as the weft. They're both part of a single tapestry. It's all one big system, honey. And you can master it, if you set aside your fear."

I could see the possibilities shimmering around me in webs of color and shadow, yet the fear remained.

"Wait. I have a connection to fire, like Mom does. We don't know how the water and fire will react. I haven't had those lessons yet." *Because of Prague,* I thought. *Because we got distracted by the hunt for Ashmole 782 and forgot to focus on the future and getting back to it.*

"So you're a switch-hitter—a witchy secret weapon." He laughed. He *laughed.*

"This is serious, Dad."

"It doesn't have to be." My father let that sink in, then crooked his finger, catching a single gray-green thread on the end of it.

"What are you doing?" I asked suspiciously.

"Watch," he said in a whisper like waves against the shore. He drew his finger toward him and pursed his lips as if he were holding an invisible bubble wand. When he blew out, a ball of water formed. He flicked his fingers in the direction of the water bucket near the hearth, and the ball turned to ice, floated over, and dropped into it with a splash. "Bull's-eye."

Elizabeth giggled, releasing a stream of water bubbles that popped in the air, each one sending out a tiny shower of water.

"You don't like the unknown, Diana, but sometimes you've got to embrace it. You were terrified when I put you on a tricycle the first time. And you threw your blocks at the wall when you couldn't get them all to fit back in their box. We made it through those crises. I'm sure we can handle this." My father held his hand out.

"But it's so . . ."

"Messy? So is life. Stop trying to be perfect. Try being real for a change." My father's arm swept through the air, revealing all the threads that were normally hidden from view. "The whole world is in this room. Take your time and get to know it."

I studied the patterns, saw the clumps of color around the witches that indicated their particular strengths. Threads of fire and water surrounded me in a mess of conflicting shades. My panic returned.

"Call the fire," my father said, as if it were as simple as ordering a pizza.

After a moment of hesitation, I crooked my finger and wished for the fire to come to me. An orange-red thread caught on the tip, and when I let my breath out through pursed lips, dozens of tiny bubbles of light and heat flew into the air like fireflies.

"Lovely, Diana!" Catherine cried out, clapping her hands.

Between the clapping and the fire, my firedrake wanted to be released. Bennu cried out from my father's shoulders, and the firedrake answered. "No," I said, gritting my teeth.

"Don't be such a spoilsport. She's a dragon—not a goldfish. Why are you always trying to pretend that the magical is ordinary? Let her fly!"

I relaxed just a fraction, and my ribs softened, opening away from my spine like the leaves of a book. My firedrake escaped the bony confines at the first opportunity, flapping her wings as they metamorphosed from gray and insubstantial to iridescent and gleaming. Her tail curled up in a loose knot, and she soared around the room. The firedrake caught the tiny balls of light in her teeth, swallowing them down like candy. She then turned her attention to my father's water bubbles as if they were fine champagne. When she was through with her treats, the firedrake hovered in the air before me, her tail flicking at the floor. She cocked her head and waited.

"What are you?" I asked, wondering how she managed to absorb all the conflicting powers of water and fire.

"You, but not you." The firedrake blinked, her glassy eyes studying me. A swirling ball of energy balanced at the end of her spade-shaped tail. The firedrake gave her tail a flick, tipping the ball into my cupped hands. It looked just like the one I had given Matthew back in Madison.

"What is your name?" I whispered.

"You may call me Corra," she said in a language of smoke and mist. Corra bobbed her head in farewell, melted into a gray shadow, and disappeared.

Her weight thudded into my center, her wings curved around my back, and there was stillness. I took a deep breath.

"That was great, honey." My father squeezed me tight. "You were thinking like fire. Empathy is the secret to most things in life—including magic. Look how bright the threads are now!"

All around us the world gleamed with possibility. And, in the corners, the steadily brightening indigo and amber weave warned that time was growing impatient.

**38**

"**M**y two weeks are up. It's time for me to go."

My father's words weren't unexpected, but they felt like a blow nevertheless. My eyelids dropped to cover my reaction.

"Your mother will think I've taken up with an orange seller if I don't show up soon."

"Orange sellers are more of a seventeenth-century thing," I said absently, picking at the cords in my lap. I was now making steady progress with everything from simple charms against headaches to the more complicated weavings that could make waves ruffle on the Thames. I twined the gold and blue strands around my fingers. *Strength and understanding.*

"Wow. Nice recovery, Diana." My father turned to Matthew. "She bounces back fast."

"Tell me about it," was my husband's equally dry reply. They both relied on humor to smooth over the rough edges of their interactions, which sometimes made them unbearable.

"I'm glad I got to know you, Matthew—despite that scary look you get when you think I'm bossing Diana around," my father said with a laugh.

Ignoring their banter, I twisted the yellow cord in with the gold and blue. *Persuasion.*

"Can you stay until tomorrow? It would be a shame to miss the celebrations." It was Midsummer Eve, and the city was in a holiday mood. Worried that a final evening with his daughter would not be sufficient inducement, I shamelessly appealed to my father's academic interests. "There will be so many folk customs for you to observe."

"Folk customs?" My father laughed. "Very slick. Of course I'm staying until tomorrow. Annie made a wreath of flowers for my hair, and Will and I are going to share some tobacco with Walter. Then I'm going to visit with Father Hubbard."

Matthew frowned. "You know Hubbard?"

"Oh, sure. I introduced myself to him when I arrived. I had to, since he was the man in charge. Father Hubbard figured out I was Diana's father pretty quickly. You all have an amazing sense of smell." My father looked at

Matthew benignly. "An interesting man, with his ideas about creatures all living as one big, happy family."

"It would be utter chaos," I pointed out.

"We all made it through last night with three vampires, two witches, a daemon, two humans, and a dog sharing one roof. Don't be so quick to dismiss new ideas, Diana." My father looked at me disapprovingly. "Then I suppose I'll hang out with Catherine and Marjorie. Lots of witches will be on the prowl tonight. Those two will definitely know where the most fun can be found." Apparently he was on a first-name basis with half the town.

"And you'll be careful. Especially around Will, Daddy. No 'Wow' or 'Well played, Shakespeare.'" My father was fond of slang. It was, he said, the hallmark of the anthropologist.

"If only I could take Will home with me, he'd make a cool—sorry, honey—colleague. He has a sense of humor. Our department could do with someone like him. Put a bit of leavening in the lump, if you know what I mean." My father rubbed his hands together. "What are your plans?"

"We don't have any." I looked at Matthew blankly, and he shrugged.

"I thought I would answer some letters," he said hesitantly. The mail had piled up to alarming levels.

"Oh, no." My father sat back in his chair, looking horrified.

"What?" I turned my head to see who or what had entered the room.

"Don't tell me you're the kind of academics who can't tell the difference between their life and their job." He flung up his hands as if warding off the plague. "I refuse to believe that my daughter could be one of them."

"That's a bit melodramatic, Daddy," I said stiffly. "We could spend the evening with you. I've never smoked. It will be historic to do it with Walter for the first time, since he introduced tobacco into England."

My father looked even more horrified. "Absolutely not. We'll be bonding as fellow men. Lionel Tiger argues—"

"I'm not a big fan of Tiger," Matthew interjected. "The social carnivore never made sense to me."

"Can we put the topic of eating people aside for a moment and discuss why you don't want to spend your last night with Matthew and me?" I was hurt.

"It's not that, honey. Help me out here, Matthew. Take Diana out on a date. You must be able to think of something to do."

"Like roller-skating?" Matthew's brows shot up. "There aren't any skating rinks in sixteenth-century London—and precious few of them left in the twenty-first century, I might add."

"Damn." My father and Matthew had been playing "fad versus trend" for days, and while my father was delighted to know that the popularity of disco and the Pet Rock would fade, he was shocked to hear that other things—like the leisure suit—were now the butt of jokes. "I love roller-skating. Rebecca and I go to a place in Dorchester when we want to get away from Diana for a few hours, and—"

"We'll go for a walk," I said hastily. My father could be unnecessarily frank when it came to discussing how he and my mother spent their free time. He seemed to think it might shock Matthew's sense of propriety. When that failed, he took to calling Matthew "Sir Lancelot" for an added measure of annoyance.

"A walk. You'll take a walk." My father paused. "You mean that literally, don't you?"

He pushed away from the table. "No wonder creatures are going the way of the dodo. Go out. Both of you. Now. And I'm ordering you to have fun." He ushered us toward the door.

"How?" I asked, utterly mystified.

"That is not a question a daughter should ask her father. It's Midsummer Eve. Go out and ask the first person you meet what you should do. Better yet, follow someone else's example. Howl at the moon. Make magic. Make out, at the very least. Surely even Sir Lancelot makes out." He waggled his eyebrows. "Get the picture, Miss Bishop?"

"I think so." My tone reflected my doubts about my father's notion of fun.

"Good. I won't be back until sunrise, so don't wait up. Better yet, stay out all night yourselves. Jack is with Tommy Harriot. Annie is with her aunt. Pierre is— I don't know where Pierre is, but he doesn't need a baby-sitter. I'll see you at breakfast."

"When did you start calling Thomas Harriot 'Tommy'?" I asked. My father pretended not to hear me.

"Give me a hug before you go. And don't forget to have fun, okay?" He enveloped me in his arms. "Catch you on the flip side, baby."

Stephen pushed us out the door and shut it in our faces. I extended my hand to the latch and found it taken into a vampire's cool grip.

"He'll be leaving in a few hours, Matthew." I reached for the door with the other hand. Matthew took that one, too.

"I know. So does he," Matthew explained.

"Then he should understand that I want to spend more time with him." I stared at the door, willing my father to open it. I could see the threads leading from me, through the grain in the wood, to the wizard on the other side. One of the threads snapped and struck the back of my hand like a rubber band. I gasped. "Daddy!"

"Get moving, Diana!" he shouted.

Matthew and I wandered around town, watching the shops close early and noting the revelers already filling the pubs. More than one butcher was casually stacking bones by the front door. They were white and clean, as though they had been boiled.

"What's going on with the bones?" I asked Matthew after we saw the third such display.

"They're for the bone fires."

"Bonfires?"

"No," Matthew said, "the bone fires. Traditionally, people celebrate Midsummer Eve by lighting fires: bone fires, wood fires, and mixed fires. The mayor's warnings to cease and desist all such superstitious celebrations go up every year, and people light them anyway."

Matthew treated me to dinner at the famous Belle Savage Inn just out-side the Blackfriars on Ludgate Hill. More than a simple eatery, the Belle Savage was an entertainment complex where customers could see plays and fencing matches—not to mention Marocco, the famous horse who could pick virgins out of the crowd. It wasn't roller-skating in Dorchester, but it was close.

The city's teenagers were out in force, shouting insults and innuendos at one another as they went from one watering hole to another. During the day most were hard at work as servants or apprentices. Even in the evenings their time was not their own, since their masters expected them to watch over the shops and houses, tend children, fetch food and water, and do the hundred other small chores that were required to keep an early-modern household going. Tonight London belonged to them, and they were mak-ing the most of it.

We passed back through Ludgate and approached the entrance to the Blackfriars as the bells tolled nine o'clock. It was the time the members of the Watch started to make their rounds, and people were expected to head for home, but no one seemed to be enforcing the rules tonight. Though the sun had set an hour earlier, the moon was only one day away from full, and the city streets were still bright with moonlight.

"Can we keep walking?" I asked. We were always going somewhere specific—to Baynard's Castle to see Mary, to St. James Garlickhythe to visit with the gathering, to St. Paul's Churchyard for books. Matthew and I had never taken a walk through the city without a destination in mind.

"I don't see why not, since we were ordered to stay out and have fun," Matthew said. He dipped his head and stole a kiss.

We walked around the western door of St. Paul's, which was bustling in spite of the hour, and out of the churchyard to the north. This put us on Cheapside, London's most spacious and prosperous street, where the goldsmiths plied their trade. We rounded the fountain at Cheapside Cross, which was being used as a paddling pool by a group of roaring boys, and headed east. Matthew traced the route of Anne Boleyn's coronation procession for me and pointed out the house where Geoffrey Chaucer had lived as a child. Some merchants invited Matthew to join them in a game of bowls. They booed him out of the competition after his third strike in a row, however.

"Happy now that you've proven you're top dog?" I teased as he put his arm around me and pulled me close.

"Very," he said. He pointed to a fork in the road. "Look."

"The Royal Exchange." I turned to him in excitement. "At night! You remembered."

"A gentleman never forgets," he murmured with a low bow. "I'm not sure if any shops are still open, but the lamps will be lit. Will you join me in a promenade across the courtyard?"

We entered through the wide arches next to the bell tower topped with a golden grasshopper. Inside, I turned around slowly to get the full experience of the four-storied building with its hundred shops selling everything from suits of armor to shoehorns. Statues of English monarchs looked down on the customers and merchants, and a further plague of grasshoppers ornamented the peak of each dormer window.

"The grasshopper was Gresham's emblem, and he wasn't shy about self-promotion," Matthew said with a laugh, following my eyes.

Some shops were indeed open, the lamps in the arcades around the central courtyard were lit, and we were not the only ones enjoying the evening.

"Where is the music coming from?" I asked, looking around for the minstrels.

"The tower," Matthew said, pointing in the direction we had entered. "The merchants chip in and sponsor concerts in the warm weather. It's good for business."

Matthew was good for business, too, based on the number of shopkeepers who greeted him by name. He joked with them and asked after their wives and children.

"I'll be right back," he said, darting into a nearby store. Mystified, I stood listening to the music and watching an authoritative young woman organize an impromptu ball. People formed circles, holding hands and jumping up and down like popcorn in a hot skillet.

When he came back, Matthew presented to me—with all due ceremony—

"A mousetrap," I said, giggling at the little wooden box with its sliding door.

"*That* is a proper mousetrap," he said, taking my hand. He started walking backward, pulling me into the center of the merriment. "Dance with me."

"I definitely don't know that dance." It was nothing like the sedate dances at Sept-Tours or at Rudolf's court.

"Well, I do," Matthew said, not bothering to look at the whirling couples behind him. "It's an old dance—the Black Nag—with easy steps." He pulled me into place at one end of the line, plucking my mousetrap out of my hand and giving it into the safekeeping of an urchin. He promised the boy a penny if he returned it to us at the end of the song.

Matthew took my hand, stepped into the line of dancers, and when the others moved, we followed. Three steps and a little kick forward, three steps and a little dip back. After a few repetitions, we came to the more intricate steps when the line of twelve dancers divided into two lines of six and started changing places, crossing in diagonal paths from one line to the other, weaving back and forth.

When the dance finished, there were calls for more music and requests for specific tunes, but we left the Royal Exchange before the dances became any more energetic. Matthew retrieved my mousetrap and, instead of taking me straight home, wended his way south toward the river. We turned down so many alleys and cut across so many churchyards that I was hopelessly disoriented by the time we reached All Hallows the Great, with its tall, square tower and abandoned cloister where the monks had once walked. Like most of London's churches, All Hallows was on its way to becoming a ruin, its medieval stonework crumbling.

"Are you up for a climb?" Matthew asked, ducking into the cloister and through a low wooden door.

I nodded, and we began our ascent. We passed by the bells, which were happily not clanging at the moment, and Matthew pushed open a trapdoor in the roof. He scampered through the hole, then reached down and lifted me up to join him. Suddenly we were standing behind the tower's crenellations, with all of London spread at our feet.

The bonfires on the hills outside the city already burned bright, and lanterns bobbed up and down on the bows of boats and barges crossing the Thames. At this distance, with the darkness of the river as a backdrop, they looked like fireflies. I heard laughter, music, all the ordinary sounds of life I'd grown so accustomed to during the months we'd been here.

"So you've met the queen, seen the Royal Exchange at night, and actually *been* in a play instead of just watching one," Matthew said, ticking items off on his fingers.

"We found Ashmole 782, too. And I discovered I'm a weaver and that magic isn't as disciplined as I'd hoped." I surveyed the city, remembering when we'd first arrived and Matthew had to point out the landmarks for fear I'd get lost. Now I could name them myself. "There's Bridewell." I pointed. "And St. Paul's. And the bearbaiting arenas." I turned toward the quiet vampire standing beside me. "Thank you for tonight, Matthew. We've never been on a date-date—out in public like this. It was magical."

"I didn't do a very good job courting you, did I? We should have had more nights like this one, with dancing and looking at the stars." He tilted his face up, and the moon glanced off his pale skin.

"You're practically glowing," I said softly, reaching up to touch his chin.

"So are you." Matthew's hands slid to my waist, his gesture bringing the baby into our embrace. "That reminds me. Your father gave us a list, too."

"We've had fun. You made magic by taking me to the exchange and then surprising me with this view."

"That leaves only two more items. Lady's choice: I can howl at the moon or we can make out."

I smiled and looked away, strangely shy. Matthew tilted his head up to the moon again, readying himself.

"No howling. You'll bring out the Watch," I protested with a laugh.

"Kissing it is," he said softly, fitting his mouth to mine.

* * *

The next morning the entire household was yawning its way through breakfast after staying out until the early hours. Tom and Jack had just risen and were wolfing down bowls of porridge when Gallowglass came in and whispered something to Matthew. My mouth went dry at Matthew's sad look.

"Where's my dad?" I shot to my feet.

"He's gone home," Gallowglass said gruffly.

"Why didn't you stop him?" I asked Gallowglass, tears threatening. "He can't be gone. I just needed a few more hours with him."

"All the time in the world wouldn't have been enough, Auntie," Gallowglass said with a sad expression.

"But he didn't say good-bye," I whispered numbly.

"A parent should never have to say a final good-bye to his child," Matthew said.

"Stephen asked me to give you this," Gallowglass said. It was a piece of paper, folded up into an origami sailboat.

"Daddy sucked at swans," I said, wiping my eyes, "but he was really good at making boats." Carefully, I unfolded the note.

> *Diana:*
>
> *You are everything we dreamed you would one day become.*
> *Life is the strong warp of time. Death is only the weft.*
> *It will be because of your children, and your children's children,*
> *that I will live forever.*
>
> > *Dad*
>
> *P.S. Every time you read "something is rotten in the state of Denmark" in* Hamlet, *think of me.*

"You tell me that magic is just desire made real. Maybe spells are nothing more than words that you believe with all your heart," Matthew said, coming to rest his hands on my shoulders. "He loves you. Forever. So do I."

His words wove through the threads that connected us, witch and vampire. They carried the conviction of his feelings with them: tenderness, reverence, constancy, hope.

"I love you, too," I whispered, reinforcing his spell with mine.

## 39

My father had left London without saying a proper good-bye. I was determined to take my own leave differently. As a result my final days in the city were a complex weaving of words and desires, spells and magic.

Goody Alsop's fetch was waiting sadly for me at the end of the lane when I made my last visit to my teacher's house. She trailed listlessly behind me as I climbed the stairs to the witch's rooms.

"So you are leaving us," Goody Alsop said from her chair by the fire. She was wearing wool and a shawl, and a fire was blazing as well.

"We must." I bent down and kissed her papery cheek. "How are you today?"

"Somewhat better, thanks to Susanna's remedies." Goody Alsop coughed, and the force of it bent her frail frame in two. When she was recovered, she studied me with bright eyes and nodded. "This time the babe has taken root."

"It has," I said with a smile. "I have the sickness to prove it. Would you like me to tell the others?" I didn't want Goody Alsop to shoulder any extra burdens, emotional or physical. Susanna was worried about her frailty, and Elizabeth Jackson was already taking on some of the duties usually performed by the gathering's elder.

"No need. Catherine was the one to tell me. She said Corra was flying about a few days ago, chortling and chattering as she does when she has a secret."

We had come to an agreement, my firedrake and I, that she would limit her open-air flying to once a week, and only at night. I'd reluctantly agreed to a second night out during the dark of the moon, when the risk of anyone's seeing her and mistaking her for a fiery portent of doom was at its lowest.

"So that's where she went," I said with a laugh. Corra found the witch's company soothing, and Catherine enjoyed challenging her to fire-breathing contests.

"We are all glad that Corra has found something to do with herself besides clinging to the chimneypieces and shrieking at the ghosts." Goody

Alsop pointed to the chair opposite. "Will you not sit with me? The goddess may not afford us another chance."

"Did you hear the news from Scotland?" I asked as I took my seat.

"I have heard nothing since you told me that pleading her belly did not save Euphemia MacLean from the pyre." Goody Alsop's decline began the night I'd told her that a young witch from Berwick had been burned, in spite of Matthew's efforts.

"Matthew finally convinced the rest of the Congregation that the spiral of accusations and executions had to stop. Two of the accused witches have overturned their testimony and said their confessions were the result of torture."

"It must have given the Congregation pause to have a *wearh* speak out on behalf of a witch." Goody Alsop looked at me sharply. "He would give himself away if you were to stay. Matthew Roydon lives in a world of half-truths, but no one can avoid detection forever. Because of the babe, you must take greater care."

"We will," I assured her. "Meanwhile I'm still not absolutely sure my eighth knot is strong enough for the timewalking. Not with Matthew and the baby."

"Let me see it," Goody Alsop said, stretching out her hand. I leaned forward and put the cords into her palm. I would use all nine cords when we timewalked and make a total of nine different knots. No spell used more.

With practiced hands Goody Alsop made eight crossings in the red cord and then bound the ends together so that the knot was unbreakable. "That is how I do it." It was beautifully simple, with open loops and swirls like the stone traceries in a cathedral window.

"Mine did not look like that." My laugh was rueful. "It wiggled and squiggled around."

"Every weaving is as unique as the weaver who makes it. The goddess does not want us to imitate some ideal of perfection, but to be our true selves."

"Well, I must be all wiggle, then." I reached for the cords to study the design.

"There is another knot I would show you," Goody Alsop said.

"Another?" I frowned.

"A tenth knot. It is impossible for me to make it, though it should be the simplest." Goody Alsop smiled, but her chin trembled. "My own teacher could not make the knot either, but still we passed it on, in hope that a weaver such as you might come along."

Goody Alsop released the just-tied knot with a flick of her gnarled index finger. I handed the red silk back to her, and she made a simple loop. For a moment the cord fused in an unbroken ring. As soon as she took her fingers from it, however, the loop released.

"But you drew the ends together just a minute ago, and with a far more complicated weaving," I said, confused

"As long as there is a crossing in the cord, I can bind the ends and complete the spell. But only a weaver who stands between worlds can make the tenth knot," she replied. "Try it. Use the silver silk."

Mystified, I joined the ends of the cord into a circlet. The fibers snapped together to form a loop with no beginning and no ending. I lifted my fingers from the silk, but the circle held.

"A fine weaving," Goody Alsop said with satisfaction. "The tenth knot captures the power of eternity, a weaving of life and death. It is rather like your husband's snake, or the way Corra carries her tail in her mouth sometimes when it gets in her way." She held up the tenth knot. It was another ouroboros. The sense of the uncanny built in the room, lifting the hairs on my arm. "Creation and destruction are the simplest magics, and the most powerful, just as the simplest knot is the most difficult to make."

"I don't want to use magic to destroy anything," I said. The Bishops had a strong tradition of not doing harm. My Aunt Sarah believed that any witch who strayed away from this fundamental tenet would find the evil coming back to her in the end.

"No one wants to use the goddess's gifts as a weapon, but sometimes it is necessary. Your *wearh* knows that. After what happened here and in Scotland, you know it, too."

"Perhaps. But my world is different," I said. "There's less call for magical weapons."

"Worlds change, Diana." Goody Alsop fixed her attention on some distant memory. "My teacher, Mother Ursula, was a great weaver. I was reminded of one of her prophecies on All Hallows' Eve, when the terrible events in Scotland began—and when you came to change our world."

Her voice took on the singsong quality of an incantation.

*"For storms will rage and oceans roar
When Gabriel stands on sea and shore.*

> *And as he blows his wondrous horn,*
> *Old worlds die, and new be born."*

Not a breeze or a crackle of flame disturbed the room when Goody Alsop finished. She took a deep breath.

"It is all one, you see. Death and birth. The tenth knot with no beginning and no ending, and the *wearh's* snake. The full moon that shone earlier this week and the shadow Corra cast upon the Thames in a portent of your leaving. The old world and the new." Goody Alsop's smile wavered. "I was glad when you came to me, Diana Roydon. And when you go, as you must, my heart will be heavy."

"Usually Matthew tells me when he is leaving my city." Andrew Hubbard's white hands rested on the carved arms of his chair in the church crypt. High above us someone prepared for an upcoming church service. "What brings you here, Mistress Roydon?"

"I came to talk to you about Annie and Jack."

Hubbard's strange eyes studied me as I pulled a small leather purse from my pocket. It contained five years of wages for each of them.

"I'm leaving London. I would like you to have this, for their care." I thrust the money in Hubbard's direction. He made no move to take it.

"That isn't necessary, mistress."

"Please. I would take them with me if I could. Since they cannot go, I need to know that someone will be watching out for them."

"And what will you give me in return?"

"Why . . . the money, of course." I held the pouch out once more.

"I don't want or need the money, Mistress Roydon." Hubbard settled back in his chair, his eyes drifting closed.

"What do you—" I stopped. "No."

"God does nothing in vain. There are no accidents in His plans. He wanted you to come here today, because He wants to be sure that no one of your blood will have anything to fear from me or mine."

"I have protectors enough," I protested.

"And can the same be said for your husband?" Hubbard glanced at my breast. "Your blood is stronger in his veins now than when you arrived. And there is the child to consider."

My heart stuttered. When I took my Matthew back to our present,

Andrew Hubbard would be one of the few people who would know his future—and that there was a witch in it.

"You wouldn't use the knowledge of me against Matthew. Not after what he's done—how he's changed."

"Wouldn't I?" Hubbard's tight smile told me he would do whatever it took to protect his flock. "There is a great deal of bad blood between us."

"I'll find another way to see them safe," I said, deciding to go.

"Annie is my child already. She is a witch, and part of my family. I will see to her welfare. Jack Blackfriars is another matter. He is not a creature and will have to fend for himself."

"He's a child—a boy!"

"But not my child. Nor are you. I do not owe either of you anything. Good day, Mistress Roydon." Hubbard turned away.

"And if I were one of your family, what then? Would you honor my request about Jack? Would you recognize Matthew as one of my blood and therefore under your protection?" It was the sixteenth-century Matthew that I was thinking of now. When we returned to the present, that other Matthew would still be here in the past.

"If you offer me your blood, neither Matthew nor Jack nor your unborn child has anything to fear from me or mine." Hubbard imparted the information dispassionately, but his glance was touched with the avarice I'd seen in Rudolf's eyes.

"And how much blood would you need?" *Think. Stay alive.*

"Very little. No more than a drop." Hubbard's attention was unwavering.

"I couldn't let you take it directly from my body. Matthew would know—we are mates, after all," I said. Hubbard's eyes flickered to my breast.

"I always take my tribute directly from my children's neck."

"I'm sure you do, Father Hubbard. But you can understand why that isn't possible, or even desirable, in this case." I fell silent, hoping that Hubbard's hunger—for power, for knowledge of Matthew and me, for something to hold over the de Clermonts if he ever needed it—would win. "I could use a cup."

"No," Hubbard said with a shake of his head. "Your blood would be tainted. It must be pure."

"A silver cup, then," I said, thinking of Chef's lectures at Sept-Tours.

"You will open the vein in your wrist over my mouth and let the blood fall into it. We will not touch." Hubbard scowled at me. "Otherwise I will doubt the sincerity of your offer."

"Very well, Father Hubbard. I accept your terms." I loosened the tie at my right cuff and pushed up the sleeve. While I did so, I whispered a silent request to Corra. "Where do you wish to do this? From what I saw before, your children kneel before you, but that will not work if I'm to drip the blood into your mouth."

"It is a sacrament. It does not matter to God who kneels." To my surprise, Hubbard dropped to the floor before me. He handed me a knife.

"I don't need that." I flicked my finger at the blue traceries on my wrist and murmured a simple unbinding charm. A line of crimson appeared. The blood welled.

Hubbard opened his mouth, his eyes on my face. He was waiting for me to renege, or cheat him somehow. But I would obey the letter of this agreement, though not its spirit. *Thank you, Goody Alsop,* I said, sending her a silent blessing for showing me how to handle the man.

I held my wrist over his mouth and clenched my fist. A drop of blood rolled over the edge of my arm and began to fall. Hubbard's eyes flickered closed, as if he wanted to concentrate on what my blood would tell him.

"What is blood, if not fire and water?" I murmured. I called on the wind to slow the droplet's fall. As the power of the air increased, it froze the falling bead of blood so that it was crystalline and sharp when it landed on Hubbard's tongue. The vampire's eyes shot open in confusion.

"No more than a drop." The wind had dried the remaining blood against my skin in a maze of red streaks over the blue veins. "You are a man of God, a man of your word, are you not, Father Hubbard?"

Corra's tail loosened from around my waist. She'd used it to block our baby from having any knowledge of this sordid transaction, but now she seemed to want to use it to beat Hubbard senseless.

Slowly I withdrew my arm. Hubbard thought about grabbing it back to his mouth. I saw the idea cross his mind as clearly as I had seen Edward Kelley contemplate clubbing me with his walking stick. But he thought better of it. I whispered another simple spell to close the wound, and turned wordlessly to leave.

"When you are next in London," Hubbard said softly, "God will whisper it to me. And if He wills it, we shall meet again. But remember this. No matter where you go from now, even unto death, some small piece of you will live within me."

I stopped and looked back at him. His words were menacing, but the expression on his face was thoughtful, even sad. My pace quickened as I left the church crypt, wanting to put as much distance as I could between me and Andrew Hubbard.

"Farewell, Diana Bishop," he called after me.

I was halfway across town before I realized that no matter how little that single drop of blood might have revealed, Father Hubbard now knew my real name.

Walter and Matthew were shouting at each other when I returned to the Hart and Crown. Raleigh's groom could hear them, too. He was in the courtyard, holding the reins of Walter's black beast of a horse and listening to their argument through the open windows.

"It will mean my death—and hers, too! No one must know she is with child!" Oddly enough, it was Walter speaking.

"You cannot abandon the woman you love and your own child in an attempt to stay true to the queen, Walter. Elizabeth will find out that you have betrayed her, and Bess will be ruined forever."

"What do you expect me to do? Marry her? If I do so without the queen's permission, I'll be arrested."

"You'll survive no matter what happens," Matthew said flatly. "If you leave Bess without your protection, she will not."

"How can you pretend concern for marital honesty after all the lies you've told about Diana? Some days you insisted you were married but made us swear to deny it should any strange witches or *wearhs* come sniffing around asking questions." Walter's voice dropped, but the ferocity remained. "Do you expect me to believe you're going to return whence you came and acknowledge her as your wife?"

I slipped into the room unnoticed.

Matthew hesitated.

"I thought not," Walter said. He was pulling on his gloves.

"Is this how you two want to say your farewells?" I asked.

"Diana," Walter said warily.

"Hello, Walter. Your groom is downstairs with the horse."

He started toward the door, stopped. "Be sensible, Matthew. I cannot lose all credit at court. Bess understands the dangers of the queen's anger better than anyone. At the court of Elizabeth, fortune is fleeting, but disgrace endures forever."

Matthew watched his friend thud down the stairs. "God forgive me. The first time I heard this plan, I told him it was wise. Poor Bess."

"What will happen to her when we are gone?" I asked.

"Come autumn, Bess's pregnancy will begin to show. They will marry in secret. When the queen questions their relationship, Walter will deny it. Repeatedly. Bess's reputation will be ruined, her husband will be found out to be a liar, and they will both be arrested."

"And the child?" I whispered.

"Will be born in March and dead the following autumn." Matthew sat down at the table, his head in his hands. "I will write to my father and make sure that Bess receives his protection. Perhaps Susanna Norman will see to her during the pregnancy."

"Neither your father nor Susanna can shield her from the blow of Raleigh's denial." I rested my hands on his sleeve. "And will you deny that we are married when we return?"

"It's not that simple," Matthew said, looking at me with haunted eyes.

"That's what Walter said. You told him he was wrong." I remembered Goody Alsop's prophecy. "'*Old worlds die, and new be born.*' The time is coming when you will have to choose between the safety of the past and the promise of the future, Matthew."

"And the past cannot be cured, no matter how hard I try," he said. "It's something I'm always telling the queen when she agonizes over a bad decision. Hoist by my own petard again, as Gallowglass would be quick to point out."

"You beat me to it, Uncle." Gallowglass had soundlessly entered the room and was unloading parcels. "I've got your paper. And your pens. And some tonic for Jack's throat."

"That's what he gets for spending all his time up towers with Tom, talking about the stars." Matthew rubbed his face. "We will have to make sure Tom is provided for, Gallowglass. Walter won't be able to keep him in service much longer. Henry Percy will need to step into the breach—again— but I should contribute something to his upkeep, too."

"Speaking of Tom, have you seen his plans for a one-eyed spectacle to view the heavens? He and Jack are calling it a star glass."

My scalp tingled as the threads of the room snapped with energy. Time sounded a low protest in the corners.

"A star glass." I kept my voice even. "What does it look like?"

.

"Ask him yourself," Gallowglass said, turning his head toward the stairs. Jack and Mop careened into the room. Tom followed absently behind, a pair of broken spectacles in his hand.

"You will certainly leave a mark on the future if you meddle with this, Diana," Matthew warned.

"Look, look, look." Jack brandished a thick piece of wood. Mop followed its movements and snapped his jaws at the stick as it went by. "Master Harriot said if we hollowed this out and put a spectacle lens in the end, it would make faraway things seem near. Do you know how to carve, Master Roydon? If not, do you think the joiner in St. Dunstan's might teach me? Are there any more buns? Master Harriot's stomach has been growling all afternoon."

"Let me see that," I said, holding out my hand for the wooden tube. "The buns are in the cupboard on the landing, Jack, where they always are. Give one to Master Harriot, and take one for yourself. And no," I said, cutting the child off when he opened his mouth, "Mop doesn't get to share yours."

"Good day, Mistress Roydon," Tom said dreamily. "If such a simple pair of spectacles can make a man see God's words in the Bible, surely they could be made more complex to help him see God's works in the Book of Nature. Thank you, Jack." Tom absently bit into the bun.

"And how would you make them more complex?" I wondered aloud, hardly daring to breathe.

"I would combine convex and concave lenses, as the Neapolitan gentleman Signor della Porta suggested in a book I read last year. My arm cannot hold them apart at the proper distance. So we are trying to extend our arm's reach with that piece of wood."

With those words Thomas Harriot changed the history of science. And I didn't have to meddle with the past—I only had to see to it that the past was not forgotten.

"But these are just idle imaginings. I will put these ideas down on paper and think about them later." Tom sighed.

This was the problem with early-modern scientists: They didn't understand the necessity of publishing. In the case of Thomas Harriot, his ideas had definitely perished for want of a publisher.

"I think you're right, Tom. But this wooden tube is not long enough." I smiled at him brightly. "As for the joiner in St. Dunstan's, Monsieur Vallin might be of more help if a long, hollow tube is what you need. Shall we go and see him?"

"Yes!" Jack shouted, jumping into the air. "Monsieur Vallin has all sorts of gears and springs, Master Harriot. He gave me one, and it is in my treasure box. Mine is not as big as Mistress Roydon's, but it holds enough. Can we go now?"

"What is Auntie up to?" Gallowglass asked Matthew, both mystified and wary.

"I think she's getting back at Walter for not paying sufficient attention to the future," Matthew said mildly.

"Oh. That's all right, then. And here I thought I smelled trouble."

"There's always trouble," Matthew said. "Are you sure you know what you're doing, *ma lionne*?"

So much had happened that I could not fix. I couldn't bring my first child back or save the witches in Scotland. We'd brought Ashmole 782 all the way from Prague, only to discover that it could not be taken safely into the future. We had said good-bye to our fathers and were about to leave our friends. Most of these experiences would vanish without a trace. But I knew exactly how to ensure that Tom's telescope survived.

I nodded. "The past has changed us, Matthew. Why should we not change it, too?"

Matthew caught my hand in his and kissed it. "Go to Monsieur Vallin, then. Have him send me the bill."

"Thank you." I bent and whispered in his ear. "Don't worry. I'll take Annie with me. She'll wear him down on the price. Besides, who knows what to charge for a telescope in 1591?"

And so a witch, a daemon, two children, and a dog paid a short visit to Monsieur Vallin that afternoon. That evening I sent out invitations to our friends to join us the next night. It would be the last time we saw them. While I dealt with telescopes and supper plans, Matthew delivered Roger Bacon's *Verum Secretum Secretorum* to Mortlake. I did not want to see Ashmole 782 pass to Dr. Dee. I knew it had to go back into the alchemist's enormous library so that Elias Ashmole could acquire it in the seventeenth century. But it was not easy to give the book into someone else's keeping, any more than it had been to surrender the small figurine of the goddess Diana to Kit when we arrived. The practical details surrounding our departure we left to Gallowglass and Pierre. They packed trunks, emptied coffers, redistributed funds, and sent personal belongings to the Old Lodge with a practiced efficiency that showed how many times they had done this before.

Our departure was only hours away. I was returning from Monsieur Vallin's with an awkward package wrapped in soft leather when I was brought up short by the sight of a ten-year-old girl standing on the street outside the pie shop, staring with fascination at the wares in the window. She reminded me of myself at that age, from the unruly straw-blond hair to the arms that were too long for the rest of her frame. The girl stiffened as if she knew she was being watched. When our eyes met, I knew why: She was a witch.

"Rebecca!" a woman called as she came from inside the shop. My heart leaped at the sight, for she looked like a combination of my mother and Sarah.

Rebecca said nothing but continued to stare at me as though she had seen a ghost. Her mother looked to see what had captured the girl's attention and gasped. Her glance tingled over my skin as she took in my face and form. She was a witch, too.

I forced my feet toward the pie shop. Every step took me closer to the two witches. The mother gathered the child to her skirts, and Rebecca squirmed in protest.

"She looks like Grand-dame," Rebecca whispered, trying to get a closer look at me.

"Hush," her mother told her. She looked at me apologetically. "You know that your grand-dame is dead, Rebecca."

"I am Diana Roydon." I nodded to the sign over their shoulders. "I live here at the Hart and Crown."

"But then you are—" The woman's eyes widened as she drew Rebecca closer.

"I am Rebecca White," the girl said, unconcerned with her mother's reaction. She bobbed a shallow, teetering curtsy. That looked familiar, too.

"It is a pleasure to meet you. Are you new to the Blackfriars?" I wanted to make small talk for as long as possible, if only to stare at their familiar-yet-strange faces.

"No. We live by the hospital near Smithfield Market," Rebecca explained.

"I take in patients when their wards are full." The woman hesitated. "I am Bridget White, and Rebecca is my daughter."

Even without the familiar names of Rebecca and Bridget, I recognized these two creatures in the marrow of my bones. Bridget Bishop had been born around 1632, and the first name in the Bishop grimoire was Bridget's grandmother, Rebecca Davies. Would this ten-year-old girl one day marry and bear that name?

Rebecca's attention was caught by something at my neck. I reached up. *Ysabeau's earrings.*

I had used three objects to bring Matthew and me to the past: a manuscript copy of *Doctor Faustus,* a silver chess piece, and an earring hidden in Bridget Bishop's poppet. This earring. I reached up and took the fine golden wire out of my ear. Knowing from my experience with Jack that it was wise to make direct eye contact with children if you wanted to leave a lasting impression, I crouched down until we were at an equal level.

"I need someone to keep this safe for me." I held out the earring. "One day I will have need of it. Would you keep it close?"

Rebecca looked at me solemnly and nodded. I took her hand, feeling a current of awareness pass between us, and put the jeweled wires into her palm. She wrapped her fingers tightly around them. "Can I, Mama?" she whispered belatedly to Bridget.

"I think that would be all right," her mother replied warily. "Come, Rebecca. We must go."

"Thank you," I said, rising and patting Rebecca on the shoulder while looking Bridget in the eye. "Thank you."

I felt a nudging glance. I waited until Rebecca and Bridget were out of sight before I turned to face Christopher Marlowe.

"Mistress Roydon." Kit's voice was hoarse, and he looked like death. "Walter told me you were leaving tonight."

"I asked him to tell you." I forced Kit to meet my eyes through an act of sheer will. This was another thing I could fix: I could make sure that Matthew said a proper good-bye to a man who had once been his closest friend.

Kit looked down at his feet, hiding his face. "I should never have come."

"I forgive you, Kit."

Marlowe's head swung up in surprise at my words. "Why?" he asked, dumbstruck.

"Because you love him. And because as long as Matthew blames you for what happened to me, a part of him remains with you. Forever," I said simply. "Come upstairs and say your farewells."

Matthew was waiting for us on the landing, having divined that I was bringing someone home. I kissed him softly on the mouth as I went past on the way to our bedroom.

"Your father forgave you," I murmured. "Give Kit the same gift in return."

Then I left them to patch up what they could in what little time remained.

A few hours later, I handed Thomas Harriot a steel tube. "Here is your star glass, Tom."

"I fashioned it from a gun barrel—with adjustments, of course," explained Monsieur Vallin, famous maker of mousetraps and clocks. "And it is engraved, as Mistress Roydon requested."

There on the side, set in a lovely little silver banner, was the legend N. VALLIN ME FECIT, T. HARRIOT ME INVENIT, 1591.

"*N. Vallin made me, T. Harriot invented me, 1591.*" I smiled warmly at Monsieur Vallin. "It's perfect."

"Can we look at the moon now?" Jack cried, racing for the door. "It already looks bigger than St. Mildred's clock!"

And so Thomas Harriot, mathematician and linguist, made scientific history in the courtyard of the Hart and Crown while sitting in a battered wicker garden chair pulled down from our attics. He trained the long metal tube fitted with two spectacle lenses at the full moon and sighed with pleasure.

"Look, Jack. It is just as Signor della Porta said." Tom invited the boy into his lap and positioned one end of the tube at his enthusiastic assistant's eye. "Two lenses, one convex and one concave, are indeed the solution if held at the right distance."

After Jack we all took a turn.

"Well, that is not at all what I expected," George Chapman said, disappointed. "Did you not think the moon would be more dramatic? I believe I prefer the poet's mysterious moon to this one, Tom."

"Why, it is not perfect at all," Henry Percy complained, rubbing his eyes and then peering through the tube again.

"Of course it isn't perfect. Nothing is," Kit said. "You cannot believe everything philosophers tell you, Hal. It is a sure way to ruin. You see how little philosophy has done for Tom."

I glanced at Matthew and grinned. It had been some time since we'd enjoyed the School of Night's verbal ripostes.

"At least Tom can feed himself, which is more than I can say for any of the playwrights of my acquaintance." Walter peered through the tube and whistled. "I wish you had come up with this notion before we went to Virginia, Tom. It would have been useful for surveying the shore while we were safely aboard ship. Look through this, Gallowglass, and tell me I am wrong."

"You're never wrong, Walter," Gallowglass said with a wink at Jack. "Mind me well, young Jack. The one who pays your wages is correct in all things."

I'd invited Goody Alsop and Susanna to join us, too, and even they took a peek through Tom's star glass. Neither woman seemed overly impressed with the invention, although they both made enthusiastic noises when prompted.

"Why do men bother with these trifles?" Susanna whispered to me. "I could have told them the moon is not perfectly smooth, even without this new instrument. Do they not have eyes?"

After the pleasure of viewing the heavens, only the painful farewells remained. We sent Annie off with Goody Alsop, using the excuse that Susanna needed another set of hands to help the old woman across town. My good-bye was brisk, and Annie looked at me uncertainly.

"Are you all right, mistress? Shall I stay here instead?"

"No, Annie. Go with your aunt and Goody Alsop." I blinked back the tears. How did Matthew bear these repeated farewells?

Kit, George, and Walter left next, with gruff good-byes and hands clamped on Matthew's arm to wish him well.

"Come, Jack. You and Tom will go home with me," Henry Percy said. "The night is still young."

"I don't want to go," Jack said. He swung around to Matthew, eyes huge. The boy sensed the impending change.

Matthew knelt before him. "There's nothing to be afraid of, Jack. You know Master Harriot and Lord Northumberland. They won't let you come to harm."

"What if I have a nightmare?" Jack whispered.

"Nightmares are like Master Harriot's star glass. They are a trick of the light, one that makes something distant seem closer and larger than it really is."

"Oh." Jack considered Matthew's response. "So even if I see a monster in my dreams, it cannot reach me?"

Matthew nodded. "But I will tell you a secret. A dream is a nightmare in reverse. If you dream of someone you love, that person will seem closer, even if far away." He stood and put his hand on Jack's head for a moment in a silent blessing.

Once Jack and his guardians had departed, only Gallowglass remained. I took the cords from my spell box, leaving a few items within: a pebble, a white feather, a bit of the rowan tree, my jewelry, and the note my father had left.

"I'll take care of it," he promised, taking the box from me. It looked oddly small in his huge hand. He wrapped me up in a bear hug.

"Keep the other Matthew safe, so he can find me one day," I whispered in his ear, my eyes scrunched tight.

I released him and stepped aside. The two de Clermonts said their good-byes as all de Clermonts did—briefly but with feeling.

Pierre was waiting with the horses outside the Cardinal's Hat. Matthew handed me up into the saddle and climbed into his own.

"Farewell, *madame*," Pierre said, letting go of the reins.

"Thank you, friend," I said, my eyes filling once more.

Pierre handed Matthew a letter. I recognized Philippe's seal. "Your father's instructions, *milord*."

"If I don't turn up in Edinburgh in two days, come looking for me."

"I will," Pierre promised as Matthew clucked to his horse and we turned toward Oxford.

We changed horses three times and were at the Old Lodge before sunrise. Françoise and Charles had been sent away. We were alone.

Matthew left the letter from Philippe propped up on his desk, where the sixteenth-century Matthew could not fail to see it. It would send him to Scotland on urgent business. Once there, Matthew Roydon would stay at the court of King James for a time before disappearing to start a new life in Amsterdam.

"The king of Scots will be pleased to have me back to my former self," Matthew commented, touching the letter with his fingertip. "I won't be making any more attempts to save witches, certainly."

"You made a difference here, Matthew," I said, sliding my arm around his waist. "Now we need to sort things out in our present."

We stepped into the bedroom where we'd arrived all those months before.

"You know I can't be sure that we'll slip through the centuries and land in exactly the right time and place," I warned.

"You've explained it to me, *mon coeur*. I have faith in you." Matthew hooked his arm through mine to anchor me. "Let's go meet our future. Again."

"Good-bye, house." I looked around our first home one last time. Even though I would see it again, it would not be the same as it was on this June morning.

The blue and amber threads in the corners snapped and keened impatiently, filling the room with light and sound. I took a deep breath and knotted my brown cord, leaving the end hanging free. Apart from Matthew and the clothes on our backs, my weaver's cords were the only objects we were taking back with us.

"With knot of one, the spell's begun," I whispered. Time's volume increased with every knot I made until the shrieking and keening was nearly deafening.

As the ends of the ninth cord fused together, we picked up our feet and our surroundings slowly dissolved.

$40$

All the English papers had some variation of the same headline, but Ysabeau thought the one in the *Times* was the cleverest.

**English Man Wins Race to See into Space**
*30 June 2010*
THE WORLD'S leading expert on early scientific instruments at Oxford University's Museum of the History of Science, Anthony Carter, confirmed today that a refracting telescope bearing the names of Elizabethan mathematician and astronomer Thomas Harriot and Nicholas Vallin, a Huguenot clockmaker who fled France for religious reasons, is indeed genuine. In addition to the names, the telescope is engraved with the date 1591.

The discovery has electrified the scientific and historical communities. For centuries, Italian mathematician Galileo Galilei had been credited with borrowing rudimentary telescope technology from the Dutch in order to view the moon in 1609.

"The history books will have to be rewritten," said Carter. "Thomas Harriot had read Giambattista della Porta's *Natural Magic* and become intrigued with how convex and concave lenses could be used to 'see both things afar off, and things near hand, both greater and clearly.'"

Thomas Harriot's contributions to the field of astronomy were overlooked in part because he did not publish them, preferring to share his discoveries with a close group of friends some call "The School of Night." Under the patronage of Walter Raleigh and Henry Percy, the "Wizard Earl" of Northumberland, Harriot was financially free to explore his interests.

Mr I. P. Riddell discovered the telescope, along with a

box of assorted mathematical papers in Thomas Harriot's hand and an elaborate silver mousetrap also signed by Vallin. He was repairing the bells of St. Michael's Church, near the Percy family's seat in Alnwick, when a particularly strong gust of wind brought down a faded tapestry of St. Margaret slaying the dragon, revealing the box that had been secreted there.

"It is rare for instruments of this period to have so many identifying marks," Dr Carter explained to reporters, revealing the date mark stamped into the telescope, which confirms the item was made in 1591–92. "We owe a great debt to Nicholas Vallin, who knew that this was an important development in the history of scientific instrumentation and took unusual measures to record its genealogy and provenance."

"They refuse to sell it," Marcus said, leaning against the doorframe. With his arms and legs crossed, he looked very much like Matthew. "I've spoken with everyone from the Alnwick church officials to the Duke of Northumberland to the Bishop of Newcastle. They're not going to give up the telescope, not even for the small fortune you've offered. I think I've convinced them to let me buy the mousetrap, though."

"The whole world knows about it," Ysabeau said. "Even *Le Monde* has reported the story."

"We should have tried harder to squash the story. This could give the witches and their allies vital information," Marcus said. The growing number of people living inside the walls of Sept-Tours had been worrying for weeks about what the Congregation might do if the exact whereabouts of Diana and Matthew were discovered.

"What does Phoebe think?" Ysabeau asked. She had taken an instant liking to the observant young human with her firm chin and gentle ways.

Marcus's face softened. It made him look as he had before Matthew left, when he was carefree and joyful. "She thinks it's too soon to tell what damage has been done by the telescope's discovery."

"Smart girl," Ysabeau said with a smile.

"I don't know what I'd do—" Marcus began. His expression turned fierce. "I love her, *Grand-mère*."

"Of course you do. And she loves you, too." After the events of May, Marcus had wanted her with the rest of the family and had brought her to

Sept-Tours to stay. The two of them were inseparable. And Phoebe had shown remarkable savoir faire as she met the assembly of daemons, witches, and vampires currently in residence. If she had been surprised to learn there were other creatures sharing the world with humans, she had not revealed it.

Membership in Marcus's Conventicle had swelled considerably over the past months. Matthew's assistant, Miriam, was now a permanent resident at the château, as were Philippe's daughter Verin and her husband Ernst. Gallowglass, Ysabeau's restless grandson, had shocked them all by staying put there for six whole weeks. Even now he showed no signs of leaving. Sophie Norman and Nathaniel Wilson welcomed their new baby, Margaret, into the world under Ysabeau's roof, and now the baby's authority in the château was second only to the de Clermont matriarch's. With her grandchild living at Sept-Tours, Nathaniel's mother Agatha appeared and reappeared without warning, as did Matthew's best friend, Hamish. Even Baldwin flitted through occasionally.

Never in her long life had Ysabeau expected to be chatelaine of such a household.

"Where is Sarah?" Marcus asked, tuning in to the hum of activity all around. "I don't hear her."

"In the Round Tower." Ysabeau ran her sharp nail around the edge of the newspaper story and neatly lifted the clipped columns from their printed surround. "Sophie and Margaret sat with her for a while. Sophie says Sarah is keeping watch."

"For what? What's happened now?" Marcus said, snatching at the newspaper. He'd read them all that morning, tracking the subtle shifts in money and influence that Nathaniel had found a way to analyze and isolate so that they could be better prepared for the Congregation's next move. A world without Phoebe was inconceivable, but Nathaniel had become nearly as indispensable. "That damn telescope is going to be a problem. I just know it. All the Congregation needs is a timewalking witch and this story and they'll have everything they need to go back into the past and find my father."

"Your father won't be there for much longer, if he's still there at all."

"Really, *Grand-mère*," Marcus said with a note of exasperation, his attention still glued to the text surrounding the hole that Ysabeau had left in the *Times*. "How can you possibly know that?"

"First there were the miniatures, then the laboratory records, and now this telescope. I know my daughter-in-law. This telescope is exactly the kind of gesture Diana would make if she had nothing left to lose." Ysabeau brushed past her grandson. "Diana and Matthew are coming home."

Marcus's expression was unreadable.

"I expected you to be happier about your father's return," Ysabeau said quietly, stopping by the door.

"It's been a difficult few months," Marcus said somberly. "The Congregation made it clear they want the book and Nathaniel's daughter. Once Diana is here . . ."

"They will stop at nothing." Ysabeau took in a slow breath. "At least we will no longer have to worry about something happening to Diana and Matthew in the past. We will be together, at Sept-Tours, fighting side by side." *Dying side by side.*

"So much has changed since last November." Marcus stared into the shining surface of the table as though he were a witch and it might show him the future.

"In their lives, too, I suspect. But your father's love for you is a constant. Sarah needs Diana now. You need Matthew, too."

Ysabeau took her clipping and headed for the Round Tower, leaving Marcus to his thoughts. Once it had been Philippe's favorite jail. Now it was used to store old family papers. Though the door to the room on the third floor was ajar, Ysabeau rapped on it smartly.

"You don't have to knock. This is your house." The rasp in Sarah's voice indicated how many cigarettes she'd been smoking and how much whiskey she'd been drinking.

"If that's how you behave, I am glad not to be your guest," Ysabeau said sharply.

"My guest?" Sarah laughed softly. "I would never have let you into my house."

"Vampires don't usually require an invitation." Ysabeau and Sarah had perfected the art of acerbic banter. Marcus and Em had tried without success to persuade them to obey the rules of courteous communication, but the two clan matriarchs knew that their sharp exchanges helped maintain their fragile balance of power. "You should not be up here, Sarah."

"Why not? Afraid I'll catch my death of cold?" Sarah's voice hitched with sudden pain, and she doubled over as if she'd been struck. "Goddess help me, I miss her. Tell me this is a dream, Ysabeau. Tell me that Emily is still alive."

"It's not a dream," Ysabeau said as gently as she could. "We all miss her. I know that you are empty and aching inside, Sarah."

"And it will pass," Sarah said dully.

"No. It won't."

Sarah looked up, surprised at Ysabeau's vehemence.

"Every day of my life, I yearn for Philippe. The sun rises and my heart cries out for him. I listen for his voice, but there is silence. I crave his touch. When the sun sets, I retire in the knowledge that my mate is gone from this world and I will never see his face again."

"If you're trying to make me feel better, it's not working," Sarah said, the tears streaming.

"Emily died so that Sophie and Nathaniel's child might live. Those who played a part in killing her will pay for it, I promise you. The de Clermonts are very good at revenge, Sarah."

"And revenge will make me feel better?" Sarah squinted up through her tears.

"No. Seeing Margaret grow to womanhood will help. So will this." Ysabeau dropped the cutting into the witch's lap. "Diana and Matthew are coming home."

# PART VI

# New World, Old World

*41*

My attempts to reach the Old Lodge's future from its past were unsuccessful. I focused on the look and smell of the place and saw the threads that bound Matthew and me to the house—brown and green and gold. But they slipped out of my fingers repeatedly.

I tried for Sept-Tours instead. The threads that linked us there were tinged with Matthew's idiosyncratic blend of red and black shot through with silver. I imagined the house full of familiar faces—Sarah and Em, Ysabeau and Marthe, Marcus and Miriam, Sophie and Nathaniel. But I couldn't reach that safe port either.

Resolutely ignoring the rising panic, I searched among hundreds of options for an alternative destination. Oxford? The Blackfriars underground station in modern London? St. Paul's Cathedral?

My fingers kept returning to the same strand in the warp and weft of time that was not silky and smooth but hard and rough. I inched along its twisting length and discovered that it was not a thread but a root connected to some unseen tree. With that realization I tripped, as over an invisible threshold, and fell into the keeping room of the Bishop House.

*Home.* I landed on my hands and knees, the knotted cords flattened between my palms and the floor. Centuries of polish and the passage of hundreds of ancestral feet had long since smoothed out its wide pine boards. They felt familiar under my hands, a token of permanence in a world of change. I looked up, half expecting to see my aunts waiting in the front hall. It had been so easy to find my way back to Madison that I assumed they were guiding us. But the air in the Bishop House was still and lifeless, as though not a soul had disturbed it since Halloween. Not even the ghosts seemed to be in residence.

Matthew was kneeling next to me, his arm still linked to mine and his muscles trembling from the stress of moving through time.

"Are we alone?" I asked.

He took in the house's scents. "Yes."

With his quiet response, the house wakened and the atmosphere went from flat and lifeless to thick and uneasy in a blink. Matthew looked at me and smiled. "Your hair. It's changed again."

I glanced down to find not the strawberry blond curls I'd grown accustomed to but straight, silky strands that were a brighter reddish gold—just like my mother's hair.

"It must be the timewalking."

The house creaked and moaned. I felt it gathering its energy for an outburst.

"It's only me and Matthew."

My words were soothing, but my voice was oddly accented and harsh. The house recognized it nonetheless, and a sigh of relief filled the room. A breeze came down the chimney, carrying an unfamiliar aroma of chamomile mixed with cinnamon. I looked over my shoulder to the fireplace and the cracked wooden panels that surrounded it and scrambled to my feet.

"What the hell is that?"

A tree had erupted from under the grate. Its black trunk filled the chimney, and its limbs had pushed through the stone and the surrounding wood paneling.

"It's like the tree from Mary's alembic." Matthew crouched down by the hearth in his black velvet breeches and embroidered linen shirt. His finger touched a small lump of silver embedded in the bark. Like mine, his voice sounded out of time and place.

"That looks like your pilgrim's badge." The outline of Lazarus's coffin was barely recognizable. I joined him, my full black skirts belling out over the floor.

"I think it is. The ampulla had two gilded hollows inside to hold holy water. Before I left Oxford, I'd filled one with my blood and the other with yours." Matthew's eyes met mine. "Having our blood so close made me feel as though we could never be separated."

"It looks as though the ampulla was exposed to heat and partially melted. If the inside of the ampulla was gilded, traces of mercury would have been released along with the blood."

"So this tree was made with some of the same ingredients as Mary's *arbor Dianæ*." Matthew looked up into the bare branches.

The scent of chamomile and cinnamon intensified. The tree began to bloom—but not the usual fruit or flowers. Instead a key and a single sheet of vellum sprouted from the branches.

"It's the page from the manuscript," said Matthew, pulling it free.

"That means the book is still broken and incomplete in the twenty-first century. Nothing we did in the past altered that fact." I took a steadying breath.

"Then the likelihood is that Ashmole 782 is safely hidden in the Bodleian Library," Matthew said quietly. "This is the key to a car." He snagged it off the branches. For months I hadn't thought about any form of transportation besides a horse or a ship. I looked out the front window, but no vehicle awaited us there. Matthew's eyes followed mine.

"Marcus and Hamish would have made sure we had a way to get to Sept-Tours as planned without calling them for help. They probably have cars waiting all over Europe and America just in case. But they wouldn't have left one visible," Matthew continued.

"There's no garage."

"The hop barn." Matthew's hand automatically moved to slide the key into the pocket at his hip, but his clothing had no such modern conveniences.

"Would they have thought to leave clothes for us, too?" I gestured down at my embroidered jacket and full skirts. They were still dusty from the unpaved, sixteenth-century Oxford road.

"Let's find out." Matthew carried the key and the page from Ashmole 782 into the family room and kitchen.

"Still brown," I commented, looking at the checked wallpaper and ancient refrigerator.

"Still home," Matthew said, drawing me into the crook of his arm.

"Not without Em and Sarah." In contrast with the overstuffed household that had surrounded us for so many months, our modern family seemed fragile and its membership small. Here there was no Mary Sidney to discuss my troubles with in the course of a stormy evening. Neither Susanna nor Goody Alsop would drop by the house in the afternoon for a cup of wine and to help me perfect my latest spell. I wouldn't have Annie's cheerful assistance to get me out of my corset and skirts. Mop wasn't underfoot, or Jack. And if we needed help, there was no Henry Percy to rush to our aid without question or hesitation. I slid my hand around Matthew's waist, needing a reminder of his solid indestructibility.

"You will always miss them," he said softly, gauging my mood, "but the pain will fade in time."

"I'm beginning to feel more like a vampire than a witch," I said ruefully. "Too many good-byes, too many missing loved ones." I spotted the calendar on the wall. It showed the month of November. I pointed it out to Matthew.

"Is it possible that no one has been here since last year?" he wondered, worried.

"Something must be wrong," I said, reaching for the phone.

"No," said Matthew. "The Congregation could be tracing the calls or watching the house. We're expected at Sept-Tours. Whether our time away can be measured in an hour or a year, that's where we need to go."

We found our modern clothes on top of the dryer, slipped into a pillowcase to keep them from getting dusty. Matthew's briefcase sat neatly beside them. Em at least had been here since we left. No one else would have thought of such practicalities. I wrapped our Elizabethan clothes in the linens, reluctant to let go of these tangible remnants of our former lives, and tucked them under my arms like two lumpy footballs. Matthew slid the page from Ashmole 782 into his leather bag, closing it securely.

Matthew scanned the orchard and the fields before we left the house, his keen eyes alert to possible danger. I made my own sweep of the place with my witch's third eye, but no one seemed to be out there. I could see the water under the orchard, hear the owls in the trees, taste the summer sweetness in the dusk air, but that was all.

"Come on," Matthew said, grabbing one of the bundles and taking my hand. We ran across the open space to the hop barn. Matthew put all his weight against the sliding door and pushed, but it wouldn't budge.

"Sarah put a spell on it." I could see it, twisted around the handle and through the grain of the wood. "A good one, too."

"Too good to break?" Matthew's mouth was tight with worry. It wasn't surprising that he was concerned. Last time we were here, I hadn't been able to light the Halloween pumpkins. I located the loose ends of the bindings and grinned.

"No knots. Sarah's good, but she's not a weaver." I'd tucked my Elizabethan silks into the waistband of my leggings. When I pulled them free, the green and brown cords in my hand reached out and latched onto Sarah's spell, loosening the restrictions my aunt had placed on the door faster than even our master thief Jack could have managed it.

Sarah's Honda was parked inside the barn.

"How the hell are we going to fit you into that?" I wondered.

"I'll manage," Matthew said, tossing our clothes into the back. He handed me the briefcase, folded himself into the front seat, and after a few false starts the car sputtered to life.

"Where next?" I asked, fastening my seat belt.

"Syracuse. Then Montreal. Then Amsterdam, where I have a house." Matthew put the car into drive and quietly rolled it into the field. "If anyone is watching for us, they'll be looking in New York, London, and Paris."

"We don't have passports," I observed.

"Look under the mat. Marcus would have told Sarah to leave them there," he said. I peeled up the filthy mats and found Matthew's French passport and my American one.

"Why isn't your passport burgundy?" I asked, taking them out of the sealed plastic bag (another Em touch, I thought).

"Because it's a diplomatic passport." He steered out onto the road and switched on the headlights. "There should be one for you."

My French diplomatic passport, inscribed with the name Diana de Clermont and noting my marital status relative to Matthew, was folded inside the ordinary U.S. version. How Marcus had managed to duplicate my photograph without damaging the original was anyone's guess.

"Are you a spy now, too?" I asked faintly.

"No. It's like the helicopters," he replied with a smile, "just another perk associated with being a de Clermont."

I left Syracuse as Diana Bishop and entered Europe the next day as Diana de Clermont. Matthew's house in Amsterdam turned out to be a seventeenth-century mansion on the most beautiful stretch of the Herengracht. He had, Matthew explained, bought it right after he left Scotland in 1605.

We lingered there only long enough to shower and change clothes. I kept on the same leggings that I'd worn since Madison, and swapped out my shirt for one of Matthew's. He donned his habitual gray and black cashmere and wool, even though it was late June according to the newspapers. It was odd not to see his legs. I'd grown accustomed to their being on display.

"It seems a fair trade," Matthew commented. "I haven't seen your legs for months, except in the privacy of our bedchamber."

Matthew nearly had a heart attack when he discovered that his beloved Range Rover was not waiting for him in the underground garage. Instead we found a navy sports car with a soft top.

"I'm going to kill him," Matthew said when he saw the low-slung vehicle. He used his house key to unlock a metal box bolted to the wall. Inside were another key and a note: *"Welcome home. No one will expect you to be driving this. It's safe. And fast. Hi, Diana. M."*

"What is it?" I said, looking at the airplane-style dials set into a flashy chrome dashboard.

"A Spyker Spyder. Marcus collects cars named after arachnids." Matthew activated the car doors, and they scissored up like the wings on a jet fighter. He swore. "It's the most conspicuous car imaginable."

We only made it as far as Belgium before Matthew pulled in to a car dealership, handed over the keys to Marcus's car, and pulled off the lot in something bigger and far less fun to drive. Safe in its heavy, boxy confines, we entered into France and some hours later began our slow ascent through the mountains of the Auvergne to Sept-Tours.

Glimpses of the fortress flickered between the trees—the pinkish gray stone, a dark tower window. I couldn't help drawing comparisons between the castle and its adjacent town now and how it had looked when last I saw it in 1590. This time no smoke hung over Saint-Lucien in a gray pall. A sound of distant bells made me turn my head, thinking to spot the descendants of the goats I had known coming home for their evening meal. Pierre wouldn't rush out with torches to meet us, though. Chef wasn't in the kitchen decapitating pheasants with a cleaver as the freshly killed game was efficiently prepared to feed both warmbloods and vampires.

And there would be no Philippe, and therefore no shouts of laughter, shrewd observations on human frailty lifted from Euripides, or acute insights into the problems that would face us now that we had returned to the present. How long would it take to stop bracing myself for the rush of motion and bellow of sound that heralded Philippe's arrival in a room? My heart hurt at the thought of my father-in-law. This harshly lit, fast-paced modern world had no place for heroes such as he.

"You're thinking of my father," Matthew murmured. Our silent rituals of a vampire's blood-taking and a witch's kiss had strengthened our ability to gauge each other's thoughts.

"So are you," I observed. He had been since we'd crossed over the border into France.

"The château has felt empty to me since the day he died. It has provided refuge, but little comfort." Matthew's eyes lifted to the castle, then settled back on the road before us. The air was heavy with responsibility and a son's need to live up to his father's legacy.

"Maybe it will be different this time. Sarah and Em are there. Marcus, too. Not to mention Sophie and Nathaniel. And Philippe is still here, if only we can learn to focus on his presence rather than his absence." He would be in the shadows of every room, every stone in the walls. I studied my husband's beautifully austere face, understanding better how experience and pain had shaped it. One hand curved around my belly, while the other sought him out to offer the comfort he so desperately needed.

His fingers clasped mine, squeezed. Then Matthew released me, and we didn't speak for a time. My fingers soon beat an impatient tattoo on my thigh in the quiet, however, and I was tempted several times to open the car's moonroof and fly to the château's front door.

"Don't you dare." Matthew's wide grin softened the warning note in his voice. I returned his smile as he downshifted around a deep curve.

"Hurry, then," I said, scarcely able to control myself. Despite my entreaties the speedometer stayed exactly where it was. I groaned with impatience. "We should have stuck with Marcus's car."

"Patience. We're almost there." *And there's no chance of my going any faster,* Matthew thought as he downshifted again.

"What did Sophie say about Nathaniel's driving when she was pregnant? 'He drives like an old lady.'"

"Imagine how Nathaniel might drive if he actually *was* an old lady—a centuries-old old lady, like me. That's how I will drive for the rest of my days, so long as you are in the car." He reached for my hand again, bringing it to his lips.

"Both hands on the wheel, old lady," I joked as we rounded the last bend, putting a straight stretch of road and walnut trees between us and the château's courtyard.

*Hurry,* I begged him silently. My eyes fixed on the roof of Matthew's tower as it came into view. When the car slowed, I looked at him in confusion.

"They've been expecting us," he explained, angling his head toward the windshield.

Sophie, Ysabeau, and Sarah were waiting, motionless, in the middle of the road.

*Daemon, vampire, witch*—and one more. Ysabeau held a baby in her arms. I could see its rich brown thatch of hair and chubby, long legs. One of the baby's hands was wrapped firmly around a strand of the vampire's honeyed locks, while her other hand stretched imperiously in our direction. There was a tiny, undeniable tingle when the baby's eyes focused on me. Sophie and Nathaniel's child was a witch, just as she had foretold.

I unbuckled the seat belt, flung the door open, and sped up the road before Matthew could bring the car to a complete stop. Tears streamed down my face, and Sarah ran to enfold me in familiar textures of fleece and flannel, surrounding me with the scents of henbane and vanilla.

*Home,* I thought.

"I'm so glad you're back safely," she said fiercely.

Over Sarah's shoulder I watched while Sophie gently took the baby from Ysabeau's grasp. Matthew's mother's face was as inscrutable and lovely as ever, but the tightness around her mouth suggested strong emotions as she gave up the child. That tightness was one of Matthew's tells, too. They were so much more similar in flesh and blood than the method of Matthew's making would suggest was possible.

Pulling myself loose from Sarah's embrace, I turned to Ysabeau.

"I was not sure you would come back. You were gone so long. Then Margaret began to demand that we take her to the road, and it was possible for me to believe that you might return to us safely after all." Ysabeau searched my face for some piece of information that I had not yet given her.

"We're back now. To stay." There had been enough loss in her long life. I kissed her softly on one cheek, then the other.

"*Bien,*" she murmured with relief. "It will please us all to have you here—not just Margaret." The baby heard her name and began to chant "D-d-d-d" while her arms and legs moved like eggbeaters in an attempt to get to me. "Clever girl," Ysabeau said approvingly, giving Margaret and then Sophie a pat on the head.

"Do you want to hold your goddaughter?" Sophie asked. Her smile was wide, though there were tears in her eyes. She looked so much like Susanna.

"Please," I said, taking the baby into my arms in exchange for a kiss on Sophie's cheek.

"Hello, Margaret," I whispered, breathing in her baby smell.

"D-d-d-d." Margaret grabbed a hank of my hair and began to wave it around in her fist.

"You are a troublemaker," I said with a laugh. She dug her feet into my ribs and grunted in protest.

"She's as stubborn as her father, even though she's a Pisces," Sophie said serenely. "Sarah went through the ceremony in your place. Agatha was here. She's gone at the moment, but I suspect she'll be back soon. She and Marthe made a special cake wrapped up in strands of sugar. It was amazing. And Margaret's dress was beautiful. You sound different—as if you spent a lot of time in a foreign country. And I like your hair. It's different, too. Are you hungry?" Sophie's words came out of her mouth in a disorganized tumble, just like Tom or Jack. I felt the loss of our friends, even here in the midst of our family.

After kissing Margaret on the forehead, I handed her back to her mother. Matthew was still standing behind the Range Rover's open door, one foot in the car and the other resting on the ground of the Auvergne, as though he were unsure if we should be there.

"Where's Em?" I asked. Sarah and Ysabeau exchanged a look.

"Everybody is waiting for you in the château. Why don't we walk back?" Ysabeau suggested. "Just leave the car. Someone will get it. You must want to stretch your legs."

I put my arm around Sarah and took a few steps. Where was Matthew? I turned and held out my free hand. *Come to your family,* I said silently as our eyes connected. *Come be with the people who love you.*

He smiled, and my heart leaped in response.

Ysabeau hissed in surprise, a sibilant noise that carried in the summer air more surely than a whisper. "Heartbeats. Yours. And . . . two more?" Her beautiful green eyes darted to my abdomen and a tiny red drop welled up and threatened to fall. Ysabeau looked to Matthew in wonder. He nodded, and his mother's blood tear fully formed and slid down her cheek.

"Twins run in my family," I said by way of explanation. Matthew had detected the second heartbeat in Amsterdam, just before we'd climbed into Marcus's Spyder.

"Mine, too," Ysabeau whispered. "Then it is true, what Sophie has seen in her dreams? You are with child—Matthew's child?"

"Children," I said, watching the blood tear's slow progress.

"It's a new beginning, then," Sarah said, wiping a tear from her own eye. Ysabeau gave my aunt a bittersweet smile.

"Philippe had a favorite saying about beginnings. Something ancient. What was it, Matthew?" Ysabeau asked her son.

Matthew stepped fully out of the car at last, as if some spell had been holding him back and its conditions had finally been met. He walked the few steps to my side, then kissed his mother softly on the cheek before reaching out and clasping my hand.

"*Omni fine initium novum,*" Matthew said, gazing upon the land of his father as though he had, at last, come home.

"*In every ending there is a new beginning.*"

## 42

30 May 1593

Annie brought the small statue of Diana to Father Hubbard, just as Master Marlowe had made her promise to do. Her heart tightened to see it in the *wearh*'s palm. The tiny figure always reminded her of Diana Roydon. Even now, nearly two years after her mistress's sudden departure, Annie missed her.

"And he said nothing else?" Hubbard demanded, turning the figurine this way and that. The huntress's arrow caught the light and sparked as though it were about to fly.

"Nothing, Father. Before he left for Deptford this morning, he bade me bring this to you. Master Marlowe said you would know what must be done."

Hubbard noticed a slip of paper inserted into the slim quiver, rolled up and tucked alongside the goddess's waiting arrows. "Give me one of your pins, Annie."

Annie removed a pin from her bodice and handed it to him with a mystified look. Hubbard poked the sharp end at the paper and caught it on the point. Carefully he slid it out.

Hubbard read the lines, frowned, and shook his head. "Poor Christopher. He was ever one of God's lost children."

"Master Marlowe is not coming back?" Annie smothered a small sigh of relief. She had never liked the playwright, and her regard for him had not recovered after the dreadful events in the tiltyard at Greenwich Palace. Since her mistress and master had departed, leaving no clues to their whereabouts, Marlowe had gone from melancholy to despair to something darker. Some days Annie was sure that the blackness would swallow him whole. She wanted to be sure it didn't catch her, too.

"No, Annie. God tells me Master Marlowe is gone from this world and on to the next. I pray he finds peace there, for it was denied him in this life." Hubbard considered the girl for a moment. She had grown into a striking young woman. Maybe she would cure Will Shakespeare of his love for that other man's wife. "But you are not to worry. Mistress Roydon bade me treat you like my own. I take care of my children, and you will have a new master."

"Who, Father?" She would have to take whatever position Hubbard offered her. Mistress Roydon had been clear how much money she would require to set herself up as an independent seamstress in Islington. It was going to take time and considerable thrift to gather such a sum.

"Master Shakespeare. Now that you can read and write, you are a woman of value, Annie. You can be of help to him in his work." Hubbard considered the slip of paper in his hand. He was tempted to keep it with the parcel that had arrived from Prague, sent to him through the formidable network of mail carriers and merchants established by the Dutch vampires.

Hubbard still wasn't sure why Edward Kelley had sent him the strange picture of the dragons. Edward was a dark and slippery creature, and Hubbard had not approved of his moral code that saw nothing wrong with open adultery or theft. Taking his blood in the ritual of family and sacrifice had been a chore, not the pleasure it usually was. In the exchange, Hubbard had seen enough of Kelley's soul to know he didn't want him in London. So he sent him to Mortlake instead. It had stopped Dee's incessant pestering for lessons in magic.

But Marlowe had meant this statue to go to Annie, and Hubbard would not alter a dying man's wish. He handed the small figurine and slip of paper to Annie. "You must give this to your aunt, Mistress Norman. She will keep it safe for you. The paper can be another remembrance of Master Marlowe."

"Yes, Father Hubbard," Annie said, though she would have liked to sell the silver object and put the proceeds in her stocking.

Annie left the church where Andrew Hubbard held court and trudged the streets to Will Shakespeare's house. He was less mercurial than Marlowe, and Mistress Roydon had always spoken of him with respect even though the master's friends were quick to mock him.

She settled quickly into the player's household, her spirits lifting with each passing day. When news reached them of Marlowe's gruesome death, it only confirmed how fortunate she was to be free of him. Master Shakespeare was shaken, too, and drank too much one night, which brought him to the attention of the master of the revels. Shakespeare had explained himself satisfactorily, though, and all was returned to normal now.

Annie was cleaning grime from the windowpane to provide better light for her employer to read by. She dipped her cloth into fresh water, and a small curl of paper drifted down from her pocket, carried on a breeze from the open casement.

"What is that, Annie?" Shakespeare asked suspiciously, pointing with the feathered end of his quill. The girl had worked for Kit Marlowe. She could be passing information to his rivals. He couldn't afford to have anyone know about his latest bids for patronage. With all the playhouses closed on account of the plague, it would be a challenge to keep body and soul together. *Venus and Adonis* could do it—provided nobody stole the idea out from under him.

"Nothing, M-M-Master Shakespeare," Annie stammered, bending to retrieve the paper.

"Bring it here, since it is nothing," he commanded.

As soon as it was in his possession, Shakespeare recognized the distinctive penmanship. The hair on the back of his neck prickled. It was a message from a dead man.

"When did Marlowe give this to you?" Shakespeare's voice was sharp.

"He didn't, Master Shakespeare." As ever, Annie couldn't bring herself to lie. She had few other witchy traits, but Annie possessed honesty in abundance. "It was hidden. Father Hubbard found it and gave it to me. For a remembrance, he said."

"Did you find this after Marlowe died?" The prickling sensation at the back of Shakespeare's neck was quieted by the rush of interest.

"Yes," Annie whispered.

"I will hold on to it for you then. For safekeeping."

"Of course." Annie's eyes flickered with concern as she watched the last words of Christopher Marlowe disappear into her new master's closed fist.

"Be about your business, Annie." Shakespeare waited until his maid had gone to fetch more rags and water. Then he scanned the lines.

> *Black is the badge of true love lost.*
> *The hue of daemons,*
> *And the Shadow of Night.*

Shakespeare sighed. Kit's choice of meter never made any sense to him. And his melancholy humor and morbid fascinations were too dark for these sad times. They made audiences uncomfortable, and there was sufficient death in London. He twirled the quill.

*True love lost.* Indeed. Shakespeare snorted. He'd had quite enough of true love, though the paying customers never seemed to tire of it. He struck out the words and replaced them with a single syllable, one that more accurately captured what he felt.

*Daemons.* The success of Kit's *Faustus* still rankled him. Shakespeare had no talent for writing about creatures beyond the limits of nature. He was far better with ordinary, flawed mortals caught in the snares of fate. Sometimes he thought he might have a good ghost story in him. Perhaps a wronged father who haunted his son. Shakespeare shuddered. His own father would make a terrifying specter, should the Lord tire of his company after John Shakespeare's final accounts were settled. He struck out that offending word and chose a different one.

*Shadow of Night.* It was a limp, predictable ending to the verses—the kind that George Chapman would fall upon for lack of something more original. But what would better serve the purpose? He obliterated another word and wrote *"scowl"* above it. *Scowl of Night.* That wasn't quite right either. He crossed it out and wrote *"sleeve."* That was just as bad.

Shakespeare wondered idly about the fate of Marlowe and his friends, all of them as insubstantial as shadows now. Henry Percy was enjoying a rare period of royal benevolence and was forever at court. Raleigh had married in secret and fallen from the queen's favor. He was now rusticated to Dorset, where the queen hoped he would be forgotten. Harriot was in seclusion somewhere, no doubt bent over a mathematical puzzle or staring at the heavens like a moonstruck Robin Goodfellow. Rumor had it that Chapman was on some mission for Cecil in the Low Countries and penning long poems about witches. And Marlowe was recently murdered in Deptford, though there was talk that it had been an assassination. Perhaps that strange Welshman would know more about it, for he'd been at the tavern with Marlowe. Roydon—who was the only truly powerful man Shakespeare had ever met—and his mysterious wife had both utterly vanished in the summer of 1591 and had not been seen since.

The only one of Marlowe's circle that Shakespeare still heard from regularly was the big Scot named Gallowglass, who was more princely than a servant ought to be and told such wonderful tales of fairies and sprites. It was thanks to Gallowglass's steady employment that Shakespeare had a roof over his head. Gallowglass always seemed to have a job that required Shakespeare's talents as a forger. He paid well, too—especially when he wanted Shakespeare to imitate Roydon's hand in the margins of some book or pen a letter with his signature.

*What a crew,* Shakespeare thought. *Traitors, atheists, and criminals, the lot of them.* His pen hesitated over the page. After writing another word, this one decisively thick and black, Shakespeare sat back and studied his new verses.

> *Black is the badge of hell*
> *The hue of dungeons and the school of night.*

It was no longer recognizable as Marlowe's work. Through the alchemy of his talent, Shakespeare had transformed a dead man's ideas into something suitable for ordinary Londoners rather than dangerous men like Roydon. And it had taken him only a few moments.

Shakespeare felt not a single pang of regret as he altered the past, thereby changing the future. Marlowe's turn on the world's stage had ended, but Shakespeare's was just beginning. Memories were short and history unkind. It was the way of the world.

Pleased, Shakespeare put the bit of paper into a stack of similar scraps weighted down with a dog's skull on the corner of his desk. He'd find a use for the snippet of verse one day. Then he had second thoughts.

Perhaps he'd been too hasty to dismiss *"true love lost."* There was potential there—unrealized, waiting for someone to unlock it. Shakespeare reached for a scrap he'd cut off a partially filled sheet of paper in a half-hearted attempt at economy after Annie had shown him the last butcher's bill.

*"Love's Labour's Lost,"* he wrote in large letters.

Yes, Shakespeare mused, he'd definitely use that one day.

# *Libri Personæ:* The People of the Book

*Those noted thus * acknowledged by historians.*

### Part I: Woodstock: The Old Lodge

Diana Bishop, a witch
Matthew de Clermont, known as *Roydon, a vampire
* Christopher Marlowe, a daemon and maker of plays
Françoise and Pierre, both vampires and servants
* George Chapman, a writer of some reputation and little patronage
* Thomas Harriot, a daemon and astronomer
* Henry Percy, the Earl of Northumberland
* Sir Walter Raleigh, an adventurer
Joseph Bidwell, senior and junior, shoemakers
Master Somers, a glover
Widow Beaton, a cunning woman
Mister Danforth, a clergyman
Master Iffley, another glover
Gallowglass, a vampire and soldier of fortune
* Davy Gam, known as Hancock, a vampire, his Welsh companion

### Part II: Sept-Tours and the Village of Saint-Lucien

* Cardinal Joyeuse, a visitor to Mont Saint-Michel
Alain, a vampire and servant to the Sieur de Clermont
Philippe de Clermont, a vampire and lord of Sept-Tours
Chef, a cook
Catrine, Jehanne, Thomas, and Étienne, servants
Marie, who makes gowns
André Champier, a wizard of Lyon

### Part III: London: The Blackfriars

* Robert Hawley, a shoemaker
* Margaret Hawley, his wife
* Mary Sidney, the Countess of Pembroke
Joan, her maid

* Nicholas Hilliard, a limner
  Master Prior, a maker of pies
* Richard Field, a printer
* Jacqueline Vautrollier Field, his wife
* John Chandler, an apothecary near the Barbican Cross
  Amen Corner and Leonard Shoreditch, vampires
  Father Hubbard, the vampire king of London
  Annie Undercroft, a young witch with some skill and little power
* Susanna Norman, a midwife and witch
* John and Jeffrey Norman, her sons
  Goody Alsop, a windwitch of St. James Garlickhythe
  Catherine Streeter, a firewitch
  Elizabeth Jackson, a waterwitch
  Marjorie Cooper, an earthwitch
  Jack Blackfriars, a nimble orphan
* Doctor John Dee, a learned man with a library
* Jane Dee, his disgruntled wife
* William Cecil, Lord Burghley, the lord high treasurer of England
* Robert Devereux, the Earl of Essex
* Elizabeth I, queen of England
* Elizabeth (Bess) Throckmorton, maid of honor to the queen

### Part IV: The Empire: Prague

  Karolína and Tereza, vampires and servants
* Tadeáš Hájek, physician to his Majesty
* Ottavio Strada, Imperial librarian and historian
* Rudolf II, Holy Roman Emperor and King of Bohemia
  Frau Huber, an Austrian, and Signorina Rossi, an Italian, women of
    Malá Strana
* Joris Hoefnagel, an artist
* Erasmus Habermel, maker of mathematical instruments
* Signor Miseroni, a carver of precious stones
* Signor Pasetti, his Majesty's dancing master
* Joanna Kelley, a woman far from home
* Edward Kelley, a daemon and alchemist
* Rabbi Judah Loew, a wise man
  Abraham ben Elijah of Chelm, a wizard with a problem
* David Gans, an astronomer

Herr Fuchs, a vampire
* Melchior Maisel, a prosperous merchant of the Jewish Town
  Lobero, a Hungarian dog sometimes mistaken for a mop, probably just
  a Komondor
* Johannes Pistorius, a wizard and theologian

### Part V: London: The Blackfriars

* Vilém Slavata, a very young ambassador
  Louisa de Clermont, a vampire and sister to Matthew de Clermont
* Master Sleford, keeper of the poor souls of Bedlam
  Stephen Proctor, a wizard
  Rebecca White, a witch
  Bridget White, her daughter

### Part VI: New World, Old Worlde

Sarah Bishop, a witch and aunt to Diana Bishop
Ysabeau de Clermont, a vampire and mother to Matthew de Clermont
Sophie Norman, a daemon
Margaret Wilson, her daughter, a witch

### Other Characters in Other Times

Rima Jaén, a librarian of Seville
Emily Mather, a witch and partner to Sarah Bishop
Marthe, housekeeper to Ysabeau de Clermont
Phoebe Taylor, very proper, who knows something about art
Marcus Whitmore, Matthew de Clermont's son, a vampire
Verin de Clermont, a vampire
Ernst Neumann, her husband
Peter Knox, a witch and member of the Congregation
Pavel Skovajsa, who works in a library
* Gerbert of Aurillac in the Cantal, a vampire and ally of Peter Knox
* William Shakespeare, a scrivener and forger who also makes plays

# Acknowledgments

So many people helped bring this book into the world.

First, thanks to my always gentle, always candid first readers: Cara, Fran, Jill, Karen, Lisa, and Olive. And a special thanks to Margie for claiming she was bored just as I was struggling with the last edit and offering to read the manuscript with her discerning writer's eye.

Carole DeSanti, my editor, served as midwife during the writing process and knows (literally) where all the bodies are buried. Thank you, Carole, for always being ready to lend assistance with a sharp pencil and a sympathetic ear.

The extraordinary team at Viking, who alchemically transforms stacks of typescript into beautiful books, continues to astonish me with their enthusiasm and professionalism. Special thanks go to my copy editor, Maureen Sugden, whose eagle eye rivals that of Augusta. And to my publishers around the world, thank you for all you have done (and continue to do) to introduce Diana and Matthew to new readers.

My literary agent, Sam Stoloff, of the Frances Goldin Agency, remains my most steadfast supporter. Thanks, Sam, for providing perspective and doing the behind-the-scenes work that makes it possible for me to write. Thanks are also due to my film agent, Rich Green, of the Creative Artists Agency, who has become an indispensable resource for advice and good humor even in the most challenging of circumstances.

My assistant, Jill Hough, defended my time and my sanity during the past year with the fierceness of a firedrake. I literally could not have completed the book without her.

Lisa Halttunen once again readied the manuscript for submission. Though I fear I will never master more than a few of the grammatical rules at her command, I am eternally grateful that she continues to be willing to straighten out my prose and punctuation.

Patrick Wyman provided insights into the twists and turns of medieval and military history that took the characters—and the story—in surprising directions. Though Carole knows where the bodies are buried, Patrick understands how they got there. Thank you, Patrick, for helping me to see

Gallowglass, Matthew, and above all Philippe in a new light. Thanks also to Cleopatra Comnenos, for answering my queries about the Greek language.

I would also like to express my appreciation to the Pasadena Roving Archers, who helped me understand just how difficult it is to shoot an arrow at a target. Scott Timmons of Aerial Solutions introduced me to Fokker and his other beautiful raptors at the Terranea Resort in California. And Andrew at the Apple Store in Thousand Oaks saved the author, her computer—and the book itself—from a potentially terminal meltdown at a crucial point in the writing process.

This book is dedicated to historian Lacey Baldwin Smith, who took me on as a graduate student and has inspired thousands of students with his passion for Tudor England. Whenever he spoke about Henry VIII or his daughter Elizabeth I, it always seemed as if they had just had lunch together. Once, he gave me a brief list of facts and told me to imagine how I would handle them if I was writing a chronicle, or a saint's life, or a medieval romance. At the end of one of my exceedingly short stories, he wrote *"What happens next? You should think about writing a novel."* Perhaps that is when the seeds of the All Souls trilogy were first planted.

And last, but not least, I am sincerely grateful to my long-suffering family and friends (you know who you are!) who saw very little of me during my sojourn in 1590 and welcomed me back when I returned to the present.